# Jesse's Renegade

## Nancy Bush

POCKET BOOKS

New York   London   Toronto   Sydney   Tokyo   Singapore

An *Original* Publication of POCKET BOOKS

POCKET BOOKS, a division of Simon & Schuster Inc.
1230 Avenue of the Americas, New York, NY 10020

ISBN: 0-671-72921-7

First Pocket Books printing June 1991

10  9  8  7  6  5  4  3  2  1

POCKET and colophon are registered trademarks of
Simon & Schuster Inc.

Cover art by Donald Case

Printed in the U.S.A.

*Kelsey tried to
edge away from him,
interpreting his heavy-lidded
gaze correctly . . .*

"Don't!" she warned as he leaned across the bed toward her.

"Don't what?" Jesse's tone was gentle and seductive as one hand curved around the back of her neck, lifting her chin and mouth to his rampant gaze, drawing her lips inexorably, inch by inch, toward his.

He hesitated, his brandy-laced breath mingling with hers. "I believe I've found the means to keep you in line," he said in amusement.

"If you kiss me, I won't be responsible for the fate that befalls you!" she threatened.

For a heartbeat, he seemed willing to listen. Then his mouth came down on hers, cool and insistent. Kelsey's heart slammed into her ribs.

In a voice muffled by her trembling lips, he warned, "Don't fight me. I'll win."

That determined tone caused her to tremble all over. He was right. This tender assault was much harder to resist than any other means of bending her to his will that he could have come up with.

Jesse deepened the kiss, his mouth moving over hers familiarly. Kelsey was momentarily frozen. She didn't want to want him, but she did, and though she knew this was Jesse's way of taking some small revenge, she enjoyed his kisses more than any she'd ever experienced . . .

**Books by Nancy Bush**

Lady Sundown
Danner's Lady
Jesse's Renegade

Published by POCKET BOOKS

Jesse's
Renegade

# Prologue

Portland, Oregon • *August 1892*

Jesse Danner grinned his devil-may-care grin and bent his head to the blond-haired beauty seated in front of the oval dressing table. Her black eyes snapped at him in total outrage, and his grin widened.

"I'll be back before you know it," he whispered in a sexy drawl.

Lila Hathaway snorted inelegantly and shrugged against the hands resting lightly on her shoulders. Damn the man. She wanted to kill him.

His teeth flashed white beneath the brim of his battered Stetson, a gift from one of his brothers years before, or so he'd explained when she'd declared the hat offensive. In the mirror's reflection his blue eyes danced with merriment. The scourge was enjoying her rage and jealousy! Yes, she wanted to kill him. She *would* kill him.

"You're a scoundrel," she hissed, combing her luxurious mane with studied sensuality. Her peignoir was silver and shimmered in the light from the overhead chandelier, outlining her sumptuous curves. Lila knew her effect on men, and with that thought planted firmly in mind she purposely stroked her long hair, hoping Jesse would succumb to her sexuality rather than leave before her plans could take effect.

She was furious. Livid! How dare he run out on her! When he'd told her he was leaving at the end of the week, he'd sealed his fate. Before that she'd been hatching plans to keep Montana from finding him, but now she hoped her husband would rip Jesse's lean body in two! Savoring her revenge, it took all of Lila's concentration not to smile. A few more minutes . . . that's all she needed.

"It won't be long—maybe a couple of weeks before I wind up everything in California," Jesse told her, oblivious to her anger. "By then I'll own that Portland park block. When I come back, we can pick up where we left off."

His voice was full of amusement. Amusement at her expense! Damn his eyes! He'd be sorry. "I don't have a couple of weeks," she said bitterly.

"Why not?"

She swung around on the stool, her chin lifting defiantly. "Because my husband will be back by then."

"Your *husband?*" Jesse stared at her incredulously. Twenty-five, successful, and worldly-wise beyond his years, Jesse was seldom, if ever, caught off guard. And never by a woman.

"Did I forget to mention him? He's due back in Portland any day now. I'm afraid he won't like the idea of you bedding his wife. He's so very puritanical about these things."

She climbed to her feet, still smiling. Jesse stepped back, staring at her as if she'd just sprouted another head. Taking advantage of his momentary stupefaction, Lila slid her arms around his waist, her hands inching up his back, pulling his shirt from his denim pants in one fluid movement.

Jesse moved so fast she gasped. He thrust her away, his strong hands gripping her forearms so hard it made her wince. He had a rule about women: no virgins and no married ones. Virgins were just plain trouble. And married women had husbands.

"You should have told me you were married," he muttered fiercely, shoving her away from him. Lila stumbled as he swung toward the door.

2

"Where do you think you're going?" she demanded, her eyes narrowing.

"I'm leaving."

"Just like that?" Lila cried desperately. He couldn't leave yet. It was too soon! "You can't!" She crowded close to him again, this time pressing her breasts against his strong back, her arms winding tightly around his waist. Jesse Danner was a fantastic lover. She wasn't going to give him up until the last moment. Now she wished she'd held her tongue about Montana. That warning may have cost her a last few minutes of ecstasy.

Jesse yanked her arms from around his waist, swearing beneath his breath. He tucked in the shirt Lila had pulled from his trousers.

But Lila wouldn't give up. She nipped at his nape and rubbed her sinuous body along his back. She was certain she would win. Jesse Danner was a slave to his senses. She'd learned that in the wonderful hours they'd spent together.

Unfortunately, she didn't know about his rules.

"Oh, Jesse," she implored, hurt. He jerked away as if her touch sickened him. "I didn't know it would matter this much."

"Didn't you?" He was scathing. "Then why didn't you tell me straightaway, when we first met?"

"All right. I was scared that you wouldn't understand. But now, after all we've shared . . ."

"All we've shared," he repeated acidly, throwing her a narrow look of disgust. Lila inwardly sighed. Even angry, Jesse was the most handsome, stimulating, sinfully sexy man she'd ever known. Tall, with thick black hair, slumberous blue eyes, a truly sensual mouth, and a strong, muscular, compact body, she'd realized she would have Jesse the moment she clapped eyes on him. Never mind that her reason for seeking him out had been because Montana had ordered it. How was she to know that Montana's latest business rival would be so damnably attractive?

And Jesse had been so willing.

Of course, that was because he was young, she thought with bitter self-honesty. Younger than herself by almost ten

3

years, though she'd taken pains that he didn't know it. The first time they'd made love was in the back of her carriage. Lord! It caused her arms to break out in goose bumps just thinking about it! Lila liked men who knew how to take charge, especially in bed. If she had one complaint, it was that Jesse didn't like it as rough as she did, although he'd kept her satisfied, heaven knew.

Now, however, he looked as if he couldn't stand the sight of her! "Nothing's changed," she said softly. "Montana doesn't have to know."

"*Montana?* Montana Gray?" Jesse stared at her in shock. "Jesus! You're married to Montana Gray?"

She nodded. "He's away most of the time. He has lots of businesses."

"You told me your name's Hathaway. This *house* is Hathaway House according to the name inscribed on the wrought-iron gate."

"I'm Lila Hathaway Gray," she admitted. "The last of the Hathaways."

If Jesse had been a resident of Portland, he would have known that. Her name was always on the society page of the *Oregonian*. Montana's main reason for marrying her had been to infiltrate Portland's upper echelons of society, and, of course, her reason for marrying an opportunist like Montana was simply for his ill-gotten money. The Hathaway fortune had dwindled over the years, until Lila had been left virtually penniless.

"Don't leave me," she begged, adding softly, "Please," as she edged a step nearer.

The cold look on Jesse's face stopped her in her tracks and she dropped her outstretched arms to her sides. Jesse was repulsed by the woman before him. When she'd approached him in the park, complaining of a twisted ankle, he'd chivalrously turned to help her. He'd been entranced by the sight of her. In a white dress with peach-colored ribbons and a low, ruffled décolletage, her white-feathered and peach-flowered hat dipped over one eye, a dainty parasol swinging from her arm, she'd looked like a confection. Sweetness and purity wrapped in a delicious package. He'd helped her to her carriage and at the door there'd been no

4

mistaking the invitation in those sultry eyes. Buoyed by his success in negotiating the park block, Jesse had followed her inside the carriage. She'd reminded him of Emerald— the Emerald who'd given him her virginity; the Emerald who'd unknowingly been responsible for Jesse's rule about virgins; the Emerald who had turned out to be as cold-hearted as she was beautiful.

Now, facing the real Lila *Gray,* Jesse realized with bitter irony that she was indeed exactly like Emerald. Scheming, selfish, spoiled, wicked. He couldn't wait to shake the dust of Hathaway House off his boots much as he'd walked away from the life he'd once known in his hometown of Rock Springs. Trouble with women followed Jesse like a bad smell, and he had a bullet scar on his right shoulder from old man McIntyre's shotgun to prove it.

"You're making a mistake!" Lila burst out when she realized her pleading had no effect on him.

"The mistake I made was three days ago when I climbed into your carriage." Lila's lips tightened, but Jesse added coldly, "Your husband's in the same business I am. He's buying property all around this city. Did you think we wouldn't meet?"

"But you already have met. You were at his office last Friday."

Jesse felt as if the breath had been knocked from him. "How do you know that?"

"Because I followed you from Montana's office to the park."

A sick feeling gathered in Jesse's stomach. Lila had followed him? Then she would have witnessed his meeting with Nell! Holy Christ, if she knew who Nell was, all hell was about to break loose!

"I didn't meet with Montana," Jesse explained, eyeing her closely, choosing his words carefully.

"Well, you met with that little mouse in the park!" Li' fury burst out as if she couldn't hold it in. "Who was Another lover?"

"Just a friend." Jesse's relief was boundless. Lila recognized Nell. She didn't know it was Nell wh Jesse the inside track on that particular piece of r

Nell who'd helped squeeze her boss, *Montana Gray,* out of the deal; Nell whom he'd planned to meet at Gray's offices, but who'd left him a note to meet her in the park.

Not a religious man, Jesse nevertheless sent up a silent prayer of gratitude for Nell's safety. If he'd had any idea Lila was Montana's wife, he never would have gotten involved with her.

"A friend?" Lila snorted, only slightly mollified. After a moment, she said in a low voice, "When I saw you at the park, I just lost my head. I wasn't supposed to take you home, but there you were and things just happened."

"You followed me on your husband's orders," Jesse realized.

Her dark gaze slid down his body. "We could still work together," she added slowly, as if turning the idea over in her mind. "Montana doesn't know anything yet."

Jesse's stomach turned at the thought of joining forces with the woman in front of him. He'd thought her a lady, and so she was. He realized he never wanted another lady as long as he lived.

He strode away from her without another word, yanking open her bedroom door. In the hall below he heard voices. Not the voices of Lila's servants. Men's voices. And one of them was Montana Gray's.

There was nowhere to run. Jesse whipped around to stare accusingly at Lila. The look on her face said she'd known, or at least guessed, that her husband would be arriving soon.

"Jesse," she implored in a whisper. "I can still hide you. There's an entrance to the attic. Tell me you'll stay with me!"

Jesse turned in revulsion and strode across the upper balcony.

"Lila!" Montana's voice boomed from below. He walked the center of the entry hall and stood in a circle of black He was huge and burly with a hard jaw and one eye rooped a bit, a relic of an earlier fight at a time when a was more interested in brawling than climbing his he top of society. Now he had money and some tion, but underneath he was still a nasty charac-

6

ter. Jesse may not have paid much attention to who Montana's wife was, but he'd committed to memory all the stories he'd heard about the man himself.

Montana looked up and saw Jesse immediately.

And Jesse saw the four other men who'd accompanied Montana inside.

"Get him," was all Montana said.

The four men swarmed up the stairwell. Jesse stood his ground. He had no pistol, no weapon at all. The first man lunged too fast and Jesse kicked him in the groin, tossing him over the rail. The second grabbed his left arm and he swung with his right, crashing his fist into the man's jaw until the fellow bellowed in pain and rage.

The third man shot Jesse an uppercut beneath his jaw. Jesse's skull exploded into stars. The fourth slugged him in the chest. He heard ribs crack and his legs buckled.

The fight was over before it had begun. They carried Jesse downstairs.

Montana barely looked at him. "Lila, come down here," he ordered.

The slam of Lila's bedroom door was her answer.

"Take him to the cellar," Montana growled. "Teach him a lesson. Then get rid of him."

He strode purposefully up the stairs.

Jesse struggled against his captors as they dragged him into a dark, dank, foul-smelling cellar. He was slugged again for his trouble. They tied ropes on his wrists, then stretched his arms straight out, lashing him to two beams so that his muscles strained from the effort. Within seconds he had no feeling left in his hands.

"What do you want to do first, Gardner?" the short one asked the taller man, who seemed to be in charge.

Gardner smiled. A thin scar ran down his left cheek. "He's awful pretty. How'd you get so pretty, son?"

"The Danner curse," Jesse replied sardonically, struggling to hide the pain of his broken ribs. It hurt to breathe, but by God, he wasn't going to let them know it. He didn't dwell on what they were planning for him. He knew he'd be damned lucky to survive it, whatever it was.

"The Danner curse, eh?" Gardner guffawed and looked

at a big man wearing a dirty black hat. He was the one who'd broken Jesse's ribs. "Want to take care of that, Al?"

A hammy fist slammed into Jesse's face, snapping his head around. His knees sagged. The ropes bit into his wrists.

"You're not gonna be so pretty now," Gardner pointed out. "Let's see. What else did the lady like about 'cha?"

"She liked him in bed," the fourth man said, the eagerness in his voice cutting through the red haze in Jesse's mind. "Maybe we should make sure he don't sleep with no one else."

That shocked Jesse to his senses. He yanked backward and kicked as hard as he could. His boot connected with Gardner's ear, ripping it open. Gardner screamed in rage. "Kill him, Al! Kill him!"

Al's fist broke Jesse's nose. Blood gushed. It took two more punches and then Jesse mercifully fell unconscious.

He awoke with a bad taste in his mouth. River water. He wanted to spit, but couldn't seem to get the muscles of his face working. In fact, he couldn't feel anything in his face. It was numb. He was aware he was alive, and that was something, but he assumed it was only for a short time. Why they should have anesthetized his pain was something he couldn't figure. But there was no other explanation for the lack of feeling.

He lifted his right hand and groaned. Hot needles of pain stabbed inside it.

"You're awake," a male voice said.

Jesse stiffened. The voice was tight and clipped. He tried to open his eyes but realized his whole face was wrapped. Gingerly, he touched his fingers to the bandages. Only his fingers hurt, not his face. "Where am I?" he asked, and his voice was so garbled he could barely understand himself.

"You're on Montana Gray's ship," the voice answered.

Hope died. He was still captured. "Why did you bother to wrap up my face?"

"What?"

8

He had to say it two more times before the man under-stood, and by that time Jesse was exhausted.

"Relax now. Take it easy," his captor said. "Someone had to put you back together."

"Why?" Jesse felt sleep taking him, but he had thousands of questions.

"I'll explain later. I'm no friend of Montana Gray's, Mr. Danner," he said, his voice sounding like watery ripples on a pool as Jesse lost consciousness again.

Jesse woke the second time to a rolling movement. The ship was under sail. He wondered helplessly if, after everything else, he was being shanghaied. But who would want him? He was useless and would be for a long while.

A sudden memory of the *other* torture Montana's men had planned made him struggle upward in fear. Hands pushed him back down, firmly but gently. "Don't move too fast," the now-familiar voice said.

"Who are you?" Jesse demanded more clearly.

"Ezekiel Thomas Drummond. My friends call me Zeke."

"Tell me—Zeke—besides my face, what other parts have been damaged?" Jesse felt no pain other than in his hands, and that's what scared him.

"You're all in one piece," Zeke assured him.

"Everywhere?"

"Gray did a nasty job on your face. That's all." He paused. "You were lucky," he added roughly, something in his tone suggesting someone else hadn't been so fortunate.

Relief washed over Jesse. He moved slightly and realized belatedly that he did have feeling elsewhere. Only his face was numb. "I can't see anything. I want to take this bandage off."

"There's nothing to see. We're on our way to San Francisco, courtesy of Montana Gray."

"He's paid you to take me to San Francisco?"

"No. I took the liberty of adding you to the passenger list. Gray thinks you're dead."

"You—saved me?"

"I fished you from the Willamette River and brought you on board. The ship's doctor was appalled at what they'd done to you. No one knows Montana's responsible but me.

9

If Montana finds you again, my friend, he'll make certain you die. I figured the safest place for you was right under his nose, so I brought you here."

"What have you got against Gray?"

There was a weighty pause. "We have a score to settle," was Zeke's cold answer.

"Stand in line," Jesse muttered.

Zeke laughed without humor. He tucked the blanket close to Jesse's neck. There was something about the way he did that that sent warning shivers down Jesse's nerves. "Are you a girly boy, Zeke?"

"Certainly not!" he declared, snatching his hands back indignantly.

"Because I don't give a damn if you are. If you save me, I'll lay down my life for you. But if you touch me, I'll kill you as soon as I'm able."

"You really don't know when you're at a disadvantage, do you?" Zeke asked with reluctant admiration.

Jesse sighed. "Another Danner curse," he muttered, sinking into oblivion once more.

*1*

## Portland, Oregon • *May 1897*

The carriage rocked slowly down the alder-lined road, moonlight bright upon the ground. Kelsey Garrett stared out the window, coldly ignoring her companion, wishing to high heaven the driver would speed up this carriage and get her home.

She felt a hand steal over hers and fought down a wave of revulsion and irritation. It wasn't that Tyrone McNamara was repulsive. On the contrary, he was attractive, humorous, and wealthy. But he was used to having his own way, and Kelsey couldn't stand men who treated her as if she had no brain. Oh, why had Charlotte talked her into accepting his invitation?

Because Charlotte's a dreamy romantic, she reminded herself. Luckily, Kelsey suffered no such illusions. Her derringer was in her black-beaded reticule. If Tyrone made a move toward her, she would shoot him right through the bag!

"Did you have a good time, Orchid?" he asked indulgently.

Orchid was Kelsey's middle name. No one knew her first name. Not even Charlotte, or Charlotte's wonderful grandmother, Lady Agatha Chamberlain, who was as starch and upright as her British heritage. And for purposes of keeping her true identity a secret, Kelsey had misled all and sundry into believing her last name was Simpson, not Garrett.

"I had an interesting evening," Kelsey answered. Lord sakes, his hand was growing sweaty. It wasn't all *that* warm in the carriage. From the way his eyes had caressed her figure all evening, she imagined his wet palm was from something else.

Tugging her cloak more closely to her body, Kelsey tried to slip her hand free. But Tyrone held on. Was he one of those that couldn't back down from a challenge? Probably. She knew, as Charlotte's companion, and Lady Chamberlain's favored friend, that the men of Portland society were intrigued by her. She was a mystery. She'd even heard one of Tyrone's friends describe her: "Orchid Simpson, beautiful, chilly, and as old a spinster as my aunt was before she took her first lover. Fair game, friends. I'll wager I can bed her before the rest of you."

Of course they hadn't meant her to overhear. But she'd been warned, and the fact that they considered a single woman sport decreased her already low opinion of men. She inwardly snorted. She should have married Harrison Danner when she had the chance. At least he'd seen her as more than a bedmate. But of course, then she'd been deluded into believing she should marry for *love* and *honor* and *happiness*. Hah. Men didn't understand those words.

Neither, anymore, did she.

"My town house is right up the street," Tyrone said smoothly. "Would you like to come in for a few minutes?"

They were nearing Lady Chamberlain's sweeping drive. Kelsey slid Tyrone a look out of the corners of her eyes. "Would we be alone?"

"Assuredly. I can just hail the driver and—"

Kelsey laid a hand on his arm, stopping him from rapping his cane against the carriage ceiling. He looked at her hand in surprise, his face lighting with expectation.

"I'm going home," she said, dashing his hopes. "Good night, Tyrone."

"You're a hard woman, Orchid. I swear, has no man ever even kissed you?"

"I've been kissed." She slipped the beaded bag from her wrist and unsnapped the clasp. She didn't want to have to display her skill with a weapon to him. Wouldn't that fuel the gossip surrounding her! On the other hand, no man would want to admit that a woman had held him at gunpoint. She was probably safe.

But she was right about Tyrone's intentions, for he suddenly grabbed her, grinding his mouth down on hers. She let him for several seconds, curling her own lips back.

"You haven't been kissed by a real man," he told her, his breath scented with whiskey. "That's what you need."

"What I need is for you to unhand me. Do it quickly, or I'll be forced to take drastic measures."

"What would those drastic measures be?"

"I might be forced to shoot you, Mr. McNamara. And what I aim at, I usually hit."

He laughed. "Is that right?"

Kelsey merely smiled. He would undoubtedly be amazed that it was her prowess with a gun that had first brought her to Lady Chamberlain's attention. They'd all been standing on the platform waiting for the train to Seattle when a thief stole the purse of the woman standing next to Kelsey. He then shot the woman's companion, an elderly gentleman, as he tried to make good his escape. Amid screams and panic Kelsey calmly pulled out her pistol. She waited until she had a clear shot, then she pulled the trigger, her bullet hitting the startled robber's gun from his hand.

She hadn't thought too much about it at the time. She'd grown up with a rifle and had never considered what effect shooting a man might have on city people. They were shocked! Astounded! Frightened! All except Lady Chamberlain, who turned to Kelsey and said simply, "I like a woman who knows how to defend herself. If you're looking for employment, miss, I'm looking for a suitable companion for my granddaughter."

Of course, most people wouldn't consider a gunslinging woman a suitable companion, but Lady Chamberlain was not most people. She was practicality itself. She knew her granddaughter would be susceptible to every fortune-hunting male around as soon as she came of age. Being in her seventies, Lady Chamberlain could protect her only so much. And she hated the thought of male bodyguards. Kelsey, or Orchid, as she had given her name to Lady Chamberlain, was "sent from heaven."

It bothered Kelsey a little that she'd falsified her identity. But she was bound and determined that her brother, Jace, and his despicable wife, Emerald, never find her. Rock Springs was only about thirty miles from Portland, after all, and news of one Kelsey Garrett could travel to Jace's ears fairly quickly. That was in fact why Kelsey had been heading to Seattle. She needed to put distance between herself and her power-wielding family.

But Agatha Chamberlain's offer had been too good to resist because Kelsey, above all else, wanted to find someone whom she could trust. Someone who believed in her. Lady Chamberlain had seen her at her worst, at least in society's eyes, and had applauded her for it. Kelsey had hired on as Charlotte's companion that very day.

The position had eased her loneliness. She'd left home in a fury, angry with her brother and his wretched, scheming wife, determined to make a life for herself somewhere else. She'd had two companions: her game little mare, Sadie Mae, and her rangy mutt, Maggie. But on Kelsey's first night riding alone she'd been accosted by two men who'd attempted to rob and kidnap her. She'd fired at them, and they'd returned fire, and Sadie Mae had bolted, Kelsey clinging to her like a burr. They rapidly outdistanced their pursuers and then Sadie Mae leapt over a narrow ravine, misjudged the distance, and stumbled. She went down, headfirst, throwing Kelsey in the process. Dazed, Kelsey awoke to the sound of pounding hoofbeats and jangling bridles—her pursuers. Before she could even understand what was happening, Maggie shot like a streak into the fray, growling and snapping viciously. She bit the nearest man in the ankle and he howled with pain and rage. A blast and the burning scent of cordite punctuated the end of Maggie's life.

After that Kelsey heard Sadie Mae thrashing and moaning in the ravine below. The first of the men's horses cleared the ravine. Through a sheen of cold tears Kelsey took careful aim. She had to force herself not to murder him in return. She blasted him in the arm, then the leg. Shrieking with pain, he raced away. The other man stayed on his side of the ravine.

Throughout that cold night Kelsey lay utterly still, waiting for one of them to return. The uninjured one did, just before dawn. Kelsey had lost her dog and her horse. She didn't feel inclined toward mercy. She leveled her rifle at the man's heart.

And then he smiled at her, raising a pistol. Even with evidence to the contrary he truly didn't believe she was an excellent shot; Kelsey could read it in his cruel, superior face. She fired a split second before he did. The look of surprise in his eyes was almost comical. His own shot went wild.

Kelsey took his horse and money and rode to the nearest town. His death was duly recorded in the city newspaper amid speculation that a bounty hunter had finally caught up with him. Why he'd been left for the buzzards was a question no one could answer.

That was four years earlier. A bitter beginning to her vagabond life. Since then, Kelsey had acquired a veneer of polish. She looked like a lady. She acted like one. She even lived like one. But she kept her rifle or derringer close at hand in case any man should make the fatal mistake of thinking she was as she appeared and then deciding to take advantage of her.

As Tyrone McNamara was trying to do at this very moment . . .

"Orchid," he murmured, tightening his grip.

Kelsey had made a serious mistake by listening to sixteen-year-old Charlotte's dreamy plans to find her a man. Her skin crawled beneath his tight grip. Even though the carriage was pulling to a stop before the grand front porch of Chamberlain Manor, and she suspected even a creature as loathsome as McNamara wouldn't attempt to rape her in view of all and sundry, Kelsey had to fight to keep herself from kneeing him in the crotch or squeezing her finger around the trigger of her pistol.

She gazed derisively at the mouth hovering over hers. "I have a derringer in my reticule."

"Really. Would you use it on me?"

"Yes," she answered honestly.

Tyrone shook his head in amazement. She was so unbelievably cool and collected. He'd fantasized about her, wondering how he could get his hands beneath her high-buttoned collar to her perfectly formed breasts, imagining what that auburn hair with its magenta lights would feel like, *look* like, if she would ever let it down from its net. And those eyes, so gray and frigid and full of mockery. Would they spark and burn with passion as he suspected?

He felt something nudge his ribs and looked down to see the barrel of the derringer placed firmly against his sternum. He was surprised, but not really alarmed. "You wouldn't shoot me," he said positively. "That would be murder."

Kelsey smiled faintly. "I won't shoot you unless I have to keep fighting you. *That* would be self-defense. I'm just warning you, Mr. McNamara."

The carriage lurched to a stop. Tyrone slowly slid away from her, unsure if she was teasing or not. But he had more than enough time to find out, he decided. Let her think she'd won this round. There was always another way to get inside a woman's drawers, and Gerrard Knight's wagered five hundred dollars was too sweet a pot to relinquish.

Ignoring the pistol aimed straight at his heart, Tyrone picked up her hand, touching it to his lips. "Will I see you again?"

"No." She swept out of the carriage and up the steps to the house, lifting a heavy brass knocker to announce that she was home. Tyrone watched her. He was too cocksure to be rebuffed by her tough stance. He would win her. It was only a matter of time.

Cora Lee, Agatha's downstairs maid, answered Kelsey's knock, swinging the door wide. "Good evenin', Miss Simpson. How was your night out?"

Kelsey yanked off her gloves and stuffed them in the

pocket of her cloak. She hated finery. She truly did. Maybe it was time to quit being Charlotte's companion and search out something else in life. She was twenty-eight. Certainly there was something out there, some vocation that would interest her. Though she didn't want a man, it did bother her to hear herself labeled "spinster." Spinsters were dried-up, passionless creatures who taught school and became librarians. God help her, she'd die before she fit that mold! There had to be more to life than just living day-to-day. Why hadn't she found her purpose yet?

Hearing Kelsey's tread on the stairs, Charlotte came bounding out of her bedroom, her blond hair tied with a blue ribbon, her lavender silk nightgown not at all the attire for Lady Chamberlain's granddaughter.

"Where did you get that?" Kelsey demanded.

"I bought it! Lord, I couldn't bear to lie in bed in a flannel gown. It ruins all my fantasies! Tell me, Orchid. What was he like? Did he kiss you? He did, didn't he? What was it like? Did it set you on fire?"

Kelsey laughed. "Not exactly. Now, give up on your matchmaking. When and if I find a man who sets me on fire, I surely won't tell you about it!"

"Why not?"

"Because you'd let the whole world know. I'd never have a moment's peace."

"I can't wait to be kissed," Charlotte told her.

Kelsey arched a brow at Charlotte's breathless tone. Agatha had sheltered her granddaughter as was the custom of her country, but Charlotte had grown up so naive that Kelsey worried over her. Most of the young girls of Portland society knew more about life than Charlotte. Some were even fast at the tender age of fifteen.

"Your time's coming. Your grandmother's invited half of Portland to your seventeenth birthday party."

"That's still two weeks away. I want something to happen now. Tell me about your kiss!" she insisted again.

"It was dreadful. He smashed his mouth on mine and his breath stank of whiskey."

"Oh."

Kelsey's eyes sparkled, but Charlotte didn't notice in the

dim light of the upper hallway. There was no harm in teasing her romantic young friend, was there? And Kelsey had suffered her share of unwanted advances. "And then he tried to stick his tongue in my mouth," she embellished.

Charlotte gasped, her hand flying to her lips. She dragged Kelsey into her room, closing the door quickly behind her. "What happened then?"

"Then he pushed me against the seat and swore he'd have me right there."

"What did you do?" she demanded, enthralled.

"I pulled out my gun and shot him. He's dead now."

"You're teasing me!" Charlotte shrieked, stamping her foot. When Kelsey started to laugh, she couldn't fight her own grin. "Okay, what really happened?"

"He did kiss me and he stank of whiskey. That's all."

"That's all? He didn't even try to kiss you again?"

"I threatened him with my derringer," Kelsey admitted.

"Oh, Orchid, you'll never get a man that way," Charlotte groaned.

"Exactly." Pointing to the clock on Charlotte's bedside, she said, "Let's get some sleep. It's late, and I know your grandmother wants to take you shopping in the morning."

"Are you coming with us?"

"Of course. Someone's got to keep you out of trouble."

The offices of Ezekiel Drummond were located on a posh corner just off Portland's Front Street. The building's staircase was marble, set off by a filigreed wrought-iron rail. Zeke's office was on the second floor at the end of the hall, where a pebbled glass window read DRUMMOND AND CO. in gold-leaf lettering. Above the door an electric light in the shape of a fluted bell left a pool of illumination on the polished marble floor. The building smelled of floor wax and money.

Sitting at his cherry-wood desk, Zeke leaned back in the chair and gazed thoughtfully at his guest. Jesse Danner stood by the inner office window, leaning an arm against the rich mahogany paneling, staring out at the street below. Zeke could tell by the harsh look on his face that Jesse was thinking about Nell again.

Little Nell, who'd run afoul of Montana Gray and died because of it.

It was because of Nell that Zeke had rescued Jesse and formed a partnership with him. It was because of Jesse that Zeke was where he was today: at the pinnacle of Portland society. Zeke belonged to the Arlington Club and the Portland Establishment. He went to all the right restaurants, and donated money to all the right charities. He was invited to parties and soirees and special events only the cream of society attended.

It was lucky that Montana Gray didn't know Zeke or remember Zeke's sister, Nell.

Clearing his throat, Zeke lifted a thin cheroot from the leather humidor on his desk, his gaze still resting on the man responsible for his change of fortune. He puffed on his cheroot. Danner's indolence was deceptive. He had an unusual grace of movement that turned women's heads. Zeke was truly envious of Jesse's innate sexuality, a trait he longed to possess himself but didn't. Zeke was too gawky and awkward. Even the trappings of wealth hadn't made up for what nature had neglected to bestow upon him.

Not so Jesse. Women were drawn to him. Like Lila Gray had been drawn to him. Like Nell had trusted him . . .

His lashes thinning against the curling smoke, Zeke allowed himself painful thoughts of his sister. When Montana found out Nell was the main reason Jesse had been able to purchase the park block away from him, he'd ordered his boys to kill her. The night Zeke found Jesse near drowned in the Willamette, he'd also found his sister's stiff, half-frozen body. Nell had been an insignificant bookkeeper at Montana's company. A nobody. Someone to remove when she became an obstacle in his path to success. Only Zeke, and Nell's desolate husband, Thomas, had mourned her passing.

And, of course, Jesse.

Zeke suffered a pang of sadness and remorse. Jesse blamed himself entirely for her death. However, Zeke didn't blame Jesse. In her own sweetly naive way, Nell had been trying to stop Montana's ruthless, and many times

19

unlawful, acquisition of real estate. Working for the man, she'd stumbled upon the avaricious cruelty of his methods, and she'd determined to stop him. She'd tried several times, with the help of others, but she'd failed. Just as she'd failed when Montana had caught her helping Jesse.

It wasn't Jesse's fault.

Zeke had said the same to Jesse hundreds—thousands— of times, but Jesse wouldn't listen. He burned for vengeance. He wanted to ruin Montana, *and* his self-serving bitch of a wife. Zeke, luckily, had talked Jesse out of killing the man outright. There were ways to trap an avaricious man like Gray without resorting to violence.

Not that Zeke wouldn't gladly see Montana strung up by a rope, but he valued Jesse's friendship too much to lose him too. Nell was gone. Sacrificing another wouldn't bring her back.

Of course, Jesse could change his mind at any moment. Lord knew Jesse was incredibly ruthless when he chose to be. He was passionate and loyal and consumed with remorse. He'd worked five long years in San Francisco to create a fortune to match Montana's. Zeke, stationed in Portland, had kept him duly informed. It had been the last straw when Montana managed to acquire the same park block Jesse had purchased on that fateful trip to Portland, the same park block Nell had died for. Now Jesse intended to ruin Montana forever by using the man's own greed against him.

Unfortunately, there was just one minor hitch.

Zeke cleared his throat again. "You should have made your move into society years ago. It'll take too long now, unless you marry somebody with a pile of money and connections. You know that." When Jesse didn't answer, Zeke added, "There's no better choice than Charlotte Chamberlain."

Jesse turned his head and scowled at Zeke, his arms crossed over his chest. From a photograph taken of Jesse when he was younger, Zeke knew Al's huge fists had permanently changed his looks. Jesse was "pretty" no longer. His jaw had been broken along with his nose. The perfect symmetry was gone, yet for all that, he was even more attractive now at thirty. He might not be pretty, but his face was still handsome, more masculine. His teeth had survived the beating except for a few broken molars, and his eyes were still sharp and clear and blue. He looked more dangerous now. Tougher. Zeke hadn't known Jesse before, but he guessed there'd been some major changes within the man as well. The humor that had emanated so clearly from the snapshot was gone. In its place was cold cynicism.

"What the hell are you talking about?" Jesse asked softly.

"Lady Chamberlain's granddaughter, Charlotte. I saw her at the concert in the park last week. She's lovely. And socially one of the best catches in the city. You should marry her."

"No."

Zeke sighed. "If you want Gray to know who's responsible for his financial collapse, you're going to have to show yourself. I don't know why you're so damned worried about your brother finding out—"

"Shut up, Zeke. I don't want any of my family to know where I am."

"They might not recognize you anyway," Zeke pointed out. "How many years has it been since you've seen them? Thirteen? And your looks have changed."

"Thanks to Montana Gray," he murmured dryly.

"Samuel Danner is fairly well known in Portland," Zeke went on, undeterred, bringing up Jesse's younger brother. "He's an excellent lawyer and businessman. You're bound to run into him sooner or later."

"I want it to be later. After I take care of the Grays."

Zeke frowned. Jesse had returned to Portland about a month before, and he'd insisted on keeping a low profile. No one knew he was the man behind Drummond & Co.

"I don't see how you can do that. Montana Gray thinks you're dead. You need him to realize you're alive and well. The ghost of retribution come back to haunt him. He needs to remember you."

"He won't." Jesse was positive. "He barely looked at

me that night. Just ordered me to be killed. Besides," he added with a faint smile, "I look different now."

"Not that different. Given a little prodding, he'll certainly remember your name. No," he went on, as if the matter were decided, "Charlotte is the best answer."

"If you're so dead set on Charlotte Chamberlain, why don't you marry her yourself?" Jesse suggested irritably. The last thing he wanted was to tangle with another society woman.

"Because you won't be able to live with yourself unless you can help make up for Nell's senseless death," Zeke said softly.

Jesse stiffened. Zeke's words stabbed into him, as they were meant to.

"Besides, *you're* the one who needs to become socially respectable," Zeke reminded him quickly, easing over the moment. "I don't know why you tried to hide out all these years anyway."

"Because I didn't want to tip off Gray." *And I didn't want any interference from my family,* Jesse added to himself.

Marry Charlotte Chamberlain? A girl less than seventeen years old? Good God! Not that he gave a damn about Charlotte. He didn't care what happened to any *lady.* He'd learned from Lila just how treacherous they could be.

"I don't need any woman to help me," said Jesse. "I'll get Gray by myself."

"You need Gray to recognize you, Jesse. Recognize you in a position of power. The only way you're going to do that is to become a part of Portland society. We've discussed all this before," Zeke added impatiently. "I can get you an invitation to the party Lady Chamberlain's throwing in honor of Charlotte's seventeenth birthday."

"I would rather cut off my right hand than go to any party Lady Chamberlain, or any other so-called lady in this town, would throw."

"Well, you need to win one of society's sweet little darlings," Zeke went on relentlessly. "If you want real revenge, you've got to do it my way. If you're powerful enough socially, you could kill Montana Gray with your bare hands and get away with it.''

Jesse swore violently. He hated being reminded of the inequities in the political and social systems. He loathed having to listen to Zeke, though he knew his friend was right. He'd spent too many years building his fortune back up to derail this plan for revenge now.

"Isn't there any way other than marriage?"

"You could buy favors from the politicians," Zeke answered as he'd done countless other times. "But the fastest way would be to marry someone with money and connections."

"Who's to say one of those sweet darlings will marry me, even if I ask?" Jesse demanded, pacing restlessly across the room.

"They'll marry you." Zeke's tone changed, causing Jesse to stop right in front of his desk. He watched Zeke puff on his cheroot. "Don't look at me like that," Zeke added, smiling. "You'll have them panting after you, and you know it."

"Go to hell," Jesse growled.

"Women want you, Jesse. All you have to do is throw out a little charm. Try not to be so cynical and impatient. Relax, for God's sake, and make a woman feel like a woman. Seduce her."

"That's your advice?" One black brow arched.

"It worked with Lila Gray, didn't it?"

"I'm not exactly sure who seduced whom," Jesse bit out harshly. "I can't do it, Zeke. I can't tie myself down."

"You don't have to be faithful."

"I don't have to be married at all!"

"Go to the party, Jesse. See Charlotte Chamberlain for yourself. She's extraordinarily beautiful, and from all accounts just waiting for a Prince Charming to come along and sweep her off her feet."

Jesse's scowl deepened and he swore a string of epithets that made Zeke grin. Finally, Jesse had heard him.

The Chamberlain party was in the ballroom of the Portland Hotel and it spilled out onto the upper balcony that overlooked the hotel's entrance two floors below. The dance floor was gray and white squares of marble and the overhead chandelier was seven levels of gaslit candles and shining, tinkling prisms. A group of musicians was assembled on a raised dais in the corner. Satin ribbons in pink and lavender and silver festooned the curtained alcoves, wall sconces, and rosewood tables clustered around the edges of the room.

Kelsey stood next to the musicians, a crystal cup of red punch cradled between her palms. Her mane of hair was pulled into its ubiquitous net, and her cream-colored dress rode high on her neck, clipped by a diamond brooch. She wore no earrings, and the cool patrician look on her face discouraged dance partners. Not that she wanted to dance. She was suffering through these hours, trying to appear entertained for Charlotte's sake, when all she really wanted to do was escape and take Justice, the Chamberlain's gray stallion, for a race across the flowing grounds of Agatha's estate.

Kelsey smiled in anticipation. Though Lady Chamberlain generally indulged Kelsey's passion for horses, she'd been in such a fluster over the party that Kelsey had been forced to delay her ride and help with the preparations. Kelsey had organized everything, from the engraved invitations to the sparkling champagne currently spewing from the mouth of the silver fish fountain on the center table, where the champagne was currently collecting in the moat around the base of the fountain and spilling over the edge in ten silvery streams into another wider receptacle.

Several people were dipping their glasses beneath the trickling champagne. Kelsey smiled to herself. She hoped Charlotte appreciated the time and effort, not to mention money, her grandmother had spent making sure the party was perfect.

"Hello, Orchid." A smooth, familiar male voice interrupted her thoughts. "May I have the next dance?"

Tyrone McNamara. Kelsey inwardly groaned. She'd had half a mind to scratch his name from the guest list, but since she'd already scratched Samuel Danner's, a necessity since Samuel would have undoubtedly recognized her, she'd left Tyrone's name on to keep Agatha from asking too many questions.

Tyrone led her onto the dance floor. Though he attempted to pull her against his chest, she kept her arms rigidly straight, her gray eyes simmering with stubbornness. Kelsey moved woodenly, skillfully parrying Tyrone's every attempt to draw her near. As soon as the music stopped, she made a beeline to the powder room. Only a few more hours and this dreadful affair would be over.

Heaving a sigh, she caught sight of her reflection in the gilded mirror hung on the flower-printed wall. She looked furious. Surprised, she purposely smoothed her brow. Tyrone and his kind got under her skin. Lord, how she wished she could be left alone!

Her mother, Lucinda Garrett, had tried to arrange marriage after marriage for Kelsey, but to no avail. From the time she was barely fifteen years old, Kelsey had endured a barrage of suitors. When Lucinda died, Jace took over the role of matchmaker. As a means of escape, Kelsey had accepted Harrison Danner's offer of marriage. She and Harrison had been friends, nothing more, but she'd thought she might be happy with him.

But that engagement ended when Harrison met up with exotic Miracle Jones, a half-breed Chinook Indian who was as wonderful as she was beautiful. Kelsey liked Miracle even after she discovered Miracle was her half sister, a product of Kelsey's philandering father's love for Miracle's Chinook mother. Unfortunately, Jace hadn't felt the same. The enmity Harrison's love for Miracle had inspired in him had been the final reason Kelsey had to leave town. She was fed up with her brother in particular, and men in general. All she wanted was peace.

Only one man had ever captured Kelsey's heart, and the memory was enough to make her twist with pain and shame. Not that she had anything to be ashamed of, far from it. She was as untouched today as she'd been when she was dreaming over Jesse Danner at the tender age of fourteen.

Kelsey groaned aloud at her foolishness. Jesse Danner. Lord sakes! Of all the men to fantasize about, why had she chosen the most shallow womanizing renegade of all? Luckily, Jesse had been totally unaware of his effect on her. The most notorious Danner son, he had provided Kelsey's thoughts with romantic visions for years—until she'd finally realized how foolish it was to pine for a man who barely knew she existed, a man who moreover had a reputation as tainted as Curley Wythecomb's homemade wine!

Jesse had been seventeen when he left Rock Springs. He'd never looked back. And he'd never looked once at Kelsey. She was a Garrett, after all, and Danners steered clear of Garretts whenever possible. But Kelsey had been smitten with Jesse, even though his philandering ways were well known, even though trouble followed him like a dark cloud, even though "scandalous" was the term generally attached to his name. Even though Alice McIntyre's father had blasted him with a shotgun for defiling his one and only daughter.

Now, as Kelsey narrowed her eyes on her mirrored reflection, she was glad she'd gotten over her adolescent infatuation. It was lucky that what beauty she possessed had come later. Jesse had known her only as a skinny, knock-kneed kid; he'd never seen her grown-up. His reputation being what it was, she wasn't at all convinced he wouldn't have used her infatuation against her, had he but known of it.

Not that he would want her now, or, God forbid, that she would still want him! She'd met other men of his ilk, like Tyrone, and couldn't stand them. And like the two bastards who'd tried to kidnap her, men were interested in only one thing.

No, she didn't want any man in her life. Ever.

Charlotte was dancing with a dark-haired gentleman in a black suit when Kelsey returned to the ballroom. Kelsey frowned, unable to see the man's face. He moved with unconscious grace, his arm wrapped possessively around Charlotte's small waist. There was something familiar about him, but she could see him only from the back.

"How do you think it's going so far?" Agatha Chamberlain asked, commanding Kelsey's attention.

"I think it's a rousing success," Kelsey told her with a smile.

"Charlotte seems to be having a grand time. You did make certain there were no fortune hunters on that list, didn't you, Orchid?"

"Every person invited possesses a healthy bank statement, I'm sure," Kelsey answered dryly.

"What about Gerrard Knight? I've heard he's a notorious gambler."

"With enough money to lose steadily for a year and still buy and sell half of Portland."

Lady Chamberlain sniffed her disdain. "And Charles DeWitt?"

"As rich as he is ugly."

"Do you really think he's ugly, my dear? His face has a certain character, don't you think?"

She sounded so anxious, Kelsey reserved her opinion that Charles DeWitt was homely enough to be mistaken for a mule. Besides, Charles *was* nice. Much nicer than most of the wealthy young men Lady Chamberlain allowed in her granddaughter's circle of friends.

"Who's Charlotte dancing with now?" Agatha asked suddenly.

The dark-haired man was leading Charlotte toward one of the curtained alcoves. Kelsey's brows rose. This was certainly not the done thing, especially in Lady Chamberlain's eyes! "I'll find out," she said in a steely voice.

Gathering her silk skirts, she swept across the room, but the dark-haired man was met by another gentleman, who spoke a few words to him, then led him in another direction, leaving Charlotte alone and bereft and looking piqued.

Her blue eyes were flashing when Kelsey reached her. "Of all the nerve! That man, Mr. Drummond, stole my dance partner from me!"

"It didn't appear that you were dancing anymore," Kelsey pointed out.

"He was going to kiss me in the alcove! He told me he was!"

"At least you were forewarned," Kelsey said, slightly alarmed. "Who is he?"

"I don't know his name yet." She spoke in a breathless voice that convinced Kelsey she was already spinning romantic dreams around this unknown lothario.

"Charlotte, I don't think it's wise to let some man take you to an alcove and kiss you when you don't even know his name."

"I don't need to know his name. I know I'm in love."

"You silly featherbrain!" Kelsey laughed in amusement. "Be careful or you'll find yourself in serious trouble. What about the other men you've danced with? Haven't you been interested in any of them?"

Charlotte's fine brow furrowed. "Well, Mr. DeWitt was very nice, but he's so—so—" She flushed.

"Ugly?" Kelsey supplied.

"Oh, I can't believe you would say that aloud! It's indecent!"

"It's the truth." Both Kelsey and Charlotte collapsed into laughter.

Across the room, Jesse Danner stared at the two women. Charlotte Chamberlain was everything Zeke had said she was: sweet, beautiful, virginal, wealthy. And she was a few other things besides: silly, naive, and way, way too young! He'd forgotten what seventeen-year-old girls were like. Lord, save him from ridiculous innocents.

The other woman interested him, however. She was a spinster, if you could believe the way she dressed. And Zeke had assured him that Orchid Simpson was indeed a spinster. God, she looked familiar. Had he met her somewhere before? Surely he would have remembered the name Orchid.

He gazed at her intently, frown lines etched across his brow. No, he didn't know her. He would have remembered. But that russet-colored hair. He wished he could see it unbound.

"Tell me more about Miss Simpson," he said now to Zeke, who was still fuming that Jesse had had the gall to actually drag Charlotte to the alcove. Well, the little lady had been willing, hadn't she? Jesse asked himself, stifling his conscience. So what if it wasn't exactly protocol. He was certain he would have saved a lot of wasted time if he'd been able to have his way with her for a few minutes. Wasn't that what Zeke wanted?

"Miss Simpson?" Zeke was looking down his nose.

"The lady with Charlotte Chamberlain."

"I know who she is. You aren't interested in *her,* are you?"

"I just wanted to know more about her."

Zeke's gaze fell thoughtfully on Orchid Simpson. Her face was truly gorgeous, he could admit that. But the woman was a dried-up, passionless thing if he'd ever seen one. He doubted even Jesse could light a fire of desire inside her.

"She's been a subject of interest ever since she became Charlotte Chamberlain's companion," Zeke said. "Lady Chamberlain dotes on her. I wouldn't be surprised if there's a sizable chunk of inheritance coming her way when the lady dies."

"Where does she come from?"

Zeke shrugged. "You'd have to ask her. She's extremely mysterious, and from what I've heard, cold as the North Sea."

"She doesn't look cold."

Zeke gazed at him in amazement, but Jesse's attention was focused on Orchid. "She doesn't?"

He shook his head slowly.

"Are you more interested in her than in Charlotte?"

"Definitely."

Zeke blinked rapidly. This was a turn he hadn't expected. "Well, she certainly should be wealthy one day, if the old lady doesn't cut her out of her will. She's also welcomed in all the right social circles. But I'd venture she won't be so easily convinced you're the man for her, if you know what I mean . . ."

"You think I'd need more than 'a little charm' to seduce her?" Jesse glanced his way, laughter in his eyes.

Zeke sniffed. "Even you have your limits."

Jesse threw back his head and laughed, drawing the attention of those around him to the deep, rolling sound. Kelsey glanced over sharply, her nerves tense, but the dark-haired man was just turning away, clapping his friend, Mr. Drummond, on the shoulder.

"I told Charlotte I would visit her soon," Jesse assured Zeke as they headed for the door. "Maybe I should stick to that plan."

"A wise idea, my friend," Zeke agreed, glancing over his shoulder to see Orchid Simpson politely shake her head in response to the request for another dance from the rakish Gerrard Knight. Zeke had the distinct feeling *that* lady was trouble.

And it bothered him the way her gaze narrowed on Jesse, almost as if she knew he was a threat.

"Blast," Zeke muttered as they walked downstairs.

"What's wrong?" asked Jesse.

"Nothing. But I think you should move rather quickly on Charlotte. Don't waste time."

"I'll take it under advisement," Jesse drawled, shaking his head. Sometimes Zeke could be fussier than a mother hen.

"And stay away from Miss Simpson," Zeke added with sudden fervor. "For your own good."

## 2

Kelsey watched in amusement as Charlotte dashed from one end of her bedroom to the other, checking her hair and her dress and her face, then her hair again. High color glowed in her cheeks. Her eyes glittered like sapphires.

"What time is it?" she asked, pacing across the carpet.

"Almost seven. I can't imagine why you're so excited over Charles DeWitt, but I'm happy for you."

Charlotte laughed and clapped her hands together in delight. "Charles isn't picking me up tonight! I just told Grandmama that to make sure she'd let me go! Since you're my chaperone, it should hardly matter anyway. Once he's here you'll love him too!"

"Who?" Kelsey demanded with growing dread.

"Jesse Danner. That's his name. He wrote me a card and told me he was Ezekiel Drummond's friend. Then he signed his name: Jesse Danner. Isn't it gorgeous!"

*"Jesse Danner?"*

Charlotte turned at the tone of Orchid's voice. My stars, but Orchid had fairly shrieked and now she looked ready to faint dead away. "Do you know him?"

Kelsey couldn't speak. There couldn't be two of them, could there? But there must be!

"Orchid . . . ?"

"No, I—uh—don't know him." But now she remembered how familiar the man at the dance had looked. Could it be Jesse? Impossible! Yet . . . yet . . .

Charlotte dashed to the door and hollered, "Maizie! Bring the smelling salts."

Kelsey took hold of herself. "For God's sake, Charlotte. I'm not going to faint."

"Are you sure?" A doubtful frown crossed her face. "You look wretched."

"Thanks." Kelsey's legs shook as she walked to the over-stuffed chair near the fireplace in Charlotte's sitting room. It was a coincidence, that was all. Jesse Danner was gone. He'd been missing for nearly thirteen years. He could very easily be dead. In any event, he was not the type of man to show up at a social function.

"You cannot go out with this Mr. Danner," she said when she'd regained her composure. At that moment the upstairs maid burst into the room, looking panicked. Kelsey waved her away impatiently. "I'm fine, Maizie. Charlotte just got hysterical." When the maid closed the door behind her, Kelsey went on. "You don't even know this man. He could be just what your grandmother fears most—a fortune hunter."

"He's not. I know he's not. And you'll be with me as my chaperone, Orchid. You can protect me if he should . . ." She blushed. "Well, you know. But I would love him to kiss me. I'm absolutely *dying* for it! You will give us a few moments alone, won't you?"

"Only if God strikes me dead," she muttered furiously.

"Orchid!"

"Charlotte, you silly nincompoop! You have no idea what this man has in mind. For all you know—"

Downstairs, the deep chimes of the front doorbell pealed through the huge three-storied manor. Cora Lee's footsteps could be heard moving steadily across the entry hall to answer the door.

Kelsey leapt to her feet, but Charlotte grabbed her arm in excitement, yanking her back down into the cushions. "What are you going to do?"

"Get rid of him." Kelsey struggled to her feet once more, escaping Charlotte's second attempt to waylay her.

"No!" Charlotte was adamant. "I won't let you! I'm going to see him and that's final."

She rushed out of the room, nearly tripping Kelsey in her haste. Hot on her heels, Kelsey fairly flew down the curved stairway, but even so she was too late to stop Charlotte, who'd forgotten every one of the manners Lady Chamberlain had drilled into her since birth and raced headlong into the drawing room at the northwest corner of the main floor.

The drawing room where Cora Lee had shown Mr. Jesse Danner.

Kelsey's heels clicked across the marble foyer. She was in a fine fury, both at Charlotte and this mysterious Mr. Danner who had won her young charge with scarcely a dozen words spoken between them. He was not the Jesse Danner of her youth, but he was most assuredly trouble.

She stopped short inside the double doors that Charlotte had thrown wide in her excitement and lifted her chin in practiced schoolmarmish style. Charlotte was hovering by the silk-draped windows on the north side of the marble fireplace, one hand laid across her bosom as if she could scarcely believe her startled eyes. She was staring unabashedly at the man who stood with one foot on the polished andiron, one arm lying gracefully across the ornately carved cream-painted mantel. When Kelsey entered, he turned toward her expectantly.

Kelsey felt the blood rush from her head so quickly her scalp tingled. Lord, it *was* Jesse Danner! He was older, tougher-looking than she remembered, but it was most definitely the same Jesse Danner from Rock Springs.

She was about to faint. She'd never fainted in her life, but she was about to now. Oh, my *God!* she thought incoherently.

"Miss Simpson?" Jesse drawled politely.

He didn't recognize her. Kelsey would have laughed if she'd had any breath left to laugh with. A soft gasp escaped her mouth just as Cora Lee closed the doors behind them. Starting at the sound, Kelsey fought her dizziness and rising hysteria. Her lungs felt constricted, unable to draw air. Lord sakes, she might truly swoon!

"Mr. Danner?" she choked out, seeking a chair with as much grace as she could muster. She sank into the depths of the green brocade cushions.

His eyes narrowed, thick black lashes pulling together, a line of puzzlement drawing between his brows. "Miss— Simpson?"

"Yes. Orchid—Orchid Simpson." Heat rushed back into her cheeks in a flood, hectic color heightening her cheekbones.

"Charlotte says you're to be our chaperone. I assure you, I won't do her any harm."

Was there laughter hidden in his words? Kelsey drew another deep breath, unable to take her eyes off him. Blue eyes regarded her evenly. He'd turned out more handsome than even she would have suspected, she realized numbly. That smile, those eyes, that arrogance. Luckily, he didn't seem to have any idea who she was.

"Mr. Danner, I never take any man's assurances."

"Orchid!" Charlotte warned desperately.

"Where did you plan to take Charlotte this evening?" she asked, recovering herself with each rapid breath she took. She ignored Charlotte's flashing eyes and angry flush.

He shrugged. "A carriage ride through the park? Or there's an excellent new restaurant on Third Street."

"Cavendish's," Kelsey agreed. "It sounds suitable. We'll forgo the carriage ride through the park, thank you."

"You don't trust me at all, do you?" he said in an amused drawl.

"Not a bit, Mr. Danner."

He laughed. The sound grated on Kelsey's nerves. She remembered his laughter. The dancing eyes and sweet flattery he'd used on every woman he ever met! Oh, he'd been accused of terrible things by scorned women. Everything from rape to robbery to murder. She'd never fully believed the rumors, but now, with Charlotte's future at stake, she let doubt creep in. She would never let him ruin Charlotte. She'd die first. And she saw no reason to keep her feelings a secret.

"Charlotte's a very wealthy young woman, prone to the scourge of fortune hunters," Kelsey remarked coolly.

"Orchid!" Charlotte shrieked.

"I won't have her taken advantage of in any way. She's an honorable young woman, and her grandmother wishes her to stay that way."

The amusement faded from his eyes, replaced by speculation and something Kelsey couldn't quite identify. That *something* sent an icy shiver of dread down her spine. Jesse Danner was dangerous.

Charlotte was apoplectic with humiliation and fury. "Orchid, how could you?" she cried.

"I won't do anything to besmirch Miss Chamberlain's honor," Jesse drawled, but the tone of his voice was edged with steel. "How could I, with a lioness guarding her so zealously? Are you ready?" he asked, turning to Charlotte. While Kelsey watched in horror, Jesse gently touched Charlotte's arm, guiding her toward the door.

"Y-yes," Charlotte stammered. "I'll get my cloak."

Kelsey rose from the chair to follow Charlotte. She could tell by the way Charlotte's shoulders quivered that she was in a fulminating rage. Kelsey couldn't blame her. She would have been furious if anyone had treated her so high-handedly.

Charlotte wouldn't look at Kelsey as she hurried down the front steps and to the waiting carriage. Kelsey strode down the porch steps, gathering her skirts at the waiting carriage. Before she could climb inside, however, a hard masculine hand spun her around.

"You can interfere all you like, Miss Simpson," Jesse's voice said quietly in her ear. "But the lady's decision is entirely up to her."

Kelsey's heart beat painfully. She pulled her elbow from his grasp with slow deliberation and shot him a glance through her lashes, just enough to read his expression. He was completely, implacably determined.

"Are you saying you're going to ask for her?"

"I'm saying she wants me, and there's not a helluva lot you can do about it."

Her gray eyes grew stormy. This was a new Jesse Danner, one who'd lost any sense of value he'd once possessed. "Isn't there? Well, you don't know me very well, Mr. Danner."

"Nor do I want to, *Miss* Simpson."

The way he said it was a slap in the face, a reminder of her spinsterhood. Kelsey could bear almost anything but a man's passing judgment on her. Especially Jesse Danner! "If you dare ask for Charlotte's hand in marriage, I'll cut you down," she warned tautly. "Lady Chamberlain listens to me. She'll refuse you."

Jesse's eyes grew hooded and he focused his gaze on her tightly set mouth. "Then maybe I'll take your advice."

"What advice was that?"

"I'll destroy the lady's honor. The good Lady Chamberlain might be begging me to offer marriage then."

Kelsey's lips parted in outrage. "You're unspeakable!"

"In fact, it might be a good idea. . . ." His gaze lifted to touch on Charlotte, whose bright face was peering anxiously through the carriage window.

"As soon as I tell Charlotte your plan, she'll never see you again!" Kelsey hissed.

"Want to bet?"

He was so utterly sure of his charms, she wanted to scream in frustration. Instead, she leveled angry gray eyes on his deep blue ones. "If that's a challenge, I'll make certain you lose."

He grinned.

"Orchid!" Charlotte rapped on the window, her voice tinny from inside the carriage. "What's taking so long?"

Kelsey's gloved hand twisted the carriage's lever handle. Jesse's hand closed over hers. Kelsey froze, yanking her fingers from beneath his. He opened the door, extending a palm to help her inside. Kelsey gathered her skirts and climbed up the two tiny steps, ignoring him.

He settled himself on the luxurious squabs opposite Charlotte and Kelsey, his gaze directed at Charlotte, sending her a smile so dangerously packed with sexuality, Kelsey could almost feel its imprint.

Charlotte's eyes grew dreamy.

Kelsey ground her teeth. How could she have ever imagined she loved Jesse Danner? He was a rogue and a rascal and he had no conscience at all! She would rather die a horrible death than let him have Charlotte. She would rather bed that horribly lecherous Tyrone McNamara than let him have Charlotte. She would rather go home to Rock Springs, and face Jace, and Emerald, and everyone else than let him have Charlotte!

She had to stop him!

Feeling Jesse's gaze on her, Kelsey leveled him an icy look. *I'm going to make your life hell, Mr. Danner,* she silently told him.

His mouth twitched in response, almost as if he were looking forward to it.

Dinner was a disaster. Jesse charmed and teased Charlotte until the poor child was so lovestruck, her lips were parted in ecstasy and her eyes were full of stars. Kelsey was sick to her stomach and had to keep her gaze centered solely on her plate. A knot of anger and determination hardened within her. She would stop him. For Charlotte's sake.

On the ride home she thought she'd go mad listening to Charlotte giggle and squeal. Several times Kelsey shot Jesse a lethal glance from the corners of her eyes, but he was being a perfect gentleman. At least his hands were where they were supposed to be. And every time he caught her look, he stared right back at her, all innocence, as if he were entirely blameless for the devastatingly miserable evening.

She wanted to wring his neck.

At Lady Chamberlain's front door Kelsey alit as if she had wings on her feet. She stormed up the walk, so furious she could scarcely see straight. But when she glanced back she found she was alone. Charlotte had stayed in the carriage with Jesse.

She swept back in fine fury, yanking open the carriage door. Jesse had Charlotte bent over his arms, kissing her passionately. Charlotte's breasts were threatening to spill from their tight bodice. Jesse's hard brown fingers surrounded her rib cage, less than an inch from the soft, velvet-covered mounds.

"Let her go!" Kelsey shouted in outrage.

Deliberately, as if he couldn't bear to unhand her, Jesse's lips slowly lifted from Charlotte's. He gazed down at her with such desire, Kelsey felt it like a physical blow. Dazzled, Charlotte exhaled a sigh of pure longing.

"You'd better get inside," Jesse told her tenderly.

"That would be a good idea," Kelsey agreed evenly.

In a daze, Charlotte floated up the walk. Kelsey didn't bother to shoot Jesse a look of loathing; battle lines had already been drawn.

She felt his gaze on her back as she marched stiffly up the walk behind Charlotte. It was like a heat wave, gathering strength, spreading across her skin. Irritated, she slammed the door behind her, then leaned against it, gathering her breath.

"If you ever do that to me again, I'll never speak to you!" Charlotte declared, her blue eyes swimming with accusations and hurt. "How could you, Orchid? How could you?"

"How could I what?"

"Discourage the only man I've ever been in love with!"

Charlotte didn't wait for an answer as her dainty feet flew up the stairs. Her bedroom door slammed.

Shaking her head, Kelsey climbed the steps on leaden legs.

\*    \*    \*

37

The following three weeks were the most infuriating of Kelsey's whole life. She was alternately boiling with rage or sick with worry. Jesse infiltrated their house like a bad smell. There was no getting rid of him. The more Kelsey decimated his character, the more staunchly Charlotte defended it.

Relations between the two women disintegrated until Kelsey and Charlotte were scarcely speaking to each other, a situation that made Kelsey's heart bleed, yet only tightened her resolve to get the better of Jesse.

Lady Chamberlain viewed the whole disaster with mixed emotions. Charlotte was so infatuated with Jesse that the fair-minded dowager didn't want to believe Kelsey's vituperative opinion. Yet, she couldn't ignore it completely.

"He's after her money. He as much as told me so!" Kelsey declared for about the thousandth time one evening as she paced rapidly from one end of the drawing room to the other.

Charlotte was not present, having locked herself in her room after another fight with Kelsey. Her brow furrowed, Lady Agatha Chamberlain looked over the top of her delicate china teacup and sighed. "Do you think there's any chance he loves Charlotte just a little?"

"No. He's a ladies' man. I've heard rumors about him!"

"Rumors aren't always the truth."

"They are in this case! Why are you defending him?" Kelsey demanded. "I thought you wanted me to protect Charlotte!"

Agatha smiled. Her skin was wrinkled and soft, a total contrast to the dynamic woman inside such a frail-looking body. "I do. It's just that the child thinks she's in love with him, and he's never been anything but the soul of courtesy and discretion when he's here."

"'The soul of courtesy and discretion.'" Kelsey swallowed the swear words that rose in her throat like bile. "That's just what he's let you see!" She snatched up a picture of Charlotte from the inlaid rosewood desk. "He said he was going to win her, even if he had to dishonor her to do it!"

Lady Chamberlain sat very stiffly, weighing her words.

She couldn't understand why Orchid was so utterly hysterical about this man. If he were a cad, time would bear that out. Meanwhile, Orchid could take excellent care of Charlotte; Lady Chamberlain depended on her to do so. "I don't believe he'd stoop to dishonoring her," she said primly.

Kelsey stared at her, aghast. "Have you fallen for his charm too?"

Her laughter tinkled. "I've lived a lot of years, Orchid, and I've met a lot of men. He cannot be as bad as you say, or I would have seen it already. No, you're blinded by emotion. Heavens, girl, you act like a woman scorned!"

"Lady Chamberlain!"

"Jesse Danner may be many things, but he's not poor. I have Ezekiel Drummond's word on that, and I've never known him to lie."

"How well do you know Ezekiel Drummond?"

"He's a member of the Arlington Club, and a long-standing supporter of—"

"I know, I know." Kelsey cut her off, her own manners deserting her in her anxiety. "So you will continue to allow Charlotte to see *him?*"

"If you mean Mr. Danner, the answer is yes. If I don't let her, I'm afraid she might find a way all on her own." She sighed. "Then she undoubtedly will be dishonored."

Kelsey swept across the room, her skirts rustling with her fury and fear. She couldn't bear it. "Please excuse me," she murmured tautly, needing some fresh air. She stormed through the double doors to the foyer. Unfortunately she ran straight into Jesse, who had just been shown inside the house by Cora Lee.

They eyed each other narrowly, adversaries locked in battle. Kelsey's glare was cold and angry; Jesse's smirkingly triumphant. Her mind devised new and imaginative forms of torture.

Hands clenched, she strode upstairs. She would prove to Agatha what a miserable scourge he was. It would be easy. All she had to do was send a wire to his family, telling them where he was. The Danners would then descend on him and reveal his past in all its ruinous glory.

Kelsey entertained that delicious notion for about ten

seconds. No. She couldn't expose him that way because the Danners would also recognize her, and then she would have to face Jace and Emerald and she just didn't have the stomach for it. Besides, what would the truth gain her? Charlotte would undoubtedly find Jesse's unsavory past romantic, and Lady Chamberlain would be delighted when she met the other Danners, who were all noteworthy citizens of Rock Springs.

Frustrated, Kelsey smacked her fist into her palm. But she could call his bluff. She could *threaten* to expose him! Since he didn't know she was a Garrett, he couldn't exact the same revenge. He would wonder how she'd come by her knowledge, but he'd never know. It would be sweet revenge indeed, to see the look of stupefaction and anger on his face!

Returning downstairs, she waited for him outside the drawing room, finalizing her plan. She could hear his low voice conversing with Lady Chamberlain. Charlotte would soon be alerted that her beloved was here, and then Kelsey would lose her chance. Ducking her head inside the room, she smiled beatifically. "Mr. Danner? Would you mind stepping into the morning room? I'd like a word with you."

His eyes narrowed instantly. He didn't trust her sudden benevolence. Realizing she'd overdone it, Kelsey let the smile fall. "I promise it won't take long."

"If you'll excuse me," he said to Lady Chamberlain.

"Not at all." Agatha frowned at Kelsey and shook her head ever so slightly when Jesse wasn't looking.

Kelsey didn't heed the warning. She was going to be as ruthless as Jesse in winning this game. She led the way to the morning room, which was cold and neglected at this time of day. No fire had been lit since early that morning and electricity, though a glorious innovation, had not found its way into Lady Chamberlain's environs yet. Agatha was slow to change.

Kelsey quietly latched the door behind them as soon as Jesse was inside.

"Please, sit down," she invited him.

"I'd rather stand, thank you," he returned politely.

He wore black, the color of his suit exactly matching his

raven hair. His collar and cuffs were snowy white. The contrast set off his swarthy good looks and heightened the dramatic blue of his eyes. He was handsome enough to take a woman's breath away, yet he looked vastly different than she remembered. His nose had been broken, she realized now, examining him carefully. And one cheek bore an indentation, as if the bone had been crushed and hadn't knit quite properly. And his mouth was more . . . more sensual than she remembered. Thinner, the lips tighter. He looked rougher by far than her childhood memories, but there was no doubt he was the Jesse Danner of her youth.

"Well?" he asked.

Kelsey clasped her hands behind her back and drew a breath. "I've tried in every way I know how to discredit you, but unfortunately no one will listen to me."

Jesse's brows shot up. It was clear he wasn't used to women speaking the plain truth. "How frustrating for you," he murmured.

She swept him with a disdainful glare before walking to the window. In the golden slanting rays from the afternoon sun, her hair glowed like fire. Jesse wanted to see that hair down around her shoulders. How long was it? To her waist? Regretfully, he supposed he would never know.

"But I know of your past, Mr. Danner. I know, in fact, that you're originally from a town called Rock Springs."

He nearly choked in disbelief. "How do you know that?"

"I've had you investigated," she lied easily. "You have three brothers, one of whom lives here in Portland, and one sister. Your mother's dead, but your father still lives on his farm outside of town."

Jesse stared at her. Despair entered his eyes before he could conceal it. Shocked, Kelsey realized she'd inadvertently scored a hit. What had she said? Oh, God, she thought with swift dismay. He hadn't known Eliza was dead.

Jesse had never had to fight so hard to cover his emotions. Could it be true? Was his mother dead? In all the time he'd been gone, he'd never once thought there might be a death in the family. They were all too tough, too invincible. He felt physically sick.

"I'm—I'm sorry," Kelsey faltered.

Jesse stared past her, through the paned windows to the rolling green lawns outside, until he collected his raging emotions. Coldly, he said, "Go on. I assume you're about to make a point."

But Kelsey had lost her momentum. She'd hurt him. She hadn't meant to do that. Now she hesitated, feeling mean. But then she remembered his plans for Charlotte. "I'll reveal your past to Lady Chamberlain. You've been accused of many crimes."

"What?" He frowned, not really listening to her.

"In your past. When you left Rock Springs there was a scandal, and talk of rape and murder."

"Rape and murder?" He snapped to attention. "What the hell are you talking about? Who did this investigation?"

"I'm not at liberty to say."

"You lying little witch," he said softly. "The facts are dead wrong and you know it."

"That's for you to prove."

The joy had gone out of Kelsey's accusations. She could tell she'd wounded him, and now he was utterly furious, and frightening. He slowly strode over to her, towering over her, his expression scathing. She wanted to shrink inside herself. Her heart thundered in sudden panic, beating so hard, she was afraid he would see its thumping through the royal blue velveteen bodice of her gown.

"You fight dirty, Miss Simpson, but it won't get you what you want. If I want Charlotte Chamberlain, I'll take her. There's not a damn thing you can do about it."

"I'll stop you—"

"I am not the fortune hunter you think I am." He cut her off in a steely voice. "I have other reasons for wanting Charlotte."

"Such as?"

He stared into her deep gray eyes. She was incredibly beautiful for such a treacherous schemer. "Respectability." He leaned even closer. "And lust."

A part of him wanted to wrap his hands around her smooth neck and shake her until she broke. She was worse than Lila. And he believed that some of her fury sprang from jealousy, whether she knew it or not. Deciding to test that theory, he cupped her chin with one hand.

Her eyes widened in horror. "What are you doing?" she hissed.

"Proving a point," he muttered.

A second later his mouth crushed hers. She tried to sweep in a breath to scream at the last second, but didn't succeed. Her arms flailed and he held them down, pinning them to her body. He leaned over her, bending her to his will.

His chest pressed against hers, his arm circling her back, his fingers digging hard against the ribs just beside her breast. Kelsey freed one arm. Her clenched fist slammed into his back. Jesse was too intent on punishing her with his kiss to take note.

Where his body touched hers, heat swarmed through Kelsey, a wave of lust so intense it thoroughly frightened her. She suddenly wanted those fingers to slide upward to her breast. She wanted to feel them pressed hard against her flesh.

His thighs were hard against hers. She was abruptly thoroughly aware of the differences in their anatomy, and her heart jumped in anticipation. She hadn't lied when she'd told Tyrone she'd been kissed; one or two rather clumsy, sexless attempts by past swains. She had, however, never encountered such raging passion and masculinity, a powerful driving force that sent her blood singing hotly through her veins, roaring in her ears.

Oh, my *God!*

With the last shreds of her self-control, she sank her teeth into his lower lip.

He shoved her away so hard that she fell across the divan, his eyes glittering with rage, a nerve jerking in his dark cheek. She'd never had anyone look at her with such unconcealed revulsion.

A tremor swept through her, part fear, part reaction. Kelsey struggled to her feet. Her derringer was still in her beaded bag upstairs. She would have given anything to have it in her hand.

Calmly, Jesse withdrew a handkerchief and held it to his bleeding lip. "And they all think you're a dried-up spinster."

"And you've just proved how despicable you are!"

"Is that what I proved? I think we both proved something entirely different."

"Get out of here!" Kelsey was fast losing her edge and she knew it.

"Gladly. A word of warning, Miss Simpson. You won't stop me."

"You may be surprised, Mr. Danner!" she declared, her voice rising as he stalked toward the door with that unconscious grace he'd always possessed.

He paused, one hand on the knob, his gaze cold on her heated face. "I'll use any means to get what I want. Any means. And since I'm a rapist and a murderer," he added sardonically, "you'd best be careful."

The click of the handle sounded behind him as he gently closed the door.

Kelsey pressed her knuckles against her cheeks, in the throes of emotions she could scarcely name. "It's you who should be careful, Jesse," she said to the empty room.

## 3

Jesse's apartment on Portland's waterfront smelled of fish and garbage and on a particularly bad morning, depending on how much liquor had been consumed by the drunks who staggered bleary-eyed down the morning-washed streets, the stench of vomit seemed to creep beneath the windowpanes.

Zeke held a handkerchief in one hand, but so far he'd resisted covering his mouth and nose. If Jesse could stand it, so could he. But thank God the time had come for Jesse to move to a better place! Returning to Portland under a veil of secrecy had been fine; Zeke had understood. Staying in this vile section of town had achieved invisibility like nothing else; Zeke could appreciate that.

But for any person of even marginal esthetic taste . . . well, this listing, worm-rotted building made the skin shiver and the stomach turn.

"Who the hell is she?" Jesse demanded with repressed violence, tossing clothes into the battered valise thrown open on that wretched cot the building manager euphemistically called a bed.

"Miss Simpson?"

"Yes, Miss Simpson. She knows my whole history and I don't know a damn thing about her! Find out who she is. Find out who sold her information on me. My God, Zeke, somehow, someone knows I'm back in Portland. If it's Montana, then what the hell are we doing fooling around with Charlotte Chamberlain and this blasted society marriage stuff?"

"She can't know about you. No one does."

"Well, Orchid Simpson does." Jesse slammed the lid shut and turned to face Zeke, his expression murderous. "She told me things about my family that no one should know. She said my mother's dead."

Zeke had heard only bits and pieces of Jesse's rather colorful past. He knew he hailed from Rock Springs and had left town under a cloud of suspicion, and he knew that Jesse's brother, Samuel, was a celebrated lawyer right here in Portland. He was vaguely aware that Jesse had several other brothers and a sister all still living in Rock Springs, but he knew nothing about Jesse's parents and hearing him speak of his mother was nothing short of astonishing.

"Why would she say something like that?" Zeke wondered aloud, his opinion of Orchid Simpson lowering dramatically. What kind of game was the woman playing? A cruel one, based on Jesse's reaction to the news.

"Find out if it's true, Zeke. Get me as much information on my family as you can without raising suspicions."

"What about Miss Simpson?"

"I'll take care of Miss Simpson," he assured Zeke grimly.

It hadn't been smart to antagonize him.

Kelsey glanced out the window of the swaying carriage and wished she'd contained herself in a more circumspect manner. Challenging Jesse had been a mistake. Two weeks of reflection and soul-searching had helped her see the light. Jesse had attacked her with his sexuality. She should have guessed that might happen. What had she expected when she'd thrown herself in his path? She was an obstacle and Jesse wasn't above using any means, no matter how low, to achieve what he wanted. He'd even said as much.

Kelsey grimaced at her own foolishness. Her reaction to his kiss flitted across her mind, and she pushed it aside. It was natural, given her girlish infatuation with him. So he'd made her lips tingle and her pulse nearly deafen her. He was an attractive man; she would be the first to admit it. And her body's sudden awakening had been but a momentary lapse, a silly last ditch effort for her girlhood crush. She'd come to her senses soon enough and now she was glad, glad, glad, that she'd bitten him!

She hoped his lip still hurt like hell.

Her lips twisted in self-deprecation. She'd also hoped she'd dissuaded him from pursuing Charlotte but had learned to her subsequent dismay that that hope was in vain. Over the last few weeks Jesse had doubled and redoubled his efforts to win Charlotte. Every time Kelsey turned around, there he was: smiling at Charlotte, caressing her hand as he helped her from a chair, gazing down into her naive, trusting face through blue eyes the shade of a tropical sea. Blue eyes that invariably met Kelsey's frigid gray ones whenever Charlotte looked the other way. Blue eyes full of smug satisfaction.

Oh, she could kill him!

Kelsey's hands clenched around the drawstring of her reticule, and she vaguely realized something was wrong. She looked down at the black bag, her heart sinking. She'd forgotten her derringer. She could visualize it on the lace-covered dressing table next to her vials of perfume.

46

Jesse Danner had her in such a state of confusion that she'd left behind her best means of protection!

"Damn," she swore softly, shifting uncomfortably against the lush squabs of Agatha's carriage. Now, here she was, on her way to Tyrone McNamara's. Good heavens, how *could* she have accepted his invitation.

It was all because of Jesse! she thought darkly. Her head had been filled with such anger and frustration that she'd scarcely paid attention to Tyrone. She'd said yes to his request for her to come to dinner with all the attention she would have shown a pesky fly she simply wanted to get rid of.

She glanced outside the darkened window. The flickering light from the lanterns kept pace eerily with the carriage. She could ask to turn back. So she would be late to dinner. So what? She didn't owe Tyrone anything, even punctuality.

The carriage jarred and squeaked as it turned off the street onto a smaller lane.

"Oh, blast."

Kelsey settled back on the squabs, snorting in disgust at her own foolishness. No, they were already heading down the drive to Tyrone's town house overlooking the city. Pride wouldn't let her turn tail and run when he'd probably already seen her carriage approaching.

Besides, Tyrone wasn't half as dangerous as Jesse was. She could survive the evening ahead.

Tyrone was waiting on the steps, elegant in a gray suit that showed off his dark good looks. Tyrone possessed Jesse's coloring: black hair, blue eyes, a swarthy complexion. But he didn't have Jesse's compact physique and broad shoulders. Because he was thin to the point of gangly, Tyrone appeared taller than Jesse, but appearances were deceptive. Kelsey suspected that were they standing side by side, Jesse might actually have an inch or two on him. Jesse certainly was more handsome, but then, Kelsey had scarcely met a man who could compare to him on either looks or charm. What they shared in equal measure was a lack of conscience that was both appalling and disgusting.

Kelsey planned to make Tyrone aware that this was their one and only evening together. She'd accepted his invitation because she'd been distracted by Jesse, and—she could admit now—she couldn't bear the thought of suffering through another evening with Jesse slobbering all over Charlotte's hand and entertaining Agatha with his dry humor and simmering sensuality. Oh, yes, Kelsey had seen the way Lady Chamberlain reacted to him too. Though she nearly managed to hide it under all that starch, the older woman's lips twitched and her eyes twinkled whenever Jesse's devilish charm was directed solely at her. Kelsey could swear that now Agatha took extra special care with her delicately coiffed white hair. And she'd been wearing her special diamond brooches and stick pins, and her most elegant dresses of the finest silk. Though her manner was just as proper as ever, and Jesse himself might be unaware of her extra preparations, Kelsey knew. Lord, yes! Lady Agatha Chamberlain, protesting that she wasn't quite certain Jesse was right for Charlotte, had nevertheless been completely captivated by him as well!

Kelsey groaned low in her throat as if in physical pain. She squeezed her eyes shut tightly, wanting to scream and rant and rage. Only she knew the black heart that beat beneath Jesse's broad chest, and while Charlotte fussed and fluttered over him, and Agatha opened her home to him, Kelsey plotted revenge. Delicious, delicious revenge!

The carriage jolted to a stop and Tyrone swept down the steps. He opened the door and took Kelsey's black-gloved hand in his own, leaning down to kiss her fingers.

Kelsey eyed his dark head ironically. What *did* he think the evening ahead would bring?

"I was afraid you'd changed your mind," he admitted with unaccustomed honesty, gazing into her eyes. "My Lord, but you look lovely."

"Thank you."

"Come on inside. The night's cool, isn't it? I'll get you a sherry and warm those cold hands."

Cold hands? Kelsey was feeling rather warm. The night was shadowed and still, cool, yes, but then, it was June and summer's heat hadn't reached the northwest yet. Tyrone couldn't feel whether her fingers were cold or warm through her gloves. He was just being overeager, Kelsey decided uneasily.

Tyrone led her into an intimate study decorated in dark-stained oak and mahogany. The fireplace was black-veined marble and an intimate fire chased away the cool night air that swirled inside as Tyrone and Kelsey entered.

"Where are the servants?" Kelsey asked, tugging off her gloves. The room was hot. Beastly. Cold hands indeed! The man was attempting to bake her in this stuffy oven.

"Well, they've retired," Tyrone explained as he lifted the lid off a crystal decanter.

"All of them?"

"Sit down. Please." He gestured to one of the buttoned, highly glossed, wine-red leather wing chairs. Kelsey hesitated, then slowly sank into the cushions, swallowed within the chair's enormous arms.

Tyrone brought her a sherry, then stood in front of her, looming over her.

"All of the servants?" Kelsey asked again, feeling faintly alarmed. "What about dinner? Are we serving ourselves?"

He grinned. "I confess, I'm going to serve you. The meal's prepared and waiting for us in the dining room."

"Maybe we should eat it before it gets cold," Kelsey suggested. It hurt her neck to look up at him, so she concentrated on the chain that hung from the watch pocket of his vest.

"Not yet. I'd rather risk a ruined meal than a ruined chance to be alone with you."

"Mr. McNamara, you've evidently misunderstood my reasons for accepting your invitation."

"Which are?"

"Boredom, mainly. I needed to get out of the house. But I can see coming here was a mistake." She attempted to rise from the chair, but his hands clasped her wrists and he very gently pushed her back down.

"Orchid, my love, we've got all night. Let's take it slowly. Dinner's warming. There's no need to rush. Have a drink." He picked up his own glass which he'd placed on the mantel and beckoned her to follow suit.

Kelsey regarded him steadily, her heart beating hard. No

servants. No derringer. It was going to be a long night and she needed her wits about her.

She lifted the glass of sherry to her mouth and pretended to swallow.

"Where's the usually skulking Miss Simpson?" Jesse asked casually, glancing around the drawing room. He and Charlotte and Agatha were the only occupants, which was highly unusual.

"She doesn't skulk," Charlotte admonished, choking back a laugh and appealing to Agatha for forgiveness at laughing at Orchid. She'd forgiven Orchid for being so dreadful about Jesse in the beginning, and she felt like a bit of a traitor enjoying a joke at her expense.

"She most certainly does. Hardly says a word, just sits around and darts me dirty looks."

"I'm certain you're imagining that, Mr. Danner," Agatha said with a shake of her head. "Orchid's only looking out for Charlotte's best interests. I'm afraid she mistrusts every man who looks either her way or Charlotte's, but she's accepted you now."

Jesse smiled, and the look he sent Agatha Chamberlain was of a man who knew when he was being conned. He liked Agatha. He liked her proper accent and fussy ways and the unconventional streak of toughness and acceptance that seemed so out of place in such a dithery-looking old lady. Lady Chamberlain was as sharp as Orchid Simpson's lashing tongue, he'd learned to his delight. She made the evenings with Charlotte nearly bearable.

Nearly.

It wasn't that Charlotte wasn't a sweet kid. She was. Adorable, flighty, breathless, naive; she was all that and more.

She just wasn't for him.

"I'm surprised Miss Simpson isn't here watching me like a hawk," Jesse pressed further. He really did want to know what had become of her.

"Actually Orchid's accepted an invitation to dinner," Agatha explained, frowning slightly. "Tyrone McNamara. Do you know the gentleman?"

Gentleman? Jesse stared at her incredulously. Tyrone McNamara was a gambler, an unconscionable rake, and in Jesse's opinion, a filthy worm. And if *he* thought that, given his own reputation, what in God's name was a prudish spinster like Orchid Simpson doing with him? Or, more aptly, what was *Tyrone* doing with *her?*

"He's called for Orchid time and time again," Charlotte said on a plaintive note. "My stars, the man has no pride. Orchid's been perfectly beastly to him, and he still won't give up. She finally accepted, though the Lord in heaven only knows why. She absolutely detests the man," she added confidentially.

"Then why . . . ?"

Charlotte shrugged prettily, her rapt gaze lovingly searching his face. Jesse felt uncomfortable. Her adoration was something he hadn't quite counted on. True, he'd set about courting her with the express purpose of marriage in mind, but the reality of this lovestruck *child* was more than he could bear.

He didn't want to hurt her.

"Charlotte, I hope you won't mind, but there's some business I need to take care of that can't wait."

"Tonight?" she cried.

"There's someone I have to meet at the club," Jesse lied easily.

"Who?" Charlotte demanded, growing piqued.

"Child, leave the man alone," Agatha inserted quickly, shooting Charlotte a quelling frown. In her part of the world, women did not question a man's comings and goings. It was not the done thing. Besides, Agatha had a pretty good idea what was actually traversing Mr. Jesse Danner's mind, and she was curious to see how the evening ended for both him—and Orchid.

"But Grandmama!"

"Charlotte, say good-bye for tonight. Good-bye, Mr. Danner," she said to Jesse herself, her eyes sharp and dancing.

"Good-bye, Lady Chamberlain. Charlotte."

Jesse reflected on Agatha's astute mind. It occurred to him that she was somehow playing as much a game as he was, and that thought left him curiously uncomfortable.

51

.As soon as he left Chamberlain Manor he forgot both Agatha and Charlotte, however. Glancing down the curving drive, he signaled Drake, the man he'd recently hired on as his driver. Immediately the *clop, clop* of the carriage horses' hooves sounded against the cobblestones. Impatient, Jesse jumped up on the seat beside Drake, surprising the rather fastidious man to the point of gasping.

"Sir, wouldn't you rather ride inside?"

"I'd rather have a fast horse," Jesse answered flatly. "You know where Tyrone McNamara lives?"

"Would that be the McNamaras off Ainsley Drive, sir?" Jesse nodded. "Get me there in a hurry."

Drake cracked the whip, and the carriage horses jumped into a trot.

"And Drake, don't call me sir," Jesse said for the uncountable time. "Jesse'll be fine."

"Yes, sir."

Kelsey couldn't decide whether to be amused or furious. If Tyrone was telling the truth—and she had every reason to believe he was—then their dinner had been drying up in a chafing dish for over an hour and a half. Not that she was the least bit hungry, but she was both annoyed and exasperated that Tyrone felt his charms were so lethal that any woman would be more than willing to forgo a meal just to spend time alone with him.

The silly ass.

She decided being amused would work more to her advantage than relying on the growing anger and dread that was working its way from the tips of her toes to the crown of her head at the realization that Tyrone intended to keep her captive until she capitulated in some way.

"It's horribly hot, don't you think?" she told him. "Could you open a window?"

"I was thinking of shedding my jacket," he answered, accomplishing the deed as if she'd *asked* him to start undressing.

With a studied manner that made Kelsey wonder if he practiced in front of a mirror, he undid his tie and began working the buttons through their confining holes.

She watched him peel off his vest and finish unbuttoning his shirt. Before he could add his shirt to the growing pile of discarded clothing on the chair, Kelsey put in quickly, "I'd rather you kept a few items on, if you don't mind. Besides, I'm too warm and I plan to open a window whether you keep your clothes on or not."

She darted from the chair before the last word was uttered, using Tyrone's moment of indecision to escape the trap where he'd kept her. He'd plied her with sherry which she'd refused to drink and sweet-talked and cajoled and insinuated until Kelsey had been hard pressed not to leap up and scratch his eyes out.

Men!

"Orchid." He whipped around, one hand grasping her arm before she could squeeze past him. Beneath his unbuttoned shirt his chest was covered with a dusting of black hair that for some reason turned Kelsey's stomach. Maybe there was something wrong with her, she reasoned. She no more wanted to touch this man's hairy skin than she wanted to return to Jace and Emerald.

"Release me or bear the consequences," she warned him coldly.

"What consequences?" Tyrone grinned lasciviously. "No derringer tonight, my love. I checked your reticule. I can only assume that's some kind of surrender."

"You are sorely mistaken, Mr. McNamara. I would think with your purported success with women that you'd realize how totally unwilling and uninterested I am. Do you seriously believe I have any desire to have you touch me?" She twisted her arm until her skin burned from his hard grasp.

The smile on her face kept her words from cutting to the bone. Still, their effect was stinging; Tyrone's expression changed from predatory to downright mean.

"I made a mistake coming here," Kelsey told him. "If you won't take me home, I'll walk. I'm not completely helpless, even without a gun."

"My dear, what you are is a stupid woman playing a stupid game. You knew why I wanted you here. You came because you wanted it too."

"If you put your stinking lips on mine, I may vomit," Kelsey said, rearing back as Tyrone moved forward, clearly intent upon crushing her mouth beneath his.

His hand snarled in her hair, yanking her head back. Tears burned in Kelsey's eyes. If he kept this up, she was going to kick him with all her strength, right where it counted the most.

"I've got money riding on you," he snarled, close enough to her face to touch noses with her. He jerked her head hard, and Kelsey clenched her teeth against the moan of pain that filled her throat. "If you don't unbutton that ugly dress right now, I'm going to rip it off. I've spent too much time thinking about what you've got hidden under there. I've tried to be patient, to treat you like a woman ought to be treated. But you don't seem to understand."

"Let go of my hair."

He responded by ripping off her hairnet and pulling the auburn strands free until they fell in a shining ripple over her shoulders. For a moment Tyrone was mesmerized by that hair. It fell to her waist and firelight bounced off reddish-purple and dark mahogany strands. With a moan of pleasure he buried his hands in its lustrous silk.

And Orchid Simpson kneed him with all the strength of her lower body.

Tyrone feinted at the last second, some latent instinct protecting him. Kelsey tried to stumble past him, but he grabbed her arms with steel hands, yanking her back until her shoulders collided with his chest. They were both breathing hard, his hot breath fanning her nape.

"Damn you, you frigid bitch. You're going to pay."

"So will you, Mr. McNamara. I'll make certain you pay dearly!" she ground out, though her heart was slamming into her ribs and she sought desperately for some means of escape.

The sound of booted footsteps ringing across the foyer brought them both up short. Joy filled Kelsey's breast. The servants. Rescue at last!

The ride to McNamara's was accomplished in haste but it nevertheless gave Jesse time for reflection—a rather painful reflection, to say the least. Orchid Simpson. He cared nothing for her. Zeke, through the services of an investigator, had learned that she'd spoken nothing less than the truth when she'd said Jesse's mother was dead. And though rationally Jesse knew Eliza's death was not her fault, Orchid's cruel insensitivity was enough to make Jesse hate her.

Clenching his fists, he fought down an unreasonable rage directed solely at the redoubtable Miss Simpson. He felt bitterly cheated, and the fact that there was no one to blame but himself—and maybe partially his father—didn't make him feel any kinder toward her.

He couldn't think of one reason to charge after her like some tarnished knight, yet he couldn't stop himself. Maybe she was leading some kind of double life, pretending to be a spinster when in fact she was McNamara's willing, wicked mistress.

No, it didn't fit. Jesse knew women, and it didn't fit.

He sighed, his mind circling back to the painful realization that Eliza was dead and changes had taken place in Rock Springs, a place he somehow expected to remain forever the same.

Jesse had left home tired of and angered by the moral restraints his father had imposed on him. Even after that wretched scandal when his mother's first husband, Ramsey Gainsborough, had held the whole family hostage; even after the sick worry that Mother might die from the fall she took off the widow's walk; even after Jesse had helped save them all—even after *that,* Joseph Danner hadn't loosened the reins on his irrepressible third son.

And Jesse had rebelled.

He'd created scandal after scandal, caused a near sensation in three counties by seducing Alice McIntyre, the ultimate virgin, then disappearing from Rock Springs and everyone he loved without so much as a by-your-leave.

He'd known then, as he knew now, that no one in Rock Springs would have believed Alice wanted to be seduced, that she'd schemed to snare Jesse Danner for a husband. A lot like Emerald had.

Unfortunately, Jesse had been too willing and eager to recognize the trap. It had taken years, and a lot of other

Alices and Emeralds and Lilas, before he'd learned to choose his partners carefully.

Jesse sighed. He had regrets; lots of them. But the freedom of doing exactly as he pleased had made up for them. Still, there were several women in Rock Springs, and the neighboring town of Malone as well, who would probably dearly love to castrate him. But he'd never raped anyone, and he'd certainly never murdered anyone.

For all his indiscretions, Jesse had spent the better part of his manhood in a, if not nobler, certainly more acceptable pursuit—amassing money. Property, real estate, land development—he had a knack for acquiring and selling huge parcels of God's green earth and making fortunes in the process. His brothers, Tremaine and Harrison, had chosen fields of medicine; Tremaine was a medical doctor, Harrison a horse doctor. His sister, Lexie, had been bound and determined to become a horse doctor too, and had succeeded, even in this man's world. Noble professions every one. The healing arts. The kind of work any man or woman could be proud of.

Jesse had no such leanings. He'd earned his first parcel of land by winning it from a drunken miner who'd thought it contained gold. The miner, after discovering it was useless, had used it as collateral, and that "useless" piece was now a part of the city. It had been swallowed up as Portland stretched its arms in all directions. Jesse had sold the land and bought more, subsequently sold it, and bought more, and so on and so on. . . .

Then in '92 he'd met Lila Gray—the most daring, sensual woman he'd ever had the misfortune to meet, and that was saying a lot. He should have known she was married; she was so careful about her past. He'd accepted her half truths and omissions only because he was careful about his past as well. But he'd made one colossal mistake: He'd told her about his property. After Montana beat and nearly killed him, then left him for dead, the lovely Lila mourned him by telling her husband about Jesse's park block. Illegally, and with the help of his many friends in the corrupt political hierarchy of Portland, Montana managed to have the deeds switched to his name. While Jesse was recuperating in San

Francisco, Montana acquired the piece of property that Nell had helped Jesse buy under his nose, along with the rest of Jesse's real estate holdings as well.

And Jesse Danner was left flat broke. But alive.

Jesse burned for revenge. It was all that kept him going. It consumed him. Zeke, though he also wanted his pound of flesh, was more respectful and fearful of Montana Gray's power. But Jesse felt no such fear. He felt nothing, in fact, but a deep-seated need for vengeance. It fueled his recovery and gave meaning to his life, and before he left this world for the next, Jesse had but one goal: the ruination of Montana and Lila Gray.

He half smiled. No, he didn't suffer from noble callings, though he did possess the single-minded determination that seemed to be another Danner curse. To earn back his fortune Jesse had started again, working as a laborer down on the wharfs in San Francisco. He'd scratched up enough money to buy a bit of property, and Zeke, his friend and savior, had given him the little money he'd saved over his years of working as a shipping clerk.

Financial recovery took years. And years. And years. Years where Jesse had to snuff his impatience and toil long hours for a miserable few cents. But his talent for real estate never deserted him, and once the first purchase was made, his fortune spiraled.

So now the time was at hand to deal the final blow. Jesse possessed enough money. He just needed clout. He could wait a few years and build up his reputation, but then the surprise would be gone. Lila would remember him even if Montana didn't. Jesse wanted to resolve the whole damn mess in a matter of weeks.

But he couldn't use Charlotte Chamberlain, no matter what Zeke said. It wasn't in him. He'd kept up the pretense these last few weeks only to annoy that stubborn, willful, and coldhearted Orchid Simpson. And now he was what? Planning to *rescue* her?

"I must be out of my mind," he muttered furiously.

"Sir?"

"Drop me off here," Jesse told the man, scarcely waiting until the carriage slowed at the end of Tyrone McNamara's long drive before he leapt to the immaculate lawns. He strode with ground-devouring strides, fueled by a self-directed anger, up the scrupulously tended drive to the front door.

He didn't knock. The door hadn't been latched properly and had swung open about a quarter of the way. Standing undecided in the foyer, he heard Orchid Simpson's lush and threatening voice.

". . . I'll make certain you pay dearly!"

No gentleman himself, Jesse strode in the direction of that voice and swung open the doors to the den without invitation.

The sight that beheld his eyes stopped him short. A half-naked Tyrone McNamara held a struggling Orchid Simpson in the bonds of his arms. They were both facing the door. Orchid's fingers were prying savagely against Tyrone's grip. Her face was flushed with fury. Her eyes wide and smoldering, both with anger and fear. She was gasping and her breasts were heaving. Tyrone was swearing viciously.

They both froze at his entrance.

"Jesse!" she cried out, shocked.

Jesse? He was momentarily diverted by the sound of his name on her tongue, then he was stopped cold by the extravagance of her unbound hair. It hung in a long, loose curtain nearly to her waist, purplish-red and brown strands flung gloriously about her shoulders, cascading like silk.

Something passed across his mind. A vision. A memory. Just outside his grasp.

"Who the hell are you?" Tyrone snarled, snapping Jesse to the present.

"I came to escort Miss Simpson home."

"I don't need an escort!" the furious beauty spat out at him, and Jesse gazed at her in amazement. Did she actually *enjoy* McNamara's less-than-loving embrace? Lila Gray had certainly enjoyed dominant lovemaking, more than Jesse could really stomach. Was Orchid that kind of woman?

But no. He was disabused of that notion a moment later when Orchid Simpson wriggled violently, desperately trying to bite one of McNamara's arms. The humor of the situation appealed to him. "Careful, McNamara, she's deadly with her teeth," he drawled in spite of her desperate struggles.

She shot him a glare of such undiluted fury that Jesse nearly doubled over with laughter.

"Unhand me, or I'll break your arms!" she let forth through her teeth.

"Get the hell out of my house!" Tyrone demanded.

Ignoring them both, Jesse crossed to the liquor cabinet, bypassing the open bottle of sherry for some of McNamara's best brandy. He poured a healthy glassful.

Behind him, the struggle abruptly ceased. Jesse glanced over his shoulder, his glass in his hand. "Are you ready to be escorted now?" he asked blandly as Orchid stared him down, her gray eyes smoky with emotion—the primary one being disgust. Tyrone looked on, completely nonplussed.

"I say, there," he sputtered. "Put that brandy down. I'll have you thrown out on your ear!"

"No, he won't." Orchid spoke to Jesse in an icy tone. "Tyrone specifically gave the servants the night off. Unless he plans to toss you out himself, you're safe, Mr. Danner."

"Well, that's a relief." Jesse swallowed a large gulp of brandy, thoroughly enjoying himself.

"Mr. Danner?" Tyrone glared, reluctantly letting his arms fall from his captive. "You're not Samuel Danner," he declared as Kelsey jerked away from him.

"He's Jesse Danner," she clarified when the space of the room divided her equally from both Jesse and Tyrone. "Samuel Danner's brother."

Jesse didn't like the way she said that, nor did he like the fact that she'd purposely linked him to Samuel. He needed time, and he didn't want her spoiling his plan. Add to that that she was too superior by far, and he wished he knew some way to set the lady down a bit. He also didn't like her knowing so much about him when he still knew next to nothing about her.

Tyrone leveled his gaze on Jesse. "You've entered my home without an invitation. If you don't leave, I'll be forced to send for the authorities. Your actions are nothing less than criminal."

"Whose actions are criminal?" Jesse lifted his brows,

deliberately letting his gaze examine Tyrone's half-dressed state. "Miss Simpson could probably cite you as well."

"I'm perfectly fine," she bit out.

As if the matter were decided, she suddenly wrapped her silken swath of hair into a bun and held it with one hand. Since she had no hairnet, however, she was forced to let it fall down her back in a loosely twisted rope. Jesse was intrigued by its beauty and wine-red richness. Why did she hide it?

"I'm ready to leave," she said abruptly.

Jesse set down his snifter. He was hard pressed to keep up with her quick, angry strides and only just reached the front door as she did. Tyrone was still sputtering but neither of them paid much attention to him. Instead, Orchid practically ripped the door from Jesse's hands.

"I don't appreciate your interference," she told him in a low voice.

"Really." He was growing annoyed with her obstinance. Jesus, the woman was bossy!

"You may think this little incident has endeared you to me, but that's not the case. I could have managed perfectly well on my own. Your timing was—opportune—but unnecessary. If you plan to keep pursuing Charlotte, I would prefer you keep out of my affairs."

"And if I don't plan on pursuing Charlotte?"

"Then, if there's any justice in this world, I'll never have to set eyes on you again, Mr. Danner."

She swept queenlike out the door. Jesse shook his head and behind him Tyrone gave a bark of laughter.

"Someone's going to have to tie her down to bed her," he complained. "She's a vicious thing." There were marks across his cheek and chest.

Jesse had no sympathy for the man. "Maybe she has reason to be," he said, though he'd be damned if he'd let Orchid Simpson know he felt the least bit empathetic toward her. Secretly, he sided with Tyrone. The woman was just plain mean-tempered. By God, though he'd planned to discontinue his courtship of Charlotte, now he reversed that decision. He'd charm the drawers off that woman if he had to, just to infuriate Orchid Simpson.

He climbed into the carriage behind her, seating himself directly across from her. Drake snapped the reins and the carriage lurched down the drive. Jesse's knees touched hers briefly, and she jerked back as if she'd been burned.

In the darkness he couldn't see her expression, but those eyes were leveled on his and he knew they were blazing.

"I don't like you much either," he told her conversationally. "But whether you can admit it or not, you're damned lucky I showed up when I did. Tyrone wasn't about to give up. He would have had you on the floor in another few minutes and there would have been nothing you could do about it."

"I'm not helpless."

Ice dripped from every word. "Not helpless. Ungrateful. You've got so much stupid pride, you can't even say thank-you. Your manners are atrocious."

"I doubt very much that I've been *saved* by the likes of you," she said sarcastically. "I've merely exchanged one intolerable situation for another."

Jesse marveled at her wicked tongue. "You're not that much of a prize, Miss Simpson," he uttered softly, dangerously.

"Neither, Mr. Danner, are you."

# 4

Charlotte fluttered nervously around Kelsey all day, as if somehow sensing it was Jesse who'd come to Kelsey's rescue the night before, Jesse who'd dragged her away from that wretched and lascivious Tyrone McNamara. Charlotte's clairvoyance was nerve-racking to the extreme, and Kelsey desperately tried to ignore her as she went about her business.

She couldn't ignore her mixed feelings about the events

of the night before, however. She was furious with Jesse, and herself, and Tyrone. Tyrone actually had *money* riding on her? He'd stooped to placing a bet on whether he could bed her? With whom, Gerrard Knight? The humiliation was almost past bearing!

It was enough to make one renounce the whole male species. Kelsey was already on the verge; one more tiny push and she'd be over the edge.

And Jesse, the way he'd acted upon finding her at the mercy of Tyrone, was almost criminal. He'd been fighting back laughter, the miserable bastard! Still, he *had* saved her from a questionable fate. Recalling those moments in McNamara's power turned her skin cold and clammy. She'd been so close to true peril. It was divine providence that Jesse had intervened. Her mind shied away from thinking about the probable consequences if he hadn't saved her.

But did he have to be so horrifyingly, disgustingly smug and self-impressed? Oh, how she wished she could have handled the situation by herself!

Hearing her own thoughts, Kelsey made a sound of disgust. How utterly stupid and prideful. Jesse had been right about that. She was a victim of her own pride and always had been.

Kelsey spent the rest of the day tight-lipped and irritable. In the afternoon she helped Agatha respond to all her mail, and in the early evening, needing to get away from Charlotte's cloying presence, she secretly pulled on her old breeches beneath her gown—the ones she'd stolen years before from her brother—then saddled Justice and gave the beautiful beast his head as they raced across the sweeping fields beyond Chamberlain Manor. Only when Justice was lathered and spent and slowed of his own free will did Kelsey rein him in. Then she walked him until he'd cooled off and brushed his satiny coat and fussed over him long past the dinner hour.

She ate in her room and for some reason, the memory of Jesse's dalliance with one Alice McIntyre entered her mind, refusing to be dislodged. Kelsey had been all of thirteen when the news had reached her tender ears, spreading as swiftly and ruthlessly as lightning, stabbing from place to place and electrifying the women in three counties. Gossip was evil, but oh so seductive, and Kelsey hadn't been immune to the tale. She'd heard the rumors, and in her innocence Jesse's seduction of Alice had seemed almost romantic. She'd placed herself in Alice's shoes, imagining Jesse's hard arms wrapped around her, his heart beating heavily against hers, his lips gently caressing hers, words of love falling sweetly on her ears.

Hah!

Now when she recalled those anxious, yearning thoughts, she wanted to wince and squeeze her eyes closed. She could scarcely stand herself! What romantic idiocy! What had happened between Alice and Jesse was little more than the rutting of a stallion with a mare. And she was only one of Jesse's conquests.

At least Alice's father had possessed the good sense to try to shoot Jesse!

Being in Jesse's embrace would be tragically similar to being in Tyrone's, she determined, completely ignoring her own reaction to Jesse when he'd had the audacity to actually kiss her.

A faint knocking sounded on her door. "Come in," Kelsey said a trifle impatiently.

Charlotte peeked inside, her blue eyes huge. "Are you angry with me, Orchid?"

"Of course not," Kelsey hastily assured her. "I was just thinking of something else."

"Don't you mean some*one* else?" Charlotte asked as she walked to the middle of the room and eyed Kelsey's dinner tray. The meal had scarcely been touched.

"What does that mean?"

She lifted one shoulder and let it fall, her unhappy gaze sweeping the floor. "I don't mean to be so horrid, but, Orchid, I couldn't sleep last night! Jesse practically ran out of here, saying he was going to his club. Then he came back with you!"

"He did *not* come back with me," Kelsey corrected her charge.

"It was his carriage that dropped you off. I saw from my bedroom window," she declared stubbornly.

"Well, then you also saw how delighted I was to be in his company," Kelsey threw back.

She and Jesse had glared at each other while standing in the circular drive in front of the house. Jesse had hoped that since he'd saved her, she would back off and let him court Charlotte in peace. But Kelsey had calmly told him she had no such intentions; she planned to prepare for war. To her consternation, Jesse had simply shrugged and agreed. Kelsey had left without a good-bye, then had spent a good two hours in high fury, pacing the confines of her room like a caged predator.

"You do like him, though, don't you?" Charlotte suggested, watching Kelsey closely.

"No."

"Yes, you do."

"Charlotte, if you're going to ask me a question and then not pay the scantest heed to my answer, this conversation is a waste of time."

"You really hate him?" she asked, perplexed. It was clear she couldn't conceive of a woman being less than dazzled by Jesse Danner.

"Yes."

"*Why?*"

"Because he's not being honest with you, you silly twit. He's making you think he's falling in love with you, but it's all an act." Kelsey's voice was kind, but Charlotte reacted volcanically.

"You're just jealous!"

Kelsey closed her eyes and counted to ten. "I don't want to hurt you, but if I don't say something, you'll be hurt much worse later on. He as much as told me he's seeing you because of your money. That's all he wants, a healthy bank account."

The color swept from Charlotte's face. Her eyes were dangerously bright. "You're making that up!" she accused. "Because . . . because . . ."

Kelsey waited, aching inside at the pain she'd inflicted.

"Because you're a dried-up spinster who can't catch a

64

man!'' Charlotte gasped out through a storm of sudden tears. Then she raced from the room, her hands over her face, sobbing as if her heart would shatter into a thousand pieces.

Kelsey gazed after her unhappily. She didn't know whether to laugh or cry herself. Instead, she did neither. She'd given up tears long, long ago, and she'd never felt less like laughing. She sat motionless at her dressing table while silence pooled around her and darkness settled in the corners of the room, and she plotted the destruction of Jesse Danner.

Jesse treated her as if she were part of the wallpaper. Neither Charlotte nor Agatha paid much attention to her at all. Charlotte, because she was still piqued; Agatha, because she was carefully concentrating on Jesse. To Kelsey's enormous relief, Agatha actually seemed to be asking herself some questions about Jesse's sincerity as well. Maybe things would work out.

So while Jesse was his most appealing, entertaining Charlotte with his razor wit and exhibiting a leashed control Kelsey wouldn't have believed possible of him, Kelsey watched and waited. She sat in a corner chair at the other side of the room and listened. Or stood by the windows and gazed outside, ostensibly ignoring him . . . and listened. Or bent her head over Agatha's correspondence at the desk . . . and listened. In her prim, high-necked gowns and exercising a control to match Jesse's own, she was demure, quiet, and simply forgotten. Charlotte sent her sizzling warning looks whenever she caught Kelsey's eye, but Kelsey was a model of propriety. Kelsey had felt Agatha's gentle perusal a time or two as well, and at least once an evening she looked up to find Agatha's gaze pinned on her. A bright smile only made the elderly dowager frown and cluck her tongue.

Agatha was harder to fool than Charlotte.

And Jesse. Had she fooled him? She didn't think so, but it was difficult to tell since anytime his gaze happened to fall on her, his eyes swept past without interest. He'd locked her out, which should have filled her with triumph but instead made her uncomfortable, edgy, and nervous.

Inside her head, Kelsey's mind whirred and plotted and planned. She would stop him, by God. Her will was as strong as his—stronger! And she had the advantage of knowing who and what he was, while he knew nothing about her. If she had to, she would reveal every sordid aspect of his past to Charlotte and Agatha. Even if it meant sacrificing her own anonymity and freedom.

But there had to be a better way. . . .

Late one night, a solution occurred to her, one so diabolically clever and risky that she sat bolt upright in bed, her heart pounding in her ears, a hand to her mouth. No, she couldn't! It was too dangerous. It would give him ultimate power, yet it would deter him like nothing else.

Lord sakes! Slowly her pulse returned to normal, matching beats with the lonely ticking of her bedside clock. But her mind churned. A chill slipped down her spine and she hugged her knees to her chest. Her plan threatened her own self-respect, her pride, her basic womanhood. But it would save Charlotte.

Moonlight lay in an elongated rectangle on her bed. Kelsey's fine brows drew into a hard line of thought. She hadn't been in such turmoil since she'd run away from Emerald and Jace.

In the cold morning hours she made a final decision. Gathering a dressing gown around her, she walked to the window, gazing despairingly at the grounds below. Her plan would take her away from Charlotte and Agatha, cut her off from them like the severing of an umbilical cord.

But it would garner her a sweet, sweet revenge. She would have the last laugh on Jesse Danner.


Jesse stood in front of the window in Zeke's office, gazing broodingly down on the rain-drenched streets below. Men in bowler hats hurried past. Women huddled beneath the awnings. Neither the electric lights lining the street nor the sparks off the trolley connection could dissipate the gloom.

The door to Zeke's inner office opened and Jesse heard

Zeke stop short in surprise as he saw him standing by the window. "Jesse!"

"Hullo, Zeke. I needed somewhere to think." He kept his eyes trained on the bustling midday traffic below.

Zeke headed to the desk and his humidor. Jesse heard him twist off the leather lid and the scent of tobacco wafted gently his way. After several minutes of silence, he asked, "How's it going with Miss Chamberlain?"

"If I asked her to marry me, she'd say yes. Her grandmother still has a few doubts, but not many." He didn't add that Orchid Simpson couldn't stand the sight of him.

"Well done," Zeke congratulated him.

Jesse glanced back. Zeke wore a black wool suit with a striped waistcoat, a far cry from Jesse's rugged denim trousers and cotton workshirt. Jesse could play the part of a sophisticated Portland businessman with ease, but he'd grown up on a farm and was just as comfortable in work clothes.

"You don't sound all that happy about it," Jesse observed, hearing the hesitation in his friend's voice.

Zeke sat down at his desk, puffing on his cheroot. He couldn't tell Jesse that the idea of him using Charlotte Chamberlain bothered his conscience a bit. No, he couldn't say that—not after he'd practically forced Jesse to pursue her! Poor Charlotte. She was a trusting child who deserved better. Now Zeke wished he'd turned Jesse's attention to that shriveled-up Orchid Simpson. She was a woman past her prime, and as mean-tempered as she was morally stringent.

Jesse would be outraged to know he was having second thoughts, so Zeke wisely kept his mouth shut. "So when are you going to get down on bended knee?"

Jesse's answer was a frustrated growl. "I don't know."

"I suppose we're running out of time."

Zeke realized his doubts had surfaced in spite of himself. The keen look Jesse seared him with burned to his soul. Abandoning any attempt at deception, Zeke lifted his palms in surrender. "All right, all right. As much as I want to get Montana"—his voice deepened with the strength of his desire for vengeance—"I can't help comparing Charlotte to Nell."

Jesse gazed at him steadily. "Your second thoughts are a tad late, Ezekiel."

"Sorry, Jesse. My mistake was when I started to think of Charlotte as a human being, not just as a means to an end."

Jesse snorted. "Well, then you'll be glad to know that I've come to the same conclusion. I can't go through with it. I can't ruin her life for the sake of revenge. And God knows, I have no interest in marriage! Not even if it'll help bring Gray down in style."

"Hmmm." Zeke wasn't exactly cheered that Jesse agreed with him. "So you haven't been courting Miss Chamberlain these past few weeks."

"Oh, yes, I have." Jesse threw his friend a sardonic smile. "But it was just to get Miss Simpson's goat. She can't bear the thought of Charlotte's marrying me."

"What about our revenge?"

"It'll have to wait, I suppose." Jesse glowered at the thought. He lived for the day when Lila Gray tasted the bitterness of financial ruin. With the added experience of five extra years, Jesse saw her for what she was and had always been: a bored woman who lived in grand style and who took lovers indiscriminately before feeding them to her shark of a husband. He had no doubt that his seduction had been a planned thing.

"Have you scrubbed the marriage plan completely?"

"I'd rather stay away from women altogether. This is business, and a woman can't be trusted to react in a businesslike manner."

"All you have to do is marry one. A socially well-connected one. You don't have to enter into a business relationship," he pointed out.

"This marriage would *be* a business relationship."

"All right, all right." Zeke waved that away. "It's still the best plan."

"Fine." Jesse stalked impatiently across the room. "So pick someone more suitable than Charlotte Chamberlain. Someone with some savvy. Someone whose heart isn't made of glass. Give me a name, Zeke."

"Orchid Simpson."

Jesse threw back his head and laughed, the sound roaring to the rafters. *"Orchid Simpson?* My God, man. Have you lost your mind? You told me yourself to stay away from her!"

"And you just asked for someone whose heart isn't made of glass. That woman is iron, through and through."

"For God's sake, Zeke, I don't even *like* her! She's hard and cold and withered inside."

"You told me she didn't look cold."

"You said she'd be too much of a challenge for me!" Jesse shot back furiously.

"Well, she is a challenge," he admitted with a shrug. "But she's got all the right connections via Lady Chamberlain."

"She can't stand the sight of me, and I can't stand the sight of her."

"You were attracted to her at Charlotte's party. You admitted that you were more interested in her than in Charlotte."

"I wasn't interested in Charlotte at all, so how could I help but be more interested in Orchid Simpson!" Jesse snapped. "No, Zeke," he warned in a tone that sliced through any further objections, "I've since learned a few things about that spinster, and I would rather swallow broken glass than so much as speak to her. I'd no more marry her than I'd sleep with Lila Gray again."

"You don't have to like her, Jesse. You don't even have to respect her. That's the point, isn't it?" Zeke said softly. "You're better off with a woman who won't win your sympathies. Someone you can use without complications. Though she may not be easily won, if anyone can do it, you can."

"You didn't have so much faith before," Jesse growled, infuriated with the conversation. The trouble was, Zeke's idea wasn't half bad.

"Well, I do now. Even bossy, small-minded women like Orchid Simpson can be won. I've seen the way she looks at you when she thinks you don't notice."

Jesse snorted. "The woman throws daggers from those gray eyes."

"Her anger masks something else."

"Your belief in my abilities leaves me humble," Jesse drawled sardonically.

"Go ahead and laugh, but I'm right on this. If anyone can find a way to get that woman to lower her guard, along with her drawers, it's you. Think of it as a—"

A short, sharp rap on the outer door stopped Zeke in mid-sentence. Through the pebbled glass he could make out a woman's figure, her head adorned by a wide-brimmed hat. Jesse started toward the inner office but Zeke stayed him with his hand as he answered the outer door.

In that split second, knowledge speared through Jesse as if it were a lance. He knew who she was before Orchid Simpson took her first step into Zeke's office. Sucking in a sharp breath, he fought back an unreasonable urge to run. Premonition left him chilled. He didn't want anything to do with her and whatever purpose had brought her to Zeke's office.

"Miss Simpson!" Zeke exclaimed in shock.

Her face was half shadowed by a gray felt hat dipped over one ear, its plume of peacock feathers trembling gently even in the still air. Her gown was gray silk, and there was a fichu of lace at her throat. The dress would have been fetching if the lines weren't so severe. As it was, even the matching lace peeking from the bottoms of her sleeves couldn't soften the overwhelming image of starched rectitude. She looked like a dowager, he thought in disgust. Didn't she have any fashion sense at all? The gown was lovely, but should have adorned an eighty-year-old grandmother, not a young woman in her late twenties. Only her black reticule had some style and verve, but it swung heavily from her wrist, weighted down. What did she have in that thing anyway? Jesse wondered. A lead pipe?

She was half turned toward Zeke. "Mr. Drummond," she greeted him coolly, as yet unaware of Jesse's silent presence. "I wanted to ask you about Mr. Danner. I need to speak to him, and even though he's spent many hours at Chamberlain Manor, I've no idea where he lives or how to reach him."

Zeke's mouth twitched. He turned a palm in Jesse's direction, and Orchid Simpson's lovely gray eyes followed

Zeke's outstretched fingers. Those eyes were luminous, reflecting the silver sheen of her gown. Her breasts were outlined perfectly, small and round and lovely. Jesse immediately revised his opinion of the dress. Were the neckline deeper, it might be ravishing after all.

"You're here!" she exclaimed in disbelief.

Jesse had positioned himself against the wall, braced by one shoulder, his arms crossed over his chest in a negligent stance. Now her gaze swept over him and he could see the nearly imperceptible tightening of her lips and a flicker of distaste in those otherwise magnificent eyes.

"Good. That will make my job easier," she added with a frown.

"Why don't you sit down?" Zeke offered, indicating the couch at the side of the room.

She moved with grace to perch stiffly on a cushion, glancing in Jesse's general direction but not focusing on him. For weeks she'd hovered around the room while Jesse had forced himself to entertain a giggling Charlotte. A silent wraith filled with malevolence where he was concerned, Orchid had made herself nigh invisible. Yet, he'd been attuned to her movements, to the glide of her skirt and the whisper of her petticoats. One day in particular he'd been fascinated by the trim ankle she'd inadvertently displayed while she'd sat silently on the windowsill. She was a woman of movement; he would swear it, yet she forced an unnatural stillness upon herself. He could picture her wild and free; he'd *seen* her in writhing fury in Tyrone McNamara's locked embrace. Inside that careful shell she must be a mass of frustration and suppressed emotion. That thought filled him with sudden passion, and Jesse was forced to look away first.

"What job have I made easier?" he clipped out.

"I've been giving your plan to marry Charlotte a lot of thought, as you know," she said, clasping her hands tightly in her lap. "And I've come to some conclusions."

"I'm just dying to hear them," Jesse murmured sardonically, regarding her through half-shut eyes, studying her face. She was gorgeous, he thought dispassionately, keeping his more dangerous thoughts well under control.

Zeke's head turned his way. He lifted his brows in a question. Jesse shook his head almost imperceptibly. *Let the lady finish,* he told his friend silently.

"I don't believe you'll give up this ridiculous, self-serving plan of yours unless you have a better offer," she continued scornfully.

Jesse asked quietly, "Meaning?"

"There are other lovely and wealthy women in this city who would easily fall in with your plans. You said you wanted respectability. Since you choose to *acquire* it rather than earn it, why don't you target one of them? I could make the introduction and—"

"No. I want Charlotte."

Zeke coughed discreetly and stared down at his hands. He was trying desperately to keep a straight face.

"Mr. Drummond, would you mind if I spoke to Mr. Danner alone?" Kelsey asked a bit desperately.

"Certainly—"

"Zeke stays," Jesse cut him off, slicing a look to Zeke, who sighed and sank back into his chair, his gaze apologetic.

Kelsey's face flushed deep red. "All right, then," she said, stiffening her spine. "I suspected that you might be unwilling to see reason," she told Jesse tautly.

"I'm a cad through and through," Jesse agreed mildly.

"So I'm prepared to offer you an alternate solution. A proposition, actually, in exchange for Charlotte."

"You've got my full attention, Miss Simpson," Jesse drawled.

Kelsey took a breath. Gazing steadily into Jesse's aquamarine eyes, she said flatly, "You can marry me instead. I have the same society connections as Charlotte, and I have a small fortune of my own. I will also make certain you receive a substantial portion of whatever inheritance comes my way when Lady Chamberlain passes on. I know I've been named in her will, and it would be money well spent to save Charlotte inestimable heartache."

Jesse's face didn't change expression one iota, but Zeke visibly brightened. "Jesse?" he asked, smiling at his friend.

"You want to marry me?" Jesse asked Kelsey slowly. She never released her eyes from the fierceness of his own.

"I would rather rot in hell first."

"So you've offered yourself like the sacrificial lamb because you're so selfless?"

Kelsey glanced away, unable to sustain that driving gaze. "Charlotte's young and impressionable. She needs someone to take care of her."

"I'll take care of her."

Her nerves scraped at his knowing tone. She glanced at him again, unsure whether to be relieved or disappointed at this juncture. She'd been so certain he would accept. Why? He'd made it clear he disliked her intensely. And she certainly disliked him. But for some perverse reason she'd still thought he might agree. "You're turning down my offer?"

"I don't know." Thoughtfully rubbing his jaw, he asked, "Have you concocted this plan because you're so tired of being a spinster that you'd poach on your girlfriend's man?"

Kelsey's lips parted and she went white. She stared into Jesse's darkly handsome face and had to fight every instinct she possessed not to bodily launch herself at him and claw his eyes out! "You're the most arrogant and conceited man I've ever met!"

"How much money have you got?" he asked, watching her tensely contained body quiver with indignation. He'd been right about her act of control. She was a volcano about to erupt!

"Twenty thousand dollars. Cash." Her eyes were cold, wintry lakes of silver.

Zeke sucked in a breath, biting his tongue to keep from screaming at Jesse to take her up on her offer. Holy Mother of God! Twenty thousand dollars!

Jesse shot him a quelling look. He had more than enough money already. He'd even told Orchid so, but the scornful look on her face said she hadn't believed him—then or now. "I'm sorry, Miss Simpson, I'm just not interested—in you."

She climbed to her feet with quiet dignity and headed toward the door without another word. "Unless . . ." Jesse drawled slowly.

"You've humiliated me enough for one day, Mr. Danner!" she declared wrathfully.

"Bring a bank draft for the twenty thousand to this office on Friday at one P.M. and prepare to be married that same day."

The order was cold and unemotional. Kelsey's chest tightened. It hurt so badly she wanted to cry out, though why that should be so she couldn't begin to figure out. What a horrible man he'd turned out to be! "You guarantee you'll leave Charlotte alone?"

"I'll never speak to her or look at her again."

Kelsey drew a trembling breath. Uncertainty flashed through her. Now that she'd gotten her wish, she scarcely knew what to do. "There's one more stipulation. This marriage would be temporary, just until you achieve the respectability you want so badly. And it would be a marriage of convenience only. You can keep the money," she added tightly.

His gaze darkened. "I no more want to sleep with you than you do with me. But the marriage lasts until I say otherwise."

"Why?" Kelsey demanded, shocked.

"Because divorce isn't good for respectability. Surely, you know that. Believe me, there's no other reason I would want to stay shackled to you, Miss Simpson. So it's on my terms. All my terms. Do we have an agreement?"

He crossed the floor in that predatory way that Kelsey was coming to know. She stiffened, prepared for anything, but all he did was hold out his hand, meaning to seal the bargain. Seal her fate.

Kelsey stared down at his hand as if it were a poisonous snake. Fighting back a shudder, she slipped her palm into the hard warmth of his fingers and met his beautifully seductive eyes.

"It will be an annulment, Mr. Danner," she stated clearly. "And yes, we have a bargain."

## 5

Kelsey sat in front of the mirror on her dressing table, her arms braced across the lace doily that covered the sculpted oak vanity as if she were preparing for an earthquake. She stared at her reflection. What had she done?

It was one thing to come up with a plan as harebrained and dangerous as the one she'd manufactured, quite another to play it out. Jesse's handshake had left her trembling with uncertainty. Oh, Lord! She pressed her palms to her hot cheeks. *What had she done?*

Pulling herself together, Kelsey walked as if in a trance to her closet. It was Friday. She'd heard the noon bells at the funny little church in the square about a half mile uphill. She would be late. There wasn't any way she could be at Ezekiel Drummond's office by one o'clock.

Maybe Jesse wouldn't wait.

Emitting a sound somewhere between a cry of despair and a snort of disgust, Kelsey pulled out the dark brown dress she saved for occasions she truly loathed. She didn't own a white gown and she wouldn't have worn one if she did. The brown dress was silk and rustled against her petticoats when she yanked it over her head. A series of dull black buttons marched upward from the tips of her black button shoes to the top of the bodice.

She examined her reflection, noticing with pleasure the heavy brown hairnet that covered the natural red highlights in her hair. "You look like a brown mouse," she told herself with a smile.

Frowning, her gaze moved to the one aspect of the dress that made it tolerable in any fashion sense at all: the square-cut neckline. Demure, it nevertheless opened her throat to view by all and sundry, cutting low enough to hint at the tops of her breasts. The unbleached lace surrounding it was an inch thick and helped hide her bosom, but Kelsey, who'd once dreamed of being a princess in beautiful gowns, now couldn't tolerate any article of clothing that reminded her of her youth.

A necklace would only emphasize the neckline, she decided, leaving her skin bare. With unusual distress, she examined her reflection critically. She was pretty; she knew that. But she'd tried so hard for so many years to squelch her identity and personality that she'd almost forgotten what she'd once been like.

Now she remembered. She'd been impulsive, active, determined, and stubborn. A proper little hellion. As free as the wailing wind except everyone had tried to mold her, or force her, or coerce her into doing what *they* wanted. When she'd left Rock Springs she'd vowed to live her own life the way she saw fit.

How could she have ever planned to marry *Jesse Danner?*

Pacing around the room, Kelsey clenched and unclenched her fists. She wouldn't go through with it! She would leave Portland! Leave Charlotte and Agatha. If she married Jesse she would be persona non grata around here anyway, so why compound the mistake?

*Because he'll marry Charlotte and make her life a living hell.*

"Miserable cur," Kelsey muttered furiously.

Grabbing her small valise, she tossed in undergarments and clothes indiscriminately, cramming the case so full she had to bounce up and down on it to get the latch closed. She didn't bother with a hat, but she threw a black cloak over her shoulders. Glancing around the room, her throat ached with despair. She would have to leave her rifle for now, along with most of her other belongings; she could send for them later.

Sighing, Kelsey closed her eyes. She didn't know what Jesse had planned, nor did she know whether she'd really see this wedding through. All she knew was that she was leaving Chamberlain Manor for good.

With a heavy heart she checked her derringer to make sure it was loaded. Picking up her black reticule, she dumped out her compact and perfume and any other feminine articles, replacing them with the gun, extra bullets, and the bank draft for twenty thousand dollars. A life savings. *Her* life savings. Her inheritance.

She was buying happiness, she thought with a painful twist of her heart. Charlotte's happiness.

What was she buying for herself?


The sun was shining beatifically as Kelsey paid the cabbie on the street outside Ezekiel Drummond's office building. The city smelled of dust and horse manure and the dank scent rolling off the Willamette. Picking up her valise, Kelsey gazed up at the brick building that housed Drummond and Company. She'd never run from a fight yet. Gripping the handle of her case with slippery fingers, she strode deliberately through the revolving doors and straight up the stairs.

Outside Zeke's office her footsteps slowed, but the pace was picked up by her erratic breathing. She felt suffocated. Near swooning. The exertion of climbing those steps was only half of it; she was terrified!

The office door was cracked about a foot. Kelsey stayed to one side of the pebbled window, gathering courage and strength. She could hear male voices: Zeke's and Jesse's. Though she hadn't planned on eavesdropping, the opportunity presented itself and Kelsey listened with straining ears.

"She's an hour late already," Zeke's anxious voice rang clearly. "She's backed out. She never meant to go through with it."

"She hasn't backed out."

Jesse's flat assessment raised Kelsey's ire. Heat flushed her face. He was so bloody sure of himself!

"She was playing some kind of game. A trick, to steer you away from Charlotte."

"She's not stupid. She's aware that if she doesn't show, I'll resume my earlier plan. She'll be here when she finally screws her courage up."

"You think she's scared?" Zeke sounded surprised.

"I think men in general frighten that poor little mouse."

Poor little mouse be damned! Kelsey stalked to the door and flung it open wider. Her gray eyes flashed with indignation. She was so angry she could hardly scare up any spit to tell Mr. Jesse Danner what she thought of him!

But then she saw that his gaze was centered on the door through which she'd entered. His eyes were full of laughter. His mouth was curved—oh so seductively, his teeth white. He'd been expecting her, the horrible beast! He'd known she was listening!

"Miss Simpson, you're here!" Zeke declared.

It occurred to Kelsey that Mr. Ezekiel Drummond was far too involved in Jesse Danner's plot to gain respectability, but she was incapable of seeing anything except Jesse's damnably handsome and amused face. He was laughing at her.

Kelsey straightened her spine. She would go through with this bloody wedding, by God, for the sheer pleasure of seeing the look on his face afterward!

"I'm sorry. I was delayed. I hope it won't make a difference."

She injected just the right amount of concern to have Jesse's expression change from enjoyment to suspicion. He was calculating just what was going through her mind. Kelsey shot him a look of pure innocence that deepened his suspicious frown.

Score one for the Garretts! she thought with uncharacteristic family pride.

"It won't make any difference." Jesse was abrupt. "We'll be man and wife by this afternoon one way or another."

"Did you bring the bank draft?" Zeke asked.

Kelsey pulled the offending envelope from her reticule, holding it between two fingers as if the touch of it sickened her. She extended it toward Jesse who, after a noticeable pause, yanked it from her palm, folded it, and shoved it into an inner coat pocket without looking at it.

He looked undeniably handsome, Kelsey thought unwillingly as he escorted her downstairs to a buggy parked behind the building. His suit was black and gorgeous. The breeze teased his hair, ruffling it across the back of his neck, tossing it in front of his eyes. He'd shaved, and something about the smoothness of his cheek and chin drew Kelsey's gaze. The snowy white shirt surrounding his sun-darkened flesh was a pleasing contrast, and she inwardly grimaced when she contrasted her own choice of clothing. Oh, well. This marriage was a sham, and there was no need to worry over silly details that wouldn't matter at all as soon as the deed was accomplished.

The day's brilliant sunlight fell over the dusty buggy in unrelenting glory, heightening the vehicle's shabbiness. Jesse scarcely had a cent to his name, Kelsey realized with a stab of something like guilt as he wiped off the seat for her. The carriage he'd used when he'd rescued her from Tyrone had undoubtedly been a hired one.

He held his hand, offering help, but when Kelsey glanced at him uncertainly, his cool, sharp appraisal reminded her who he was and what his morals were.

She gathered her skirts and brushed past his hand, climbing onto the seat and staring forward, her jaw set.

The place Jesse had chosen for the wedding was a tiny chapel perched on the edge of Portland's teeming, seedy, and notoriously wicked waterfront. Out of her peripheral vision Kelsey saw Jesse turn her way as he pulled the buggy up to the curb. He was waiting for her reaction.

She stared at the chapel appraisingly. It was a sorry sight. The doors were opened invitingly, but grizzled, lice-ridden human specimens lay about the place, asleep or in stupors. Portland's loose drinking laws had turned every corner into a tavern—the building next to the chapel being no exception. Off-key singing—a raucous tale of a young maiden stowaway found by the lusty crew—was the processional music as Jesse mockingly gestured that she enter the chapel ahead of him.

Having grown up in Rock Springs, and being well acquainted with its Half Moon Saloon (Jace owned the damn thing, whores and all, for God's sake!) there was little in the way of decadence and depravity that could shock Kelsey.

As she swept past Jesse into the chapel she decided to

get a bit of her own back. She shot him a look from beneath her lashes. "Is there any chance the minister will be sober?" she asked softly.

Her candor surprised him. He jerked slightly. "No."

"Well, just as long as this marriage is legal and binding. Charlotte must think you're actually wedded to me."

"We will be. Trust me."

He held her gaze for a long moment. Kelsey, for reasons she couldn't explain—and which infuriated her enormously later—was temporarily mesmerized. That gaze dropped to her mouth, hung there explosively for a heartbeat, then sank yet farther, to the neckline of her gown. If it was a deliberate means to make her aware of her own femininity, her locked-up sexuality, it surely worked.

Kelsey dragged her eyes away and blinked against the dimly lit interior.

"Mr. Danner?" a booming voice called.

"Reverend Cleaves," Jesse greeted him, extending a hand.

The minister was a short, spare man with a loud voice and an energetic way of moving that suggested he could single-handedly, cheerfully, rid the world of sin and sorrow if given half a chance.

He pumped Jesse's hand, then clasped one of Kelsey's within both of his, gazing at her as if she were the luckiest woman alive.

"I have two witnesses," he told them. "Mrs. Reynolds plays the organ, if you'd like some accompaniment."

"No," Jesse answered flatly.

"Yes," Kelsey said at the same time.

She challenged him with a look that said, Why not? This is my wedding too.

"Tell Mrs. Reynolds thank-you," Jesse capitulated.

They were ushered into a small chamber with two tiers of candles in gleaming brass stands. How the stands had escaped being pilfered for cheap wine was anyone's guess. Reverend Cleaves draped a white satin shawl over his black suit, took a Bible lovingly from the plump, smiling woman on his right, then gestured Kelsey and Jesse to come forward.

Curiously, it was Jesse who hesitated. The look he sent to the reverend down that short aisle was one of a man caught in the throes of a powerful dilemma.

"Orchid," he murmured uneasily under his breath.

"Have you changed your mind?" she asked softly.

For an answer he clasped her hand, placing it on his arm, tucking her close. But his stiff actions spoke more of a man facing a firing squad than one about to be married. He didn't look at her, just stood there, a muscle jerking in his jaw.

Kelsey glanced at his finely sculpted face, focusing on the nose that had been so drastically changed. She remembered the last time she'd almost been a bride. With Harrison, Jesse's older brother. She'd been left at the altar that time through circumstances beyond Harrison's control. She'd be damned if she'd be left at the altar again, especially by another Danner.

"I'll give you time to think it over," she said coolly. Walking straight down the aisle ahead of him, she smiled at the concerned reverend. "Could I have a few moments alone with you? There's something I need to talk about before Jesse and I are married."

"A confession, my dear?" he asked kindly.

"Of a sort," she answered after a moment of hesitation.

He beamed at her. Kelsey realized wryly that he thought he was going to hear her confess to some terrible wrongdoing. Well, maybe he was.

Jesse was hot and stifled and uncomfortable. This situation was fast getting beyond his control. The little chapel reeked of sour scents from the river and the street that even the gently flickering beeswax candles couldn't override. It was the middle of the day and it was too hot. He wanted to yank off his coat and tie and head straight to the corner bar and drink himself into a stupor.

Hell, where was the woman? She'd grabbed the reverend and practically dragged the fellow from the room. Mrs. Reynolds was waiting patiently at the organ and the other woman, the one with the smile permanently engraved on her portly face, had opted to sit down on the front pew and rest her feet.

It took all of Jesse's concentration to remember *why* he was going through with this and *what* the rewards would be. Instinctually, he wanted to bolt from the room and let Orchid Simpson rot in this miserable little chapel with Reverend Cleaves, Mrs. Reynolds, the fat lady, and anyone else who cared to join in this ridiculous travesty.

Deep in his gut he knew this was a mistake. And Orchid, the lovely witch, had engineered this situation to make him sweat. He was fast growing beyond mere sweating, however; he was cooking! His own anger and impatience had combined with the summer weather to lift his temper into dangerous territory.

The door behind the altar opened and Orchid and the reverend returned. She stopped in front of the altar, glanced back, and lifted one fine brow. "Are you ready?" she asked him sardonically.

With a control he'd mastered only in these past few years of his life, Jesse stowed his flickering rage to the farthest corners of his mind. "Yes," he bit out, stalking down the aisle.

This time she held out her palm, enjoining him to take it. He clasped it in his own. Her hand was cool; icy, really. He was hot and she was cold, and he wondered if that was a prophetic start to their life together.

"Your—fiancée—suggested signing the papers after the wedding," the reverend said in a befuddled manner. He seemed peculiarly at a loss. "In case either of you has a—change of heart."

"Fine." Jesse almost admired her forethought. He was surprised she'd let things go this far.

The ceremony began. Jesse was detached. He stared past the reverend to the green velvet drapes drawn across the back of the church. The drapes hid the scarred, broken bricks that made up the back wall. A touch of elegance in squalor. He'd chosen this chapel deliberately, a macabre touch to frame this silly pomp and circumstance. But Orchid wasn't the least bit shocked. She was more amused, and yes, nervous: He could practically hear her knees knocking together. But when he glanced her way, her gray gaze seemed to say, You needn't have bothered, you silly ass. You can't surprise me. You can't even interest me.

Holy Christ! She was going to be his wife if he didn't do something drastic right *now*.

"Do you, Jesse Danner, take this woman, Kelsey Garrett, to be your lawfully wedded wife?"

He didn't hear it for a long, pregnant moment. He was concentrating too hard on what his answer would be. Do you take her? *Do* you? But then he heard it, heard it in the pit of his soul. *Kelsey Garrett!*

He stared at her in blank incredulity.

Amused and scornful gray eyes gazed back at him.

"Kelsey?" his voice shook slightly.

"Kelsey Orchid Garrett," she qualified.

"Oh, *hell!*"

"Mr. Danner," the reverend admonished with a shake of his head.

Jesse's jaw slackened, increasing the shining mirth in those silvery eyes. The rushing inside his head sounded like a Pacific storm. No, it was the sound of her laughter. Only she wasn't laughing aloud. She was laughing *inside!* This was the other Orchid he'd only guessed at. The one with restless fire, and, it appeared, a macabre sense of humor.

And she was enjoying every god-awful moment of his shock!

"Kelsey Garrett." He shook his head to clear it.

She hated him because he was Jesse Danner, he realized in dawning wonder. Not because he'd tried to marry Charlotte. Because he was Jesse Danner from Rock Springs and she knew every blasted detail about his past.

Well, he knew a thing or two about her too. She was a *Garrett*, for God's sake. Jace Garrett's younger sister. And that made her a liar, a schemer, and a grafter, and he'd had the dubious pleasure of witnessing some of those traits firsthand already.

"Mr. Danner?" the reverend asked. "Do you take Kelsey Garrett to be your—"

"Yes," he answered swiftly. "I do."

"To have and to hold?"

"Yes."

"For richer for poorer?"

"Yes," he answered intensely, his gaze slicing to Kelsey.

"In sickness and in health?"

Her health was deserting her, Jesse thought, watching the color drain right out of her face. "Yes, yes, yes!" he declared impatiently.

"Until death do you part?"

"Until death. Right." He smiled tightly into Kelsey's now-widened eyes. "Your turn," he said softly through his teeth.

"Kelsey Garrett, do you take this man, Jesse Danner, to be your lawfully wedded husband?"

An engulfing wave crashed over Kelsey's head. She was drowning. Drowning, drowning, drowning. She felt a hand on her arm, hard and hurting. It was Jesse. Holding on to her to keep her from fainting.

She opened her mouth to say no. This was a ridiculous game and she had to end it. But then she caught sight of his expression. He knew she wouldn't be able to go through with the ceremony. Pride kept her from forming the word; she couldn't do it.

"Yes," she whispered above her thundering heart.

"Yes?" Jesse asked sharply, amazed, before the reverend could continue.

Knowing she'd sealed her fate, Kelsey swallowed and said in a stronger voice, "Yes. I do. . . ."

"Oh, *hell!*"

By the time they left the chapel the heat of the day had turned the streets to baked cobblestones and dry, throat-catching dust. Kelsey was wilted. She wasn't as good at emotional confrontations as she was at physical ones, she'd learned to her dismay. She felt wrung out, and when Jesse suddenly grabbed her, slamming her against the vestibule wall with the hard and tensile strength of his entire body, she nearly cried out from pain and surprise.

"Kelsey Garrett?" he said through his teeth. Then, softer, "Kelsey Garrett?"

"Let go of me, Jesse."

"Not until you tell me what this is all about. You're my wife now. You realize that, don't you? My *wife*," he muttered furiously, clenching his fists as if fighting the urge to strangle her.

"Just temporarily."

"You're damn right!"

He flung himself away from her, eyeing her as if he expected her to sprout another head. But he couldn't rip his gaze away, as if her appearance were fascinating in some repulsive way.

Kelsey didn't know what to say, so she kept quiet, staring back at him warily. Jesse's temper was explosive. She wouldn't be surprised if he tried to do her bodily harm.

He couldn't seem to take it in. He just stared at her while the heat and smell from the street mingled with the cloying atmosphere of the church.

"I married a Garrett," he finally said blankly.

"Just temporarily," Kelsey repeated.

Jesse regarded her murderously. "You knew all along who I was. Why didn't you just come out with it? Charlotte would have never been allowed to marry me if my past came to light."

"I couldn't be sure of that."

"Oh, couldn't you? You wanted this marriage for some other reason. What?"

Kelsey's lips tightened. She tried to stoke up her anger, but she just felt too tired. Suddenly Jesse grabbed her shoulders and shook her so hard her neck ached.

As soon as he released her she doubled up her fist to slug him in the stomach, but he grabbed her wrists, glaring at her, his nose a hairbreadth from hers. Fury simmered in those blue eyes. Blind fury.

"Answer me," he said in a dangerously soft voice.

"I married you to turn you away from Charlotte. I know what you are, and I'm better prepared to handle you than she is."

"What am I?" he demanded.

"You're a wastrel. A liar, an opportunist, and a womanizer. You've always gotten by on shallow charm, even when you were fifteen!''

''Well, that's a pretty detailed list, Mrs. Danner. Want to know what you are?''

''No. Let go of my wrists. You're hurting me.''

He snorted, tightening his grip cruelly. Kelsey sucked in a breath, her mind churning in an effort to thwart him.

''You're an empty, envious, mean-spirited woman who would rather sell herself to a man like a whore than risk winning a husband on her *feminine qualities*.'' His voice rasped in her ear. ''Don't be hurling the first stone, Mrs. Danner. Lest you want to be buried under a rockfall!''

She hated him. She hated the way he said, ''Mrs. Danner,'' as if it tasted bad on his tongue. She hated the way he looked. She hated his touch!

''I paid for this marriage with my inheritance,'' she told him in a tight, flat voice that warned of her escalating temper. ''We made a bargain. So take your dirty hands off me and let's get on with it. You want respectability, start acting respectable. You're a social disaster, Jesse, and unless you change, and change quickly, you'll be laughed out of Portland's elite circles before you've even begun!''

His eyes narrowed. ''You don't know everything about me,'' he declared cryptically, releasing her so suddenly she nearly lost her balance.

He strode into the baking sunlight. Kelsey glanced down at her wrists, which were red and hurting, the skin still burning where he'd twisted it. She thought of her derringer. She'd never shot a man in the back but, my Lord, she itched to take out her gun and blast him!

Drawing a calming breath, she followed her new husband to the dust-shrouded black buggy, a niggling worry taking root as she realized the truth to his last statement: She didn't know everything about this Jesse Danner. Her opinion was based on what she knew of his past. She knew next to nothing about his present.

But, she thought with renewed panic and desperation, she was about to find out.

# 6

The apartment was swept clean, but that was its only saving grace. It was small and the noxious scent of it was enough to make Kelsey gag. She stood in the center of the living room, trying desperately to hide her alarm. This was where Jesse intended her to stay?

He'd disappeared through the doorway to another room. The bedroom, she presumed. She didn't have the courage to follow him. Bedsprings groaned. What *was* he doing?

Kelsey's hands were like ice even though the air was so stale it seemed to have the substance of pudding every time she took a shallow breath. She could taste the squalor. Her mind was too jumbled to think why he'd brought her there; this was hardly the place to start scaling the heights of society. But she'd be damned if she'd pose a question. He'd been silent since the chapel, deathly silent, and she'd shared that silence with relish. She could outwait him, outplay him. She had no doubt.

His booted footsteps rang across the plankwood floor and she realized the sound of the bedsprings was only from him flinging her valise on the bed. Small comfort.

He stopped short, about six feet to one side of her. Keeping a rigid posture, Kelsey slowly turned to confront him.

"Lovely," she said.

He didn't make any response, either verbally or by the merest flicker of expression. His gaze seemed to move past her, to the window, as if his mind were elsewhere.

That irritated her. She didn't believe anyone could be so supremely unaffected by the events of the past few hours. He looked, she realized belatedly, totally nonplussed.

"I have to leave," he said. "I put your valise in the bedroom."

"Where are your clothes?"

"I haven't brought them here yet. I'll go get 'em."

"No, wait." Kelsey moved between him and the door. "You really intend for us to *live* here? Where *are* your clothes? Do you have some other residence?"

"I'll be back."

"If you leave without answering some questions, don't expect me to be here when you return," she declared imperiously.

His gaze sliced to hers. A smoldering fury turned those aquamarine eyes a chilling blue, and Kelsey straightened away from him in spite of herself. "Suit yourself," he told her icily. "But don't meddle in my plans. You bought me, and I bought you."

Kelsey's mouth dropped open in outrage.

"Consider the twenty thousand your dowry. It's the only way any man would have you."

Kelsey couldn't answer him. His cruelty shouldn't surprise her, but it did, and she was supremely aware of how pathetically weak her defenses were against that kind of hurtful remark.

He gazed at her a few nerve-stretching moments longer. Without another word he quietly shut the door behind him, but there was more suppressed emotion in that gentle closing than if he'd slammed the thing so hard it'd rocked off its hinges.

Kelsey walked into the bedroom and sat on the edge of the bed. Because she had nowhere else to go, she decided not to leave. Closing her eyes, she thought about how Charlotte would take the news of her recent marriage. A bubble of hysteria rose in her chest, and she had to gulp several times to keep it down.

"You've made a mess of everything," she told herself dismally, and the words seemed to echo back at her like some hellish prophecy for her future.

Portland's waterfront was seamy, smelly, dangerous, and full of the kind of people the Women's Temperance Society tried its futile best to save. Jesse wandered among them, drawing curious stares because of the elegant black suit he wore. He was out of place, and might have been the recipient of pickpockets and thugs except for the controlled look on his face and the coiled fury that emanated from him like a supernatural force.

The waterfront scum left him alone. Only one whore even dared approach him, and his terse words of rejection were enough to send her scurrying back to the safety of her friends.

At ten o'clock that evening Jesse had found his way to a noisy tavern called Briny's. He sat at the bar, oblivious to the fights and colorful language that swirled around him. Smoke hovered like a cloud. The bottles behind the bar were coated dark gray with it. The bartender wore an apron stained with God knew what. He kept refilling Jesse's glass with his own particular brand of rotgut whiskey and silently signaling the group of men playing poker at a relatively quiet nearby table against the rear wall.

The bartender, who called himself Sal, was proud to declare himself a personal friend of the establishment's owner, Briny himself. He'd seen all kinds come in for a drink, seamen and waterfront scum, dirty whores and fashionably dressed women, gentlemen seeking a little anonymity. But he'd never seen a man show up in such an elegant suit before, and he wasn't quite certain how to read the man inside the clothes, drinking with such blatant determination. Drowning his sorrows, probably, the poor fool. Except he didn't look like a fool, and he sure as hell wasn't poor. Too much arrogance, and not enough desperation. A businessman, maybe. Or a preacher? Or maybe even a groom, Sal decided, judging the man by his choice of clothes rather than by his personality. It was easier. The man wearing the suit was just a bit too tricky to pigeonhole.

"Ya got a good reason to drink, fella?" Sal asked, showing unusual concern by swiping down the scarred bar in front of Jesse.

Jesse glanced up at Sal, assessing him with a pair of the sharpest, bluest eyes Sal had ever seen. It unnerved him slightly.

"How bad do you want to know?" Jesse asked.

"Huh?"

"How bad do you want to know the reason why I'm drinking?" he repeated patiently. Glancing at the table of poker players, he added, "Bad enough to keep your dogs off me?"

Sal didn't answer.

The man at the bar emptied his pockets. There was about fifteen dollars and some coin there, a relatively inexpensive pocket watch, and a crumpled piece of paper that bore an address. "That's all I have with me. I went to the bank today and deposited twenty thousand dollars, my bride's dowry. But I didn't bring any with me, so you can beat me up if you want, but it's not gonna change anything."

Sal looked at the money, then at the man. "What's your name, fella?"

Jesse smiled thinly. "Call me Duped."

"Duped?"

"I've been duped for about eight hours now."

Sal grinned, showing off an incredible set of beautiful teeth. He was one of those lucky people who never faced cavities and who'd been providential enough to hang on to those choppers through all the fights of his boyhood.

He poured his newfound friend another shot of whiskey. "It weren't be the bride with the dough, would it?"

"Yes, it would." Jesse tossed back the whiskey.

"Boys, leave this here Mr. Duped alone. He ain't got much money on him. If'n we treat him right, he might come back with more though. Lots more!" Sal laughed heartily, his great belly shaking beneath the soiled apron.

Jesse suddenly found himself surrounded by "friends." They weren't menacing, but they felt bound and determined to let him buy them all drinks. He was glad to help. Whiskey flowed and talk grew bold, and through a haze of self-indulgence Jesse felt the grip on his anger loosen a little.

"Wha'd she pay so much to get the likes of you for?" someone asked, clapping him on the back.

"She needed a husband. I was available." It took a great deal of effort to keep from slurring. Jesse was proud of himself, until he fell backward off the stool. His friends picked him up and plunked him back down on it.

"She ugly?" one asked, leaning forward to send reeking, whiskey-sour breath into Jesse's face.

"Stupid?" another voice suggested. "Dumb as horse-meat?"

Jesse considered. "Nope. Not ugly or stupid."

"What's wrong with her, then?" a voice by the door bellowed.

"She's ornery. And she's uppity. And she hates men."

There was a moment of silence, as close to a prayer for their brother as these men ever came to. Jesse half expected to hear choir music.

"You're a sorry bastard," someone commiserated.

"You know what ridin' her's gonna be like, doncha? Better check out Mamie at the boat."

"Mamie'll treatcha right. Or one o' her girls."

"Don't go back to that tight-legged bitch tonight. You need some fun."

"Mamie?" Jesse asked foggily.

"Best damn madam this side of the Willamette. All the way to the coast. None better."

There was a general consensus that this was true, although a lone voice in the corner insisted a woman named Patricia Lee could give Mamie a run for her money. This created a ruckus that left three men with broken teeth and blood-smeared mouths. Since Jesse had no interest in Mamie or Patricia Lee, he decided not to get involved.

"What's 'er name?" a skinny guy in a black bowler asked. He was leaning over the bar, clinging to it for support.

"My wife? She's Mrs. Duped. She duped me. I duped her." Jesse grinned.

"Ya did? How?"

"Don't know yet." Jesse staggered off his chair, swaying slightly. His friends plunked him down once again, none too gently, but it was more from lack of finesse than any malevolence on their part.

"Get this fella 'nother drink!" Skinny demanded. "He ain't goin' home to that ornery bitch sober!"

Jesse, who rarely let himself get so shit-faced that he couldn't see danger coming, decided he owed himself this belated bachelor party.

"Keep 'em comin', Sal," he suggested with a dopey grin. "I'd rather be drunk than married."

"Looks like you're a little of both," said Sal, breaking out a bottle of his best whiskey in a magnanimous gesture to toast the new groom.

Kelsey managed to wait decorously for Jesse the space of exactly one hour—well, almost an hour. That was long enough for her to swallow back her melancholy and then decide there was no earthly reason to do anything he said.

She slammed out of the apartment and clambered down the narrow stairway to the street, where she walked ten blocks before she felt safe enough to keep her hand outside of her reticule and away from the protection of her gun.

She hailed a carriage for hire and directed the driver to Chamberlain Manor. It was evening and Agatha and Charlotte should both be home by her reckoning. Unless, of course, some other young swain was squiring Charlotte around. She wished she could encourage Charlotte to wait for romance, but given the fact that everyone—Jesse Danner included—felt Kelsey was eaten up with jealousy over the fact that she couldn't land a husband, Kelsey felt her advice would fall on deaf ears.

"Miss Simpson, you're home!" Cora Lee declared in delight. "We've been sorely missin' you these past hours. Lady Chamberlain is powerful worried."

"I'm sorry. Where is Lady Chamberlain?"

"In the drawing room, ma'am."

Kelsey walked down the hall, her footsteps slowing with dread. What she was about to tell Agatha and Charlotte weighed heavily on her mind. She'd never been the kind of woman who stole another's man, and the enormity of what she'd done was nearly unbearable.

Grimacing, she let herself into the drawing room. Agatha's head turned at her approach. "Orchid!" she exclaimed in relief.

Charlotte whipped around. Kelsey hadn't seen her at

first, for her green brocade gown was nearly the exact shade as the curtains she'd been standing next to while she stared out the windows. She was tense, her blue eyes filled with a nameless anxiety.

Kelsey drew a deep breath. "Agatha, there's something I have to tell you."

"Is it about Jesse?" Charlotte asked quickly.

"Mr. Danner hasn't called here all week," Agatha explained as Kelsey crossed to the fireplace.

Kelsey looked down at her fingers. No wedding band. Jesse hadn't bothered to buy her one. "I know. I'm the reason. I made a bargain with him."

Charlotte stared at her uncomprehendingly.

Miserably, Kelsey admitted, "I said I'd marry him if he stopped chasing after you, Charlotte."

Charlotte's gasp was torn from her soul.

"Orchid," Agatha said crisply, sitting erectly. "Whyever did you do such a thing?"

"Because I know Jesse. I knew him when he was a boy. He's a renegade, a womanizer, and by all accounts, a rapist. I think he's murdered some men. By the time he was fifteen he'd been in enough trouble to make every mother in three counties pray he wouldn't set his sights on her daughter." Her voice faltered and her troubled gaze encountered Charlotte's white face. "I couldn't let him use you, Charlotte."

"Use me?" Hectic color invaded Charlotte's cheeks. "He was getting ready to marry me!"

"I know. But for all the wrong reasons. He admitted to me that—"

"How do you know Mr. Danner so well?" Agatha interrupted. She picked up the silver bell on the table beside her and rang for Cora Lee. The downstairs maid appeared so quickly, Kelsey wondered if she'd been listening at the keyhole. "Tea, please, Cora Lee. And maybe some brandy."

When the maid disappeared, Kelsey half sat, half fell into the chair next to Agatha's. The starch had drained straight out of her. "I haven't been completely truthful with you, Lady Chamberlain. My name isn't Orchid Simpson, it's

Kelsey Garrett. My family and Jesse's live in Rock Springs and they've been feuding for years."

"You deceived us!" Charlotte's lips trembled. Her eyes were glassy, full of horror and betrayal.

"I couldn't let my family find me," Kelsey said painfully.

"You didn't trust us to keep your secret?" This was from Agatha, whose pallor was a frightening gray color.

"Not at first, and then later you all thought I was someone else and it just seemed easier to keep up the deception."

"Why are you telling us now?"

"Because of Jesse!" Kelsey shook herself, angry all over again that he'd created so much trouble and turmoil. "Because he'd targeted Charlotte as his next victim. He needs social respectability, and he chose to take it rather than earn it!"

"Why does he need social respectability?" Agatha asked tartly.

"I—don't know." Kelsey blinked rapidly as the door opened and Cora Lee brought in the elegant silver tea set. A delicate, flowery scent, Agatha's favorite jasmine tea, filled the air.

"I don't care why he wants to marry me, I love him!" Charlotte declared in a high, passionate voice. "I love him!"

"You don't even know him," Kelsey said gently.

"You just can't bear the idea that he might love me too!"

"Shush, Charlotte." Agatha's voice was like the crack of doom. She turned to Kelsey, and none of the affection Kelsey had grown to depend on was evident in her stern expression. "He's agreed to marry you, then? He'll stop courting Charlotte in exchange?"

"Yes."

"He won't marry her! He won't. He *hates* her! He told me so."

Kelsey died a little inside at the soul-sick misery in Charlotte's outburst. It was a plea. She was begging Kelsey to say it wasn't true.

"Have you agreed to marry him?" Agatha's eyes searched Kelsey's drawn face.

"Yes."

"You don't have to now, dear. If what you say is true, and I believe it is, I won't allow my granddaughter anywhere near the man."

Kelsey regarded the older woman blankly. Charlotte rustled angrily across the room, stopping three feet in front of Kelsey's chair, her fists clenched, her bosom heaving. "You can't stop me from seeing him!" she declared. "Either of you. I'll see whomever I damn well please!"

"Charlotte!" Agatha was furious.

"You can't stop me!" she wailed in growing hysteria.

"I've already married him."

For a heartbeat Charlotte didn't comprehend Kelsey's words. Then she let out a weak cry and clapped her hand to her mouth. Tears welled in her velvety blue eyes. She fled the room, fighting back tortured gasps. Her footsteps clambered on the stairs. A door slammed. Silence followed. Dreadful silence.

"Tea?" Agatha asked in a dry, papery voice. She handed Kelsey a cup.

Kelsey accepted it as if in a dream. She even tried to drink a little. She couldn't look at Agatha. She was a traitor. A Judas. Though her reasons were right and sound, she knew neither Agatha nor Charlotte would ever be able to truly forgive her.

"I suspect you'll be moving out now," Agatha said, her voice so normal and pleasant that Kelsey felt hysteria bubble up inside her again.

"Yes." Choking back a sob, she set her teacup down and managed to say in a voice that trembled only a little, "I'll send for my things."

"I'm sorry, dear."

"So am I," she said through a shaky smile.

It was well past midnight by the time Kelsey arrived at Jesse's horrible, mean little apartment. She was alone. Her erstwhile husband hadn't returned. Kelsey was too distraught to worry unduly about either Jesse's whereabouts or her own surroundings. She deserved this miserable hovel. She deserved worse! This whole disaster wasn't even Jesse's fault. It was hers. *Hers!* She'd brought it all on herself.

For the first time in recent memory, she had no idea what to do next.

She shoved her valise off the bed in a fit of rage. The case sprang open eagerly and clothes tumbled to the floor. Kelsey fought the urge to snatch them up and rip them to shreds. Instead, she flung herself on the moth-eaten wool blanket that served as a coverlet and laid her arm across her eyes.

She drifted off to slumber, certain even as she relaxed that she would never be able to fall asleep. Her dreams were filled with images of Jesse and Charlotte, and a deep, deep anxiety that brought her sharply awake, bathed in sweat, sometime near dawn. She watched the gray skies lighten through the window. She wrinkled her nose in disgust as daylight coldly revealed the dilapidated ruin Jesse Danner had brought his bride to.

*Why am I still here?* she asked herself. Who said she had to stay in these sorry rooms? *Jesse?*

The thought galvanized her into action. She leapt from the bed, ripped off the hated brown wedding dress, and flung it against the wall, where it hit the windowsill and hung there like some drunken curtain.

In her drawers and camisole, her hands on her hips, Kelsey surveyed the room with disfavor. Auburn hairs fell across her eyes and she blew them away with restrained fury. She ripped the net from her hair, letting the lustrous red-brown mane tumble over her shoulders. Yearning for the clawfoot bathtub at Chamberlain Manor, she wondered if she had the nerve to wander down the hall and find the bathing facilities. Were they even designated for men and women? The thought of some hairy, lustful beast interrupting her was enough to make her stomach turn.

A scrape of a key in the lock caused Kelsey to freeze where she stood. Since she herself had no key, she'd been forced to leave the door open but had bolted it upon her return. Now, realizing her new husband was undoubtedly about to make an appearance, she raced to the living room, grabbed the one and only chair, and shoved it under the doorknob, making it impossible for Jesse to enter.

The scraping sounds stopped. He tried to shove his shoulder against the door. Wood groaned. Kelsey eyed the doorjamb with dismay. Could termites have infested this neglected building? Undoubtedly!

Suddenly furious, Kelsey yanked the chair out of the way, slid the bolt herself, and flung open the door. "I was just about to leave," she said icily as Jesse, who'd been about to shove his shoulder against the panels one more time, tumbled into her, knocking them both to the floor.

Kelsey gasped, shocked and stunned by the feel of his hard body atop hers. She wriggled furiously, kicking and flailing and muttering unintelligible threats. "Get your blasted hide off me!" she shouted, sinking her fingers into his thick hair and yanking his head up to meet her blazing eyes.

Jesse grunted and knocked her arm away. " 'Scuse me," he murmured, lifting himself on his palms until his chest was raised above her heaving breasts.

"You're drunk." Kelsey could taste his whiskey-laden breath.

"You're undressed," he said in surprise, his gaze centering on the milky white crests of her breasts.

She instantly covered her exposed flesh with her hands. "If you don't get off me this instant, I'll scream and scream until someone comes to take you to jail!"

Jesse shook his head, as if he were having trouble concentrating. "No one's gonna help you here, Mrs. Danner," he pointed out.

*"Get off me!"*

Instead of complying, the beast had the nerve to actually bend his head and kiss her. With thoughts of paying him back as she had before, Kelsey unclamped her locked teeth. Before she could bite into his lower lip, he said softly, "Remember, I'm a rapist and a murderer. I've also been known to beat women on occasion, and I'm feeling more in the mood for delivering a sound thrashing by the second."

"You're not drunk," she breathed against his lips.

"Not drunk enough," he assured her.

His mouth covered hers in a searing kiss that turned Kelsey's bones to liquid and did wild things to her pulse. Her emotions were so torn and confused that she didn't resist. Nor did she willingly participate.

As soon as Jesse realized she wasn't going to fight, his lips gentled, moving over Kelsey's with an almost irresistible appeal, while an awful, treacherous warmth seeped through every pore of Kelsey's body.

Her lips parted involuntarily, her mouth clinging to his, softly greeting his kiss with one of her own. Confusion and curiosity made her want to experience more. This was nothing like the timid pecks or sloppy kisses of Kelsey's past swains. Nor was it like Tyrone McNamara's overpowering smashing of mouths together. This was . . . wonderful.

Jesse lifted his head, eyeing her narrowly. Reality washed over Kelsey and she could have cried out at her susceptibility. "You're not the only one in the mood for a sound thrashing," she declared, punching one fist into his chest.

"Oh, hell!" he muttered, rolling off her at the same moment. He clunked his head against the hard floor. He was less sober than he sounded, she realized with some relief as he groaned and grimaced.

"Serves you right, you bastard!" Kelsey scrambled to her feet. "I'm not staying in this stinking hole one more minute! I'm getting out of here. If you want me, I'll be at the Portland Hotel."

"No, you won't."

His total lack of concern ripped aside the last vestiges of her thin veneer of sophistication. Kelsey reacted like the Rock Springs hellion she'd once been. She grabbed him by the lapels of his once-black—now dusty gray suit—and tried to haul him to his feet.

Unfortunately, she miscalculated. She was strong, but not that strong. Not strong enough to lift a man who outweighed her by over eighty pounds. She managed to get his head off the ground, then drop him. Jesse groaned again.

"I'd like to kill you!" she shouted, kicking him in the thigh.

He swore and struggled to get up.

"You're so drunk you can't see straight! What were you doing all night? Where were you? If you wanted to drown your sorrows in liquor, you should have taken me with you. I'm the one who's got something to cry about! Look at you! *You haven't changed one bit.*"

"Stop screaming like a fishwife. You want to drink yourself into oblivion, be my guest."

He staggered to his feet, running a hand through his hair, eyeing her as if she were some noxious insect. She suddenly felt self-conscious. Hearing noises in the hallway—doors creaking open, stealthy footsteps—she slammed closed the door to their apartment and bolted it.

Only she'd bolted herself in with Jesse.

Beneath the scent of liquor she could smell a tawdry feminine perfume. "You've been with a woman," she said in disbelief.

His gaze took in her camisole and drawers. "Yes," he admitted.

Kelsey wouldn't have believed she could feel worse than she already did, but his complete lack of guilt nearly buckled her knees. It had been her wedding night, such as it was, and Jesse, the black-hearted scoundrel, had been making love to some *other woman!*

"Mamie," he said, sounding slightly baffled, as if he couldn't quite believe it himself.

Kelsey couldn't speak. She twisted her head back and forth, trying desperately to control the wounded emotions that seemed to fill up every space inside her.

"I understand she's a whore, and a damned good one too."

"You miserable cur!" Kelsey choked out.

"I didn't bed her, if that's what you're thinking," he said, knowing full well that that was exactly what she was thinking. "I just slept on her floor."

"Oh, *hell!*" she blasted him with one of his own favorite expressions. "When I think about what you are, words fail me."

"That would be a first. You know how to talk sharper and meaner than any female I know, Mrs. Danner."

His tone was more teasing than angry and that worried Kelsey. Worried her, because she inadvertently responded to it. "Don't call me Mrs. Danner," she said.

"It's your name," he pointed out dryly.

"It's an insult, the way you say it."

"You'd prefer I call you Kelsey?"

She didn't like the sound of her first name on his tongue any better. In fact, it sent goose bumps down her arms. "No."

He lifted one brow. "I'll have to call you something."

They stared at each other and Kelsey grew ever more conscious of her state of undress. It took all her strength of will—which her brother had complained bitterly on numerous occasions was an awesome burden on his attempts to find her a suitable husband—not to cross her arms over her chest again. She was unable, unfortunately, to stem the crimson wave that swept up from her breasts and neck and stained her cheeks.

Jesse's gaze followed that blooming tide. His expression was detached. A frown creased his brow. For some reason his very lack of interest bothered Kelsey far more than if he'd suddenly yanked her against him and ravaged her mouth and body.

It was humiliating—no, *mortifying!*—that a man of his dubious temperament—especially where women were concerned—could stand there so *uninvolved,* so utterly *disinterested!*

"I spent last night getting used to the idea that you and I are married," he said.

"Oh, yes?" Fire burned in Kelsey's blood. "It took a night with a damned good whore to help you?"

"If I'd known who you were, I wouldn't have gone through with the wedding," he said, ignoring her.

"I told you who I was before the ceremony."

"You staged the whole thing on purpose," he pointed out. "I merely played my part. So, now we're stuck with each other—at least for the time being. Since being my wife is part of the bargain, you're going to have to play it to the hilt."

She could not *believe* his cool detachment. "Meaning?" she asked in a dangerous tone.

"You're going to have to learn a bit more self-control. A true lady doesn't sputter and scream and challenge her husband. Meekness would be a nice change. 'Blessed are the meek,' " he reminded her.

Was he laughing at her? "You could take some lessons yourself. Your idea to become respectable by setting up house in this cheap, dirty apartment is shocking. And then a night with a whore? Either buy a home—preferably a prestigious one around the park blocks—or move us to a hotel." She smiled faintly as she eased toward the bedroom door and the rest of her clothes. "Since *your wife* is moving to the Portland Hotel, perhaps you'd like to take rooms there as well. My twenty thousand should help pay the cost," she added in a voice that dripped ice.

Kelsey snatched up her nearest gown: the ugly brown wedding dress. She heard Jesse stop at the bedroom doorway, but she kept her back to him as she buttoned up her dress. Only then did she turn around.

He looked murderous, and as sober now as a country parson. "Meekness," was all he managed to say. Kelsey took that to mean he was acquiescing to her suggestion.

She didn't have a chance to ask all the other questions hovering on her tongue. Jesse threw her remaining clothes in her valise and started to take it downstairs. She did question him on where his own belongings were, and he tersely commented that he didn't have any.

Two hours later, when Kelsey was ensconced in a suite of rooms at the Portland Hotel, she realized there were several bags already there with at least three men's suits already hanging in the closet looking freshly laundered and pressed. When Jesse offered no explanation, she bit her tongue, deciding she didn't want to know anyway. Since the suits were in the west-end bedroom and he'd dumped her valise on the four-poster bed in the east-end room, she decided it scarcely mattered from where and when he'd moved his clothes.

The rooms were gorgeous. Done in sky blue and gold, the upholstery and curtains and sinfully thick carpet were so luxurious Kelsey had to fight to keep from demanding how long they could possibly afford such opulence. Her twenty thousand dollars was a lot of money, but it was all she had. She'd given it to Jesse to prove a point. Now a streak of thriftiness she'd never quite been able to staunch made her worry if he intended to squander the whole amount. Surely not. Even Jesse wouldn't be that irresponsible.

Would he?

Kelsey gazed anxiously at Jesse's bedroom door which was closed and locked. She'd grown up wealthy—by Rock Springs standards—but she couldn't abide waste. Now she wished she'd stemmed the recklessness and impulsiveness that had led to this debacle.

Kelsey paced in front of Jesse's cream-colored paneled door, her high-button shoes sinking into the carpet, leaving tracks. Her hair was still unbound, floating like a wild cloud around her shoulders and down her back. She hadn't had time to do more than throw on the hated wedding dress before Jesse had been snapping the reins on the back of the horse who'd drawn their buggy through the teeming streets to the hotel.

Grabbing her unruly mane in an impatient hand, Kelsey muttered furiously beneath her breath and headed to the bathroom. Yes, their room was equipped with a clawfoot tub with its own hot and cold running water. The luxury only made Kelsey more concerned. Jesse Danner or no Jesse Danner, she didn't want to come out of this adventure penniless because of blatant waste.

She bound her hair into a net, splashing her face with water from the beautifully hand-painted porcelain sink in front of the gilt-edged mirror. White porcelain knobs painted with the matching floral pattern in blue, gold, and the faintest peach—a color so lovely it looked as if it might taste delicious—flanked the brass faucet. Every touch of grace and elegance tightened Kelsey's chest.

She stood undecided in the bathroom for long moments. She wanted a bath, but was determined to straighten out this financial situation with Jesse at the first opportunity.

Returning to the main salon, she was astounded to see his bedroom door was now open.

"Jesse?" she called softly, knocking against the opened panels.

The blue and gold color scheme extended to his room. Her eyes darted to every corner. She was afraid she'd discover him half dressed, or fully naked, and a thrill of something like panic slipped down her spine.

But the room was empty. Unless he was waiting in the closet, ready to pounce on her, he'd already left. Throwing open the closet door, Kelsey braced herself, already knowing that Jesse had left their suite of rooms as he had left her alone the night before. No explanation. No word about when or if he might return.

In a fulminating fury she unbuttoned her shoes and threw them the length of the elegant salon. They crashed against the veined marble fireplace; one ended up on the carpet, the other sat straight up on the grate, as if someone had placed it there for that evening's fire. Swearing with all the couth of a logger, she then twisted on the taps of the beautiful bathtub, ripped off her "wedding gown" for the last time, and sank into the depths of the water, plotting a dastardly revenge, all the while knowing she was as much to blame as Jesse for the impossible situation they'd put themselves in.

# 7

Jesse watched Zeke chew thoughtfully on the tender morsel of veal he'd laid on his tongue. Zeke ate with enjoyment, but a certain decorum. His tastes were refined in spite of the fact that he'd spent most of his life in tenements and backwater shanties. Through his own indomitable will, he'd raised his and Nell's social status and acquired a polish and well-bred sensibility along the way. Jesse had surprised Zeke's lowly roots from him on only two occasions: the first being during Zeke's daring rescue of Jesse beneath Montana Gray's ubiquitous nose; the second being when Jesse had nearly killed a man who had been publicly slapping around his wife. The wife's name had been Nell, and Zeke had yanked Jesse from his antagonist's hammy fists, explaining coldly and precisely (and inaccurately) that Zeke's sister's name had been Nell and she'd met a terrible fate at the hands of a brutal bully. Zeke's intervention had been so spontaneous and out of character that Jesse had nearly missed the opportunity to fell the bastard with a well-placed blow to his paunchy midsection.

Otherwise Zeke had been the epitome of a gentleman, in his thinking, in his actions, and in his overall view of the economy and his place within it. It was Jesse who had more difficulty with his "gentleman" persona. He could accomplish it with ease, but inside, where it counted, he never felt like he truly belonged. Never wanted to truly belong.

"How's the missus?" Zeke asked, hiding a smirk while he chewed.

"A model of discretion."

The choking noises emitting from Zeke's throat drew the attention of more than one table of diners at Sinclair's Eating Establishment, one of Portland's more elegant restaurants. Jesse fingered his crystal goblet of water. He itched to get out of this gray wool suit. The collar rubbed against his throat. Hot, stifled, and frustrated, it was all he could do to sit there and share a civil conversation. A part of him blamed Zeke for the mess he was in.

"You're at the hotel?" Zeke asked, gulping water and swiping at the tiny tears that had formed at the corners of his eyes.

"Yes."

Jesse's tone was cold with disgust. He'd planned to take his new bride directly to their suite of rooms, not for the purpose of seducing her—heaven forbid!—but simply to set up residence and begin the charade he was bound and determined to play for Montana Gray's benefit. But before he'd had a chance to reveal his intentions to the starchy Miss Simpson, the reverend had called her by name. *Kelsey Garrett!* Kelsey goddamned Garrett! Jace Garrett's little sister, who'd been betrothed to the mayor of Malone—what was his name again? Oh, yeah. Warfield. The spurious old lecher, Jesse thought in disgust. Now he remembered. Warfield had taken one look at the unusual young Kelsey with her rich burgundy hair and wide gray eyes, and he'd asked for her hand. Apparently Kelsey had somehow squeezed out of that arrangement. Or else she was a widow.

That thought struck Jesse hard. He tried to imagine a coupling of the sexually stifled Kelsey and the round-bellied and lascivious Warfield, and failed. Which was lucky, he decided. He didn't want to think of Kelsey and Warfield, or Kelsey and anyone, and why that should matter at all was enough to increase his frustration and make him want to slam his fist down on the table with impatience.

It had taken monumental self-control for him not to wring Kelsey's lovely neck when she'd berated him about the conditions of the apartment. He'd taken her there on purpose. Punishment for tricking him. He hadn't intended on staying, but she'd made him so furious he'd wanted to bring her to heel.

And then, in bewilderment and an overwhelming sense that things had definitely gotten out of control, he'd left for the bar and subsequently Mamie's whore's den of satin sheets, red feathers, and heavy perfume. Only Jesse had slept off his drunken binge on the floor. He'd woken to the sounds of rather disinterested lovemaking; one of his "friends" from Briny's taking advantage of what Jesse had paid for and then never bothered to receive.

Jesse had stumbled out of the place and taken a deep lungful of dank Willamette River air, clearing his head before he returned to the apartment where he'd stashed Kelsey hours before.

He'd been surprised that she was still there. He'd half expected her to bolt. And then she'd stood there in a pair of drawers that outlined the curve of her hips and the shape of her thighs, and a camisole that fell loosely from the soft mounds of her breasts. Her hair had billowed, soft and feminine in the breeze from the open window, and he'd suddenly, fervently, wanted to push her down on the bed and bury himself inside her.

She hadn't noticed. He was certain of that. She hadn't seen his involuntary reaction, and years of practice had kept his feelings from showing on his face. He'd had to focus on those frigid gray eyes to keep his sanity.

He wouldn't make that mistake again. The last time he'd been suckered by a woman was when Lila Gray's husband had had him beaten nearly to death. He'd be damned if he'd be suckered by Kelsey.

But what the hell was she doing parading around as Orchid Simpson? Clearly she didn't want the Garretts to find her just as much as he didn't want the Danners to find him. They had that in common, he thought ironically.

Zeke speared another morsel of veal. "Gray's having a party. A charity auction in the ballroom of his home. It's slated for the Saturday after next. I don't know if I can wangle an invitation, but I'll try. You do want to go, don't you?"

"With Kelsey?" Jesse made a sound of disbelief. He would never trust her in such august company.

Zeke's brows lifted. "With Orchid," he admonished.

Jesse wondered if he had the energy to explain that Orchid was Kelsey. Kelsey Orchid Garrett, he thought bitterly.

"How much are you going to tell her of your plan?" Zeke asked, frowning.

"Just enough to insure she'll help me. Not enough to cause me trouble."

"Oh?"

"I don't know how I'm going to accomplish it," Jesse admitted. "I'm sorry I ever took a bride. I want this to be over so Nell's avenged and Gray's buried in his own muck!"

"It'll take a little time. Just a little more."

"Easy for you, Drummond. You're not living with that hellion."

Jesse's uncharacteristic bitterness caused Zeke pause. "The woman is that impossible?"

"Damn near impregnable," he muttered, unaware of how that sounded.

Zeke cleared his throat and rubbed the end of his nose. "As I understood it, this was to be a marriage of convenience."

"It is a marriage of convenience." Jesse's retort was swift. "In a physical sense anyway. Nothing else is convenient about it in the least."

Zeke had to hide a smile. Jesse had been the one who'd fancied Orchid over Charlotte. Zeke wasn't above thinking the handsome, irresistible Mr. Danner was getting a bit of his own medicine back.

"If I can get you an invitation, will she behave at Gray's party?"

Jesse scowled. "What about Samuel? Will he be invited?"

"Quite possibly," Zeke said unhappily.

Jesse's scowl deepened.

The two men sat in silence for a few moments, each absorbed in his own thoughts. People drifted by. Some smiled at Zeke, whom they knew from his carefully constructed social climbing, and looked curiously at Jesse. Surfacing from his dark thoughts, Jesse realized it was past time for him to get moving on his plan to ruin Montana Gray. He was going to have to make some compromises.

"I'll take care of Kelsey," he said, ignoring Zeke's confused gaze. "But I'll need your help to approach Samuel. I don't know my brother very well. He's a wild card. Years ago, when my mother's life was threatened by Ramsey Gainsborough, Samuel grabbed a gun and started calmly and cold-bloodedly trying to shoot Gainsborough's guards."

"Samuel Danner?" Zeke asked in disbelief. "The lawyer?"

"One and the same. Before that mess with Gainsborough, Samuel had always seemed kind of—I don't know—studious, I guess. Quiet. Reserved. Cautious. But then he just started blasting and all hell broke loose." Jesse shook his head. "It wasn't long afterward that I left."

"Well, the Samuel Danner here in Portland is reserved, and maybe you could call him quiet. He doesn't waste words. But you know all this; I've talked about him before," Zeke added, frowning.

"I don't know *him*. Just because he's my brother, I'm not sure I can trust him. I don't want him running off to Rock Springs and giving me away."

Zeke now knew a great deal about Rock Springs and Jesse's absolute obsession over keeping away from it. The investigator he'd hired to learn about Eliza Danner had been very specific. The way Zeke saw it, Montana Gray had obliterated Jesse's past. There was the Jesse from before, and the Jesse after. The "after" Jesse wanted nothing to do with the "before" one.

"Maybe it's time to meet Samuel face-to-face and find out what he's like," Zeke suggested. "If we have to, we can force him into going along with us."

Jesse eyed Zeke with raw skepticism. "How?"

"Everyone has a secret past. I doubt even the illustrious Mr. Samuel Danner could escape a serious investigation. If so, we can always manufacture something. . . ."

"You're totally unscrupulous when it comes to Nell," Jesse said. "You know that, don't you?"

"Yes." Zeke was fully aware of his own obsession.

"Just don't underestimate Samuel." A rakish smile faintly curved the corners of Jesse's mouth. "I made that mistake once, but when I saw the way he handled a rifle, I decided Samuel was a man to be reckoned with—and he was only thirteen at the time."

"Well, he's twenty-eight or nine now, but I doubt he's handled a rifle since."

"Zeke," Jesse admonished his friend. "Be careful. Don't tell him why you want to see him, just get him to your office. I'll take it from there."

Zeke met Jesse's direct gaze. "You really think there's reason to worry?"

"He's a Danner."

"Good point," Zeke conceded without hesitation.

Mrs. Jesse Danner peered through the fronds of an enormous potted plant, pleased that it gave her a direct view of the hotel lobby. She was seated in the lobby restaurant, which consisted of groups of sofas, chairs and small tables. Piano and harp music tinkled softly in the background, giving the impression of an intimate soirée. Kelsey, whose taste for the aesthetics was similar to Jesse's—she'd learned what she needed to know to survive and play a convincing part, but had yet to understand half of the musical or artistic endeavors she'd been introduced to—couldn't help thinking the arrangement was rather thin and unappealing. It was all she could do to keep still in her chair. She wanted to fidget like a schoolgirl. She hated waiting, but she had no idea where her husband was, and until they sat down with some plain talk about what his plans were, Kelsey was at his mercy.

A white-coated waiter bent over her, smiling benevolently. "More tea, madam?"

Kelsey had barely choked down the tepid brown liquid. One taste she *had* acquired was for English tea, the way Lady Chamberlain insisted it be prepared. Nothing else came close. "No, thank you."

"Cakes?"

The silver tray was loaded with confections, some oozing cream and topped with meringue, others swirled with miniature frosting roses in shades of pink, peach, and yellow.

Kelsey shook her head again. She was in the wrong place at the wrong time. A sudden urge to grab her rifle and ride to open places was so strong, she had to willfully fight it back, gritting her teeth in the process. While she'd worked for Agatha she'd never felt this stifled. Perhaps it was because she'd always known she could flee the gilded cage. Or perhaps it was because she'd been playing a part; Orchid Simpson was an entirely different personality from Kelsey Garrett. But whatever the case, now, with her marriage feeling like an ever-tightening noose around her throat, she couldn't bear the restraints of high society.

She wanted to leap to her feet and scream as loudly as she could!

While Kelsey, the hellion, inwardly battled Kelsey, the proper lady, Jesse Danner strode through the revolving doors and crossed to the desk. Kelsey was so caught up in her own frustration, she almost missed him. But suddenly spying his familiar figure jolted her heart. Where had he been? What was he doing now?

What should *she* do?

The clerk delivered him a note which he read without interest and tossed into the trash as he strode to the stairs.

Kelsey's heart lifted. Well, now here was an opportunity. She had no faith that Jesse would level with her, but she could garner some information on her own. Consumed with curiosity, she gathered up her rustling skirts and hurried to the trash can, plucking the letter from the other slips of paper.

"Ma'am?" the head clerk asked coolly.

"I've lost my only photograph of my brother," Kelsey improvised with a faint trembling smile. "I've searched and searched and now he's missing and I'm—I'm afraid I'll never see him again!"

Concern for decorum rather than a damsel in distress prompted the clerk to offer in an undertone, "Let me help you."

A broad, bejeweled dowager leaning on an elegant ebony cane entered the lobby as Kelsey rummaged through the waste can. The woman was gasping at the effort of walking, and her expression was thunderous. An entourage of followers held back, as if afraid of her wrath. Spying her, the clerk snapped to attention, shot Kelsey a confused glance, then swung around the desk and went to the wealthy dowager's aid.

"Here it is!" Kelsey declared joyously, hugging Jesse's message to her chest. "Glory be! Saints be praised! God has smiled on me today!"

"Yes, ma'am," the clerk shushed Kelsey coldly. All his attention was on the new arrival. "Good afternoon, Madame Duprés. Let me call Bentonhurst to help you to your rooms. What a lovely gown!" he raved effusively. "It's been ages since we've had the pleasure of your company. Are you in Portland for long?"

The old lady snorted and, with surprising agility, hit him straight across the thigh with her cane. "Get my bags!" she ordered in a voice that rang with ill temper.

The clerk bustled past the lady's entourage and was

gone. Kelsey was sorry she would have to miss the rest of this spectacle, but she was determined to learn what Jesse was up to. She scurried to a safe corner behind a massive marble pillar and smoothed out the crumpled note.

One Henry Connors was interested in discussing a sale. A phone number was listed, along with an address.

What kind of sale? Kelsey wondered. And only the very well-to-do possessed telephones. Was it a business number, or could this Mr. Connors actually have a telephone in his own home?

Shoving the note into the pocket of her dress, she headed up the stairs. At the door to her room, she hesitated, feeling absurdly as if she should knock. Then remembering it was *her* money that had afforded such wasteful opulence, she used her key and swept imperiously into the room. The door to Jesse's bedroom was closed. Kelsey could hear water running. He was either bathing or shaving.

Ten minutes later Jesse appeared in the main salon. He wore a shirt, open at the throat, and a pair of gray trousers. A towel was wrapped around his neck. He had indeed been shaving, and she could smell the scent of soap even from six feet away, which is where he chose to stand right in front of her.

Kelsey had changed into a black dress that emphasized her paleness. Its collar was tight white lace that nearly reached her chin. The only relief were the mother-of-pearl buttons on her leg-o'-mutton sleeves.

Jesse regarded her with displeasure. "This afternoon we're buying you some new clothes," Jesse said by way of a greeting.

"I don't need any new clothes."

"Nevertheless, you're going to get some."

"I prefer the ones I have."

"I don't really care what you prefer. You look terrible in black. It's time we put you in something that'll make you look better." Jesse strode toward the cabinet against the wall and pulled down a door that revealed a stocked bar. He poured a glass of brandy for himself, then sank negligently onto the gold brocade chaise longue.

His indolent form infuriated Kelsey. He looked so . . .

111

*animalistic!* At his throat she could see dark chest hairs, and the breadth of his shoulders made her wonder at his strength. She found she detested those beautiful all-seeing eyes. And she detested his face, even though the structure was different from the youthful Jesse. Age had changed him dramatically. He'd been almost pretty as a boy, sporting the thickest lashes and most beautiful smile she could remember. But he wasn't approachable anymore. He was dangerous and coldly masculine and what had once passed as youthful high jinks could be termed only cruelty now. He got what he wanted, when he wanted it, from whom he wanted it, and the devil take those who didn't comply.

Well, she wouldn't comply. If he wanted something, *anything,* he was going to have to take it by force.

"As I recall you wanted a wife who could place you in society. Her appearance, pleasing or otherwise, was not part of the bargain." Kelsey's eyes were stormy.

"I remember what you looked like once. You were the most unusual woman around. You had all the old lechers drooling over you without even trying."

Kelsey stared. "Your memory's faulty! When you left, I was still a child."

"My memory's excellent."

They eyed each other silently for several moments. Kelsey couldn't credit his conclusion. She possessed some beauty; she knew that. Once upon a time she'd even cultivated her beauty. She'd worn elegant gowns at some of the Rock Springs dances. She'd fixed her hair and let it fall down her back. She'd even flirted a bit with Harrison, her one-time husband-to-be. But those moments had been fleeting, a brief slip into fantasy before Kelsey had learned men couldn't be trusted. Her brother, Jace's, repeated attempts to marry her off to the highest bidder, her prospective suitors' drooling, lustful looks, and then Harrison's breaking their engagement had taught Kelsey well.

Except it wouldn't be truly fair to blame Harrison for that. They'd been friends, not passionate lovers. They'd agreed to marry more to end the feud between their two families than out of any blinding love. And though Kelsey had been left standing at the altar, it was only because

Harrison had been wounded and unable to make it to the church. He would have married her if he could have; she knew Harrison wouldn't have purposely humiliated her. No, the hurt she felt owed more to the fact that no man had ever loved her—really loved her—like Harrison Danner ended up loving Miracle Jones Danner, his current wife, an exotically beautiful half-breed Chinook medicine woman who just happened to be Kelsey's own half-sister . . .

"I want you to look like that Kelsey Garrett again," Jesse said. He regarded her moodily, as if the mere sight of her displeased him. "I'm meeting a man this afternoon who's interested in selling me one of his homes. I want you with me, playing the part of the adoring, *beautiful* wife."

"Buying a house!" Kelsey was aghast. "We can't afford it! We can't afford these rooms! The way you spend money, my inheritance will be gone before next Tuesday!"

"Your inheritance?" he bit out.

"I should have never handed you that money. I should have insisted I keep hold of it. You're reckless and fool-hardy! We'll be penniless in the space of three weeks!"

Jesse slammed down the brandy snifter, spilling drops onto the table from the force. He sprang to his feet and advanced upon her, staring down at her through blazing eyes. "I have enough money to take care of us for a lifetime," he declared in a voice that hissed with muted fury. "Your *inheritance* is safely stashed away."

"But—"

"Be quiet," he slashed through her sputtering. "And change into something you can take on and off without spending three hours about it. We're going to a seamstress, then to Mr. Connors's office, then to Zeke's office. . . ."

"Henry Connors?"

"You know him?" Jesse demanded swiftly.

"We've—never actually met." Kelsey felt the note in her pocket burning through the fabric. She decided it was to her benefit not to let Jesse know her penchant for getting information her own way.

"Well, take care. Everyone still thinks you're Orchid Simpson. We'll stick with that."

"I'd like to know what you meant about having more than enough money," Kelsey said.

"I hate to disillusion you, Mrs. Danner, but I'm wealthy. It's a fault of mine, making money. I'm afraid you'll just have to get used to the idea. Now, go change."

"I'm not buying more clothes. I—"

"Go change, or I'll change you."

The threat in his voice was unmistakable, and it raised Kelsey's ire like a match to dry tinder. "Lay a hand on me and I'll scream bloody murder!"

"Go change." He glanced at the clock on the mantel above the fireplace. "You have twenty minutes."

Kelsey's face flamed with pent-up emotion. She sat stiffly beside Jesse on the buggy seat. Not for a moment did she believe his protestations of wealth. Hah! This buggy was proof of his financial woes. Dusty, dirty, its blacking chipping away—Agatha would have berated the stable groom up one side and down the other for such inattention!

But if Jesse's pride were so enormous that he couldn't admit he was penniless, she, Kelsey Garrett, would button her lip. He could fall on his face at some public event and make a spectacle of himself and that would be revenge enough.

He sat stonily beside her, the reins loose in one gloved hand. Clouds threatened rain and Jesse kept glancing skyward. Kelsey wondered what he planned to do if a sudden deluge caught them. Her bonnet was more stylish than functional. Gray, with a lush pheasant tail feather curling under the chin, Kelsey had picked it because it was her nicest. Not that she wanted to do *his* bidding, but, well, the idea of Jesse undressing her was enough to make her swallow her pride for a short time.

Her dress was a soft dove gray also. Jesse had eyed it with distaste before they left their rooms, which had made Kelsey feel better. Small victories were all she had, and she was determined to enjoy every one of them.

The seamstress Jesse took her to was in a posh area of town, a lovely little shop with gorgeous hats in a rainbow of colors in the window and several dressmaker's models wrapped in flowing gowns. This was not a place for minor

*114*

heiresses from Rock Springs, with or without their twenty-thousand-dollar inheritances. Kelsey glanced anxiously at Jesse and plucked at her gray kid gloves. Was he so hellbent on proving a point that he would spend her every cent, making her conscience writhe with every foolishly purchased extravagance?

"Mrs. Honeycutt?" Jesse asked when the bell above their heads tinkled, announcing their arrival.

A lady with a beaming smile in a dark green satin gown swept toward them. "Good afternoon. Could I be of some help today?" Her gaze passed over Kelsey, a slight frown marring her brow.

"My wife needs to be measured for some new gowns," Jesse told her. "Something with more—color."

The frown disappeared as if someone had magically wiped it away. "Oh, something in blue! Or green. I have the most wonderful emerald-colored silk. Straight from the Orient. It's divine. Utterly, sinfully divine." She clasped her hands to her chest in ecstasy.

"I'm sorry, I can't—" Kelsey began.

"We'll take the green silk," Jesse cut her off. "Show me the blue, too, and she needs some more clothes. Show it all to me."

"Jesse . . ." Kelsey said between frozen lips.

"Indulge me, precious," he answered, squeezing her arm lovingly and tucking it through his. His grip was like iron.

"I don't think we should be so extravagant all at once," she murmured.

"I haven't had a chance to really spoil you," he returned with a smile so utterly charming that Kelsey wanted to spit in his eye.

"Ah, a man who appreciates a well-turned-out young woman," the dressmaker sighed. "Right this way, Mr. . . . ?"

"Danner. And this is Orchid. She's so careful with a penny, it's all I can do to get her to treat herself."

"How unusual," she said, clucking her tongue as if Kelsey had so much to learn about being a woman. "Let me help."

Kelsey was torn between fury and an undeniable longing for a gown out of one of those wonderful, brilliant silk fabrics. She glanced at Jesse, whose eyes danced with suppressed laughter. Grinding her back teeth together, she said through a tight false smile, "By all means, show me your most gorgeous and most *expensive* fabrics." Blast and damn, she would rather squander all of her money than suffer his superiority one more instant. "I want scores of dresses, and hats, and shoes, and a bounty of silken undergarments worthy of a princess!"

One hand on her hip, she flung Jesse a triumphant look.

To Kelsey's consternation, he smiled slowly and for a heartstopping moment she saw again the rakish charm of the Jesse Danner of her youth.

*8*

Jesse had never been known for possessing a long fuse on his temper, and therefore he truly believed he'd been positively saintly in his forbearance where Kelsey was concerned. He vacillated moment by moment between wanting to strangle her and wanting to kiss her, touch her, drag her off to his bedroom and make love to her until they were both senseless with passion.

His blood stirred at the thought which only added to his mounting frustration. He swirled his snifter of brandy, then knocked it back as if it were water. Clenching his teeth against the hot burn, he glared across the room at her closed bedroom door. His sudden desire for his wife was not supposed to happen.

The fact that Kelsey had chosen to battle over how many dresses she should possess, making him practically physically force her to accept them (an anomaly since most women would sell themselves into marriage to be in her pricey new shoes) exasperated and infuriated him to no end.

After three hours of fighting which had left Mrs. Honeycutt frazzled, bewildered, and with her nose clearly out of joint, Jesse had grabbed his wife's unwilling arm, marched her back to the buggy and, heedless of the rain that now came down in buckets, drove her to the hotel and dragged her upstairs.

Ominous silence issued from behind the closed door to her bedroom. He'd half expected to hear the sound of a tantrum; he'd known women who would break every valuable item they possessed to infuriate their husbands or lovers. But Kelsey, so far, had confined herself to pointed isolation.

Which was fine with him. Glancing at the clock on the mantel, he sighed, set down his brandy snifter, and walked to her door. "I'm meeting Mr. Connors now," he told her. "Be ready by the time I get back."

He expected her to ask, "Ready for what," but he only received more of that accusatory silence.

Muttering impatiently, he let himself out of the suite. It was all for the best anyway. He couldn't trust Kelsey to give the performance of a loving, trusting wife. The fact that she was his wife was like a jolt with a branding iron every time it crossed Jesse's mind. He burned with disbelief and resentment, and, he could admit it though it tore his gut to do so, a certain amount of lust.

She was gorgeous, whether she tried to cover it up or not. And she was full of spirit and pride, qualities he admired in a woman. But she was also pigheaded, stubborn, untrustworthy, and full of her own brand of self-righteous justice.

Kelsey heard the outer door close with a soft thud. With a sigh of self-disgust, she let herself out of the bedroom and into the main salon. Eyeing the liquor cabinet, she wished she enjoyed spirits more. If there was ever a time she would have liked a bracing shot of whiskey, this was it.

Instead, she drew herself a bath, washing the rain from her hair and soaking in the fabulous lavender- and carnation-scented bath salts donated by the hotel. "Be ready," he'd ordered just before he'd left. Ready for what? Was

Jesse already setting his plan into motion? They'd scarcely been married one full day!

She dressed in a hurry, finding no solace in the dull dark-blue dress with its chokingly high collar. Combing her hair dry, she settled her heavy mane in another hairnet, then drew a strengthening breath of courage.

Ten minutes later Kelsey was striding impatiently back and forth across the blue and gold carpet of the salon, wondering how long Jesse would be with the real estate man. She ended up in the center of the room, her hands clasped together so tightly her knuckles showed white.

Inwardly berating herself for compounding mistake after mistake, she asked herself if she could truly go through with this marriage, even for a little while. Could she truthfully stand by while Jesse insinuated himself in Portland society, knowing, as she did, that he was social-climbing for some nefarious purpose of his own?

She shook her head. Jesse Danner had married her for her connections. The more she thought about it, the less sense it made.

Why should she honor their bargain? she asked herself belatedly, surprised that it had taken her this long to consider the obvious plan of action. She would leave. Right now. Disappear without a trace. She owed Jesse nothing, and she was worried and alarmed that she'd been blinded by some pointless sense of duty and hadn't left earlier.

Spurred to action, Kelsey grabbed her valise and repacked it once more. She checked her derringer once again and was reassured to see it was loaded and ready. She thought of her other belongings, her rifle and the rest of her clothes, and was washed by a wave of poignancy. She'd treated Agatha and Charlotte shabbily, and for what? True, Charlotte was beyond Jesse's reach, or, rather, he was beyond hers, but Agatha had said herself that if Kelsey had just been honest, none of this would have happened.

"Blast," she murmured unhappily, gathering up her case and heading downstairs to the hotel foyer.

The bejeweled and garishly bedecked dowager was standing near the bottom steps as Kelsey descended the stairs. The woman was leaning heavily on her cane and being aided by a young man whose expression suggested perpetual boredom. Upon spying Kelsey, the woman's dark, beady eyes traveled over her in a thoroughly insulting inspection and Kelsey, who'd had her fill of being someone else's pincushion, leveled a cool, imperious gaze back at the woman.

"I've seen you before," the dowager declared in her commanding way.

Kelsey was taken aback. "I don't think so, madam. I would have remembered you."

"At Lady Agatha Chamberlain's," she stated. "You were one of the servants, I believe. Agatha was having a soiree, and you were serving canapes. Your name escapes me, child."

Clearly she expected Kelsey to bow and scrape and behave like the lower classes. "It's Orchid Simpson, and if I was passing around a tray of canapes, it was out of politeness, not servitude, Madame Duprés."

"Ah, you do remember me."

"I heard the desk clerk call you by name. I'm sorry, but as much as it surprises me, too, I don't recall your being at any of Agatha's functions."

"Your mind was elsewhere. I recall very clearly. You were there only briefly and you kept looking out the window. I remember thinking that if my servants acted so dreamy and lost, I would dismiss them on the spot."

Kelsey suddenly knew which soiree Madame Duprés was referring to. She'd been homesick after a bout with influenza, and all she'd wanted to do was saddle up Justice and ride far, far away from the social silliness of some of Agatha's acquaintances. Vaguely she recalled several older women who seemed to blur together in a blend of silvery hair, too much rouge, and overly bright and garish gowns.

"As I said before, I was not a servant. I was Charlotte's companion."

"Was?"

"I left Lady Chamberlain's when I got married."

The sadness in Kelsey's voice didn't escape Madame Lacey Duprés, who was as devious as she was boorish. Though she had been married only once, briefly, in her

119

youth, to a Confederate soldier, she'd been desperately in love once—with someone else. She knew what Orchid was feeling all too well.

But then, the money from her deceased husband's wealthy Southern family had helped her get over her pain and enabled a lowly chorus girl to become mistress of the manor. Lacey—whose real name was Myrtle Cummings—had used her own sharp, business-oriented mind to encourage those funds to multiply. The result was that she was outrageously wealthy and completely ignorant of protocol. The only reason she'd been at the eminent Lady Chamberlain's soiree at all was that a "friend" owed her a favor. Lacey had loaned the blue-blooded and financially straited woman a hefty sum of money and had been paid interest in invitations to *the* events happening in Portland. Lacey, who currently resided in San Francisco, used her "friend's" connections whenever she was in Portland. Unfortunately, the friend had had the bad sense to die last winter and Lacey was left without anything but her enormous wealth.

For reasons of her own she was planning to move to Portland, and now, sensing that this impudent chit might help gain her entry into Portland's most snobbish homes—specifically Lady Agatha Chamberlain's again!—Lacey decided to make herself indispensable to the young woman.

"Your name?" she said again, irritated that the girl was so ridiculously proud. After all, she'd been a *companion* to Agatha Chamberlain's granddaughter. If that wasn't a servant, Lacey certainly didn't know what was.

"Orchid. Orchid Simpson Danner," said Kelsey as she tried to step past the woman.

"Are you leaving the hotel?" Madame Duprés's snapping black eyes rested on Kelsey's valise.

"Er—yes. I have somewhere else to go," Kelsey answered vaguely.

"Mrs. Danner, I feel so close to you." Lacey grabbed Kelsey's arm, which was quite a feat while balancing herself on her cane. "Agatha is a dear, dear woman, and I've left my card with her. Please join me for afternoon tea, so we can get reacquainted."

"Thank you, Madame Duprés," Kelsey answered, hiding

a smile. "But I'm afraid I'll have to decline. I've got an appointment I just can't miss."

"But I insist. Jeffrey, we'll be going to the Veranda Restaurant," she announced grandly to her bored companion, gesturing Kelsey to follow in their wake.

Kelsey couldn't decide whether to honor the wretched woman's demands or sail past the group of onlookers who'd witnessed this scene as if nothing had happened. The problem was, Madame Duprés had brought attention to Kelsey, and anyone would be able to describe her to Jesse and pinpoint the exact moment of her departure.

*Do you seriously believe he'll chase after you?*

The answer to that was a resounding yes. He needed her. It was she who did not *need* him.

Tightening her grip on her valise, Kelsey aimed instead for the revolving doors ahead of her, only to see Jesse's familiar physique being spewed out of them. He spied her instantly, but apart from a lifting of one sardonic brow, appeared not in the least worried that his wife was about to bolt.

She stopped short and he strode up to her. Lifting her chin, Kelsey regarded him steadily, her knees trembling only a little at the scathing glance of contempt he rained on her.

"I've had all I can bear of this," he told her flatly.

"We agree on something, then, for I've also had about all I can—" Kelsey's outraged voice ended in a gasp as Jesse's hand suddenly dug into her scalp, ripping the hairnet off her burnished auburn locks. Her hair tumbled down in a torrent.

"Close your mouth, Mrs. Danner," he suggested. "You could catch flies. And the net stays off."

Her teeth clamped together. Gray eyes shot icicles at him. "I was leaving," she bit out. "Kindly, step aside."

To her intense surprise, he did exactly as she'd bid him, moving out of her path with one graceful step. "Just be back by six," he said to her retreating back. "Remember, we have an appointment."

"Appointment be damned," she flung over her shoulder.

"I'm not coming back at all. I'm leaving town and there's nothing you can do to stop me!"

She barely made it to the revolving door when strong arms seized hers, pinning her shoulders back. She nearly cried out in surprise. The strength of his grasp numbed her arms and she dropped her valise.

"Don't push me," he whispered harshly in her ear. "I'm at the end of my tether with you. Tonight we're meeting Samuel, and by God, you're going to be there if I have to wrap you in burlap and haul you there over my shoulder. I don't like this arrangement any more than you do, but you're the one who suggested it," he reminded her, biting off each word as if it tasted bitter. "You could have told me who you were, but since you didn't, here we are. You promised to act like my wife. I suggest you start making good on your promise. The sooner we're through this, the better. So stop pushing me," he added in a calmer but no less dangerous voice.

His breath against her ear sent quivers of emotion racing through her veins. He was threatening her, but surprisingly, fear was not one of those emotions she felt. Apprehension, yes. And smoldering rebellion. But she didn't feel afraid of him because Jesse Danner, damn his gorgeous hide, inspired far different emotions than terror. She still suspected him capable of all the worst crimes he'd been accused of, but Kelsey was painfully aware that like all his other conquests, she wasn't immune to Jesse's charm. It didn't seem to matter that he was a plunderer. Her every nerve thrummed with something akin to passion at his touch. *That* was what frightened her!

"Samuel?" she asked, picking out the one part of his threat that should have bothered her the most but somehow seemed the least worrisome.

"Good old brother Samuel," Jesse admitted sardonically, loosening his hold. Kelsey rubbed her arms automatically. She could still feel the impression of every one of his hard fingers. "I can't avoid him any longer."

Kelsey turned around to face him, her brow furrowed. "I can't see Samuel. Maybe you didn't know who I was, but it hasn't been that long since he's seen me. He'll know who I am.''

"I'm sure of it.''

"You don't care?''

Jesse shrugged. "No,'' he answered flatly. "I don't know why the hell you've hidden out as Orchid Simpson, but it doesn't matter. We're going to run into Samuel whether we like it or not. We've just got to convince him to keep quiet about us. I don't want him talking to Pa and my brothers and Lexie.''

He didn't mention his mother. Remorse stabbed through Kelsey at the way he'd learned Eliza was dead. "Jesse . . .'' she said uncertainly.

"I think we should go back upstairs and get ready, hmmm? I need to decide how to deal with Samuel. I don't really know him very well.''

"I'm sorry—about the way you learned—about how I told you that Eliza was—''

"Is this valise all you took?'' he asked. He didn't look at her and she was left staring down at his blue-black hair as he bent to pick it up.

At that moment Madame Duprés stumped through the glass-paned doors that led from the lobby restaurant, her face red with annoyance. "Mrs. Danner!'' she all but bellowed. "What has detained you?''

Jesse stared at her incredulously, then his blue eyes turned to Kelsey. She all but laughed at the look of disbelief hovering in their depths. "My husband,'' she said, her lips twitching.

Twenty minutes later Kelsey sat on the salon divan, her feet tucked beneath her, an unasked-for snifter of brandy in one hand. Her hair still hung loosely, a cloud of rich brown-red silk against her navy dress. Catching a glimpse of Jesse's vulnerability had lessened her starch, and instead of being furious with him, she couldn't help feeling unhappily responsible for his current moodiness. She'd been unwittingly cruel and now it had come back to haunt her.

"Why are you so determined to blast your way into Portland society?'' she asked him.

He was standing in front of the windows, his back to her. His feet were planted apart, his shoulders tense beneath his suit. For some reason he hadn't poured himself a brandy as he had for her. His hands were at his hips and she realized that he often stood just that way when he was thinking hard.

She was coming to know him, she thought uneasily.

"I've got a score to settle."

Kelsey's upturned face was full of questions as Jesse swung around to face her. Clearly she couldn't believe he'd been so open with her.

"A score to settle with whom?"

In that goddamned dress she looked like a schoolmarm. As he had with the net that bound her hair, he wanted to rip it off her and see once again the lush curves and soft mounds that made up her womanly body. He was furious with himself for his own thoughts. Of all the women in the world, she was the worst. Not as conniving as Lila Gray, perhaps, but so determinedly stubborn that his frustration mounted with every passing second. He couldn't trust her, but he *wanted* her. No one—not one single female since Lila—had made him feel that way.

"With a man named Montana Gray."

Kelsey's eyes widened. "Montana Gray?"

"You've heard of him."

"I've met him. Once."

"And?" Jesse was curious to know her impression of the man.

"Lady Chamberlain was wary of Montana's reputation and never invited him to the house. I was introduced to him at a charity event," Kelsey answered, her delicate winged brows drawn into a frown. "He'd donated a vast sum of money."

Jesse snorted. "I made the man wealthy enough to become a philanthropist," he muttered beneath his breath in disgust.

"*You* made him wealthy?"

The laughing note of disbelief that crept into her voice irritated Jesse. "Montana Gray stole a fortune from me. I mean to get it back."

"I thought you said you were wealthy."

"I am. This is revenge, pure and simple."

"How did he steal your money?"

Jesse gazed at Kelsey's vibrant hair. Several silken strands lay against the smooth skin of her cheek, and as he watched, she lifted a hand to brush them aside. It was a surprisingly erotic gesture. "He had me beaten and thrown in the Willamette. I'd be dead now if it weren't for Zeke. Zeke pulled me out and put me back together. Gray helped himself to my money and land with the help of some of his friends in high places after I 'died.' He still doesn't know I survived," Jesse finished. "I've kept a very low profile these last five years."

"And now you plan to appear like some unearthly visitor come back to seek vengeance?"

Her lightning thinking intrigued him. "He might not even recognize me. Our initial meeting was—brief."

Kelsey heard the tension in his voice. *He had me beaten and thrown in the Willamette*. She shivered a little. Jesse's tone was matter-of-fact, but Kelsey could read between the lines. "Was he the one who changed your face?" she asked.

"It's that obvious?" Jesse was surprised. He'd grown so used to his looks he sometimes forgot how different he appeared now.

"I knew who you were the first time we met, but your face is different. It's . . ."

Jesse waited, his curiosity growing.

"It's—just different."

"But someone who knew me fairly intimately will be able to recognize me?"

"Yeees." How intimately? she wondered.

"Good." His eyes narrowed thoughtfully.

"So once Montana sees you, how do you propose to get your money back? From all I know, he's hardly the type to just fall on his knees in repentance, spectral vision or no."

"You're enjoying this, aren't you?"

Kelsey straightened. She eyed Jesse warily, but he sounded more curious than angry. "I'm just trying to get the facts straight."

"The only facts you need to know are one: I plan to hit the Portland social swirl dead on, with you by my side. You're the one who's going to open the right doors. Two, once I confront Montana, you're going to act like a doting wife. A loving wife. An *adoring* wife," he stressed. "In fact, even before Montana and I renew our acquaintanceship, so to speak, you've got to play your part."

"You expect me to fawn all over you just for the sake of revenge?" Kelsey looked down her nose.

A vision of Nell as she'd last looked flashed across Jesse's mind. Sweet, innocent, concerned . . . Zeke had told him that she'd ostensibly died from a broken neck after a fall from a horse. But Jesse knew Montana Gray had instigated the "accident" and he also knew it was because of him—because of his meeting with her. He didn't mention Nell to Kelsey. He didn't care if she thought his reasons for revenge were noble or not. "That was the bargain."

"Oh, no." Kelsey stalked across the room and set her brandy glass down on the mantel with a thump. "I became your wife and I'll help you get invited to the right circles, but I will *not* pretend to care about you. I will *not* bend and scrape and subjugate myself. I will *not* be your chattel."

His thoughts centering on Nell, Jesse growled, "Oh, yes, you will." Kelsey regarded him stubbornly, her small nose tilted in the air. "If you don't," he said in a reasonable voice, "I'll expose you."

"Expose me?" She tossed back her hair, and it swirled around her shoulders in a shimmering brown-magenta veil. "I've already told Agatha and Charlotte who I am and what I've done. You can't expose me, for I've done it myself."

Her triumph was short-lived. "I'll send a wire to Jace and tell him where to pick you up. We can get an annulment, then Jace can sell you to the highest bidder. Maybe someone older and uglier than Warfield. Someone interested in a passionless creature like yourself."

His words hammered hotly in Kelsey's brain. Her chest heaved, her breasts tight against the bodice of her gown. "You can't expose me without exposing yourself! You won't have to worry about Samuel keeping your whereabouts a secret; you'll have let your family know all on your own!"

126

"You want to test that theory?" He took a step closer, his face harsh with some indefinable emotion.

Kelsey hesitated. She didn't believe him. He wouldn't risk so much. He wanted this revenge too badly.

Revenge.

Of all the loathsome qualities Jesse possessed, she'd somehow never suspected him of being vengeful. He was too charming and careless and self-indulgent. Or at least he had been. Now she wasn't so sure. . . .

"No," she answered after the moment stretched endlessly. "I'd rather play out this charade than deal with Jace and Emerald. You're the lesser of two evils, so I choose you."

Jesse rubbed his nose thoughtfully. Her capitulation surprised him. "Then try to find something decent to wear. The least offensive garment of your Orchid Simpson collection. No, never mind. Let me choose." He stalked across the room and through her bedroom door before Kelsey could react. She scurried after him, affronted.

Jesse glanced at the empty closet, then snatched up her valise and popped the catches. Her clothes, tumbled and tossed inside with haste, were now dumped unceremoniously on the bed. While he rummaged through them, Kelsey's temper escalated.

"I can pick out my own clothes!"

"Yes, I know. You just don't do it very well."

He was studying a lavender silk, his handsome face a mask of concentration. Kelsey tried to rip the gown from his hands, but his grip was too strong and she succeeded only in yanking on the garment, knocking herself off balance, and tumbling onto the bed. She still held her end of the dress, however, and she glared up at him.

"Let go," she said through her teeth.

"Lavender's a color for old ladies."

"Lavender's a spring color worn by ingenues and dowagers alike."

"So which end of the scale are you?" he asked pointedly. "Ingenue or dowager?"

"I can hardly put the dress on if you're going to hang on to it so tightly," Kelsey pointed out.

"Why don't you have any pink dresses? Or light blue? Or green? What in God's name happened to turn you into a spinster?"

He was leaning over her, his blue eyes examining her in a thoroughly aggravating way, as if she were an inanimate piece of property without feelings, one whose flaws he could correct if he just studied her closely enough.

She yanked the dress from his grip. "I discovered very early on that a woman doesn't need a man. Marriage is a convenience of men. I grew tired of Jace's attempts to marry me off, so I left. I enjoy being on my own."

"That doesn't explain the change," he pointed out, nodding his head in the direction of her other clothes.

"When you're not in the market for a husband, you might as well make it very clear," Kelsey said, folding her hands atop her lavender gown. "My choice of clothing reflects my state of mind."

"Reflected. You're married now. You don't have to worry about a parade of suitors."

"I've grown used to looking a certain way and—" She broke off in a muffled gasp when Jesse suddenly leaned his face closer to hers, so close she could see the striations of deeper blue in his eyes.

"Put on the lavender dress. Leave your hair down. The appointment's at six. I'll expect you dressed and ready and waiting in the salon at five-fifteen. Think you can manage that?"

"Do you really expect me to act like your loving wife in front of Samuel?" she asked sarcastically, drawing back and tilting her head to hold his gaze. "Someone who knows us both?"

Jesse suddenly cupped her chin with one hand. He saw fear in the widened depths of her gray eyes even though she was trying desperately to hide it. Fear of him, and the impossible situation he'd thrust her in. She wasn't half as brave as she'd like him to believe.

"Just don't act like you'd like to cut out my liver and feed it to the wolves," he said dryly. "That'll be progress enough."

## 9

Samuel Danner had lived in Portland most of his adult life. He'd attained his law degree and earned a position with one of Portland's most prestigious law firms. The three years he'd been in their employ had made him realize that the only way he could advance was either to bring in a bevy of wealthy clients or to marry one of the senior partners' daughters.

He chose neither alternative. He went into practice for himself and fell in love with the daughter of his very first client, Cedric McKechnie. Cedric was a Portland merchant specializing in buggies and carriages and all forms of deluxe conveyances. He was a widower with an only daughter, Mary, who was both the apple of his eye and his most dependable, level-headed partner in business. But Cedric had gotten himself into trouble over a custom-ordered coach. The wife of one of his customers, as spoiled and willful and petulant a woman Samuel had ever had the misfortune of meeting, had complained to her wealthy, powerful, and somewhat shady husband that Cedric had quoted her one price, then demanded twice the amount when the coach was finished. Cedric had come to Samuel for legal help, and Samuel had helped resolve the mess by buying the coach himself, even though the petulant wife had ordered the interior done in pink and silver, the silk curtains embroidered with shining silver cupids. The woman's demands had in fact run Cedric way over budget.

Mary McKechnie had been intrigued by any man who would buy such a ridiculously opulent rig. Samuel had done it because he needed transportation, and it seemed a good way to start his reputation. He'd intended to redo the interior of the coach as soon as possible, but Mary's amusement over seeing him inside such a garish, nauseatingly feminine vehicle had kept him from immediately changing it. He'd fallen in love with her at first sight.

They were married for less than six months when Mary lost control of the team Samuel had bought for the coach. The horses, newly trained, bolted at the screech of a factory whistle and ran headlong into Main Street and a Portland trolley. Several people were injured. One of the horses broke its leg and had to be destroyed.

Mary was thrown from the driver's seat and crushed beneath the coach's wheels.

Initially, there was some mystery surrounding the accident. Several eyewitnesses swore she wasn't alone in the driver's seat when the coach plowed into the trolley, but there was so much confusion no one knew for sure. Samuel didn't care. His beloved Mary was dead.

He threw himself into his practice and very quickly built it up to respectable proportions, respectable enough to gain him an invitation to the Arlington Club and the homes of Portland's most socially prominent homes. But there was no joy in it. In fact, there had been little joy in Samuel Danner's life since the death of his wife, and when Ezekiel Drummond requested an urgent meeting with one of his investors, Samuel felt only mild irritation. He wanted to go home and work on a pressing battle over land rights that looked as if it might end up in the court of one Judge Barlowe, who could be bought for the right sum, but Drummond had been so insistent that Samuel had agreed to see Drummond's client if he came to his office.

Glancing down at the sheet of paper in front of him, Samuel thought of Judge Barlowe. His only defense was to tie the issue up in such legal knots that Barlowe would grow impatient with the length of proceedings and endless court dates and hand the thing over to some lesser and more ethical judge. It all depended on how big a fish Barlowe considered the other party in this deal. Samuel stared down at the inked-in name: Montana Gray.

Not good. Not good at all.

The buzzer outside his office door sounded. He could

see the figures of a man and a woman through the glass. Drummond's investors. Heaving a sigh, he thrust back his chair and swung open the door.

The sight that greeted him left him speechless.

"Hello, Samuel," Kelsey Garrett said almost apologetically. In a high-necked lavender gown, her hair flowing like a warm red waterfall over her shoulders and down her back, her gray eyes full of soft humor, she was as lovely as a dream.

But it wasn't Kelsey who struck Samuel dumb. It was the man beside her.

"Jesse," he said hoarsely, recognizing his brother instantly even though Jesse had definitely changed. He wore a dark blue suit with a snowy white shirt. He looked tougher and harsher than Samuel's adolescent memory of his wayward brother. His nose was less perfect, broken, undoubtedly in some fight. His cheeks were bladed and harder. There was nothing boyish about Jesse now.

"Good Lord, where the hell have you been?" Samuel heard himself ask as Jesse shook his extended hand.

"In and out of trouble," Jesse drawled.

"And what are you—" He turned back to Kelsey in bewilderment. "What are you doing here—together?"

Kelsey suddenly reached for his hands, squeezing them between her gloved ones. "It's so good to see you," she said with genuine delight. "How's Harrison, and Lexie? And Joseph?"

"I—fine." Samuel's emotions had been so long dead, buried alongside his wife, that the stirring of nostalgia inside him made him suddenly draw Kelsey close and hug her. She hugged him back just as warmly. "Good Lord," he murmured hoarsely again. "Come on in. I was waiting for a client, but I'll just reschedule. How long have you been in Portland?" This was for Jesse, who moved into the room with that fluid grace Samuel recognized again. A Danner trait, but strongest in Jesse.

*Jesse!*

"We're that client," Jesse told his flabbergasted brother. Samuel looked as if he'd been struck by a sudden illness. The color washed out of his face and he stared at first at

Kelsey, then Jesse, then Kelsey, as if he couldn't believe his eyes.

Jesse would not have immediately recognized Samuel as the little brother he'd left behind. He'd filled out to look like all the Danners, except that he alone had inherited the dark Danner eyes. Jesse, Harrison, and Lexie had all taken that aspect of appearance from their mother. So had Tremaine, come to think of it, though his mother hadn't been the same as theirs. But Samuel's eyes were dark, nearly black, and his hair was lighter than Tremaine's and Jesse's, which was black as pitch, and darker than Harrison's and Lexie's blond locks. Samuel's was a dark russet—a brown shot with faint streaks of red. Not as lush and wildly beautiful as Kelsey's reddish-brown. Darker, deeper, and smooth against his head. Controlled. Just like Samuel looked, totally controlled.

This was his little brother?

The way Kelsey was eyeing Samuel stirred the embers of jealousy. Her reaction to him was warm and loving, and Jesse remembered vaguely that she'd always been an open, giving, and sweetly genuine child. He'd thought she'd just radically changed, and so she had. Some. But that other side was still there and apparently available to Samuel.

It annoyed the hell out of him.

"You're the client Ezekiel Drummond insisted I see tonight?" Samuel was nonplussed.

"Yes." Jesse stalked across the room to his favorite spot near the window, any window. Samuel's view wasn't as imposing as Zeke's; over the tops of the nearest buildings could be seen Portland's waterfront complete with its den of whorehouses and taverns and sailing masts.

"You wanted to see me on a business matter?" Samuel was having great difficulty getting a handle on this odd situation. He glanced again at Kelsey, sensing correctly that she was the more approachable of the two. "Both of you?"

"It's a rather involved story." Amusement lurked around the corners of her mouth as she tugged off her gloves. "Oh, Samuel, it's so good to see you. I've spent months, *years*, it seems, trying to avoid you, and now all I want to do is hug you and tell you how much I've missed your whole family!"

"Well, you found one of them," he pointed out dryly.

"Yes . . . well . . ." She slanted Jesse a look beneath her lashes.

"How did you two link up? And why were you avoiding me?" Samuel asked Kelsey.

"Because you'd recognize me and I didn't want to be recognized. I've been hiding out in Portland, living under a false name," she confessed. "I don't want Jace and Emerald to know where I am. You've got to *promise* you won't tell them."

"I promise," Samuel said automatically.

"Can we count on you for that?" This was from Jesse. Said without his turning around.

Samuel crossed his arms over his chest and leaned his hips against his desk. The waters were muddy and they weren't growing any clearer. "For keeping Kelsey's whereabouts a secret? Yes."

"For keeping *our* whereabouts a secret," he said, finally turning to face Samuel. "I don't want Pa or Harrison or Tremaine or Lexie knowing I'm in Portland."

"Why not?"

"I've got my reasons."

"Better spell a few out," Samuel suggested easily, "if you want my silence."

"I don't want them interfering with what I have to do until it's done."

"What do you have to do?"

"Jesse has to reclaim some stolen property," Kelsey inserted quickly.

"What property? Stolen by whom?"

Kelsey looked to Jesse, waiting. Samuel followed her gaze, eyeing the brother who was so much a stranger with both curiosity and wariness. Kelsey's greeting had been warm. Jesse was cold as the Alaska frontier.

"Montana Gray."

Samuel started. Gray was the man uppermost in his own thoughts these days.

"What?" Jesse asked, seeing Samuel's reaction.

"I have a client who's run up against Gray. There's legal action pending."

"What client? What legal action?"

The questions came thick and fast. "As his lawyer, I can't discuss my client's situation."

"Well, if he needs help," Jesse said coldly, "give him my name."

What kind of help? Samuel wondered. By the color creeping up Kelsey's neck, he suspected it might not be quite within the law either. "Why are you involved?" he asked Kelsey.

"She's my wife," was Jesse's blunt answer.

Samuel couldn't have been more shocked if his own wife had suddenly risen from the grave before his very eyes. "Your *wife?*" he gasped, gazing in disbelief at Kelsey.

"We're newlyweds," she admitted through a too-bright smile.

"Okay, that's it." Samuel levered himself from the desk and grabbed his coat and hat. "We're going out to dinner, and you're telling me this story from beginning to end, top to bottom. Don't leave out any details."

"You might not want to hear it all," Jesse drawled.

"If you want my support, you won't omit a single word."

He waited for the both of them. Jesse looked at Kelsey, who stared right back with what could be described only as absolute challenge.

Deliberately placing her arm through his, Jesse said, "Looks like it's time for the truth, my love." He brushed his lips against her cheek.

Kelsey linked her free arm over his. "Yes, darling."

Samuel had never before heard such loathing expressed in endearments.


Two hours later he knew a great deal more about both Jesse and Kelsey, yet neither had explained the actual circumstances of their marriage. He knew that Kelsey had married Jesse to protect Charlotte Chamberlain from him, and that Jesse had wanted to marry someone—anyone—of social significance to allow him into the upper echelons of Portland's inner circle. He also knew they both truly believed those were their motivations, but Samuel suspected there was considerably more at work here. Fact one, Kelsey, as Orchid, would have merely had to tell Agatha Chamberlain the truth from the beginning and she would have extricated herself from the whole damn mess. Fact two, if Jesse truly were interested in using someone to social-climb, why not use *him,* Samuel Danner, his own brother? It struck Samuel that both Kelsey and Jesse were bent on their own pursuits and the rest of the world be damned. They were two of a kind, whether they knew it or not.

And that cold hatred they displayed to each other every time they thought he wasn't looking was all an act. He'd bet money on it.

But did *they* realize it? he wondered. It amused him to think they probably hadn't even gone to bed together yet, and they were married, for chrissake!

"Is something funny?" Jesse asked acidly when Samuel couldn't control a chuckle.

"So what do we do next?" Samuel fought back a smile, but his eyes danced with laughter as he turned to Kelsey.

Kelsey couldn't help smiling in return, even though she had the sinking sensation that Samuel saw far more than either she or Jesse wanted him to. "My husband's the one with the plan," she said with a lifting of her shoulders.

Jesse ground his back teeth together and stared over their collective heads to a space at the back of the restaurant where Samuel had directed them. The place was paneled in walnut, dark and clublike. Though the place apparently allowed the female gender, the maître d' clearly did not, looking down his long nose at Kelsey as he took their order.

It irked Jesse that Kelsey had warmed to Samuel as if they'd once been lovers. And it irked him even further that they shared a history—a history where great gaps were missing for Jesse. He'd left Rock Springs of his own free will, yet now it bothered him when they spoke fondly of a certain time, or person, or place that he knew enough about to make him wish for more.

In the lamplight Kelsey's hair shone richly. Her gown

lay smoothly on her figure, and the vision of her as he'd seen her the morning after their wedding, wearing only drawers and a scanty camisole, left him with a huge ache and a dawning passion.

He wanted her. Wanted her in a way it was becoming increasingly difficult to deny.

She laughed at something Samuel said, and Samuel smiled slowly. Then Jesse nearly fell off his chair at his brother's next words.

"Harrison blames himself for your leaving," Samuel told Kelsey gently.

"I didn't leave because of him. Or because he deserted me." Her smile disappeared, but her eyes were gentle. "Or even because of Miracle."

"Deserted you?" Jesse demanded.

"Kelsey and Harrison had planned to be married," Samuel explained.

Dazed, Jesse let the news sink in slowly, feeling an irrational anger toward his older brother. Harrison and Kelsey had been engaged? "What miracle?" he asked.

Kelsey's laughter rang gaily through the quiet club. Several men turned and frowned, and Samuel's smile broadened into a rich chuckle. Jesse merely glared at the two white-haired gentlemen with the disapproving looks sitting closest to their table.

"Miracle is the name of Harrison's wife, Miranda 'Miracle' Jones Danner, to be exact," Kelsey enlightened him.

She didn't seem too distraught about being thrown over for another woman, Jesse decided, instantly cheered. "Harrison's married?"

"To a half-breed Chinook medicine woman," Samuel explained. At Jesse's look of disbelief, he added, "You'll have to meet Miracle. She's quite a lady."

"She's also my half-sister," Kelsey put in, drawing Jesse's attention back to her. "My father apparently had a long-running affair with Miracle's mother," she explained with a faint trace of bitterness. "Infidelity seems to be an affliction of all the Garrett men." Her cool gaze leveled on Jesse and he knew she was thinking it would be an affliction of one of the Danner men as well.

"Miracle sounds—interesting," was all Jesse said. The topic was rapidly becoming dangerous.

"How long have Harrison and Miracle been married now?" Kelsey asked, her gaze swinging back to Samuel.

"About four years?" Samuel shrugged. "It wasn't long after you left Rock Springs. They have a daughter now."

"Do they?" Kelsey asked quietly. "I'd like to see her."

"You were really engaged to Harrison?" Jesse asked in spite of every instinct he possessed, all of which were crying out to him to steer clear of Kelsey's life.

Her lashes swept her cheeks, their curling length creating shadows against her alabaster skin. He'd embarrassed her. "Yes," was her only answer.

Jesse revised his initial impression that Harrison's defection hadn't bothered her. It had hurt deeply, perhaps even been the cause of her descent into spinsterhood.

Scowling down at his drink, Jesse fought back an unreasonable spurt of jealousy against his older brother. Harrison hadn't married Kelsey. He had. And it wasn't Harrison's fault if Kelsey still longed for him.

Holy Christ, first Samuel, now Harrison. The only brother he wasn't jealous of was Tremaine.

"The Grays are sponsoring a charity auction," Jesse said into the silence that had fallen over the table. "It's by special invitation. Only those people who they know will donate and donate heavily have been invited. Zeke's on the list."

"So am I," Samuel said, though he knew it was a testing of loyalty where Montana Gray was concerned. Gray would like to buy him off, as he had Judge Barlowe. Samuel had planned to refuse the invitation.

"I'm going to attend that auction if I have to gate-crash," Jesse continued. "Zeke's working on an invitation, however. I don't think it'll be a problem. My wife's an excellent reference."

Jesse's dry tone didn't escape Kelsey. "Agatha and Charlotte will be invited," she said in a low voice. The thought of walking into the auction on Jesse's arm and having to face them made her feel uneasy and miserable.

"I wasn't planning on going," admitted Samuel, "but

137

now I wouldn't miss it for the world. How do you want me to act when I see the two of you?"

"Samuel, I'm determined to get Gray," Jesse warned solemnly. "It might not be in your best interests to claim a relationship with me."

"If you don't mind admitting you're my brother, I don't mind," Samuel assured him.

"It could get"—Jesse hesitated—"sticky."

"I'm not worried." Samuel was calm. "But what about Kelsey?"

"She's Orchid Simpson Danner." Jesse glanced at Kelsey.

"I told Agatha who I really am," Kelsey said.

"Will she keep your secret?"

"I—don't know. I had to explain, after the marriage, and I'm not sure she'd want to lie for me."

"Hmmm." Jesse frowned. "Does Charlotte know?"

Kelsey nodded.

"Damn," Jesse muttered with repressed fury. "Well, it can't be helped. I signed the papers on a house along the park blocks tonight, and we'll be moving in soon. I suppose we've already bought enough respectability, no matter what your name is." Jesse downed his drink with finality, regarding his new wife soberly. Some changes were going to have to be wrought in the few weeks they had before the charity auction. Some changes Kelsey Orchid Garrett Danner was going to undoubtedly object to strenuously.


Three nights later, after a surprisingly enjoyable dinner with her usually impossible new husband, Kelsey strode imperiously across her luxurious bedroom carpet, threw open the door to her room, and demanded in a carefully controlled voice, "Where are my clothes?"

Jesse was stretched out on the chaise longue, reading the paper in so thoroughly engrossed a manner that Kelsey was certain he was putting on an act. "They're gone."

"Gone?" Her voice trembled faintly. *"Gone?"*

"I had the maid take them and give them to the underprivileged."

"I don't have the courage to ask what I'm supposed to

wear until Mrs. Honeycutt finishes those gowns you ordered."

"She's sending the first one over tomorrow afternoon."

"Did you leave me some underclothes?" Kelsey asked sarcastically. "The room is swept clean!"

"There should be some in the bureau drawer."

"What about a nightgown?"

"Sleep in your drawers. Or naked, if you prefer." He glanced her way.

She envisioned creative ways to murder him. Garrotting would be nice. No, better yet, she would like to string him up by his—his—his— Her mind shut down at this rather colorful image, and she glanced away, plotting new destructive ways to make his life as miserable as he'd made hers.

Speechless with rage she returned to her room. The outline of her derringer was clear inside her soft suede reticule. Snatching up the bag, she considered holding him at gunpoint until he ordered the maid to return her clothes. But that was hopeless, she realized instantly, helplessly. It had been hours since the maid had cleaned their room today. There was no chance she would get her belongings back; Jesse would have seen to that. In fact, before dinner he'd taken her with him on a pleasant sight-seeing trip which had surprised and pleased her. Now she realized he'd had ulterior motives.

"What are you doing?" he demanded.

She gasped at the voice so close to her ear. Whipping around, she was overcome by renewed anger at the sight of his handsome form leaning negligently in the open doorway.

"I'm going to kill you," she said flatly. "I've never really wanted to kill someone in cold blood before. It's quite a new experience. Frankly, I like it."

"How are you going to kill me?" His gaze drifted to the weighted bag swinging from her hand. "Bash me over the head with your purse?"

"I'm going to shoot you," she said calmly, drawing out the derringer and checking the chambers. How dare he stand there and mock her!

"Do you really know how to use that thing?"

He sounded curious, interested. So he'd forgotten her prowess with a rifle, Kelsey realized with grim humor. He knew nothing about her. *Nothing!*

"Actually, no," she lied, sounding a bit worried. "Let's see. Lift . . ." She raised the derringer and held it in front of her, letting trepidation cross her mobile face. "Aim . . ." She centered the barrel just to the left of Jesse's face. "And pull the trigger."

Jesse's body slammed hard into Kelsey's, knocking them both to the floor. The force knocked Kelsey's hand, and a shot exploded into the wall, blasting a rain of plaster over them as the derringer skidded from her grasp and under the bed.

"You crazy fool!" he shouted in shock. "Damn you! God *damn* you!"

"I didn't—mean—to—"

He was shaking her so hard her teeth rattled and her neck felt like it would snap. She couldn't catch her breath. Dazed and frightened, she was stunned the pistol had actually discharged.

"Let—me—go—" she gasped out, closing her eyes against the sickening whirling inside her head. Oh, Lord, she was going to be sick! His weight was crushing her chest. Her lungs screamed for air. Her head ached where it banged against the floor.

"The hell I will. You bloodthirsty witch! If you ever try anything like that again, I'll kill *you!*"

"You're—hurting—me."

"I'd like to break your neck!"

He released her so swiftly her shoulders thumped to the ground. Turning her head to the side, she gulped air, fighting back the dizzying nausea rising in her throat. She could have killed him.

He was supporting his weight on his hands, staring down at her, his expression ferocious and malevolent. Kelsey's eyes fluttered closed, both to block out his murderous face and to keep from succumbing to nausea.

"I wouldn't have pulled the trigger," she said in a small voice. "Surely you know that."

"Oh, really?" he asked nastily. "That's how people get killed. Surely you know that."

Harsh pounding sounded against the outer door. Jesse rolled to his feet and away from Kelsey. She heard him answer the frightened queries of other guests in a hard, uncompromising tone, assuring them that yes, they'd heard a gunshot and no, no one was hurt.

Kelsey was shaking all over from the aftermath. It had been a stupid, stupid thing to do. She should have guessed he'd defend himself rather than trust that she was simply baiting him. And he was right. That *was* how people got killed. She'd never before done something so irresponsible in her life.

The hotel manager rang the bell a few minutes later and Kelsey heard Jesse offer him more assurances as well. When the manager entered the bedroom to examine the damage, Kelsey had collected herself enough to take a seat on the edge of the bed. She didn't dare meet Jesse's eyes; the fury emanating from him came off in waves.

Then they were alone again. Kelsey watched his booted feet come to a stop three feet in front of her. "That was a stupid, reckless thing to do," he told her coldly. "There's nothing more dangerous than a woman who carries a gun and doesn't know the first thing about how to use it. Who gave that derringer to you? Why the *hell* do you carry it around all the time? You're lucky it was me you shot at, instead of someone else. You could have landed in jail, or worse." His tone was dire, filled with repressed fury and fear for her safety and his own.

"I'm not—unskilled," Kelsey admitted, feeling slightly better now that the world had stopped bucking and weaving. She could breathe and she did so in great gulps. Color had returned to her gray-washed cheeks.

"Not unskilled?" Jesse was scornful. "It's only by the grace of God that I didn't get my head blown off."

"No, I—"

"Shut up, Kelsey. Just shut up and admit that for once in your life you were wrong!"

She turned her head away from him, but he reached out and yanked her chin back, forcing her remorseful gaze to meet his determined one. The pure folly of her recklessness filled her with deep distress. "I was wrong," she admitted in a quiet voice.

He stared at her and the moments ticked by. Tense moments. Reaction made her weak and emotional. All her life she'd let pride and recklessness overcome her better sense. In these last four years with Agatha and Charlotte, she thought she'd learned forbearance and maturity, but in a matter of weeks—ever since Jesse had barreled into her life again—she'd reverted to the wild child she'd once been. Pride, and a need to show off, had made her aim at him. Though she was too good a marksman to actually hit him even if she'd pulled the trigger, he could have startled her into making a mistake. After all, she hadn't planned for the gun to discharge. They were both lucky to escape injury.

The gamut of her emotions played across her face. Her mouth trembled and she heaved a sigh. "I'm sorry."

The sudden transition from wild assassin to tremulous woman melted Jesse's fury. He didn't trust the change, however. He'd underestimated her once; he wouldn't do it again. "Not until I have your word that you'll never touch a gun again. Any gun. Any type of firearms."

"If I give you my word, will you believe me?"

"If you give me your word and mean it," Jesse countered, certain, and rightly so, that there was a catch somewhere.

Kelsey could never promise something so ingrained in her overall personality. But she wasn't above lying. "I give you my word."

Jesse searched her eyes—eyes now filled with innocence instead of remorse. Too much innocence. "You'll try it again, won't you?" he said in wonder. "The next time you get your hands on a gun, or any other kind of weapon, you'll try to murder me!"

"No, I won't." Kelsey was sincere. "I didn't intend for the gun to fire at all."

"Liar," he whispered softly, entranced by the sight of those soft, lying lips. "You would think I'd have learned my lesson," he muttered.

"About what?" Kelsey tried to scoot across the bed,

interpreting his heavy-lidded gaze correctly. "Don't!" she warned as he leaned toward her, his hands on her shoulders.

"Don't what?" His tone was gentle and seductive as one hand curved around the back of her neck, lifting her chin and mouth to his rampant gaze, drawing her lips inexorably, inch by inch, toward his.

"If you kiss me, I'll—I'll go back on my promise!"

He laughed softly. "You didn't mean it anyway."

"I mean it now, Jesse," she breathed in fright. "I will never, ever, pick up a gun. Ever. For the rest of my life."

He hesitated, his mouth a hairbreadth away, his brandy-laced breath mingling with hers. "I believe I've found the means to keep you in line," he said in amusement.

"If you kiss me, I won't be responsible for the fate that befalls you!" she threatened.

Challenging him was her gravest error, Kelsey realized later. For a heartbeat, he'd seemed willing to listen, but flinging that threat in his face had forced his decision—and cost her dearly. His mouth came down on hers, cool and insistent. Kelsey's heart slammed into her ribs.

In a voice muffled by her trembling lips, he warned, "Don't fight me. I'll win."

That cold, determined tone caused her to tremble all over. He was right. She found this tender assault much more frightening than any other means of bending her to his will that he could have come up with.

Jesse deepened the kiss, his mouth moving over hers familiarly. Kelsey was momentarily frozen. She didn't want to want him, but she did, and though she knew this was Jesse's way of taking some small revenge, she couldn't deny that she enjoyed his kisses more than any others she'd ever experienced.

Until Jesse, in fact, she'd never wanted to kiss anyone back. She'd always wondered why women looked as if they were about to swoon when a man glued his lips to theirs. Kelsey had often asked herself what magic occurred at that moment to glaze over the couple's eyes and elevate their breathing. She'd been certain she was immune and was perplexed and relieved and slightly dismayed that this was so.

Now, however, she knew differently. The melting sensation that was starting somewhere in her abdomen was spreading to her thighs and stomach, and her head felt both fuzzy and light. The hard pressure of his mouth was welcome. When he slid the tip of his tongue along the crease of her lips, seeking entrance, she had no compunction about honoring that request. As soon as her mouth parted, his tongue plunged into the sweetness within, then slowly withdrew, then plunged again in a blatant imitation of the act he was beginning to make her crave.

Kelsey was dazed, pliant, utterly bemused. When he lifted his head to gaze down at her, she reacted on instinct, her hands curving around his neck in helpless ardor, bringing his mouth back to hers. Jesse's kisses became more demanding, his tongue more insistent, his hands sliding down her rib cage and over her hips, possessively exploring each tender curve and trembling contour.

A war was waging inside his head. An insistent beat hammered at his brain: *She's my wife . . . she's my wife . . . she's my wife.* He had every right to take what she so sweetly offered. He wanted to. Every fiber was straining right now to finish what had been so innocently begun.

Jesse had never stood on principle. He'd taken whatever came his way, and, by God, something as right as *this* would never be questioned. But there was more going on here than just sex. He wasn't even sure he liked Kelsey, and though that had hardly mattered in his past, it mattered now. They were stuck with each other for the time being; he needed her as a partner. He didn't want to get tangled up with other man/woman problems until he'd resolved things with Montana once and for all. Maybe not even then.

But God she felt *good.*

His hand slid restlessly up her midriff. Through the lavender silk he caressed the mound of her breast. Through the lavender silk he felt her nipple crest into a hard bud. In the dark recesses of his brain he recalled the shape of those breasts beneath her soft camisole. He wanted to see her again and reached for the buttons at her throat at the same instant he reseized her lips in a devouring kiss.

Kelsey watched through the veil of her lashes as Jesse

systematically undid the line of her buttons. His concentration was so fierce it left her breathless. He was undressing her. *Undressing her!* And she was letting him.

"Wait." She stilled his hand with one of her own. Beneath their tightly clasped fingers she could feel her wild and rampant heartbeat.

He gazed down at her a long moment. There was no teasing light in his eyes now. He was deadly earnest and intent. Kelsey was shattered by that look. She was powerless to do anything but stare back, wide-eyed.

His attention shifted to the buttons. Beneath her gown she wore only the thin camisole, and when Jesse pulled open the bodice of her dress, exposing her breasts, the dark buds of her nipples stood erect against the shiny satin.

He lowered his mouth to one and sucked the bud right through the camisole. Kelsey gasped in surprise and pure pleasure. She hadn't expected such a blatant assault. Her back arched upward, and the moan in her throat was raw and trembling with awakened desire.

Jesse was startled by the tormenting sweetness of her response. He'd expected her to scream, or panic, or beat her fists against his back—*something* besides this passionate surrender. He'd told himself he would go on until she stopped him, knowing that her frigid, albeit currently belated, nature would undoubtedly surge forward as soon as he began taking too many liberties. He'd expected it and counted on it. There were dozens of other women he could use for sex, but not Kelsey. Their situation was just too damned complicated.

So why wasn't she objecting? Where was that upright, rigid, thoroughly sexless Orchid Simpson *now?*

Her hands slid tentatively down his back to his hips. He was lying half atop her. Her exploration shattered his senses and he moved fully atop her, fast losing sight of anything but the need to be inside her, buried deeply within her essence, stroking her, pleasuring her. His knee nudged her legs apart and he pressed himself against her, forcing her into vibrant awareness of his rigid hardness. It was now or never, he thought, a tremor of need shaking him.

Kelsey dreamily realized what was happening. She willed

herself to fight back but was devastated by the raw need emanating from him. She wanted to pull his hips against her as hard as she could, wrap her legs around him, demand he give her that ultimate reward, even while her mind was screaming at her to wake up and fight.

She didn't have to. Jesse made the decision.

"Oh, *hell*," he muttered, rolling away from her and onto his feet, his back to her, his shoulders so tense they seemed to shake. She lay as he'd left her, on her back, shocked and devastated, for several long, long moments: wanton, rejected, and full of unrequited desire. Embarrassed, Kelsey emitted a cry of humiliation and pain and rolled into a ball.

Before she could invent some conceivable reason why she'd reacted so passionately, her husband strode out of the room, closing the door softly behind him.

# 10

Lights blazed across the sweeping circular brick drive as carriage after carriage lined up in front of Montana Gray's imposing three-story manor. A hot July breeze offered little relief to the auction patrons swathed in elegant finery. The day had been blistering—a rare cloudless, airless, breathless summer misery. Kelsey, in burgundy velvet, had felt limp and ragged while her new maid, Irma, had dressed her. Now, with the prospect of three hundred people crushed inside the Grays' ballroom facing her, she wanted to run as far away as possible as soon as the carriage door opened.

It was Jesse's carriage. His own. He hadn't lied about his abundant finances, Kelsey had subsequently learned. He'd been systematically planning his revenge for years, and all the pieces were now in place. The purchase of their new home, every inch as elegant as Montana Gray's, had been his last and final move. Now Jesse Danner, and his lovely, obedient wife, Orchid, were settled into their new, highly prestigious neighborhood, and were on the brink of becoming one of the socially elite's favorite couples. Invitations had begun to arrive, a trickle that was fast becoming a deluge. As it turned out, Zeke hadn't needed to wangle an invitation to the charity auction. Jesse and Kelsey's popularity had begun before they'd attended their first function together; people who'd seen them strolling through the parks or around the quiet, oak-lined neighborhood liked the way they *looked* together.

It was enough to make any intelligent person retch.

"Are you ready?" Jesse asked in his deep baritone.

Kelsey dragged her gaze from the carriage window and the scores of elegant patrons climbing Montana Gray's tiered brick stairs to look at her husband. He wore black from head to toe except for the stark white collar of his ruffled shirt.

He was hatless, like herself, and his hair was black as midnight, combed back and brushing the white collar of his shirt. In the half light of the carriage, his eyes were shadowed, but she knew just how blue they were, just how intense. In the three weeks since he'd kissed her and nearly made love to her, she'd felt those eyes assessing her sharply whenever she was in his presence. Sharply and disparagingly. Apparently he regretted those passionate moments as much as she did. Neither one of them had spoken of the incident since.

"I'm ready," she answered coolly.

Drake brought the carriage to a smooth stop. Jesse opened the door, leapt lightly to the ground, then extended his hand to Kelsey. Her gloves matched her dress and reached past her elbows, and as Jesse's fingers closed around hers, she was glad for their small barrier. She didn't want to touch him at all, but tonight she would be forced to—at least for the sake of appearance.

As soon as her feet touched the ground, his hand curved possessively around her waist. Kelsey's head snapped back. "What are you doing?"

"Escorting my new bride inside," he said through his teeth.

Since the incident with her derringer, he'd treated her like a stranger. Kelsey supposed she should be glad, but if Jesse expected this charade to succeed, he should have put aside his own differences with her and tried to coach her a bit more. Now her legs quivered as she walked up the porch stairs, and her heart fluttered. How did he expect her to act like a loving wife when they could scarcely bear the sight of each other?

A black-coated butler opened the door and they entered the foyer. Noise from hundreds of excited voices met them like a wall. Colors swirled in front of Kelsey's eyes—hundreds of jewel-toned gowns. Light glanced off diamonds and emeralds and sapphires circling women's throats and wrists and sometimes even wound in ropes throughout their hair.

Kelsey's hair was braided. Jesse refused to allow her to net it, but she stubbornly refused to wear it down. They'd compromised. Her lush mane was pulled loosely back from her forehead, then braided in a thick rope that swung gently between her shoulder blades. The arrangement was starker than Jesse wanted, but still attractive, soft wisps of sun-streaked auburn curling near her ears and across her smooth forehead.

She'd given in on the ruby necklace at her throat. Of all the gowns Mrs. Honeycutt had fashioned, the burgundy was the least provocative. The neckline dipped low, but came in close to her neck so only a rectangle of skin showed. When Jesse realized which dress she planned to make her debut in, he bought the necklace. Kelsey had protested its cost and had succeeded only in irritating her new husband. She'd given in, finally, for two reasons: the necklace covered more skin, and it was too stunningly beautiful to resist.

Two black-suited attendants guided the crowd into the ballroom. Chairs were arranged in neat rows beneath three monstrous crystal chandeliers. After the auction the room would be used as it was meant—for dancing. Kelsey

148

planned to escape before she was forced to move into Jesse's arms.

"How long will it take you to accost Montana Gray?" she murmured. His hand had shifted and was now in the small of her back, guiding her through the crush.

"I'm not certain. He obviously doesn't remember my name, or I'd have been *accosted* myself."

Jesse wondered how Lila had forgotten him. Lila was too clever and self-preserving to ignore a threat like Jesse Danner. Montana might not remember his name, but Lila would have seen it on the guest list and known exactly who he was. He'd half expected her to contact him in advance, but the fact that she hadn't intrigued him.

Kelsey half turned to gaze curiously around the room, offering Jesse her lovely profile. Beneath his hand, the velvet was soft and crushable. Beneath the velvet, the small of her back curved gently. These last few weeks had been hellish torture, he thought angrily. When she'd aimed her pistol at him, he'd reacted on instinct and by God, they were both damn lucky to still be alive! Any sane man would have considered that grounds for divorce at the very least, but half the time he fantasized about consummating their marriage and getting her out of his system once and for all.

*If* that would work, he admitted darkly, and he had the terrible feeling it would backfire on him.

For the first time since Montana Gray had ordered him killed and stolen his life out from under him, Jesse felt deterred from his goal. Deterred by a *woman*. His own *wife!*

Her rope of hair swung against his arm. His gaze traveled upward, following one glowing wine-red strand that wound through the rich brown braid. Her nape was white as moonlight, the curve of her jaw so enticing that he had to look away or let his tongue explore it.

God *damn* it!

Jesse released Kelsey so abruptly she stumbled. Glaring at him, she strode into the ballroom alone and settled into a chair in the back row. Expecting him to follow her, she was slightly dismayed when he took up a position at the back of the room, his hands thrust into the pockets of his trousers, his broad shoulders leaning against the crushed-velvet-paneled wall.

The devil take him! Kelsey thought in a huff. Between the shoulders of the men seated in front of her, and the coiffures of the women, Kelsey's gaze was drawn to a familiar white-haired woman and her young companion: Agatha and Charlotte.

Her heart wrenched. So they'd come. She wondered painfully if it was because they suspected she might be here. Maybe that was why they'd accepted the invitation. Agatha detested Montana Gray and would never willingly attend one of his affairs unless there was another reason. But would they even care to see her? No. Charlotte positively loathed her, so they had to be there for something else.

Movement caught her eye. Directly across from her, and several seats in from the aisle, Samuel Danner was motioning to her. There was an empty seat next to him.

Kelsey glanced back at Jesse and caught him staring at her. He lifted one brow. Kelsey gave him a sweet smile, gathered her skirts, then excused her way down the row until she was next to Samuel.

"You look incredible," Samuel told her.

Kelsey flashed him a grateful smile as she settled herself into the seat. "So do you," she said, meaning it.

Like Jesse, Samuel's suit was pitch black. With his dark hair and eyes, he looked harsh and forbidding, and only his slow smile reminded Kelsey that Samuel was more easygoing than his elder brother.

"What's Jesse got planned?" he asked, inclining his head to where Jesse stood.

"I neither know nor care. Revenge isn't my cup of tea."

"I'm surprised it's Jesse's."

Kelsey gazed at him with interest. "Why?"

"Well, you must remember Jesse about as well as I do. He was careless and tended to buck authority. He and Pa were at each other's throats half the time. But he was also honorable, in his own way. He certainly possessed family loyalty the one time it was really needed."

Kelsey knew why Samuel's voice deepened in memory. He was thinking of the night Eliza Danner's first husband had reappeared from the grave, so to speak. The Danners had rallied to Eliza's rescue, Harrison had nearly been killed, Lexie and Tremaine had saved Harrison's arm and life, Jesse had been injured, and Samuel, the youngest, had chased one of Gainsborough's men away with a shotgun.

It wasn't long after that incident, however, that Jesse had left town and Alice McIntyre had cried rape.

"Jesse was a rake and a libertine and I don't believe he's changed except now we can add ruthless and vengeful to his list of qualities."

Samuel snorted skeptically.

"What is that supposed to mean?"

"It means you married him, Kelsey my girl. There must be something about him you like and admire."

"I was *forced* to marry him."

Samuel just shook his head and smiled, annoying Kelsey to no end. The auctioneer rose to the podium and his assistants held up an original painting by a renowned East Coast artist, so Kelsey was forced to hold her tongue. That Samuel believed she'd married Jesse for other reasons than the ones she'd named was unthinkable.

Throughout the auction, Kelsey's gaze continually strayed to the back of the room. People stopped to chat with Jesse from time to time. Especially gorgeously turned-out women, one of whom had the pompous nerve to offer her hand to be kissed, which he did so with considerable enjoyment.

By the time the auction came to a rousing end, and thousands of dollars had changed hands, Kelsey's temper was simmering. Her eyes were narrowed on a distant point, her thoughts focused on murder. Except Jesse—blast him!—had hidden her derringer and now she was defenseless.

What she wouldn't do to get her hands on an honest-to-goodness rifle! She was going to have to approach Agatha and ask that her belongings be sent to her new home.

She swept out of the ballroom ahead of Samuel and felt

a hard hand grab her arm. Furiously, she shook off Jesse's grip, never bothering to look at him.

That sparked Jesse's anger.

He caught up with her in the small anteroom off the foyer. "Where the hell are you going?" he demanded.

"I need some fresh air."

"Well, I need a loving companion. Take a few deep breaths out on the balcony and get back here quick. Montana's waiting to meet you."

"To meet me? You mean you've already talked with him?"

"We've been introduced. He doesn't remember me." Jesse's tone was dry. "Yet."

Kelsey hadn't seen Montana, and he was not a man to be easily missed. "Mr. Gray will just have to wait." She picked up the folds of her skirt and aimed toward the nearest balcony exit until Jesse's hand caught her elbow, spinning her around.

"I'll accompany you," he said flatly.

"Really, there's no need. I'm perfectly capable of catching my breath by myself."

"Humor me," was his imperative response.

The balcony was a small one on the south end of the house. It overlooked a garden closed on all sides by a laurel hedge, and a stone fountain with a statue of a maiden filling a bucket placed squarely in the center. In the lambency from the house lights, the colors were blurred and darkened and shadows lurked in the corners. Nevertheless, its loveliness struck Kelsey and, for the first time since she'd moved into her new house, she felt a pang of regret that she wouldn't be staying long enough to make it a real home.

"You're very tense," she told him when they were standing alone. Behind them, the house was a cacophony of noise with the faintest violin music sounding hauntingly above it all.

"Yes, well, it's all I can do to keep from breaking Montana's fat neck."

"You hate him that much."

"I owe him."

"For stealing your land and your money." Her mocking tone was full of reproach.

Jesse's lips tightened. Revealing Nell's fate at Montana's hands was on the tip of his tongue; however, before he could utter one word, the reason he wanted to tell her entered his brain: He wanted her to think well of him. "Yes," he answered shortly before he lost what little control of his senses he still maintained and did something as foolish as tell her the truth.

"I don't understand you, Jesse," she said, perplexed, reminding him vividly of the Kelsey of his youth.

"Understanding isn't part of the bargain, Mrs. Danner," he answered lightly. "Are you ready for the performance?"

"I suppose so," she sighed, so full of reluctance that Jesse almost smiled.

"Do you think—" she began, but his hands fell on her shoulders, startling her. Her eyes widened as Jesse's head descended toward hers. Her intake of breath was an aborted gasp. She jerked backward and he cupped her nape, drawing her lips upward, her sweet breath fanning his face in rapid terror.

His mind was only half on the kiss. Lila Gray's face was imprinted on his mind—Lila Gray's curious face as it peeked around the French doors of the balcony.

Recovering herself, Kelsey squirmed beneath the pressure of his embrace and kiss. He dare not let her up for air or she would blast him. Squeaks of protest sounded. Her hands clenched in his lapels, thrusting against—no, *battering*—his chest.

Lila's vituperative face disappeared and Jesse ended the kiss, crushing Kelsey's face to his ruffled shirt at the same moment. "Shhh," he warned in a whisper.

"You son of a . . ." The rest was lost as he pressed her face closer. He grinned to himself. Kelsey tried to kick him in the shin and he pulled on her braid, snapping her head back so that he caught the end of her furious diatribe. ". . . black-hearted scoundrel with no conscience!" she gasped, jerking backward, practically tearing her dress from his grasp in her attempts to free herself.

Jesse wrapped one hard arm around her and squeezed her to his chest once again. "Stop it."

"You have no right to manhandle me, and by God, I won't *stand* for it!"

He increased the pressure against her rib cage and Kelsey choked. "You said you were ready to play your part," he hissed in her ear. "We were being watched."

Instead of bringing her to her senses, his revelation had the opposite effect. "Watched?" she shrieked in a whisper. "You kissed me while someone was watching?"

"Because someone was watching," he explained. "Lila, Montana's lovely wife, nearly fell on her nose trying to get an eyeful."

Kelsey regarded him with undiluted outrage. "In case it's escaped your notice, you and I are husband and wife. We don't need to paw over each other in public. In fact, it'll only worsen our bid—*your* bid!—for acceptance. You astonish me, Jesse. Sometimes you act like you've had lessons in manners and breeding, other times you're a Rock Springs hick! I ought to slap you. That's what a lady would do."

"Wives don't slap their husbands unless they expect to be treated the same way," he retorted, annoyed because she was right about the public display of affection. He'd done it purely for Lila's benefit. Or maybe his own, he thought with an inward wince, knowing he'd been dying to kiss Kelsey all night. "Besides, you're no lady." He grabbed her arm and propelled her back toward the ballroom. "Ladies don't shoot *anybody.*"

Lila Hathaway Gray thought about having an attack of the vapors in the center of the ballroom. She could swoon in her partner's arms, a jelly-stomached gent with noxious breath who had a habit of squeezing her right breast when he thought no one was looking. Her freezing glare didn't work on him either. He was Judge Barlowe, one of Montana's paid "friends."

But the odious Barlowe wasn't the reason she wanted to create a scene. She was mad as spit and could scarcely contain herself. If she didn't find some release soon, she'd explode!

Jesse Danner, *her* Jesse Danner, practically had his tongue down that gorgeous bitch's throat, and he'd done it on purpose! He'd known she was watching, the filthy bastard!

Lila steamed. Surely a woman of her supposed breeding would faint dead away upon witnessing that vile scene on the balcony. She could spread rumors. Ruin him.

That thought stopped her short. Ruin him? How on *earth* had he gotten an invitation to the auction? She'd thought he was dead, for God's sake, and now here he was, as virile and handsome as ever. No, *more so!*

"Excuse me," she said, peeling Barlowe's fat hand from her overripe chest. Sailing through the crowd in layers of blue chiffon, she caught the eye of her husband, who was flanked by his hard-eyed bodyguards, Gardner and Al.

Montana watched her approach. "You should have let me read the guest list," Lila spit at him. "We've got a gate-crasher."

"Who?" he grunted, his pig eyes darting around the room. Montana didn't give a damn about social niceties, but he knew that his enemies weren't above attacking him in his own home.

"Jesse Danner and—friend." She curled the last word on her tongue.

"Don't know him."

"You should. You were supposed to have killed him five years ago!"

"Use that tone with me, woman, and you'll find yourself locked in your room for a week on bread and water."

Lila reined in her fury, clenching her teeth to keep from screaming. Five years ago, when Montana had caught her with Jesse, he'd nearly beaten her to death. The only good thing to come out of that was that she'd been rendered incapable of having children. Now she could indulge her taste for men without fear of pregnancy. And Montana had been kind enough not to damage her face.

Stewing, Lila stalked away. Over her initial shock, she began to regret her hasty words as she recalled the lovemaking she'd experienced with Jesse. She didn't want Montana to murder or castrate him. Not yet, anyway.

Suddenly the scene with Jesse and the beautiful red-haired woman brought a wave of weakness to her lower limbs. Now she viewed the whole thing over again as a voyeur, not as a jealous one-time lover. Excitement crawled over her skin as she envisioned the passion of that kiss; the hard, determined way Jesse had held his feminine companion; the fierce sexual tension of the moment. Oh, Lord, she thought in fear, seeing the way Montana's men were fanning out across the room. She had to stop them from harming him!

"Wait!" she ordered, grabbing her husband's arm. "We need to find out what he knows. We can't just kill him."

Montana was as determined and ruthless a man as had ever walked the earth, but he wasn't stupid. He gazed coldly at his wife. "Leave it to me," was all he said, but Lila was convinced that he'd listened to her.

Jesse's hand was in the small of Kelsey's back, guiding her back inside the main ballroom. He half expected her to bolt, but her hand was on his forearm as if she were a willing partner. He shot her an amused look, uncomfortably aware of the hot color that still stained her cheeks and made her gray eyes shimmer with emotion. Much as he wanted a gorgeously turned-out wife, he wished he were immune to her incredible beauty. It would sure as hell make life a lot easier.

He spotted Lila and Montana together, both of their expressions tight-lipped and stony. Whatever they were discussing was repugnant to both of them. "This way," he murmured in Kelsey's ear, his breath fluttering the reddish curls.

The throng of people was a hot crush of bodies. Jesse's arm circled Kelsey's back, pressing her to his side. They'd taken only three steps before Tyrone McNamara and Gerrard Knight blocked their path. Both men ogled Kelsey, their expressions comical in their surprise.

"Miss Simpson?" Knight croaked out, his eyes bulging as his gaze traveled almost indecently down her neck, the front of her gown, to her feet, then settled on her lusciously outlined breasts.

Jesse's grip tightened as Kelsey extended a hand. Knight slobbered over her fingers just long enough to spark Jesse's temper. He was saved from smashing Gerrard's buck teeth down his throat by Tyrone's intervention.

"I see you're still together," he said, eyeing Jesse carefully.

"Together," Jesse agreed. He threw a glance at Kelsey, expecting her to inform McNamara and Knight about their marriage, but when she merely stood silently by his side, he was forced to take matters into his own hands. "Orchid's my wife."

"Your wife!" Tyrone exclaimed.

"So your little wager is off," Jesse said in a controlled, pleasant voice.

"Wager," Knight blustered. "I don't know what you mean."

"You know exactly what I mean," Jesse countered, the pressure on Kelsey's back increasing as he practically pushed her away from the two men.

"Stop it," she bit out once they were out of range. "I'm perfectly capable of walking on my own two feet. Keep pushing me and I'll trip and make a scene."

"You could have helped out with your friends back there," he said dryly, "instead of leaving me to explain."

"You did fine as the jealous husband," she answered with a toss of her head. "I swear, you should have taken up a theater career."

"Polish your own acting skills. We're about to meet Montana and Lila Gray. . . ."

Kelsey gazed straight ahead of her to where Montana Gray and his elegant, beautiful blond wife stood side by side. They almost seemed to be waiting for them. Lila wore a royal blue chiffon dress that wrapped across her waist and pressed the tops of her breasts nearly out of the tight bodice. Her eyes were a bright, deep, glacial blue. In contrast to her peacock brilliance, Montana looked tough and deadly and somber in his dark gray suit. His face showed the remnants of his brawling days. Kelsey focused on the eye that drooped because the stare from his other one made her feel naked.

Jesse's hands were deep in his pockets. He made no gesture of politeness, friendliness, or even greeting. "Remember me?" he asked in a soft voice.

"Yes, Mr. Danner. Now I do." Montana moved slightly, indicating Lila. "You remember Mr. Danner, don't you, darling?"

Lila drew a deep breath, her bodice tightening until Kelsey was certain the seams would rip wide open, spilling out those globes of flesh for all the world to see. "Yes." Her voice was strained.

"I didn't expect to see you again," Montana had the gall to admit.

"I was born under a lucky star." Jesse smiled. "In fact, I'm back in Portland to do some business. Real estate business."

Montana kept up his one-eyed stare.

"Since we're bound to cross paths time and again, I thought you should know I've all but forgotten the past. Who knows? We might even be able to do business together, being as we're both in real estate."

Kelsey could scarcely hide her astonishment. Montana would never believe him! Oh, Jesse was excellent! A consummate actor. But no one could possess the egomania to truly believe anyone could forgive an attempt on their life! Especially one as ruthless as Montana had made on Jesse's.

Montana didn't change expression. Lila, however, fairly quivered at her husband's side. The glimmering rope of sapphires around her neck refracted dazzling pinpoints of light with each tiny shiver Lila couldn't control.

A stab of jealousy shot through Kelsey, unexpected and hot as a branding iron. She didn't need a crystal ball to discern this woman's thoughts. Lila Gray was in an absolute panting state over Jesse!

"Who's your lovely companion?" Montana suddenly asked.

"Orchid Simpson Danner. My wife."

Lila smothered a gasp. Her black eyes bored into Kelsey's gray ones. Kelsey eased closer to Jesse, who draped his arm over her shoulders as if it were the most natural thing in the world.

Montana clasped one of Kelsey's hands. He actually bent down to kiss it. She steeled herself, repulsed beyond measure. Jesse tensed beside her. His lips were dry and papery.

"How long have you been married?" Lila's voice was low.

"A few weeks," Kelsey answered.

"I feel we've met before, but I'm sorry, Mrs. Danner, I can't place you."

"I was companion to Lady Agatha Chamberlain's daughter, Charlotte," Kelsey explained.

"Ah, yes. A lovely, lovely woman, Lady Chamberlain. We must have you to dinner soon." The words tripped off Lila's tongue as if she'd spoken them a hundred times this evening. Meaningless invitations between bored socialites.

Kelsey's heritage reared up. Forgetting everything she'd learned in Lady Chamberlain's employ, she stated with a smile, "I really doubt that would be in the best taste, don't you? I mean, considering the past. It's hard for one to forgive being nearly beaten to death. I'm sure Jesse would—"

Jesse coughed into his hand. "Excuse us, please," he interrupted, practically carrying Kelsey to a remote corner of the room. "Are you finished?" he asked in an ominous tone.

"I couldn't stand it one more minute," Kelsey defended herself in a harsh whisper, forestalling the lecture she was sure was coming. "That woman's a viper. She practically wrapped herself around you and flicked her tongue in your ear."

Jesse's head snapped around and he gazed at her in incredulity. "You sound like a jealous wife."

"I *am* a jealous wife. That's what you wanted me to act like, wasn't it?"

"You're not acting."

Kelsey wanted to swipe the pleased look off his face. "You may charm the leaves off the trees, and the drawers off other women, but I know you. I haven't forgotten what

159

you did to Alice McIntyre, and God knows how many other silly girls in Rock Springs.''

"What did I do to Alice McIntyre?" Jesse's voice was the crack of a whip.

"Seduced her. Maybe even . . . probably even . . . I mean, people said . . .''

Jesse waited with growing impatience, but Kelsey couldn't force the words past her lips. She didn't truly believe he'd taken any woman against her will. Lord sakes, he wouldn't *have* to! They practically fell at his feet. "After you left town, there were dozens of rumors about you. Terrible stories. Your name is infamous in Rock Springs.''

He dropped her arm, glancing past her as if he'd suddenly grown tired of her company. "Are you ready to leave? Montana's got the message, so my business is finished here.''

Kelsey was as eager as he was to leave the stifling, opulent home. She squeezed past a chattering throng of latecomers and nearly ran smack into Charlotte. "Charlotte!" She greeted her with surprise and delight.

"Hello, Orchid." Charlotte gazed past Kelsey to Jesse, who was standing slightly behind her. "Jesse," she said bitterly, inclining her head.

Kelsey's heart squeezed. "Is Agatha here?"

"Yes, but she doesn't want to speak to you." Charlotte's mouth was tight but her lips trembled ever so slightly. In a lacy white gown that hinted at her full bosom, she looked young and fresh and innocent. Kelsey wanted to drag her into her arms and beg her forgiveness.

But Charlotte brushed past them just as Agatha entered the room. Tears burned Kelsey's eyes. She fought them back and put on a brave smile. "Hello, Agatha," she greeted her.

Agatha gazed at the young beauty who'd hurt her granddaughter. Kelsey's eyes begged for forgiveness, but over Jesse Danner's shoulder she caught Charlotte's misery-filled gaze. "Hello, Orchid," she said coolly, moving into the room with regal bearing.

Kelsey was shattered. She'd thought Agatha understood.

A hand dropped on her shoulder. "Come on," Jesse said softly in her ear.

In the carriage Kelsey swayed against the luxurious squabs, so filled with her own misery that she didn't notice the speculative way Jesse was watching her. Her hands were clenched in her lap; her unhappy gaze directed out the window to the breathless night beyond.

At their house she barely registered the light feel of Jesse's hand as he guided her down the steps to the cobblestone walk. At the door, Irma took their coats, shooting anxious glances from Jesse's dark countenance to Kelsey's pale one.

"Would you like a brandy?" Jesse asked as Kelsey turned automatically toward the stairs and their upstairs bedroom suites.

"No, thank you."

"You need one."

"I'm perfectly fine." She moved up the deep blue carpeted stairs as if in a dream.

She removed her gown and fumbled with the clasp on her necklace. A sudden breath of air made her glance to the door. It was open and Jesse stood there with a brandy snifter in his hand.

"Drink this," he ordered.

Dressed in a camisole and drawers, Kelsey felt positively naked. She froze at her vanity table as he set the glass down beside her perfumes.

Jesse finished removing her necklace and eased it down in a coil. He met her gaze in the mirror. "Charlotte will get over it."

"Will she?" Kelsey's mouth quivered. She fingered the coil of rubies, afraid to meet his gaze for long.

"Yes."

Kelsey swallowed. "And will Agatha ever forgive me?" she asked miserably.

"Someday you can tell them the whole truth."

"I already told her. It doesn't seem to help." She pinned on a bright smile. "You don't have to try to cheer me up, Jesse. It's really a little thing. I'll be fine."

In the mirror's reflection she saw his dark head nod.

Then she felt his fingers brush her hair lightly, and to her enormous surprise he bent down and laid a kiss on her nape.

Twenty minutes later she lay in bed, staring up at the canopy. She couldn't remember the last time she'd cried, but tears hovered in the corners of her eyes. Scrunching up the pillow, she buried her face in it, willing away the anguish that threatened to engulf her.

# 11

The bright lights of the chandeliers beamed down on Kelsey with malevolent heat. She'd thought July was hot, but August was an oven. She was sick to death of women in fine gowns and men in tuxedos and people of both sexes trying to outwit, outcharm, and outmaneuver one another at social event after social event.

Tonight they were at the home of Margaret and Walter Fuller, acquaintances of Agatha's, friends of Montana and Lila Gray's, and as glamorous and morally bankrupt a couple as one would ever hope to meet. The Fullers had extended the invitation to their luxurious home to a scrupulously edited guest list; yet the party had swelled to enormous proportions as social climbers and gate-crashers alike (she and Jesse had been lucky enough to be honored with one of the gilt-edged vellum invitations) packed the ballroom.

Yes, Kelsey knew more about the goings-on of Portland's upper classes than anyone had a right to. She knew, for instance, that Margaret Fuller was pregnant, but the child wasn't her husband's. She also knew that Walter Fuller had a cozy little hotel room set up for his mistress, Eunice Winterton, who just happened to be Tyrone McNamara's married sister. Since Richmond Winterton was fifty, and looked a hundred, and spent most of his time gambling with Gerrard Knight, no one much blamed Eunice. And anyway, she might be a widow soon, since Richmond, and Gerrard too, for that matter, were rumored to owe their very souls to Montana Gray. It was becoming well known that those who couldn't pay their debts suffered rather unlucky fates, though it was heresy to even whisper that Montana Gray might be to blame. . . .

And Montana Gray was as pervasive as a bad smell. Kelsey's skin crawled whenever he was nearby, which lately had been often, since he and Jesse were now close business associates. Lord sakes, but she didn't see how Jesse stood it! She knew how much Jesse hated Montana, but he was a master at hiding his emotions. Zeke was much less effective at this. He actively loathed the man but was smart enough to keep his distance so that Montana and he were rarely in close contact.

Lila Gray drove Kelsey to distraction. The looks she passed over Jesse were sinfully avaricious. Kelsey was consumed with the desire to rip every blond hair out of her head and hold her at gunpoint and see how long it took before she cracked. She'd accepted this jealous side of her nature as inevitable. Jesse was her property, at least temporarily, and Lila had no right to be so openly eager to crawl between the sheets with him.

Now, tonight, they were all together for another evening of dining and dancing and gossiping. It was all in the name of revenge, and Kelsey was damned near at the end of her tether. But anytime she asked Jesse how his business was progressing, he dismissed her with a "fairly well" or "don't worry about it" or "I'll let you know soon."

It was enough to send a girl from Rock Springs straight for her rifle.

Over the rim of her champagne glass, Kelsey glared darts at the broad back of her husband. If he didn't level with her soon, she would have to take matters into her own hands. She'd started already, as a matter of fact. Whenever Jesse was out of the house she practically ransacked the papers and drawers of his desk, searching for some clue to the exact means he'd chosen for this revenge. To date, she'd been unsuccessful, but sooner or later Jesse would inadvertently leave some clue lying about.

And even if her efforts failed, she might yet squeeze the information from either Samuel or Zeke. They seemed to at least credit her with a brain, and she'd caught the sympathetic looks Samuel had sent her way whenever Jesse had been particularly short-tempered with her questions.

Either way, she refused to be kept in the dark much longer. This purgatory marriage was enough to drive her out of her mind. She was ready to end it, completely ready in fact. For the interim, however, she'd contacted Agatha and requested that the rest of her belongings—including her rifle—be sent to her new home. Jesse had been out with Zeke when the package had arrived so Kelsey had been able to secrete the rifle in her bedroom closet.

Lila Gray's sultry laughter sounded from somewhere near the dais at the end of the room, where the band members were warming up. Kelsey's gray eyes narrowed. What a treat it would be to hold Lila down the barrel of her rifle until she shriveled up with fear.

It was a delicious dream and it kept Kelsey entertained for nearly an hour while she avoided the dance floor and the throngs of spoiled, self-appointed aristocrats.

Her solitude was abruptly interrupted by a familiar dowager who, upon spying Kelsey, charged toward her like a steam engine. Madame Lacey Duprés, Kelsey thought with an inward groan, glancing around for an avenue of escape. The woman had been at several of the balls, soirees, and charity fund-raisers where Kelsey and Jesse had played out their highly social, mad-about-each-other charade. Madame Duprés had made a terrible pest of herself, but she apparently had enough money and connections to keep her name on at least some of the social lists, for she invariably turned up like the bad penny she was.

And she'd targeted Kelsey—or more accurately, Orchid—as her next victim for reasons that were beyond Kelsey's ken.

"Mrs. Danner!" she bellowed as Kelsey searched desperately for some means of escape. "How wonderful to see you again. Our paths seem destined to cross. Jeffrey!" She glanced around for her loyal servant, who immediately snapped to attention. "Send the waiter with more champagne."

"Yes, Madame."

Kelsey ducked her head to hide a smile. "Excuse me, Madame Duprés. I believe I see my husband signaling me."

"Wait just a moment," she ordered imperiously. "I'm having an intimate affair at my suite at the Portland Hotel next Sunday afternoon, and I positively insist that you be there."

"I—don't think I can."

"You and your husband have put me off twice now. I'm beginning to think you're deliberately avoiding me. Does a more important invitation keep you from attending?"

For once in her life Kelsey's fertile brain seemed to stall. She didn't have an excuse. The thought of another lavish affair, especially one hosted by Lacey Duprés, was singularly depressing. Also, Jesse would have no interest in attending if Montana Gray wasn't invited; he loathed these parties as much as Kelsey did and accepted invitations only to keep up appearances. Kelsey suspected Lacey Duprés wouldn't be on the top of Gray's "must-see" list, so Jesse would refuse to go.

And it would probably irritate the hell out of him if she accepted an invitation for them, she realized, deciding it was time to take action. "Thank you, Madame Duprés. I'll be there even if my husband can't pull himself away from his latest business venture."

"And Lady Chamberlain? I expect you to convince her to accept my invitation also."

"I can't speak for Lady Chamberlain." Kelsey involuntarily glanced around the room, searching for Agatha. So that was why Lacey Duprés was so interested in her. To get an "in" with Agatha. Fresh pain welled inside her, and she focused again on Jesse's strong back halfway across the room. Jesse, who was consulting with Zeke and Samuel and . . .

Lila Gray.

Lila stood on the periphery of their circle, one hip thrust

forward provocatively. She wore ice blue—blue appeared to be her trademark color—and the gown dipped scandalously low in back. Only Montana's tremendous grip on Portland industry kept her from being publicly shunned, for she was as outrageous and bold as any harlot.

"Excuse me," Kelsey said, stalking toward the group.

It struck her when she was almost upon Lila that she should be glad some other woman was so interested in Jesse. Knowing her husband, his forced celibacy was bound to create problems. Kelsey didn't want those "problems" to turn his attention to her. Since the fight over her derringer, and the aftermath, and those tense, passionate moments on the Grays' balcony, Jesse had left her alone. The only kiss he'd given her was the tender one the night she'd been so hurt and lost after Charlotte had snubbed her.

Samuel spied her first, coughing discreetly into his hand to smother a smile. Jesse turned around and Lila, who'd placed her lily-white fingers on his arm, circumspectly drew back her hand.

Kelsey swept her husband a loving look that smoldered with repressed fury. His mouth twitched and he slid an arm around her, pressing her close to his side, an intimate, affectionate pose for husband and wife. Kelsey's elbow dug like a knife into his rib cage while she ostensibly returned the hug.

"Are you ready to leave, darling?" she said through a brilliant smile.

"In a minute. Lila says Montana wishes to speak to me." Jesse's grip tightened around his wife's slender waist until Kelsey's intake of breath was a choked gasp.

"Let's dance," Samuel inserted, clasping one of Kelsey's gloved hands and leading her away from Jesse's constrictive embrace.

"How are you feeling?" he asked once they were on the dance floor.

Kelsey shot him a quizzical look. Samuel was grinning like a devil.

Realizing he'd seen through their little battle of wills, she snorted in disgust. "Please keep it a secret, but I'm afraid

I've married a boa constrictor. One day he'll squeeze the life out of me."

He chuckled. "The two of you remind me of something I'd almost forgotten."

"What's that?"

"There is some fun left in the world."

"Fun." Kelsey cast him a disparaging glance as he swept her across the floor. Unlike Jesse, who could scarcely dance the waltz without counting the steps in his head, Samuel was an excellent partner. Beneath Jesse's sophisticated exterior beat the heart of an outlaw, but Samuel possessed the true polish of a gentleman.

"Lila's fit to be tied," Samuel observed. "Jesse will scarcely even look at her."

Kelsey couldn't stop herself from craning her neck to see her husband. He was talking to Montana now, the picture of gentlemanly civility. But his posture was tense.

"Lila is a married woman," Kelsey said unnecessarily.

"And Jesse's a married man."

"Oh, no. He's not. I mean"—she stumbled over her words—"not that way."

"What way?" Samuel's gaze was all innocence.

"You know full well our marriage is temporary, Samuel," she retorted evenly. "Jesse and I made a deal."

"It's still a marriage."

Kelsey simply shook her head. She had no wish to further this conversation, as it was quickly veering into dangerous territory.

She and Samuel moved to the punch bowl, and it was then that Kelsey saw Charlotte Chamberlain. Her young friend was flirting outrageously with Tyrone McNamara, acting the part of the coquette. Fear stabbed Kelsey's heart, and before she could consider her actions, she excused herself from Samuel and strode anxiously toward the couple, her mouth set.

". . . you really are bad," Charlotte was cooing, slapping Tyrone's arm lightly with her hand.

"And you are a gorgeous tease," Tyrone returned. Charm oozed from him like a noxious odor.

They both looked up at Kelsey's sudden appearance.

Charlotte's expression turned sour and Tyrone's gaze swept down Kelsey's dark green gown, focusing on her sumptuous bosom. Kelsey hated the dress. Rich emerald silk ruffled her nape, then dipped scandalously low over her bosom, revealing more of her breasts than Kelsey felt comfortable with. She wouldn't have worn it at all except her treacherous mind remembered the one comment Jesse had made when she'd consented to put it on just after it had arrived from Mrs. Honeycutt.

"That color suits you," was all he'd said, and Kelsey, who'd eyed the neckline with worry, had nevertheless worked up the nerve to wear the gown tonight. Now she regretted it.

"Where's Agatha?" Kelsey asked.

"She's seated at one of the tables," Charlotte announced airily, inclining her head in the direction of the musicians.

"Could I speak to you alone?" Kelsey requested humbly.

"I don't think so."

"Miss Chamberlain and I were just about to dance." Tyrone clasped Charlotte's arm and drew her toward him.

Only Charlotte's slight resistance, a resistance she tried to mask, saved Kelsey from ripping her young friend out of Tyrone's slimy hands. It was all an act, Kelsey realized with a pang. For her benefit. Because she'd stolen Jesse away.

Agatha was seated alone, drinking a cup of tea and fighting back a look of distaste as the weak fluid passed her lips. Upon seeing Kelsey, her expression grew guarded. "Hello, Orchid," she greeted her.

"Agatha." There was a wealth of feeling in Kelsey's tone. She couldn't hide it. It filled her throat and choked her. "Thank you for sending my things to me."

"You're welcome, my dear."

"How—have you been?"

Agatha gazed at her thoughtfully. "Fine, although if I have to attend one more event in the interest of furthering my granddaughter's social circle, I may consider Charlotte a candidate for a nunnery."

Kelsey smiled. "Would you mind if I sit down?"

"No, dear. Please do."

While music floated over the heads of the crowd and Charlotte moved into their line of view, pretending to revel in Tyrone's embrace even while her arms held him stiffly at bay, Kelsey let Agatha's gentle company soothe her. She hadn't realized how much she'd missed her these past few weeks. She ached inside for the friendship she'd lost.

"Jesse's taken Portland by storm," Kelsey murmured in an attempt at polite conversation. "This sham of a marriage should be over soon."

"What will you do then, my dear?"

"I don't know. Leave, I suppose."

"Leave the city?" Agatha regarded Kelsey somberly.

Kelsey drew a breath and nodded. It was time to find herself a real life. Near time, anyway.

"I'm sorry," Agatha said.

"No sorrier than I."

The music ended and the guests clapped politely. Kelsey stood to excuse herself, but Madame Duprés suddenly thumped up to them in all her glorious splendor.

"Lady Chamberlain," she said in her dramatic voice, leaning intimately toward Agatha on her cane. "I hope you'll accept my invitation."

Agatha's brows arched.

"Madame Duprés is having a soiree this Sunday," Kelsey explained. "She asked me to make certain you knew how much she wanted you to attend."

Humor twinkled in Agatha's blue eyes. "Ah, yes."

"Do say you'll come. Your lovely companion has delighted me with her acceptance. I would so enjoy introducing you to some acquaintances of mine."

Agatha looked bemused by Madame Duprés's gushing insistence. Kelsey half expected the woman to fall on bended knee and kiss Agatha's hand. "I'm afraid I'm otherwise engaged," Agatha murmured politely. "Perhaps another time."

Annoyance flared the nostrils of Madame Duprés's rather sumptuous nose. "Yes," she snapped out. "Another time." She pounded away in a fit of pique, Jeffrey fluttering behind her.

Kelsey shared a moment of silent mirth with the woman she considered as close as a grandmother. Then Charlotte appeared, her face flushed with ill temper. She flopped into the chair beside Agatha and looked ready to cry.

"What's wrong, dear?" Agatha asked sharply.

"He's just so—so—" She glanced toward Kelsey, fighting back her feelings in front of her adversary. *"Awful,* Grandmama!"

"Yes, Charlotte." Agatha's voice was dry.

Charlotte glared at Kelsey as if it were all her fault. "And he said terrible things about you!" she flung out. "He said that you and he had actually—"

"Actually what?" Kelsey prodded gently while anger ran like molten lava through her veins. So help her, she was going to take care of Tyrone McNamara once and for all!

Charlotte blushed to the roots of her hair, shooting her grandmother an anxious glance. "Never mind."

"He loves to shock, Charlotte," Kelsey told her. "Beware of the man. Whatever he says about me, he would have no compunction to say about you either."

The color drained as quickly from her face as it had appeared. "Grandmama," she whispered in a shaking voice.

"Don't worry, dear," Agatha soothed gently. "Orchid will take care of everything."

Three hours later, as she unbound her hair, sending the fashionable coil of curls Irma had fussed over cascading down her nape, Kelsey smiled at the memory, knowing it was Agatha's way of forgiving her. And Charlotte, the silly ninny, had actually *learned* something from Tyrone's outrageous and shocking manners.

Filled with a glow of happiness, Kelsey headed downstairs in search of Jesse. She wanted to talk to him, to share her joy. She wanted to share something with someone, and he was all she had.

Her face rapt, she threw wide the doors to his den and strode into the room.

Jesse was seated at the desk, reading through sheaves of

correspondence. He glanced up at his wife's unexpected entrance, then slowly set down the papers and laid his arms across the desk.

This was something new, he thought. Kelsey invariably went straight to bed as soon as they returned from any outing. Frowning, Jesse wondered what had caused the color in her face and the sparkle in her eyes. A man, he thought sinkingly. She had the look of a woman in love.

"Jesse," she said with undiluted delight. "I had the most wonderful time tonight!"

"Really."

"I was dancing with Samuel and feeling awful and eager to leave. I was hoping you would finish with Montana soon and say it was time to go. But then . . ." She clasped her hands together, smiling with genuine joy.

"But then?" Jesse prodded coolly.

Her lovely eyes lifted to meet his harsh gaze. "But then something wonderful happened. I had a few moments alone with Agatha, and Charlotte, and I think Agatha's forgiven me."

Jesse didn't immediately answer, and Kelsey felt utterly foolish that she'd expected him to understand. Even though he'd sympathized with her feelings once, he couldn't know what this meant to her. He would think her a silly featherbrain that Agatha's friendship mattered so much.

"I just enjoyed the moment, that's all," she finished lamely, clasping her hands together.

Jesse dragged his gaze away from the vision Kelsey presented in that gown. Her hair was loose. She'd let it down, and it fell in ribbons of purplish-red to her waist. The green silk shimmered and whispered when she moved. The tops of her breasts glowed milky white in the soft light from his desk lamp. Vividly he recalled the touch of her close to him, the gentle smell of her perfume, the taste of her lips.

He stared at the papers in front of him. Papers representing the deal Montana was willing to make with him. Papers he would soon sign. Papers that represented the culmination of his revenge.

But between the lines of print he saw Kelsey Garrett's luminous gray eyes and curving pink lips.

"Do you have time to talk?" she asked uncertainly. "I'm not tired, and I've got thousands of questions about your—plans."

"Have a seat." He gestured to the grouping of leather chairs on the other side of the desk, but she moved in a soft rustle to the window seat, curling her legs beneath her on the dark blue chintz cushion.

"Thanks. Have you come to any decisions about Montana Gray?"

Jesse glanced down at the papers. He'd deliberately kept her uninformed, but now that the deal was set, he couldn't see what harm telling her would do. "We're starting a shipbuilding business together."

"Shipbuilding?" Kelsey looked at him in surprise. "That sounds almost legitimate."

"It *is* legitimate," he responded dryly.

"That doesn't sound much like revenge."

Jesse flicked a glance out the window to the black sky beyond. It was a moonless night. He was starting to lose sight of what was important, he realized. A thirst for vengeance could be doused, he thought sardonically. Lust certainly obscured other emotions. No one knew that better than he did.

"Tell me about your engagement," he heard himself ask.

"To Harrison?" Kelsey looked startled.

"Unless you were engaged to someone else too," he answered sardonically, then suddenly lifted a hand as he remembered. "Oh, wait. I forgot about Warfield."

"That wasn't an engagement. That was disgusting."

"What happened between you and Harrison?"

"I already explained: He was in love with Miracle, not me."

"You didn't say how you felt about him," Jesse pointed out, walking around his desk and leaning his hips against its polished surface.

Kelsey looked down at her hands, then out the window, then back at him. "I wasn't in love with him either."

"But you were going to marry him," Jesse persisted.

172

*"Yes,"* she admitted a bit testily. "To end the feud."

"You agreed to marry Harrison as a means to end the feud?" Jesse asked in disbelief.

"Harrison and I liked each other. The arrangement seemed to—make sense. But that was before he met Miracle." When Jesse didn't immediately respond, Kelsey said with spirit, "I don't see what my history has to do with the situation we're in now. I didn't marry Harrison, I married *you.* And all I really want to concern myself with is getting out of *this* marriage before something—awful happens."

In the lamplight her skin looked soft and sleek as satin. Frustrated with her—and himself—Jesse was compelled to learn more about her. For reasons he didn't want to explore, she absolutely fascinated him. "You said Harrison deserted you."

"Yes, I did." She lifted her chin and gazed at him coolly. Jesse waited, and she finally relented. "He left me at the altar. It wasn't his fault. He was injured in a fire and Miracle helped save his life. Unfortunately, she didn't know who he was, so none of us knew why he didn't show up at the church." Her voice grew brisk at the memory. "It was very embarrassing. You can probably imagine the gossip that followed: Kelsey *Garrett* left at the altar by Harrison *Danner.* Jace was apoplectic!"

Jesse lowered his lids. Inside, he winced with sympathy. It had been hard enough for him to be labeled the black sheep of the family, and he'd *deserved it!* Kelsey had been an innocent victim. "I'm surprised it didn't set off another Danner/Garrett war," he said blandly.

"Oh, it did. Not directly, but indirectly. And then when it was discovered that my father had been carrying on a secret affair with a Chinook woman, well, you can imagine the uproar. Jace and Emerald were livid! They wouldn't acknowledge that Miracle was even a human being, let alone that she was Garrett kin!" Kelsey smiled and shook her head. "They're such prigs!"

Jesse marveled at the change in Kelsey. He would have labeled her much the same after their first few meetings. "Who's Emerald?"

"Jace's wife," Kelsey answered promptly. She shot him a sideways glance, her lips twitching with mirth. "A real lady, much like Lila Gray."

Jesse's blood froze. Emerald? Not *his* Emerald! "I'm surprised your brother actually married," he murmured. "I thought he'd never get over Lexie. How did he meet— Emerald?"

"She's from Malone. You remember my mother, Lucinda?"

"Of course." Jesse's expression grew harsh. He was sure now that Jace's wife was one of the women—the virgins—he'd seduced, or in Emerald's case, been seduced by.

"My mother wanted at least one of us to marry someone wealthy and important. Jace dutifully followed through, though he and Emerald never had children. At least they hadn't by the time I left Rock Springs. Mother died several summers before Harrison and I were to be married," Kelsey added quietly. "She was thrown from a horse."

"And my mother died of diphtheria."

Kelsey looked ashamed. "I'm sorry, Jesse. I never meant to hurt you with that news."

"It doesn't matter," he dismissed gruffly. "It's all long over now."

Silence pooled in the room, their spate of conversation ending as if turned off by a spigot.

"Are you ever going back to Rock Springs?" Kelsey asked at length.

"I don't know," he said softly, thoughtfully.

"What about after this situation with Montana's over? What do you plan to do?"

"I have no idea," Jesse admitted honestly.

"Do you know," she said, her voice shaking with suppressed laughter, "what our families would do if we showed up together, married? Jace would have an attack!"

"Truly," Jesse agreed with a smile. "You're on a downward spiral with the Danner men. I'm sure he'd much prefer you to have married Harrison."

Kelsey gazed at him through her wide gray eyes, and he

didn't like the look of compassion written across her face. "Is that why you haven't been back? Because of what people said about you?"

"Hell, no." Jesse was disgusted with himself that he'd given her the wrong impression. "I was in trouble with my father, practically my whole family. It was too constraining. I don't want to rake it up again."

"Don't you miss them though? Sometimes?"

Against his will Jesse remembered parts of his youth he'd purposely repressed: the sweet scent of newly mown hay, Harrison's uncomplicated grin, his first taste of homemade wine—which he'd choked on and therefore had caused Pa to struggle to fight back laughter—the ring of Lexie's joyous, musical laughter, and the hard sting of Tremaine's hand when he'd slapped Jesse on the back for taking good care of his horse, Fortune.

He shook his head.

"Not ever?" she asked tentatively.

"Not ever." Uncomfortable with this whole conversation, Jesse said dryly, "You haven't told me why you left. You said it *wasn't* because Harrison deserted you, or because he married someone else. So why was it?"

Kelsey blinked several times, her lovely brows drawing into a delicate frown. "Actually, I suppose it was just as you said. Only I was in trouble with my brother, and Emerald. They wanted to marry me off to somebody. And they wanted to stir up trouble with your family. They *were* stirring up trouble with your family." She wrinkled her nose in remembrance. "A lot of things happened and I just— left."

"By yourself?"

"I had my horse, and my dog . . ." Her voice trailed off.

Jesse wasn't certain what caused that cloud of melancholy to sweep across her face. He wanted to ask her, but this illuminating conversation had helped him come to some other, disturbing conclusions. "Was it because of Harrison that you formed your current opinion about men?"

"What do you mean?" Kelsey straightened. "I've already told you *twice* that I didn't want to marry Harrison. I wasn't in love with him. We were just going to end the feud. What do you mean my *current opinion?*''

"Well, it's clear you take a pretty dim view of my sex. I assume something happened to create this impression.''

"Jesse . . .''

He smiled, loving the sound of his name on her tongue, even when she was about to revile him as her tone suggested.

She couldn't seem to get any more words out. They were stuck in her throat. Finally, she said, "Not all men are horrid lustful beasts. Harrison wasn't.''

He heard the sideways slur clearly. Just as she'd undoubtedly intended. And because it was maybe partially deserved, it infuriated, and hurt, all the more deeply. "Haven't you ever wanted to make love?'' he demanded. "Haven't you ever wanted someone to hold you and touch you and tell you you're beautiful?''

Kelsey had enjoyed this unexpected truce between her and Jesse right up to this very moment. But now she knew it was over. "I think I'll go to bed,'' she said uncertainly, correctly interpreting Jesse's mood as somehow dangerous. She'd made a mistake in even thinking he might be a friend. Slipping from the window seat, she walked past him toward the open doorway.

"Wait!''

His commanding tone stopped her dead in her tracks.

Kelsey's pulse fluttered in her throat. "Thanks for talking with me awhile,'' she said. "It's really helped me unwind. For heaven's sake, I can hardly keep my eyes open any longer. I'm sorry I interrupted you. I can see you're busy and—''

"You know I'm not busy,'' he bit out. "There's something else I need to talk to you about.''

Kelsey looked over her shoulder cautiously. "Can it wait until morning?''

The corners of the room were dim, shadowing his face until he looked hard and alien. His arms were folded across his chest, but she had the impression his control was very thin.

"Things can't go on this way much longer," he said softly, sending warning bells ringing in Kelsey's head.

"What things?" Kelsey edged toward the door.

"Our marital situation, such as it is. Don't go," he commanded, seeing how poised she was for flight. "Come here."

She shook her head, keeping her gaze trained steadily on his hooded eyes. "Whatever you have to tell me, you can tell me from a distance."

"No, actually I can't."

"I know what you're going to say anyway," Kelsey rushed in. "Your ploy worked splendidly! Better than anyone could have wished for! You have the cream of Portland society falling all over themselves to get you to accept their invitations. And now you've got Montana right where you want him," Kelsey babbled on. "We don't have to pretend anymore."

"What do you mean?" His voice sliced through the room, and Kelsey jumped involuntarily.

"We can end our marriage now," she pointed out reasonably. "You're Montana's business partner."

"This marriage isn't over until I say so." Jesse stalked toward her. "*That* was our bargain."

"But you don't need me anymore!" Kelsey sputtered, alarmed at the proprietary way he was acting.

"Don't I?" he asked silkily.

Kelsey had never been a coward in her life, but she sensed this explosive situation was fast getting out of control. Without a word she spun around, gathered her skirts, and ran upstairs, down the hall, and into the security of her room. She slammed the door behind her, desperately wishing she could bolt it. Then reality struck her. Jesse didn't want *her*. Good heavens, she was acting like a ninny, worse than even Charlotte! She was a business arrangement for Jesse, nothing more. He certainly didn't want her virtue. Good heavens, he'd made love to that wretched waterfront whore when he'd wanted sex. On their wedding night, no less! That was not the act of a man lusting for his wife.

The door crashed inward against the wall and Kelsey

shrieked. "Jesse!" she gasped, infuriated, a hand to her chest. "You nearly scared me to death!"

"We weren't through talking," he informed her coldly.

"Maybe you weren't through, but I was." Kelsey recovered herself, her eyes flashing fire. "Please, get out of my room."

"I'll leave when I'm damn well good and ready." He shut the door with a soft warning thud. "This marriage ends when I say so, not before. I'm not finished with Montana yet, and I don't want anything, or anyone, threatening me."

"Threatening you?" Her mind flew to the rifle in her closet. He didn't realize how threatening she could be!

He crossed the space between them so quickly, Kelsey scarcely had time to draw a frightened breath. "Jesse," she warned.

"I've been thinking things over, and I've decided I was wrong."

"Wrong?" She couldn't keep up with the lightning changes in this conversation.

"I do want to make love to you," he said conversationally. "And since you're my wife, I can't think of a single reason not to."

Kelsey stared at him in utter disbelief. "How about the fact that I *loathe* you!" she sputtered in sheer terror and outrage.

"You don't loathe me." He smiled, then his hands encompassed her upper arms like velvet manacles. His fingers were hard and determined, the look on his face implacable.

"Don't," she said even as she watched his mouth slowly descend to hers. At the last moment she tried to turn away, but one of his hands captured her chin. The next instant his lips found hers, and she braced herself, hoping against hope that she wouldn't respond this time.

His kiss gently explored her lips, terribly potent in its promise of wondrous, exciting things to come. Kelsey emitted a squeak of protest, knowing she was powerless against this tender assault.

Jesse had kissed her from curiosity, and anger, and overriding need. But he'd never kissed her like *this*, and Kelsey's inexperience made it impossible to discern that he was purposely, persuasively, seducing her. Her own curiosity, and a growing inner need, made her hesitate, her thoughts crashing about inside her head.

His lips were cool and hard and strangely thrilling. His arms gathered her closer, until her heart fluttered like a frightened bird, and her breath came in shortened gasps. His mouth explored hers, and the tip of his tongue touched the trembling corner of her lips. Kelsey jerked in surprise and he lifted his head. Dazed, she stared into his hooded eyes, but then he bent his head to her cheek, trailing soft, slow, long kisses across the arch of her cheekbone to the sensitive curves and crevices of her ear.

"Please . . . don't . . ." she murmured, her hands clenched tightly around his shoulders.

For an answer his hands swept down her back, dragging her into intimate contact with his rigid thighs. The groan torn from his throat shattered Kelsey's resistance. He *did* want her. And she wanted him too, she dimly realized. Jesse Danner. Her husband.

Meltingly, achingly, she molded herself against him.

"Let me," he said in a shattered voice.

He'd never asked for anything from her before. She gazed up at him dazedly. His mouth returned to hers, crashing down with possessive elemental force. One hand swept up the front of her dress, across the hardened peak of the nipple thrusting against the green silk. He brushed his hand over it lightly several times, until she pressed herself against his palm, wanting to cry out with need for something he seemed to purposely keep out of her reach.

"You don't loathe me," he said huskily.

His fingers began systematically unbuttoning her gown. Kelsey trembled, watching in disbelief as the fabric fell away and Jesse's hands swept the thin straps of the camisole down her arms. In the lamplight her breasts quivered, but it wasn't until she saw and *felt* his dark brown hand caress one that her dreamy conscience shot awake.

"No!" she burst out, clutching the bodice to her breasts.

*"Yes."* He yanked the fabric from her hands. Kelsey pushed against his chest, gathering the folds of green silk to her once more, taking a step back.

"I refuse to make love to you."

"You seemed willing enough several moments ago," he pointed out dryly.

"No, I was just—waiting to see how far you'd go."

"The hell you were. Come here . . ."

She twisted, but she was too late. His hard arms enveloped her. She sought to hang on to her bodice, but he swept her hands aside, crushing her bared breasts against his shirt. Her breath came in-short gasps. She was truly afraid.

"I want you," he told her, and the low, possessive timbre of his voice sent goose bumps rising along her arms. Her chest rose and fell against his. Slowly, carefully, he loosened his death-tight grip, his gaze sweeping down the swell of her trembling breasts.

"You're beautiful," he said, mesmerized by the sight of her.

Kelsey couldn't listen. Seizing her chance, she jerked herself free of his embrace, jumping nimbly away from him and lunging for the closet in one fluid move. Quick as lightning, she snatched the rifle from its hiding place and leveled it at her husband's chest. Jesse stared down the barrel.

"I'll put a bullet in your chest if you try to rape me," his wife assured him coldly. Given the fact that she was stripped to the waist, it took Jesse a moment or two to gather his wits. Then her words hammered in his brain.

"Rape." His face darkened. Swift as a cobra, he reached out and yanked the barrel of the rifle, nearly ripping the gun from her hand. Kelsey gasped in shock. One more hard jerk and the rifle was his.

"You're crazy! I could have really killed you!" she yelled at him, frightened.

"The hell you could. I unloaded the damn thing yesterday when I found it."

"You've stooped to searching through my things?"

"No more than you go through mine," he said mildly, his blue eyes narrowed.

Kelsey glared into his harsh, angry face. "I thought it was Irma who'd unloaded the rifle." She reached out a hand for the rifle. Jesse hesitated, half expecting her to bash him over the head with it, but then he let her yank back her rightful property.

With skilled fingers she emptied the chamber into her hand. Jesse's gaze was incredulous at the firepower lying in her small palm.

"I reloaded it," she told him coolly. "I'm in the habit of checking my rifle every morning."

"You're the most hellish woman I've ever met," he told her, shocked.

"Touch me again and you'll be sorry."

Jesse'd had enough. He didn't know what the hell he wanted with her anyway. "Mrs. Danner, I would rather let Montana Gray get himself elected mayor of this fair city than even look at you again. What I need is a woman. A *real* woman."

"Why don't you go after Lila Gray?" Kelsey suggested, shoving her arms through the sleeves of her gown. "She's obviously willing. Or have you already slept with her? I'm surprised you haven't thought about that way of getting to Montana. It is your usual method, after all, and I—"

Jesse's sudden silence was as loud as a gunshot. Kelsey stopped in mid-sentence, aware she'd inadvertently landed on the truth. "Oh, no," she murmured, hurt beyond bearing, furious with herself for even feeling the slightest tingle of desire.

"It was a long time ago. Before Montana took everything from me," he bit out tersely.

"I don't want to hear any more." Kelsey swept across the room, needing space. Her knees had turned to rubber, and she felt sick.

"I have no interest in Lila Gray anymore."

Kelsey shook her head. "That's what this is all about, isn't it? This *revenge* of yours. He found out about you and Lila and he beat you up and left you for dead and now you want to get even!"

"That's partly true," Jesse admitted stiffly. "But Lila isn't the issue between me and Montana."

"Yes, she is." Kelsey was fast realizing what a complete and utter fool she'd been. "It's Lila you want, isn't it? My God, you're a better actor than I realized. You made me believe that you could scarcely stomach her!"

"Tonight, Mrs. Danner, I wanted you," Jesse pointed out ruthlessly as he strode to the door. "I think that was painfully obvious. And no matter what you'd like to make yourself believe to preserve your misplaced sense of honor, it wouldn't have been rape!"

## 12

Madame Lacey Duprés's top-floor suite at the Portland Hotel was incredibly posh. Cream-colored wainscotting framed pink and spring-green flowered wallpaper. The carpet, a dreamy shade of pastel peach, was thick enough to sleep on. Windows on all sides of the salon looked over the balcony and grassy parklike grounds. While the musicians gently played at the soiree, the notes floated out the open windows to the crowd of Sunday strollers below.

Kelsey, standing beside the windows, yearned to be with the multitude on the grounds. Children with hoops and bicycles and men and women strolling arm in arm made a pretty picture. In contrast, the guests Madame Duprés had managed to round up were a sorry, pinch-faced lot. They tended to be of renowned families who, by one disaster or another, had fallen on hard times. Kelsey wouldn't have been surprised if Madame Duprés had somehow coerced them into coming today; they looked singularly unhappy and eager to leave.

Luckily, there were so many guests that Kelsey had been

relatively unnoticed since her grand entrance when Madame Duprés had swept one hand skyward and announced "Lady Agatha Chamberlain's most favored companion, Orchid Simpson Danner!" Lacey had then demanded where Jesse was, and Kelsey had told the plain unvarnished truth: She had no earthly idea.

Since that wretched evening nearly a week earlier, Jesse had been a shadow. He'd left the house, slamming the front door behind him, and hadn't returned until the following morning. Kelsey, who'd suffered a dreadful sleepless night, alternating between helpless fury and the painful realization that Jesse had been right—she *did* want him and it *wouldn't* have been rape—had run across him just as he was entering the house in the early dawn hours.

They'd stared at each other across the length of the entry hall: Jesse, unshaven, sober, and emanating sexuality (a result of his night with a woman? *Lila Gray?*) and Kelsey, circles under eyes, mouth set, and dressed in the only dress left over from her days of spinsterhood.

And that was just the first of such mornings. Kelsey tried her best to stay out of his way, but she could nevertheless hear him when he entered his adjoining suite of rooms and shaved and bathed. She refused to eat breakfast with him, then wondered how he spent the rest of his hours when he invariably took off in the buggy, with Drake in the carriage, or on horseback. Her fertile mind imagined him locked in feverish embraces with not only Lila, but all the other women she'd caught casting him yearning glances from across the dance floor at whatever party they were currently attending when they thought she wasn't watching.

Then last Thursday she'd learned that during daylight hours, at least, Jesse was behaving like a gentleman. Zeke and Jesse had closeted themselves in Jesse's den, and Kelsey, who had resorted to listening at the panels and drawing a "cluck" of disapproval from Mrs. Crowley, the cook, who happened to catch her eavesdropping, had overheard them discussing the past week's meetings with Gray at his offices, or down at the shipyards.

She also heard that Jesse had apparently put up a staggering amount of his own money—the amount made

Kelsey's blood drain straight down to her toes—and that a certain park block had been thrown into the deal as well.

Since Jesse's deal to ruin Montana was moving forward, it wouldn't be long before their marriage would be over, Kelsey realized. A few more weeks at the most. All she had to do was be patient and wait. So here she was, passing another afternoon without him and wishing there were something she could *do* to stop caring about him.

"A canape, madam?" one of Lacey's waiters asked at Kelsey's elbow. Absently she took a tiny pastry shell filled with something that looked like grape jelly. One bite and she gagged. Caviar. Ugh. She detested it.

Clapping her hand to her mouth, she frantically searched for the waiter with the champagne tray. Spying him, she waved frantically until she caught his attention. Her flailing arm also inadvertently caught the attention of a rather nondescript man seated at a corner table.

As Kelsey gratefully drank her champagne, the man eyed her from head to toe, a thorough inspection he automatically made of everyone he met. Kelsey was noticed, judged, and catalogued within the space of thirty seconds. The man, who'd arrived late and been lucky enough to escape Madame Duprés's heralding boom announcing his arrival, circumspectly asked Kelsey's name of another guest.

"I believe it's Danner," the man answered him. "Orchid Danner."

Danner! *Danner!* He was electrified by the name, staring at Kelsey as if he'd seen a ghost.

"You don't like caviar, hmmm?" an elderly woman asked Kelsey sympathetically. "I can't abide the deadful stuff myself."

"Are you a friend of Madame Duprés's?" Kelsey asked politely.

"Hardly." She sniffed. "And I simply won't believe that you are."

Kelsey smiled enigmatically, unwilling to admit that the only reason she'd accepted this invitation was to defy, and get away from, Jesse.

Jesse. Everything she *did* seemed to revolve around him.

Hating someone took as much energy as loving him, maybe more. Although, she could admit with painful candor, she didn't really hate him. Not when her pulse took off at a rollicking gallop when she just recalled his kisses and caresses. Not when a treacherous part of herself longed to have him make love to her . . .

She knew now that he was no rapist. Good Lord, he didn't have to be! He could win it all on charm and sexuality. Look at Lila Gray. *She* clearly didn't have any qualms about wanting Jesse, no matter how unsavory his past was.

*I have got to get out of this marriage soon.*

"Lady Agatha Chamberlain!" Lacey Duprés's voice rang loudly and triumphantly over the heads of her guests.

Kelsey jerked around, astounded. It was indeed Agatha who was being shown into the main salon. Charlotte wasn't with her. Another astounding discovery.

What in heaven's name was she doing here?

Kelsey's gaze clung yearningly to her, and as if feeling its weight, Agatha caught her eye—and smiled conspiratorially.

Filled with delight, Kelsey weaved through the crowd toward her, clasping Agatha's dry hands within the shelter of her own.

"I can't believe you're here," Kelsey whispered in her ear.

"No more than I can," Agatha said. "But I wanted to see you, dear."

"You did?"

"If there's one thing I've learned in my advanced years, it's that friendship's too precious to throw away."

"Oh, Agatha!" Kelsey gazed at her with undiluted pleasure.

Patting her hand, Agatha said more for Lacey Duprés's benefit, since that curious dowager was avidly eavesdropping on their conversation, "I truly am in the mood for some entertainment. Madame Duprés, is there any chance you might be serving tea?"

Eight blocks away Montana Gray gazed coldly at his wife. Not with hatred, Lila thought, alarmed that her husband had sought out her company. Montana didn't feel emotions like hatred and jealousy and love. He didn't *feel* anything as far as she could tell, which was both a blessing and an annoyance. It was a blessing because his punishments were meted without the heat of passion, and Lila reckoned that was the only reason she was still alive. It was an annoyance because she was a passionate person herself, and every once in a while she would have liked a rousing good fight, or some wild, erotic lovemaking. Oh, he would beat her if she asked him. Once in a while he'd really whip her. Like that time over Jesse. But more often than not, he treated her with total disinterest.

"What do you want?" she demanded cautiously, glancing over her shoulder to her vanity mirror. She'd just gotten back from a ride in Gerrard Knight's carriage, and she hoped the effects didn't show. Land sakes, the man was a total wastrel as a lover. All he'd done was cry about how much money he owed Montana, as if *she* might somehow help him out of his troubles!

"You lied to me."

Lila didn't move. "I did no such thing."

"Mr. Danner is as wealthy as I am. Maybe wealthier. You said he was broke."

"Well, how was I supposed to know that?" she demanded impatiently. "I am not his mistress!"

"But you were." Montana didn't betray any emotion, not by the flickering of an eyelash. Since this was old news, Lila couldn't see how it would harm her, but just to be on the safe side she kept silent, watching him warily. "And you will be again."

Her breath caught. "You want me to become his mistress?"

"I want his money. I want his life in my hands." He held his thick palms as if he were begging.

Lila understood. Jesse was a living reminder that even the powerful, invulnerable Montana Gray could make a mistake. It was only a matter of time before Montana would order him put to death.

"Give me a few weeks," Lila said huskily, a delicious thrill shooting up her spine.

\*     \*     \*

What had seemed like a lonely, miserable future for Kelsey suddenly opened into a vista of lovely dreams. She sat beside Agatha on Madame Duprés's pink-and-green flowered divan and shared a pot of reasonably good jasmine tea.

"Justice is acting like an absolute tyrant," Agatha said with a smile. "He threw Smithers off him last week and yesterday he nearly unseated Merriweather. I actually think the dreadful beast misses you."

"I miss him too. I haven't ridden since I left Chamberlain Manor."

Agatha cocked a brow at Kelsey's wistful tone. "When do you expect to extricate yourself from this marriage?"

Kelsey drew a long breath. "Do you mean you'd like me to come back?" she dared to ask.

"Of course. Justice isn't the only one who misses you."

A lump filled Kelsey's throat, and she ducked her head to hide the emotion that crossed her mobile face. She'd been a Judas and yet Agatha was willing to take her back. "And Charlotte?" she murmured. "What will she say?"

Agatha patted her hand. "Don't worry, my dear. You always have a home with us, Orchid. Excuse an old woman's forgetful mind, *Kelsey*," she corrected herself in self-annoyance. "But I don't truly expect to see you on my doorstep with your bags in hand."

"You don't?"

"You're married to a very handsome, complicated man, and I suspect," she added on a long sigh, "a somewhat dangerous one. But somehow—"

"I've already told you about Jesse's unsavory past—"

"Don't interrupt, dear," Agatha said, committing the sin herself. "It only makes the man more romantic. I also suspect you've felt tugs on your heartstrings yourself."

Kelsey shook her head vigorously. "Jesse Danner means less than nothing to me! He's a vengeful, arrogant, seductive scoundrel. If I've learned anything at all, it's that no man—not even the good ones—can be trusted to be faithful, loving, and true." She laughed shortly. "And Jesse Danner can't even brush *good!*"

\* \* \*

187

Twenty paces directly behind Kelsey and Agatha, to the left of the musicians, the man in the brown suit pretended to be absorbed in the painting hung at the north end of the salon. It was a mediocre representation of a field of daffodils, done by a local, and soon to be entirely forgotten, artist.

At least that was Victor Flynne's opinion.

Kelsey's soft laughter floated to his ears. He'd eavesdropped with consuming interest on her conversation with Lady Agatha Chamberlain. Lady Chamberlain had called her Kelsey, and that made no sense to him at all.

He knew exactly who the lovely red-haired beauty was: Jesse Danner's new bride. And, by his own association with the Danner family as a whole, and Tremaine Danner in particular, Victor Flynne knew nearly everything there was to know about Jesse Danner.

The assignment had fallen into his lap. Ezekiel Drummond had paid him a call. Of course Drummond, and everyone else in Portland, thought his name was Victor Flannigan. Tremaine Danner had seen to that!

Drummond wanted information on the Danner family of Rock Springs. When Victor had heard the request, the blood had rushed from his head and he'd had to excuse himself and break open a stick of smelling salts in the back room. It was true what they said about dying men, he reflected now. His past, in all its lurid detail, had flashed before his eyes. Tremaine had finally caught up with him, he thought. Over ten years past he'd run afoul of the famous Danner temper by trying to capitalize on a passion-filled scandal the entire family had been hiding. Victor had exposed their secret, but instead of handsomely capitalizing on it, he'd unfortunately been singled out by Tremaine Danner, Jesse Danner's eldest brother, and literally run out of town on a rail.

Tremaine had wanted blood. Since Victor had been the one to stir up the sleeping tiger, Tremaine had determined that Victor would be the one to pay!

Victor had been forced to flee Portland in the middle of the night, had altered his name, and had set up business in

Seattle. But his ties were in Portland. He knew the city's officials. He knew who wielded power. Victor Flynne Investigations had grown fat with success in Portland. He wanted that back.

Three years ago he'd returned—and nearly tucked his tail between his legs and scurried away again when he learned Samuel Danner, the youngest Danner brother, was an up-and-coming young Portland attorney. But Samuel didn't know Victor Flannigan was Victor Flynne. And Victor now suspected that the name Victor Flynne might not mean anything to him anyway. Samuel had been a kid during Victor's blackmail attempts on the Danner family; they'd probably kept it from him.

Still, having a Danner residing in Victor's fair city hadn't sat well. Besides, the few times Victor had seen Samuel, he'd reminded him so much of Tremaine Danner that Victor had been filled with rage and injustice and a certain amount of gut-shaking fear. So Victor had decided to make Samuel's life hell—tit for tat—and he'd chosen Samuel's wife, Mary, as the means.

He'd decided to scare the silly girl senseless first, and so thinking, had sent one of his men to frighten her when she was alone. One cold afternoon Mary McKechnie Danner had very congenially taken out her carriage by herself. Victor's man had intercepted her. But then something had gone awry.

"She just din't scare right," the man told him later. "Wasn't afraid at all! I had to fight 'er for the reins and then she fell and was crushed under the rims."

Icy fear had speared Victor's heart. If the truth ever came out, he knew Samuel Danner would never let him live. The Danners were just made that way. All of them.

But luckily Samuel Danner had no idea that Victor was involved. He believed, as did everyone else, that his wife's death had been an accident, and gradually Victor got over his fear. He gave up his fight against the Danners and concentrated instead on his plummy life. The people that counted in Portland came to him, sometimes for matters within the law, sometimes not. And Victor, who knew more secrets than anyone rightly should, kept files on everyone, even those who considered him a friend, because one never knew when one might need some extra *persuasion*.

Lacey Duprés was a case in point. Victor had done work for her. She was determined to break into Portland society, no matter whom she had to trample over. Because it was his nature, Victor had conducted his own investigation on the disgusting old dowager even while he helped her learn secrets about others. He'd followed the threads of Lacey's past and now he knew more about her than she probably knew herself. He half suspected she'd killed that husband of hers after coercing him to leave his money and property to her. She told a soul-stirring story of his dying in the war to anyone who would listen, but Victor, who had a sense of such things, could picture her slowly poisoning the poor fool, then bringing him back to health, just enough to win his gratitude. There were rumors to that effect, disgruntled relatives who'd been left out in the cold when the Duprés money found its way to Lacey's purse.

Yes, Lacey Duprés could be blackmailed, if the need arose. And she was smart enough to know it. She kept Victor nailed to her side. She'd targeted Portland as her city because she'd been spurned long ago by a wealthy, respected patriarch of one of the city's most powerful families. Victor knew the whole story, though Lacey wasn't aware he did. Another means of blackmail.

Victor strolled through the crowds to find his hostess now. She, too, was eyeing the mysterious Kelsey and Lady Chamberlain. Since Lady Chamberlain was a personal friend of Lacey's ex-lover, Victor could practically see the gears clicking in Lacey's unscrupulous little mind.

"The woman with Lady Chamberlain," Victor said without preamble.

Lacey jerked to attention, nearly forgetting that she was supposed to be half crippled and practically lifting the cane off the floor. She quickly leaned her bulk against it again. "Yes?" she asked cautiously.

"Jesse Danner's wife. I overheard Lady Chamberlain address her as 'Kelsey.' "

"Kelsey?" Lacey narrowed her eyes. "Her name's Orchid Simpson Danner."

"Jesse Danner's from a small town called Rock Springs. His brother is Samuel Danner. I've had more than my share of dealings with the family, and their closest neighbors, the Garretts. Jason Garrett is head of the Garrett family. His only sister's name is Kelsey."

"Why are you telling me all this?" Lacey demanded.

"If your bid for acceptance into Lady Chamberlain's circle of friends fails, well . . ." Victor flicked imaginary dust off his lapel. "There are other routes of entry. I can help you buy your way in through a back door."

"And what would you require in return?" Lacey asked wryly.

"The terms are negotiable. I owe Tremaine Danner a debt, and I'm willing to pay it through any of the Danners—Samuel, Jesse, or Jesse's wife. What I need from you, Lacey, is to be ready to jump when I tell you to," he added in a silky whisper.

"Vile snake," she harrumphed when he was out of earshot.

Kelsey returned home in lighter spirits; in fact she was whistling as she crossed the foyer. The sweet sound filtered into the den, where Zeke sat in one of the leather wing chairs and Jesse stood by the window, his face shadowed in the growing twilight.

Jesse glanced around. The lilting melody sharply reminded him that he was married to a paradox. Kelsey could be sweet and gentle and thoroughly entertaining when she felt like it; he'd witnessed the transformation. But with him she was a barbed-wire fence. He couldn't get close. She wouldn't let him, and invariably, her good mood faded whenever her husband entered the room.

Now, listening to her light footsteps hurry up the stairs, he felt a powerful frustration. "Are we ready, then?" he growled at Zeke.

"The money's been transferred into a new account. Montana can just reach his greedy hands in and take it. The park block now belongs to both of you."

"Nell's park block."

Zeke nodded. "Nell's park block," he repeated softly.

Jesse shot Zeke a knowing look. "Montana won't be able to stand it. It won't be long before his new 'partner' is booted out—permanently."

"Be careful, Jesse."

"Montana and Judge Barlowe and all their other 'friends' won't be able to get away this time. The contracts are signed and I've got my copy sealed away."

"And if your body should turn up floating in the Willamette?"

"Then you'll be there to pull me out again. Stop worrying, Zeke. We've got nothing to lose. Nothing that matters." Jesse's face was harsh in the deepening shadows. "Montana's had to put up a lot of his own money. He wants to break me, and he's matched me dollar for dollar in the shipbuilding venture. He's close to his limit."

"As are you," Zeke pointed out. "You'll be as broke as he is."

Jesse shrugged. "Like I said, it doesn't matter."

Zeke turned thoughtfully in the direction of the den's double doors. He could still hear Kelsey's gentle whistling. "What do you plan to do afterward?"

"Leave town. Disappear." Jesse shrugged. "I don't want anything more to do with Rock Springs or Portland." Interpreting Zeke's glance, he added, "Kelsey will have her annulment, so she'll be happy. I'll make certain she's well provided for beforehand, just in case."

"Just in case?"

"Just in case," Jesse repeated deliberately, but he was determined that nothing would go wrong. Nothing.

Kelsey's whistling changed to out-and-out singing. Her voice was surprisingly clear and lovely, the sound drifting down from the upstairs hall like a gentle waterfall.

Nothing, Jesse reminded himself sternly, dismissing the tightening in his chest as a premature case of nerves.

## 13

Rain poured in a deluge, gathering in the eaves and running off the roof in silvery sheets outside Jesse's den window. Yesterday had been a beast, the air breathless and heavy with thick August heat. Jesse had expected a storm to break the oppressive blanket of air, but throughout the night and most of the day it had been the same: the air laced with a weighted expectancy, as if something would surely happen soon.

Then without warning the rain had started, a pounding, saturated mass that swirled with the dust and blanketed the sky in shades of gray. It dampened Jesse's mood. He'd been planning to leave again tonight. He couldn't bear being in the house with Kelsey, and though he knew his leaving would mean her opinion of him would ebb still further—did she truly believe he was spending each night with Lila?—it was better than being forced to think about *her*.

He spent his nights at Briny's, his days with either Zeke, Samuel, or Montana Gray. Tonight was the eve of Gray's destruction, the culmination of Jesse's dreams of vengeance.

He should feel elated. Triumphant. Victorious.

Instead, he felt restless, unsated, and uncertain for the first time that he'd chosen the right path. He hadn't anticipated the complications of bringing Montana to ruination. He hadn't anticipated his *wife!*

Jesse strode impatiently across the foyer, his footsteps deadened by the horrendous torrent of rain slashing down outside the windows. The lights flickered and he paused to look up the sweeping staircase. Kelsey was talking to Irma;

their female voices murmured faintly beneath the loud music of the rain.

After tomorrow there would be no need for her to be his wife. She could leave. Disappear. Start over wherever she chose.

Jesse climbed the stairs with purposeful strides and knocked on the door to Kelsey's room.

"Yes, Mr. Danner?" Irma asked, opening the door a crack.

"I'd like to talk to my wife. Alone," he told the skittery maid wryly.

"Yes, sir."

She fled down the hall as if he'd ordered her put to death if she didn't make haste. Shaking his head, Jesse entered Kelsey's sitting room.

She was standing in the center of the room wearing a blue-flowered dress, her small hands fisted against her hips, looking for all the world as if she'd like to murder him. "What do you want?"

"We have some things to talk over."

"Well, you can jolly well talk them over with yourself. We have nothing else to say to each other." With that she swept up a black woolen cloak with a hood and thrust her arms inside the heavy folds.

"Where do you think you're going?"

"Out." She tucked her braid inside the hood.

"Tonight? In this weather?" Jesse was more amazed than angry.

"I have plans."

"Well, you'll have to break them. I haven't seen you for over a week, and we've got to get a few things straight."

"Write me a letter. I'll read it tomorrow."

Her arrogance got under his skin. As she swept toward the door, he grabbed the crook of her arm. "The hell you will. This isn't up for argument!"

She jerked her arm away and Jesse had to control the impulse to yank it right back. Her eyes blazed with gray fury. "I'm not in the mood for a conversation with you, Jesse. If you're really so desperate to talk to someone, try Lila Gray. I'm sure she can provide that service too."

"You wicked-tongued devil," he breathed, half in admiration, half in exasperation. "You're not leaving here if I have to lock you in this room to keep you from going."

He could see her eye the distance between him and the door as if she were planning to bolt. He tensed, ready, but Kelsey was no fool. She could see she would lose that contest.

"Oh, all right!" She seated herself on the edge of a chair and gazed up at him angrily. "Please deliver whatever's so all-fired important so I can get on with what I'm doing."

"First of all, you're not going anywhere," he told her again. What *had* she been doing all these nights he'd been away? Had she left on other occasions? Visions of Kelsey in all sorts of nefarious situations with all sorts of ill-intentioned characters made Jesse's blood boil. "Second of all, my deal with Montana's set. Soon this will all be over and we'll be finished with each other. You can go your way, and I'll go mine."

"You'll give me my annulment?" she asked slowly, watching him.

The words stuck in his throat. "When I'm ready."

"I'm ready now."

Seated on that stool, her hands folded primly in her lap, Kelsey was as austere and remote as a cold star and Jesse wanted to shake her. Remembering the trembling, pent-up passion of her response when they'd embraced, his loins tightened in automatic response. He wanted to toss her down on the bed and yes, force her, if necessary. The woman could try the patience of a saint, and he was far from that.

"I'll wait until you're in a more approachable mood to talk," he growled, heading for the door. "Don't go anywhere."

He headed straight for Briny's bar.

Four hours later, filled with Sal's whiskey and still as sober as morning, Jesse unlocked the front door of his home. He'd had enough drinking and he'd had enough pretending. He wanted Kelsey and by God, if that meant telling her that he'd spent the last few weeks in celibacy, unable to even think about bedding another woman, well, to hell with it, he'd do it. He couldn't think of one goddamn reason why he shouldn't sleep with her.

Water dripped off his rain-soaked jacket, puddling on the upstairs carpet as he strode to her door. Pushing it open, he hesitated, peering into the darkness and running his hands through his wet hair.

"Kelsey," he said softly, switching on the light.

The room was empty, the air quiet with the emptiness of long hours.

Anger scorched through him. She'd deliberately disobeyed because he'd ordered it! She'd done it to spite him.

Or she'd done it to meet a lover, an irrational voice inside his head suggested.

Coldly determined, Jesse returned to the rainswept street. Drake was nowhere in sight. He'd already driven to the carriage house. Jesse sloshed through the mud puddles to find him. The buggy, he noticed, was gone.

"My wife's gone visiting," Jesse told the smaller man. "I'm afraid I'm going to have to find her."

"Yes, sir." Drake immediately began rigging up the team to the carriage once again, but Jesse laid a hand on his arm.

"No, I'll take the chestnut mare. And please, Drake. Don't call me sir."

"Yes, sssi—Mr. Danner."

Sodden, tired, and filled with growing concern and anger, Jesse left the company of Lady Agatha Chamberlain and her granddaughter, Charlotte. He'd expected to find Kelsey there, expected it so much that when he learned she hadn't visited the Chamberlains, his initial worry about her taking a lover had turned into an out-and-out certainty. He rode slowly through the tireless rain toward Portland's city center.

She couldn't. She wouldn't. Not unless she was madly in love with someone, and Jesse was certain Kelsey didn't love anyone. There was not a man in Portland she would even look at twice; she'd scorned his sex one and all.

Except Samuel.

A weight settled on Jesse's heart. No, even Kelsey

wouldn't be reckless and foolhardy enough to fall in love with his own brother! And Samuel, well, Jesse didn't know him well, but Samuel struck Jesse as a man of honor. Certainly of family honor.

Still, once lodged, the idea refused to be ignored, and Jesse rode through the downtown city streets to Samuel's office building. There was a livery around the corner, a rather sorry-looking site, but the groomsman seemed to know his business as he took the mare and began brushing the rain from her hide. Jesse was soaked through and through, and his mood was as dreary as he looked. On the threshold of Samuel's office he realized there was probably no chance his brother would be at work this late at night, but at almost the same moment he was struck by the line of light emanating from beneath the door.

He rapped loudly and within ten seconds Samuel swung open the door. "Jesse!" Samuel declared in surprise. "You look as if someone threw you in the river."

Samuel wore a vest and shirt, the sleeves rolled up his forearms. He smelled like dusty tomes, and it was clear that he'd spent the night working.

Jesse's relief was instantaneous and immense. "Not this time," he drawled. "I just got caught in the rain."

"Come in. I'll get you a brandy."

While Samuel poured a crystal glass nearly full of the aromatic liquor, Jesse leaned against the wall next to the window.

"You're always on the lookout, aren't you?" Samuel said with a slight smile.

"Maybe." Jesse shrugged, regarding his younger brother critically. They had next to nothing in common except their heritage. "Kelsey's missing. Have you seen her?"

"Yes."

It was about the last thing he'd expected to hear. Jesse gazed at Samuel, lost.

"She surprised me here, at the office. She left about an hour ago," Samuel continued. "She wanted me to help her arrange an annulment."

"That woman is the limit!"

Samuel smothered a smile. "She said her husband bullies

her and even threatened to lock her in her room if she should disobey him.''

"Well, she doesn't apparently take his advice since she's gallivanting all over the city." He slammed his half-empty glass down on the windowsill. "Those were her exact words?''

"Uh-huh."

"Good-bye, Samuel."

"Good-bye, Jesse." A thread of humor laced his words and mocked Jesse during the long ride back to the house.

Lights blazed from the upper floor windows, cutting through the pelting rain and gloom as Jesse guided the mare down the lane to the carriage house. Impatiently, he snapped the reins against the horse's sweating flanks so that she picked up her feet smartly the last few feet to the stable door.

"Take care of her," he ordered the stable boy, sliding off in one fluid motion. He strode to the back door, slamming it behind him. The sound echoed and re-echoed throughout the spacious house, announcing his arrival as completely as a pair of buglers. Taking the stairs two at a time, Jesse planned to stride into Kelsey's room uninvited, but since the door was locked, he practically ripped the knob off with his bare hands.

At least his wife was home.

"Open this door," he said in an ominous voice.

No answer.

"So help me God, I'll break it down if you don't—"

The door flung inward so quickly he sucked in a startled breath. Kelsey stood in the aperture, her wildly beautiful hair cascading to her waist, a silver silk robe covering a matching peignoir. She looked as cool as a spring breeze. Jesse's gaze clung to the outline of her breasts until he realized that a silver gun, a derringer, was held between her hands.

"I bought another one," she explained, as if firearms were as mundane a purchase for ladies as new drawers or petticoats. "And I know how to use it."

"God *damn* it, Kelsey!" he bit out, stalking toward her.

"I mean it, Jesse. I can shoot a gun as well as any man, probably better than you can."

"Then, by God, you'd better aim and fire, because I'm sick to death of looking down a gun barrel.'

His implacability pierced through her resolve. Inside, Kelsey wasn't nearly as controlled as she wanted him to believe. Her knees were veritably knocking together.

"You've pointed a gun at me too many times for me to believe you really intend to kill me. If I'm wrong, pull the trigger; otherwise put that damn thing away."

"I'm—I'm getting an annulment, Jesse. No woman should feel compelled to hold her husband at gunpoint."

"Put it away," he said calmly, reaching out without a qualm and pulling the derringer from her unresisting fingers.

"You can carry on this dreadful revenge without me. You said it was almost over. I want my freedom now. I've played out this travesty long enough. Let me go, Jesse."

If she'd thought she could appeal to his better nature, she found out she was wrong. He simply unloaded the derringer, put the bullets into his pocket, then tossed the gun on her dresser. Then he crossed the space left between them and placed his hands around her upper arms, drawing her forward into the heat and shelter of his arms.

He looked down at her and there was no love in his face, no lust either. Just annoyance, and anger, and a desire for revenge. Revenge against her?

"Jesse, I—"

"Shut up," he told her softly, and accomplished the deed himself by pressing his cold lips to hers. He was soaked to the skin, she realized. He'd been out, what? *Searching* for her? "I made a mistake by ever agreeing to enter into this marriage," she said in a breathless voice when the kiss finally ended. Her pulse was pounding in her ears.

"So did I."

"Well, then we can end it before something terrible happens," Kelsey said eagerly. "There's no need to pretend that we care about each other. I mean, in *that* way."

Jesse's blue eyes were knowing. "What way?"

"You know what I mean." Kelsey sought to free her arms but his grip was too tight. "Jesse, you're hurting me."

"God, I hope so!" he muttered through his teeth. "I want to shake you until your teeth rattle."

"What have *I* done?" Kelsey demanded. "If you're mad because I left when you *ordered* me not to, then you don't know women very well!"

"I *am* mad. I'm bloody furious. And I know women very well. I know, in fact, that you'd like nothing better than to make love to me no matter what you say to the contrary. All *ladies* are the same," he said in a scathing voice. "Even you, Kelsey Garrett."

"Your high opinion of your sexual attraction leaves me speechless," she snapped.

Jesse's sense of humor—an attribute that had been sorely missing since this sham of a marriage had begun—returned full force. He chuckled. Then he laughed outright, throwing back his head and letting the laughter roll from his chest.

Kelsey eyed him suspiciously. "I don't see what's so funny."

"Don't you? You're hardly speechless, my love. In fact, I'd venture to say you're one of the most annoyingly talkative females I've ever met."

The hands that had been gripping her so tightly loosened a bit, but before Kelsey could make another bid for escape, one of them cupped her nape, turning her face up to his.

"I am not going to let you kiss me," she hissed.

"Go ahead and stop me," he challenged, crushing her mouth beneath the power of his.

She clamped her lips together tightly and felt him grin against them. She struggled, her efforts making his chest shake with silent laughter. She preferred him angry, she realized with despair. This Jesse was too dangerous! Desperately, she sought for a way to change his amusement to fury. With vague thoughts of how she'd tried to render Tyrone helpless, she lifted one knee, but he twisted agilely, taking her with him, and before she knew it she was flung onto the soft down comforter covering her bed.

Kelsey sprang upward, leaping to her feet and away from the treacherous bed. Jesse stood back, his arms across his chest, grinning like a devil.

"Get out of here!" she ordered.

"I've spent the last weeks with you alternately furious or frustrated," he answered as if he hadn't heard a word she'd uttered since he'd barged his way into her room. "I've told myself it's because Montana Gray has taken much too long in completing my deal with him."

"What deal is that?" Kelsey burst out, suddenly certain the best way to handle Jesse was to divert him.

Jesse, however, was not to be diverted. "But Montana's foot-dragging hasn't been the reason. It's you, Mrs. Danner," he said conversationally. "It's not knowing what to do with you."

"You don't have to do anything with me," Kelsey answered quickly. "Our bargain is nearly complete. A few more days . . . you said so yourself."

"I'm not interested in that bargain. We made another agreement. A pledge. That's the one I'm interested in."

"I don't know what you're talking about," she declared, but, with growing dread, she realized she did.

"Our wedding vows," Jesse clarified. "I believe there are certain rights that come along with them."

Kelsey backed away a step even though Jesse made no move toward her, her courage deserting her in a flood. "You said you had no interest in sleeping with me."

He held up his palms. "And then I said I changed my mind."

"Jesse, don't, please." Kelsey switched to pleading without so much as a second thought. Desperate situations called for desperate measures. She would have done anything, *anything,* at that moment to change his mind about her.

Her gaze swept the room for her gun. Her rifle was in the closet, but her derringer was on the top of the bureau. Unloaded.

"Don't," Jesse ordered softly, correctly reading her mind.

"I am fully aware that you can overpower me and that no one will come to my aid," Kelsey said, her gaze clinging desperately to the derringer as if it were a drink of water just out of reach of a drowning man. "But if you have any honor at all, then—"

"I don't," he said without compunction, and crossed the space between them so quickly that Kelsey scarcely had time to take in a breath.

"You can't bear to back down from a challenge!" she accused him angrily, sidestepping him. "You don't really want me. If I were throwing myself at you, you wouldn't even look my way, would you? *Would* you?"

Jesse shook his head. He was impressed by the different arguments she could devise to keep him at bay. At this rate, they'd be fighting until sunrise. "Of course I would," he pointed out. "I can't resist any female."

Kelsey narrowed her eyes. "You're just saying that to get me to be quiet."

He laughed again. "Yes," he admitted with a grin. "Yes. I'm through fighting with you. Now, come here . . ."

Kelsey evaded his hands and swept to the door, but he caught her lithely around the waist, pulling her back against his hard thighs, one arm squeezed hard beneath her breasts, his mouth near her ear.

"I want you," he said in a harsh voice, the tone of which turned Kelsey's muscles to water.

And at that moment she remembered all the silly, tormented dreams of her youth, how she'd wanted him, wanted him to kiss her and touch her and tell her *she* was the woman he loved. There had been years of wanting Jesse. And then there had been years of deliberately crushing his memory and trying to convince herself that she'd suffered from youthful fantasies all of her own making.

And then there had been years of man-hating, where men were rapacious monsters who used women without compunction. Used women like Jesse used woman.

Except that all those conclusions jumbled and blended together and ran away like water down a cliffside, until all that was left was the wanting. That tiny ember of desire that Jesse's touch was fanning to flame. Against her better judgment she still wanted him. Wanted him to tell her she was beautiful and special and that he'd waited his whole life for someone like her.

His hand cupped her breast as his mouth pressed against her neck, his tongue hot and sweet and wet as it caressed her skin. Kelsey's eyes fluttered closed. Her conscience fought through a haze of luscious sensuality and awakening passion. It was a losing battle. He was her husband. Her *husband*. Maybe none of her dreams were reality, but there was no getting around the fact that she had every right to make love to him—and he had every right to make love to her.

He turned her slowly, until her eyes were captured by the intensity of his. She'd resisted her feelings. She'd resisted him. But now, for the life of her she couldn't think of a single reason to resist any longer. She didn't *want* to resist, and when he drew her against him, she let her arms glide around his neck, let her cheek rest lightly against his, let her heart thunder with increasing passion and fear at the realization of what that ragged tempo of his breathing meant.

He kissed her senseless, sweetly, and with restraint, a deadly combination. Had he been forceful, she would have balked. She could have half believed the tales of plunder and rape she'd both heard and manufactured about him herself. But no . . . He was holding back his own passion, letting her find her own herself. And it didn't take long.

Kelsey longed to press herself against his hard body. She ached for it. And finally, because he wasn't going to help her, she leaned closer, feeling his rocklike thighs and the bold evidence of his own passion.

Her clothes disappeared as if by magic. In a dream she felt him unbutton her dress and slip it down her hips. Her camisole and drawers followed in swift abandon, and when she was completely naked he cradled her in his arms and lay her down on the cover. The rain beat heavily outside the window, cutting through the heat, cooling the air that touched her skin, awakening her from her dream in time to see Jesse stripping off his wet clothes.

In the dim cast of the lamp by her bed, the room's only illumination, the muscles of his shoulders and back looked like oiled bronze, rippling smoothly as he reached for the buttons of his breeches. Swallowing, Kelsey clutched the comforter, her nakedness, her vulnerability, hitting her like a sledgehammer. She sat up quickly, drawing his swift, piercing gaze. Her hands fluttered to her breasts, and Jesse simply stared at her, waiting to see what she would do, his hands poised on the buttons of his breeches.

"Oh, my *God!*" Kelsey declared on a shattered breath.

"Her voice returneth," he said with drawling amusement. "For a moment I thought maybe you were right. You were struck speechless."

She tried to scramble off the bed, but he sank down on it beside her, the look on his face telling her it was much too late for maidenly second thoughts. Pride forced her to remain where she was, but she wriggled down protectively between the cool sheets, drawing the covers to her chin—hardly a dominant position, but Kelsey was too rattled to care. Besides, Jesse still had his breeches on and he was on the other side of the covers.

He stretched out beside her, letting her enjoy the security of the covers—for the moment. From his point of view there was no need to rush, no need to storm her defenses. Even if Kelsey wasn't ready to admit what she wanted, he knew. And knowing turned his voice lazy and helped him keep a rein on his desire.

"I don't suppose you might change your mind about this," Kelsey asked in a quiet voice.

"No." She'd hidden herself from him; a self-protective measure that he'd let himself be fooled by. Yes, he'd suspected her passion, but he hadn't expected her intelligence, and vulnerability. She'd wrapped herself in layers of defenses and now, with her own desire too recently exposed to deny, she'd resorted to gentle pleading, trying to appeal to his better nature.

"What can it possibly matter to you?" she whispered. "It matters only to me."

"It matters to me."

She shook her head, her rich magenta-streaked hair tumbling riotously across the pillow. Jesse captured her chin with one hand and kissed her, leisurely exploring her lips. Kelsey's eyelids fluttered closed. She luxuriated in the kiss, heat swarming through her at the way his arms circled her, his hands at the small of her back drawing her closer, intimately closer, until the blankets were an impediment that she wanted to thrust aside.

Her hands slid up his back, over those hard muscles. She wanted to dig her fingers into his skin, clutch him closer. He must have sensed her need, for he swept aside the blankets impatiently, pressing his heavy body down on hers. Kelsey moaned. Her pulse beat in her temple like a pagan drum. Her fingers flew to his waistband, but he gently brushed her hands away, pulling the breeches off himself with a muscular twist, sliding his lean, hard body next to hers, turning her so they lay face-to-face.

"Open your eyes," he ordered softly. There was no amusement in his voice any longer, and for that Kelsey was glad.

Slowly, she lifted her lids, just a tiny little bit. His mouth quirked, but it was more a recognition of her fear than amusement at her expense. He wasn't laughing at her. He wasn't lording it over her that yes, she *had* been susceptible to his charms. That *yes* she was just like all the other *ladies* he'd known.

Other ladies . . . Knowing she was just the same hurt, ached, deep in her soul. She'd known it all along. Had denied it vehemently. Had placed herself above the carnal cravings other simpering women ensnared themselves in. But it was a lie. All a lie.

"Don't turn away," he said gently when she twisted her head away from him.

Slowly, she obeyed, watching him through smoky gray eyes that were Jesse's total undoing. With a groan he captured her lips again, his tongue probing their trembling curves. She opened her mouth and the stab of his tongue echoed through her deliciously, touching every nerve ending. His hand slid over the curve of her hip, drawing her against the rigid shaft of his manhood. Kelsey gave a shuddering gasp that turned to a groan of disbelief and embarrassment when he placed her hand around that swollen member.

"Jesse . . ." she protested.

"Kelsey," he answered in a harsh breath.

Except for the day he'd learned her true identity he'd

never called her by her first name before. The sound reverberated in her head. It emboldened her. And suddenly she didn't want to be a passive partner. She touched him with gentle fingers and felt the shudder that rocked his hard frame, heard the hiss of breath he dragged between his teeth.

Her exploration lasted less than five heartbeats before he pulled her hand away. Confused, she stared at him, unaware that her innocent, tentative caresses were far too intoxicating.

Instead, his hands explored, sliding down her neck and breasts and abdomen to the juncture of her thighs. Kelsey made a choked sound and reared backward, but Jesse held her tightly. "Let me," he said thickly.

She fought to relax and then his skillful fingers worked a new kind of magic. She melted, shocked by the amazingly pleasurable feeling of him inserting his fingers into her wet warmth. His movements caused her acute embarrassment and immeasurable pleasure. She moaned and turned her face into his shoulder, her nails digging across his shoulders, her body twisting to his, demanding release.

"Jesse," she murmured low in her throat.

His body was then covering hers, his face above hers harsh with passion. Kelsey dragged his lips down to hers, meeting his kisses fiercely with unbridled desire. His knee wedged itself between her thighs and he moved into position above her. He lifted her hips. She felt his hot hardness probing entrance. She wasn't quite certain what she wanted, but she sensed he could give it to her, and she waited breathlessly, expectantly, while her mouth clung passionately to his and her body tensed in poised anticipation.

"Relax." His voice was taut with pent-up passion.

"I am relaxed."

Languorous laughter filled his tone. "No, darling. You're not. I don't want to hurt you."

"You're not." She was breathless.

"Not yet."

Jesse hadn't expected to feel so tender toward her. That this was Kelsey Garrett, his *wife*, left him feeling unsure and incredibly possessive. He inched himself inside her, his senses jolted by her tight heat. When he reached the fragile barrier that proclaimed her innocence he drew a deep breath—he was shocked. A virgin? Who in God's name had she been saving herself for?

"Kelsey," he murmured unsteadily.

She didn't answer. Her trembling hands were at his hips, and she softly pulled him tighter. Her trust shattered his control and he drew back and thrust deep, deep inside her.

She gasped in pain, the sound cut off almost instantly as she bit down on her lower lip.

To Kelsey it was a moment of reckoning. This pain was what women spent long hours giggling over, gossiping over, rhapsodizing over? *This?*

Her eyes flew open. It wasn't horrible, certainly, but it wasn't nearly as glorious as the lovemaking that had come before. If he would just kiss her again, touch her again—that's what she craved.

She was convinced the sex act was vastly overrated.

"Well," she said in a voice of one who's been sorely disappointed.

The beast actually started to *laugh!* Convinced the joke was on her, Kelsey did her utmost to dislodge his heavy body from atop her, but Jesse held her down with his superior weight. It infuriated Kelsey that they were still joined in such an intimate fashion and she gazed up at him through angry silver eyes.

"Now that you're finished, I insist you let me up!"

"Who said I was finished?"

"Oh, Lord, there isn't *more,* is there?"

For an answer he moved within her, just a little bit, and the sparks of pleasure that burst inside her jolted a moan from Kelsey's lips. "Yes, Mrs. Danner, there's more," he murmured, moving again with deep rhythmic thrusts.

She would resist it, whatever it was, she determined, fighting back her astonishment at the building pressure that seemed to be rising inside her like a tidal wave. Closing her eyes, she gritted her teeth as stabs of piercing pleasure jarred through her.

"Don't fight me," he told her in a voice like rough velvet. "There's no need."

But there was a need. If only she could remember what it was. If only her pleasure-drugged mind could assimilate the fragments. But she couldn't. All the things that mattered seemed to spin away, flung to the far corners of the universe as she concentrated on that mounting, hot desire that engulfed her, taking her over like a deadly spirit.

Jesse moved deliberately, checking his own passion, fighting the sweet torture of her own instinctive movements, movements she wasn't aware she was making. Her body arched and writhed, but still she held back. He could sense it. A battle of wills it was, where neither of them could be the winner. He wanted to shatter her resistance. He wanted to drive into her as deeply as he could, but it would be too soon. He didn't have as much resistance as she apparently had. So he moved slowly, tortuously, amazed and humbled by the pleasure she was giving him even while she fought against it.

Heat burst through Kelsey, so hot, so vital that she cried out, clutching Jesse's sweat-dampened shoulders, her body racked by spasms. He groaned and pushed forward, increasing the pressure, and then he thrust fast and furiously, reaching his own climax in seconds.

She floated back to earth an eternity later. Gradually, reality returned and she saw she was in her bedroom, her gaze trained on the arched canopy above her head. She could scarcely breathe. Jesse's weight crushed against her chest. She wanted to push him away, yet a part of herself didn't want to move. In fact, when Jesse rolled to his side, her lips automatically formed a protest, but he brought her with him, cradling her against his chest in a loving, protective way that stole the words from her tongue.

*I love him,* she thought inconsequentially.

It was a shattering realization, made more so by the next conclusion: *I always have.* How could she love someone she despised? she thought with uncharacteristic despair.

"I didn't want to hurt you," he said in a quiet voice.

There was no love in his tone. No feeling of any kind. If he was purposely holding back his emotions, he was successful, because she had no idea what he was feeling. That thought increased her despair.

Jesse *was* purposely holding back his emotions. In truth, his feelings for Kelsey bordered on proprietary. She was his wife and, by God, he wasn't going to let her go! He found the thought of being without her so terrifyingly empty that he said the first thing that entered his head, "Well, there'll be no annulment now."

It was a blow to Kelsey. She'd been dreaming of love and desire and a fulfillment of her fantasies, and then he told her *why* he'd made love to her. It was all part and parcel of the game. His need to conquer, to have his own way. He wasn't going to release her from this marriage until he was damn good and ready, and now she'd played right into his hands! Divorce was her only option. A stigma no "good woman" could hope to overcome.

He'd slept with her on purpose. And it hadn't been because he couldn't bear the thought of not having her— Kelsey Garrett—his wife—the woman he loved. . . .

She slapped him. Hard. Straight across the cheek. She took him completely by surprise.

He froze. Kelsey, in a moment of true insight, realized she'd just done something irrevocable.

Jesse shoved himself out of bed and yanked on his clothes. Kelsey watched in sadness and growing dread. "Where are you going?" she asked when it was clear he was getting the hell away from her. And fast.

The look he sent her withered something inside her. Protectively, she pulled the covers around her breasts.

Jesse hadn't been slapped since Lila Gray set him up. The astonishing pleasure he'd felt in Kelsey's arms disintegrated when he realized she was no different from any other woman. How had he ever convinced himself she was? Without a word he left the room and headed downstairs, uncertain whether he wanted to drink himself into oblivion or find someone to brawl with; uncertain whether he hated his willful wife or was half in love with her.

# 14

Victor "Flannigan" sat in his black leather desk chair in the corner of his cramped office and sourly contemplated his future. Samuel Danner was encroaching on his territory. The young attorney had appointed himself savior to the masses and he'd begun winning cases—cases where Victor had dug up dirt for his clients and assured them that *they* would prove victorious.

People were losing faith. Judge Barlowe was having to rule in favor of Samuel's clients or lose his position. And now this damned trial over one of Montana Gray's deals looked as if it might go Danner's way too.

And Montana Gray didn't care to lose.

Victor swallowed hard. Light from his desk lamp filtered through the amber liquid of his whiskey. Victor's den was also his main living space; he'd been staying in these rented rooms for far too long, forced to keep a low profile.

The Danners were the bane of his very existence.

Setting his glass down with resolution, Victor came to a long overdue conclusion: It was time to finish what he'd begun, and Lacey Duprés was the woman to help him.

He would start with the other Danners—Jesse and Kelsey—and then work his way up to Samuel. There could be no connection between him and the fate that would befall Jesse and Kelsey, or he'd have not only Samuel after his neck, but Tremaine Danner as well, and Victor still harbored a deep abiding fear of the eldest Danner. Not that Jesse or Samuel wasn't challenging in his own right, but he and Tremaine shared a history, an unpleasant history.

And then there was the matter of Samuel Danner's wife . . .

Victor shuddered. He didn't like thinking about the repercussions if that were ever to come to light. No matter what, he had to keep the truth about Mary McKechnie Danner's death a secret.

Crossing to his desk, he penned a note to Lacey Duprés. All he needed was one night—a night where he knew the whereabouts of every Danner—a night where Lacey invited them one and all to her hotel for some special event that none of them could resist. And then he would take care of them, starting first with the easiest: Kelsey Garrett Danner.

Across town, Montana Gray was sharing similar sentiments. He stood on the loggia of his home, his gaze focused across the park grounds, past the firs and oaks and grassy knolls to the space in the blackness beyond where he knew Jesse Danner's home to be. The trees obscured it from view, but it was there, a mocking edifice to failure. His failure.

Grinding his teeth, he clenched his fingers into hammy fists. He didn't like Danner's style. He didn't like the way he smiled whenever they met, as if he were enjoying some great joke at Montana's expense. He didn't like the harsh, determined slant to Danner's chin when a business deal was struck. He didn't like knowing Danner had the upper hand.

"Get my wife," he ordered the servant who was busying around inside the upper salon.

The young girl scurried out as if he'd threatened her bodily harm. Lila glided in a few moments later, her expression wary.

"I thought you said you could seduce Danner."

Lila's eyes widened. "I can. These things take time," she said, rankled. The fact that Jesse had studiously ignored each and every advance she'd made struck her in her most vulnerable spot, her vanity.

"I've wasted enough time. I want you to do something else."

"What?" she asked, years of living with Montana keeping her from committing herself until she knew all the details.

"The next time Danner leaves his home alone, I want to know about it."

She tossed him a cool look. "You ask the impossible. I can't watch his every move."

"You already are," Montana said softly. "You should know by now you can't hide anything from me."

Lila stood still as a stone. So he knew she'd hired someone to report on doings at the Danner household. Did he also know about her clandestine meetings with Gerrard Knight? "What are you planning to do with Jesse?"

"Strike another deal. One that suits me better."

Lila twisted a strand of blond hair between her fingers, then drew it thoughtfully across her lips. She saw no harm in dropping a plum into Montana's lap. "Jesse's alone at a bar on the waterfront this evening, drinking himself into oblivion, I understand." Satisfaction filled her voice at the thought that marital bliss was sorely lacking at the Danner household and Jesse went out into the evening alone again.

"Where?"

"A place called Briny's." Her nose twitched in distaste.

Seconds later Lila was alone. Montana left without so much as a good-bye. A chill settled over her, and she wondered if she'd made a vast mistake.

Kelsey awoke slowly, a vague feeling of doom making her want to keep her eyes tightly closed in spite of the late morning sunlight streaming across her bed. She turned slightly, and an unaccustomed soreness brought her eyes open in a snap. She and Jesse had made love last night!

"Oh, my *God!*"

She lay perfectly still, almost afraid to move, as if pretending she were a statue could somehow make reality fade. Her inertia lasted about forty-five seconds. Throwing off the covers, she jumped to her feet, then realized she was stark naked.

With a strangled sound she headed straight for the bath, washing herself vigorously. She stopped halfway through these rather rough ministrations, suddenly weak, fully aware that she didn't really want to wash away the remnants of last night.

Drawing several deep breaths, Kelsey finished getting dressed, brushing her hair with long, meditative strokes. She left it loose to her waist, her mouth twisting at the realization that it was because Jesse liked it that way. Annoyed, she braided it and hastily wound it at her nape. Loose wisps curled against her nape, softening the effect. Kelsey stared into the stormy depths of her eyes and wondered how she was ever going to get over Jesse Danner.

"Has Mr. Danner returned?" Kelsey asked Mrs. Crowley thirty minutes later as she swallowed a bite of fresh peaches swimming in cream.

Mrs. Crowley clasped her hands beneath her sumptuous bosom and harrumphed. Since this was as close to conversation the taciturn cook ever allowed, Kelsey interpreted that to mean no, Jesse hadn't returned.

The peaches, delicious as they were, felt permanently stuck in her throat. Excusing herself, Kelsey walked down the hall and out the front door. The soothing caress of the afternoon breeze feathered her cheeks and neck. Glancing down at her cotton day dress, Kelsey felt an irresistible urge to slip on her old breeches and head to Lady Chamberlain's. Justice could use a run, and she was dying for some speed.

But in the back of her mind lay a nagging worry. Jesse. He'd never stayed gone this long. He'd always returned by morning.

Instead of following her instincts, Kelsey remained at home, pacing the house like a caged animal. She drove Irma to distraction, the maid seeking desperately to please her mistress in some way, failing at every turn, for as the afternoon stretched into twilight, and twilight to evening, and evening to night, Kelsey's nagging worry about Jesse turned to out-and-out concern. The fifth time she snapped unnecessarily at Irma, she decided the waiting was finished.

"Drake," she called to the groomsman. "I need a horse. A fast horse."

"You're certain you wouldn't like the carriage, ma'am?" he asked anxiously.

Kelsey gave him a faint smile. Drake, like Irma and probably Mrs. Crowley too, assumed since she rarely rode that she was incapable of it. "Certain as the blackest midnight on a moonless night."

"But it is a black night, madam. Dark as hell." Hearing himself, Drake blinked in shock, his mouth dropping open.

"Dark as hell is exactly what it is," Kelsey reassured him with a pat on the arm. Honestly, the groomsman-cum-driver was so stiff he looked as if he should be oiled. "Please bring me a decent horse, not that nag Jesse tried to get for me once."

"Yes, madam." Drake's mouth quirked.

"And Drake . . ."

"Yes, madam?"

"Please don't call me madam. Kelsey, er, Orchid will be fine."

"Yes, madam."


Samuel rocked back in his desk chair and pressed the palms of his hands to his eyes. A vision of Mary appeared in his mind followed by a yawning ache so huge he could practically fall inside it and never come out.

He dropped his hands and opened his eyes. It was still his same office. It was still 1897 and he was still alone. He thought about the rooms he'd lived in since Mary's death, and realized he had absolutely no desire to ever return to them.

A shadow slipped through the light streaming beneath his office door. He waited for a knock. It was late. Too late for clients.

The figure of a woman was silhouetted. Kelsey, he realized, pleasantly surprised. Then with a burst of insight, he knew something had happened to Jesse.

Samuel leapt to his feet as the door swung inward. Kelsey, her hair unbound and tangled in an unruly and totally bewitching mass, stepped inside. "Samuel," she said in relief, coming straight toward him.

He gathered her in his arms. "It's Jesse, isn't it? What's wrong? Where is he?"

She flinched at each question, then drew herself away from him, inhaling a long, trembling breath.

"He left without a word last night. Well, not exactly without a word," she amended hastily. "But he left."

The blush that pinkened Kelsey's neck and traveled to her cheeks made Samuel wonder what exactly had transpired between her and Jesse. "I suspect I'm pointing out the obvious, but Jesse does disappear occasionally."

"He was very angry with me, but the situation isn't—usual." Kelsey moved stiffly across the room.

"What's changed?"

She took so long in answering, Samuel almost rephrased the question. "Nothing's changed," she said finally. With a sound of frustration she raked back her hair in a shimmering red wave. "Oh, I don't know. Samuel, something's wrong! I can *feel* it. I made Jesse furious, but that's hardly a headline. And anyway, I would have at least seen some trace of him by now. I went to Zeke's, but Jesse missed an appointment with him. Even Montana stopped by the house to return some signed papers and Jesse didn't show up to look at them."

"That's odd." Samuel frowned.

"And Jesse and I crossed a threshold last night," Kelsey admitted obliquely. "He wouldn't just run out on me now. There are too many unsolved problems. He said he's close to finishing his deal with Montana. As soon as that's done, he'll give me my divorce."

"Last night it was an annulment," Samuel pointed out with sudden understanding.

Kelsey stopped short, her lips parted in dismay as she realized what she'd given away. "I—just want the marriage to end," she said, swallowing.

"How does Jesse feel about this?"

"He wants to be free as much as I do," Kelsey answered vehemently. "He's just unwilling to let me have my way."

Samuel had his own doubts about that. Though Jesse refused to talk to him about his feelings for Kelsey, Samuel had a pretty fair idea that his brother was unwilling to let her go for entirely different reasons. Maybe reasons he hadn't yet realized himself.

But telling Kelsey that would be throwing oil on the fire. Besides, there was a more immediate, troubling issue at stake. "Where would Jesse have gone?"

"I don't know."

"What kind of mood was he in?"

"Angry. Very angry."

"At you?"

Kelsey nodded.

"Why?" Samuel asked bluntly.

"Because I . . . because he purposely made it impossible for me to have an annulment and I . . . slapped him." Her cheeks flamed. "I would have shot him if I could have gotten my hands on my gun," she added quickly, as if that were more acceptable behavior. "But as it was, I just hauled off and hit him."

"Are you saying he forced you?" Samuel asked quietly.

"Oh, good heavens, no!" Kelsey's mobile face was earnest. "Oh, no. I'm saying he's absolutely impossible, and half the time I want to murder him with my bare hands!"

"And the other half?" Samuel asked with a half grin.

"I'd like to murder him with a bullet."

A lightness filled Samuel's dark soul. Jesse and Kelsey helped make him forget. "Let's go find Jesse," he suggested, snagging his coat from the brass stand by the door. "And then you can kill him."

It was three A.M. by the time Samuel, with Kelsey tightly gripped beside him, entered the shadowy environs of a place called Briny's. Briny was the word for it, Kelsey thought, wrinkling her nose at the dank, fish-rotting smell that seemed to seep through the cracks in clouds off the nearby Willamette River.

Conversation stopped and dozens of pairs of eyes stared at Kelsey as if they'd never seen a woman before. She held her reticule tightly, wondering if she should remove her derringer right now and establish herself.

Samuel, however, smoothed over the moment. "Yes, it's a woman, and no, she's not interested in anything but finding her husband."

"Husband?" a voice snorted from the rear. "Whoever he is, he ain't here!"

A chorus of male voices agreed.

"His name's Jesse Danner," Kelsey said coolly. "We were married about two months ago." Her face reddening with humiliation, she added, "I believe he spent our wedding night with a woman called Mamie."

"No, it were Patricia Lee!" a drunken man hollered from the back.

"You know him?" Kelsey turned swiftly to the man who'd spoken.

Silence.

"This isn't just a case of a scorned wife searching for her errant husband," Samuel said dryly. "Jesse's been missing for about a day and we're afraid he may have run into trouble."

"I don't know his name," the man behind the bar said, wiping his hands on a towel thrown over his shoulder. "Called hisself Mr. Duped."

"Mr.—Duped?" Kelsey asked, disheartened. This couldn't be Jesse.

"Said he'd been duped into marriage. He's been here a time or two. Was here last night for a while."

"And?" Samuel asked, interested.

Kelsey shot him a glance. "You don't think this is Jesse, do you?"

"And he left with the cap'n, and he ain't come back," the man continued. "Neither's a few others."

"The captain?" Samuel asked with dread.

"The captain?" Kelsey repeated, her mind jumping ahead to the same horrible conclusions Samuel had drawn. "Captain of a *ship?*"

"Aye," a voice murmured mournfully from the shadows.

"You think he may have been shanghaied?" Samuel asked in a quiet, deadly voice that made Kelsey shiver.

More silence. Uneasy silence.

It was common, if unspoken knowledge that men and boys and women sometimes disappeared without a trace, kidnapped and taken to ships bound for the Orient. The unlucky were used for slave labor, then tossed overboard

217

into the vast Pacific when the ship neared its destination. No one was left alive who could plead for help. It was easier to simply snatch someone else off the waterfront when the ship docked at Portland again.

The bartender flicked the bar with his towel, his expression gloomy. "That particular captain don't come off his ship unless he's got hisself a reason."

"Damn it all," Samuel breathed.

"Which ship?" Kelsey asked. "Is she still docked?"

"Don't know."

"Which *ship?*" Kelsey ground out through her teeth.

"The *Lady Lee,*" the mournful voice from the back of the room answered. "Cap'n Randolph's the man yer want to see. . . ."

The hot August wind felt cooler, almost chilly, at the edge of the river. The *Lady Lee* was berthed next to a darkened ship that was the last on the pier. Beyond them was a slow-moving blackness, the southward-flowing Willamette. Stars hung low in the sky, nearly touching the water, and a strip of moonlight shivered and swirled, lighting the end of the *Lady Lee*'s deck.

"Stay here," Samuel ordered softly.

Kelsey watched the yellow glow from the portholes below deck. Lantern light moved eerily across the water with the sway of the ship. "No."

"This isn't Rock Springs," he said through his teeth. "Do you know what they'd do to a woman?"

Kelsey eyed Jesse's brother squarely. "I'm not afraid."

"Foolhardy is closer to the truth," he muttered, beginning to realize why Jesse found Kelsey so aggravating.

"If Jesse's on board that ship, I'm going to help rescue him."

"The hell you are." Samuel stripped off his suit jacket and tie and rolled up his sleeves. Kelsey withdrew her derringer and checked the chamber. "You're not going on board," he told her.

"You'll have to try to stop me then."

"Kelsey . . ." Samuel laid his hands on her shoulders. "I need someone to stand guard. In case something should happen and I can't get off the ship, you've got to run for help."

"Then you stay here and—"

"No." His voice was implacable.

"Why aren't you afraid for me here?" she argued, glancing over her shoulder to the shadows and figures moving around the crates and boxes lining the docks. "Something could just as easily happen to me here as on the ship."

"Unlike my hotheaded brother who can't seem to remember the Kelsey from Rock Springs, I know just what kind of excellent shot you are." He gave her a light shake, smiling. "I wouldn't like to try my trigger hand against yours. I tried to tell Jesse the same one evening, but he's too pigheaded to listen."

"Since I'm such a crack shot, it makes sense that I should be the one to save my husband from whatever mishap he's gotten himself into."

"We could argue all night and it wouldn't solve anything." Samuel strode toward the gangway and the burly sentinel who was on watch. "Stay put." His voice drifted softly back through the velvety darkness.

"He's probably not even on board," Kelsey grumbled, wishing she'd brought her rifle. Sighing, she glanced again at the uncertain golden lantern light shimmering from the portholes, decorating the water like a row of glittering topaz gems. Where are you? she asked Jesse silently, wondering if he hadn't fooled them all and was at this very moment bedding down with Mamie, or Lila, or any other willing woman, knowing in her heart that that just wasn't so. Womanizing rake that Jesse was, his main motivation was revenge on Montana Gray, and his plan would have been finished by now if Jesse had been home this afternoon.

No, something had happened to him. Something terrible.

The metallic taste of blood filled Jesse's mouth. He lay perfectly still on the narrow bunk, his hands tied behind his back, his wrists numb. Stupidity had brought him to his current fate. His wits were all that would save him.

His head was clear. Pain had a nasty way of sharpening

219

every sense. At least it kept him awake. One should be thankful for small favors, he thought grimly.

He opened one eye to squint narrowly at Captain Randolph, a huge blond-haired man with the strong, wide chest of a sailor and arms thick from the pulling and lashing of ropes. Randolph was conferring with his first mate. It seemed to Jesse that they couldn't decide what to do with him. They kept turning to stare at him. He was not their usual type of victim, if you counted the other Briny patrons who'd been unwillingly recruited for the *Lady Lee*'s next voyage. The other men looked like lost souls, but Jesse didn't fit the mold. Clearly Randolph and his first mate were concerned about him, concerned about what kind of hornet's nest his disappearance might stir up.

He'd never thought the trappings of wealth would suit his purposes on the docks, but it was clear his expensive clothes had them wondering about him. It gave him a few extra minutes to think. And for them to think about him.

The first mate held a towel to his mouth, courtesy of Jesse Danner's right fist. Two of the man's half-rotten teeth had given in one easy blow. Jesse had fared better. His jaw ached miserably, but his teeth had proved to be strong as a horse's once again.

There was a third man on the floor, unconscious. Jesse had aimed two well-placed kicks at him before the first mate had subdued him: the first to the groin, the second to his head. Unfortunately that's when Randolph had reappeared and thrown Jesse onto the bunk as easily as if he were a sack of potatoes. The good news was that they hadn't tied his ankles. Feigning unconsciousness, Jesse had managed to listen to their conversation while they ignored him—and the hapless man lying on the floor—but he had yet to come up with some plan of escape.

Jesse sighed inwardly, berating himself harshly for falling into this trap. He'd been too angry with Kelsey to think straight. The way she'd delivered that slap had brought back unpleasant memories of Lila and the beating she'd caused him. And it had also brought back memories of Emerald, and her wicked taunting ways. Of course it could hardly matter now, he reminded himself with furious self-honesty. He'd certainly fared a lot worse at the hands of Randolph and his crew. He just hadn't expected it from Kelsey, and it had wounded him in a way he couldn't truly fathom.

When Randolph had entered Briny's Bar Jesse had been too immersed in his own problems to bother to look around and discover why the place had suddenly grown silent as a corpse. And even the resultant scuffle of bodies out the front door had only mildly interested him. He'd only forsaken his drink and painful reflections when he'd heard the sound of a blow.

And then he'd made the fatal mistake of asking Randolph what the hell the captain thought he was doing by choosing these derelict specimens of humanity to crew his ship. He'd capped that announcement with another: "You'll be lucky to make it to the Columbia River without running aground. Can't you even find a decent sailor to shanghai?"

The captain's answer had been swift and silent. Jesse had caught a brief look at a wooden stick that looked something like a billy club before the instrument crashed against his skull, dazing him and bringing him to this current state.

Stupidity. Jesus, he probably deserved this.

Randolph strode up to the bunk, his knees at Jesse's eye-level. He slammed a hammy fist against Jesse's shoulder, trying to wake him. Pain exploded through every sinew. Jesse fought to keep his eyes closed but couldn't prevent a groan of pain.

"He's out," the captain said, satisfied, jabbing Jesse once more for good measure.

"Kill 'im," the first mate garbled fiercely through the cloth pressed to his mouth.

"Later." Randolph was unconcerned as he headed for the steps to the deck. "Make sure he stays like that."

"I'll smash 'im over the head with the lamp!" Lifting a lantern, the first mate hefted it toward the narrow ceiling.

"Cap'n!" a voice hailed from above. "Someone's here!"

Randolph's bootsteps clamored up the steps. Before he'd topped the deck stair, Jesse thrust himself off the bunk and rolled across the floor. The lantern crashed inches from his head. He hit the first mate's legs and knocked him off balance. The man yelped in surprise and fell on Jesse, hard. Stunned, Jesse couldn't breathe for a moment. He wondered if his ribs were cracked.

Before the first mate could recover, Jesse kicked backward, the heel of his boot connecting with the man's back. The first mate squealed in pain. Oily smoke filled Jesse's nostrils. He jerked around. The lantern had caught the rug on fire!

"I'll kill ya! I'll kill ya!" the first mate screamed somewhere to Jesse's left.

With an effort Jesse staggered to his feet, squinting through the haze. Flames were racing across the cabin carpet. Smoke was rising, filling the air. The first mate was struggling upward. The other man was still out cold. Jesse's brain whirled dazedly. He shook his head to clear it, just as the first mate came at his legs. The toe of Jesse's boot connected beneath the man's chin. The first mate went down without another sound.

His lungs burned. Jesse stumbled blindly toward the stairs, the muscles of his arms screaming with pain as he tried to free his wrists. No use.

Fresh air hit him like a cool breeze. He drew several deep breaths, coughing. Near the gangway, Randolph and his men were greeting a newcomer. A man. Dressed in a white shirt and slacks.

Jesse didn't have time to discover who this new arrival might be. Within seconds the smell of smoke would reach them. He had to escape and escape now. Being shanghaied was certain death. It was a sad fact of the seagoing trade, and Jesse wasn't foolish enough to think he could escape such a fate.

Five steps and he was at the rail. A shout rang out. Inelegantly, Jesse tumbled over the rail and threw himself into the water.

The Willamette hit him hard and cold. He sank, water closing over him, entombing him. Memories crashed together. He'd been tossed into this very river once before. A deep abiding fear chilled him to the bone.

He propelled himself away from the ship, his lungs screaming for air. It took every ounce of will he possessed to keep from surfacing too soon. He felt dull, dumb; only the frigid water kept him from blacking out. He couldn't use his arms. He couldn't *breathe,* for God's sake. He was drowning, but there was no other choice. None.

No more time. He couldn't last. Shooting upward, he broke the surface just as he gasped air into his starved lungs. Water and air entered together. He choked violently and fought to keep his face above water.

He opened his eyes, shaking hair from his vision. He was next to a darkened ship, not far enough away. Glancing back at the *Lady Lee,* he was surprised to see the deck was empty. They weren't looking for him. Yet.

Gulping air, he sank beneath the water, swimming through the blackness to shore. His head bumped against scum-slickened planks and he surfaced again. About thirty feet to his right was a makeshift plank ladder built into the pier. He drifted toward it, wondering how in the hell he was going to climb up it.

He heard noises. Something was going on aboard the *Lady Lee.* Jesse glanced again to the deck but no one seemed the least bit concerned about an escapee in the water. But there were shouts and loud talk and someone was shoving someone else. He could make out dark figures topside.

His shoulder brushed the ladder. He turned his back to the rungs, fumbling with fingers he could scarcely feel for a hold. Inch by inch he backed his way upward, panting with exertion and pain, pausing every few seconds to keep himself from fainting.

He half tumbled onto the pier, choking, dripping wet, certain he'd be discovered by the *Lady Lee*'s sentry before he had a chance to get his bearings.

The cocking of a pistol sounded like the rattling of the gates of hell. Every muscle turned to stone. It's true, he thought inconsequentially, knowing he was going to die. The past truly does pass before one's eyes. He saw Kelsey as clearly as if she were standing above him. Her hair down and wild. Her eyes full of concern and fear and undisguised love.

She was sighting him down the barrel of her pistol.

It had to be a vision. "Kelsey," he murmured.

"Good Lord in heaven," she answered in a shaking voice. "Jesse!"

And then she gathered him in her arms and Jesse sank into oblivion.

## 15

Dimly Jesse awakened to the sound of a woman's voice, Kelsey's voice, and it was running on and on in a desperate dialogue. "Don't you dare die on me. Don't you dare! I've got too much to tell you. I'm sorry. I'm sorry, Jesse. Please, please don't do something foolish like this! I need you. I need your help."

She was shaking him too. His head felt as if it were splitting.

"Wake up, for God's sake!" she whispered harshly. "What's wrong with you? Come on, Jesse. We've got to get out of here."

They were on the dock, still right where he'd collapsed. She had his head in her lap and her hands were shaking him. He tried to answer. The scent of her pushed the odor of the river away. It was pleasant and he wanted to just lie there and smell it.

"Jesse," she said in a heartbroken voice. "I'm sorry. I didn't mean to hurt you—last night."

Hurt me? Foggily, he tried to concentrate on what she was saying. The slap, he realized. His reaction to it had been dramatic, to say the least.

She stopped shaking him long enough to take several trembling breaths. Jesse's head cleared and he lifted his eyelids. Joy swept across her face when she realized he was awake.

"Jesse!" She bent down and kissed him hard.

"Lila . . . ?" He couldn't resist.

*Wham.* His head hit the docks so swift and hard he saw stars. He chuckled, then choked up more water, turning onto his side. No matter what she said, she cared, at least to some degree.

Her face appeared above him. She was regarding him with a thoughtful, measuring look. "You did that on purpose, didn't you?" Before he could answer, she cried out, "Your hands are tied!"

He felt her warm fingers try to free him. She'd laid the derringer down in front of his nose, and as he contemplated it, he wondered if Samuel might not have been right after all. His lovely wife had a penchant for firearms. She'd said she was well versed in the use of them. Maybe she was.

"I can't get these knots undone. I'll have to cut you free."

"I suppose you have a knife in your purse as well," he murmured.

"No. Sorry. You'd have to rely on Miracle for that."

"Miracle . . . oh, yes . . . is she handy with a knife?" Jesse was fading.

"Very handy. Lethal."

"As you are with a gun?" he asked from what seemed like a long, long distance.

"Yes." There was a smile in her voice.

His revival in the icy water was only temporary, he realized. The cold was seeping into his marrow and he couldn't stop shivering.

"Jesse, you've got to stay awake!" Kelsey whispered urgently in his ear.

*Slap.* His face stung from another healthy blow by his wife.

"Samuel went to look for you on the *Lady Lee,*" she went on, peering down at him anxiously. Jesse fought to focus on her.

"*What?*"

"He left me here just in case I needed to get help. Oh, Jesse. You've got to stay awake!"

He opened his eyes to stare at the bright pinpoints of stars in the velvety black sky. "Samuel's in trouble," he mumbled.

"Yes, I think so. He's been gone a long time." He heard the scrape of metal against metal. Kelsey was checking the chamber of her derringer. "You've got to sit up so I can untie these knots," she told him.

Jesse struggled upward as Kelsey pulled on the water-logged lapels of his jacket, helping him into a sitting position. His mind grasped one significant fact: *Samuel*. Now he knew why Captain Randolph hadn't been looking for him. Randolph had been forced to pretend Jesse didn't exist in front of Samuel.

Jesse gulped air, clearing his head. Randolph may have decided to capture Samuel in his net. A neat exchange. Jesse for Samuel. It depended on how desperate Randolph was for a crew.

He leaned against Kelsey. Her nimble fingers worked against the swollen ropes binding his hands. Frustrated, she cursed like a sailor, causing Jesse to smile.

Suddenly he wanted to hold on to her and never let go.

"Are you really all right?" she asked in a worried voice as she finished untying his hands.

"Yes."

"Maybe it would be better if you stayed here and I—"

"No! Just help me up."

"All right . . ." she murmured uncertainly.

She leaned toward him. Jesse gripped her forearms and they rose together. Jesse felt her staring at him and he stared right back.

"Your lip's split," she told him. "And your left eye's half shut."

"They weren't pleasant company. I don't think you should go with me."

"Jesse," she sighed, shaking her head. "I'm in far better shape than you are."

He wanted to order her to stay on the pier, but the

226

stubborn slant to her jaw made him think better of it. Arguing with her didn't work; he'd learned that from hard experience.

"I'm an excellent shot," she said softly, as if reading his mind. "You need me. You *need* me."

He thought about the fact that he would be taking a woman on board a ship swarming with dozens of tough, randy sailors. A woman he cared for deeply. His mouth was dry.

"Samuel needs me," she added for good measure.

"Oh, *hell*. You'd better be a damn good shot," he bit out harshly as Kelsey tucked herself close to his side, offering support, and they made their way down the gangway.

"I am," was her cool response.

The hot breath of wind that swept the decks of the *Lady Lee* portended danger. Kelsey felt its fingers run across her nape. The chill of Jesse's soaked clothing dampened through her dress to her already clammy skin, yet she clung to him for emotional support—just as he leaned on her for physical.

The young sailor on guard, who couldn't have been more than thirteen, had stared slack-jawed at the sight of Kelsey and Jesse. He'd burbled something about getting the captain, his Adam's apple bobbing in his throat, then run across the deck to the steps leading down to the cabins.

Smoke wisped lazily above the deck; its strong, oily scent permeating the air. Kelsey wondered what had been burning, or maybe still was burning, but her thoughts were cut short when a blond giant appeared at the top of the steps and then strode determinedly their way. Kelsey felt Jesse tense and release his hold on her. He moved several feet away. She shot him a worried look, but he was staring at the approaching man, his expression hard and controlled. His muscles seemed coiled, as if he were preparing for a fight. Either his strength had returned or he was a consummate actor. She prayed it was the former.

"You," the captain sneered, stopping six feet in front of Jesse.

"I want my brother. Bring him topside now or I'll kill you."

Kelsey's heart slammed into her ribs. Jesse was bluffing. He had no weapon. Nothing. And she knew every breath he took hurt him.

The captain knew it too. He smiled acidly. "Your brother, eh? That who he is? Another Mr. Danner?"

Jesse didn't answer. All along the deck rail the captain's men stood like statues, waiting for a signal or sign from him. Kelsey felt their presence keenly. A woman's sense of danger in the company of so many men.

The blond man's gaze turned speculatively to Kelsey. Her heart rose to her throat. Samuel hadn't minimized the danger to her person. She could feel it in that stripping glare.

"Your brother was not part of my deal, Mr. Danner," the captain said, confusing Kelsey. "I'd be willing to make an exchange."

Kelsey drew a sharp breath. "Don't do it, Jesse," she said flatly. "He means to kill you."

"Oh, I don't want him, young lady. I'd much rather have you."

"I'm certain that's true," Jesse answered, his own smile deadly. "But she's not part of the bargain."

"Then there is no bargain."

Tension heightened. The captain glanced at his followers.

"Wait!" Kelsey called out. "If you bring Samuel topside, and let him and Jesse go, I'll take your bargain."

"The hell you will!" Jesse growled, never taking his eyes from Captain Randolph's menacing form.

"Are you a man of your word?" Kelsey asked the captain, knowing she wouldn't believe him if he said yes.

Jesse grabbed her arm hard. "Don't play this game, Kelsey!"

"You'll have to chance that, won't you?" the captain leered at her. "Starky, bring me the gentleman who's in my cabin," he threw over his shoulder to one of his men.

Kelsey could feel the waves of animosity coming off her husband. She dared not look at him. She could gamble as

228

well as any man, and he was just going to have to trust her on this.

Samuel was shoved onto the deck, stumbling to his knees before regaining his feet. Other than a bleeding right fist, he looked none the worse for wear. "Jesse!" he said in relief.

"This bastard thinks he can make an exchange—you for Kelsey," Jesse said coldly, pointing at the captain.

"What the hell—?"

"We're all leaving," Jesse rasped between his teeth, poising on the balls of his feet. Kelsey sensed he was about to launch himself full body at the captain. The captain felt it too. He turned his head, an almost imperceptible move, signaling his men.

Kelsey, with the calm surety of true talent, pulled her gun from the pocket of her skirt, aimed, and shot the captain in the foot.

A screech of pain and rage rose to the heavens and mixed with the smell of gunpowder. Bedlam broke loose. Jesse's hard hand grabbed her upper arm, nearly yanking her off her feet. A body plowed into her, knocking her against her husband. Vaguely, she saw Samuel clip an uppercut to a sailor's jaw with his bleeding hand.

She was on the gangplank. Jesse was half dragging, half carrying her, swearing a blue streak. A sea of humanity was after them. Bouncing against her husband's shoulder, she aimed the derringer as best she could, squeezing the trigger. The shot went wide, missing the sailor's ear and splitting into the ship's hull with an explosion of wood.

The sailor stopped as if he'd been hit in the chest, his eyes bulging. Samuel nearly ran him down as he shouldered his way past the stupefied fellow.

Jesse didn't put her on her feet until they were three blocks off the pier, in the black shadow of a mean-looking tenement. "God *damn* you!" he spit in fury. "You don't have the sense of a mule!"

"Mules have a lot more sense than horses," Kelsey pointed out just as furiously.

"And they're a hell of a lot more stubborn. Christ, Kelsey! I'd love to wring your neck myself! Do you have *any* idea what kind of trouble you could have gotten into with *him?*"

"You mean sexual trouble? With Captain Randolph?" Kelsey asked with feigned innocence.

"Yes, goddammit!" He slammed her against the wall, holding her pinned there as if planning to show her what he meant.

"I'm not as naive as you'd like to believe. Certainly not anymore," she reminded him on a hard swallow. "And what kind of plan did you have for saving Samuel? Did you truly think you could overpower that man? Especially when you're half dead yourself?" She shoved gently at his chest, making him wince in spite of his burning fury.

"I'd have given him a run for his money," Jesse said through his teeth.

Footsteps sounded behind them in the gloom. Kelsey stiffened, twisting her head. "Samuel," she murmured in relief.

"What the hell kind of man are you?" Samuel demanded coldly, striding straight up to Jesse and wrapping his arm around his neck. "Bringing a woman on board with you? If you care the least little bit about her, why don't you protect her? My God, man. She could have been killed and raped and a dozen other atrocities I don't even want to think about!"

"If you think it's so easy telling her what to do, go ahead." He drew a breath made painful by bruised ribs. Samuel slowly released him. "Tell her. Go ahead. Tell her never to take such risks again or by God you'll take her over your knee and thrash the life out of her!"

"I'd like to see you try," Kelsey hissed at Jesse through her teeth.

Samuel stared from one to the other of them, then he buckled over and began to laugh. He laughed and laughed until he was gasping for breath and leaning against the wall, wiping tears of mirth from the corners of his eyes. Kelsey and Jesse stood by in silence. Kelsey didn't see what in God's name was so blasted *funny!*

"Let's go home," Samuel suggested, slapping his brother lightly on the back. "You look like hell, Jesse."

"I feel like hell."

"I don't suppose either of you would like to thank me for saving your hides," Kelsey said sardonically.

To her surprise and consternation, her husband pulled her into his arms and kissed her soundly on the mouth. "Don't ever do it again," he warned her, and he and his brother broke into howls of laughter.

"Maybe the doctor should look at this cut," Kelsey suggested, examining Jesse's injured mouth. She dabbed at the dried blood with a damp cloth.

"Nah." He waved that suggestion away.

She was sitting on the edge of his desk, trying desperately to get him to go upstairs and lie down and take care of himself. But Jesse was more interested in talking to Samuel, and Kelsey's frustration was increasing by degrees.

"The *Oregonian* needs to hear about this," Samuel insisted again. His swollen right hand was wrapped in a cold, wet towel. "You want to stop Captain Randolph and his kind? There's no other way. The authorities won't do anything unless people speak up."

"You can talk to the *Oregonian* until you're blue in the face after I get Montana."

"Your obsession with this man will get you killed," Samuel threw back at him. "Let me handle him in court."

"Handle him in court all you want. I'm doing this my way. Christ! Dammit!" He sucked air between his teeth at Kelsey's not so gentle ministrations. "Enough," he told her roughly.

"And have you suffer?" She smiled. "Never."

Jesse's gaze narrowed on her lovely face. The fact that Samuel seemed to get intense enjoyment out of Kelsey's never-ending twisting of the knife irritated Jesse.

"Get away from me before I do something we'll both regret," he warned her.

Amusement flickered in the gray depths of her eyes and twitched at the corners of her mouth. Jesse was intrigued in spite of himself. The creamy whiteness of her skin and the soft scent, the essence of her, filled his mind. Last night's lovemaking had surprised him; his emotional reaction had surprised him even more.

His gaze dropped involuntarily to her smiling lips. He wanted to kiss her, and he didn't much care that Samuel would be a witness. As if divining his thoughts, Kelsey suddenly stepped back, gazing at him nervously. The cool, capable woman who'd shot Captain Randolph in the foot was shaky facing her husband.

"Leave Montana Gray to me." Samuel interrupted Jesse's contemplation of his wife. His authoritative tone snapped Jesse back to the matter at hand.

"You think I can't handle this myself?" he asked in a deceptively soft voice.

Samuel sighed. "Past history would suggest you don't always make the best choices."

"Montana's mine," was Jesse's quiet answer, and the way he said it sent a chill down Kelsey's spine.

"Did Captain Randolph discuss *why* you'd been brought on board in front of you?" Samuel wanted to know, not in the least disturbed by Jesse's call to vengeance. "Someone wanted you shanghaied. Someone who bears you a mighty grudge."

"Montana?" Kelsey inhaled sharply.

"Undoubtedly," Jesse answered with a frown. He didn't want to discuss this in front of Kelsey.

"Unless you have other enemies as well," Samuel added blandly.

"If anyone's behind my being knocked unconscious and dragged out of Briny's and onto Randolph's ship, it's Montana. Our deal's done. Montana decided to make himself a full owner in the way he knows best: elimination of his partner." Jesse smiled coldly. "All I need is a few more days, Samuel."

"And what about Kelsey?"

"I don't want her to leave the house."

"Whoa," Kelsey inserted quickly. "I'm perfectly capable of making my own decisions."

Jesse sent her a look from beneath his lashes that said quite clearly what he thought of her declaration. Kelsey's mouth tightened. This from the man she'd practically rescued single-handedly!

"Randolph seemed perfectly willing to exchange me for

you," Samuel said to Jesse, following his own train of thought. "That's not how Montana would feel."

Jesse turned toward his brother. "Randolph simply made the best of a bad situation. He'd failed to capture me, so he decided to use you. You were there. You were obviously coming to rescue me, and he couldn't have you around to raise a hue and cry. Besides, he had a whole voyage ahead of him to come up with a way to explain to Montana why the wrong Danner had been shanghaied." Jesse turned to Kelsey. "You're not going anywhere until I'm through with Montana. Understand?"

Kelsey's eyes flashed fire.

"I'm not through talking about this, Jesse, but"—Samuel glanced from Kelsey's stubborn face to Jesse's implacable one—"for now I'll leave and let you two work things out."

As soon as he was gone, the temperature in the den seemed to drop ten degrees. Kelsey eyed her husband with mistrust. He'd changed from his soaking wet clothes into a pair of tan buckskin pants and a cotton shirt. The sight of him casually dressed disarmed her, reminding her of the Jesse of her youth. In fact, everything about him disarmed her now, which could be extremely dangerous.

"I think I'll go change," she said. The skirt and blouse she'd worn to the pier were still damp.

"Wait."

Kelsey hesitated at the door, glancing back uncertainly.

"Last night . . ." he began, a deep frown marring his brow.

She stiffened.

Jesse swept a hand through his hair, his expression inscrutable. "I'd like you to move into my room."

Oh, Lord. Kelsey drew a strengthening breath. "What makes you think I'd agree to that?"

"Because you enjoyed last night as much as I did."

Through the east window she could see the sun just cresting the horizon, its rays lightening the dark corners of Jesse's office a dull gray. "*Last* night I rescued you from certain death," she parried softly.

"All right. The night before last. You enjoyed *the night before last* as much as I did."

She shook her head mutely.

"You're such a lovely liar," he laughed.

"I don't want to—repeat—what happened between us."

"I've instructed Irma to put your clothes in my closet."

His audacity sent a flood tide of renewed anger rushing through her veins. "You can take everything I own and put it in your blasted bedroom, but I'm not going to be there!"

He sobered, drawing a breath that must have caused him some pain because air hissed through his teeth and he froze. "We'll move you in tomorrow. Tonight—*today*—" he corrected himself. "We both need some sleep." When she didn't answer, he added softly, "It's only for a few more days."

"Why are you doing this, Jesse?" Kelsey asked. "We'll be free of each other soon enough."

He didn't answer and Kelsey resisted the sudden wild desire to press herself against him and beg him to reconsider the ending of their marriage. She didn't want to leave him. She didn't want to lose him. But she had to remind herself that he didn't belong to her and never would.

"Any husband who leaves his wife's bed to go to a whore doesn't deserve even a kind word," she told him in an effort to work up some anger.

"I did not go to a whore last night, nor on our wedding night, nor any other night since we've been married. Neither have I been with Lila Gray. In fact, since our wedding I've been completely celibate—except with you."

Kelsey's breath quickened. She didn't want to believe him, but she knew he was telling the truth. And that made him all the more appealing. "I'll—see you later."

"Yes," he agreed softly, "you will."

# 16

Kelsey awakened late in the afternoon following Jesse's ultimatum to move into his bedroom. Her husband, she was told by Irma, was waiting for her in the den. Curious, Kelsey dressed and headed downstairs, her heart fluttering with both anticipation and dread. But instead of bringing up their parting conversation, Jesse launched directly into the rules of the house, the main one being that she could not leave without an escort.

It was too dangerous, he told her. He was certain Montana was behind his abduction, and he didn't want the same to happen to her. For the next few days she would have to do as he said.

He was reasonable, concerned, and completely detached. Kelsey could scarcely believe this was the same man who'd warned her in his husky voice that he wanted to make love to her.

She determined to ignore his orders entirely, especially when Lila Gray showed up on the doorstep that evening, white-faced and trembling, only to cry out with relief and fling herself in Jesse's arms when she realized he was alive and well. Kelsey, unable to bear this particular scene, had climbed the stairs on leaden feet, locking her door behind her.

Unfortunately, in the intermittent hours, Irma had dutifully moved her belongings to Jesse's bedroom. The canopied bed, however, still resided in the center of the room. It seemed to mock her efforts, but Kelsey was too tired and hurt and discouraged to go back downstairs and try to work things out with Jesse. She decided, instead, that she would sleep in her clothes rather than step one foot inside her husband's room.

If he wanted her, he'd have to come get her.

"The *Lady Lee*'s still in port," Samuel told Jesse quietly when he'd closed the double doors to the den behind him. "It appears Captain Randolph suffered a gunshot wound last night and is missing several toes."

Jesse, who'd spent the day in a black mood, couldn't help smiling at his wife's handiwork. "Lila was here. When she saw me, she acted as if she'd seen a ghost."

"Gray won't stop," Samuel said soberly. "You know that."

"All I need is a little more time."

"You'll get yourself killed, and Kelsey too!"

Jesse paced the confines of the room, sick with worry himself. The papers were filed on his new shipping business with Montana. The money was being transferred. "Gray's mortgaged his house for this. He's sunk his entire fortune into this venture."

"And so have you!" Samuel reminded him furiously. "You're waiting for the right time to steal him blind; meanwhile he's planning to murder you to control the whole company. It's a deadly game of who will slit whose throat first!"

"I'm not planning to steal him blind, or slit his throat," Jesse argued mildly.

"What the hell are you planning?"

"As soon as the money's been used to buy lumber, and the warehouse, and ships to be refurbished, I'm going to burn it all down. It'll happen before Montana can even consider insurance."

Samuel gaped at him. "You're going to destroy everything? Jesse, you'll ruin yourself. You'll be penniless and you'll have the law on your neck. Montana will know it was you. You'll go to prison."

"All you have to do is keep Kelsey safe," Jesse replied as if he hadn't heard a word his brother had uttered. "Zeke's got his own funds, and I've set aside some for

Kelsey. I want a week, Samuel. And then Montana Gray and his whole network of thugs'll come crashing down."

"You're a bloodthirsty fool," Samuel said angrily.

"Do I have your word?"

"Yes!" he hissed, striding from the room as if he couldn't stand the sight of his brother.

The light rap on her bedroom door sent Kelsey shooting off the bed. Jesse opened her door and switched on the light, eyeing her rumpled skirts and hair with something akin to amusement. Kelsey planted herself in the center of her room, hiding her fears and misgivings behind a frigid demeanor and furious glare.

"If you could patent that look, you'd be the richest woman this side of the Atlantic, because every man in the country who could still take a breath would *pay* you to keep it to yourself!"

"What do you mean?" she asked warily.

"I *mean* you're about as approachable as a cobra and just as warm and loving." He inclined his head toward the hall. "The door to my room's that way."

She carefully crossed her arms over her chest, and had Jesse not noticed the way those arms trembled slightly, he would have bodily thrown her over his shoulder and carried her to his bed out of sheer frustration. But that tremor was telling.

"I'm quite aware of the direction of the door. But I'm not walking past it."

"Don't fight me, Kelsey. Not tonight."

"Jesse, you're not well enough to—"

"To?" he demanded, crossing the distance between them and gently clasping her arm.

"You've got a cut above your eye and I know your ribs hurt you. You need sleep. Rest," she amended hurriedly. "You don't need me."

"You're exactly what I need," he said in a low voice that sent frissons of awareness down her spine.

"I won't give in this time, Jesse. I mean it."

"Fine." He expelled an impatient breath. "You're welcome to play this game if it makes you feel better. Lots of women do."

"You'd be an expert on that, wouldn't you?"

"Yes!" She'd made him angry and his gentle persuasion turned to out-and-out force. He grabbed her arms and dragged her across the polished oak floor, her high-button shoes actually sliding across the planks. Kelsey sputtered in outrage. It would have been farcical if she hadn't been so mad and terror-stricken.

At the door to his room, Kelsey managed to yank herself free. Before she could move a muscle, his hard hands encircled her upper arms, squeezing hard. "Why are you fighting something we both want?"

"I don't want—"

"The hell you don't. What happened was good between us. I want you and you want me."

"There're only a few days left! You said so yourself! Why do you have to make this so complicated?" Kelsey blasted at him.

Jesse glared at her, his mouth thin. "Because I don't like anything easy."

His dark head bent to hers, the kiss hard and full of fierce need. *I love you,* she thought miserably. *And if I don't stop you now, the hurt will be so much worse later on.*

"Jesse, please. Be reasonable," Kelsey begged, dragging her mouth from the torment of his. "I want to get out of this marriage with some pride left. A few more hours. A few more days. It's not going to last much longer. Neither one of us wants it to. All right. You win. You've got what you want. A society wife and Montana Gray. But you don't need or want your wife any longer. And she doesn't need or want you," she added achingly. "Let's not make this worse. Please. *Please.*"

She'd never seen him look so darkly handsome. Perhaps it was the intense way he listened to her, the shadowed depths of his eyes, and the tension of his lips. He didn't want to hear what she had to say. He didn't want to admit she was probably right.

"All right," he said at length, taking Kelsey by surprise.

She nodded, stunned and relieved by his capitulation. When he leaned down for a last kiss, she lifted her mouth willingly, wryly disgusted by the twinge of regret that stabbed through her.

He kissed her lightly, sensuously, his palms cupping her chin like a lover. The sweetness of the kiss arrested Kelsey, and her lips parted beneath the teasing pleasure of his lips. Time spun out. Kelsey's hand found his nape of its own volition, holding him to her.

When he finally lifted his head, it was to gaze down at her seriously, somberly, and with a smoldering passion she sensed he'd purposely leashed. "Don't leave the house without me or Samuel," he told her softly. "Promise."

Kelsey nodded.

"No, say it. Promise me."

"I promise not to leave the house without you or Samuel."

His mouth quirked unhappily. "You can have your divorce in a week's time."

Three days later the *Oregonian* reported that Montana Gray had invested a huge amount of his vast fortune in Pacific Shipping Ltd., a partnership venture with Mr. Jesse Danner. Mr. Danner had also invested an exorbitant amount. The news made the society column as well: It was rumored that Mr. Danner had also invested the considerable inheritance his wife, Orchid Simpson, had brought to their marriage.

Kelsey didn't need to read about it in the paper. Tongues were wagging all over Portland and the men of the Establishment (those that *mattered* in the city) discussed the unlikely partnership over cards and drinks, while the women of the Establishment (the wives, mistresses, and daughters of those that *mattered* in the city) gossiped about it at their volunteer meetings, afternoon teas, and even while they promenaded the plaza blocks.

Kelsey slammed the paper down onto her vanity table, annoyed and anxious about this latest article. Her chest tightened at the realization that Jesse had put everything on the line. Every dime he'd scraped together. Everything he owned and cared about. Everything!

Well, almost everything. Her inheritance he'd placed in her very own bank account and given her the passbook. Next week, when they signed their divorce papers, she would be completely independent.

"Are you goin' to Madame Duprés's band concert?" Irma asked as she fussed over the gown Kelsey had carelessly tossed across her bed.

"Excuse me?" Kelsey murmured, lost in thought.

"The band concert this afternoon, ma'am. Right across the way. Four hundred people's invited into them tables."

"Four hundred of Lacey Duprés's closest friends," Kelsey said wryly. "Yes, I'm going."

"With Mr. Danner?"

"I think so."

She had no idea. She wouldn't even care to attend, except that Agatha had sent a note saying she was looking forward to seeing Kelsey this afternoon and that Madame Duprés had been kind enough to seat them all at the same table.

Madame Duprés, Kelsey thought with an inward snort. Since Kelsey was fully aware that Lacey used her only as a means to cultivate Agatha's friendship, she was both amused and irritated by the arrangement. She, too, wanted to see Agatha, and hopefully Charlotte, but did it have to be by Lacey Duprés's invitation?

And what about Jesse? He didn't seem the least bit interested in escorting her to Madame Duprés's outdoor affair; there was no need to keep up social pretenses now. But since he absolutely refused to let her go anywhere by herself, she was stuck unless she could find an escort.

"I wish I could have accepted Agatha's offer to ride Justice before now," Kelsey sighed to herself, feeling a bit like a caged animal.

"Ma'am?" Irma was fluffing the pillows on her bed.

"I said I'm dying to get out of the house, with or without Mr. Danner."

"He's lookin' much better, ma'am," Irma said earnestly.

Kelsey had to fight back a laugh. Irma had been rendered

speechless with horror at Jesse's physical appearance after his escape from the *Lady Lee*. His swollen eye had turned horrifying shades of purple and green. Along with the other bruises and cuts, even Jesse's extraordinary good looks had suffered. Now the bruises were a sickly yellow and the swelling had subsided, but he still moved stiffly. Kelsey was sure he was nursing bruised, if not broken, ribs.

It amazed her he'd even wanted to sleep with her that first night. In any event, he'd certainly left her alone since and now the deal was done, the final ink laid down. . . .

Three hours later Kelsey, who'd dressed for Lacey's affair with care, then worried herself sick that Jesse would forget she wanted to go and would make her stay home and honor her beastly promise to him, stood impatiently in the foyer, slapping a pair of white kid gloves against her mint-green gown.

When she couldn't abide waiting a moment longer, she made a sound of impatience and let herself out of the house, waving off Drake's insistence that he drive her to Lacey Duprés's social extravaganza.

"It's only a few blocks, Drake. I'll walk," she told him.

"But madam, Mr. Danner doesn't want you to go alone."

"Then you can accompany me," she said on a sigh.

She was lonely and depressed. Jesse had done it again, a chronic habit, and though she shouldn't have expected anything more, the thought that he cared so little for her feelings was like a weight on her shoulders.

She walked through the sycamores, oaks, and elms that towered over the prestigious city blocks with Drake at her side. On pleasant Sunday afternoons like this one, the sidewalks teemed with people and bicycles. Lost in thought, Kelsey paid scant attention to the clusters of men, women, and children, and she was oblivious to the fact that a pair of narrowed eyes watched her every move with scrupulous detail.

Two blocks west, the white picket fence that surrounded Lacey's private party stood out starkly against the green parkland grass and lush trees. A red, white, and blue beribboned bandstand stood at an angle to the umbrella-topped tables whose draping edges snapped in the breeze. Lacey's guests grouped around the tables, lifting glasses of champagne and punch. Even from this distance Kelsey thought they looked bored.

Kelsey drew a deep breath and stopped for a moment, willing herself to relax. Jesse's worries for her safety must have taken their toll, she mused a bit sheepishly. She felt exposed and was glad Drake was standing stiffly by her side.

"Damn." Jesse swore softly, glancing from the sheaf of papers in his hand to Zeke's office clock. "It's after two."

"What's wrong?" Zeke had been staring pensively at Pacific Shipbuilders Ltd.'s ledger of monetary transactions. Now, though he looked up and regarded his friend and partner, his expression was still distracted.

"Kelsey wanted to go to a party this afternoon. Madame Duprés's outdoor concert. I forgot to ask Samuel to take her, and now I'm late. Blast," he muttered, dropping the papers on Zeke's desk as he strode rapidly toward the door.

"You don't think it's safe for her to go by herself?"

"It wasn't safe for Nell, and this pretty face I've got testifies to Montana's yen for violence."

Zeke examined the yellowish bruises on Jesse's bladed cheeks. "Be careful," he advised.

"You too."

Twenty minutes later Jesse threw open the front door to his house and strode to the center of the foyer. The place was a tomb. "Kelsey?" he called loudly.

Irma appeared at the upper banister, looking frightened as a doe. "She left, Mr. Danner. Just a few minutes ago. With Drake."

"With Drake? You're certain?" he snapped out.

She nodded her head vigorously.

Relief ran through him. At least she'd heeded his advice and hadn't gone out alone. He would meet her there, he determined, taking the stairs two at a time and striding toward his bedroom. He had time to change and could still be there by half past three. Although attending one of Madame Lacey Duprés's parties was the last way he wanted to spend his afternoon, the thought of meeting his wife filled him with anticipation.

He dressed in record time and headed for the stables as the hallway grandfather's clock bonged three times. At the door to the carriage house he stopped short. The carriage was still there.

She and Drake had walked, he realized. If he hadn't been late himself, he would have done the same. As it was, he took the buggy, snapping the reins impatiently on the back of the horse the groomsman had put to the harness.

He circled the park blocks, arriving at the party from the north side. Tossing the reins to one of the stable boys, he strode past the roped-off area for carriages, buggies, and horses, and toward the white garden arch festooned and woven with red and pink petunias.

"Your invitation, sir," the attendant guarding the entryway intoned, holding out a white-gloved palm.

"My wife has it. She's already here. Excuse me." Jesse brushed past him to the man's choked indignation, searching the crowd for Kelsey. His gaze landed on Lila Gray, whose backless Delft-blue gown glittered with tiny blue beads. She saw him at the same moment, moving toward him like a bright wave, clasping his hands in hers as if they were long-lost lovers. Jesse stifled his irritation, wondering if she'd come with her husband.

"Your face," she said softly, her eyes studying him with disconcerting interest. Excitement flickered in those icy orbs, and Jesse felt his stomach turn to witness her undeniable reaction to violence.

"Excuse me," he said, jerking backward when her fingertips lightly brushed his cheek.

"She's not here," Lila told him deliberately. "You bastard, you're in love with her, aren't you?" Jesse didn't answer, but she clasped his elbow tightly when he tried to push past her into the sea of bodies. "What is it about her you find so compelling? She isn't even that pretty. She's bold and uncouth and a lump of coal in bed, just ask Tyrone McNamara. What *is* it you like about her?"

"She isn't you," he said caustically, pulling away from her, forgetting her just as quickly. His gaze roved anxiously over the crowds. Kelsey could be here. Chances were Lila was lying, just to be difficult. But as his glance swept from the red, white, and blue beribboned bandstand to the white picket fence around the perimeter which clearly marked the line between the socially accepted and the uninvited, he had to admit there was no sign of Kelsey.

However, Samuel was standing by one of the tables, and as Jesse worked his way toward his brother, he saw that Lady Agatha Chamberlain, Charlotte, and their hostess, Madame Duprés, were all seated beneath the royal blue umbrella, sipping tea and champagne.

Samuel jerked his head in recognition as Jesse approached.

"Mr. Reevesworth and I are personal acquaintances," Lacey Duprés was saying. "I've been meaning to call on him."

Agatha was eyeing Lacey with carefully concealed suspicion. "Are you certain we're discussing Mr. Evanston Reevesworth? Evanston and his wife, Beatrice, have been friends of mine since I first arrived in Portland. He's never mentioned you knew each other."

"We know each other very well," Lacey maintained through tightened lips. "He's a Southerner, like myself."

"Well . . . yes, that's correct," Agatha agreed.

Charlotte's gaze froze on Jesse. "Grandmama . . ." she murmured in distress.

"Hello, Lady Chamberlain, Madame Duprés, Charlotte." Jesse inclined his head in greeting, wishing he could avoid this scene and get Samuel alone.

"Mr. Danner." Lady Chamberlain tilted her coiffed white cotton-candy head regally.

"Jesse," Charlotte squeaked out painfully.

"Where's your lovely wife?" Lacey Duprés broke in perfunctorily, looking beyond him.

"I thought she was already here." He glanced at Samuel, who slowly shook his head from side to side, his expression changing from mild exasperation to worry.

"She's not alone, is she?" Samuel asked quickly.

"She's with Drake."

He expelled a breath of relief, but Jesse's nerves tightened. Where was she? Montana was nowhere to be seen, and although his presence at this party would scarcely mean he wasn't sending one of his men out to do his dirty work, Jesse would feel better just having the big man in his sights.

Kelsey, Kelsey, he thought with growing uneasiness, checking his pocket watch.

"Jesse?" Charlotte spoke up in a small voice. "Could I speak to you alone?"

Stifling his impatience, he nodded, leading her away from the table to a relatively quiet spot by the picket fence. Fear was crawling through him, and he heeded it, trusting his own intuitive nature.

"I have to know something for my own peace of mind," Charlotte said in a strained voice, clutching her hands together as if afraid they might betray her if she let them go. "When you were—seeing me"—her voice softened, becoming barely audible—"was it just because I had money, or social connections. That's what Orchid, I mean, Kelsey, said. I just have to know if it's true. . . ."

People had lined up to gawk outside the gates. Jesse's eyes moved from place to place, hoping for some sight of her, of her lovely hair and mischievous eyes and smiling mouth.

A waiter held out a silver tray laden with champagne glasses sparkling in the late afternoon sunlight. Jesse shook his head. Beer, or brandy, or bourbon was all he wanted.

"Jesse . . ." Her voice had changed to a breathy whisper of embarrassment.

He snapped his attention back to her. "Yes, it's true," he said gently, unable to lie and be kinder. For all his experience with women, he had little with young innocents whose hearts were on their sleeves and whose eyes reflected their anguish.

"Oh . . ."

"But I like you, Charlotte. For what it's worth, I couldn't go through with my plan, whether Kelsey was there or not. I'd already determined to give it up. You trusted me, and I couldn't use you."

"Are you in love with Kelsey?"

Jesse was baffled by women's obsession with *love*. "She's my wife."

"But are you in love with her?" Charlotte insisted with the fervency of a true romantic.

"No," he growled out, stalking away, quickly surrounded by glittering peacocks of women and black-suited men, wishing his wife would suddenly appear. Memories of Nell's cold, stiff body slashed across his mind, and he couldn't wait one moment longer.

Thrusting his way back through the crowd, he felt someone's gaze like a knife between his shoulder blades. Glancing back, he encountered the watchful eyes of a man in a brown suit. As soon as the man caught Jesse's stare, however, his eyes slid away and he engaged himself in a conversation with a young blond woman standing next to him. Jesse's skin crawled with premonition. Was he one of Montana's men?

"Kelsey," he muttered through his teeth. "Where the hell are you?"

"Are you ready to continue, madam?" Drake asked.

Kelsey jerked to awareness. She'd been gazing off into space, reliving those moments of fear when she'd realized Jesse had been shanghaied. She wasn't the only one who had to watch her back these days, and she fervently wished her husband would give up this dangerous game of revenge.

She wanted a chance, she'd realized during this moment of reflection. A chance to be a real wife to him. A chance to love him. As silly and heart-breakingly risky as that was, she knew it was what she desperately craved: to admit her love and hope, pray, that he might be able to return that love.

"You idiot," she told herself furiously an instant later.

"Madam?"

"No, Drake, I was reviling myself." What a dreamy imbecile she was! Lord sakes, her heart was in danger of being shattered into a million pieces. She smiled achingly at her starchy companion. "Please, Drake. Can you call me Kelsey?"

"I don't believe so, mada—"

A shrill cry suddenly rent the air, the terrified scream of a woman. Drake's mouth was still open in surprise. Kelsey half turned. A flash of black thunder clattered across the cobblestones straight toward her: an enormous stallion the color of midnight.

"Madam!" Drake yelled, stepping forward.

But he was too late. Kelsey threw up her arms to shield her face, her shoes slipping on the cobblestones. A shriek pierced the quiet sky. A bridle jangled and clangled. The horse hit Kelsey's shoulder, spinning her backward. She stumbled, falling. A whip bit into her back and she cried out, her cheek crashed into the street, stunning her. Hoofbeats rang like angry, discordant bells all around her. Something hard struck her right hand and jagged streaks of pain shot up her arm.

The horse wheeled and reared high above her. Dimly Kelsey turned her face protectively to the ground. Then the animal gathered to leap over her prone body, its hoofbeats crashing past her, receding into the now-empty silence.

"Oh, my heaven!" the woman next to Jesse declared as screams rent the somnolent afternoon air. Jesse whipped around, in time to see a black horse racing hell-bent through the towering oaks that lined the eastern side of the park, scattering shrieking cyclists and couples and children strolling along in its wake.

"Damn fool!" Jesse muttered. The rider, bent low over the withers, slapped his reins against the horse's flanks. Shaking angrily, the horse leapt away.

The skin on the back of his neck prickled. He glanced back. There was no one watching him. Everyone's gaze was riveted to the drama played out beyond the white picket fence. Even the man in the brown suit.

A crowd was gathering on the other side of the grassy knoll, which obscured Jesse's view of the road where the horse had crashed by. He could see the tops of men's bowlers and women's feathered hats. Someone must be injured, he determined, and without pausing to consider what his own thoughts might be about who and what had occurred, Jesse dashed through the gates in aid of the victim.

Halfway to the accident he spied the mint-green gown and lustrous fall of hair of the woman lying on the ground. His heart constricted. Drake was bent over the woman, his normally taciturn face a mask of horror.

"Oh, God, no. No, no!" He ran with all his strength.

Kelsey lay on the street. Blood ran in rivulets down her white cheek to mingle with the dust between the cobblestones. One hand was thrown outward, as if beseeching him to help her.

"He ran her down, sir," Drake said in a choked voice as Jesse bent to her side, almost afraid to touch her.

He gently checked the pulse at her neck. It was strong and sure. "Thank God," he murmured, heartfelt.

A hand touched his shoulder. "I'm going after him," Samuel's voice said determinedly.

Jesse nodded. He could scarcely breathe. "I'm going to kill Montana for this."

"We'll kill him together."

"Get a doctor," Jesse ordered Drake, gathering Kelsey in his arms. "Meet me at the house."

"Yes, sir."

Drake disappeared. Jesse drew a slow breath. Beneath Kelsey's cold skin he could feel the slow throbbing beat of her heart. He stared down at her, consumed with pain. This was his fault. *His fault.* Just like Nell. Only this hurt a thousand times worse. He'd never believed it could hurt worse than Nell, but he'd been wrong.

Montana Gray would pay with his life.

## 17

"Kelsey." Jesse's voice sounded faraway and watery. She moaned and turned her head into the pillow. She was in his room, she realized, inhaling his masculine scent deep into her lungs.

"Kelsey, can you hear me?" he asked, his voice strained. She felt his hand cover hers.

Lifting one eyelid, she saw the room was nearly dark, the bedside lamp dimmed. Jesse's beloved face swam into view. His blue eyes were naked with concern, and she wanted to reach out and assure him she was all right.

"I'm sending you home," he told her. "I've got to get you away from here."

Home? What did he mean by home? This was her home, here with him.

"You've got a concussion, and several fingers on your left hand are broken," he went on.

So that was why her hand felt so strange. She twisted to look at the splinted fingers, and pain exploded inside her skull.

"Don't move, love," he whispered. "Tremaine'll take care of you when you get to Rock Springs."

*Rock Springs!* Kelsey uttered a protest, every muscle tightening.

"Shhh." Jesse warned, smoothing hair away from her forehead in such an intimate, loving way that Kelsey's throat filled with unshed tears.

"Don't . . . make . . . me . . . go," she whispered.

"Jace doesn't know. No one's going to tell him unless you want them to," he said, misinterpreting her reasons for not wanting to leave. She wanted to be with *him*, with her husband. "Tremaine and Lexie will be here tonight. They're taking you with them."

She squeezed her right hand, holding on to his like a lifeline. He squeezed back reassuringly.

"It's going to be all right," he added in a voice consumed with dark emotion. "I'll take care of everything. You just need to rest."

"I want you . . . with me . . ."

Kelsey wasn't certain she'd actually said the words aloud or if they were only in her mind. But Jesse's sudden silence cued her that she'd indeed used her voice.

"I'll be there as soon as I can," he murmured hoarsely. Then he released her hand and she heard his booted foot-steps leave the room.

"She's coming around again," a familiar male voice said into the gray gloom.

Kelsey slitted open her eyes, expecting another wave of pain. Tremaine Danner was eyeing her with the profession-alism of a doctor. He smiled when he saw her eyelids rise. "Hello, there."

"Hi," Kelsey struggled to get out.

"You've got a concussion. Did Jesse tell you?"

"Have you seen Jesse?" Kelsey asked anxiously.

"Actually, no. My brother seems to have disappeared on some mysterious mission."

"Trust Jesse to turn the whole family upside down with his first message in *years,* then make certain he's absent when we come to see him!"

Kelsey turned her head, experiencing only a few sharp twinges of pain. Lexington Danner, Jesse's half sister and Tremaine's wife, regarded her with amusement and curios-ity. Kelsey smiled at the dynamic blond-haired woman. Though Tremaine was also Jesse's half brother, Lexie and Tremaine had been related only by marriage: Lexie's mother, Eliza, had married Tremaine's father, Joseph, when Tremaine was a small boy and while already pregnant with Lexie from a previous marriage.

"He said in the wire that you and he were married," Lexie added in a voice filled with disbelief.

Kelsey tried to nod but the pain hiding around the edges shattered into her skull. She closed her eyes and bit back a moan. Lord, her head *hurt*.

"I'm going to give you some laudanum for the pain," Tremaine told her briskly. "Jesse insisted we take you back with us. He doesn't seem to trust any of the Portland doctors. If you feel well enough, we'll leave tomorrow morning."

Thirty minutes later Kelsey felt floaty and detached from her body, and her head seemed stuffed tight with cotton. She didn't want to go to Rock Springs. She certainly didn't want to go without Jesse.

"I . . . won't . . . go . . ." she struggled to breathe out.

"There's a man downstairs, a Mr. Drummond, who explained in no uncertain terms that your life may be in danger," Lexie said. "He hinted it was Jesse's fault, which, I must say, comes as no surprise."

"Lex . . ." Tremaine warned.

"So, we're taking you away whether you like it or not," Lexie went on, undeterred. "And sooner or later I'll get to see my brother again and tell him what a pain in the"— she hesitated a moment—"*neck* he is," she finished humorously. "My God, Kelsey, you're his *wife?*"

"Leave her alone," Tremaine said on a chuckle. "You're going to be fine, Kelsey. But you'd better be aware that as soon as you're able, you're going to have to tell the tale of how and why you ended up wedding my brother. We're all waiting with bated breath."

"It was—a bargain," she murmured. The laudanum was working its pain-killing magic too quickly.

"Did she say a bargain?" Lexie asked. "Tremaine, she's fading away again!"

"It's all right. Let her. We'll see you in the morning, Kelsey. Sleep well."

"I had nothing whatsoever to do with your wife's unfortunate accident," Gray said with smooth disdain. "We're business partners, Mr. Danner, and I'd hoped our—past association—wouldn't interfere with our present dealings. You were the one who suggested we could work together,

251

I believe. What you're accusing me of is nothing short of criminal!"

Jesse stood squarely in the center of Montana Gray's den, his feet planted apart. He seethed with frustration and powerless rage. "Hurt her again, and I'll kill you. I might just anyway."

Gray linked his hands over his expanding girth and leaned back in the creaking chair. "You still have more passion than good sense." He smiled coldly. "Unfortunate accidents occur all the time."

"To the best of us," Jesse rejoined meaningfully.

"We do not have a good atmosphere for our business relationship, do we, Mr. Danner?"

"I suspect our partnership is about to dissolve," Jesse answered. It was all he could do to keep from squeezing his hands around Montana's thick neck. But that would serve no purpose except a momentary thirst for vengeance. It might finish Montana, but Lila would step right in and Jesse already knew how ruthless and cutthroat she could be.

Gray's smile grew colder. "I'm not responsible for what happened to your wife. I'm very sorry she was injured. Will she recover?"

"If she doesn't, you'll be the first to know."

Victor Flynne watched in distaste as the dirty-smelling man at the bar deliberately counted his money. He took an inordinate amount of time about it while Victor fairly squirmed inside with the need for haste. The stupid sod. He probably hadn't suffered through the least little bit of education.

The stench of him was almost worse than his appearance, which was disgusting in the extreme. A filthy beard spotted with food from forgotten meals covered his mouth. Close-set pig eyes capped a flat, fighter's nose. His arms were thick as tree trunks and mapped with scars and tattoos.

But the odor emanating Victor's way . . . Lord, he would rather smell an unmucked stable!

The man, whose name was Pete, moved his lips as he counted the stack of bills. He licked his thumb. Victor shuddered. He found even the man's tiniest gesture repulsive. But Pete had done the job and now he was leaving Portland.

"Looks like it's all here," Pete pronounced, wadding up the bills and stuffing them inside his shirt pocket.

"You've been paid handsomely. Now we're finished." Victor slid off his stool.

Pete's gaze wandered to the back of the bar, riveting on the lusty outline of a woman silhouetted against the thin red curtain covering the doorway to the back rooms. While Pete rubbed his hand over his beard, his tongue darted between his dirty whiskers to lick what Victor could only presume were his lips.

"Ya didn't tell me that the whole damn town'd be after me," he complained. "It weren't this way with that other lady."

His reference to Mary Danner's death nearly unhinged Victor. Pete knew far too much, and Victor didn't trust the man's simple brain to keep his knowledge to himself. Only meticulous weekly payments had kept Pete in line thus far. Victor was growing distinctly tired of this "employment" contract with a man he could barely stand to be in a room with. He'd considered permanently removing Pete, but unfortunately, the other men he sometimes employed would know who precipitated and why Pete had met an early demise.

No, it was best to send him on his way. Victor had promised him work in Seattle. All he had to do was make certain Pete got there in one piece. Then later, after six months or a year or so, if Pete should say, cease to hang around the usual spots, there might be a bit of talk, but nothing anyone could point back to him.

For now Victor had to bide his time. And live in fear that he may have made an irrevocable mistake with those god-awful, ubiquitous Danners!

"I need me a little bit of time, understand?" Pete said with a leer toward the silhouetted figure. "Who were that last one, anyway? The mayor's daughter?" He guffawed, showing worn-down, brown-stained teeth.

"It's better if you don't know."

He slitted Victor a sly look. "The name's Danner, jes' like that other one. You got a powerful hatred for that family. I know."

Maybe three months, Victor thought, fear stealing through him like a thief in the night. The merest breath of his involvement in Mary's death and Kelsey's accident would lay him wide open. Samuel Danner would kill him. An eye for an eye; Victor had never underestimated the youngest Danner. Jesse Danner . . . He was too unpredictable to even contemplate what horrors might await any man who deliberately set out to frighten and hurt his wife.

Belatedly, but with true insight, Victor realized attacking the Danner women had been a mistake.

"Leave tonight," he ordered Pete harshly. "If the lady's husband, or brother-in-law, should catch you, they'll cut off the most well-used and treasured part of your anatomy and stuff it down your throat! Understand?"

"I ain't afeared a' no one." Pete licked his lips again and swallowed.

"Then you're a man waiting for death to find him." A cold chill cut through Victor as he considered that he'd chosen the same path as his disgusting companion. And he'd heard via one of his sources that Tremaine Danner was in Portland at this very moment. He wished with the fervency of a religious zealot that he'd never embarked on this damned course. He was speeding down the road to ruin at breakneck pace himself. His crimes loomed up before him: He'd led Ramsey Gainsborough to the Danner farm, putting Lexie and Tremaine and the whole family in mortal jeopardy; he'd arranged the death of Samuel Danner's wife. A mistake, yes, but none of the Danners would see it that way. And now he'd purposely injured Jesse Danner's wife. To get them to leave. Leave him alone. *All of them!* That's all he wanted!

And this ugly cur beside him was willing to risk everything—everything Victor had staked his very life on—for a quick tumble with a whore in a dirty back room.

It was past bearing!

"If you walk out that door now and onto the late train

tonight, I'll pay you double. Wire me from your destination. I'll send you the money.''

"Hah! You ain't sendin' me nothin'. I know the likes a' you. As soon as I'm gone, no more cash. I'll be lucky to have a job waitin'.''

"I'll pay you half now.'' Victor scrambled through his pockets for the money, stuffing it into the man's shirt pocket with the rest of his booty. "Wire me from Seattle, that way I'll know you're gone.''

The man looked dazed by his good fortune. "I reckon I might find me a better whore in 'nother town after all.''

"At least you'll have the equipment to do something about it,'' Victor pointed out with perfect clarity. "Understand?''

Pete nodded, his gaze drifting regretfully to the silhouette one last time.

"Tremaine and Lexie have picked up Kelsey by now,'' Jesse told Samuel as they stood side by side down at the docks, gazing out toward where the *Lady Lee* was still rocking gently on the water.

"You didn't even want to see them?'' Samuel shook his head in wonder.

"I'm going to Rock Springs. Soon.''

Samuel was surprised. "Why?''

"I told Kelsey I would.''

His heart twisted with remembered pain. Samuel carefully concealed his feelings, unwilling to share the agony of losing Mary even with Jesse, whom he was growing closer to by the day. His brother's love for Kelsey was clear as spring rain, and it reminded him sharply, too sharply, of what he'd felt for Mary.

"I wish I'd found out more about that horse and rider,'' Samuel said, narrowing his eyes on the *Lady Lee*. "It's funny, but it didn't matter who I questioned, or followed, or paid off—everyone adamantly claimed Montana had nothing to do with it.''

Jesse didn't respond.

Samuel flicked him a look. "You're still going to burn down the shipping company?''

"It's not enough." Jesse's jaw was hard. "I owe Montana more. For Nell, and now for Kelsey."

"Nell?"

"Zeke's sister," Jesse admitted reluctantly. Samuel was staring at him, the same way Tremaine stared at him, the same way his *father* stared at him when nothing less than the truth would suffice. Briefly, Jesse explained what had happened to Nell.

"So that's what this revenge is all about," Samuel said, shaking his head. "You should tell Kelsey. She deserves to know."

"This has nothing to do with Kelsey."

"Oh, the hell it doesn't. You're so sick in love with her, you're afraid to let her know you might have some bit of good in you. It's easier to be the black sheep. Then no one expects anything from you."

"You know you have a disturbingly strong resemblance to Tremaine," Jesse grumbled.

"You're the one like Tremaine," he argued good-naturedly. "I'm more like . . ."

"None of us," Jesse said, frowning at his brother. Samuel was difficult to understand. "Or maybe all of us."

Samuel shrugged.

Jesse trained his gaze on the *Lady Lee*. "You don't think one of Randolph's crew was the rider?"

"Hard to say. I'm glad you sent Kelsey to Rock Springs. If Montana was behind her accident, that's bad enough. But if it's something entirely different, then we're completely in the dark. Do you have any other enemies you can think of?"

"None like Montana."

"I don't know. I have a bad feeling about this." Samuel drew a long breath. "When are you leaving for Rock Springs?"

Jesse expelled a breath in frustration. "I can't leave until I square things with Montana once and for all."

"Why don't you leave that to Zeke? Nell was his sister, after all. He wants Montana as much as you do."

"Zeke's no arsonist," Jesse said on a humorless smile. "No, I've got to take care of things myself."

"Let me do it."

Samuel stared at his brother through the darkness. Jesse shook his head. "And have that on my conscience too?" he asked softly. "Not a chance."

"I can get him legally. I'm this close." He squeezed his hand into a fist. "I've got people willing to testify if they can be promised Montana will be jailed."

"You can't promise them that. Montana'll find a way to silence them, or their families, first!" Jesse was adamant. "It won't work!"

"Have a little faith, brother. Go to Rock Springs. Kelsey needs you."

"She doesn't even like me," he revealed sardonically.

Samuel snorted. "Let Zeke and me take care of Montana for a while."

"It's my responsibility. I can't—"

"Oh, shut up, Jesse!" Samuel barked in annoyance. "Kelsey's your responsibility. I was married once. I know. And it was when my wife was alone that she had an accident and died. You want to risk that? You want to take a chance that Montana could get to Kelsey when you're not there? Then what good will it do you to finally bring the man down? You won't have anyone waiting for you."

"That's not how it is between Kelsey and me," Jesse bit out, growing angry with Samuel's assumptions. "It sounds like you loved your wife."

"And you don't love yours?" At Jesse's silence, Samuel expelled a furious breath. "For once in your life, get the hell out of it, Jesse. Kelsey loves you. If you can't see that, you're blind as well as stupid."

Jesse marveled at his brother's blunt talk.

"Give me this chance," Samuel said insistently. "Do it for me. And do it for Kelsey."

"Oh, *hell!*"

Kelsey examined her splinted fingers, moving them gingerly. It was only her little finger and ring finger and Tremaine had bound them together. They didn't even hurt. Luckily it was her left hand, she thought. She could still hold a rifle if necessary.

She sat up in the bed Tremaine insisted she stay in, disgusted that the Danners were treating her like an invalid. Hell's bells, a concussion wasn't about to send her to the grave!

Kelsey closed her eyes and sighed in exasperation. She *had* been lucky, she admitted to herself reluctantly. She could have been seriously injured or even killed. Being run down by a thousand pounds of horseflesh was no laughing matter. She was grateful that she was still alive.

But where was Jesse?

The question entered her mind even though she'd sought for two days to keep it at bay. He'd promised to come to Rock Springs as soon as he could. He'd promised.

Kelsey threw off the covers and paced around the room: Lexie's old bedroom at the Danner home. Frustration gnawed at her. Jesse wasn't coming. He was in Portland, chasing after his ignoble dream, dropping her out of his life like so much garbage.

Not fair, her conscience argued. He's worried only about your safety. He'll be here.

Kelsey stopped short in the center of the room in dawning horror. She'd asked Samuel to draw up divorce papers. She'd gone to his office specifically for that purpose. Was Jesse even now signing those papers, giving her her freedom, thinking he was giving her what she wanted?

The door to the bedroom opened. Elsie, one of the Danner housemaids, bustled inside bearing a silver tray with soup and biscuits.

"Mrs. Garrett—er—*Danner!*" she cried in surprise. "What'er ya doing outta bed?"

"Stretching my legs. I really can't bear another moment in this room!"

"Oh." Elsie set the tray on the bedstand, glancing over her shoulder nervously. "I heard 'em talking, ma'am. Downstairs about you."

Kelsey could well imagine. Lexie, Tremaine, Joseph, Harrison, and even Miracle, had besieged her with questions about Jesse and their unexpected marriage. Kelsey had answered as best she could, leaving out the real reason Jesse and she had wed. She couldn't bear for them to think she'd been a charity case, especially after what had happened with Harrison.

"What are they saying?"

"Well, it's about Mr. Jesse," she admitted, flustered. "About you being married and all."

"And . . . ?"

"There's talk that he forced you into that marriage, ma'am! And I wouldn't be surprised! He done and got Alice McIntyre with child, didn't he?"

Kelsey gazed at her with a mixture of exasperation and sympathy. "Alice McIntyre never had a child."

"Only 'cause the good Lord helped her out. Saved her from having to face all them folks that knowed what happened."

Jesse's reputation was well documented, Kelsey thought tiredly. "Elsie, Jesse Danner is not nearly as bad as everyone thinks. He couldn't have forced me into marriage if I wasn't willing. Anyway, from all the stories about him, doesn't it seem like he would try to *avoid* marriage? He didn't force me," she said again, wondering how this somewhat sideways version of the truth had been discovered. "I married him because I wanted to."

Elsie's blue eyes were round with disbelief. At sixteen she was still so very young and impressionable. Remembering her own foolish fantasies from her youth, Kelsey winced.

"You really married him 'cause you wanted to?" Elsie looked doubly horrified.

Kelsey didn't think she had the strength to continue defending Jesse. He'd sowed his wild oats long ago. He could damn well reap this harvest himself if and when he ever returned to Rock Springs.

A light knocking sounded at the door, and Elsie hurried to admit the caller. Lexington Danner, wearing mud-spattered boots, a denim skirt and blouse, her blond hair braided down her back, peeked into the room. "Do you know you look absolutely terrible?" she said, frowning when she saw that Kelsey was out of bed.

"Yes," Kelsey admitted with a smile, glancing down at the flannel nightgown someone had found for her. Whoever had packed her clothes—Jesse, maybe?—had neglected a lot of necessary items.

"Are you really feeling all right?" Lexie asked. She smelled of hay and animals and Kelsey knew she'd been working. She was a horse doctor around these parts, as was Harrison. She glanced at the hovering maid and said, "Shoo, Elsie. And mind you don't eavesdrop at the door."

"I wouldn't!" Elsie sputtered. "Mrs. Danner, God would surely strike me deaf if I should—"

"Be careful He isn't eavesdropping Himself when you say things like that," Lexie admonished, hiding a grin as the terrified maid bolted from the room. "She's the most gullible girl I've ever run across," she said, turning to Kelsey with laughter in her eyes. "Now, about you . . ."

Kelsey waited expectantly.

"You actually married a Danner," Lexie said, shaking her head in wonder. "And not Harrison, *Jesse!*"

"Have you heard from him?" Kelsey couldn't prevent herself from asking.

Lexie's look was knowing and Kelsey, feeling her emotions were naked, couldn't sustain her sister-in-law's gaze.

"Not yet. He's truly a phantom, isn't he? The whole household's in an uproar, hoping he'll show up. Pa and Jesse left on bad terms, and I think he's hoping they can settle some things."

"What about you?" Kelsey asked curiously.

"Me? I?" she corrected herself, shooting Kelsey a sheepish glance. "Miss Everly's School for Girls taught me good, didn't it?" Kelsey laughed and Lexie went on. "I miss Jesse. He used to drive me crazy. He reminded me too much of Tremaine. And he was wild." She smiled fondly. "But he's my brother, and I wish he'd come home."

"I do too."

"You're happily married, then?"

There was such caution in Lexie's voice that Kelsey suddenly couldn't bear the explanations—the humiliation—that would follow when she told her the truth. Kelsey Garrett, the spinster, had to bargain herself a husband. "Yes, happily," she said on a swallow.

Lexie suddenly was all business. "Do you feel up to

coming downstairs? Everyone's still got dozens of questions. And Miracle wants to know if you drank her special tea."

"That's what that terrible stuff was? One of Miracle's Chinook recipes?"

"She did say it was a little bitter." Lexie grinned.

"Miracle's a master at the art of understatement."

Lexie laughed.


The Danner parlor was full of people: Tremaine, Lexie, and their two nearly grown sons; Harrison and Miracle and their infant daughter, and Joseph Danner, the family patriarch. Kelsey could feel their curious gazes on her from time to time, but they kept the conversation general until Miracle finally declared, "I'm dying to meet Jesse. If he's half as notorious as his reputation, he'll be memorable."

"Don't believe everything you hear," Joseph Danner said gruffly. He sat stiffly in a chair, a cane across his lap. His right leg had suffered from an accident several years before and now he was lame.

"Why not?" Harrison asked with a faint grin. "Jesse's lucky to be alive. He undoubtedly still bears the scar from old man McIntyre's bullet."

"Jamie, Seth," Lexie said to her sons. She hooked her thumb toward the door, and the two teenage boys grumbled about how unfair life was as they stomped out of the room. "Do you mind?" Lexie said to Harrison. "They don't need to hear about their uncle's sexual exploits."

Kelsey suddenly knew exactly why Jesse didn't want to come back to Rock Springs. He was infamous, and though now, knowing Jesse as well as she did, she believed a lot of the stories had been fabricated, there was no way he could live this down.

"I'm sorry, Kelsey," Lexie said, hearing herself.

"It's all right."

"Has he changed much?" Tremaine asked into the awkward silence.

"Yes and no."

"I think Kelsey's been questioned long enough," Miracle put in quietly. "It's good to see you again," she added in a low voice, and Kelsey knew she was thinking back to that time when Harrison had chosen her over Kelsey. That time when Kelsey had learned Miracle was her half sister. That time when Kelsey's world had disintegrated, and she'd left everything she knew behind in the plume of dust created by Sadie Mae's hooves.

"My brother still doesn't know I'm here, does he?" she asked.

"Jace and Emerald have been kept in the dark, per Jesse's written request." This was from Harrison. "Unless you want us to tell him . . . ?"

"No." Kelsey was positive. "I don't care to ever see him, or Emerald, again."

"He'll throw an absolute fit when he realizes we've been hiding you here," Harrison said with laughter in his voice. "And when he learns about Jesse—"

"The god of stupefaction will strike him dumb," Miracle intoned in the orator's voice she sometimes assumed to sell her tinctures and elixirs.

"Hear, hear!" Lexie proclaimed, making a mock toast.

Laughter filled the room and the tense moments passed. But Kelsey knew if Jesse did come home, the whole town wouldn't give him a moment's peace.

"I can't wait to see him again," Joseph Danner said, as if reading Kelsey's thoughts.

Kelsey smiled, suffused with a new happiness. She was with her family and friends and they loved her. She'd forgotten that in her quest for freedom, in the desire to find a new life. She'd left Jace and Emerald, but she'd also left the Danners and Miracle. She was glad she was back. Glad fate had found a way to send her home.

"I can't either," she admitted quietly. "And if I were dying, I'd make sure I lived long enough to see the look on my brother's face when he finds out I'm married to Jesse Danner!"

Everyone broke into laughter.

"Lord in heaven," Jace Garrett muttered, words as close to a prayer as anything that had ever passed his lips. The men seated next to him at the Half Moon Saloon's bar craned their necks to see what cataclysmic event was transpiring to startle someone as jaded and cynical as Jason Garrett.

Above the half curtains adorning the saloon's front windows, a dark-haired man was tying his horse to the railing. He was dusty, travel worn, and weary looking, but each movement was sharp and fast, as if he was inwardly furious about something. When he pushed through the swinging doors, conversation stalled. His gaze leveled on Jason Garrett, who was actually *gaping* in surprise.

"You sure as hell aren't Tremaine," Jace said, staring at the newcomer as if he'd risen from the dead. "So you must be Jesse Danner."

A trace of amusement flickered across the hard lines of his face. "Always a pleasure, Jace. You haven't changed a bit."

Jace collected himself with an effort. He hated the Danners in varying degrees: Tremaine the most, next Harrison and Miracle, followed by Samuel, and then Lexie, whom he would have liked to hate with the kind of passion he'd once loved her with but for whom he still carried a softly glowing torch. Jesse Danner, however, had never been considered. He'd left at too young an age, and the trail of broken hearts and fallen women he'd left in his wake had made Jace feel almost friendlylike toward him. Jace had always believed Jesse was a kind of kindred spirit. Jesse was the black sheep, the renegade, the troublemaker. If anyone could get under Tremaine Danner's thick, self-righteous skin, it was this brother who looked so much like him it was enough to freeze the blood!

"*You've* changed," Jace said, easing behind the bar as Jesse leaned one hip against a stool. The glossy oak bar separating them didn't feel like enough protection, somehow, though Jace didn't have the slightest idea why he should feel so threatened. "But you're still the spitting image of your brother."

"Tremaine?"

"You sure don't look like Harrison." Harrison Danner had taken after his mother's side of the family, as had Lexie. They were both fair with jade-green eyes and a wicked sense of humor. But Jace would bet a year's salary that Jesse was like Tremaine, a Danner through and through: tough, unbending, cheerfully threatening, and a veritable pain in the ass.

His feelings toward Jesse nose-dived just by looking at the man.

"You still own this place, huh?" Jesse inquired, gesturing to the fact that Jace was planted firmly on the other side of the bar.

"Yes. It's been a long time."

"Years," Jesse agreed. "Quit staring at me and get me a bourbon," he added with that Danner arrogance that so set Jace's teeth on edge.

"Conrad!" Jace bellowed, bringing the Half Moon's manager scurrying from the back room. "Get Mr. Danner a drink. On the house."

"I'll pay," Jesse said with quiet determination, throwing Jace's gesture of friendship back in his teeth.

"Your family know you're here?" Jace asked when Jesse'd been given his drink.

"I believe they're expecting me." He swallowed half of the glass, gritting his teeth as the bourbon burned a trail of fire to his gut. He was filled with anxiety over Kelsey. Her accident had been no accident. Seeing her torn, bleeding, and white as snow, he'd felt as if Montana Gray had ripped out his heart. A shudder swept through him at the thought of how Kelsey had looked, how easily he could have lost her. Jesse had stared death in the face and thought he'd known fear. But nothing compared to the all-consuming horror and debilitating terror he'd felt when he'd first seen her lying on the cobblestones.

Kelsey could die, he'd thought, his mind numb with pain. *Die*. All because of his vendetta with Gray.

Sending for Tremaine had been an easy decision: He wanted the best for his wife, and the best was his oldest brother, Dr. Tremaine Danner. Kelsey had been seen by another physician first, but Jesse hadn't trusted the man. Anyone could be in Montana's employ. *Anyone*. Jesse had practically sworn the doctor to write in blood that the bottle of medicine he left for her was only a painkiller, but he still hadn't been satisfied.

He'd prayed that first night. Gotten down on his knees and *prayed* that she would live. And God, surprisingly, had apparently listened to his prayers, for Kelsey's injuries had been relatively minor.

So now Kelsey was safe, and mending, and he, Jesse Danner, was back in Rock Springs. While Samuel and Zeke took care of things in Portland, Jesse was being forced to face his past.

Maybe it was time.

"You've been gone a long time," Jace said, eyeing Jesse's empty glass and lifting his brows in a question.

Jesse shook his head and threw some coin on the counter. "A long, long time," he agreed. "I hear you're married now, Jace."

"Afraid so."

"That bad, huh?" Jesse grinned. Jesus, Jace would have a shit-fit when he realized they were brothers-in-law.

What, he wondered to himself, would Jace do if and when he realized it was Jesse who'd taken Emerald's virginity from her? Obviously Jace didn't know yet, or he'd hardly be this friendly. And would he ever believe that Emerald had practically forced herself on him, much the same way Alice McIntyre had?

Not a chance, he decided quite accurately. Jace had the understanding and compassion of a rattler, and he was just as nasty. He wouldn't be easy to convince that Jesse Danner—the rebel Danner who'd been tried and convicted of both murder and rape in the minds of many Rock Springs residents—had simply taken what Emerald had so generously offered.

Kelsey would never believe him either, if the whole sordid tale should ever come to light.

Nope, Jesse thought. His marriage to Kelsey wouldn't breach Danner/Garrett hostilities. It would undoubtedly create wider and more immediate problems.

Deciding life was far too complicated, Jesse turned to leave.

"What made you decide to return after all this time?"

Jace called after him. "Half the town thinks you're dead or in jail."

Jesse flicked Jace an assessing look over his shoulder. "I'm meeting my wife."

"Your *wife?* You're married?" At Jesse's nod, Jace hooted with laughter. "Then I guess I won't offer you one of the women upstairs."

"Did'ja finally end up at the wrong end of a rifle?" a wheezing drunk chortled from his place at the end of the bar. He was so inebriated, his body was poured all over the stool as if he were a pool of water.

"It wouldn't be the first time," Jace answered for Jesse. "McIntyre's been saying for years that he blew your right arm off. Guess the man's a liar."

Jesse turned back to the bar, thinking maybe he could use another drink after all. "I guess he is. I've changed my mind, Jace. I'll take another one."

Jace got the bourbon himself this time, sliding it across the bar to Jesse. "Your wife's already here with your family, then?"

"That's right."

"So how'd she talk you into marriage?" Jace persisted.

Jesse rubbed his nose, hiding a smile. He drank some of the bourbon, considering. "She offered me twenty thousand dollars. Her entire inheritance."

"Whoa, lordy!" the drunk exclaimed. "That's a whole lotta money. She an heiress, or somethin'? Your wife?"

"She's an heiress," Jesse agreed.

Jace didn't like the way Jesse was staring him down. Those blue eyes were too knowing, just like Tremaine's. And they were simmering with some inner amusement, as if a joke had been played at Jace's expense. Damn unnerving, it was.

"You haven't seen her, then?" Jesse asked when he'd finished his second drink.

"Well, maybe I have and I just don't know it yet," Jace hedged. He determined right then and there that he had to set eyes on Jesse Danner's bride as soon as possible. Good God, this would set the Rock Springs biddies' tongues wagging for months!

"If you saw her you'd know it," Jesse assured him.

"She pretty, then?"

"Beautiful." A slow smile spread across Danner's handsome face. "Downright breathtaking."

Jace snorted. The Danners had a knack for marrying beautiful women. "So how come she hasn't been to town?"

"She's been in an accident. Tremaine's taking care of her."

Jace's curiosity was itching. The Danners had obviously been playing host to Jesse's wife for some time and not a word had been breathed about her, otherwise the whole of Rock Springs would be in an uproar, everyone wanting a peek at the woman who'd managed to drag Jesse Danner to the altar.

"This a love match?" It would tickle him to death to learn Jesse'd been trapped into matrimony. Jace himself had discovered just how cold and cruel wedded bliss truly was. He hoped the same for Jesse, especially since Lexie, Tremaine, Harrison, and Miracle all seemed to be so revoltingly happy.

Jesse set down his glass. "Jace, I really don't think you want to know."

"Why's that?"

"Because I married your sister," he answered, smiling. "Kelsey is my wife."

# 18

The lights from the Danner homestead glowed like welcoming yellow beacons through the windows on the first floor. Electric lights, Jesse realized with a start. When he'd left home, the place had been illuminated by oil lamps. It appeared progress had reached even Rock Springs.

The widow's walk above the portico was a ghostly white square refracting the faint moonlight. Jesse pulled up his mount about a hundred yards from the front door. He didn't want to be here. The sensation of a noose around his neck was one he'd fought for years whenever he thought of his family. It was there now, ever tightening. Yet, Kelsey was here and he'd walk through fire to make certain she was all right, even though he knew the best way to ensure her safety was to stay as far away from her as possible.

His moments of amusement at Jace's expense had been a coward's reaction to this homecoming, he decided with brutal honesty. He'd put off this meeting because he didn't want to face them. Any of them. He'd stayed out of Tremaine and Lexie's way when they'd come to Portland because he didn't want to see them.

And yet . . . and yet, he did.

"Hell with it," he muttered, leading the horse to the stables. Inside the familiar building he breathed the scents of hay and dust and animal sweat. His gaze flicked ironically to the box at the end: He'd slept with Annie, the maid, there on more than one occasion. Lexie had even caught him once.

He closed his eyes and drew a deep breath. No wonder he was such a pariah in Rock Springs.

Rubbing down his horse, Jesse then fetched it some water, and threw a handful of oats in the bin next to the manger of hay. He walked out into the star-studded night, belatedly wishing he'd done something worthwhile in his misspent youth.

There were outdoor stairs that led to the second floor of the house. Deciding cowardice was the only way he would have a few moments alone with Kelsey, Jesse climbed the steps, as lithe and quiet as a cat, and let himself in on the upper floor. Voices rumbled from downstairs, and the scent of roasted chicken still clung in the air. Dinner was over. He could imagine his family seated in the den, sharing drinks.

His family.

Jesse shook his head in disbelief. Which room would she be in? he asked himself, and because there was only one answer, he strode silently to the corner room at the end of the hall. Lexie's old room.

Twisting the knob, Jesse gazed inside. At first he thought the room was empty, but then he realized Kelsey lay against the pillows, her eyes closed, her face so white it tightened Jesse's heart. Her hair was fanned around her in its usual glorious abandon. She looked so incredibly delicate and touchable that before he considered what her reaction might be, he'd crossed the room and sat on the edge of her bed.

Fear scored deep ridges on his soul. He could have lost her. The emotions he felt at that moment ripped at him. He had to clench his teeth against a cry of anguish that Montana Gray could hurt her so badly.

"I'm going to kill him," he whispered, taking her right hand in his own. Her left hand was splinted, he realized with an aching wrench. "As soon as I go back, I'm going to kill him. For you. For *this*," he hissed furiously, his gaze sweeping over her inert form.

"You'll end up in prison, then," she answered, opening her eyes to reveal how very wide awake she was. "And stop squeezing my hand. Are you trying to break it as well?"

Relieved, Jesse grinned down at her soft lips. "Are you all right?"

"I'm well enough to be sick to death of this room. Actually, I went downstairs this evening until your brother insisted I take to my bed again like an invalid. So I've been lying here awake for about an hour, until you crept in. They don't know you're here yet, do they?"

"No." He reluctantly relinquished his hold on her fingers.

In the darkness he couldn't quite read her expression, but he sensed that she was glad to see him. And he was terribly glad to see her. "Mrs. Danner, didn't anyone ever tell you it's suicide to step in the path of a running horse?" he asked gently.

She searched his eyes. "Suicide, or murder . . . ?"

Jesse wanted to gather her into his arms and never let go. "It wasn't an accident," he answered.

"Montana?"

He nodded.

She closed her eyes, her fingers plucking nervously at the bedcovers. "I'm surprised you're even here. You're so—set—on getting even."

"More now than ever," Jesse agreed soberly. "But you asked me to come."

He didn't realize how much those words hurt. *You asked me to come.* Not, "I wanted to."

"Kelsey," he whispered, cupping her chin.

His soft voice brought her to tears. "Don't call me that," she said, turning her head away, hating her sudden weakness. "Just go away, Jesse. Please. You didn't have to come. I—I don't want to see you, now or ever. I just want to be left alone. . . ."

In the darkness that followed Jesse's departure, Kelsey stared in misery at the white-painted ceiling where moonlit shadows danced like demons. She was embarrassed by her outburst, embarrassed and humiliated.

She'd been delighted that he'd come to Rock Springs to be with her. Humbled that he would risk seeing his family again because she was there. But then he'd called her by name in that achingly loving tone and a dam had burst inside her, and now, oh, God! She wanted to die.

Much more of this and she would put her fate in the keeping of his cruel hands forever. A fate worse than death. Unthinkable. Her worst nightmare and fondest dream.

A sharp wave of sound—deliriously excited voices from the floor below—swept through the bedroom.

Jesse Danner, the prodigal son, the scoundrel whose self-indulgent youth had left women's reputations in shambles, had returned home.

The den looked just the same as he'd remembered it— Pa's mahogany liquor cabinet with its diamond-paned windows glittered like Christmas tinsel in the slow gleam of the firelight. Crystal decanters sparkled against the dark wood, illuminated by electric lamps, dimmed this evening for atmosphere.

What Jesse had seen of the rest of the house showed the passage of years, however. The distinctive woman's touch Eliza Danner had brought to the place was missing. Only a few reminders remained of her starchy, upright ways—the highly polished silver, the glossy patina of the dining room table, the ornate wall sconces, the heavy, glittering chandelier. But the carpet was threadbare in places, notably from the foyer to the den. And Jesse's father, Joseph Danner, was grayer, his shoulders stooped, one hand wrapped tightly around the handle of a gnarled wooden cane.

He sat in a straight-backed chair in the den, staring at Jesse with that same expression of disfavor he remembered from his youth. The only real change that Jesse could discern was that Joseph still wore his boots even though he was inside the house. A cardinal sin during the strict reign of Eliza I.

Jesse stood by the fire, one arm stretched across the mantel. He hadn't felt so ill at ease since the days his father had taken a switch to him for his less than noble pursuit of Annie. Jesse hadn't waited around for whatever punishment Joseph Danner would have meted out over his "affair" with Alice McIntyre. He was lucky Joseph hadn't known of all the others.

Absentmindedly, he rubbed his scarred shoulder at the memory of Alice's righteously indignant and miserably aiming father. He was damned lucky to be alive too.

Lucky . . .

*I don't want to see you, now or ever.*

So lucky.

Tremaine caught the movement of Jesse's hand rubbing his shoulder, and the corners of his mouth lifted sardonically. Lexie snorted inelegantly, and Jesse glanced her way. Apparently, she, too, had witnessed his reaction to that memory.

If he'd had any illusions about meeting up with his family again, they were certainly shattered now. All of his youthful indiscretions hovered like ghosts in the room. Even Harrison, who'd been less critical of his younger brother, seemed remarkably restrained and careful as he looked at Jesse through wary green eyes.

271

And then there was Miracle. Jesse's gaze kept returning to her in spite of himself. He marveled at her beauty. Long black hair and blue eyes, and a razor-sharp tongue that was as lethal as her reputed prowess with a knife.

Quite a collection of relatives. He fit right in.

"So you married a Garrett," Joseph said, closing his eyes, as if this and this alone were the cardinal sin.

Since Harrison had married a Garrett also, Jesse rightly felt this was hardly an issue. "Yes," he said in a careful voice.

"Oh, for God's sake, Jesse, stop looking like you're facing a firing squad," Lexie declared happily. "We're just all completely undone over seeing you again! And then to find you're married. And to *Kelsey Garrett!*" She clapped her hand to her shaking head and laughed.

"I understand Harrison almost married her," Jesse pointed out.

Harrison looked surprised that he knew so much. "Well, yes, but I was—detained before I made it to the altar." He threw a glance at his wife.

Miracle's gaze was direct and, for some reason, filled with the most curiosity. "Harrison once told me you were one of Rock Springs most infamous stories. You don't look like such an evildoer."

"Is that right?" Jesse sent his brother a speaking look, but Harrison shrugged, smiling a bit sheepishly.

"You look unhappy," Miracle continued, breaking into Jesse's thoughts.

He was taken aback. Unhappy? He frowned, consciously facing the heavy weight lying on his heart. Yes, he was unhappy. Unhappy over how things stood with his wife. Over how he'd jeopardized her life by embroiling her in his own plot of vengeance.

"Is Samuel coming home?" Joseph asked.

"No." Jesse glanced at his father. "He's following up on who tried to run down Kelsey."

"Have any idea who that might be?" asked Harrison, frowning.

"Nope," Jesse lied. He would take care of Montana his own way. He didn't want any interference from his family.

272

There was time—time for Kelsey to mend and for his and Montana's shipbuilding venture to suck up every bit of capital each of them had invested. Then he would sabotage the whole operation. Burn the place to the ground if necessary. Anything to cripple Gray financially and have him thrown out of Portland society. The man had bought his way in; it would be interesting to see how many friends stood by him when he was penniless.

Montana Gray's blind greed would work against him; Jesse was counting on it. If Gray was foolish enough to believe that Jesse wouldn't risk losing every cent he himself possessed, he was being incredibly shortsighted. Jesse didn't care how much it cost—in dollars. But a life, specifically Kelsey's life, was an entirely different matter. Jesse would sell his soul to the devil before he let Montana hurt Kelsey again.

Pain slashed through him at the remembrance of Kelsey's reaction to him. She blamed him for this, and rightfully so: It was his fault. For a moment she'd seemed almost happy to see him, but then those tears. When had he ever seen her cry? It had shaken him down to his boots.

"Well, it's bound to be interesting to have you home, Jesse," Tremaine drawled.

"What about Garrett?" Joseph Danner frowned, etching deep lines in his forehead. "When Jace finds out Kelsey's here, all hell will break loose."

"He—er—knows."

"*What?*" the whole family chorused.

Remembering the look on Jace's face brought a grin to Jesse's face in spite of everything. It had been priceless! "He'll probably be by to see Kelsey soon. Probably tonight," he guessed, though it was well past midnight now.

"You told him?" Lexie gasped in disbelief. "You told *us* to keep it a secret!"

"I wanted him to know," Jesse revealed. "I kept it from him only because Kelsey didn't want him to know, but I *wanted him to.* So I stopped by the Half Moon and gave him the good news."

"You're really in love with her, aren't you?" Lexie said, her smile deepening.

Jesse didn't answer. First Samuel and now Lexie had told him how he felt. He didn't believe he could feel romantic love, not the kind where two people share everything, two people plan a life together.

"She's my wife," he finally said, as if that answered everything.

Seconds later the door chimes rang loudly through the house. Since Elsie had gone home hours earlier, Lexie jumped up to answer the door. In the uncertain porch light, Jace, accompanied by his wife, Emerald, stood in tight-jawed conspiracy.

"I want to see my sister," Jace demanded coldly. "I want to make certain she's all right, and I want her to come home."

Upstairs, Kelsey heard the doorbell and stopped short in the center of the room, where she'd been fretfully pacing for the past hour. She'd given up trying to sleep, torn between the desire to race downstairs and throw herself into Jesse's arms and the equally strong need to stay detached, keeper of her own person.

Cracking open the door to her bedroom, she eavesdropped shamelessly and heard her brother's ringing ultimatum.

Jace!

"Good evening, Jace," Jesse drawled in a tone guaranteed to send Jace's blood pressure through the roof. "It's a little late tonight. Kelsey's sleeping. I'll talk to her and maybe you can see her tomorrow."

"The hell with that!"

"Jace." Emerald's tight voice sent goose bumps skittering up Kelsey's arms.

"In fact, why don't you wait for an invitation?" Lexie added with mock pleasantness. "From what she's told me, Kelsey's not that eager to see you again."

This eavesdropping was the height of cowardice. Kelsey threw a dressing gown over her flannel nightgown and drawing a deep, fortifying breath, headed for the stairs.

At the top of the sweeping staircase she could see her brother's familiar, autocratic face, and Emerald's once-beautiful one, now older and pinched with fury. Lexie was regarding them with hostile amusement, her arms crossed over her chest. Jesse was gazing straight at Emerald, and the look on his face was unfathomable.

"Hello, Jace," Kelsey said, taking the stairs on legs that were undeniably shaky. Too much of her life had been spent under her brother's control.

Jesse's dark head swung her way in surprise. He flicked a look at Jace that could be described only as savage, then took the steps two at a time, meeting Kelsey at the halfway mark. She gazed at him in wonder. Chivalry she didn't expect, especially now, as she recalled the searing words of rejection she'd cried just a few hours earlier. But Jesse knew how she felt about her brother, and even though he was certain he hadn't forgotten she'd ordered him out of her life, he gathered her right hand in his and squeezed gently. She squeezed back, silently thanking him for his support.

The rest of the Danners had gathered around the foyer with Jace and Emerald standing squarely in the middle, sparkled with light refracted off the myriad bulbs on the new overhead chandelier. Upon hearing Kelsey's voice they all looked upward, witnessing Jesse's reaction to Kelsey with varying degrees of surprise: Miracle and Harrison looked pleased; Tremaine and Lexie shot each other knowing glances; Joseph frowned as if Jesse had committed some notorious act; Jace stared in stupefaction; and Emerald's face was white and stripped naked with pain. Kelsey, who'd rarely seen her sister-in-law at such a loss, was amused that Emerald was so blatantly upset with Kelsey for marrying a Danner.

"Why don't we all step into the parlor," Joseph said, gesturing to the room opposite the den. "Tremaine, bring the bourbon and sherry."

"Is this all right?" Jesse asked Kelsey in an undertone as they descended the rest of the stairs and followed the group into the parlor. His gaze was now riveted on Jace.

"Yes," Kelsey said, realizing with a start that she spoke the truth. Jace had no hold on her any longer.

"You're sure?" His blue eyes regarded her searchingly and with a touch of wariness. Kelsey was unaware that her eyes were wide with a slow, simmering terror. Before she could answer, he said, "Just a minute," and left the room just as Tremaine appeared with a tray of crystal decanters and glasses.

Jesse's sudden disappearance left Kelsey bereft. She hadn't realized how dependent she'd become on his support until she stood alone near the doorway. Suddenly she was aware of her state of dress, and the travesty of her marriage, and the circumstances that had led to this unusual meeting.

"Just in case Jace gets out of line," Jesse's voice murmured from behind her. Kelsey swung around as he pressed a rifle in her right hand.

Kelsey's eyes filled with gratitude and love. If they hadn't had an audience, she would have flung her arms around her husband's neck and told him how sorry she was for the hurtful things she'd said.

"What in God's name did you give her a rifle for?" Jace demanded incredulously. "Kelsey! You've got a lot of explaining to do. And now is not the time to do it. Certainly not while your *husband* feels threatened enough to stick a rifle in the hands of a woman!"

"Oh, Jace," Kelsey said in a voice laced with amusement. "Shut up."


An hour later Kelsey was back in her room, deliciously recalling every moment of the scene downstairs. Jace had been absolutely livid! He'd bounded to his feet, demanding she listen to reason, and Jesse had told him in plain words that she was *his* wife, that Jace had no hold on her, and that unless he started exhibiting a more neighborly attitude, maybe he ought to just ride on back to Garrett land.

That stopped them in their tracks. Jace and Emerald looked around the room and realized the odds were stacked against them. No one, not even any of the Danners, had expected Jesse to take such a proprietary stand. Even Kelsey had been surprised and delighted. From the instant she'd been reunited with Jesse's family, she'd realized how little they believed her marriage to Jesse would last. She herself knew it was destined to end, and end soon, but she'd wanted the Danners to believe that Jesse loved her, at least a little. And tonight Jesse had fulfilled that lovely dream.

Of course it was temporary; she knew that. Just because she'd faced her love for him didn't mean he felt the same way. But he cared enough to help her deal with her overbearing brother, and for that she was grateful.

Kelsey was cuddled in the window seat, her knees drawn up, her gaze through the window to the moon-washed fields and woods behind the Danner house. The house was quiet now. Everyone had gone to bed. Everyone except Jesse, that is, since he wasn't in the bedroom the Danners all expected him to sleep in. But Kelsey knew Jesse wouldn't join her in the bedroom even if they didn't know it. He had, however, given them all the impression that he and Kelsey were happily wedded, so she was curious about how he intended to keep up this farce if he took to sleeping on the downstairs couch.

A moment later she heard footsteps muffled by the upstairs runner, footsteps heading her way. Mouth dry, she watched the knob turn and then Jesse stepped inside the room, closing the door softly behind him, his gaze sweeping the room until he found Kelsey in the window alcove.

"Well, Mrs. Danner," he said softly. "How much do you want to keep up this masquerade?"

"Very much," she answered without hesitation. "And thank you for helping me out downstairs."

He nodded, passing his gaze over the room, stopping at the doily-covered armchair next to the vanity table. Neither of them said what they were both thinking. Kelsey thought of Jesse sleeping in that chair while she lay in bed and knew she'd never be able to sleep a wink.

Jesse was thinking much the same thing. He'd waited until the members of his family had either gone home or to bed, then found he didn't know quite what to do next. If he had any sense at all, he'd just leave. Her tears and anguished words of rejection had hurt. He hadn't expected them. She'd blind sided him. In his own mind they'd made love and that was definitely progress, whether Kelsey realized it or not, and now, *now*, to be ordered to leave was enough to make Jesse want to throw her down on the bed, kiss her senseless, and squeeze out the words of love, and torment, and need that were deep inside her.

Except she didn't want this marriage at all. She'd told him countless times how much she wanted to end it.

He took off his coat and tossed it over the vanity, unbuttoning his shirt at the same time.

"What are you going to do?" she asked.

"Don't worry. Much as you don't believe it, I haven't stooped to rape yet. I'm tired and I want to go to sleep."

He stripped down to his pants and Kelsey scurried off the window seat and handed him the feather comforter from the bed. Across his right shoulder was a faded scar. Catching her gaze, Jesse said sardonically, "That wasn't rape either."

"I never believed it was. Alice McIntyre was undoubtedly trying to rope you into marriage. As were most of the others."

Jesse gazed at his wife in amazement. "The last person I'd expect to come to my defense is you."

"Why?" Kelsey asked automatically.

"You know why. You've been pretty vocal about what you think of my past. Now, good night, Kelsey," he added pointedly when she still hovered by the chair. "Excuse me. I forgot. Good night, Mrs. Danner. Or isn't that acceptable either? Maybe you ought to tell me what you'd like to be called."

"Kelsey will be fine," she said sheepishly. She dragged her eyes away from his sun-bronzed chest, hurrying to switch off the lamp by her bedside. The room was plunged into darkness, but as her eyes adjusted, she could make out shadows and shapes in the thin stream of moonlight coming through the window.

Long, quiet moments passed while Kelsey lay beneath the blankets and stared at the ceiling. She could hear him breathing, but she refused to look his way. It was too tantalizing. Desperately, she wanted to curl against his chest, feel his arms around her, glory in the joy of his lovemaking. But she couldn't. She *couldn't*.

"Oh, hell," he muttered suddenly, crossing to the bed. Kelsey stiffened, her heart racing crazily.

"What are you doing?" she demanded when the bed sank beneath his weight.

"Crawling in beside my wife."

"No, you're not!"

"Yes, I am," he countered, his arms sliding possessively around her waist, drawing her close to him, her back to his chest, his mouth near her ear.

Tenderly, he brushed back her hair, turning her chin in order to examine every beloved curve and plane of her beautiful face. His finger traced her skin's smooth, delicate texture.

"Don't, Jesse," she said softly.

"I know you don't want this marriage to continue. Neither do I," he said, dousing the flare of sudden hope in her breast. "But while it's lasting, I can't sleep on the other side of the room, thinking about you here, wanting you."

Kelsey closed her eyes and sucked in a long breath. "Jesse . . ."

"When I saw you lying on the street, and I didn't know whether you were—mortally—injured or not, it made me realize how short life is." His voice was husky, deep with emotion.

Kelsey swallowed, her pulse beating light and fast. Charm, specifically Jesse's fatal charm, had been sorely missing since they'd become reacquainted. But now it washed over her in drowning waves. "Your life probably will be short," she murmured, seeking desperately to derail the thrust of this conversation. "Since you're bound and determined to throw it away for the sake of vengeance."

His face was somewhere near her nape, buried in her hair. His hand stole gently upward, cupping her breast. His breath was torn and ragged. "Montana Gray killed a friend of mine. A woman," he admitted, the words pulled from within him. "Nell. She's the main reason I set out after Gray."

Kelsey heard one thing. "A woman," she repeated, hurting inside.

"Gray killed her. He fashioned it to look like an accident, but he killed her. He killed her because she'd passed on information to me about his business dealings."

Kelsey slowly turned in his arms, the enormity of his admission sinking into her brain. She searched his shadowed eyes, the lines of his face, for some evidence that he was lying. But he gazed at her impassively, and except for the passion smoldering in those aquamarine depths, she could discern no other emotion. If he were anyone else, she would swear he was telling the truth.

"Are you saying your motives were noble?"

"I don't know what I'm saying," he muttered. "But it's the truth, and I wanted you to know. And I don't want to wait any longer," he added, his hands bunching her nightgown and pulling it over her head, tossing it to a distant corner of the room. "I don't want to wait for *this*."

He bent his head to her breast, sucking her nipple between his teeth with controlled savagery. Kelsey moaned, her own wanting such a building pressure she couldn't think straight. She plunged her hands in the thickness of his midnight hair, desire raging through her veins in pinpoints.

"And," he added against her skin as he placed soft kisses against her quivering breasts and up the slope of her neck, "since you're certain my life might end at any moment, I might as well take advantage of the few hours left to me." He swept back her thick red-brown mane, his hand lingering in the rich silken strands. "I'm going to make love to you."

She drew a trembling breath. "I can't do it, Jesse. I don't want to."

"Yes, you do," he breathed against her mouth.

"No . . . not if . . . not when I know we're bound to . . . we will . . . divorce. I can't . . ."

"I think that's exactly what you want," he argued softly. "To be with a man who has no holds on you. Your husband. Someone society won't frown on you having an affair with. But you're happy there's no future ahead of us. It's what you really want."

He couldn't be more wrong about her. "No!"

"I'll give you your divorce," he murmured achingly, uttering words he knew she wanted to hear. "But right now I want my wife."

She thrust her hands against his broad chest and pushed,

but Jesse's mouth had captured hers. She fought to tell him the truth, but struggling was no use; his kiss was devastating, his tongue teasing the inside of her mouth until Kelsey's reason melted along with her resistance. He held her crushingly tight against him, his arms like iron bands. When he freed her mouth to trail fiery kisses across her cheek to her ear, Kelsey managed to say, "This is going to hurt later. I can't bear it. Please, don't, Jesse," she pleaded, adding for good measure, "I'm—I'm not well enough—to do anything like this."

"Like this?" he said on a regretful chuckle. His tongue traced the curves and crevices of her ears and Kelsey shuddered with pure longing

"You can't . . . please, Jesse . . . don't . . ."

"You'll have to be a hell of a lot more convincing than that, Mrs. Danner."

"You'll have to force me," she babbled.

"Oh, horseshit," he said on a laugh, and Kelsey lowered her gaze from his beloved face because she knew he was right.

Surrendering was not in Kelsey's nature, however. And she'd learned too early and too well that she could trust no man, not even her husband, *especially* not her husband, the man whose sexual prowess had attracted and won even the most chaste, most sheltered women. "All right. You win. There's a part of me that wants you. I guess it's ridiculous to keep lying about it."

"Completely ridiculous," he agreed, capturing the hands still thrusting against his chest and wrapping them around his back. "Don't, Kelsey," he said softly, staring into her mutinous, terror-stricken eyes. She was afraid of getting hurt, hurt by him, and that knowledge burned like nothing else. He didn't even ask himself why she was so paralyzed with fear; it was simply a fact. Rarely had he encountered a woman who so clearly wanted nothing to do with him. Yes, she was attracted to him, but it was only for the moment, and distantly Jesse realized that it wasn't what he wanted. Not now. What he *wanted* was Kelsey: mind, body, and soul. And if he had any hope of winning her, he had to stop *now,* while she still possessed some modicum of respect for him.

But even as he realized what he had to do, her lips, red from his kisses, lifted upward; her magnificent eyes fluttered closed. Cursing himself for his one vast weakness, he took what she now willingly offered, plundering her mouth with his tongue, caressing her quivering body with his hands.

Kelsey gave in with unbridled ardor, her self-control buried beneath an avalanche of primal need. She'd sampled lovemaking once, Jesse's lovemaking, and it had left her confused, shocked, and full of a longing she could not, and would not, let herself face. But it was here now, wild and beautiful and out of control. Mere words of denial were nothing beneath the weight of her own discovered passion. She simply had reached a point where she didn't want to fight anymore.

With a moan of surrender Jesse covered her body with his own. Kelsey wrapped her arms around him, holding him close, attuned to every hard and fluid muscle. In the darkness, the fervency of his kisses and thrusting hardness splintered her thoughts, sending her to a faraway ecstasy. She suddenly wanted to please him as he pleased her, and when she touched him his groans of laughter and desire returned that pleasure.

"Kelsey," he murmured in her ear. Then more harshly, "Kelsey, Kelsey, *Kelsey!*"

His hands, in turn, discovered all her feminine secrets, leaving Kelsey clutching the bedcovers, her body aching for release. His expert touch brought her to the trembling brink of fulfillment time and again before he finally pushed himself full length inside her, driving with a need so great, even Kelsey sensed how much the moment meant to him before her body exploded in primal ecstasy the same time Jesse reached fulfillment.

But afterward, while he lay beside her, his face buried in her red-brown hair, his arm tucked protectively beneath her breasts, his body warm and relaxed, one leg swung possessively over hers, she lay awake long into the night, watching as moonlight faded into the unwelcoming gray light of dawn.

She loved Jesse, had always loved him, and seemed destined to always love him. His past didn't matter. Nothing mattered. Love didn't listen to reason, she realized with dull, thudding pain. Her heart didn't care that he couldn't feel the same. She simply loved him.

Inhaling a shuddering breath, Kelsey squeezed her eyes closed. Hearing about Nell had been the final nail in her coffin. Before that she could almost believe he was a vengeful womanizer without a noble or heroic fiber in his body. But she'd recognized the ring of truth when he'd explained about Nell; his very reluctance in admitting it attested to how much the issue mattered.

Her emotions had gone wild, as if a gate were slowly raised and her feelings had been released in a turbulent, ravaging flood. There was no hope for her pride now. She'd succumbed, heart and soul.

And Jesse was more than willing to give her what she'd begged for, *demanded,* all these weeks. Now that she didn't want it. Now that it was the last thing in the world she wished for. Now that she'd faced the fact that her husband was the most important part of her life and she would do *anything* to keep him.

Jesse Danner was about to grant his wife a divorce.

# 19

There was a bite of fall in the breeze that rattled the still-green leaves on the trees and brushed against Kelsey's cheek as she leaned her elbows against the rail and gazed across the waving fields beyond. She was alone, mainly because she'd craftily engineered some time without the accompaniment of any of the Danners.

She needed time alone to think. Making love to Jesse

seemed to turn her brain to mush, she'd discovered to her disgust and horror. Was that what other women felt? Was that what made him so irresistible to the opposite sex?

"Blast the bastard," she muttered under her breath.

Footsteps sounded against the dry ground behind her. Kelsey stiffened but didn't turn around, wishing with all her heart that her well-meaning in-laws would give her some much-needed space.

"Thinking about Jace?" Jesse's voice asked, low and quiet.

Kelsey turned to stare at him in surprise. Apart from some passionate nocturnal visits, he'd kept her at arm's length. In fact, Kelsey was absolutely livid over the way he'd made it clear to all and sundry that she might be his wife, but she had no chance of entering his heart. His moments of tenderness had been for Jace's benefit, she now knew, and though she was grateful that he'd put her irritating brother in his place, she wished he would treat her the same way in front of his family.

Instead, Jesse had reverted to his old self: aloof, sardonic, and even testier than usual—a result she attributed to the fact that his family couldn't seem to quit teasing him about his reputation. In any case, Jesse was as cold and distant as the moon.

Except in bed.

"Actually, I was thinking about you," she told him flatly, tossing her head.

He leaned his muscled forearms over the rail, his shirtsleeves shoved up to his elbows. "What have I done now?" he asked lazily.

"As if you don't know. I don't like the way you're treating me."

He threw her a sideways glance and smiled. "Would that be during the day, or at night?"

"Both!" Kelsey declared, annoyed because she invariably responded when he looked so damnably attractive. Turning away from the appeal of his sexy smile, she asked, "Was there something you wanted? Or is it that we're alone and so therefore you can be nice to me?"

"There's something I wanted. I thought we could go for a ride up to the hot springs or over by Silver Stream, if you felt up to it."

"I think I'd rather stay right here."

"Suit yourself."

He started to turn away, but she placed her hand on his muscled forearm, conscious of the warmth of his skin. He waited.

"Tell me why you've been so cool toward me."

"Would you rather I acted like a doting lover?" He searched her face. "I don't know what your future plans are, Kelsey, but if you ever come back to Rock Springs, it'll be easier for you if people don't think our marriage was a happy one."

"Is our marriage a happy one?" she asked softly, turning away from his assessing eyes, squinting across the fields.

"Are you reconsidering divorcing me?"

The words sounded dreadful to Kelsey's ears. "We have a bargain," she said through a tight throat. "I'll stick to it."

Jesse frowned. "Kelsey . . ."

She ached inside, and she didn't know how to make that ache disappear. The thought of racing across the grounds, her hair flying behind her, the wind burning across her skin, was more than she could bear to forsake in the name of pride. "I'd like very much to go for a ride with you," she said in a small voice, turning blindly toward the stables.

He caught up with her as she was struggling to place a saddle onto the back of a black mare with dainty hooves. "Stop that," he commanded, his voice so dire that Kelsey froze, the saddle held in her hands. He finished saddling the eager mare, then turned to Kelsey, examining her left hand in careful detail.

"Nothing was seriously broken," she assured him, moving the splinted fingers slightly. His hard fingers softly examining and caressing hers bothered her. "I'm nearly as good as new."

He suddenly pulled her into his arms, shocking her so much she actually gasped. Then he released her and, without a word, saddled up the chestnut gelding in the box next to the mare's, then led both horses outside.

He didn't comment on her rejection of a sidesaddle, Kelsey noted as she swung herself astride with Jesse's help. Her skirts hiked scandalously upward, around her knees. Apart from a sideways glance, Jesse seemed oblivious to the fact that his wife was behaving like a wild hooligan.

For that she was grateful. She thought longingly of Joseph Danner's well-oiled Winchester hanging on the north wall of the stables. She wanted to test her skill again, but suspected Jesse wouldn't be as eager to go riding with her if she insisted on bringing along firearms.

Jesse opened the gate to the fields, swinging himself lithely onto the chestnut's broad back. "Ready?" he asked.

"Almost." Before he could react, she slid from the saddle, raced back to the stable and plucked the rifle from its hook on the wall. When she reappeared, she kept her gaze focused on the chamber, assuring herself the rifle was loaded even while she felt Jesse's stripping gaze. With lithe grace, and only a twinge of discomfort from the lingering bruised muscles of her shoulder, she climbed onto the mare's back, steadying the rifle across the mare's withers with one hand.

"It appears we're going for a walk," Jesse said with scarcely veiled sarcasm. "Unless you plan on galloping with that weapon in one hand."

"I don't want my skill to atrophy."

Jesse couldn't decide if he was irritated or amused by his wife's insatiable obsession with firearms. Considering the danger he'd embroiled her in, maybe she was right to be so cautious. "Just don't aim the damn thing at me," he growled.

She grinned. "I'll try to be careful."

Jesse found himself wanting her so badly he could scarcely keep his hands from reaching out and yanking her to him. Instead, he guided his horse across the field to the banks of Silver Stream, the dividing line between Garrett and Danner property. He thought of the last few nights of passion with his fiery wife and was consumed with an ominous fear for the future. He wanted her too much, and though she was now willing, even eager, to sleep with him, the sense of urgency he felt, as if it were all going to be snatched away from him, seemed to consume her as well. Their lovemaking was intense, but no words of love were spoken—by either one. Jesse had never experienced the feelings Kelsey was awakening in him and certainly didn't trust them. Love? That was a word women used to absolve themselves from the baseness of lust. Women couldn't be honest about their feelings—especially society women—and he mustn't forget that Kelsey Garrett Danner *was* a society woman now.

Except she toted a rifle and let her skirts ride above her knees like a carefree child.

What did she feel for him? He couldn't help wondering. She wanted out of their marriage; she'd been clear about that. But what if she were to become pregnant? What if she was already?

Jesse's mood darkened as he realized he *hoped* she was—hoped it because it would mean Kelsey would have to make some kind of choice—a choice heavily weighted in his favor!

Coercion was hardly the way to win a woman's heart, yet he'd been coercing her from the moment they met. And he'd choose getting her with child as a means to keep her even now.

"What has put you into such a foul mood?" she asked when they stopped by the side of Silver Stream, its banks strewn with a riotous profusion of late summer wildflowers in red and blue and gold.

"Our marriage," he admitted, throwing her a look as he dismounted.

"Oh." Kelsey tethered her mare next to Jesse's gelding, looping the reins around the scraggly branch of a low-growing bush. Then she walked several yards away, raised the rifle to her eye level, and sighted across the fields toward a distant lone oak tree.

"How soon do you want those divorce papers signed? The ones Samuel's drawing up," he added a bit testily when she gave him a startled look. "The ones you asked him to draw up."

She thought about their lovemaking these past few nights. "As soon as possible," she said, her chest tight. "We can't really stand each other, you know," she pointed out lightly.

"Except at night, when we're alone in bed."

Kelsey swiftly turned back to her rifle. The intimate turn of this conversation was too dangerous. "You see that one branch that dips downward? If I hit it just right, I can break off the end."

"Impossible," he said. "Do you still want a divorce?"

"I just told you—"

"You said you'd keep to the bargain, I know," he cut in swiftly. "But do *you* still want a divorce?"

Kelsey's hands shook as she took aim. Carefully, she inhaled a long breath and expelled it. "Yes." She squeezed the trigger and the shot rang out in the still September air. The tiny branch broke neatly and fell to the ground.

Jesse was astounded by her accuracy. She was a better marksman than he was.

"Don't you?" she asked.

Her gray eyes were regarding him seriously through a small cloud of cordite. "No," he admitted baldly, deciding honesty was the only answer.

"Why not?" Kelsey questioned cautiously.

"Because I don't."

"I see," she said slowly, though by her troubled brow she clearly didn't see at all. Not that Jesse understood his own possessiveness either.

"I just don't want to, yet," he qualified, glancing toward the oak tree so that he missed the hurt that crossed Kelsey's features.

"When will you want to?" she asked, opening the chamber and examining it as if it held the key to all life's mysteries.

"I don't know . . ." *Maybe never,* Jesse thought.

"What if I were to fall in love with someone? Would you be willing to end this farce of a marriage then?"

He stiffened. "I suppose it would depend on who he was," he answered without thinking.

Kelsey clicked the chamber shut and aimed at another branch. "You mean he'd have to be worthy of me, as, for instance, you are," she declared sardonically.

As soon as she lowered the rifle it was jerked from her hands. Kelsey gasped as Jesse tossed it on the ground, then grabbed her by the shoulders, glaring at her. "Has it been so terrible? Has it?"

"Yes!" Kelsey declared recklessly. "You've used me, and deceived me, and treated me like a possession. You refuse to acknowledge to your family that we're husband and wife except when it's time to go to bed. How do you think that makes me feel?"

"If you want me to act like a husband, I will."

"*Act* like a husband. You *are* my husband! At least for the moment. And don't tell me you're trying to spare me future heartache, because I don't believe it. The only time you really want me is in bed, and that's only because I'm the most available woman!"

"That's not true."

"Yes, it is, Jesse."

"I don't want any woman but you," he admitted suddenly.

Kelsey gazed at him doubtfully, but with growing hope. Kicking herself, she shook her head slowly, then ever faster, refusing to listen to this.

"What do you want from me?" Jesse demanded. "Would it help if I said I love you? Would it make that much difference?"

She swallowed hard. "It wouldn't make any difference at all," she admitted. "Because you wouldn't mean it."

"Kelsey, for God's sake, don't do this!" he muttered in a tortured voice.

"While we're here in Rock Springs, I'd just like you to be a little nicer to me. In front of your family."

Gathering her close, Jesse closed his eyes and inhaled through his teeth. "Whatever you want," he murmured, knowing how easy it would be. Knowing that very easiness was what had made him push her away.

"Kelsey," he murmured, cupping her face between his palms, wondering what was happening here to make him feel so utterly helpless and anxious.

With an eagerness that seared him with regret, Kelsey dragged his mouth down to hers, wrapping her arms around his neck as they both sank into the wildflowers beside the flowing stream.

## 20

Kelsey lay against her husband's chest, breathing deeply of his masculine smell mingled with the dry dust of Indian summer, the delicate scent of wildflowers, and the musty, dank odor emanating from the riverbank. A bird dipped overhead, its shadow sweeping across Jesse's shoulder before disappearing.

"It's true, you know," she said softly, slightly shame-faced.

"What?" he asked lazily, his hand twining in her hair.

"You are an"—she swallowed on a choking, desperate laugh—"accomplished—lover."

"And you would know so much about it?" he teased, pulling her atop him until her breasts were hot against his chest.

"I'm learning," she admitted, blushing furiously in spite of her need to prove herself capable, independent, and in control.

"Yes, you are," he replied, his smile widening.

Deciding conversation was more dangerous than silence, Kelsey closed her usually voluble mouth and lay her cheek against Jesse's bare chest. Her gaze followed the trail of clothes: his boots, her camisole, her cotton socks, his shirt, her wrinkled calico dress, his breeches.

His chest hair tickled her nose and she smiled, savoring the moment, for she knew it wouldn't last. Then her eye spied a white envelope sticking from the pocket of his butter-soft buckskin breeches. She opened her mouth to ask what it was, then thought better of it. Dealing with Jesse was still tricky, and she was fully aware he wouldn't tell her more than he wanted her to know.

She would simply lift the missive from his pocket before he put his breeches back on.

"I feel well enough to make the trip home," she told him a few minutes later when the breeze swept her shoulders and caused her to shiver.

"Home?" He eyed her sardonically.

"To Portland," she clarified.

"Oh, no." He shook his head. "It's too dangerous. You need to stay in Rock Springs until it's safe."

"When will that be?"

He shrugged, and said instead, "Let's get dressed before we turn blue."

Their interlude of peace was apparently over. Kelsey scurried to clutch her camisole and drawers to her chest, lifting Jesse's breeches at the same time and expertly plucking the telegram from his pocket before handing him his clothes.

"Thanks," he said, trying to fathom her mood.

Dressing hastily, Kelsey turned her back to him and shoved the purloined missive inside the front of her gown. It felt hot against her chest. Her penchant for trickery would undoubtedly be her downfall someday, yet who could blame her for resorting to such methods when her husband was so unwilling to play fair with her?

"I'm almost certain I could ride a horse all the way to Portland. I feel as good as new."

"You're not going back to Portland," he said again, buttoning his trousers and shoving his arms through his shirt.

"I'd like to go back with you."

"I want you to stay here until I'm finished with Montana. Please," he added as an afterthought.

"What exactly are you planning to do?"

He frowned at the buttons of his cuff, as if the task were one which required infinite concentration.

"You won't tell me anything, will you?" she declared in exasperation. "It would help if I knew something. I could help you."

"No." He was adamant.

"Let me make my own decisions," she threw back in growing anger. "You may be my husband, but you have no right to tell me what to do."

"Oh, don't I?" Now Jesse was furious too.

"No, you don't. I'd rather walk through a pit of rattlesnakes than let some man tell me what to do!"

"Meekness," Jesse reminded her, inflaming her further.

"You can't stop me, Jesse."

They glared at each other, the sweet somnolence of the afternoon forgotten beneath the heat of their anger. "A few more days," he bit out. "Maybe a couple of weeks. I've already said I'll give you your divorce. Just stay here in Rock Springs until I send for you. Then we can finish this."

Her breath was trapped in her lungs. Depressed, she fought back the unreasonable pain of rejection. "Thank you," was all she said, and she stepped past him, collected the rifle, and swung herself into the saddle before the conversation could deteriorate further.

The telegram was brief, pointed, and more confusing than enlightening: GRAY AND FRIENDS UP TO SOMETHING NEW STOP ZEKE WATCHING THEM STOP DON'T WORRY STOP SAMUEL.

Jesse had received the telegram yesterday morning. He hadn't received one yet today, but since he'd been delivered one every day since his arrival, it was only a matter of time until today's missive appeared. Kelsey was going to have to make certain she got her hands on today's as well, because she had no intention of being left in Rock Springs, and she knew her husband was likely to steal away without so much as a good-bye if he felt it would keep her safe.

If Jesse was facing down Montana, she wanted to be there. His fight was now her fight.

Dinner was served at eight with the entire Danner clan in attendance: Lexie and Tremaine and their two sons; Harrison and Miracle and their four-month-old daughter, Elena; Joseph and Jesse.

To Kelsey's surprise and delight, Jesse acted as promised, lavishing her with attention in a way that had everyone trying hard not to stare. He held her chair, let his hand linger a moment or two longer than necessary against her back, and brushed her hair away from her cheek in a tender gesture it was impossible to misinterpret.

Except that Kelsey knew—*knew!*—it was an act and therefore every sweet touch only deepened her resolve to thwart him.

When he left Rock Springs, she would follow.

The doorbell rang right before dessert. The Danners collectively looked up as Elsie swung open the front door. The succulent pork roast turned to ashes in Kelsey's mouth as she saw again the russet hair of her brother, Jace, and the thin, mean-lipped beauty of her black-haired sister-in-law, Emerald.

"Kelsey, there's some family business we need to discuss," Jace told her. "Emerald and I would like you to come back home for a few hours."

"No," said Jesse.

Jace's face turned brick-red at Jesse's insolence. He strode around the room, reaching for Kelsey's arm, intending to yank her from her seat.

Kelsey snatched her arm back, but there was no need. Jesse was already on his feet, his body taut and ready for battle.

"Touch her and I'll break your arm," Jesse snarled.

"Jesse!" Lexie admonished on a strangled laugh. She tried to adopt a stern face for her sons, who stared wide-eyed across the table at their uncle, hero-worship shining from their eyes.

"Let's all relax," Tremaine suggested, lifting a decanter of red wine. "Sit down, Jace, Emerald. Have you eaten? We'd love to have you for dinner."

"Yes, sit down, Jace," Harrison added with a grin. "Miracle and I were just talking about how long it's been since we've seen you.''

Miracle was delicately cutting a piece of roast with her knife. She glanced up, meeting Kelsey's gaze across the table, the look in her eyes saying clearly that Harrison was a bald-faced liar. Kelsey felt a giggle of nervous laughter bubble in her throat as Jace's gaze swept to Miracle, then froze on his half sister's knife, as if he expected her to draw it across his throat.

Emerald was staring at Jesse. Kelsey's brows knit at the strange look on her face.

Seeing Jace was distracted, Jesse turned to Kelsey, gazing down at her with undiluted adoration. She had to remind herself it was an act, but her lips parted involuntarily anyway.

"Kelsey, get out of that chair right now. We're leaving," Jace warned sternly.

She dragged her gaze away from the hypnotic emotion of Jesse's eyes. Her brother's mouth was a line of fury and contempt. Rage surged through Kelsey's blood. "If you want to discuss family business, send me a letter. I'm staying with my husband and his family," she informed Jace determinedly. "And unlike the Danners, I don't care to have you stay for dinner. You and Emerald can leave the way you came."

"By broomstick?" Lexie asked Emerald innocently.

"Lexie." Joseph Danner frowned sternly while Lexie's sons struggled to maintain serious faces.

"Dessert's ready, Dr. Danner," Elsie announced to the room at large, supremely unaffected by the tension radiating in all directions. "And Mr. Jesse's got another telegram." She handed the envelope to Joseph, still unwilling to approach Jesse. "One of the Cullen boys just brung it," she added, eyeing the envelope with blatant curiosity as Joseph handed it to Jesse.

Kelsey looked over his shoulder, in time to see: TROUBLE STOP GET BACK HERE NOW STOP SAMUEL before Jesse crumpled the telegram in his hand.

"Excuse me," he said, shouldering his way around Jace and Emerald.

Kelsey tossed her napkin down on the table, gathered her skirts, and raced after him as Elsie held the front door open for the departing Garretts. By the time she reached their room, Jesse had gathered up the few belongings he'd brought to Rock Springs and was preparing for a quick exit.

"You're not going with me," he said.

"I know," Kelsey said calmly. "Gray and his friends are up to something new."

Jesse stared at her, then jammed his hand into the pocket of his breeches, searching for yesterday's telegram. His gaze was accusing.

"There's something you don't know about your wife, Mr. Danner. She has a troublesome penchant for thievery." Kelsey's knees started trembling at the harsh severity of his unrelenting gaze. "You might not let me come with you, but you can't keep me here, especially if you're gone yourself," she said reasonably.

"I'll have you put under lock and key if necessary."

"Oh, yes." Kelsey was sardonic. "That's just the kind of thing your family would do."

"Then I'll have your brother take you away," he declared in an ominous tone that sent apprehension skittering up her spine.

"You need me, Jesse."

"I need you *safe!*"

"I can handle a rifle better than all women and most men. Maybe even better than you—"

"Goddammit, Kelsey! I've got one woman's death on my conscience. I refuse to have another. *Stay out of it.*"

"You were the one who brought me in it," she reminded him with damning logic.

"No more." He dropped his hands to her shoulders, then dragged her close against him. "No more, Kelsey," he added in an agonized voice.

He kissed her hard and she wrapped her arms around him, somehow hoping this pitiful attempt to delay him would keep the inevitable from happening. But he gently removed her arms and slipped through the door, his bootsteps deadened by the runner on the stairs.

She heard him murmuring his good-byes to his family.

295

Dashing around the room, Kelsey gathered up her own belongings, the ones she couldn't do without. Luckily, there weren't a lot.

Sweeping down the stairs in Jesse's wake, she bypassed the dining room and sneaked out the kitchen door, hurrying to the barn. Unfortunately, she couldn't tell the Danners good-bye without raising a hue and cry.

Thievery was fast becoming second nature, she thought with a pang as she saddled the prancing black mare and snatched the Winchester down from its wooden hooks. She would explain later in a letter. Lexie and Tremaine would understand, and, she reminded herself hastily, Joseph Danner had always liked her.

She was halfway down the lane, just short of the turnoff to Garrett property, when she heard voices. A man's and a woman's. Jesse's and Emerald's.

Kelsey reined in the mare so quickly, the poor thing nearly stumbled. Luckily Emerald's voice was such an outraged screech that Kelsey's approach was virtually soundless.

"Damn you to hell, Jesse Danner!" Emerald hissed viciously. "You married her on purpose, didn't you? Because I married Jace!"

"I didn't realize you were married to Jace until I came back to Rock Springs," Jesse said bitingly. "And I wouldn't have cared if I'd known."

"You used to care. Remember? Back in Malone . . ."

Kelsey shivered in the crisp night air. She had no jacket and her bones felt chilled. She heard a rustling—Emerald's reams of petticoats—and realized her sister-in-law had moved closer to her husband.

Nausea tightened Kelsey's stomach. Jesse and Emerald? Realization slammed into her like a battering ram. *Jesse and Emerald!*

Oh, no! she moaned inwardly, her hands to her mouth. She'd accepted his past because she loved him, letting that love drive out of her head the one truth she'd learned about men: They were untrustworthy, philandering beasts! Hadn't her father been just the same way? Her father and

Jesse Danner, the most influential men in her life, were the same. And yet she'd loved Jesse! *And still did!*

Even though behind the screen of oaks and firs and under-brush, Emerald was tight within Jesse's hard arms at this very moment.

She closed her eyes, pressed the heels of her hands close against them, blotting out the vision.

"When I was younger, I made a lot of mistakes." Jesse's voice rang out coolly in the night air. "I still make a lot of mistakes, but they're different ones. I have no intention of making the same one with you."

"You wanted me. You—you *forced* me to sleep with you! You stole my virginity!"

"Your memory's faulty," he stated crisply. "I remember it being the other way around."

"You bastard!" she cried, but Kelsey heard the unmistakable sound of Jesse swinging himself into the saddle. "You ruined my life!"

Thundering hoofbeats sounded, leaves whirled upward in Jesse's horse's wake, settling noisily against the dry ground. Emerald was breathing hard. Kelsey couldn't tell if she was sobbing or swearing or both. She had no love for her scheming sister-in-law, but in this case, she almost felt sorry for her. Kelsey had always wondered what mystic force had brought Emerald and her brother together; they seemed to almost detest each other. Jace she'd understood more; he'd been licking his wounds after Lexie had refused to marry him. He'd turned to Emerald because she was from a wealthy family—a good match for one of Rock Springs's most influential businessmen.

But Emerald's interest in Jace had been less easy to understand. She'd told all and sundry of the endless offers for her hand that she'd turned down, intimating that only Jace had been able to capture her heart. A cold heart it was, too, for Kelsey, who'd once lived with them, had never seen a shred of love inside it for Jace. Nor passion. Nor caring of any kind.

So why had she married Jace? Now, years later, Kelsey finally knew the answer. Emerald had chosen Jace because he was a Garrett—and the Garretts lived next door to the

Danners. And the Danners' third son was Jesse Danner, the one man Emerald desired.

What a sad, sick, pointless existence. It chilled Kelsey to the bone.

And Jesse . . . ?"

*You are an accomplished lover.* . . . Kelsey winced in humiliation as she remembered her own breathless infatuation. Lord, she'd only declared aloud that she, too, had fallen under his spell. That she, too, lay awake in restless hunger for him night after night. Oh, God, what had she done?

Kelsey hunched her shoulders. She'd worried about this long ride to Portland, remembering the last time she'd traveled it. She'd lost her horse and her dog. But now she had a lot to think about. It was a long, dreary ride, made more so by the facts that she was so newly mended from her fall, that the night was nearly pitch black, and that a cold, persistent rain had begun to fall. But Kelsey scarcely noticed her discomfort. She had the Winchester. She wasn't afraid. She was just cold, tired, and sick with an inner misery that threatened to consume her. The depths to which Emerald had humbled herself in order to be with Jesse shook Kelsey to her very soul.

She would never, *never* let that happen to her.

Soaked to the skin, Jesse swept the Stetson from his head as he headed up the back porch steps and let himself in the kitchen entrance. It was predawn. The house felt cold as morning ashes. He strode down the hall and toward his den, stopping short when he saw the doors were open and a light was on.

Samuel was seated at his desk, his eyes closed, his hands squeezing the back of his neck as if he were in pain.

"Samuel?"

His eyes opened wearily. "Jesse. Damn it all, I'm glad you're back."

"What's wrong?"

"Zeke's dead. There was a fire down at the shipyards. . . ."

"*Zeke* set the fire?"

Samuel's eyes were glazed with lack of sleep and worry.

"I don't think so. I think Montana knew what was up. I think—he did it."

Jesse's pulse pounded in his head. "Zeke. How did he die?"

"In the fire. I helped pull his body out. It was Zeke."

"God."

Jesse strode slowly to the window, staring out at the black shapes of the trees just visible against the dark night sky.

"Montana was supposed to show for a court date yesterday," Samuel went on. "He didn't. I was elated." Bitterness edged his voice. "I thought, 'Now, I've got him!' But he was busy sowing the seeds of destruction. I'm sorry, Jesse. I was wrong. I thought I could handle him through the legal system, but he's just as diabolical as you've said all along."

Jesse was silent, numb. Zeke was dead. Just like Nell. "Why would Montana burn down the shipyards? He lost everything."

"No. You lost everything. He got his money out. There was some illegal handling of the money. Zeke figured it out. He came to my office and told me Montana and his friends had set you up. He wouldn't wait until you got back. He was after blood."

"Goddammit!" Jesse expelled in pain.

"I know. I tried to stop him. I sent you the wire as soon as I could, but I never dreamed he'd get himself killed before you could get here."

"Montana's mine," Jesse muttered, crossing to the desk in jerky strides. He yanked open a drawer and pulled out a pistol. "Enough of this."

"Wait!" Samuel grabbed Jesse's wrist. "This is what he's expecting. All you have to do is wave this gun in front of his face and he can shoot you dead and claim self-defense. Think, Jesse," he spit out through his teeth.

"You think. I'm through thinking."

"What about Kelsey? Is she still in Rock Springs?"

Jesse nodded. "When I said my good-byes, Tremaine promised me he'd keep her there." He glanced down blankly at the Stetson still in his hand, rain dripping from

299

the brim onto the carpet. "Harrison gave me another hat," he added reflectively. "I lost the first one when Montana ordered me killed."

"The man deserves to die," Samuel agreed, punctuating every word to get through to his hotheaded brother. "As long as Kelsey's safe, you've got time to do it right."

"What would you suggest?" Jesse demanded acidly.

"I've got an idea. Now, listen . . ."

The porch lights sent out welcoming yellow rays as Kelsey slid off the weary mare's back and led her to the stables beside the carriage house. She startled the sleeping groom.

"Mrs. Danner!" he sputtered. "Ma'am!"

"Please brush her down and feed her," Kelsey said in a tired voice.

"Yes'm! Right away."

She let herself in the back door, surprising Mrs. Crowley into dropping her rolling pin. "Mrs. Danner!" the cook exclaimed in shock, clutching her massive bosom.

"I'm fine," Kelsey quickly assured her. "I'm just glad to be home. I'll just go to my room and take a bath and be good as new," she added, aware of her bedraggled state.

"Irma," the taciturn cook said.

"No, please. I'd rather be alone. I just need some time to myself. Is—er—Jesse upstairs?"

She shook her head, frowning. "Gone out, he has."

Kelsey's spirits plummeted. "I see. Well, maybe that's for the best," she said more to herself than to Mrs. Crowley.

Excusing herself, she hurried upstairs, every muscle aching. It seemed to take forever to fill the tub, and when she slipped into its steaming depths her eyelids drooped in response to her complete emotional and physical exhaustion. Promising herself she would stay in the bath only a minute before slipping into her bed, Kelsey lay her head against the porcelain rim and closed her eyes.

Strong hands hauled her from the water, yanking her upward so quickly her neck hurt.

"Jesse!" she sputtered, choking. She couldn't breathe!

"What the hell's the matter with you?" he demanded fiercely. "Are you trying to drown yourself? You were underwater when I got here!" He slapped her on the back, hard, as she continued to choke water from her lungs. "You're damn lucky I came back and saw the door to your room open. Holy Christ, Kelsey!" he added in a shaking voice. "I've got enough to worry about without you scaring the liver out of me! What the hell are you doing here? How did you get—oh, God. You *didn't!*"

"I'm—okay," she managed to croak out, her eyes tearing.

"You rode back here alone, didn't you? You sneaked out of the house. Jesus, Kelsey!" He shook her shoulders, concern turning his voice hard. "You could have been killed!"

"I had—Joseph's Winchester."

"Oh, God!" Grabbing her under the arms, he hauled her completely out of the bathtub, staring at her with fury and some other emotion she couldn't name. "You're going to be the death of me," he muttered, snatching a towel from the counter and tossing it over her shoulders.

"You mean if Montana isn't first?" she asked, beginning to shiver.

He suddenly pulled her close to him, kissing her hard on the mouth. His shirt was damp. He was wearing the same clothes he'd left Rock Springs in. Whatever mission had sent him out of the house early that morning must have been important.

"It's not safe for you to be here," he said as if divining her thoughts. Gently, he pushed her away. Kelsey awkwardly wrapped the towel around herself, feeling suddenly embarrassed at this intimacy. It was one thing to make love to Jesse in the dark, she discovered. Quite another to stand naked in front of him.

"Gray's left town," Jesse said. "He's made things hot for himself around here, and he's taken off for a while."

"Where did he go?"

"San Francisco, I think. That's the *Lady Lee*'s first stop before she sets sail for the Orient. Montana's on board."

"What about your shipbuilding venture?" Kelsey asked, tugging on the towel.

"Burned to the ground. Montana's doing, not mine," he added, seeing the look on her face. "But Montana managed to get out with his money," he added bitterly. "So, I've got to go after him."

"To San Francisco?" Kelsey was suddenly alarmed.

"Uh-huh. For Nell, and Zeke . . ."

"Zeke?" Kelsey asked in a small voice.

Quietly, and emotionlessly, Jesse told her about Zeke's fate. Jesse's seemingly utter detachment worried Kelsey. Not because she believed it, but because she knew it hid his inner turmoil.

"Don't go," she begged. "It doesn't matter anymore. He's gone. Let him be."

Jesse stared at her as if she'd lost her mind. "It doesn't matter anymore?" he repeated incredulously. "It matters more than ever. I don't care what it costs, I'm going to kill that man."

"No, Jesse. It'll backfire," Kelsey babbled hurriedly. "Nothing's worked so far. He's a bastard, and a murderer, and he should be swinging from a rope, but let the authorities handle it! You can't be a one-man army!"

"Samuel's got a plan," he said as if he hadn't heard a word she'd uttered. "I'm going to confront Montana. I've got an ultimatum for him."

"No." Kelsey shook her head. Premonition lifted the hairs on her arms. "You can't go."

For the first time, a trace of something besides driven fury crossed his face. He almost smiled. Almost. "Nothing's going to stop me, Mrs. Danner."

"Nothing?" Kelsey eyed him steadily, her gaze dropping to his sensually curved mouth.

Sensing the direction of her thoughts, Jesse shook his head. "Not even sex is going to work on me," he said, half amused, half baffled by his wife's change of attitude.

Kelsey's heart was thudding so hard it almost hurt. She'd never once considered herself in the role of seductress; she was too embarrassed, too careful of her feelings. But Jesse was her husband, and for better or worse, she loved him.

And she had a terrible sense he was on a path to certain death.

Lowering her eyes, she unwrapped the towel, gripping it tightly in her hands. Then, shooting a somewhat frightened glance upward, she encountered the cold, wary blue of his eyes. He wouldn't give in, she realized, disheartened, but a panicked voice inside her told her not to give up.

Carefully, she wound the towel around his neck, drawing his face down to hers.

"Kelsey," he said on a half laugh, his voice smothered beneath the demanding pressure of her kiss.

"I want you to stay. I want you to make love to me," she whispered urgently.

"Later. When I get back."

"*Now*."

She pressed her damp body against his, her hands deliberately pulling his shirt from his breeches. Jesse shook his head, but he didn't resist completely. Encouraged, Kelsey trailed kisses along his jawline and flicked her tongue in his ear.

He thrust her away from him, holding her at arm's length, his eyes no longer cold. A hot flame fired their blue depths. "This isn't going to work. Besides, it would only be temporary. I'm going to San Francisco."

"Not yet," she whispered seductively.

"*Dammit*, Kelsey!"

"Give in, Jesse." A smile twitched at her lips. Cautiously, half afraid he would win this battle and therefore send her opinion of her femininity down another notch, she reached for the buttons on his breeches, undoing them one by one. A detached part of her mind marveled at her own composure. A few months ago she would never have been able to even *think* of herself in such a position!

She slid her hands inside. Jesse lasted about twenty seconds.

"Oh, *hell!*" he muttered, sweeping her into his arms and carrying her to his bedroom.

## 21

If wishes were horses, then beggars would ride, Kelsey thought a week later. She'd wished and wished and *wished* that Jesse would cable her, or show up in person, or somehow alert her to his plans, but she'd heard nothing from him. Not a word.

She'd awakened to a cold, lonely bed, and a cold, lonely house, and though his conscience had smote him enough to leave a note, it hadn't kept him from chasing after Montana to San Francisco.

That note was crumpled inside her reticule: *I've sent a wire to Tremaine, telling him you're safe. Don't leave the house alone. Montana may still have someone watching you. Be careful. Jesse.*

A coolish September breeze pulled at her hair and rattled the branches of the trees overhead as Kelsey hurried along the street to Samuel's office. She'd taken the buggy, sneaking around Drake, whose loyalties would be torn between her and Jesse if he knew she wanted to leave the house unaccompanied. Still, she couldn't stay housebound one more moment; it wasn't her way. And if Montana was threatening anyone right now, it was her reckless husband. Whenever she thought of what Jesse might be doing at any given moment, she broke out in gooseflesh, sick with concern.

A horse whinnied shrilly somewhere behind Kelsey's back. Gulping back a cry, she whirled around, a hand to her thudding heart. But there was no black destrier thundering toward her, no clattering hooves, no sweating flanks. A horse harnessed to a carriage had simply given his partner a nip.

Kelsey's pulse slowed and she swallowed in relief. She could rationalize all she wanted; she hadn't forgotten the throat-choking fear she'd felt the moment before she'd been run down.

Samuel's office was dark. Kelsey leaned her forehead against the wall and counted to ten. It was lunchtime. Surely he would be back soon. Unless he was in court.

In court. Hours to wait.

"Blast!" she muttered. She couldn't bear it. The waiting would drive her insane.

Hurrying back to her buggy, she wrapped her skirts around her knees and climbed up to the hard board seat. She would visit Agatha and Charlotte and maybe even take that long-delayed run on Justice.

Anything was better than suffering through the endless minutes of worry over Jesse.

The sense of being followed kept touching Samuel like unseen fingers even with his mind occupied with something else. Now he felt it like a whisper on the back of his neck and he whipped around, surveying the street through sharp eyes: Men strode by in somber business suits; women pushed navy blue baby carriages, or strolled along dangling dainty parasols; drunks staggered or stretched out numbly in shadowed doorways.

No threat.

Half an hour later, as he unlocked his office, he was still unable to shake the feeling that someone was watching him, dogging him. Someone working for Montana Gray? It didn't make sense. Jesse was stirring up a hornet's nest down in San Francisco all by himself; he sent telegrams to that effect daily. There was no one in Portland who would care about the movements of one Samuel Danner, Attorney-at-Law.

"Mr. Danner?"

Samuel inhaled sharply, startled at the sound of the scratchy female voice. The woman standing in the doorway was of indeterminate age, but she looked as if life had been a long, hard road. Her makeup was heavy: kohl-blackened eyes, bloodred lips, and cheeks turned hectic with some kind of vile fuchsia rouge. She wore a tight, blue-beaded dress, and her hair was blond, brittle, and pulled beneath a black-veiled hat. She kept touching her lips, as if afraid her lipstick had smeared.

"Can I help you?" Samuel asked a trifle impatiently.

"The name's Patricia Lee," she said, holding out one black-gloved hand as she sailed across the room. Samuel accepted her outstretched hand and, realizing she expected him to kiss it, dutifully bent over her and laid a kiss on the somewhat soiled silk. "You're Samuel Danner, then? The one what's a lawyer?"

"Yes," he answered, his interest piqued in spite of himself.

"I been not knowin' what to do. But I've got some information. I thought about sellin' it," she said, a real blush now flooding beneath the fake one. "It's the kinda thing would make a blackmailer's day, if'n ya know what I mean."

Samuel hesitated, assessing her. She was from a lower class than his usual clientele: Her dress, her demeanor, her language, suggested she had little or no education. "And you think I'd be willing to pay for this information, is that it?"

"Oh, no, sir! It's just you're involved, and I been strugglin' with my conscience. But when a man tells me he murdered someone, I can't keep it to myself. You understand?" she asked anxiously, peering at him through the screen of her veil.

Baffled, certain he would be sorry for asking, Samuel inquired, "Someone confessed a murder to you?"

"Yes, sir, Mr. Danner. He did." She clutched her bosom as if expecting her hands to encounter a cross, but her fingers closed around a cheap-looking bauble meant to look like a ruby.

"You want me to defend him?" Samuel hazarded, groping through the dark.

"I should say not!" Her lips tightened in exasperation as if she deemed him completely dense. "There was a man what's name was Pete. He came to me though he shoulda left town. Had lots of money. Wavin' it in front of everyone's noses. Said murderin' was the quickest way to get rich."

"Why don't you have a seat, Mrs. Lee," Samuel suggested, gesturing to the chair. He leaned against his desk and crossed his arms over his chest, resigning himself to the fact that this was bound to be a lengthy interview.

"Lee's my middle name," she said, daintily arranging her skirts around her as she settled into Samuel's one comfortable chair. "I don't go by no last name."

"Who was this Pete?"

"I don't ask too many questions. None of my business. Good way to get yourself murdered, if'n ya know what I mean. But he was braggin' somethin' fierce, and then he said he shoulda killed her like the first one. He was drunk, y'see. Babblin' away." Her lips curved in remembered distaste. "A man gets like that, he don't have any sense left on how to treat a gal."

Memory flashed on inside Samuel's head. Kelsey's voice, quiet and humiliated. Inside Briny's bar. "He spent our wedding night with a woman named Mamie."

And then another voice, a man's voice, responding from the back of the room: "No, it were Patricia Lee. . . ."

"Was this Pete—a customer of yours?" Samuel asked as delicately as he could.

"Just the one time," she assured him quickly. "Just that once."

"You said I'm involved somehow," Samuel reminded her.

"Well, Danner's the name he said. Knocked her down with a horse. She be your wife, Mr. Danner?"

"Wait a minute." Samuel stared at her, gathering his thoughts. "Kelsey Danner? Did he say her name was Kelsey?"

"No, sir." Patricia Lee screwed up her face in intense concentration. "I thought he said it were Mary."

Lady Chamberlain beamed at Kelsey as if she were a long-lost relative come home to the manor—which, in an absurd way, she was. "My dear, I'm so glad you're all right," Agatha said for about the tenth time, shooing Cora

307

Lee out of the way as the downstairs maid hovered by Kelsey, her own face wreathed in smiles as if she, too, had received some bountiful gift from the gods.

"I'm glad too," said Charlotte, who was nervously arranging and rearranging the flowers on one of the drawing room tables. She could scarcely meet Kelsey's eyes.

"But what dreadful news about Mr. Drummond," Agatha said with distress.

Kelsey nodded. She didn't like thinking about what had happened to Zeke. It reminded her too much of what could happen to Jesse.

"Was there a funeral?" Charlotte asked, moving a brilliant orange chrysanthemum behind a sprig of Oregon grape.

"No. A memorial service." Kelsey had sat by Samuel. They'd hardly spoken a word to each other, just held hands, both wrapped in worry over Jesse.

"I'm really sorry," Charlotte said, swallowing.

Kelsey met Charlotte's misery-filled gaze, and her heart turned over with a painful flip. Teasingly, she said gently, "And here I thought you'd rather see me drawn and quartered."

"Oh, Orchid!" Charlotte wailed, her eyes filling with tears. "I can't bear it! I can't bear it one more minute! Can you ever forgive me?"

"Forgive you? Can *you* forgive *me?*"

"No, it's my fault. I've been an absolute beast!" Charlotte suddenly made a beeline toward Kelsey, who opened her arms to her young friend.

"Charlotte, you silly nincompoop," Kelsey whispered fervently, hugging her. "Don't you know the last thing I ever wanted to do was hurt you?"

"I thought I loved him," she said in a muffled voice. "I really thought I did." She disengaged herself from Kelsey and stepped back, swiping angrily at the tears collecting in her eyes. "But he was a fake! A fraud! Just like you said. You simply must get out of that marriage, Orchid!"

"Charlotte," Agatha remonstrated on a sigh. "Let Kelsey make her own decisions."

"We're planning to end the marriage," Kelsey admitted with an effort, the words sticking in her throat.

"Good," said Charlotte, lifting her chin in justified indignation. This posture lasted about ten seconds, and then she asked anxiously, "It is good, isn't it?"

Kelsey nodded firmly, her heart aching. "It's for the best. Jesse and I both got what we wanted out of this marriage, and now he's in San Francisco, finishing up some business. When he gets back, then we'll—divorce."

Agatha lifted a delicate flowered teacup to her lips, her snow-white brows arching. "No annulment?"

Kelsey lowered her lashes, slanting Agatha a look. "No."

"My stars . . ." Charlotte's voice was so low and breathy, Kelsey could scarcely hear her even though she was standing less than five feet away. "You're in love with him, aren't you? You're really in love with him. I knew it! I knew it!"

Kelsey regarded her in distress. "Charlotte, it isn't what you think."

"Yes, it is!" For a moment she looked as if she would cry, then she suddenly clapped her hand to her mouth and broke into peals of laughter. "Who's the silly nincompoop now? You *love* him, Orchid . . . Kelsey. You do, you do, you do!"

"Charlotte!" Agatha sighed wearily.

"Jesse Danner is not the kind of man to fall in love with," Kelsey corrected Charlotte quickly. "He's a womanizer, and a renegade, and doesn't know the meaning of true romantic love." She glanced to Agatha for confirmation, unaware that her feelings were naked on her face.

Agatha gazed at her fondly. "Your opinion of him's elevated somewhat. I believe you called him a rapist and murderer before as well."

"You're in love with him," Charlotte insisted. "You just can't admit it!"

Kelsey stared from one to the other of them. They were her dearest friends. They'd taken her into their home, loved her, and forgiven her her misdeeds, and now all they expected was a bit of honesty.

"Yes, all right, I'm in love with him!" Kelsey declared, sinking into one of the chairs and throwing up her hands in surrender and misery. "But it doesn't alter anything. I can't live with him. He'd be the last man on earth I'd want for a husband."

Agatha took another sip of tea. "The last man on earth? I believe you've forgotten about Tyrone McNamara, my dear."

"And Charles DeWitt." Charlotte gave a mock shudder. "Your children would be downright *ugly*."

*"Charlotte!"* Agatha laughed.

Kelsey shook her head. "I'm really glad you've both forgiven me," she said softly, the moment of hilarity fading. "When I leave Jesse, I'll probably leave Portland, but it'll be good to know I still have friends here."

"Don't say that." Charlotte knelt down by Kelsey's chair. "You can't leave. I've just got you back. I can't bear to lose you again! I need you. I need your advice." She sent a mischievous glance at her grandmother and added daringly, "Now that you're married and have more experience in—matters of lovemaking, you can help me make some decisions."

"Child, you'll send me to an early grave," Agatha said with a shake of her regal head. "If we were in England, fresh words spoken from a young girl's mouth could ruin her reputation. Kelsey, didn't you say you wanted to take that temperamental Justice for a run? Now would be an excellent time, as Charlotte and I have some things to discuss."

Kelsey grinned at Charlotte's crestfallen expression. "Be smart," she told her as she headed for the door.

"When I marry, it'll be for love. Just like you," Charlotte declared.

As Kelsey reached the drawing room doors, they suddenly swung inward. Cora Lee tiptoed nervously into the room, knowing that Agatha was a woman set in her ways who absolutely abhorred unexpected interruptions.

"Yes?" Agatha demanded, tipping her head without looking at the maid.

"Madame Lacey Duprés to see you," Cora Lee announced diffidently.

"Hell's bells," Charlotte muttered, drawing daggers from her grandmother's eyes. Kelsey smothered a smile.

Lacey Duprés thumped into the room without further ado. She wore a bilious green caftan that flowed around her heavy frame unattractively, looking the exact shade of sewer water. Spying Kelsey, Lacey's expression changed to one of consternation, even, Kelsey thought fancifully, fear. Jeffrey, her faithful companion, hovered outside as Cora Lee closed the doors.

"Lady Chamberlain," Lacey intoned gravely. "I just learned about Mrs. Danner's terrible accident, and I—I wanted to express my worry and sympathy." Her hands worked the end of her cane as if she were under terrible stress. "I'm so glad you're all right," she said to Kelsey. "Truly."

Thinking the woman's distress was out of character, Kelsey smiled away her concern. "I'm right as rain," she said. "It was really more frightening than debilitating."

"No aftereffects?" Lacey asked anxiously. "You're fully recovered?"

Kelsey glanced down at her now-unsplinted fingers. She hadn't been able to stand the damn nuisance of having them tied together. "Fully recovered," she agreed.

"Your concern is well taken," Agatha murmured, her gaze skating over Lacey as if she, too, were wondering why the woman was so shatteringly upset.

"I would hate to see anything happen to you," Lacey said with difficulty. "I would like you to know that I've been extremely worried. That I—feel responsible."

"Responsible?" Kelsey gazed at her uncomprehendingly.

Perspiration formed on Lacey's powdered brow. "It was one of my servants who ran you down, Mrs. Danner. A man in my employ, I regret to admit. He lost control of that black devil. He should have never trusted that miserable piece of horseflesh on a city street! Mrs. Danner, it was all a terrible error. A horrible mistake, and—and—" She drew herself upright. "And a horrible, horrible man! He's gone now. I fired him without pay, and he's left town. So, there's no need to search farther. You're safe now."

Kelsey stared at her in complete bewilderment. "You're sure the man was employed by you?"

"Positive." She drew a fortifying breath. "I'm leaving Portland," she added stiltedly. "This unfortunate incident has—ruined my plans."

"Ruined your plans?" Kelsey repeated blankly. Was the woman daft? "No one will blame you personally, Madame Duprés."

"You told me yourself how much you wanted to be reacquainted with Evanston Reevesworth and his wife, Beatrice," Agatha put in softly, eyeing the colorful dowager with something approaching amusement. "You were terribly insistent about it, as I recall."

Lacey stiffened, nearly lifting her cane off the rug. "Circumstances have changed," she stated tightly. For a moment, Kelsey thought the upset dowager might actually topple over and faint. "I'm moving back to San Francisco. Jeffrey!" she practically screamed, sending him scurrying to her side. "Good afternoon, Lady Chamberlain, Charlotte, Mrs. Danner . . ." She seemed about to say something more to Kelsey. Her lips moved and the muscles of her throat worked. But then she shook herself and left, moving with surprising speed across the foyer for a woman who relied on a cane.

"Well," Agatha said thoughtfully.

"I don't think she really needs that cane!" Charlotte declared in a hushed whisper of excitement. "What do you think, Kelsey? What was that all about?"

"I don't know." Kelsey was reflective. "I thought I knew who was responsible for my accident, and it wasn't anyone associated with Madame Duprés. After my ride, I think I'll have a talk with my brother-in-law about this."

Samuel was waiting on the front porch, slapping his gloves impatiently against his thigh as Kelsey drove the buggy around the back to the carriage house. He followed her, catching up with her at the back door, practically dragging her into the privacy and seclusion of Jesse's study.

"What is it?" Kelsey demanded fearfully. Then she added in sudden comprehension, "Oh, my God, it's Jesse, isn't it?" Her heart began thumping the death knell. "Is he all right? Is he hurt?"

"It isn't Jesse. Not directly. It's . . ." He closed his eyes and drew a breath. "I'm glad you're safe."

"Where is Jesse?" Kelsey demanded, her hands lifting to her lips. "Have you heard from him?"

"Kelsey, sit down. Please." Samuel paced the room in jerky strides. Belatedly, Kelsey noticed his chalk-white pallor.

"You're scaring me, Samuel."

"Have you ever heard the name Victor Flynne? Actually, Victor Flynne Flannigan? He's an investigator here in Portland."

"Investigator?" Kelsey asked blankly.

"Sit down, please." He clasped her arms and gently forced her into one of the chairs, but Kelsey sat stiffly and as soon as Samuel walked away she rose to her feet.

"I don't understand," she murmured anxiously.

"Flynne's an old enemy of Tremaine's."

"Tremaine? What does this have to do with Jesse?"

"I think he's after revenge, and he's chosen Jesse and me, and anyone associated with us, as targets. It wasn't Montana's man who ran you down. It was Flynne's. I'm positive of it. He's got a longtime grudge against my brother, and probably Lexie, and so he went after you. And he went after my wife," Samuel added in a hard, chilling voice. "Jesse has no idea Flynne's even out there."

Kelsey's head was spinning. She held out a hand to stop him. "Your *wife?*"

"I was married once," Samuel bit out tersely. "She's dead now."

"Dead?" Kelsey's heart went out to him. "Oh, Samuel, why didn't you say something before?" She tried to touch him, but this time he turned away.

"Jesse's playing a bluffing game with Montana," he said shortly, deliberately changing the subject. "We concocted it together, but now I'm not so sure it's going to work. I didn't know about Flynne. *Dammit,*" he bit out through his teeth with repressed violence, stalking to the window, reminding Kelsey poignantly of her husband. "If he isn't back by Friday, I'm going after him."

"Then I'm going too."

"Oh, for God's sake, Kelsey!" he exploded. "You should still be in Rock Springs with Tremaine and Harrison and the rest of the family. Someone needs to keep an eye on you."

"I'm not afraid. You know I can defend myself."

Samuel ducked his head in weary acceptance. "We've got two factions working here: Montana Gray and Victor Flynne. Maybe they're working together, I don't know. But you stay out of it!"

The front door creaked open, sending a waft of cool September air through the crack beneath the den's double doors. Kelsey automatically turned toward the sound, wondering if Drake had let himself in.

Then the den doors were thrown wide and Jesse stood between them, dark and dangerous and so wonderfully familiar that Kelsey forgot everything she knew and simply ran across the room and threw herself into his strong arms.

"Mrs. Danner," he murmured in surprise.

"Jesse, thank God!" Samuel clasped one of Jesse's palms in a hard handshake.

Kelsey buried her face in his neck, drawing in deep drafts of his scent. She hadn't realized she'd been so viscerally frightened until this moment, until she could hold and touch and feel him again. She never wanted him to go away again, she realized dully. Never.

"How are you?" Kelsey asked, collecting herself slowly.

"Fine. A little tired, but—satisfied." Jesse's gaze sliced to Samuel. "Montana went for it."

Samuel released a pent-up breath. "He did? Good."

"Went for what?" Kelsey demanded, disengaging herself from her husband's arms as she realized he must be wondering what had possessed her to act so lovingly.

The look on his face said exactly that, but then he dragged his gaze from her and grinned slyly at his brother. "I told Montana I had evidence against him, written evidence linking him to all his crimes. At first he didn't believe

314

me, but I guess he figured I wouldn't be half so bold to follow him to his lair, so to speak, if I didn't have some kind of proof.''

"Did he give you much trouble?" Samuel asked.

"Some," Jesse admitted, remembering how Montana's henchmen had flanked their leader as if they were guards to some unholy king. In truth, they'd looked rapaciously eager to take him apart, but Montana hadn't given them the chance. He'd listened to Jesse whether he'd wanted to or not, his face drawn in lines of intense concentration. All the while Jesse had stood in the hallway of Montana's luxurious San Francisco home, he could practically hear the wheels turning in Montana's villainous mind as he tried to finagle a route of escape.

"I told him there was an incriminating paper that would find its way to the proper authorities—not Montana's paid ones—if anything should happen to me," Jesse went on. "He had to listen to me. I then told him to pay me my half of the Pacific Shipbuilders Ltd. money if he wanted immunity. He agreed.''

Kelsey found herself staring at her husband as if she'd never seen him before. "You mean, you let him buy you off?" she asked in disbelief.

"I let him think he could," Jesse drawled, smiling at his wife's horror.

"There's another problem," Samuel said quietly.

"What?"

"Does the name Victor Flynne mean anything to you? He goes by Victor Flannigan now, but from what Patricia Lee said, I think his real name's Flynne.''

"Patricia Lee?" Jesse gazed at him uncomprehendingly. "Victor Flynne sounds somewhat familiar. Flynne," he added musingly.

"He's the private investigator Tremaine was after. The one who helped Gainsborough find our mother and Lexie. He may be working for Montana too." Seeing Jesse's still-blank look, Samuel shook his head. "I don't have all the information yet, but I will. I owe Flynne.''

"You mean Tremaine owes him," Jesse said. "If anyone's got a debt to pay Flynne, it's—''

315

"No," Samuel cut him off, a muscle working in his jaw. "Leave Tremaine and Lexie out of it. You let them know, then the whole family, Harrison and Miracle too, will charge to the rescue. This is my battle."

Jesse suddenly remembered the Samuel of his youth, standing in the doorway of the farmhouse, calmly shooting the bastards who'd threatened Lexie, his mother, and their whole family. Samuel'd clipped one too. If he'd been older, he'd probably have aimed a little steadier, a little stronger, and he'd have killed him outright. If he wanted this to be his own private war, Jesse believed he would prevail.

"Okay," Jesse said.

Kelsey had been practically forgotten during this whole exchange. Now she put in tensely, "In case either of you is interested, Lacey Duprés told me today that one of her men was responsible for the attack on me. She said it was an accident, that the horse was uncontrollable. She fired the man responsible and he's since left Portland."

Samuel's dark gaze fastened on Kelsey. "It's either a lie, or she's covering up for someone else."

"Montana?" Jesse suggested crisply.

"Only if Flynne's working for Montana."

Memory hit Jesse like a bullet between the eyes. He inhaled sharply. *"Flannigan?* Victor Flannigan. Jesus," he whistled between his teeth. "Zeke used an investigator named Flannigan, I believe it was *Victor* Flannigan, to find out some information about our family. I wanted to know if Mother was really dead, and Zeke handled the whole thing."

"And I'm the reason you hired that investigator," Kelsey said with dawning horror.

"It doesn't matter." Samuel's voice was the crack of doom. "Flynne was already after the Danners before either of you got involved."

"How do you know?" Jesse asked, aware Samuel was keeping back some sort of vital information.

"Let me handle Flynne," was all he said as he strode determinedly for the door. Jesse followed in his brother's wake, dissatisfied with Samuel's ambiguous remarks.

"This isn't over yet," Jesse told him tersely.

"You're damn right it isn't over." Samuel managed a cold smile that chilled Kelsey's blood. She'd never seen this side of him. "I've got a score to settle. You were right, Jesse. The newspapers, the police, the justice system—none of it's going to work. And it wouldn't be enough anyway," he said, his voice lowering threateningly. "If I need you, I'll let you know," he added as a parting farewell.

"What do you think he'll do?" Kelsey asked when they were alone once more, standing beneath the foyer chandelier.

Jesse didn't answer. His face was pulled into a frown of concentration, his hands on his hips, his gaze locked on the doorway that Samuel had just passed through. Time seemed suspended. The only sounds were those of Kelsey's rapid heartbeats, and Jesse's slow, rhythmic breaths. When his gaze touched on hers it was sober, considering. Jesse, who moments before had treated her like a partner, an equal, and whom she'd treated like a long-lost lover, now regarded her with the eyes of a distant stranger.

The moment of decision had arrived, Kelsey realized instinctively. This was it. The next course of action. The next hurdle. He was about to end their marriage.

*I'm not ready!* she cried inside, suddenly afraid. Now that the issue was at hand, she couldn't bear to face a decision that would only cause her deep misery.

Jesse seemed to understand what she was feeling. He gestured toward the den, and Kelsey preceded him stiffly. She walked to the window and Jesse crossed to the bar, poured himself a drink, and lifted one eyebrow at her, silently asking her what she wanted. Kelsey was about to refuse, but then decided if she'd ever needed to stoke her courage, it was now. "Bourbon," she said, causing her husband to choke out a laugh.

"When have you ever drunk bourbon?" he asked ruefully as he handed her a glass.

"Never," she admitted, tasting the amber liquid. It filled her throat with fire, nearly choking her.

He nodded. "You seem to be expecting some kind of scene. I'm not going to fight you, Kelsey. I already told you that."

"I know." She nodded jerkily. "We've threatened each other, and ordered each other around, and maybe even pleaded with each other a bit," Kelsey said, staring into the depths of her drink. "But we've never really said how we feel about this marriage."

"You've said how you feel. You want a divorce." He gulped down a third of his drink.

His tone suggested he didn't believe she might have changed her mind. Hope flared in her breast, but was quickly doused as reality crashed down on her with devastating ruthlessness. "I overheard your conversation with Emerald that night," she admitted in a pained voice. "I wasn't that far behind you when I left your father's house. I caught up with you in the lane."

This clearly wasn't what he'd expected to hear. Jesse paused, staring at her in consternation, his drink halfway to his lips. "What did you determine from that illuminating discussion?" he asked flatly.

"That every rumor about you was probably based in truth. And then I thought of my father, and how his philandering nearly ruined my life, and even Jace's to some degree. And I felt—miserable."

"I see."

She could feel him pulling away from her. His brain was muddled. She didn't want to make things worse, but she couldn't deny what she knew to be the truth. "Did you love Emerald, Jesse?" she asked in a small voice, hoping in some absurd way that he'd admit he had.

"No."

"Or Alice, or any of them?"

He sighed and set down his glass on the desk, the rest of his drink untouched. "No."

"Do you think you're—capable of love?" Kelsey fought to get out, dying inside.

His blue gaze was somber, regretful. "No. Probably not. Not the way you mean. Is that what you want?"

"I think that's what every woman wants," Kelsey admitted sadly.

Jesse took a long breath, realizing with needle-sharp clarity that he'd dreaded this day because he'd known the truth would devastate her. He'd known it would be the end of their marriage. The simple truth would kill any chance they might have had.

"When I met you, you were a challenge, *Orchid.*" He stressed her alias with a faint smile. "And I wanted you, not Charlotte. Wanted you like a fire in my blood."

"Like all the rest of the women you've known," she said, the color draining from her face.

"Like a man wants a woman," he agreed.

Kelsey lifted her shoulders protectively, glancing away. "I think I wanted something more," she admitted. "Maybe not at first. I mean, you didn't even know my real name."

"When you turned out to be Kelsey Garrett, I thought you'd hoodwinked me into marriage. But I was wrong. You never wanted to marry me. It was a necessary evil, or so you thought. And now it's not what you want either."

"I want to be married to someone I love," she said in a voice so low he could scarcely hear her.

"You left Rock Springs to get away from the bonds of a forced marriage," Jesse said with near-painful accuracy. "You wanted freedom. A chance to find that someone to love all on your own. Unfortunately, I got in your way."

"Jesse . . ."

"Shhh." He smiled regretfully. "I'll sign those divorce papers tomorrow. I've got money set aside for you; you've got the passbook. And you can have whatever else you want. The house . . ." He glanced around the room as if viewing it for the first time. "I don't really give a damn."

"No, Jesse, that's not what I want—"

"I always told myself I wouldn't get involved with a *lady*. A society lady. I felt, with some rightfulness, that she would suck me dry financially, and be an albatross around my neck. But it isn't true with you," he added, seeing the misery in Kelsey's beautiful silvery eyes. "It was never true with you."

"I think we're working at cross purposes," she choked out desperately.

"You want to marry someone who'll love you. For better or worse. Richer or poorer. Till death do you part. Isn't that what you want?"

"Yes."

He crossed to her, staring down at her face, deep into her soul, for several long, distressing seconds, where Kelsey fought to tell him it didn't matter. She didn't care that he didn't love her. She *loved* him. But her damnable pride was like a rock in her throat, suffocating her, cutting off the truth.

"Good night and good-bye, Mrs. Danner," he said gently. "You were a truly remarkable wife."

# 22

The two forty-five train to Denver was late. Anxiously scanning the face of the rail station clock, Victor Flynne considered what would happen if Samuel Danner caught up with him before he could realize his travel plans. Victor's network of informants had been explicit about the youngest Danner's intensely focused campaign to learn his whereabouts. In fact, his informants had been all too eager to give Victor the news; in truth, the vicious, traitorous bastards had been downright smug. *Hopeful* wasn't even too strong a word.

So far none of them had given him away, but Victor had taken no chances. He'd been forced to live like a sewer rat these past few weeks to keep Samuel from catching him before he could get away.

Fury was a cold and constant companion. How *could* this happen to him again? Injustice beat inside his head, driving like a hammer. Once again he'd been forced from the life he knew by a *Danner*. Mary McKechnie Danner's death had been an accident—an *accident,* by God! Yet Samuel would never believe it. That bloodthirsty Danner spawn was just as ruthless and determined as his eldest brother,

Tremaine, and Victor would be as good as dead himself if Samuel ever caught up with him.

It was enough to give an innocent man nightmares.

Victor swallowed, wondering if his mouth would ever form spit again. He lay awake nights now, afraid to fall asleep, envisioning all the terrible nightmares he'd warned Pete about. Pete! That slimy cur! Pete had given him away. Pete was the only one who'd known the truth about Mary Danner's death.

Pete and Lacey Duprés.

Victor's lip curled in disgust. He'd misjudged Lacey also, but the woman was a coward. She'd turned and run at the first sniff of danger. Victor had thought her need for vengeance against Evanston Reevesworth was as great as Victor's own against the Danners. But no! The ugly old bitch had scurried away, frightened of the trouble she would be in if it ever were discovered her gala party had been instigated in part to lure Kelsey Danner into a trap.

Too bad Pete didn't manage to kill Kelsey that day, Victor thought, feeling very put-upon by his unhappy fate. Maybe that would have sent Jesse Danner thirsting for more vengeance against Montana Gray and kept Victor in the clear.

The unfairness of it was choking, galling! Remembering how polished and controlled he'd once been, Victor tasted bile in the back of his throat. He almost hoped Samuel Danner found his trail. He'd lead the bastard on a merry chase, and when it was over, Victor would be in control once more. Samuel was only one Danner, after all. Jesse Danner, for reasons Victor could only guess at, didn't seem to be involved in Samuel's single-minded revenge. He suspected it was because Samuel hadn't been completely honest with Jesse.

Typical Danner arrogance, Victor thought with a superior sniff. Samuel wanted Victor all to himself. And that would be Samuel's fatal mistake.

A rush of air and an ear-splitting whistle announced an arriving train. The black monster rushed into the station with a deafening roar. Victor leapt to his feet, clutching his briefcase, his only luggage, tightly in his hand. Inside the case were names and information, the remnants of a once-titanic blackmail industry, one Victor intended to resurrect once Samuel Danner was removed forever.

Victor shuffled into the center of a crowd of travelers, unable to prevent himself from a last glance over his shoulder. But there was no sign of the russet-haired devil chasing him.

Smiling to himself, Victor set his sights on the future. He would leave for a while. A few months, maybe a year. This time it wouldn't take ten years, by God! He'd murder all the Danners in their beds first. All he had to do was bide a little time, and put enough distance between himself and his past so that if Samuel finally found him, the youngest Danner would be dead months before word got back to the rest of that hornet's nest of a family.

"Where ya headed?" a friendly freckle-faced young man asked him as Victor dusted off his seat.

"East."

As far east as he could get, he thought, relief flooding through him as the great wheels of the locomotive began to circle, the train building up steam. London! Victor thought with sudden inspiration. He knew a fellow there. A goddamn blueblood. An earl with a pedigree long enough to choke a horse, and a voracious need for cash, no questions asked.

A good place for business. A great place.

And far enough away for Samuel Danner to seek vengeance on Victor's terms.


A chill wind blew through the trees and numbed Kelsey's hands as she sat beside Drake on the driver's seat. She clutched her shawl more closely to her shoulders, crumpling the papers folded in her right hand even more thoroughly than two weeks of worrying them had.

True to his word, Jesse had signed away their marriage. He'd handed her the papers that Samuel had reluctantly handed him. She'd stared at his bold scrawl for hour upon hour until she'd heard Irma whispering to Mrs. Crowley how "dreadful unhappy the poor missus is over the way that scoundrel broke her heart. Ah, but he's a handsome devil. Don't blame her for hopin' it would be different . . ."

*Handsome. Scoundrel. Devil.*

She'd certainly thought of Jesse in those terms. The Danner curse, he would declare sardonically anytime his particular charms were noted. Kelsey closed her eyes and drew a breath into pain-tightened lungs. She, Kelsey Orchid Garrett, keeper of her own heart, the dried-up spinster who was as cold and passionless as morning ashes, had fallen for those celebrated charms body and soul.

"Damn."

"Ma'am?" Drake asked, shooting her a glance in an anxious way.

"I'm fine, Drake."

She stared at the line of carriages and buggies traveling ahead of them to the downtown corner where Samuel's office building was located.

"Are you certain you wouldn't be more comfortable inside, ma'—Mrs. Danner?"

She smiled, knowing how difficult it was for Drake to unbend even that much. "I've spent half my life on a horse, Drake. Outside. Racing across fields, generally with a rifle as my companion. Riding inside a carriage still isn't my favorite way to travel."

There was silence for several blocks, then Drake worked up the courage to ask, "Will you be staying with the house, then—er—Mrs. Danner?"

Tears rose in her throat at his worried tone. "No," she murmured unsteadily.

At Samuel's office building she abandoned Drake without a word as to her intention. The loyal driver simply waited at the curb, as dedicated to Kelsey as he was to Jesse. This split in their marriage bothered him deeply, and unbeknownst to either Kelsey or Jesse, the servants had spent many hours together worrying over the fate of their new master and mistress, concurrent in their belief that the two young people were both too stubborn and full of pride to see that they were meant for each other.

Kelsey hesitated outside Samuel's office. She was angry

with Jesse for putting her in this position. No. She was angry at herself for putting her in this position!

She glanced down at the papers in her white-knuckled hands. With sudden fervor she ripped them straight down the middle, then ripped their halves, and fourths, until tiny shreds of paper scattered like rain to fall at her feet and drift across the waxed floor.

Drawing several deep breaths, Kelsey stared off into space. She'd won many battles by relying on a rifle or pistol as a means of defense. She'd also barricaded herself behind a facade of frigidity. For a woman who prided herself on taking control of her life, she'd certainly run away and fought from an inferior position enough times.

But it was time to face her feelings and do a new kind of battle. It would hurt terribly if he rejected her. Hurt a thousand times worse than being humiliated by Harrison in front of her whole hometown. Hurt more because she was far more vulnerable. Hurt more because she loved Jesse so desperately.

With a newfound determination, and a rollicking pulse, Kelsey retraced her steps down the narrow stairway that led to the first floor of Samuel's office building. On an impulse at the second floor landing she looked over the rail and spied a man's polished black shoes. Someone was waiting in the building foyer.

Slowing her steps, Kelsey held the stranger's gaze as her footsteps landed on the cracked marble floor of the street level. He didn't smile at her or approach her in any way. Through the open transom she could hear the beat of the city, and she thought about Drake.

She opened her mouth to call when the man suddenly struck like a cobra, grabbing her hair and clapping a hand over her mouth, taking her completely by surprise. Kelsey bit into his palm and drew blood. He hit her so hard her teeth rattled.

Then he hit her again and she went limp.

The blackened remains of what had once been Pacific Shipbuilders Ltd. looked like lonely skeletons in the fading twilight. Jesse stood beside Samuel and stared across the ruins of what could have been a thriving business.

Would he have had the courage and lack of conscience to actually burn this place down? he asked himself now. Would it have been a fitting revenge? Though he wanted Montana Gray to pay for his crimes, he saw with the clear vision of hindsight that the methods he'd chosen hadn't, and wouldn't have, ever worked.

The ending to his vengeance hadn't been quite satisfactory either. He felt frustrated and unsettled. He wanted something *more*. Some kind of finish. A fire and brimstone apocalypse to send Montana and his murdering ways straight to hell.

*Damn you, Kelsey.*

Jesse lifted his face to the cloud-covered sky, drawing the scent of charcoal and ashes deep into his lungs. He didn't want to lose her.

He already had lost her.

"I'm taking the train to Seattle tonight," Samuel said, dragging Jesse's thoughts back to the present. "The man who worked for Flynne—this Pete person—has a job there."

"Let Tremaine help you. Christ, let *me* help you," Jesse muttered in frustration.

Samuel didn't bother to respond. Jesse shot his brother a look, struck again, as he had been time and again over the past several weeks, how much Samuel had reverted to the quiet, cold, reserved stranger he'd been accused of being by Portland society. This was the Samuel from Rock Springs. The one who'd fought off Gainsborough with a rifle at age thirteen.

Something had drastically changed since Samuel had learned about Flynne's involvement, and now Jesse's little brother was as close-mouthed as a confessional priest.

"I'm leaving Portland too," Jesse said. "Might as well join you in Seattle."

"I don't want you to."

"What the hell is it, Samuel?" Jesse demanded in frustration.

Samuel shook his head and asked, "Why are you leaving Portland?"

"Because Montana's gone. Because my whole purpose for being here is finished."

*Because Kelsey's here*.

"Isn't Lila still in Portland?"

Jesse slid his brother a sideways glance. "So?"

"You said yourself, it isn't over. I was wondering what you planned to do about her."

"Now who's lusting for vengeance?" Jesse muttered, slapping his Stetson against his thigh to shake off some of the black dust that swirled with each fitful breeze. "I don't give a plug nickel what happens to Lila Gray."

Samuel kept his own counsel on the buggy ride back to his office building. He'd shut Jesse out as clearly as if he'd slammed a door in his face. They entered the lobby in shared silence, each consumed with his own dark thoughts, but as the door started to close, Jesse thought he heard someone on the street call his name.

He glanced at the open transom as Samuel mounted the stairs. The sounds of the city met his ears: the crackle of electricity and hum and clatter of the trolley; horses' hooves clip-clopping against cobblestones; people's voices.

With a shake of his head he mounted the stairs after his taciturn brother and was surprised to find Samuel standing outside his office, staring in puzzlement down at the pile of confetti-like squares of paper that littered the hallway.

"Where's Kelsey?" Samuel demanded tersely without looking up.

"How the hell should I know? At the house. Or at the Chamberlains, or God knows where else. I don't monitor her movements," Jesse reminded his brother flatly. Samuel knew the state of their marriage. He knew about the pending divorce. Hell, he'd drawn up the papers Jesse had signed and given to Kelsey. He also knew that for the past few weeks Kelsey and Jesse had practically closeted themselves in opposite corners of the house whenever they happened to be home at the same time, which wasn't often since Jesse had taken back his worm-infested apartment— a reminder of the good old days.

"These are your divorce papers," Samuel enlightened him, scooping up a handful of scraps.

"Let me see that!"

Jesse snatched up several pieces, enough to witness part of his own signature. "Who did this?" he demanded, already aware that it had to be Kelsey. His pulse beat heavily, thunder pounding inside his head.

"Looks like maybe she's changed her mind," drawled Samuel.

Jesse gently crushed the papers in his right fist. There had to be some other answer. "If she'd wanted the marriage to continue, she would have said something earlier."

"Did you give her any clue to how you feel?"

Jesse sent Samuel a scornful look. "She knows exactly how I feel."

"The hell she does!" Samuel exploded furiously, showing the first spark of emotion he had in weeks. "Because you're too damn stubborn to tell her. Have you ever told her you love her? No, of course you haven't. You don't believe in love."

Since Jesse had never told his brother his feelings on the subject, he was amazed and thunderstruck at Samuel's unerring accuracy.

"I've got a good idea about you, brother," Samuel said in the voice of a man who has long since lost patience with the situation. "You won't trust a woman to play fair. Well, some do. Kelsey does. And you know it, if you'd ever pay attention to your feelings long enough to see the truth.

"But Kelsey doesn't trust men. She certainly doesn't trust *you* to possess any deep feelings about *her*," Samuel hammered on. "So you don't believe in love and she doesn't believe you can love her. Stalemate. Except that you do love her, and if you told her, you might learn something about your wife: Behind that carefully built wall, she longs for you too. If you don't want a divorce," Samuel ordered, striking his index finger against Jesse's chest for emphasis, "then for God's sake, say so!"

"After two weeks of near complete silence, you certainly know how to speak a mouthful," Jesse drawled.

"That's all you can say? That's the extent of your feelings for Kelsey?"

Samuel's impatience gave Jesse pause. "No," he admitted through tight lips.

"Then what the hell are you doing here talking to me?"

They glared at each other. Jesse turned on his heel, furious with Samuel and himself. He needed air, or so he told himself, and he burst onto the street in full stride—and collided with another man's chest.

"Mr. Danner!" Drake cried in distress as Jesse held on to the smaller man's shoulders, righting him.

"What the hell are you doing here?" Jesse growled.

"It's Mrs. Danner. She disappeared inside hours ago, but hasn't come out." He darted a nervous glance toward the door that was closing behind Jesse. "Is she still at your brother's office?"

"Kelsey came here to see Samuel?" Jesse bit out.

"Yes, ssss—Mr.—Danner—Jesse," Drake fumbled in distress.

Samuel stepped onto the street, taking in the situation in a glance. "Something's happened?"

"Did you go into your office?" Jesse was terse. At Samuel's nod, he demanded, "Was there anyone inside? Kelsey?"

"My office was empty."

"Then . . . then . . ." Drake couldn't form the thought.

"Drake, take me back to the house," Jesse ordered tensely. To Samuel, he said, "You take the buggy. I'll pick it up at the train station."

"No, I'll help you. I can leave tomorrow. I want to make certain Kelsey's all right."

Jesse punched his index finger against Samuel's chest in direct imitation of his brother's arrogant actions. "You take care of your problems, I'll take care of mine. Kelsey's my wife. She's my responsibility. Besides, I *love* her," he added with sardonic mirth.

Samuel shook his head. "I never listened to you when we were kids. I'm not listening to you now."

"Jesus! Drake, let's go!" Jesse bellowed, jumping onto

the driver's seat of the carriage and grabbing for the reins as Drake scrambled up beside him.

"I'll go to the Chamberlains," Samuel said, striding toward the buggy. "If she's there, I'll send her home within the hour. If not, I'll take other measures."

"What other measures?" Jesse cracked the reins against the team of grays harnessed to the carriage.

"I have friends who won't let it happen again," Samuel muttered cryptically.

Jesse didn't hear the rest. The grays jolted forward. Drake hung on to the seat with both hands, his face a mask of horror at the reckless way Jesse drove the team through the streets.

By the time they reached the house, Drake was perspiring freely and when Jesse helped him to the ground he leaned against the carriage for support. Jesse strode inside the house.

*"Kelsey? Kelsey!"*

The place was a tomb. Irma and Mrs. Crowley appeared from the back of the house to stare at him blankly. No, Mrs. Danner hadn't returned since she left with Drake, they assured him. No, she'd left no message. *No, no, no!*

"But you received a message, sir," Irma managed to squeak out when she'd collected her scattered wits. "An invitation. Hand-delivered by special messenger. To Hathaway House."

Hathaway House. Jesse froze. Lila's one-time residence, the home she and Montana had shared five years earlier, the last remnant of her once-wealthy and prestigious family.

Jesse turned on his booted heel and stalked from the house without another word.

Hathaway House had been freshly painted. There was a garland of dried fall flowers adorning the front door, and through the three diamond-shaped windows he could see the veined-pink marble foyer and the staircase to the second floor. The staircase to the cellar was beneath the sweeping stairway. Remembering, he could practically smell the dust and mildew and scent of his own blood.

He opened the door without knocking and stood at the

bottom of the steps, envisioning Lila's bedroom. A maid appeared, dressed in a black uniform with a starched white collar. She gaped at him.

"Lila's expecting me," Jesse said, mounting the stairs, dread creeping along his spine as memories assailed him.

He turned toward her bedroom by rote. The door was slightly ajar and inside he could see the same rose wallpaper and pink pillows. Pushing the door wider, he encountered Lila's somewhat startled gaze as she sat at her vanity, a rope of sapphires held up to her neck, ready to clasp.

Her lips parted. "Jesse!"

"Someone sent me an invitation. You, or your husband?"

"Didn't you read it?" she asked, her breath fluttering in her throat. At his deadly silence she swooped her lashes over her cheeks and said softly, "I was afraid that—I didn't really expect you to come."

Crossing the expanse of thick carpet between them, Jesse lifted the sapphires from her nerveless hands. The last time he'd fastened a necklace around a woman's neck it had been Kelsey's. Fighting back the desire to choke Lila, he adjusted the clasp, meeting her gaze in the vanity mirror. Her blue eyes were wary. She didn't trust him any more than he trusted her.

"I've been doing some thinking," he said, fighting to keep his loathing for her out of his voice. Lightly, he rested his hands on her smooth shoulders. "Your husband would like nothing better than to put a bullet in my back, but he can't take the chance. Because I've got him by the throat."

Lila's own throat was long and white. "You broke him, Jesse. You did it." She smiled. "All that money—you got it from him, didn't you? The rest went up in smoke with Pacific Shipbuilders, and you *did it!*"

"He needs a bargaining chip," Jesse went on. "Something that matters enough to me to make me willing to trade."

"Trade?" Lila asked blankly. "Trade for—the money?" She looked stricken.

"The hell with the money. He wants my evidence." Jesse's fingers touched the sapphires flowing against her skin. They were cold. Blue. Lila's favorite color. "And I think he's got my wife as a bargaining chip. You're going to tell me where she is."

Lila was affronted. "I don't know what you're talking about."

"Yes, you do." Jesse twisted the necklace around his fingers, pulling it ever so gently up to her white throat. "Maybe your memory's just a bit faulty, Lila. Think hard."

Her fingers scrabbled for the necklace. She clutched it desperately. "Jesse, don't. Please." Her chest heaved and light refracted off the sparkling blue stones.

"Where is she?"

"I've already told you I have no idea what you mean! If you can't keep track of your—"

Her words ended with a jerk of the sapphires. Gasping, horrified, she gazed up at him beseechingly. Relaxing the pressure, Jesse said, "He's got her, doesn't he?"

Lila coughed in exaggerated pain. Her eyes flashed with hurt and anger. "I don't know."

"Don't make me hurt you. I will."

She believed him. Initially she thrilled to the prospect, but something made her hesitate. He had the same look of determination Montana sometimes wore. "I don't know where she is, but Montana's back in Portland," she added hurriedly before Jesse could increase the pressure. "Honestly," she added in a vexed voice when he relinquished his hold on the gems. "You're scaring me."

Twisting on the stool, she faced him. "Tell me where Montana is, Lila," Jesse ordered, his patience all but gone.

A smile teased her lips. "Oh, come on now, Jesse." She slid her hands up his chest. "All you have to know is that he isn't here."

Jesse pulled her hands off his chest. "Your vanity amazes even me, Lila."

From far below, a door softly closed. The cellar door. Men's booted footsteps slapped across the marble foyer and headed for the stairs.

"Montana?" Jesse asked sardonically.

"No . . . it's Gardner . . . and Al . . ." she burbled.

"Jesse, don't leave. I'll stop them. I'll say you've left! You can hide!"

Jesse turned in disgust, meeting Al and Gardner at the top of the stairs. Anticipation lit their mean, crevassed faces.

"Mr. Danner, you don't learn too good," Al said with an ugly smile.

"Oh, yes, I do." Jesse pulled Kelsey's derringer from the pocket of his jacket and aimed it at Gardner's wide chest. "It's a Danner curse."

She'd left the house without her gun, lulled into the belief that Montana was gone and she was safe, too upset over delivering the divorce papers to check the chamber and put the damn thing back in her reticule.

Her cheek hurt. He'd hit her hard and now she lay against a plankwood floor where the nails were working their way out of the wood. Her line of vision encountered two pairs of boots and a polished set of men's shoes: her abductor who was complaining bitterly about the teeth marks she'd left in his palm.

"She's awake," an unfamiliar voice said.

"Put her on her feet."

That voice she recognized: Montana Gray's.

Kelsey's head cleared as if she'd been given smelling salts. Rough hands pulled her to feet that danced beneath her as if detached from her ankles. With an effort she balanced on her feet. Her black skirt was covered with dust, and the once-white sleeve of her blouse was gray and torn.

"Your husband's been bedding my wife," Montana said emotionlessly.

The sting of his words was followed by the realization that he wanted only to hurt her. Kelsey didn't gratify him with an answer. Instead, she glanced around, trying to discern her whereabouts. This room looked like the back room of a bar. Briny's? No. She couldn't smell the river, and the wood paneling was rich and refined even if it looked decayed from neglect; Briny's had been roughly hewn, a sailor's haven. She surmised she was closer to the heart of the city, probably in a part of town she generally avoided.

"Did you hear me?" Montana demanded.

"You said my husband's been bedding your wife," Kelsey responded calmly. "I'm not surprised. And if any of the rest of you would be lucky enough to have a woman"—she passed her eye over the other men in the room, her tone suggesting this was entirely doubtful—"he's probably proved to them what a real lover is like as well."

Silence rained down upon them. Kelsey fought the trembling in her hands and the pain in her cheek and concentrated on her false bravado. It had taken a lot to make that speech, but it had been even more effective than she'd hoped for. The other two men in the room, the men who'd captured her and another she'd never seen before, looked as if they'd been thoroughly slapped.

Montana almost smiled. "Relax, my friends. Mrs. Danner has a sense of humor, that's all. I believe that sense of humor's about to fail you, however. You see, your husband is dead. Jesse Danner is *dead,*" he reiterated with satisfaction. "I killed him myself."

Kelsey kept her gaze trained on his drooping eye. She didn't believe him, but her heart leapt in fear nonetheless.

Montana's chair creaked as he shifted his bulk to his feet. He stood right in front of Kelsey. She could smell garlic on his breath. "I stuck a knife in his throat right here." He touched the hollow of her neck. "And I waited till he stopped breathing. Then I threw him in the Willamette, where he should have stayed five years ago."

"You're lying."

He slowly wagged his head from side to side, watching her.

The edges of the room seemed to recede. For a moment Kelsey almost believed him. *It's not true, Jesse. It's not true! I love you. You're all right. I know you are, and when I get out of here, I'm going to tell you how I feel. I promise.*

"And now I need something from you," Montana went on. "A piece of evidence your husband threatened me with. He followed me to San Francisco just to make certain I knew it existed. I think you know where it is, or even *if* it is . . ."

She was quaking inside. *Don't show it. Don't show it.*

*Keep calm. For Jesse.* She didn't believe him. She *didn't* believe him.

Montana's burly hand cupped her swollen cheek. Revolted, Kelsey maintained a costly outer calm. "Turnabout's fair play. He's bedded my wife. I'll bed his. I owe him that."

"I would rather be dead than have you lay one dirty finger on me," Kelsey said in a surprisingly strong voice.

"Looks like I'm going to have a fight on my hands," Montana said on a chuckle. He jerked his head, motioning his thugs to leave. They disappeared reluctantly, hovering by the door, enthralled with Montana's cat-and-mouse game. He shot them a furious look and they were gone.

Kelsey measured the distance to the door. She looked past her captor to every shadowed corner and dim recess of the room. Montana was strong. Too strong for her to overpower, but she'd been in tough situations before, and she'd be damned if she'd give in easily. He might win, but he'd sure as hell remember the battle. With a longing nearing physical pain, she wished for her derringer.

"Where's your husband's evidence, Mrs. Danner?"

"There is no evidence," Kelsey said truthfully, never changing expression.

"You're as foolhardy as he is. If I have to break your arms to get the truth, I will!" So saying, he clamped his meaty fists around her upper arms, squeezing until she had to bite her lip to keep from crying out. "Tell me where it is. Tell me!" He ground his mouth down on hers. Kelsey's head swam, and she broke into a sweat of revulsion.

She was like a wooden doll in his arms. Montana's eyes narrowed. She could almost hear the churning of his brain. "Your husband didn't cry for mercy either," he said. "He fought. He was tough."

Her lashes swept her cheek, regret tearing through her. She *didn't* believe him!

"A hero to the end," Montana whispered nastily. "His last words were, 'I love you, Kelsey.'"

"Mr. Gray," she said through colorless lips, her eyes opening to gaze into his with a cold hate that even brought

Montana up short. "My husband isn't dead. You just told me so yourself."

Gardner and Al liked to talk a lot more when they weren't looking down the barrel of a gun, Jesse discovered as he stretched the arms of first one, then the other, and lashed them to the same beams used when he was their captive five years earlier. Tightening the ropes, he bound them face-to-face, about five feet apart. Jesse then sat on a chunk of fir used for a chopping block and leaned his chin on his hand, curbing his own mounting impatience and dread.

"You know, there was a time when I looked different," Jesse said reflectively. "My nose was different. And my cheekbones. Even my jaw."

Gardner and Al didn't speak. Jesse could see the way their muscles strained against the ropes. He gave them thirty minutes to crack. He prayed Kelsey had thirty minutes left.

"Then I ran into some trouble. It's a habit of mine," he confided. "I got in trouble with a lady's husband, and he told his friends to take care of me. Which they did." Jesse climbed to his feet. Kelsey's derringer hung slackly from his right hand, as if he'd somehow forgotten it. Gardner and Al hadn't, however; their eyes kept darting nervously back and forth to the gun that swung negligently by Jesse's side.

"They thrashed the living tar out of me," Jesse said. "Threw me in the river and left me for dead. Don't that beat all?" he drawled.

"You won't get away with this, Danner," Gardner said in a thin, scratchy voice. His scar was purple against his white cheek. "Lila's gone for help."

"Lila is tied to her bed. A favorite position of hers," Jesse added sardonically. "And she forgot to tell the maid it was her day off. In fact, the entire household staff is now gone." He tucked the barrel of the gun under Al's chin. "You know, you look a lot like the fellow who broke my jaw and my nose." He pulled back the hammer, easing his thumb in the space between.

335

Al was sweating like a pig and smelling just as bad. "They're at a bar downtown," he burst out. "Near Chinatown. You know where."

"Al!" Gardner blurted out in fright.

"The name of this establishment?" Jesse asked, wiggling his thumb just the tiniest bit.

"Jesus Christ!" Al was gasping so hard he could scarcely summon air into his lungs to breathe. "The—the—the—"

"Come on, Al." Jesse was a model of patience.

"The Silver Nickel!"

Jesse jerked his thumb free. The hammer clicked harmlessly against the chamber. Al sank to his knees, hanging from his wrists, blubbering like a baby. An acrid stench filled the room. Gardner had passed out, a puddle of urine forming on the dirt floor below him.

Jesse exchanged Al's dirty black hat for his Stetson, a meager disguise but all he had time for. Harrison was going to have to stop giving him gifts, he determined regretfully as he propped his Stetson on Al's head.

"You'd better hope she's still alive," Jesse told them in a dire voice. "If she's not . . ."

He left the thought unfinished.

# 23

The Silver Nickel was on a desolate corner, mixed in among Chinese laundries and outdoor produce vendors. The dregs of both societies, whites and Asians, collected there, and the thought that Kelsey was somewhere behind those mean-looking walls made Jesse's blood run cold.

It was a prime location for nefarious deeds. The front doors were at an angle to the street. The side door, to the back rooms, was certain death for the hapless victim who

into the room, dropping on one knee, the derringer held between his hands with deadly intent.

The sight that met his eyes made him go weak with relief. His wife, her hair wild to her waist, her gray eyes measuring Montana like cold steel, her blouse torn and one cheek swollen and faintly blue as if she'd been struck, was sighting down the barrel of a rifle aimed point-blank at Montana, who was lying on his back amid shattered glass and an overturned table.

"I will kill you if you twitch a muscle," she told him, hazarding Jesse only one small glance. "Mister, you'd better leave by the count of ten," she said through her teeth to Jesse. "Or you're next."

"Al! Al!" Montana gasped out. "Get her! Hit her!"

Very carefully Jesse tilted back the black hat that had shadowed his face. Montana's already chalky face turned alabaster. Kelsey darted a sideways glance at him, which turned to a double take, the expression on her face one of relief and shining love.

"Jesse," she choked out, pressing the barrel of the gun tight to Montana's chest when he suddenly moved. Montana lay still, his arms and legs spread-eagle, his gaze riveted on the rifle.

Kelsey's hands started to shake, as did her knees. Reaction hit with such overwhelming force she felt dizzy. Jesse was alive and well and here to help! She wanted to tell him she loved him. Now, before it was too late. But she couldn't find her voice.

"You're right where I want you," Jesse told Montana softly.

"She won't pull the trigger," Montana sneered.

"I wouldn't be so certain. I've seen what she's capable of."

"He left the rifle against the wall," Kelsey said, feeling as if she were in a trance. "I don't think he believed I would grab for it."

"A costly mistake," observed Jesse with some degree of humor.

"Her hands are shaking," Montana said through dry lips. "She's shaking. She won't do it."

Jesse smiled coldly. "Go ahead and pull the trigger, Kelsey. It'll be self-defense. I'll see to it."

Montana choked unintelligibly.

Kelsey could scarcely think straight. "Jesse . . . ?"

"No!" Montana shrieked, his eyes bulging as her finger tightened on the trigger. "No, for God's sake! *No!*"

"Hold it," Jesse ordered Kelsey tautly, realizing Montana's nerve had finally broken. So had his daring wife's, he deduced with a pang of regret. "Relax, my love. Hand me the rifle." Tucking the derringer in his belt, he added in a snarl to Montana, "Get on your feet and lead the way out of here. Do it now, before I change my mind."

Montana stumbled onto his knees, staggering to his trembling legs. He stared in shock at the two of them.

A commotion sounded outside. Jesse pinned Montana against the wall as the door suddenly flew open and Samuel burst inside, his gaze slicing from Kelsey to Jesse to Montana and back again.

"Okay," he said to the group of men rushing in behind him. "Looks like it's over already."

Two hours later Kelsey sat on the settee in the drawing room of her home, a cold compress held to her throbbing cheek. Jesse had explained about Lila, and the men he'd left tied up in her cellar, and how Samuel had followed his tracks after learning Kelsey hadn't been to the Chamberlains, stopping only long enough to ask Cedric McKechnie and a band of his friends to join in the fight. Samuel and Jesse had then delivered Montana to the authorities, and had listed complaints that ranged from murder to kidnapping to attempted rape. Montana's paid "friends" might be among those Samuel and Jesse had talked to, but his fate was in the hands of the law now, and Jesse felt confident that one way or another, Montana's stranglehold on Portland business would be broken. Nell's death, Zeke's death, and Jesse's near death would be hard to put down to a series of unfortunate accidents by even the most gullible, or grafting, on the police force, and when Samuel had suggested Judge Barlowe be excluded from Montana's case, owing to the fact that they were friends and had been seen together numerous times at numerous parties and benefits, the chance for Montana to win in the courts was greatly lessened.

"Personally, I'd rather see him lynched," Jesse finished as Irma came in with a silver teapot and several china cups. Jasmine tea, Kelsey noted. A gift from Agatha after her first brush with death.

"And Lila? What will happen to her?"

"The balance of Montana's money has been seized pending this investigation." Jesse shrugged. "She's facing poverty. Knowing Lila, she'll find some way to keep herself in jewels and furs."

"You're very cynical about women." Kelsey lay back on the couch, cushioning her head.

"Not all women."

Closing her eyes, Kelsey let the warmth of his voice wash over her in welcome waves. "He told me you were dead. That he'd killed you. I didn't want to believe him, but a part of me did." Her voice lowered to a strangled whisper. "I couldn't help it and then I thought—I thought what it would be like if it were true, and I didn't want to think about it. I couldn't. I was afraid—"

"I'm not dead."

"I know. I know." She nodded quickly, fighting to cover up her emotion. "Montana told me you weren't."

"He told you I wasn't?" Jesse's brows blunted in surprise.

"He told me that your last words were, 'I love you, Kelsey,' and I knew then that it was a lie."

Silence fell like a curtain. Kelsey's emotions were so raw she couldn't look at him. She didn't want him to feel sorry for her. That wasn't what she'd meant.

"Kelsey . . ." Jesse reached for her hand, his tone tender.

"Oh, Jesse." The tears she'd fought back most of her life seemed destined to fall regardless of how desperately she wished them away. This was the worst moment. A time when she needed to be strong and in control. A time to state her feelings, but without the drama she knew would send him away from her.

One sparkling tear slid over the hill of her cheek. Jesse's blue eyes tracked its progress, then he gently smoothed it aside with his thumb, gazing down at her through emotion-filled eyes.

"I love you, Jesse," she managed to choke out. "I promised myself I'd tell you the truth. I love you. I always have."

"You always have?" he asked with an amused lift of his brow.

"Don't tease me now. I can't bear it."

His expression changed and he looked regretful. Kelsey panicked. She closed her eyes against the rejection she knew was coming.

"I was wrong about not being able to love," he said. "I've spent a hell of a day getting accustomed to the idea. It's an entirely new experience, and not a very comfortable one."

She opened one eye, gazing up at him in puzzlement and distrust.

A rueful smile touched the corner of his mouth. "I love you, Kelsey," he said soberly, truthfully. "I don't want a divorce."

"Jesse . . ." Kelsey couldn't believe her ears.

"I've never met another woman like you," he went on. "One whose interest in firearms surpasses her interest in needlepoint, or gossip, or childbearing. Yet, you're not interested in vengeance."

His gaze lowered tenderly to her inviting lips. "You're what I want. What I've always wanted. No woman has ever treated me with less respect and with more honesty. You're not a society lady, yet you have more grace than the lot of them. You're a renegade." Burying his face in her fragrant hair, he muttered hoarsely, *"And I love you."*

Kelsey melted against him, shocked and thrilled and utterly humbled that her dreams had been answered, that the one thing she'd never, ever believed she could obtain had been handed over with such sweet selflessness.

Kelsey's tears flowed with happiness and she grinned against the warm, musky-scented skin of his neck. "I meant what I said, Jesse Danner. I've *always* loved you.

Even when I was a skinny kid without a lick of sense. I loved you even then."

Jesse slowly drew back to look into his wife's smiling, tear-stained face. "No, you didn't."

"Yes, I did. The scandalous tales about you were romantic. And then when I saw you again, I wanted to hate you, but I couldn't. There you were . . ." She shrugged lightly, her eyes shining, her bottom lip trembling. "The only man I ever loved."

"Oh, *Kelsey!*" He squeezed her close, reveling in the feeling that somehow, for reasons he couldn't begin to understand, they'd been granted each other.

"I tore up the divorce papers. I left them in the hall outside Samuel's office."

"I know." His voice was muffled.

"I was so afraid this wouldn't happen. That you would leave and I'd have to live without you."

He shook his head, kissing the slope of her chin fervently, as if she were a gift he'd been unexpectedly given. "I wouldn't live without you."

"Jesse . . ."

"Hmmm?"

Kelsey cradled his handsome face between her palms, her silvery eyes shining with passion and happiness. "I was wrong about one thing too. I *do* like the way you say my name."

He laughed, kissing her upturned nose, then the sweetness of her lips, then the shadowy curve of her lowered lashes. "Good," was his drawling answer as he slowly drew his wife, the wife he loved fully and completely, into the shelter of his arms and helped her forget anything but the touch and feel and love of the man who was her husband: Jesse Danner, Rock Springs's most scandalous, notorious womanizer whose heart had been captured by the only woman strong enough, passionate enough, and sweet enough to make him believe in the power of love.

"Kelsey Orchid Garrett Danner," he whispered.

# — The Bicyclist's Guide —
## to the
# Southern Berkshires

5/2/93

alec,

Happy Cycling!

Steve

# The Bicyclist's Guide to the
# Southern Berkshires

## Steve Lyons

Freewheel Publications
P.O. Box 2322
Lenox, MA 01240

Freewheel Publications
P.O. Box 2322
Lenox, MA 01240

Photographs by Steve Lyons and others as noted.
Maps by Charlotte Zanecchia
Cover designed by Deirdre Antes
Book designed by Michael Vuksta
Copyfitting by Eileen M. Clawson, Custom Typography
Edited by Kali Lew

Library of Congress Catalog Card Number: 92-71085

ISBN 0-9632585-5-9

Printed in the United States of America

Bill Raymond

# BERKSHIRE BICYCLING BUDDIES

*"When I see an adult on a bicycle, I do not despair for the future of the human race."*

— H. G. Wells

# ACKNOWLEDGEMENTS

Well, lots of folks had input on this book. I want to thank them all and I'll start with the Carleton brothers: Dave, John and Frank. They reintroduced me to cycling as an adult about 13 years ago. I had the good fortune to be living in the same house with them at the time, and many offers to go out riding came my way. I resisted their enthusiasm at first but gave in when they generously offered to put a bike together for me out of good spare parts they'd accrued from upgrading their cycles over the years. That bike has thousands of miles on it now and I'm still riding it (even though my "tech-weenie" biking buddies rib me about it). Next, hats off to Rudi (Fred) Peirce, master bike trip planner/co-ordinator, for the superb male-bonding, overnight rides he puts together each summer, and for finding great places to eat on the road. Barbara Edison encouraged me to go ahead and do the book when I was sitting on the fence vacillating. Her light-hearted optimism pushed me over the edge. My good friend Eric Knudsen rekindled the natural joy of exploring I'd lost somehow over the years since my boyhood. (Peeling off on side roads just to see where they'd go led me to many of the "special attractions" in this book.) He gave me excellent feedback on the manuscript and pointed out ways it could be improved, as did his wife Connie. My friends Britt Fanney, Betsey Hallihan, Dane Silcox, Mort Davis, David Sands and Paul Carleton also read the manuscript and improved it with their comments.

Kali (Karen) Lew helped me clean up the manuscript with her excellent editing skills, and showed me how to find my way around inside my Macintosh computer when the territory was unfamiliar and overwhelming. She is a real pal, and I thank her for the excitement and childish glee we shared while working on *The Bicyclist's Guide*. I admire the boldness of her lifestyle, and I wish her the best as she continues her exploring, in the Berkshires and beyond. The manuscript was further refined by Pepper Trietley and Carol McGlinchey who did the proofreading. Much thanks to Charlotte Zanecchia, who drew all the maps and managed to do it gracefully between her community outreach work for Mahaiwe Harvest Community Supported Agriculture at Sunways Farm in Housatonic, and raising a family with four young boys. Michael Vuksta designed the book. His sense of humor blends the absurd and the obvious, and we had many hearty laughs working together. I'm grateful for his friendship and his enthusiasm for the project. Thanks to Eileen Clawson for fitting the copy to the design. Glenn Zaderecki and Harriet Miekeljohn supported me with good-natured encouragement and valuable, inside knowledge of the printing trade. Thanks also to Gerry White and Mark Pugsley for their excellent darkroom work with the photographs and to Louis Ravez for the "fun-time" captioning sessions.

And last but not least, I want to thank all my cycling buddies, some of whom appear in photos in this book, for many happy hours of free-wheeling in the Berkshires.

# TABLE OF CONTENTS

# TABLE OF CONTENTS

# TABLE OF CONTENTS

## Chapter Four (continued):

# TABLE OF CONTENTS

## Chapter Four (continued):

Colonel Ashley House
Mission House
Oldest Covered Bridge in Massachusetts
West Cornwall Covered Bridge
Indian Burial Ground
Nathaniel Hawthorne's Little Red House
Beckley Furnace
General Stores

# Southern Berkshires Map

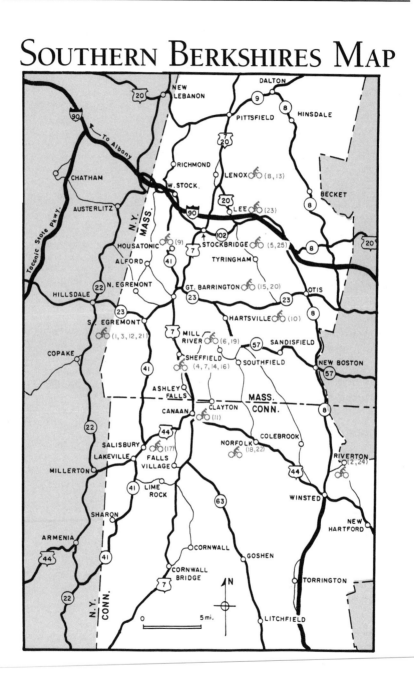

# TOUR/RATING CHART

| Tour # | Rating | Distance (miles) | Time (hours) | Start |
|---|---|---|---|---|
| 1 | easy | 15.3 | 1–1½ | Sheffield |
| 2 | easy | 8.6 | ½–1 | Riverton |
| 3 | easy | 11.2 | ¾–1¼ | South Egremont |
| 4 | easy | 11.7 | ¾–1½ | Sheffield |
| 5 | easy | 6.0 | ½–1 | Stockbridge |
| 6 | easy | 16.6 | 1–1½ | Mill River |
| 7 | easy | 24.6 | 1½–2½ | Sheffield |
| 8 | mod | 5.8 | ½–¾ | Lenox |
| 9 | mod | 14.2 | 1–1½ | Housatonic |
| 10 | mod | 30.5 | 1¾–3 | Hartsville |
| 11 | mod | 17.2 | 1¼–2¼ | Canaan |
| 12 | mod | 9.4 | ½–1 | South Egremont |
| 13 | mod | 17.0 | 1–2 | Lenox |
| 14 | mod | 35.2 | 2½–4 | Sheffield |
| 15 | mod | 11.4 | ¾–1¾ | Great Barrington |
| 16 | mod | 38.6 | 2½–4 | Sheffield |
| 17 | mod | 31.4 | 2–4½ | Salisbury |
| 18 | mod | 8.4 | ½–1 | Norfolk |
| 19 | mod | 16.0 | 1–2½ | Mill River |
| 20 | chal | 27.0 | 1½–2½ | Great Barrington |
| 21 | chal | 24.4 | 1½–2½ | South Egremont |
| 22 | chal | 15.8 | 1–2 | Norfolk |
| 23 | chal | 27.4 | 2–3½ | Lee |
| 24 | chal | 38.4 | 2½–4 | Riverton |
| 25 | chal | 106.0 | 7 hrs–3 days | Stockbridge |

*Generally, you can ride at least three times as long (in time) as your average training ride. If you've been cycling regularly for several months, use this rule of thumb to estimate the maximum distance you can currently handle.*

—*"Ride Longer and Stronger," Bicycling Magazine*

# INTRODUCTION

One spring morning, I awoke early and looked out the window. A brilliant sunrise was topping the silhouetted October Mountain range to the east. It was my "day off," and, with all the joy and anticipation of an eight-year-old on Saturday morning, I dressed, pulled my road bike off its hook, stuffed a couple of muffins and a banana in my bike pack, filled my water bottle and wheeled out of my home and onto the road. Soon, I was pedaling through the dawn shadows toward the valley to the south. The hum of the tires on the pavement vibrated up through the bike like the purr of a cat. The air felt fresh and clean on my face as my body began to warm from the exercise.

An hour later I was coasting down a road that follows the Konkapot River. To my left, just off the road, the fast water seemed to match my rambling pace. Golden sunlight from the rising sun played on the rocks and among the riffles, as hand-sized leaves on the maple branches overhead waved with the gentle breeze. The birches in their whiteness seemed to step forward out of the shadows of the firs and hemlocks.

I realized I hadn't seen a car or a person along this country lane in quite some time. It seemed everyone was elsewhere — busy with the "doing-ness""of life — the road, the river, the valley, and this magnificent day belonged to me alone.

Just then, I rounded a bend and came upon three white-tailed deer in a farmer's field. They ambled easily, single-file, along the stone fence row, then bounded, sleek and graceful, across the road in front of me. I let out my breath and laughed as they disappeared among the trees.

I continued wheeling over the countryside at a comfortable 15-miles-per-hour clip, passing old, weathered farm houses and horses grazing in the fields. I worked up a good sweat climbing the twisting turns of Hatchery Road, breezed through the one-store town of Monterey, crested the hill north of town, and downshifted for the mile-long descent through the forest into Tyringham Valley.

An hour later, I pulled off the road at Cold Spring. The water, lively and crisp, went down easily. I gulped my fill, topped off my water bottle, and splashed my face. All right!

Back in the saddle, I ate up 25 more miles of valley road around Beartown Mountain before stopping at Umpachene Falls for a swim. If you had been sunning on the rocks along the cascades you'd have heard my hoots of delight when I plunged into the pool below the falls.

As I sat on a boulder drying off in the sun, I thought, "Why not share this with others? There must be plenty of cyclists who would enjoy riding this country as much as I do."

Well . . . I mulled it over. And I continued thinking about it after I finished my ride. Why not, indeed? I'd been exploring the Berkshires by bike for the last nine years: I'd ridden thousands of miles, with buddies and alone. I knew the scenic, untrafficked roads, the challenging hills, and the long, open flats. I knew of lake beaches and hidden swimming holes. I knew springs, fountains, and faucets for water. I knew safe places to park a car. I even knew a few good places for serious carbohydrate-loading! Why not put it all together and share it? *Why not write a book?*

Yeah, great idea. But my life was filled with obligations. Where would I get the time?

Unbeknownst to me, the universe was conspiring for the production of this *Bicyclist's Guide to the Southern Berkshires*. Several months after my original inspiration, a major lifestyle shift gave me the time I needed. With the time and desire, it was a only a matter of getting it all down on paper.

However, once started, I realized cyclists could use information other than just the routes and scenic attractions. They might want to know where to find a good bike shop or organized rides and races, where to stay, weather considerations, etc. This meant research — and I did it.

Everything I could find, culled and selected, is in the book you're holding.

## How the tours are rated

Using this book, picking a tour to match your fitness and skill level is easy. Each tour in the *Bicyclist's Guide to the Southern Berkshires* is rated by degree of difficulty: easy, moderate, or challenging. To establish these ratings, I measured the total distance climbed on each route — after all, the hardest part on any ride is the climbing. Physical fitness, stamina, experience, and technique separate the beginner from the accomplished athlete-cyclist, and these attributes are brought into stark relief when the rider meets the hill.

I used an Avocet 50 Altimeter cyclocomputer as my measuring tool. It accurately measures the distance each time the bike climbs, adding all the measurements to give a total at the end of the ride. The total feet climbed divided by the number of miles gives a "climb-per-mile" figure. This is an excellent, objective measurement of a route's difficulty.

Tours with a 0 to 40 feet-per-mile climb are rated "easy"; those with 40 to 60 feet-per-mile climbed are considered "moderate"; and tours of 60 feet-per-mile (or more) climbed are rated "challenging." A tour's distance was *not* used to determine the degree of difficulty. Thus, there are "easy" tours varying from six to 24 miles and "moderate" and "challenging" rides as short as six miles. In the case of a tour with long stretches of flat, moderately rolling, or downhill terrain with one or two hunker-down-and-stoke inclines — a route which requires more conditioning and technique than a rating of "easy" would indicate — I gave the ride a more difficult rating and explained why in the tour description. I've also given an estimated time range for each ride. It's intended as a general guide, as cyclists have different styles, speeds, and interests. If you're going for a fast, no-stop ride, figure on the shortest time; use the longest time if you like to stop for rests or sightseeing.

**What's in this book**

If you're a beginning or intermediate cyclist, this book offers a variety of easy to moderate rides, both long and short. Scattered throughout the book are tips from professional cyclists, which you can use to develop your style, skill, and endurance. Then choose progressively more demanding tours as you become a stronger biker.

If you are a racer-in-training, triathlete, or an athlete who enjoys challenges, check out the cycling course for the Josh Billings Runaground Triathlon and the Manu-Sudama Century-Plus, as well as the Bash Bish–Breezy Hill and Tyringham Valley loops.

The Tour Chart lists each tour's rating, distance and point of origin. You can start any tour at its stated beginning or anywhere along its route; the directions and maps make it possible to jump right in at any point.

In the "Special Attractions" chapter are descriptions and locations of places you might like to stop for a swim, picnic, or sightseeing. These range from the likes of Bash Bish Falls to the Norman Rockwell Museum. The tours that pass each special attraction are listed with the site's description.

If you want to find an organized ride, a race, or a good county map or need information about bike rentals, a good bike shop, or local cycling clubs, look to the "Resources" chapter. You can get the low-down on Berkshire climate in "When to Ride." This chapter also includes phone numbers for the latest Berkshire weather forecasts and tips for catching the autumn–color season.

If you are coming from somewhere beyond the Berkshires, the chapter, "How to Get to the Southern Berkshires," can help you make your way via several modes of transportation. Telephone numbers of all the transportation services are included, as are tips for transporting your bike. And accommodations — from campgrounds to plush country inns — are listed in "Places to Stay."

I scattered quotes from Southern Berkshire personalities, and others, throughout the book. I got a kick out of them and thought you might, too.

I hope you enjoy using this book and find the information helpful and satisfying. If you know of a Southern Berkshire cycling event, new route, place to eat, or other bike-touring-related information you'd like to pass on for future editions of this book, drop me a line. I can be reached at the following address.

Happy cycling!

Steve Lyons
Freewheel Publications
P.O. Box 2322
Lenox, MA 01240

# How to Get to the Southern Berkshires

# How to Get to
# the Southern Berkshires

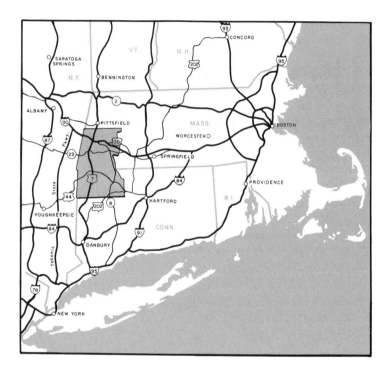

## BY CAR

The chart below shows driving times and mileages to Sheffield, Massachusetts, which is located at approximately the middle of the Southern Berkshires.

| City of Origin | Driving Time | Miles |
|---|---|---|
| Albany | 1 1/4 hrs | 67 |
| Boston | 3 hrs | 142 |
| Hartford | 1 1/4 hrs | 50 |
| New Haven | 1 1/2 hrs | 80 |
| Montreal | 5 1/2 hrs | 295 |
| New York City | 2 3/4 hrs | 135 |
| Philadelphia | 4 1/4 hrs | 215 |
| Springfield | 1 hr | 45 |
| Washington, DC | 6 3/4 hrs | 335 |

**From Manhattan:** Take Major Deegan Expressway or Henry Hudson Parkway to Saw Mill River Parkway. Proceed to Taconic Parkway. For the southernmost towns in the Southern Berkshires, take exit for Rte. 44 east; for mid-northern towns, take exit for Rte. 23 east.

**From New Jersey, Pennsylvania, and south:** Take I-84 east to the Taconic Parkway. For the southernmost towns in the Southern Berkshires, take exit for Rte. 44 east; for mid-northern towns take exit for Rte. 23 east.

**From the New York Metro area:** Take I-684 north to I-84 east. At Danbury, CT, pick up Rte. 7 north. This runs through the heart of the Southern Berkshires. Rte. 7 is an official scenic highway and parallels stretches of the Housatonic River.

**From Connecticut:** If coming from the southwestern corner of the state, follow the preceding directions for the metropolitan New York area. If coming from further east, take Rte. 8 north, then Rte. 44 west from Winsted. Rte. 44 crosses Rte. 7 in Canaan. Proceed on Rte. 7 for destinations north.

**From Boston:** Take I-90 west. For Lenox, Lee, and Stockbridge, stay on it until Exit 2 at Lee. For a very scenic route to points further south (Great Barrington, Egremont, Sheffield), pick up Rte. 202 south at Exit 3, eight miles west of Springfield. Go south to Rte. 20 west and pick up Rte. 23 west at Woronoco. If going to towns in Connecticut, take Rte. 8 south where it intersects with Rte. 23.

**From Hartford:** Take Rte. 44 west through the towns of Norfolk and Canaan. If going further north, take Rte. 7 north, when it intersects with Rte. 44 just east of Canaan.

**From Montreal:** Leaving Canada, take I-87 (known as "The Northway") south to Albany. Go east on I-90, exiting at Lee, MA.

**From Albany and points west:** Take I-90 east to the Taconic Parkway south. Exit on Rte. 23 and go east for the towns of Egremont, Great Barrington, Sheffield, and those in Connecticut. For Lee, Lenox, and Stockbridge, continue on I-90 to the exit at Lee, MA.

# By Bus

Several commercial bus lines serve many of the towns in the Southern Berkshires. Call for details and schedules.

*Peter Pan Bus Lines, Inc.* — (800) 322-8995
*Bonanza* — (800) 343-9330
*Arrow Line* — (203) 547-1500
*Greyhound* — (617) 423-5810
*Greyhound* leaving from Montreal — (514) 843- 4231
*Greyhound* leaving from Albany — (518) 434-8461

*Greyhound* will transport bikes at no additional charge, but they must be disassembled and boxed (see bike boxing tips in the appendix).

*Bonanza* will transport bikes at no additional charge. Bikes do not have to be boxed; however, Bonanza will not be responsible for damage.

*Arrow Line* requires a bike be disassembled and boxed (see boxing tips in appendix). There is an additional charge of $10, and the bike is considered one of the two pieces of allowable baggage to be carried in the storage compartment.

# By Train

*Amtrak* has trains, which will accommodate bikes, leaving from Boston, New York City, Montreal, and other cities to Pittsfield, MA, Albany, NY, and Hartford, CT. Call the number listed for information on leaving from other cities.

Bikes can be loaded and unloaded only at stations which have baggage handlers, and there is a $5 handling fee for a bike each time it is checked. You must be at the station one hour before departure time, with your bike boxed (see appendix for bike boxing tips). Some stations have boxes available. Call (800) 872-7245 for more information.

## BY AIR

**Bradley International Airport, (203) 292-2000,** in Windsor Locks, CT, just north of Hartford, serves many domestic and international flights, so you can fly to Bradley from almost anywhere. Then, you can charter an air service, catch a bus, or rent a car to get to your destination in the Southern Berkshires.

**Albany County Airport, (518) 869-9611,** in Albany, NY, just west of the Southern Berkshires, also serves many domestic airlines. From the airport, you can charter an air service, catch a bus, or rent a car.

Several airlines come into both airports and have varying bike-transporting policies and costs. Call for information and reservations. (When making reservations, if you are taking your bike and want to use an airline's box, let them know so a box will be held for you.)

*Continental* — (800) 525-0280 — $30 additional each way; bike must be boxed (see appendix for boxing tips). Boxes available at some airports for an additional $10.

*American* — (800) 433-7300 — $45 additional each way; bike must be boxed or bagged (see appendix). Boxes available at airport for $15; bags $10.

*US Air* — (800) 428-4322 — $45 additional each way; boxes available at no charge. Bike may go unboxed if pedals are removed, handlebars are turned sideways, and handlebars and the crank arms are encased in plastic.

*United* — (800) 241-6522 — $45 additional each way: boxes available for $10. Bike can be either boxed or bagged (see appendix).

*Northwest* — (800) 225-2525 — $45 additional each way; boxes available for $15 at airport on first-come-first-served basis (see appendix for boxing tips). Bike may go unboxed if you turn handlebars sideways, remove pedals, and wrap parts of bike in plastic. Liability form must be signed no matter how bike is packed.

*Delta* — (800) 241-4141 — $30 additional each way; must be boxed (see appendix for boxing tips). Boxes available at no charge; when making reservation, just ask that one be held for you.

## AVOID A HASSLE

You can avoid the hassle of taking your bike apart and packing it at the airport (a time-consuming and awkward job — particularly if you're doing it for the first time) by doing any of the following:

1. Get a bicycle box from your local bike store and pack up your bike ahead of time. Bike stores generally have a surplus of boxes, as their stock comes in boxes. Pack the bike (following the instructions in the appendix) at your leisure and bring it to the airport ready to go.

2. Ship your bike, ahead of time, to your destination via United Parcel Service (UPS). It's cheaper — between $10 and $25 each way, depending on distance. Overnight and Second-Day Air UPS are also available. The United Parcel Service toll-free number is (800) 535-1776. When you make arrangements for a place to stay in the Berkshires, ask if the lodging will accept delivery of your bike. Most places will do so gladly, if you have a reservation.

3. Purchase a commercially made case or bag specifically designed for protecting your bike during transport. A number of bike equipment companies that handle these are listed in the appendix.

## GETTING AROUND IN THE BERKSHIRES

**Charter flights** are available from
> *Page Flight* — (518) 869-0253 — in Albany, NY
> *Berkshire Aviation* — (413) 528-1010 — in Great Barrington, MA
> *Lyon Aviation* — (413) 443-6700 — in Pittsfield, MA
> *Direct Airways* — (800) 357-9424 — in Hartford, CT
> *Dawn Flight Aviation* — (800) 637-9781 — in Hartford, CT

**Car Rentals**
> from Bradley International Airport, Hartford, CT
> *Hertz* — (800) 654-3131
> *Avis* — (800) 331-1212
> *National Car Rental* — (800) 227-7368
> *Budget Rent-A-Car* — (800) 527-0700

> from Albany County Airport, NY
> *Hertz* — (800) 654-3131
> *Avis* — (800) 331-1212
> *National Car Rental* — (800) 227-7368
> *Budget Rent-A-Car* — (800) 527-0700

from Pittsfield, MA
*Avis* — (800) 331-1212
*National Car Rental* — (800) 227-7368
*Rent-A-Wreck* — (413) 447-8117

from Great Barrington, MA
*Caffrey Motors* — (800) 698-0848
*Condor Chevrolet* — (413) 528-2700
*Larkins Enterprises* — (413) 528-2156

from Canaan, CT
*Ugly Duckling Rent-A-Car* — (203) 824-5204

**Taxi Service**

in Pittsfield, MA
*Rainbow Taxi* — (413) 499-4300
*Aarow Taxi* — (413) 499-8604
*Berkshire Limousine* — (800) 543-6776

in Stockbridge, MA
*Stockbridge Livery* — (413) 298-4848

in Lenox, MA
*Aarow Taxi* — (413) 499-8604

in Lee, MA
*Abbott's Limousine & Livery* — (413) 243-1645

in Great Barrington, MA
*Taxico* — (413) 528-0911

in Litchfield, CT
*Litchfield Livery* — (203) 567-9438

# WHEN TO RIDE

# WHEN TO RIDE

*"Hey, guys, I see blue skies and sunshine rolling in —
just like* The Farmer's Almanac *predicted."*
Fred "Rudi" Peirce, master bike trip planner

## WEATHER

*One of the brightest gems in New England weather is the dazzling uncertainty of it.*

— Mark Twain
Summer resident of the Southern Berkshires

What Mark Twain said about New England weather is borne out by the weather patterns in the Berkshires — they change a lot.

Fortunately, the summers are usually quite mild (as shown in the average-temperature chart below), due to the elevation. Because the air is clean and dry, high humidity doesn't usually last long. Wind is light during the summer months, averaging six to seven mph, and comes mainly out of the west-southwest (compared with 12-14 mph from the north-northwest in winter). The hills and forests deflect the wind, so you don't have the blasts and buffets you'd have in less protected areas — such as along the coast or on the plains.

Another advantage of the hilly Berkshire terrain is that the temperature fluctuates with the elevation — as much as 15 degrees between the high and the low points on a tour. If it's a hot day, you'll welcome the coolness at the top of a climb. Evaporation of the sweat you work up climbing the hill will cool you off at the top. Of course, you can also run into even cooler weather unexpectedly, especially if it turns cloudy or wet. I keep a light windbreaker in my bike pack all the time for surprise weather changes.

About three to four inches of rain fall in the Berkshires in any given bicycling month (precipitation is fairly consistent year round). You'll get one day out of three with some measurable precipitation — anything from an early morning mist to a downpour. In the late spring and during the summer, you may be treated to a thunderstorm (some are spectacular, with thunder booming and rolling across the mountains and lightning flashes you can see from miles away). These storms are most common at this time, although they can occur any time of year.

This temperature chart shows the normal average highs and lows (in degrees Fahrenheit) for each bicycling month:

|      | April | May | June | July | Aug | Sept | Oct | Nov |
|------|-------|-----|------|------|-----|------|-----|-----|
| High | 57    | 68  | 75   | 81   | 79  | 71   | 61  | 50  |
| Low  | 33    | 43  | 53   | 60   | 55  | 48   | 38  | 28  |

## WEATHER FORECASTS

*The Old Farmer's Almanac* is in its 201st year of publication. It's been around that long for good reason — it's useful! Considered by many to be more accurate than official weather stations, it has the added advantage of providing the weather forecast up to a year in advance — very helpful for planning a trip. This publication has a reliability rating of 80% overall, which is so good that the U. S. Army Corps of Engineers is considering using the forecasts in its planning of flood-control releases each year. State highway departments, which must plan for the amount of salt needed in the forthcoming winter, also use these forecasts.

*The Old Farmer's Almanac* weather forecasts are determined both by a secret formula, devised by the founder of the almanac in 1792, and by modern scientific calculations based on solar activity.

The almanac has regional forecasts, including — of course — New England and the Berkshires. My good friend and bike-trip planner, Rudi (Fred) Peirce, swears by the almanac. I was skeptical the first few times he disagreed with me about the dates for an upcoming trip (the almanac predicted rain). I disregarded the predictions and ended up, on several occasions, slogging for hours through a downpour. Needless to say, I began to soften up my skepticism and soon started consulting the almanac myself. I now recommend it highly.

*The Old Farmer's Almanac* is available for $3.95 in bookstores, convenience stores, drugstores, and other outlets, or call (toll-free) 1-800-733-3000 to order by phone.

## WEATHER REPORTS

Call these numbers to get up-to-date weather forecast information:
in Massachusetts: (413)
>Great Barrington — 528-1118
>Lenox — 637-3292
>Lee/Stockbridge — 243-0065
>Pittsfield — 499-2627

in Connecticut: (203) 936-1212

## FALL-COLOR SEASON

*According to Native American legend, the red leaves of autumn symbolize the dripping blood from the killing of the Great Bear of the Heavens, and yellow leaves represent the flames from the sacrificial fires in which his flesh is cooked.*

The Berkshires are covered with trees, shrubs, and plants that change color. Black cherry, pin oak, sumac, and white oak leaves turn brilliant red, while American elm, beech, willow, birch, silver maple, and Norway maple turn vibrant yellow. Add to this the scarlets from the maples and scarlet oak, the dark purple of ash trees, and the brilliant oranges of sugar maples, and you've got a spectacular visual feast through which to cycle.

Foliage season in the Southern Berkshires usually starts in mid-to-late September and ends in mid-to-late October. While the complete phase takes about three weeks, peak color lasts for a week. At the "peak," all the trees have turned, and the colors are most vibrant. This frequently happens near Columbus Day.

Many factors affect the length and intensity of the foliage season: temperature, rainfall, sunlight, wind, etc. The best color appears after a rainy spring and summer and during an autumn with warm, sunny days and cool nights.

A free booklet, entitled "The Spirit of Massachusetts Fall Foliage Guide," is available from the Massachusetts Division of Tourism. The Division of Tourism and the Department of Environmental Management also have a Fall Foliage Hotline — at the same toll-free number. By calling, you can find out the percentage of color and the expected peak dates. From Massachusetts, call 1-800-632-8038. From other northeastern states, call 1-800-343-9072. From all other states, call (617) 727-3201.

There's a Norman Rockwell Fall Foliage Bicycle Tour, in Stockbridge, MA, in the autumn. For dates and times, call the Norman Rockwell Museum at (413) 298-4239.

## WEEKENDS VS. WEEKDAYS

During the area's "busy season," between the first of July and Labor Day, all the roads in the Berkshires get more vehicles, and weekends get the heaviest. For the tours in this book, I've selected roads with low automobile traffic. However, occasional stretches do use the larger, more trafficked roads. For the sheer joy of having long stretches of open road to yourself, I recommend riding on weekdays.

If you plan to stay at a bed-and-breakfast or an inn, you can save as much as 30% on the room rates if you come during the week.

# THE TOURS

# TOUR #1

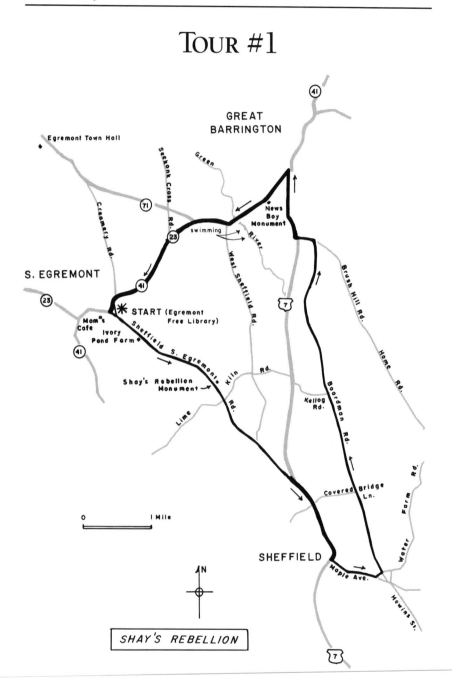

# SHAY'S REBELLION TOUR

**Mileage:** 15.3
**Time:** 1 – 1½ hours
**Rating:** Easy. 15.7 ft. per mile climbed. Total climbed: 240 ft.

**Description:** This is a mellow, easy ride with long stretches of flat-to-mildly rolling road. There are no significant climbs. Outstanding scenery includes panoramic views of the Housatonic Valley, Mount Everett, and the Mount Washington Mountain range. All are well paved roads with the exception of one two-mile stretch of flat, somewhat rough, dirt road between Kellogg and Brush Hill roads. (You can take an alternate, less scenic, paved road if you want to avoid the dirt one.)

**Options:** See llamas and alpacas grazing at Ivory Pond Farm. Visit Shay's Rebellion stone monument, the oldest covered bridge in Massachusetts, or the Newsboy Monument. Swim or picnic at Green River. (See Special Attractions chapter for descriptions.)

**Food and Drink:** Mom's Cafe, on Main St. (Rte. 23/41) in the middle of South Egremont, serves blueberry pancakes and sandwiches. It's an excellent place for breakfast or lunch, and you can eat out on the deck, shaded with maple trees and overlooking the creek that flows behind the restaurant. For snack food, Mom's Convenience Store is next door.

There are two markets in Sheffield and PJ's Convenience Store (on the south end of town) for snacks, drinks, and water-bottle fills. PJ's has deli sandwiches and is open seven days a week. There's also a diner in town which serves breakfast and lunch. It has a small-town atmosphere, and mediocre food. You can fill your water bottle with potable city water at the Newsboy Monument on the last leg of the tour.

**Parking:** The town of Egremont has generously offered use of South Egremont Free Library parking lot on Button Ball Ln., just south of Rte. 23/41, for cyclists' parking on weekends. On weekdays, however, please park elsewhere because the space is needed for library patrons. An alternative is the Egremont town hall parking lot on Rte. 71 (see map). It has ample space, and town officials are happy to have you park there.

### SHIFT GEARS
Join the fun!

## DIRECTIONS

**0.0 Mile**     **Starting from corner of Rte. 23/41 and Button Ball Ln., head south on Button Ball.**

**0.1 Mile**     **Swing left onto Sheffield/Egremont Rd.** You'll pass Egremont Inn on the right. About half a mile further, on the right, is the Ivory Pond Farm, with alpacas and llamas grazing or sleeping in the shade. Some 1.8 miles from the start of the trip, there's a five-foot-high stone, which marks the site of the last battle of Shay's Rebellion. It's on the left, just before you come to the corner of Rebellion Rd., and may be partially hidden in the weeds at the corner of a cornfield . . . so keep an eye out. Just past Shay's Monument, there's a wide open view of Mount Washington and the valley to the west.

**3.8 Mile**     **Turn right onto Rte. 7** when you come to the stop sign. On the left, 0.3 mile from the turn, you'll see a sign for the "oldest covered bridge in Massachusetts." It's across the road from a big artillery gun sitting in a yard. To see it, go left down a little dirt lane called Crook Rd. There's also a picnic table beside Housatonic River, just below the bridge.

**5.0 Mile**     **Go left onto Maple Ave.** at the north end of Sheffield; it's 1.2 miles from the turn onto Rte. 7 and the first left past Crook Rd. (If you want something to eat or drink go straight into Sheffield. There are two markets just a stone's throw down the road.) You'll cross the Housatonic River less than a mile further on Maple Avenue.

**5.7 Mile**     **Take the first left immediately after the bridge.** It's Atwater St., but there's no road sign.

**5.8 Mile**     **Turn left onto Boardman St.**, the crossroad you come to 0.1 mile from the turn onto Atwater. From Boardman, you can see the Mount Washington range on the western horizon. See if you can spot the lookout tower on the top of Mount Everett.

Kellogg St. goes off to the west 2.5 miles from the turn onto Boardman St. There's no road sign, but if you look north you may see a "Road Closed" sign on the continuation of Boardman. (It may be gone by the time you have this book in your hands.) If you have a regular touring bike, hybrid, or off-road bike and don't mind taking it on some semi-rough dirt road, continue straight on Boardman for a more scenic ride than the alternative route up Rte. 7. (If you have a road-racing bike, or don't want to do this dirt stretch, go left on Kellogg St. Take a right on Rte. 7 and continue to Rte. 23/41, where you'll rejoin the tour directions.)

**8.3 Mile**    **Continue straight on Boardman Rd.** There's another "Road Closed" sign further down. The paved road gets patchy and deteriorates. Although the road is not closed, the next two miles are bumpy and rough in spots. The road becomes dirt after a mile or so and passes near the Housatonic River.

**10.7 Mile**    **Take a left onto Brush Hill Rd.**, the next paved road you encounter. You cross the Housatonic River and come to a stop sign at Rte. 7.

**10.9 Mile**    **Go right onto Rte. 7** and continue one mile. (For something to eat or drink, continue straight on Rte. 7. There's a Popeye's Convenience Store and The Deli sandwich shop on the right just past Searles Castle, less than 0.2 mile from the intersection.)

**11.9 Mile**    **Turn left onto Rte. 23/41.** You'll pass the Newsboy Monument fountain on the left after 0.4 mile. If you're thirsty, stick your water bottle under the satyr's head and fill up; it's good, potable city water.

About a mile further on, the road goes over Green River. There are great places to picnic and cool off all along this waterway. Look for a fire hydrant off the road to the left just before you come to the bridge, and follow the trail that winds from it to the south, going along the river. There are several pools, a rock to sun on, and stretches of pebbly beach.

Continue on Rte. 23/41 to the east end of South Egremont.

**15.3 Mile**    **Turn left onto Button Ball Ln.,** and you are back to the parking lot at the library.

## HELMETS SAVE LIVES
Consider those who love you.

# TOUR #2

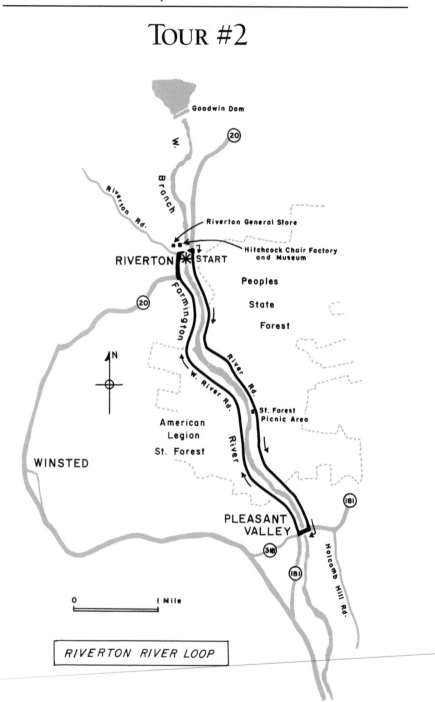

Goodwin Dam

(20)

W. Branch

Riverton Rd.

Riverton General Store

Hitchcock Chair Factory and Museum

RIVERTON ✳ START

Peoples

State

Forest

(20)

Farmington

N

River Rd.

W. River Rd.

St. Forest Picnic Area

American Legion St. Forest

River

WINSTED

(181)

PLEASANT VALLEY

(318)

Holcomb Hill Rd.

(181)

0                    I Mile

RIVERTON RIVER LOOP

# RIVERTON RIVER LOOP

**Mileage:** 8.6
**Time:** 1/2–1 hour
**Rating:** Easy. 18.6 ft. per mile climbed. Total climbed: 160 ft.

**Description:** This is a  mellow ride (my favorite short ride) on gently rolling road along an outstandingly scenic stretch of the rocky, swiftly moving Farmington River. This portion is designated as a Wild and Scenic River by the National Park Service. The route goes through Peoples State Forest and the American Legion State Forest, and there's lots of shade from maples, firs, and pines. There are also many rocks along the river for meditative sitting or picnicking. The route is all well paved road.

**Options:** Many boulders and rocky places by the river to picnic or rest. Peoples State Forest on River Rd. has a picnic area with tables in a maple and hemlock grove on the river.

**Food and Drink:** The Riverton General Store on Rte. 20 has made-to-order deli sandwiches as well as a good selection of snack food, and the friendly folks there will fill your water bottle if you ask.

**Parking:** In the parking lot at Riverton Park on Rte. 20 in Riverton, across from the Hitchcock Chair Factory (see map).

## DIRECTIONS

| | |
|---|---|
| **0.0 Mile** | **Starting at Riverton Park, go east over the bridge.** |
| **0.1 Mile** | **Take a right onto River Rd.** The road rolls through the forest and along the boulder-strewn river. If you want to picnic at the tables in the hemlock grove, stop at the state forest parking lot and walk back to the river. |
| **4.2 Mile** | **Go right onto Rte. 318 when you come to the stop sign.** You'll go over a big steel bridge. |
| **4.3 Mile** | **Turn right onto West River Rd. after crossing the bridge.** This leg takes you through the American Legion State Forest. |

**8.3 Mile**   **At the stop sign, take a right onto Rte. 20.** There's no road sign. You'll go over the river and around a sharp bend, then pass the Riverton General Store.

**8.6 Mile**   **You're back at Riverton Park, where the tour began.**

*"Improvement makes straight roads; but the crooked roads without Improvement are roads of Genius."*

William Blake

## ME AND MOTHER NATURE

*"When bike touring I'm vulnerable to the elements, breathing deeply, endorphins lifting me to a natural meditative high. The wind and the sun hit me directly. And I bathe in the energy of a place and take it in."*

Reid Saunders

# TOUR #3

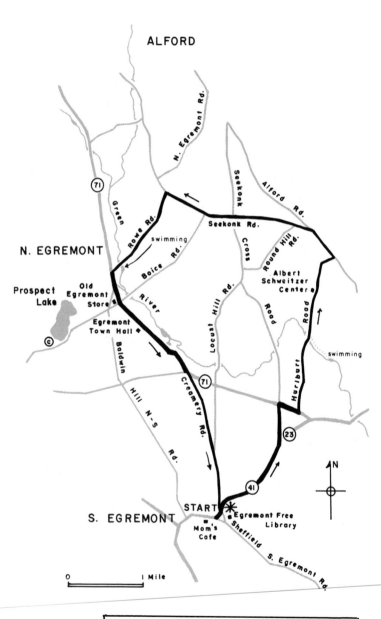

ALBERT SCHWEITZER - GREEN RIVER

# ALBERT SCHWEITZER – GREEN RIVER

**Mileage:** 11.2
**Time:** 3/4 – 1¼ hour
**Rating:** Easy. 24.1 ft. per mile climbed. Total climbed: 270 ft.

**Description:** This ride is mostly flat, with occasional mildly rolling hills. There are only two significant climbs; both are short and on Seekonk Rd. You can see views of mountains across Alford Valley, and you'll pass country horse and cattle farms. All the roads are well paved.

**Options:** Take a tour of the Albert Schweitzer Center on Hurlburt Rd. (See Special Attractions chapter for Albert Schweitzer Center tour information.) If you'd like, you can picnic in the nature preserve, a pine-shaded glen beside the Green River, near the center. It's a short walk, and a sign at the entrance shows you how to get there. You can also cool off in the Green River on Hurlburt Rd. south of the Schweitzer Center or at Rowe Rd.

**Food and Drink:** Before this ride, my friends and I like to eat blueberry pancakes out on the deck at Mom's Cafe on Main St. (Rte. 23/41) in South Egremont. Mom's serves lunch as well as breakfast. There are a couple of other restaurants in town as well. Mom's Convenience Store is next door, if you want to get pretzels, Gatorade®, or other snacks and drinks. Old Egremont Country Store has deli sandwiches made fresh on request, as well as snack food and drinks. The friendly folks there will be happy to fill your water bottle.

**Parking:** The town of Egremont has generously offered use of South Egremont Free Library parking lot on Button Ball Ln., just south of Rte. 23/41, for cyclists' parking on weekends. On weekdays, however, please park elsewhere because the space is needed for library patrons. As an alternative, the Egremont town hall parking lot on Rte.71 (see map) has ample space, and town officials are happy to have you park there.

## DIRECTIONS

| | |
|---|---|
| **0.0 Mile** | **Tour begins at the intersection of Rte. 23/41 and Button Ball Ln. in South Egremont.** Go northeast, toward Great Barrington, on Rte. 23/41. |
| **1.2 Mile** | **Take a left onto Seekonk Cross Rd.** Seekonk Pines Bed and Breakfast is on the corner. In less than 0.5 mile, you'll come to Rte. 71 (the first cross street). |
| **1.6 Mile** | **Go right onto Rte. 71.** Ride 0.3 mile. |
| **1.9 Mile** | **Turn left on Hurlburt,** the first road. A sign points to the Albert Schweitzer Center, and there's a road sign in the bushes on the southwest corner. About a mile up Hurlburt you'll cross the Green River. If you'd like to cool off, you can pull off at the bridge and wade up the river (it's shallow with a sand and pebble bottom) to quiet, secluded pools. You'll pass the Albert Schweitzer Center on the left 1.5 miles from the corner. You can stop for a picnic in the nature center or take a tour of the Albert Schweitzer Center. The view of the valley is excellent from here, and there's a great view of Tom Ball Mountain to the north. |
| **4 Mile** | **Take a left when you come to the stop sign at Alford Rd.** You'll pass Simons Rock College on your right just beyond the turn. |
| **4.4 Mile** | **Go left onto Seekonk Rd.** Note the view of Alford Valley to the north. Seekonk Rd. changes to Green River Rd. as you pass Boice Rd. The only two hills you'll climb on this tour are on Seekonk Rd. The first is shortly after you turn onto Seekonk Rd., and the other is about 0.3 mile long, ending at Boice Rd. |
| **6.4 Mile** | **Take a left onto Rowe Rd.** A mile down Rowe Rd., just before coming to Rte. 71, you'll cross a bridge over Green River. On the left side is a pebbly beach — good for picnicking and cooling off. |

*"Man can no longer live for himself alone. We must realize that all life is valuable and that we are united to all life. From this knowledge comes our spiritual relationship with the universe."*

Albert Schweitzer

| | |
|---|---|
| **7.7 Mile** | **Turn left at the stop sign on Rte. 71.** There is no road sign on the corner, but you'll see one a short way down the road. Old Egremont Country Store is on the right less than 0.5 mile from the turn. |
| **9.4 Mile** | **Go right onto Creamery Rd.** a little more than a mile past the store. Just before the turn is a sign that says "Rte. 41," with an arrow pointing to the right. Baldwin Hill Rd. comes into Rte. 71 just before Creamery Rd., so go past Baldwin Hill and make a sweeping right onto Creamery. |
| **11.1 Mile** | **Go straight onto Rte. 23/41 when you come to the intersection.** |
| **11.2 Mile** | **Take a left onto Button Ball Lane,** less than 0.1 mile from the intersection. |

# TOUR #4

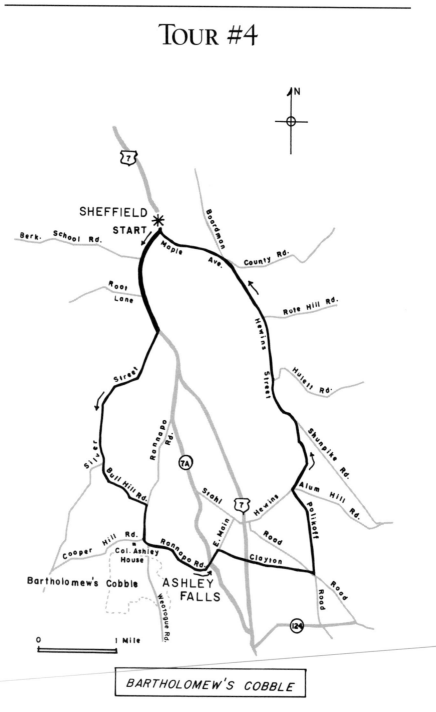

BARTHOLOMEW'S COBBLE

# BARTHOLOMEW'S COBBLE

**Mileage:** 11.7
**Time:** 3/4 – 1½ hours
**Rating:** Easy. 18 ft. per mile climbed. Total climbed: 210 ft.

**Description:** This tour passes cattle farms and country homes as it goes through the Housatonic River valley. It's mostly flat, with only a couple of small hills. There are views of the Mount Washington range and other mountains to the north and west.

**Options:** Hike, picnic, or visit the museum at Bartholomew's Cobble Nature Preserve. Tour Colonel Ashley House, the oldest house in Berkshire County. (See Special Attractions for descriptions.)

**Food and Drink:** In Sheffield, there are two markets, two restaurants, and PJ's Convenience Store (on the south end of town). PJ's has deli sandwiches and is open seven days a week.

**Parking:** Main St. in Sheffield.

## DIRECTIONS

**0.0 Mile**    **Go south on Rte. 7 (Main St.), beginning in Sheffield.** The road is flat all the way to Silver St.

**1.2 Mile**    **Turn right onto Silver St.** at the sign indicating Cooperhill Farm to the right. Cross the railroad tracks. This stretch of road is patched pavement and good asphalt. The scenery includes corn fields, maple-shaded country homes, and mountain views to the west.

**3.1 Mile**    **Take a left on Bull Hill Rd., the first dirt road to the left.** There's no road sign, but it's a shady dirt road and the first road you can take to the left.

**3.9 Mile**    **Go right onto Rannappo Rd. when you come to paved road.** There's no road sign on this corner either. Along this stretch, there are good views of the Housatonic River valley.

**4.3 Mile**    **Colonel Ashley House.** Turn right at the grassy triangle at Cooper Hill Rd. if you want to visit the Colonel Ashley House; it's just up the road on the left.

**4.4 Mile**    **Bartholomew's Cobble Nature Preserve** is only a short way down Weatogue Rd. and well worth a visit.

Go across the river, past the cow-grazing pastures on the river-bottom land, and up the mild climb into the town of Ashley Falls.

**5.3 Mile** **Go straight across Rte. 7A to East Main St. at the stop sign across from the Ashley Falls post office.** You'll cross the railroad tracks and go through a residential section.

**5.6 Mile** **Turn right onto Clayton Rd. at the first intersection.** No road sign on the corner. This very flat stretch passes the cemetery and crosses Rte. 7.

**6.7 Mile** **Take a left onto Polikoff Rd.** The ride's flat and easy.

**7.8 Mile** **Head north on Hewins Rd. when you come to the intersection of Polikoff, Alum, and Hewins roads.** Along Hewins, note the views of the Mount Washington range to the west. There are a couple of small hills on this stretch through farm country.

**10.8 Mile** **Go left onto Maple Avenue when you come to the yield sign.** Cross Housatonic River and continue to the stop sign at Rte. 7.

**11.7 Mile** **Turn left onto Rte. 7, and you are back in Sheffield.**

*"We are used to thinking of bicycling as a way to stay fit, compete, see the countryside, or commute. But it can be a means of self-discovery, too."*

Scott Martin, Editor, *Bicycling Magazine*

## HIGH PERFORMANCE CYCLIST
*"I can go from 0 to Bliss in 2.4 minutes."* — Betsey Hallihan

# TOUR #5

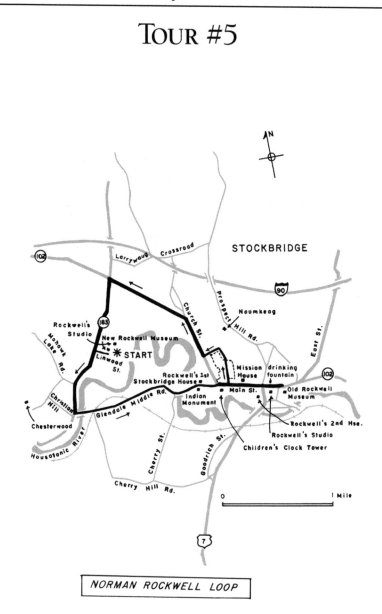

NORMAN ROCKWELL LOOP

# NORMAN ROCKWELL LOOP

**Mileage:** 6
**Time:** 1/2 — 1 hour
**Rating:** Easy. Less than 10 ft. of climb per mile.

**Description:** Norman Rockwell liked to bike, and this tour follows one of the loops he enjoyed with his wife Molly and friends. The route is gently rolling to flat, with one short, steep climb. It goes through the village of Stockbridge and past places Rockwell used as backdrops for his paintings.

**Options:** See the collection of original Norman Rockwell paintings at the Norman Rockwell Museum in Stockbridge (or at the new museum on Linwood St. off Rte.183, scheduled to open in 1993). Also, see the Indian Burial Ground or tour the Mission House which belonged to the man who founded the town. (See Special Attractions chapter for descriptions.) During the warmer months, there are "Tour de Rockwell" bicycle tours led by experienced Rockwell Museum guides. See description in Resources chapter under "Organized Rides."

**Food and Drink:** There's a drinking fountain on Main St. in Stockbridge, as well as many restaurants and several markets within a block of Main St.

**Parking:** In the parking lot of the new Norman Rockwell Museum on Linwood St. off Rte. 183 (see map).

## DIRECTIONS

**0.0 Mile**   **Starting at the intersection of Linwood St. and Rte. 183, go south (left) on Rte. 183.** It's downhill to the little town of Glendale.

**0.5 Mile**   **Take a left onto Glendale Middle Rd.** You'll cross the Housatonic River, then there's a short, steep climb just past the bridge. The road sweeps left over the river again further on and runs through the Stockbridge Country Club. Just past the golf course, there's a house on the left, across from the Indian Burial Ground Monument, which Norman Rockwell, his wife, and sons rented when

Courtesy of Norman Rockwell Museum

## CRUISIN' MAIN STREET
Norman Rockwell and friend in Stockbridge.

they first moved to Stockbridge from Vermont. Around the bend, you'll pass the Children's Clock Tower on the right. You are now on Main St. in Stockbridge.

The section of Main St. from the corner where The Red Lion Inn is located to the old Rockwell Museum is the scene of Rockwell's famous centerfold painting, *Main Street at Christmas*. The house the Rockwells lived in for many years is opposite the back of The Red Lion Inn, south on Rte. 7, one block from the corner. The building has "1794" on the chimney.

Above Stockbridge Center Market, you can see the large picture window of Rockwell's old studio. The nearby court house was the site for his famous painting, *Marriage License*. The old Rockwell Museum is on the corner, just past the marble fountain with a water spout in the shape of a satyr's head. (By the way, the water coming from its mouth is drinkable city water.)

| | |
|---|---|
| 2.5 Mile | **Turn around at the old Rockwell Museum and head back down Main St. to the Stockbridge Cemetery.** |
| 3.1 Mile | **Turn right into the cemetery.** At the north corner are the graves of Norman Rockwell and his wife Molly. **Exit the cemetery on Church St. (Rte. 102) and go right.** |
| 4.5 Mile | **Take a left onto Rte. 183.** |
| 5.3 Mile | **Turn left onto Butler Rd.** just past Linwood St. |
| 5.7 Mile | **Go left onto Linwood Dr.** just before the bridge. To the south of the Linwood estate sits Rockwell's last studio. To the west is the new Norman Rockwell Museum. |
| 6 Mile | **Ride around the stone mansion on the little dirt road, returning to the parking lot where the tour started.** |

# TOUR #6

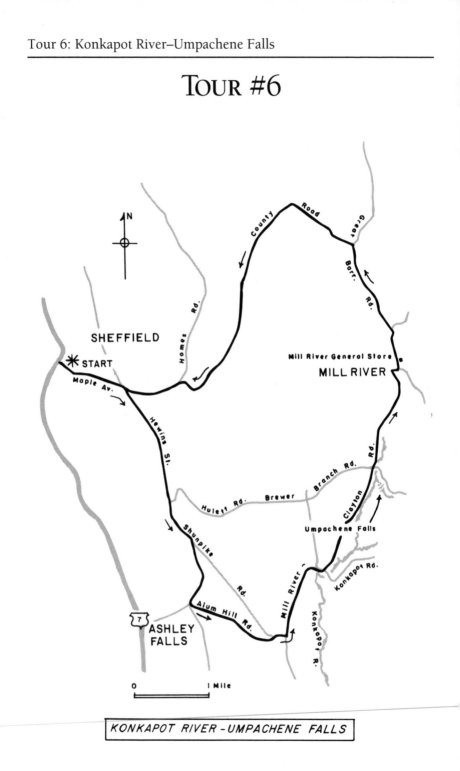

KONKAPOT RIVER - UMPACHENE FALLS

# KONKAPOT RIVER –
# UMPACHENE FALLS

**Mileage:** 16.6
**Time:** 1 – 1½ hours
**Rating:** Easy. 37 ft. per mile climbed. Total climbed: 610 ft.

**Description:** The route is on mostly flat to gently rolling, paved road through the Housatonic River valley and along the swiftly flowing Konkapot River. There are good views of the Mount Washington range to the west and the Canaan Mountains and Rattlesnake Hill to the south. Expect one moderately challenging, one-mile climb over Alum Hill.

**Options:** Swim, picnic, or sun on the rocks at Umpachene Falls.

**Food and Drink:** Sheffield has two markets, two restaurants, and PJ's Convenience Store. PJ's has deli sandwiches and is open seven days a week. There are no other places to get food or drink until you reach the Mill River General Store, where you can get fresh fruit, drinks, or made-to-order deli sandwiches. The folks at both stores have always gladly filled my water bottle when I've asked.

**Parking:** Main St. in Sheffield, in front of stores, next to median.

## DIRECTIONS

**0.0 Mile** **Starting on the corner of Maple Ave. and Rte. 7 in Sheffield, go east on Maple.** In less than a mile, you cross the Housatonic River. The first right past the river is Hewins Rd.

**0.9 Mile** **Take a right onto Hewins Rd.** A short distance further on, you'll pass Balsam Hill Farm. To the west are views of Mount Washington and Mount Everett (the one with the lookout tower). Looking straight south, you can see knobby Rattlesnake Hill. This section of road through the valley is flat to gently rolling. Three miles from the turn onto Hewins, the road splits three ways. Alum Hill Rd. is on the left, Polikoff Rd. is the middle fork, and Hewins continues to the right.

| | |
|---|---|
| **3.9 Mile** | **Go left onto Alum Hill Rd.** It's a short, moderately steep climb (100 feet of vertical climb over a distance of one mile) followed by an equally moderate descent. |
| **5.2 Mile** | **Turn left onto Mill River-Clayton Rd.** when you come to the stop sign at the bottom of the hill. A mile past Alum Hill Rd., Mill River-Clayton Rd. swings to the left and Konkapot Rd. bears right. (There's a white wooden road sign in the grassy triangle.) Stay left on Mill River-Clayton Rd. You'll pass a sheep farm as you continue on the rolling, well paved road, and further on you'll parallel the swiftly flowing Konkapot River. |
| **7.8 Mile** | **If you want to stop at Umpachene Falls, take a right onto Umpachene Rd.** Look for a plain, white, wooden 4x4 post marker stuck in the ground at the corner on the right side. (It's easy to miss if you're not watching closely.) Umpachene Rd. is the dirt road across from Brewer Branch Rd. Follow it over the bridge. Immediately after the bridge, turn into the parking lot on the right. Follow the sound of water to the falls. |
| **9.1 Mile** | **Continuing on Mill River-Clayton Rd., swing right over the bridge, then take an immediate left** in the middle of the town of Mill River. The sign on the corner has an arrow that points left toward Sheffield. |

Mill River General Merchandise store is immediately on the right. It's open 7:30–5:30 weekdays, 8:00–5:30 on Saturday, and 9:00–noon on Sunday. There you'll find essentials such as Gatorade®, sandwiches, and bananas.

The road is a steady, moderately uphill climb north of town. A half mile out of town, Hartsville-Mill River Rd. splits off to the right. Continue to the left, following the sign to Great Barrington. You'll go over the

*"But what will be left for our children?"*

Chief Umpachene upon hearing his co-chief, Konkapot, agree to sell Mahican tribal land — almost all of what is now south Berkshire County — to white settlers for 460 English pounds, 30 quarts of rum, and three barrels of cider.

Konkapot River, the site of several old mills. There's a historical marker on the right, just before the bridge, which gives the mill's history.

**10.9 Mile**    **Turn left onto County Rd.** when you come to a white wooden sign in a grassy triangle. The sign points to the left to Sheffield.

There's a short uphill ride at the beginning of County Rd. As you continue west, the road levels, then heads downhill. Now you've got a smooth, exhilarating, descent on good pavement for almost four miles! The rest of the route into Sheffield is flat.

**16.6 Mile**    **Back to the corner of Maple and Rte. 7,** where the tour started.

*"You can observe a lot by watching."*
Yogi Berra

# TOUR #7

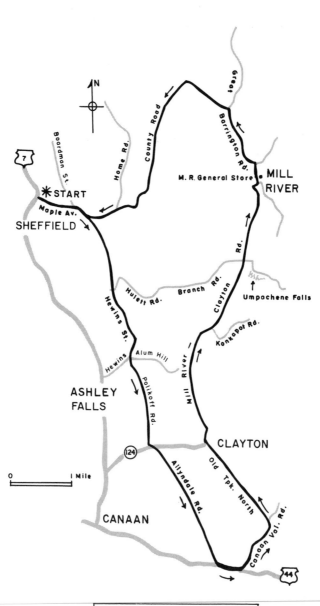

SHEFFIELD - MILL RIVER

# Sheffield – Clayton – Mill River

**Mileage:** 24.6
**Time:** 1½ – 2½ hours
**Rating:** Easy. 33.3 ft. climbed per mile. Total climbed: 820 ft.

**Description:** This is an extended version of the Konkapot River–Umpachene Falls loop, adding eight miles of scenic, mostly flat, valley riding, with a couple of moderate climbs. It's all on well paved roads.

**Options:** Swim, picnic, or sun on the rocks at Umpachene Falls.

**Food and Drink:** Sheffield has two markets, two restaurants, and PJ's Convenience Store (on the south end of town). PJ's has deli sandwiches and is open seven days a week. There are no other places to get food or water until you reach Mill River General Store (17 miles into the trip), which has deli sandwiches, fruit, and drinks. The folks there always gladly fill my water bottle when I ask.

**Parking:** Main St. in Sheffield.

## DIRECTIONS

**0.0 Mile**  **Starting at the intersection of Maple Ave. and Rte. 7 in Sheffield, go east on Maple.** In less than a mile, you'll cross the Housatonic River. The first road on the right after the river is Hewins Rd.

**0.9 Mile**  **Take a right onto Hewins Rd.** After a short distance, you pass Balsam Hill Farm. To the west are excellent views of Mount Washington and Mount Everett (the one with the lookout tower), and straight south you can see knobby Rattlesnake Hill.

This section of road through the valley is flat to gently rolling. Three miles from the turn onto Hewins Rd., the road splits three ways. Alum Hill Rd. is on the left, Polikoff Rd. is in the middle, and Hewins Rd. continues to the right.

**4 Mile**  **Go south onto Polikoff.** Ride down this flat, straight

## POWER SNACKIN'
Phillip May at Umpachene Falls.

|          | stretch with patched pavement and cross Clayton Rd. |
|----------|------|
| **5.7 Mile** | **Continue across Rte. 124.** Polikoff changes its name to Allyndale, and the road passes dairy farms, small homes, and a little air strip. Rattlesnake Hill rises immediately on the right. There's a split in Allyndale Rd. after 2.2 miles. The arrow on the yellow road sign points to the right. |
| **7.9 Mile** | **Turn left while Allyndale sweeps to the right.** There's no road sign on the corner. You pass a sand pit on the right and, a little further on the left, a mining operation. Ride around a tight turn, and you come to a stop sign at Rte. 44. |
| **8.3 Mile** | **Go left onto Rte. 44.** The road passes a cemetery, cattle barns, and Blackberry River Farm. |
| **8.9 Mile** | **Take a left onto Canaan Valley Rd.** and follow the road up the valley for 1.3 miles before coming to Old Turnpike North Rd. |
| **10.2 Mile** | **Turn left onto Old Turnpike North Rd.** There's no street sign on the corner, but it's the first left you can take off Canaan Valley Rd. The road climbs to the left, and there's a 35-mph sign on the right. Immediately, you have a steady, 0.4-mile climb through heavily shaded woods, followed by a long, even, moderate descent. Cross the Konkapot River, and it's downhill all the way to the stop sign at the crossroads. |
| **12 Mile** | **Go right when you come to the stop sign.** There's a white wooden sign in the bushes on the corner. Follow the arrow to Mill River, biking through the little town of Clayton. There's a fork in the road 0.3 mile from the turn; look for another white, wooden sign. |
| **12.3 Mile** | **Take a left onto Mill River-Clayton Rd.** Now there's a flat stretch through the valley, and you pass a huge corn |

*Bananas are an all-time favorite cycling food. A banana is easy to peel, provides more than 100 calories of carbohydrate, replaces potassium lost through sweat, comes in its own biodegradable container, and fits easily in the pocket of a bike jersey.*

field. A mile past Alum Hill Rd., Mill River-Clayton Rd. swings to the left, and Konkapot Rd. goes right. There's a white, wooden sign in the grassy triangle. Stay left on Mill River-Clayton Rd. You'll pass a sheep farm as you ride this rolling road, and a little further on you'll pedal along the Konkapot River.

**15.6 Mile** **If you want to stop at Umpachene Falls, turn right onto Umpachene Rd.** There's just a plain, white, wooden, 4x4 post marker stuck in the ground at the corner on the right side, and it's easy to miss if you're not watching closely. Take the dirt road across the bridge and turn into the parking lot immediately on your right. Follow the sound of falling water to the falls.

**17.2 Mile** **Continuing on Mill River-Clayton Rd., bear right over the bridge, then take an immediate left** in the middle of the town of Mill River. The sign on the corner has an arrow pointing left toward Sheffield. Mill River General Merchandise store is immediately on the right. It's open 7:30-5:30 weekdays, 8:00-5:30 Saturday, and 9:00-noon on Sunday. It carries essentials such as Gatorade®, sandwiches, and bananas.

The road is a steady, moderately uphill climb north of town. A half-mile north of town, Hartsville-Mill River Rd. splits off and goes right. You continue to the left, following the sign toward Great Barrington and crossing the Konkapot River. This is the site of several old mills, and there's a historical marker just before the bridge, which gives the mills' history.

**19 Mile** **Take a left onto County Rd.** when you come to a white, wooden sign in a grassy triangle and see a road coming in from the left. The sign points left to Sheffield.

*"Wake up to where you are. Then you're current! The greater the concentration on the moment, the greater the pleasure!"*

Davis Phinney
U.S. professional road-race champion and
stage winner of the Tour de France

There's a short uphill at the beginning of County Rd. As you continue west, the road levels, then heads downhill. Now there's a smooth, breezy descent on good pavement for almost four miles! The rest of the road is flat into Sheffield.

**24.6 Mile** **Back to the corner of Maple and Rte. 7,** where the tour started.

# TOUR #8

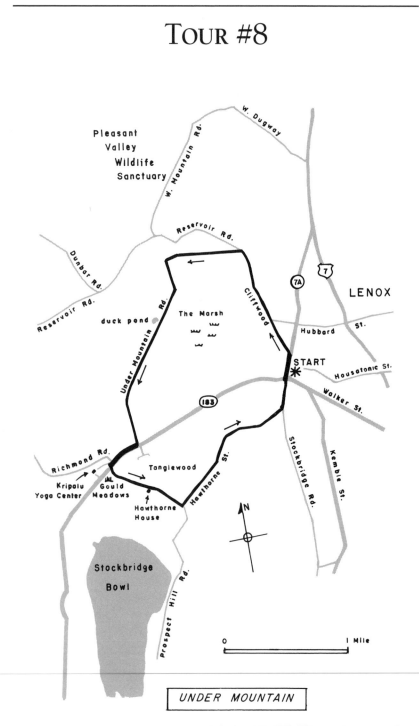

Pleasant
Valley
Wildlife
Sanctuary

W. Dugway

W. Mountain Rd.

Reservoir Rd.

Dunbar Rd.

Reservoir Rd.

duck pond

The Marsh

Under Mountain Rd.

Cliffwood

7A

7

LENOX

Hubbard

St.

START

Housatonic St.

Walker St.

183

Richmond Rd.

Tanglewood

Hawthorne St.

Stockbridge Rd.

Kemble St.

Kripalu
Yoga Center

Gould
Meadows

Hawthorne
House

Hawthorne St.

N

Stockbridge
Bowl

Prospect Hill Rd.

0                    1 Mile

UNDER MOUNTAIN

# UNDER MOUNTAIN

**Mileage:** 5.8
**Time:** 20 – 50 minutes
**Rating:** Moderate. 65.5 ft. per mile climbed. Total climbed: 380 ft.

**Description:** Mostly gently rolling with two short, steep climbs — all on paved roads. From the hill above Under Mountain Horse Farm, there is an excellent view of Rattlesnake Mountain and the wetlands known as The Marsh. Across Gould Meadow and Stockbridge Bowl, there's a panoramic view of seven mountains (including Monument Mountain, Mt. Everett, and Mt. Washington).

**Options:** You can take a walk through the grounds of the Tanglewood Music Festival, summer home of the Boston Symphony Orchestra, or check out Nathaniel Hawthorne's Little Red House across from Tanglewood's Lion Gate on Hawthorne Rd.

**Food and Drink:** There are several restaurants and two small markets within two blocks of the center of Lenox. Clearwater Natural Foods on the corner of Church and Housatonic Streets in Lenox has sandwiches and a wide selection of snack foods.

**Parking:** Main St. or Walker St. (Rte. 183) in Lenox.

## DIRECTIONS

| | |
|---|---|
| 0.0 Mile | **Starting at the monument, at the intersection of routes 183 and 7A in Lenox, go north on 7A.** |
| 0.1 Mile | **Turn left onto Cliffwood St.,** the second road on the left, which goes through a residential section and then changes name to Under Mountain Rd. as you leave town. Just past the Under Mountain Horse Farm, there's a short (0.7 mile), steep climb. From the top of the hill, looking south, there's a good view of the valley and Rattlesnake Mountain. You can see another range of mountains further east and, to the southeast, the wetlands known as The Marsh. |

Continue past the duck pond until you come to a crossroad. This is Rte. 183. Across the road is Tanglewood Music Festival's main gate. (If you want to walk

## NOT A SHOPPING MALL IN SIGHT
Rattlesnake Mountain across Stockbridge Bowl.

through the grounds, go straight across and up to the entrance. The gate is left open when there is no performance, and you're welcome to take a stroll. (Leave bikes out front.)

**3.4 Mile** **Turn right onto Rte. 183 and go 0.2 mile (past the entrance to Kripalu Center) and turn left on Hawthorne St.** From the corner, across Gould Meadows, there's a spectacular view of West Stockbridge Mountain, Mt. Everett, Mt. Washington, and Monument Mountain.

Down Hawthorne St. 0.4 mile is Nathaniel Hawthorne's Little Red House. The author moved here to recover his self-esteem after being fired from his Customs House job in Boston. He wrote *House of Seven Gables* and *The Wonder Book* while living here. The building now serves as practice space for Tanglewood musicians.

**4.5 Mile** **Take a left on the first road, which is actually a continuation of Hawthorne St.** You'll have a short downhill ride on a well paved road.

**5.5 Mile** **Turn left when you come to the stop sign at Stockbridge Rd.** Now you've got a grunt of a hill back up to the monument where the ride started. It's very short — but steep. Don't be embarrassed to walk your bike if necessary. I've seen athletes get off their bikes on this one.

**5.8 Mile** **You are back at the monument in Lenox.**

*"Happiness is not a destination; it is the attitude with which you choose to travel."*

Yogi Amrit Desai
Founder of Kripalu Center for Yoga and Health

# TOUR #9

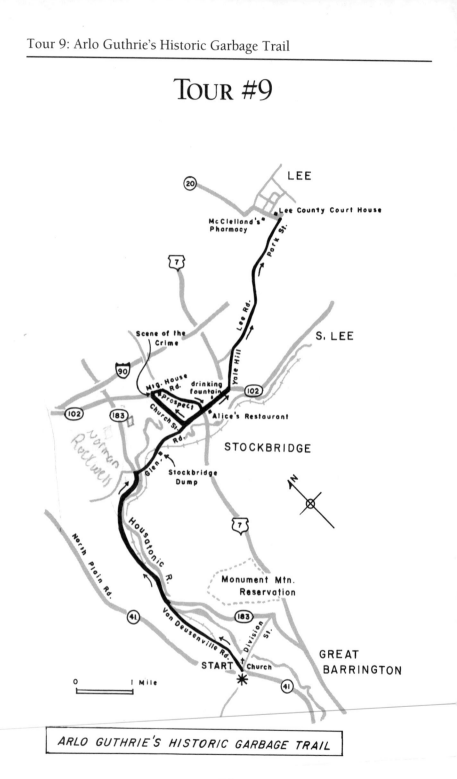

ARLO GUTHRIE'S HISTORIC GARBAGE TRAIL

# Arlo Guthrie's Historic Garbage Trail

*You can get anything you want at Alice's Res-tau-rant.*
*You can get anything you want at Alice's Res-tau-rant.*
*Walk right in. It's around the back, just a half a mile*
*from the railroad track.*

— Arlo Guthrie

If you grew up in the late '60s, *Alice's Restaurant* is bound to bring a flood of memories. It was a time of change: a time of hippies, long hair, granny dresses, wire-rimmed glasses, questioning authority, the American Dream, the Vietnam War, the draft — and the movie *Alice's Restaurant* captured the essence of those times.

The movie was filmed right here in Stockbridge, Massachusetts, after Arthur Penn, producer and Berkshire resident, heard Arlo Guthrie's account of the "Alice's Restaurant Massacree" on the radio and decided to make a movie of it. (If you want a full hit of the nostalgia, watch the video.)

The route, which follows the "Arlo Guthrie Garbage Trail," starts at the church in Housatonic where the infamous Thanksgiving Day party took place. From here, the route follows Arlo and his friend as they loaded the resulting garbage in a bright red Volkswagen microbus and took it to the Stockbridge town dump, which was closed for Thanksgiving. Then the route follows the microbus's trail as, "with tears in our eyes, we drove off into the sunset, lookin' for another place to put the garbage," passes the 15-foot cliff — scene of the "crime"— and returns to Stockbridge Town Hall, where Arlo was jailed.

The tour passes the site of Alice's Restaurant and on to the Lee County Court House, where Officer Obie presented the "twenty-seven 8x10 colored glossy pictures with circles and arrows and a paragraph on the back of each one explaining what each one was," to the blind judge.

It was here that Arlo was convicted for "littering and being a public nuisance," a crime that ultimately made him unfit for military service in the Vietnam War.

**Mileage:** 14.2
**Time:** 1-1 ½ hours
**Rating:** Moderate. Several short, steep climbs.

**Description:** The tour is over moderately rolling hills, with several short, steep climbs. The roads are paved except for one dirt stretch of about a mile. This is a point-to-point ride instead of a loop. Arrange for someone to drop you off at the church and pick you up in Lee; or, you can park near the church and make it an out-and-back by retracing the route. The church, where the tour starts, now belongs to Arlo and is headquarters for his musical tours, mail-order business, and a museum for his father's musical memorabilia. You're welcome to stop in for a visit.

**Food and Drink:** Drink or fill your water bottle at the drinking fountain across the street from the market, next to the tourist booth, in Stockbridge. There are several restaurants in Stockbridge and two markets, all within a block of Main St.

McClelland's Pharmacy, in Lee, has a soda fountain from the 1950s era, where you can hang out with the locals and "carbo-load" on Haagen-Dazs or Ben & Jerry's ice cream. There are several convenience stores, a grocery store, and restaurants along Main St. (Rte. 20) in Lee.

**Parking:** On Van Deusenville Rd. just north of Division St. in Housatonic, there are several cleared areas just off the road next to the railroad tracks.

# DIRECTIONS

| | |
|---|---|
| **0.0 Mile** | **Starting at the infamous church, scene of the Thanksgiving Day party in the movie *Alice's Restaurant*, at the corner of Van Deusenville Rd. and Division St., go north on Van Deusenville.** The road is flat and parallels the railroad tracks. You'll cross the tracks several times before you go through the main part of the sleepy little town of Housatonic. |
| **1.8 Mile** | **Go straight across to Rte. 183 when you come to the stop sign in Housatonic.** On your left is the school playground, and on your right are the old paper mill buildings and train station. Just outside town, you'll start following the Housatonic River. The road goes away from the river and then comes back to a beautiful stretch of boulder-strewn white water. |

**4.7 Mile**   **Take a right onto Glendale Rd.** It's the first paved road you can take after climbing the hill by the pumping station on the river. You'll cross the Housatonic River at the bottom of the hill and climb another little grunt of a hill. Just beyond the top, the road levels out. On your right, at 5.1 miles, just before you cross a bridge over the railroad tracks, there's a house with a dirt drive. Beside the drive is a dirt lane with a steel-screen fence. This is the scene of the "THIS-DUMP-CLOSED-ON-THANKS-GIVING" sign where Arlo and friend went to dump the party garbage. Since then, the dump site has moved.

Continuing on Glendale Rd., swing left over a bridge across the river and through a golf course. At the corner of Church St. and Main St. in Stockbridge, you'll see the sandstone-colored Jonathan Edwards monument in the median on your left.

**6 Mile**   **Take a left onto Church St.** at the monument. The Stockbridge cemetery will be on your right.

**6.5 Mile**   **Turn right onto North Church St.** at the first bend in the road. The road becomes dirt and then forks almost immediately. **Take Field Rd. to the right.** After a short distance, you'll come to Meeting House Rd.

**Go right onto Meeting House Rd.** Going up the road, on your right is a "15-foot cliff." (A recently built, light brown house and garage are at the bottom of it now.) On the fateful day, Arlo found a pile of garbage already at the base of the cliff and decided "that one big pile of garbage was better than two little piles; and rather than bring that one up, we decided to throw ours down." They did. Thus the infamous garbage-dumping deed and initiation of Arlo's criminal record.

**7.1 Mile**   **Take a right onto Prospect Hill Rd.** when you come to the stop sign at the paved road. Just down the road, you'll pass Naumkeag Estate on your right.

**Officer Obie:** *Kid, we found your name on an envelope at the bottom of a half a ton of garbage, and I just wanted to know if you had any information about it.*

**Arlo:** *I cannot tell a lie. I put that envelope under that garbage.*

Courtesy of Arlo Guthrie

Arlo:  *Obie, I can't pick up the garbage with these here*
       *handcuffs on.*
Officer Obie:  *Shut up, Kid, and get in the back of the*
               *patrol car.*

---

**8 Mile**          **Go right onto Main St.** (Rte. 102) when you get to
                    the corner. At the end of town, you'll come to the
                    Stockbridge Cemetery. Across the street, east of the
                    Children's Clock Tower, is the big, white Stockbridge
                    Town Hall. **Cross the street and ride through the**

**parking lot.** The town hall houses the police department offices and the jail where Arlo and his friend were incarcerated after admitting to the dastardly garbage-dumping misdemeanor. Here Officer Obie took their belts: "Kid, we don't want any hangin's," and Arlo replied, "Obie, did you think I was gonna hang myself for litterin'?" Officer Obie also removed the seat from the toilet in their cell so they "couldn't hit themselves over the head and drown." This is where Alice came and, with "a few nasty words to Obie on the side," bailed out Arlo.

**8.4 Mile** **Turn around and head back down Main St.** toward the center of town. You'll pass the Red Lion Inn on your right. Just beyond it is an alley between the Stockbridge Center Market and the Seven Arts Building. At the end of the alley ("walk right in; it's around the back") on the right, is the site of Alice Brock's restaurant (now the Fête Chez Vous food shop).

**9.3 Mile** **Head east on Main St. and take a left on Yale Hill Rd.** The white Berkshire Festival Theatre building is on the northwest corner. There's a short (0.4-mile), steep climb on Yale Hill. Halfway up, you'll pass a scenic old mill wheel on your right.

**11 Mile** **Take a right onto Lee Rd.** when you come to the stop sign. There is no road sign at the corner. Continue until you come to a stop sign at the corner of Rte. 20 in Lee. Across the street, to the north of the village green, is a brick building — Lee Court House — where Officer Obie presented the "twenty-seven 8x10 colored glossy pictures with circles and arrows and a paragraph on the back of each one explaining what each one was" to the blind judge. This is where Arlo was tried and convicted of "littering and being a public nuisance."

**14.2 Mile** **Go left onto Rte. 20.** Across the street from the Court House is McClelland's Pharmacy. If you have worked up an appetite, grab a shake, float, frappé, or sundae at the soda fountain. Seltzer water is free for the asking. This is the end of the trip. If you want to make it an out-and-back, just retrace your tracks back to Arlo's church in Housatonic.

# TOUR #10

Adsit Crosby Rd.

(23)

Konkapot River Pool

START

River Rd.

(57)

HARTSVILLE

Roadside Store

Fish
Hatchery

Bidwell Park

MONTEREY

Monterey
General Store

Green
Park

Tyringham Rd.

N. Marl. Hill
Rd.

NEW
MARLBOROUGH

Lake
Garfield

N. Marl.
Southfield
Rd.

Sandisfield Rd.

(23)

Main Tyringham Rd.

S. Sandisfield Rd.

Sandisfield
State Forest

Street

West

Sandisfield New Hartford Rd.

SANDISFIELD

Hubbard

Town Hill Rd.

W. OTIS

(23)

Cold Spring Rd.

Lower
Spectacle
Pond

N

W. Otis Rd.

swimming
hole

Hawley
Rd.

(8)

W. Branch Farmington River

NEW BOSTON

0          1 Mile

New Boston
General Store

HARTSVILLE - NEW BOSTON - MONTEREY

80

# HARTSVILLE – NEW BOSTON – MONTEREY

**Mileage:** 30.5
**Time:** 1¾–3 hours
**Rating:** Moderate. 59 ft. per mile climbed. Total climbed: 1,800 ft.

**Description:** This very rural tour passes old farms with horses or cattle grazing and goes through several small, one-store country towns, including Monterey and New Boston. There are long stretches of open road through the woodlands, some moderate climbing, and an easy, breezy, four-mile descent through Sandisfield. You'll also bike along scenic stretches of the Buck and Farmington rivers. The boulder-filled, white-water stretch of the Farmington is famous for kayaking competitions; you may even see kayakers in early spring. Auto traffic is very light on back roads, but there is more on the Rte. 8 stretch. All are paved roads, most in excellent shape with some patched pavement.

**Options:** You can swim or picnic at the Buck River pool, Spectacle Pond, and Konkapot River pool. There's also picnicking at Bidwell Park. Tour the Berkshire National Fish Hatchery, where Atlantic salmon are milked for their eggs. (See the Special Attractions chapter for descriptions.)

**Food and Drink:** Fill your water bottle before you leave home, as the first fill-up stop is the New Boston General Store, about 13 miles into the ride. The store has a good selection of snack foods, Gatorade®, and prepackaged sandwiches. The folks there will be glad to fill your water bottle; if you come when the store is not open (such as Sunday afternoon), you are welcome to fill your bottle from the outside faucet near the bulletin board on the front porch.

You can also get snacks, drinks, and made-to-order sandwiches at the Monterey General Store. There's a drinking fountain behind the baseball diamond in Monterey's Greene Park.

The Roadside Store, just west of Monterey on Rte. 57, has great home-cooked food. This is where my biking buddies and I fill up on outstanding blueberry pancakes with maple syrup and fresh, home-baked bread before long rides. It's one of our all-time favorites and a good place for breakfast or lunch before, after, or during the ride.

RAPIDS ON THE KONKAPOT RIVER

**Parking:** on the side of the road, Rte. 57, next to the Umpachene Grange Hall in Hartsville; it's on the corner of Rte. 57 and Hartsville-Mill River Rd. (see map)

## Directions

| | |
|---|---|
| **0.0 Mile** | **Starting at the corner of Rte. 57 and Hartsville-Mill River Rd. in Hartsville, go south on Rte. 57.** The road is patched pavement and rolling, with a fair amount of climbing. You'll go through the tiny town of New Marlborough 3.3 miles from the start, but there's not much to see there other than the white church and The Old Inn on the Green. |
| **8.3 Mile** | **Rte. 57 takes a very sharp left turn.** A green and white sign on the corner reads "New Boston 4 Miles." All the climbing you've done is now rewarded with four miles of downhill. On your way down, 2.6 miles from the bend and just after you pass the Sandisfield School on your |

left, there's a fine swimming hole on the right just after the curve. You'll see a row of two- to three-foot-high rocks lining the road. Then the road widens where cars have parked. Stop here. Hop over the rock embankment and down to the small set of rapids. At the bottom of a gnarled boulder outcropping you'll find an eight-foot deep pool with clean, clear water. Enjoy!

**12.9 Mile**  **Take a left onto Rte. 8** when you come to the stop sign. On your left is the New Boston Inn. (If you want snacks or drinks, go right on Rte. 8. A stone's throw down on your left is the New Boston General Store.) Going north on Rte. 8, the road follows the scenic West Branch of the Farmington River. This is a famous whitewater stretch where kayakers compete in the spring when water is high. Along here, there are two side pull-offs with picnic tables along the river — good places to picnic or stop to cool your feet.

**17.7 Mile**  **Go left onto Hawley Rd.** 4.8 miles from the turn onto Rte. 8. It's the first left you can take past the Earth Camp. You start to climb immediately, and it's patched pavement. For the next 2.5 miles, it's uphill and rolling. Then it levels out some, followed by a rolling, winding downhill past beautiful old farms.

You'll come to Spectacle Pond — surrounded by maples, beeches, and pines — about three miles from the turn onto Hawley. On the right, just before the road goes over a creek feeding the lake, there's a grassy area near the shore, a dilapidated picnic table, and a stone fire circle. This is a comfortable spot to take a break, and you can swim here, too, if you don't mind the darkness of the water. (It's caused by the tannin from the pine needles and other decaying vegetation.)

Past Spectacle Pond, the road name changes from Hawley (West Otis Rd.) to Cold Spring. You have a short downhill stretch before you come to Rte. 23.

**23 Mile**  **Turn left onto Rte. 23** and bike the 3.8 miles of rolling, winding, predominantly downhill road to Monterey. The Monterey General Store is on the left on Main St. There you can get deli sandwiches made to order, then take your food down to Bidwell Park. It's just past the store on your left, down a little dirt lane. This is a relax-

## BE KIND TO YOUR THIGHS
Niti Seip stretchin' out at Spectacle Pond.

ing place to take a picnic; it's quiet, has a picnic table and the soothing sounds of laughing water.

If your water bottle is dry, fill up at the fountain behind the baseball diamond at the other park in town, Greene Park. It's across the street from Bidwell Park.

Continuing east on Rte. 23, you'll pass the Roadside Store about 1.5 miles east of Monterey. For lunch or breakfast, this is the place for home cooking. It's said by many — including me — to have the best breakfast in the Berkshires.

**28.7 Mile**    **Take a left onto River Rd.** 0.3 mile past the Roadside Store. There's a green and white sign on the corner that reads "Hartsville 4 Miles." It's all down hill from here. You'll ride across the Konkapot River, and less than 0.2 mile further down on the right is a widening of the road where cars have pulled off. From there, follow the trail down to the swimming hole hidden away beneath the pines at the base of a water chute and rapids formed by jagged rock ledges. The water's cool all summer, and there's even a rope swing.

A mile further on River Rd., on the left, you'll see the sign for the Berkshire National Fish Hatchery. (See Special Attractions chapter for details.)

**30.5 Mile**    **Turn left onto Rte. 57** at the stop sign at the bottom of the descent. Go a hundred yards, and you're back at the grange hall where the tour started.

*Don't ride the brakes on a long descent. It will heat the rims and could cause a clincher tire to blow off. Instead, apply the brakes briefly and firmly to slow your speed, then coast until you want to slow again. This way the rims and brake pads will cool between applications.*

— 600 Tips for Better Bicycling,
by the Editors of *Bicycling Magazine*

# Tour #11

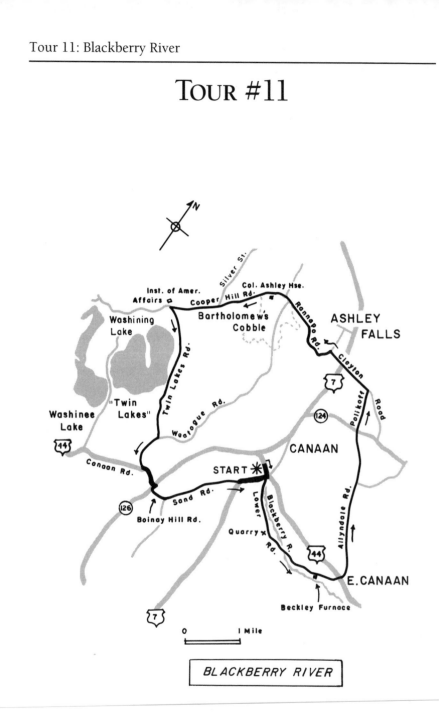

BLACKBERRY RIVER

# BLACKBERRY RIVER

**Mileage:** 17.2
**Time:** 1¼ – 2¼ hours
**Rating:** Moderate. 33.7 ft. per mile climbed. Total climbed: 580 ft.

**Description:** This route has long stretches of level or gently rolling road through farm land, horse ranches, and river-bottom country. There are mountain views to the north, east, and south. The route follows Blackberry River past the Pfizer Limestone Quarry and the ruins of the Old Beckley Furnace. It then goes through the valley around Rattlesnake Hill. There's a rolling, pleasantly winding, and well-shaded stretch along the shore of Washining Lake. The challenging 0.8-mile climb up Cooper Hill makes this otherwise easy tour a moderate one. It has two breezy descents and is all on paved road.

**Options:** Look into the huge pit at Pfizer Limestone Quarry. Check out the historic ruins of the 19th century Beckley Furnace. Hike or picnic at Bartholomew's Cobble. Tour Colonel Ashley House, the oldest house in the Berkshires. (See Special Attractions chapter for descriptions.)

**Food and Drink:** Fill your water bottle and get snack food before you start; there are no places to buy food after the first 0.1 mile, but you can get a water bottle fill at the Colonel Ashley House if you ask.

**Parking:** At the baseball diamond parking lot on the south side of Rte. 44, east of Canaan (across from McDonald's) and just west of the intersection of Rte. 44 and Rte. 7 (see map).

## DIRECTIONS

**0.0 Mile**    **Starting at the parking lot, go east on Rte. 44.**
**0.1 Mile**    **Take a right onto Rte. 7 at the light.** Almost immediately, you'll cross a bridge over the Blackberry River.
**0.2 Mile**    **Turn left onto Lower Rd. just past the bridge.** (There's no road sign on the corner.) The road is gently rolling, with views of the Canaan Mountains to the south. Less than a mile along is the **Pfizer Limestone Quarry.** This pit was originally begun to mine magnesium for the Manhattan Project — to create the first atomic bomb — during World War II.

You can pull your bike over and walk up the rise of land for a look into the pit. (But don't cross the fence. This is private property, and it is against federal regulations for non-authorized personnel to be on the grounds. Besides, it's dangerous!) The equipment may look like Tonka® toys down there, but they are real trucks and bulldozers! If you are susceptible to poison ivy, be careful; there's a lot of it growing along the road here.

**2.3 Mile**    **Beckley Furnace.** The remains of the big, stone Beckley Furnace is off to the right down a little dirt road. This historical monument is an industrial relic of the 1800s — a time when carpenters, farmers, shipwrights, and railroads were in a growth cycle and needed iron. Fast-flowing Blackberry River turned the turbines to provide energy for the air blast to the furnace. A sign in front of the furnace gives detailed information and history about the furnace and the iron-smelting era.

A little trail goes up past the furnace to the dam. Hike up it if you want to see the dam or look for pocket-sized, hundred-year-old pig iron ingots and slag glass along the banks. There are a couple of picnic-blanket-sized rocks in and along the river.

**3 Mile**    **Turn left onto Rte. 44 at the stop sign. Go right immediately onto Casey Hill Rd.** You'll pass a sand and gravel processing operation and come to a stop sign at the end of the road.

**Go straight onto Allyndale Rd.** This flat-to-gently-rolling stretch has panoramic views of the mountain and valley to the north.

**5.7 Mile**    **When you come to the stop sign, go straight across Rte. 124 onto Polikoff Rd.**

**6.3 Mile**    **Take a left onto Clayton Rd. at the intersection and bear left almost immediately to stay on Clayton.** You'll cross Rte. 7 further on.

**7.5 Mile**    **Go left onto East Main St. at the crossroad in the residential part of Ashley Falls.** There's no road sign on the corner, but it's the first crossroad you come to after crossing Rte. 7. (Take a right on this corner if you need bike supplies. The Bike Doctor and his bike shop are just up the road, less than a block.)

**7.7 Mile**    **Cross Rte. 7A to Rannapo Rd. at the stop sign in Ashley Falls.** Now you'll go through open farm country and river-bottom land. Shortly after crossing the

Housatonic River, you'll see signs for Bartholomew's Cobble Nature Preserve on the left.

**8.6 Mile** **Take a left onto Cooper Hill Rd., just past Weatogue Rd.** The Colonel Ashley House is on the left a short way down. You can get your water bottle filled here, if you ask. Further on, the climb begins. Hunker down — Cooper Hill is the meanest climb of the day. It's a 0.8-mile thigh-burner. (If you enjoy this climb, you've got to try the Greylock Century tour. See its description in the Resources chapter under "Organized Rides.")

**Turn left at the yield sign at the top of the hill to stay on Cooper Hill Rd.** You've got a long downhill with great views of the Washington Mountain range to the west.

**10.9 Mile** **Go left onto Twin Lakes Rd., across from the Institute of American Affairs.** The route now rolls and winds through shaded forest and along the shore of Washining Lake. Further on, you'll pass two horse farms: El Hamil Arabians and McGariage Morgans.

**14.4 Mile** **Take a left onto Canaan Rd. (Rte. 44) when you come to the stop sign.**

**14.6 Mile** **Turn right onto Rte. 126 immediately after crossing Housatonic River.** There's no road sign on the corner, but it's the first right you can take after the bridge.

**14.7 Mile** **Turn left onto Boinay Hill Rd., the first paved road to the left.** There's no road sign on this corner either. You'll climb a small hill and be rewarded at the top with a view to the west of the Canaan Mountains across Robins Swamp.

**15.2 Mile** **Take a left onto Sand Rd. at the stop sign at the bottom of the hill.** The next stretch is flat, easy biking along the valley floor.

**16.4 Mile** **Go left onto Rte. 7 at the stop sign.**

**17.1 Mile** **Take a left onto Rte. 44 when you come to the traffic light.**

**17.2 Mile** **Back to the baseball diamond parking lot, where the tour began.**

# TOUR #12

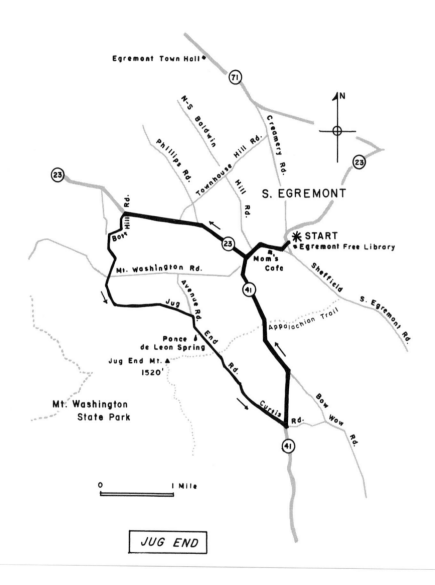

# JUG END — PONCE DE LEON SPRING

**Mileage:** 9.4
**Time:** 1/2 –1 hour
**Rating:** Moderate. 51 ft. per mile climbed. Total climbed: 480 ft.

**Description:** Rolling roads, with views of Jug End Mountain to the south and Tom Ball Mountain to the north. There are a few moderate climbs on Jug End Rd. and Rte. 41. The tour crosses the Appalachian Trail near Ponce de Leon Spring. There is a 1.5-mile stretch of dirt road; the rest is well paved.

**Options:** Drink cool, pure water coming right out of a cleft in the rock at Ponce de Leon Spring. (Even though the local folks have been drinking from this spring for generations, I must caution you to partake at your own risk because the water is not monitored by health officials.)

**Food and Drink:** Mom's Cafe, on Main St. (Rte. 23/41) in the middle of South Egremont, is an excellent place to have breakfast or lunch. Mom's Convenience Store is next door, if you want to get pretzels, Gatorade®, or other snacks and drinks. You can fill your water bottle at Ponce de Leon Spring.

**Parking:** The Town of Egremont has generously offered use of the South Egremont Free Library parking lot on Button Ball Ln., just south of Rte. 23/41, for cyclists' parking on weekends. On weekdays, however, please park elsewhere, because the space is needed for library patrons. As an alternative, the Egremont town hall parking lot on Rte.71 (see map) has ample space, and town officials are happy to have you park there.

## Directions

| | |
|---|---|
| **0.0 Mile** | **Start at the intersection of Rte. 23/41 and Button Ball Ln. in South Egremont.** Bike west on Rte. 23/41 through South Egremont. At the west end of town, Rte. 41 goes south, and Rte. 23 continues west. Follow Rte. 23 over the gently rolling hills. |
| **2.2 Mile** | **Take a left onto Botthill Rd.** There's an empty red wooden building on the southwest corner. |

**Swing left onto Jug End Road at the bottom of the hill.** After the turn, there's a view of Jug End Mountain to the south.

**3.2 Mile**  **Go straight across Mount Washington Rd.** Looking north from the road after it swings east, you can see Egremont Valley and Tom Ball Mountain; further to the east is Monument Mountain.

**4.6 Mile**  **Jug End Rd. sweeps to the right and turns into a dirt road.** Approximately 0.3 miles further along, there's a sign marking where the Appalachian Trail crosses the road. About 0.2 further down on the right, you'll find Ponce de Leon Spring. It's hard to see unless you're looking for it, so keep your eyes open for a narrow, rocky riverbed. Follow the path going up into the woods and listen for falling water. You can fill your bottle from the pipe or follow the pipe back up to where water comes right out of a cleft in a rock.

**6.5 Mile**  **Turn left onto Rte. 41 when you come to the stop sign,** about 1.6 miles after the spring. This 2.3-mile paved stretch of road is rolling with some uphill.

**8.8 Mile**  **Turn right onto Rte. 23/41** at the stop sign and ride through South Egremont.

**9.4 Mile**  **Go right onto Button Ball Ln.** at the east end of town and into the library parking lot to complete the ride.

*Fossil fuels are fueling future fossils.*

## PASSING THROUGH
Alford, Massachusetts

# TOUR #13

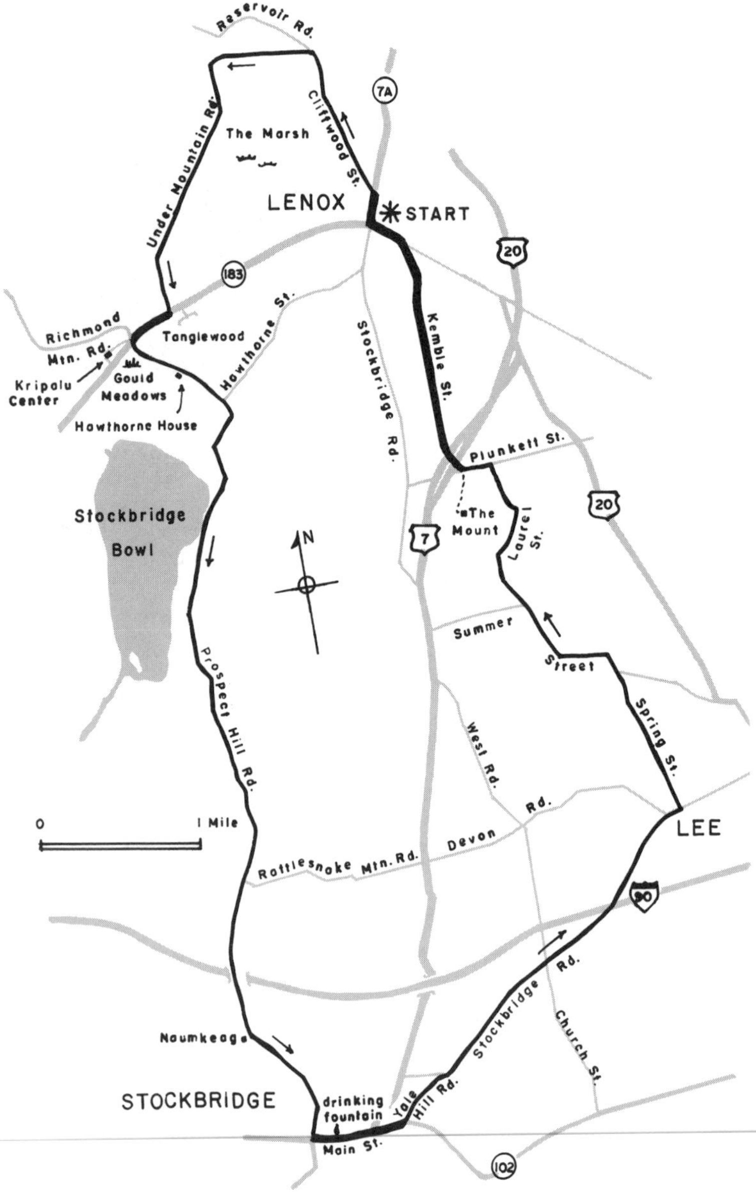


TANGLEWOOD-NAUMKEAG-THE MOUNT

# TANGLEWOOD –
# NAUMKEAG – THE MOUNT

**Mileage:** 17
**Time:** 1-2 hours
**Rating:** Moderate. 53.5 ft. per mile climbed. Total climbed: 910 ft.

**Description:** Mostly rolling road with two short, steep climbs and several moderate climbs. Except for a one-mile stretch of dirt road, it's all on well-paved roads. There is an excellent view, from the hill above Under Mountain Horse Farm, of Rattlesnake Mountain and the wetlands known as The Marsh. There's also a panoramic view of seven mountains (including Monument Mountain, Mt. Everett, and Jacob's Ladder) across Gould Meadow and Stockbridge Bowl, and good views of The Pinnacle and the October Mountain range. The tour passes through the town of Stockbridge.

**Options:** If you like, take a walk through the grounds of the Tanglewood Music Festival or check out Nathaniel Hawthorne's Little Red House across Hawthorne Rd. from Tanglewood's Lion Gate. You can experience a relic of the "Gilded Age" by touring Naumkeag Estate mansion and gardens, sightseeing in the town of Stockbridge, or touring Edith Wharton's summer home, "The Mount." (See Special Attractions for descriptions.)

**Food and Drink:** Drink up or fill your water bottle at the drinking fountain on Main St. in Stockbridge. There are many good restaurants in both Lenox and Stockbridge. Clearwater Natural Foods on the corner of Church and Housatonic Streets in Lenox has sandwiches and a wide selection of snack foods. There's a market off Main Street in Stockbridge.

**Parking:** Main St. or Walker St. (Rte. 183) in Lenox.

## DIRECTIONS

| | |
|---|---|
| **0.0 Mile** | **Starting at the monument in Lenox at the intersection of routes 183 and 7A, go north on 7A.** |
| **0.1 Mile** | **Turn left onto Cliffwood St.**, the second road on the left. It goes through a residential section, and then the name changes to Under Mountain Rd. when you leave |

town. Just past the Under Mountain Horse Farm, there's a short (0.75 mile), steep climb. From the top of the hill, there's a good view of the wetlands known as The Marsh to the southeast and Rattlesnake Mountain to the south. Continue past the duck pond until you come to a "T" intersection. This is Rte. 183. Across the road is the main gate of Tanglewood Music Festival and the summer home of the Boston Symphony Orchestra. (If you want to walk through the grounds, go straight across and up to the entrance. The gate is left open when there is no performance, and you are welcome to take a stroll. Leave bikes out front.)

**3.4 Mile**  **Turn right onto Rte. 183, go 0.2 mile (past the entrance to Kripalu Center), and take a left onto Hawthorne St.** From the corner, look across Gould Meadows for a view of West Stockbridge Mountain, Mt Everett, Mt. Washington, and Monument Mountain.

Down Hawthorne St. 0.4 mile, you'll see Nathaniel Hawthorne's Little Red House, across from Tanglewood's Lion Gate. The author moved here to recover his self-esteem after being fired from his Customs House job in Boston. He wrote *The House of the Seven Gables* and *The Wonder Book* while living here.

Continuing south, the road swings down by Stockbridge Bowl (Lake Mahkeenac). If you look north across the water, you can see a huge, brick building on the side of the mountain. This is Shadowbrook, home of Kripalu Center, largest holistic health facility on the East Coast. It houses a unique organization whose members live a yogic lifestyle. The center offers year-round programs open to anyone who wishes to learn how to live a healthier lifestyle via yoga, conscious

*"Summer afternoon — summer afternoon; to me those have always been the two most beautiful words in the English language."*

Edith Wharton,
Author and Southern Berkshire resident

## NOT JUST ANOTHER HORSE TROUGH
This fountain in Stockbridge has been quenching the
thirst of travelers since the 1880s.

eating, stress-reduction, and healing arts. Great place to visit! (I'm putting in this plug 'cause I know about Kripalu; I lived there as a resident staff member for more than nine years.)

Looking west, you can see the ridge of West Stockbridge Mountain. To the northeast is the large white mansion of Seranac, used by the Boston Symphony Orchestra during the Tanglewood season.

4.9 miles from Rte. 183, you come to the Naumkeag mansion, a relic of the "Gilded Age." It's on your right across from the Congregation of the Marians of the Immaculate Conception. (Tours of Naumkeag are available. See Special Attractions chapter for details.)

Continue south on Prospect Hill Rd. (The name changes from Hawthorne St. to Prospect Hill just past Hawthorne's Little Red House.). At the bottom of the hill, past the tennis courts, there's a stop sign at Main St. (Rte. 102) in Stockbridge. On your left is a Civil War monument with an eagle at the top. Across the street, on the corner, is the famous Red Lion Inn.

**9.2 Mile**    **Turn left onto Main St.** Just past the tourist information booth (check it out if you want to sightsee in town), on your left in the middle of the block, is a drinking fountain. Across the street and down a bit, on the corner of Elm St. and Main, is another fountain — a bronze satyr's head emerging from a marble slab, with potable water pouring out of the satyr's mouth. This fountain has been around a long time; horses used to drink from the trough beneath the head. Follow Main St. east, past the junction with Rte. 7, to Yale Hill Rd.

**9.8 Mile**    **Take a left onto Yale Hill Rd., the first left past Rte. 7.** The big, white Berkshire Playhouse is on the corner, and there's a road sign in the small grass triangle. Yale Hill has a fairly steep, 0.2-mile climb and follows a delightful little brook up to the top of the hill. Part way up, on the right side, you can see a little mill and water wheel, with the brook flowing underneath. When you come to a stop sign, you're at the corner of Lee Rd. There is no road sign.

**10.6 Mile**    **Take a right onto Lee Rd.** About 0.8 mile from the turn, there is a good view of the Beartown Mountains to the southeast.

| | |
|---|---|
| **12.5 Mile** | **Go left onto Spring St.** Spring St. is gently rolling and goes past a golf course and graveyard before it comes to a "T" at Summer St. |
| **13.2 Mile** | **Turn left onto Summer St.** There is a moderate, 0.4-mile climb up to Highlawn Farm. To the east, across from the farm, you have a good view of the October Mountain range. |
| **14 Mile** | **Take a right onto Laurel St.** It's dirt and the only road to your right. There is no road sign on the corner, but you'll see a swimming pool to the north. Laurel St. goes immediately downhill. At the bottom, look across Laurel Lake. The knobby mountain you can see is called The Pinnacle. |
| | Further up the road, off to the right, is a road sign saying, "Laurel Lake ext." Don't take it. Continue straight on Laurel Lake Rd., and you'll come to a stop sign on Plunkett St. There's no road sign at the corner. |
| **15.1 Mile** | **Go left onto Plunkett St.** Just before you come to the intersection with Rte. 7, you'll see "The Mount," a mansion built during the "Gilded Age" by the famous writer and interior designer Edith Wharton. It is now the home of the Edith Wharton Restoration and Shakespeare & Co., and it's worth a tour if your interests lie in that direction (see Special Attractions for details). |
| **15.4 Mile** | **Continue across Rte. 7, and you're on Kemble St.** Kemble St. is also Rte. 7A north. Canyon Ranch Spa is on your right about 0.7 mile from the intersection, and Berkshire Performing Arts Center is to the left a little further on. After a moderate, 0.4-mile climb, you come to the stop sign at Rte. 183. |
| **16.8 Mile** | **Take a left onto Rte. 183.** You are in Lenox village. |
| **17 Mile** | **You are back at the monument where the tour began.** |

*"There are two ways of spreading light; to be the candle, or the mirror that reflects it."*

Edith Wharton

# TOUR #14

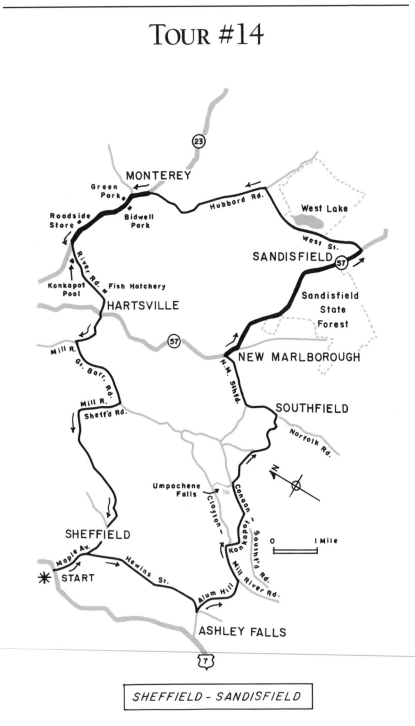

SHEFFIELD - SANDISFIELD

# SHEFFIELD — SANDISFIELD

**Mileage:** 35.2
**Time:** 2½ – 4 hours
**Rating:** Moderate. 54 ft. per mile climbed. Total climbed: 1,890 ft.

**Description:** This route has long stretches of flat to gently rolling hills and several moderate-to-challenging ascents. It's a very scenic tour, with valley and mountain views to the south and west. Stretches of the road follow the swift water of the Konkapot River and babbling Umpachene Brook. There's an especially smooth, easy, four-mile descent on very good pavement toward the end of the ride.

**Options:** Picnic and/or cool off at Umpachene Falls or Konkapot River pool. Picnic at Bidwell Park; tour the Berkshire National Fish Hatchery, where Atlantic salmon are milked for their eggs. (See Special Attractions chapter for details.)

**Food and Drink:** Sheffield has two markets, two restaurants, and PJ's Convenience Store (on the south end of town). PJ's has deli sandwiches and is open seven days a week. There are no places to get food/drink until Southfield (10 miles). There you'll find a restaurant, and the Southfield General Store has made-to-order deli sandwiches and a good selection of drinks (it's not open Sunday afternoons).
The next place to get food or drink is 12 miles further in Monterey at the Monterey General Store (also closed Sunday afternoon). I like to pick up a sandwich and fruit at the Monterey General Store and take it down to Bidwell Park (a stone's throw down the road).
There's a drinking fountain behind the baseball diamond in Greene Park, across the street from Bidwell Park, for water-bottle filling. The Roadside Store, just west of Monterey, serves home-cooked meals and is a favorite stop for my biking buddies and me.

**Parking:** Main St. in Sheffield.

## DIRECTIONS

| | |
|---|---|
| **0.0 Mile** | **Start on the corner of Maple Ave. and Rte. 7 in Sheffield. Go east on Maple.** In less than a mile, you'll cross the Housatonic River. The first right past the river is Hewins Rd. |
| **0.9 Mile** | **Turn right onto Hewins Rd.** A short distance further |

## THE ROADSIDE STORE IN MONTEREY

on is Balsam Hill Farm. Check the views of Mount Washington and Mount Everett (the one with the lookout tower) to the west, and straight south you'll see knobby Rattlesnake Hill. This section of road through the valley is flat to gently rolling.

Three miles from turn onto Hewins, the road splits three ways. Alum Hill Rd. is on the left, Polikoff Rd. is in the middle, and Hewins continues to the right.

**3.9 Mile** **Take a left onto Alum Hill Rd.** Now there's a short, moderately steep climb (100 feet of vertical climb over a distance of one mile), followed by an equally steep descent.

**5.2 Mile** **Go left onto Mill River-Clayton Rd.** when you come to the stop sign at the bottom of the hill. A mile past Alum Hill Rd., Mill River-Clayton Rd. swings to the left, and Konkapot Rd. goes right. There's a white wooden sign in the grassy triangle.

**6.3 Mile** **Turn right onto Konkapot Rd. when you come to a "Y" in the road.** You'll cross the river after another 0.1

mile. On the right side, there is sandy beach, if you want to take a breather or cool off in the water. Past the river, the road climbs to a "T" at Canaan-Southfield Rd.

**7.1 Mile**    **Take a left onto Canaan-Southfield Rd. at the stop sign.** This stretch is generally uphill to Hadsell Rd.

If you'd like to go to Umpachene Falls, turn left on Umpachene Rd. when you come to the bridge over Umpachene Brook. The falls are 0.6 mile down this dirt road. There's a parking lot on your left just before the wooden bridge.

Continue on Southfield-Canaan Rd., biking along Umpachene Brook. There's some uphill, and the last 0.25 mile to Norfolk Rd. is a fairly steep, winding climb.

**10.3 Mile**    **Go left onto Norfolk Rd. at the stop sign and follow it into Southfield.** Southfield General Store is on the left, past the Buggy Whip Factory. **Continue north on Norfolk Rd.** The patched-pavement road is rough with some potholes, and it's downhill until you cross the metal-grate bridge and come to Southfield Rd.

**10.9 Mile**    **At the stop sign, take a right onto New Marlborough-Southfield Rd.** This is also patched pavement. Now you have one half-mile climb coming up to New Marlborough-Sandisfield Rd.

**12.2 Mile**    **Turn right onto New Marlborough-Sandisfield Rd. (Rte. 57) when you come to the stop sign.** This stretch goes through sparsely populated forest country, much of which is Sandisfield State Forest.

**16.6 Mile**    **Take a left onto West St.** You have to keep your eyes open for this one; it's easy to whiz right by. The corner is nondescript and difficult to distinguish because the sign is old and rusty and you can barely read "West St." on it. Look for a grayish-brown house with cedar shingles on the left.

About a mile and a half up West St., on the right, you'll see the abandoned West Lake Headquarters of the Massachusetts Department of Environmental Management. It's an old brown barn with a tin roof. Go

*"When you come to a fork in the road, take it."*

Yogi Berra

down the little dirt drive if you want to visit the lake for a breather or swim. It's a pretty little lake, but there isn't much of a beach.

**19.4 Mile** **Follow the pavement where the road bends sharply to the left. West St. changes its name to Hubbard Rd. here.** This portion has the roughest road surface of the whole tour — a two-mile stretch of pitted asphalt with chuck holes and patches.

**22.7 Mile** **Take a left onto Rte. 23 at the stop sign.** Now it's winding and rolling into Monterey. The Monterey General Store is on the left. You can fill your water bottle at the fountain behind the baseball diamond at Greene Park. Bidwell Park is right across the street from Greene Park.

Outside of Monterey, it's downhill. At 24.6 Mile, you pass the Roadside Store.

**24.9 Mile** **Go left onto River Rd.** Past the Roadside Store about 0.3 mile, there's a green and white sign on the corner which reads "Hartsville 4 Miles." It's all downhill from here. Cross Konkapot River. Less than 0.2 mile further on the right, there's a widening of the road where cars have pulled off. If you want to take a break or swim, follow the trail down to the swimming hole hidden away beneath the pines. It's at the base of a water chute and rapids formed by jagged rock ledges. The water's cool all summer, and there's even a rope swing.

A mile further on River Rd., on the left, is the sign for the Berkshire National Fish Hatchery. Visitors are welcome.

**26.7 Mile** **Take a left onto Rte. 57 when you come to the stop sign in Hartsville, then immediately go right on Hartsville-Mill River Rd.** Almost a mile down the road, there's an abandoned wooden building on the right and a sign, in the grassy triangle, which reads "Mill River 4 miles."

*On bumpy pavement, put all your weight on the pedals and lift your buttocks slightly off the saddle to use your legs as shock absorbers.*

"Faster, Longer, Stronger!"
*Bicycling Magazine*

CARBOHYDRATE LOADING
Eric "Mega-thighs" Knudsen cuts into a
large blueberry pancake at The Roadside Store.

| | |
|---|---|
| **27.6 Mile** | **Turn left onto Mill River-Great Barrington Rd.** This stretch is even and rolling. |
| **29.5 Mile** | **Swing right onto Mill River-Sheffield Rd. when you come to the fork.** There is a sign, in the grassy triangle, which points to "Sheffield 6 miles." To the west on this stretch, there are excellent mountain views. After an initial climb, you've got a superb, smooth, four-mile descent on nicely paved road. The road then levels into Sheffield. |
| **35.2 Mile** | **Go left onto Rte. 7,** and you're back to the starting point. |

# TOUR #15

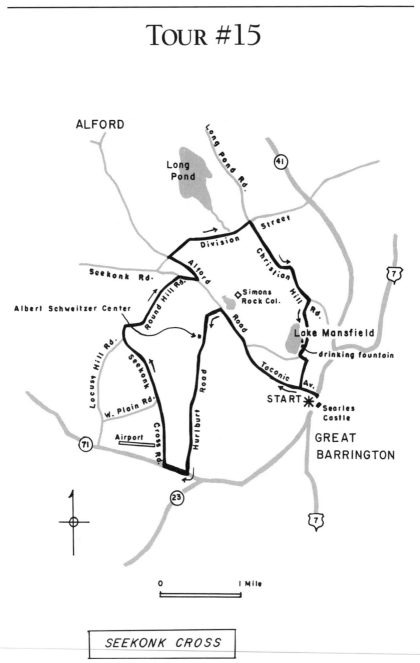

ALFORD

Long Pond Rd.

Long
Pond

41

Street

Division

Christian

Seekonk Rd.

Alford

Hill

7

Round Hill Rd.

◇ Simons
Rock Col.

Rd.

Albert Schweitzer Center

Road

Lake Mansfield

Locust Hill Rd.

Seekonk

drinking fountain

Toconic

Av.

Hurlburt Road

W. Plain Rd.

START ✳ Searles
Castle

Airport

71

Cross Rd.

GREAT
BARRINGTON

23

7

0          I Mile

SEEKONK CROSS

106

# SEEKONK CROSS

**Mileage:** 11.4
**Time:** 3/4 — 1¾ hours
**Rating:** Moderate. 52 ft. per mile climbed. Total climbed: 590 ft.

**Description:** This tour offers lots of flat riding through Alford Valley, with views of Tom Ball Mountain to the north and Mount Washington to the south across the spacious valley. Three significant climbs make this otherwise easy route a moderate one. All roads are well paved.

**Options:** Swim, cool off, or picnic at Green River or at Lake Mansfield's beach. Take a tour of the Albert Schweitzer Center. (See Special Attractions chapter for descriptions.)

**Food and Drink:** There is a drinking fountain at the Lake Mansfield beach. Many restaurants and places to buy snacks are in Great Barrington.

**Parking:** Main St. in Great Barrington.

## DIRECTIONS

| | |
|---|---|
| **0.0 Mile** | **Start on the corner of Taconic (St. James Place) and Main St., across from Searles Castle, in Great Barrington. Go west on Taconic Ave.** under the railroad overpass. Veer left and climb through Great Barrington's residential section with its many beautiful, old homes. (This mile-or-so climb is the first of three significant climbs on the tour.) Then it's easy downhill all the way to Hurlburt Rd. |
| **1.7 Mile** | **Take a left onto Hurlburt Rd.** You'll see a big, red barn/house complex on the northwest corner across from Simon's Rock College. A sign points to the Albert Schweitzer Center. The road is well paved and mostly flat. Note the view of Mount Washington to the south. |
| **2.2 Mile** | **Albert Schweitzer Center is on your right.** Another 1.4 miles and you pass the Great Barrington airport. |
| **3.8 Mile** | **Turn right at Rte. 71 when you come to the stop sign.** |
| **4.1 Mile** | **Go right at Seekonk Cross Rd.**, the first road on the right. This is the flattest stretch of the tour. |

## YOU CAN SMILE AT A FLAT TIRE
... if you've brought along a patch kit and tire irons.

| | |
|---|---|
| **4.8 Mile** | **Green River.** After you cross Green River, you'll see where cars have pulled off the road. Explore along the trails, and you'll find a good place to take a breather or cool off in the crystal clear water. |
| **5.9 Mile** | **Take a right onto Round Hill Rd.** when you come to newer pavement. After you pass through a heavily wooded section, you'll have beautiful valley views to the east and Tom Ball Mountain to the north. |
| **6.9 Mile** | **Go right onto Seekonk Rd. at the stop sign.** There's no road sign. Go down the hill and across Seekonk Brook. **Swing left where the road forks after the brook.** |
| **7.1 Mile** | **Turn left onto Alford Rd. when you come to the stop sign.** |
| **7.5 Mile** | **Take a right at Division St.** — that's the first paved road. Now you're on the second significant climb: a moderate, one-mile push to the blinking yellow light at Christian Hill Rd. |
| **8.6 Mile** | **Go right onto Christian Hill Rd.** After a short downhill, the road alternates between ascending and level stretches as it winds past country homes. |
| **9.9 Mile** | **Take a right onto Lake Mansfield Rd.** There's no road sign, but it's across from a wooden house with metal flashing on the roof. Tall spruce trees, with their lower branches cut off, line the northwest corner of the intersection. |
| **10.3 Mile** | **Lake Mansfield Park.** This small park has a swimming beach, picnic tables, and a drinking fountain (near the parking lot). |
| **10.8 Mile** | **Turn left onto Castle Hill St. at the intersection.** Ride downhill through the residential section and past the railroad station. |
| **11.3 Mile** | **Go left onto Taconic at the stop sign,** back under the railroad trestle to the traffic light. |
| **11.4 Mile** | **You're back at the starting point in Great Barrington.** |

*"A human being is never a total and permanent stranger to another human being. Man belongs to man."*

Albert Schweitzer

# TOUR #16

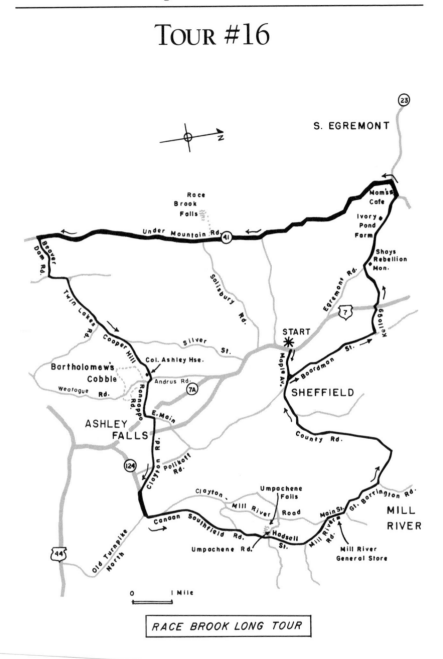

RACE BROOK LONG TOUR

# RACE BROOK LONG TOUR

**Mileage:** 38.6
**Time:** 2½ – 4 hours
**Rating:** Moderate. 42.5 ft. per mile climbed. Total climbed: 1,640 ft.

**Description:** This is a great tour if you want a long ride with outstanding scenery and don't mind a few moderate-to-challenging climbs. There are panoramic valley vistas and many views of mountains, including the East Mountain range to the east, the Mount Washington range to the west, and the Canaan Mountains to the south. See alpacas and llamas grazing at Ivory Pond Farm, plus many horse or cattle farms, country homes, and woodland brooks and rivers. The route varies from wide open valley to forest, and all is on paved roads with very little automobile traffic.

**Options:** Visit the Shay's Rebellion stone monument; hike to Race Brook Falls; tour the Colonel Ashley House, oldest house in Berkshire County; walk the nature trail, visit the museum, or picnic at Bartholomew's Cobble; swim, picnic, or sun at Umpachene Falls.

**Food and Drink:** Sheffield has two markets, two restaurants and PJ's Convenience Store (on the south end of town). PJ's has deli sandwiches and is open seven days a week.

My biking buddies and I like to eat at Mom's Cafe on Main St. (Rte. 23/41) in the middle of South Egremont (seven miles into the tour). Mom's Convenience Store is next door for snacks and drinks. If you ask first, you can fill your water bottle at the outside tap at the Colonel Ashley House (21 miles into the tour). The next place for food and drink is the Mill River General Store (31 miles into the tour). There you'll find deli sandwiches, fruit, and Gatorade®, and the folks there have always been glad to fill up a water bottle.

**Parking:** Main St. in Sheffield.

---

## DIRECTIONS

**0.0 Mile**     **Starting at the intersection of Rte. 7 and Maple Ave. in Sheffield, head east on Maple Ave.** After crossing the Housatonic River, Atwater Rd. is on the left immediately after the bridge. There is no road sign on corner.

| | |
|---|---|
| **0.7 Mile** | **Take a left onto Atwater Rd.** and go a short distance to the stop sign at Boardman Rd. |
| **0.8 Mile** | **Turn left onto Boardman Rd.** It's an easy, gently rolling ride, with sweeping valley vistas and great views of the Mount Washington range to the west. |
| **3.2 Mile** | **Go left onto Kellogg Rd.** You'll cross the Housatonic River. |
| **3.9 Mile** | **Take a right onto Rte. 7 and an immediate left at Rebellion Rd.**, the first left turn you can make. Now there's more flat, easy riding through the valley. |
| **5.2 Mile** | **Turn right onto Sheffield-Egremont Rd.** and follow it to Rte. 23/41. Just past the turn onto Sheffield-Egremont Rd., on the right at the corner of a cornfield, you can see a rough stone monument commemorating the last battle of Shay's Rebellion. (See the "Special Attractions" chapter to find out why Shay was rebelling.) Keep a lookout for the monument, as the weeds grow high around it in summer. |
| **7 Mile** | **Go left onto Rte. 23/41** and continue through the town of South Egremont. Mom's Cafe is on the left in the middle of town; next door is Mom's Convenience Store. West of town, Rte. 23 and Rte. 41 split, with Rte. 41 going south. |
| **7.5 Mile** | **Take a left onto Rte. 41.** There are some great views of the mountains to the east, west, and south at different points along the route. The road is rolling with occasional flat stretches all the way to Beaver Dam Rd. |
| **11.8 Mile** | **Race Brook Falls.** For a hike to Race Brook Falls (see "Special Attractions" chapter for description), look for the sign and paved turn-out on the right before you get to Salisbury Rd. |
| | Further on, look sharply for Beaver Dam Rd.; it is not well marked. There is no road sign on the corner, but at the intersection, there's a white plywood sign which says "Taconic" and points to the left. |
| **16.9 Mile** | **Take a left onto Beaver Dam Rd.** and follow it east to Twin Lakes Rd. You pass Fisher Pond almost immedi- |

*Drink plenty of water on a long ride. If you dehydrate, not only will you get fatigued, you'll take longer to recover.*

ately (you can see mountain peaks across the pond to the north), then climb a short hill.

**17.8 Mile**    **Turn left onto Twin Lakes and head north.** A short distance on, the road swings right, past the Taconic village green. You'll pass Taconic's post office on your left just beyond the green. There's moderate climbing on this stretch of well-paved road.

Across from the Institute of American Affairs, Twin Lakes Rd. makes a sharp right. Don't take it.

**19.8 Mile**    **Go straight onto Cooper Hill Rd.** It's a fairly steep climb. At the top, the road splits: Silver Rd. goes left, and Cooper Hill goes right.

**20.8 Mile**    **Make a right on Cooper Hill Rd.** As you descend on Cooper Hill Rd., you can look over the sweeping valley between the East Mountain range to the northeast and the Mount Washington range to the west. At the bottom of the hill, on the right side, is the Colonel Ashley House. Stop in if you'd like a tour (see Special Attractions chapter for details). If you need water, ask to fill your bottle here.

**22 Mile**    **Take a right onto Rannappo Rd.** when you come to a "Y" in the road.

**22.1 Mile**    **To visit Bartholomew's Cobble** (see description in the Special Attractions chapter), **go right on Weatogue.**

**23 Mile**    **Continue straight across Rte. 7A and onto East Main St. when you come to the stop sign near the Ashley Falls post office.** You'll bike through the residential section of Ashley Falls.

**23.3 Mile**    **Turn right onto Clayton Rd.,** the first road that crosses East Main St. There's no road sign at the corner. (The Bike Doctor's bike shop is just a little further up East Main, if you need bike supplies.) Cross Rte. 7 and continue down Clayton.

---

*For long-distance comfort, keep your elbows loose. Riding with stiff arms is not only fatiguing, but also dangerous, because it limits your ability to make subtle changes in direction. Try steering with your elbows locked, then relax them and feel the difference.*

*"Faster, Longer, Stronger!"*
*Bicycling Magazine*

## EVER HEAR THE GRASS SING?
Mort Davis listens closely.

Continue on Hadsell Rd. to the intersection with Lumbert Rd. and Mill River-Southfield Rd. This is a three-way intersection, with Mill River Rd. going to the left.

**30.2 Mile** **Turn left on Mill River Rd.** and follow the road into town.

**31.2 Mile** **Go right onto Main St. when you come to the town of Mill River.** Mill River General Store (and post office) is on the right.

A half mile north of town, Hartsville-Mill River Rd. splits off to the right. You'll continue to the left, following the sign toward Great Barrington, crossing Konkapot River. This is the site of several old mills, and there is a historical marker on the right, just before the bridge, which describes the mills' history.

**32.9 Mile** **Take a left onto Mill River-Sheffield Rd. (County Rd.)** when you come to a white, wooden sign in a grassy triangle. The sign points to the left to Sheffield. There's a short uphill at the beginning of County Rd., but as you continue west, the road levels, then heads downhill. Now you're in for a treat. It's a smooth, even, exhilarating descent on good pavement for the next four miles! The rest of the road is flat into Sheffield.

**38.6 Mile** **Back to the start of the tour in Sheffield.**

# Tour #17

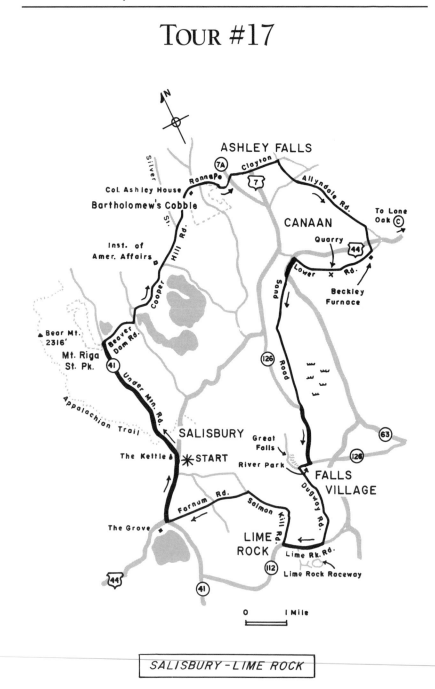

SALISBURY - LIME ROCK

# Salisbury — Lime Rock

**Mileage:** 31.4
**Time:** 2 – 4 ½ hours
**Rating:** Moderate. 35 ft. per mile climbed. Total climbed: 1,100 ft.

**Description:** There are spectacular mountain/valley views on this route. It passes cattle farms, horse ranches, country homes, and beautiful river stretches, including the Housatonic River — with an option to visit Great Falls — and the Blackberry River. One long, flat section on Sand Rd. parallels Robins Swamp. The long stretches of level, gently rolling road, with a few moderate downhills, make this, for the most part, an easy ride. However, there are several moderately difficult climbs, which is why the tour gets the moderate rating. All the roads are well paved.

**Options:** Look into the huge pit at the Pfizer Limestone Quarry. Visit the ruins of the 19th century Beckley Furnace. Hike or picnic at Bartholomew's Cobble Nature Preserve. Tour Colonel Ashley House, the oldest house in the Berkshires. Swim or picnic at The Grove in Lakeville. Visit Great Falls and picnic there or at the nearby park on the Housatonic River outside Falls Village. The Village Store on Main St. in Salisbury has a bike shop, if you need cycling supplies.

**Food and Drink:** Fill your bottle with pure spring water from The Kettle (an outside stone basin) on the corner next to the Salisbury Town Hall. There are several restaurants and markets in Salisbury. Except for a water-bottle fill at the Colonel Ashley House (8 miles into the ride), there are no food/drink places until Lakeville (29 miles into the tour). Lakeville has several restaurants, a convenience store, and a market. My favorite is On The Run Coffee Shop, because I can get freshly made sandwiches to go, then ride the short distance to The Grove park for a picnic and swim. You can also fill your water bottle at the faucet at the park.

**Parking:** In the parking lot behind the Scoville Library at the west end of Salisbury (see map)

## DIRECTIONS

| | |
|---|---|
| **0.0 Mile** | **Starting in Salisbury, at the corner of Library and Main St. (in front of town hall), go east on Rte. 41 through town.** |
| **0.1 Mile** | **Take a left onto Rte. 41 North (Under Mountain Rd.) at the east end of town.** The road rolls gently past a cemetery, elegant country homes, and horse pastures. |
| **3.6 Mile** | **Go right onto Beaver Dam Rd. Keep your eyes peeled for this one;** there's no road sign at the corner, but there is a white plywood sign saying "Taconic" and pointing to the right. You'll pass Fisher Pond almost immediately before climbing a short hill. Take a look at the mountain peaks across the pond to the north. |
| **4.6 Mile** | **Turn left onto Twin Lakes and head north.** After a short distance, the road swings right past Taconic village green. You'll pass the Taconic post office on your left just beyond the green. There's moderate climbing on this stretch of winding road. Across from the Institute of American Affairs, Twin Lakes Rd. takes a sharp right. Don't go that way. |
| **6.6 Mile** | **Go straight onto Cooper Hill Rd.** It's a fairly steep climb. At the top, the road splits, with Silver Rd. going left and Cooper Hill going right. |
| **7.6 Mile** | **Take a right on Cooper Hill Rd.** As you descend, there's a sweeping view of the valley between the East Mountain range to the northeast and the Mount Washington range to the west. At the bottom of the hill, on the right, is the Colonel Ashley House. Stop in if you'd like a tour (see Special Attractions chapter for details). If you ask first, you can fill your water bottle at the outside tap. |
| **8.6 Mile** | **Turn right onto Rannappo Rd.** when you come to a "Y" in the road. |

*Whether you should sit or stand on climbs is a matter of personal preference. But generally, stay in the saddle on long, steady hills to conserve energy. On short ones, stand and jam to maintain speed.*

600 Tips for Better Bicycling,
by the Editors of *Bicycling Magazine*

**If you want to visit Bartholomew's Cobble** (see description in the Special Attractions chapter), **take a right on Wheatogue Rd., just past the turn.**

**9.6 Mile**  **At the stop sign near the Ashley Falls post office, continue straight across Rte. 7A to East Main St.** and bike through the residential section of town.

**9.8 Mile**  **Take a right onto Clayton Rd.**, the first road that crosses East Main St. There is no road sign at the corner. (The Bike Doctor's bike shop is just a little further up East Main.) Continue on Clayton after you cross Rte. 7.

**11 Mile**  **Turn right onto Polikoff. It's the first paved road to the right.** This section is flat, patched pavement.

**11.6 Mile**  **At the stop sign, go straight across Rte. 124 to Allyndale Rd.** The road passes dairy farms, small homes, and a small air strip. Rattlesnake Hill rises immediately on the right. You'll come to a split in the road some 2.2 miles down Allyndale. The arrow on the yellow road sign points to the right. Go that way.

**14.1 Mile**  **Go straight across to Furnace Hill Rd. when you come to the stop sign at Rte. 44.**

**14.4 Mile**  **Take a right onto Lower Rd. at the stop sign.** Less than 0.1 mile on your left are the remains of the big, stone Beckley Furnace. This historical monument is an industrial relic of the 1800s — a time when carpenters, farmers, shipwrights, and railroads were in a growth cycle and needed iron. Fast-flowing Blackberry River turned the turbines to provide energy for the air blast to the furnace. A sign in front of the furnace gives a detailed history of the furnace and the iron-smelting era.

Past the furnace, a little trail winds up to the dam. The rocks in the river are an okay place to picnic on a sunny day. If you look, you may find pig iron ingots and slag/glass along the bank of the river.

About a mile further on, you'll pass the Pfizer Limestone Quarry. This huge pit was originally begun to mine magnesium for the Manhattan Project — to create the first atomic bomb — during World War II. A hundred yards or so after you've passed the quarry buildings, pull your bike over to the side of the road and walk up on the rise of land for a look into the pit. (But don't cross the fence. It's private property and against federal regulations for non-authorized personnel to be on the grounds — plus it's dangerous!) The equipment may look like

Tonka® toys way down there, but they're real trucks and bulldozers. If you are susceptible to poison ivy, be careful; there's a lot of it growing along the road here.

**16.5 Mile**    **Take a left onto Rte. 7 at the stop sign.** There's no road sign on the corner.

**17 Mile**    **Go right onto Sand Rd. when you come to the first bend, just past the Canaan Country Club sign.** This ride is relaxing, even, and flat past the farms and corn fields bordering Robins Swamp.

**20.4 Mile**    **When you come to a stop sign, turn left onto Rte. 126.** There's no road sign at the corner. You'll pass over railroad tracks and the river.

**21.9 Mile**    **Go straight on Point of Rocks Rd. at the fork. Go right and under the bridge on Water St., less than 0.1 mile from the fork.** The road passes a power plant and goes over a one-lane bridge.

**Take a left onto Dugway Rd. after crossing the river.** There's no road sign on this corner either. Immediately on the left is a little park with picnic tables and an outhouse. Kayakers and canoeists often launch here. The slalom gates used by kayakers for practice when water is high can be seen hanging over the rapids downriver. Dugway Rd. follows the river.

When the water is high, the falling water at Great Falls fills the gorge beneath it with a thundering sound. The Rattlesnake Slalom Kayak Race is held there in the spring. At other times of the year, the water table drops so low there's almost no water going over the falls at all. But in either case, the rocky gorge beneath the dam is interesting to explore, and the boulders offer good places to picnic. If you'd like to check it out, you can either hike up the dirt trail (it's a section of the Appalachian Trail) that winds up along the river on your right immediately after you cross the bridge, or bike

*"Our Creator would never have made such lovely days and given us the deep hearts to enjoy them . . . unless we were meant to be immortal."*

Nathaniel Hawthorne
Author and resident of the Southern Berkshires

up Housatonic River Rd. 0.5 mile and then take the path down to the falls.

**24.2 Mile**    **Turn right onto Lime Rock Rd. (Rte. 112) when you come to the stop sign at the end of Dugway.** Lime Rock Race Track, world famous for automobile racing, is across the road from this corner. In the summer, a bicycle race is also held there — the Minoso Rock and Roll Classic, a race sanctioned by the United States Cycling Federation and organized by the Minoso Cycling Club. New riders are welcome. If you'd like to do the race, contact the club. Details are in the Resources chapter under "Bicycling Clubs."

**25.6 Mile**    **Take a right onto Salmon Kill Rd.** You've got a winding, fairly steep hill on the first part of this stretch, then the road is rolling to level.

**27.6 Mile**    **Go left on Farnum Rd.** The road rolls pleasantly, with a couple of short climbs.

**29.8 Mile**    **Turn right onto Sharon Rd. at the stop sign in Lakeville.** If you want to stop at The Grove park for a picnic or a swim, don't turn right — go straight across to Ethan Allen Rd. Pass the On The Run Coffee Shop, Brothers Pizzeria, and the old train station, then follow the road (to the right) a short distance to the end. The park is on the lake. (See the Special Attractions chapter for more information about the park.)

**Go right on Rte. 44 when you come to the traffic light** and ride through town.

**31.4 Mile**    **Back to the library in Salisbury. End of tour.**

# TOUR #18

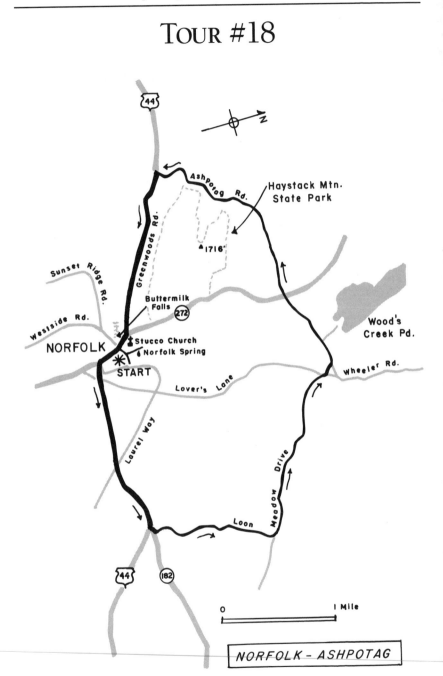

# NORFOLK-ASHPOHTAG

**Mileage:** 8.4
**Time:** 1/2 – 1 hour
**Rating:** Challenging. 68 ft. per mile climbed. Total climbed: approximately 570 ft.

**Description:** This tour features rolling hills through untrafficked, wooded countryside, with several moderately challenging climbs. A curving downhill goes along Norfolk Creek. All paved roads in good shape.

**Options:** Picnic or rest at Woods Creek Pond or at Buttermilk Falls.

**Food and Drink:** Fill your bottle with spring water at Norfolk Spring on Shepard Rd.

**Parking:** Park on the side of Shepard Rd., by the field in Norfolk (see map).

## DIRECTIONS

For cool, natural spring water, fill your water bottle at Norfolk Spring. You can see the spring along the drive bordering the north side of the field where you parked on Shepard Rd. The water comes out of a waist-high, square, stone block, located just before the townhouse parking lot.

| | |
|---|---|
| 0.0 Mile | **Starting at the corner of Rte. 272/44 and Shepard Rd., go east (left) into Norfolk.** |
| 0.1 Mile | **Take a left onto Rte. 44 at the light, on the corner of the village green.** This stretch of the route is a major road and has the most traffic. |
| 1.4 Mile | **Turn left onto Rte. 182, then take another immediate left on Loon Meadow Rd.** You'll have several climbs over the next 2.5 miles. |
| 2.6 Mile | **Go left on Loon Meadow Rd. when you come to the "T" in the road.** |
| 4.1 Mile | **Take a left onto Ashpohtag Rd. after the stop sign at the fork.** If you'd like to stop at Woods Creek Pond, |

JUST WHERE ARE WE ANYWAY?
Norfolk Green, Connecticut

look for a little paved road on your right as you descend a small hill. There's a sign, but it will be facing away from you, so you won't be able to read it.

**5 Mile** **When you come to the stop sign, go straight across Rte. 272.** Ashpohtag Rd. winds downhill in comfortable curves and follows Norfolk Creek.

**6.7 Mile** **Turn left onto Green Woods Rd. (Rte. 44) when you come to the stop sign.** The road, with a well paved shoulder, is a long, moderate, uphill climb into Norfolk.

**8.2 Mile** For a good place to picnic or relax, check out Buttermilk Falls. To get there, turn right on West Side Rd., just past where Rte. 272 goes north. The half-stone/half-stucco Immaculate Conception church is on the left. About 0.1 mile down West Side Rd., just before you come to a narrow bridge, there's a grassy patch on the right, with stone steps going down to the base of the falls.

**8.3 Mile** **Go left onto Shepard Rd., and you're back to the start of the tour.**

*"Soap and education are not as sudden as a massacre, but they are more deadly in the long run."*

Mark Twain
Summer resident of Norfolk, Connecticut

# TOUR #19

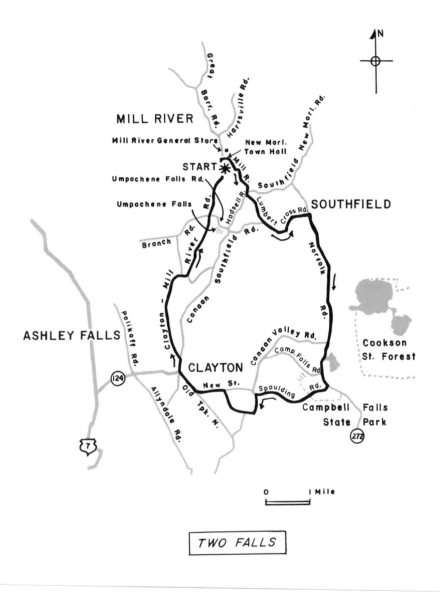

TWO FALLS

# TWO FALLS

**Mileage:** 16
**Time:** 1 – 2½ hours

**Rating:** Moderate to challenging. 50 ft. per mile climbed. Total climbed: 800 ft.

**Description:** If you enjoy waterfalls, two of the best in Berkshire County — Campbell Falls and Umpachene Falls — are on this tour. You'll bike along babbling Umpachene Brook on the first leg and up the Konkapot River on the return. Rolling hills and some moderate-to-challenging climbs make up the first half of the loop, with the second half being easy miles of flat to gently rolling terrain. The route includes some rough, but easily ridable, stretches of cracked and broken pavement on Norfolk Rd. The rest is well paved.

**Options:** Picnic or cool off at Umpachene or Campbell falls. (See Special Attractions chapter for descriptions.)

**Food and Drink:** Mill River General Merchandise Store (and post office) is the only place on this tour to get food or drink, so load up. It has fresh fruit, Gatorade®, made-to-order deli sandwiches, and snack food. The folks there have always been glad to fill my water bottle when I've asked. Store hours are 7:30-5:30 weekdays, 8:00-5:30 Saturday, and 9:00-noon Sunday.

**Parking:** In the parking lot behind the New Marlborough town hall in Mill River (see map).

## DIRECTIONS

**0.0 Mile**   **Start at the New Marlborough town hall. Turn right out of the parking lot onto Mill River Rd.** There's a 0.3-mile climb with some cracks and broken pavement. You'll come to an intersection of three roads: Southfield, Lumbert Cross, and Hadsell.

**0.8 Mile**   **Take Lumbert Cross Rd., the middle road.** It follows Umpachene Brook. Further on, you come to another three-road intersection. Keyes Hill (dirt) goes to the far left, and Cagney goes to the right. Stay on Lumbert Cross Rd., the middle road. The pavement is cracked and has some frost heaves but is still easily ridable.

**2.9 Mile**   **Go right onto Norfolk Rd. when you come to the stop sign.** It's patched pavement with rough spots. There are several moderately steep climbs on this stretch.

**6.6 Mile**   **If you want to visit Campbell Falls, turn right on Campbell Falls Rd.** On the corner, there's a white, painted 4x4 post with "Campbell Rd." written on it and an old rusty sign with an arrow pointing to the right. (You'll also notice that just beyond Campbell Falls Rd., it's no longer patched pavement, but newer asphalt.) Campbell Falls Rd. is dirt. Go about 0.4 mile, and there's a parking lot to the left. From there, follow the trail down to the falls.

**6.7 Mile**   **Take a right on Spaulding Rd.,** the first right you can take after Campbell Falls Rd.

**8.6 Mile**   **Swing left on Emmons Ln. when you come to the "Y" in the road.** There is no road sign for Emmons Ln. Bear right when you come to the next bend. All the major climbing is over, and the rest of the ride is gently rolling to flat.

**9.2 Mile**   **Go straight across to Meade Rd. when you come to the stop sign at Canaan Valley Rd.** and follow Meade to the first intersection.

**9.9 Mile**   **Turn left onto New St. at the intersection.** Follow New St. to the end where it joins Old Turnpike North.

**10.2 Mile**   **Take a right onto Old Turnpike North.** There's a short, smooth downhill to the intersection.

**10.5 Mile**   **Go right onto Mill River-Clayton Rd. at the stop sign.** Watch for a white, wooden sign in the bushes on the corner. Follow the arrow to Mill River. About 0.3 mile

*You can improve your climbing technique by keeping your back flat and your elbows bent. A curved back restricts the diaphragm and limits your intake of oxygen. Keeping the spine relatively straight and your arms flexed away from your chest facilitates breathing.*

*"Faster, Longer, Stronger!"*
*Bicycling Magazine*

from the turn, you come to a fork in the road, with another white, wooden sign. Stay on Mill River-Clayton Rd. (to the left). This is a flat stretch through the valley.

About 2 miles further down, Mill River-Clayton Rd. swings to the left, and Konkapot Rd. goes right. There's a white, wooden sign in the grassy triangle. Stay left on Mill River-Clayton Rd. You'll pass a sheep farm, and then parallel the Konkapot River.

**13.8 Mile**      **If you want to stop at Umpachene Falls, go right onto Umpachene Rd.** There's just a plain, white, wooden 4x4 post marker stuck in the ground at the corner on the right side. It's easy to miss if you're not watching for it. Look for a dirt road across from Brewer Branch Rd. and follow it across the bridge. Immediately on your right is the parking lot. Follow the sound of falling water to the falls.

**15.4 Mile**      **Continuing on Mill River-Clayton Rd., swing right across the bridge and into the town of Mill River.** Continue straight, following the road as it bears to the right to take you to New Marlborough town hall. Or take the first left, if you want to stop at Mill River General Merchandise Store.

**15.7 Mile**      **Back at the Marlborough town hall, where the tour began.**

# Tour #20

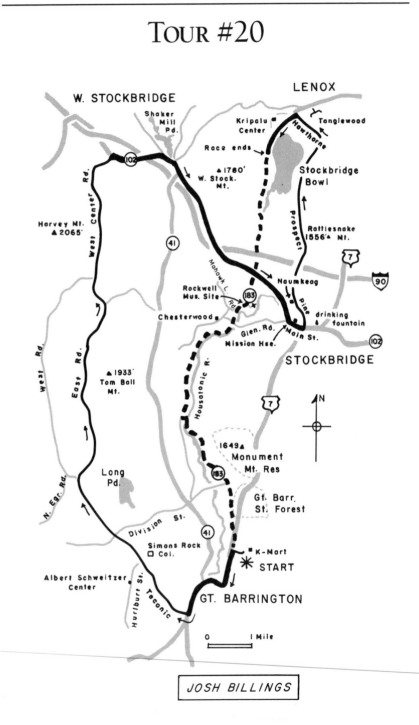

JOSH BILLINGS

# JOSH BILLINGS RUNAGROUND RACE COURSE

*Be sure you are right, then go ahead; but in case of doubt, go ahead anyway.*

— Josh Billings

Josh Billings (the pen name of Henry Wheeler Shaw), born and raised in the Berkshires, was a popular humorist during the 1800s. The origin of the word "josh" — or jest — has been attributed to Josh Billings. He was a hayseed philosopher with something to say about almost everything. Of his Berkshire neighbors, he once remarked, "Human nature is the same all over the world, except in New England, and there it's according to circumstances." Many, including President Abraham Lincoln, admired Josh Billings for his perspicuity, and Lincoln said, "Next to William Shakespeare, Josh Billings is the greatest judge of human nature the world has ever seen."

The Berkshires' biggest athletic event, named in Josh's honor, is a bike-canoe-run triathlon which draws thousands of participants and spectators to the Stockbridge/Great Barrington area every September. As a matter of fact, it's the largest and longest-running triathlon of its kind in New England. In 1991, more than 500 teams competed, with competitors ranging from top semi-pros to just-for-funners.

There's more Josh Billings Runaground Race information in the Resources chapter under "Organized Rides."

**Mileage:** 27 for race course; 37.9 for loop
**Time:** 1½ – 2½ hours for course; 2¾ – 4 hours for loop
**Rating:** Challenging. For the course, 56.3 ft. per mile climbed. Total climbed: 1520 ft. For loop, 44.9 ft. per mile climbed. Total climbed: 1,700 ft.

**Description:** The Josh Billings Race course was picked because of great scenery and good road conditions. It winds over rolling hills, goes up several challenging grades, and passes through the quaint New England towns of Alford, West Stockbridge, and Stockbridge. The first half of the race is through the Alford valley on well paved, but little trafficked, roads. The middle section, on the larger Rte. 102, has a wide shoulder. And the last leg, on Prospect Hill Rd., is well paved, passing mansions, country homes, and farms. There are views of the West Stockbridge Mountain range and other mountains to the west.

There are two ways to do this tour: the official race course, which is a point-to-point ride; and a loop, which follows the race course and then continues on to take you back to the starting point. The return portion of the loop ride goes along two beautiful stretches of the Housatonic River. The entire route is on well paved roads.

**Options:** Points of interest include Albert Schweitzer Center. Norman Rockwell Museum. Old Mission House. Naumkeag Estate mansion and gardens. Chesterwood Estate and Museum are on the return portion of loop. Monument Mountain is a short side trip away toward the end of the tour. (See Special Attractions chapter for descriptions.)

**Food and Drink:** There are restaurants and convenience stores along Rte. 7 in Great Barrington. There are no food/drink places on the course between Great Barrington and West Stockbridge (about 15 miles), so start with a full water bottle. West Stockbridge has two markets and two restaurants.

Stockbridge has several restaurants and markets within a block of the center of town. Fill up your water bottle at the drinking fountain on Main St. in Stockbridge, because there are no food/drink places between Stockbridge and Housatonic (14 miles).

Christina's Just Desserts in Housatonic has soft drinks, juice, ice cream, and pastries. The Pleasant St. Market, also in Housatonic, has a limited selection of snack foods and a grill.

**Parking:** In the parking lot in the K-Mart shopping center, just north of Great Barrington on Rte. 7 (see map).

## DIRECTIONS

| | |
|---|---|
| **0.0 Mile** | **Starting in the parking lot of K-Mart on Rte. 7, take a left on Rte. 7 and head south toward Great Barrington.** You'll go across Housatonic River a mile down. Bear left after the bridge and stay on Main St. through town. |
| **1.8 Mile** | **Turn right onto Taconic St. (St. James Place) after you pass St. James Episcopal Church,** a big, grey, stone church with a red door. Go under the railroad |

Courtesy of *The Berkshire Eagle*

## JOSH BILLINGS
(Henry Wheeler Shaw)

overpass and swing left, staying on Taconic. Now you're on the first climb of the race. It's a winding, 0.9-mile climb. There's a good view of the West Stockbridge Mountain range as you come down off the first hill.

**3.5 Mile**    **Albert Schweitzer Center.** To visit the Albert Schweitzer Center, go left on Hurlburt St. The center is on the right about half a mile.

At 5.8 miles, you enter village of Alford; at 6.0 miles, you pass tall pine trees in a lovely yard to the right. Just beyond the white house, the road splits with West Rd. to left and East Rd. to the right.

**6 Mile**    **Turn right onto East Rd.** You'll start to climb shortly after the turn. After the first climb, it's rolling with more up than down. There are excellent views of the mountains across the valley to the west.

**10.1 Mile**    **Go left onto West Center Rd. where the road splits.** It's winding and generally downhill from here.

**14.1 Mile**    **Take a right onto Rte. 102.** You'll climb a hill and cross an overpass above the interstate highway.

**Take a right when you come to the blinking light, then follow Rte. 102 through West Stockbridge.** On Rte. 102 south of town, you'll start to climb. From the highest point, it's a smooth 1.5-mile descent followed by level road into Stockbridge.

**20.3 Mile**    **Turn left onto Main St. (Rte. 102) at the stop sign across from the Children's Clock Tower.** If you're touring, you may want to stop and see the Old Mission House, Rockwell Museum, and Naumkeag Estate, or eat at the famous Red Lion Inn.

**20.7 Mile**    **In town, take a left on Pine St., kitty-corner from the Red Lion Inn.** There's a sandy-red obelisk, with an eagle on top, in the median at the corner of Pine and Main streets. Pine St. swerves to the left past the tennis courts

---

*"I have finally come to the conclusion that a good reliable set of bowels is worth more to a man than any quantity of brains."*

Josh Billings

Mark Mitchell

## HEY, WAIT FOR ME!
Josh Billings racers round the curve into Great Barrington.

and its name changes to Prospect Hill. At the top of the hill, on the left, is Naumkeag Estate. At about Mile 25, you'll come to Lake Mahkeenac. To the north across the lake, the big, brick building is Shadowbrook, home of Kripalu Center for Yoga and Health, the largest holistic health center on the East Coast. The center offers a wide range of health and personal/spiritual growth programs, as well as a rest-and-renewal option for those who want to relax, unwind, and enjoy the wholesome vegetarian food. Quite an amazing place — I should know: I lived there as a staff member for more than nine years. Visitors are welcome. Stop in for a look around if you're curious.

Just past the lake there's a short, steep grunt of a hill.

**26.2 Mile**    **Take a left onto Rte. 183 when you come to the stop sign.** From this corner across the valley, there's a view of seven mountains, including Jacob's Ladder, West Stockbridge Mountain, Monument Mountain, and Beartown Mountain.

**27 Mile**    **Go left into the public boat-launch area, just past Berkshire Country Day School, to finish the race course.** If you were actually doing the race, this is where you'd hand off the official wristband to your canoe team.

To make a loop that will take you back to the K-Mart parking lot, **continue on 183**. It's a scenic rolling road with more down than up. Larrywaug Swamp is on your right before you pass under the interstate highway.

**30.1 Mile**    **Cross Rte. 102 at the blinking traffic signal.**

**30.8 Mile**    **Norman Rockwell Museum.** Go left on Linwood if you want to visit the new Norman Rockwell Museum.

**31.1 Mile**    Here there's an optional side trip to the **Chesterwood Estate**. Go right at Mohawk Lake Rd. and follow the signs. It's less than a mile.

Continuing on Rte. 183, you'll bike along a stretch of rapids in the Housatonic River.

**34.2 Mile**    **Go left on Rte. 183 when you come to the stop sign across from Pleasant St. Market in Housatonic.** This goes under the railroad overpass, across the river, past old mill buildings, along a widening of the Housatonic River, and past Rising Paper Company.

**37.2 Mile**   **Take a right onto Rte. 7 at the stop sign.** The K-Mart
parking lot will be further down on your left.

**37.9 Mile**   **Back to the K-Mart parking lot to complete the trip.**

*"Some folks are so contrary that if they fell in a river,
they'd insist on floating upstream."*

Josh Billings

# Tour #21

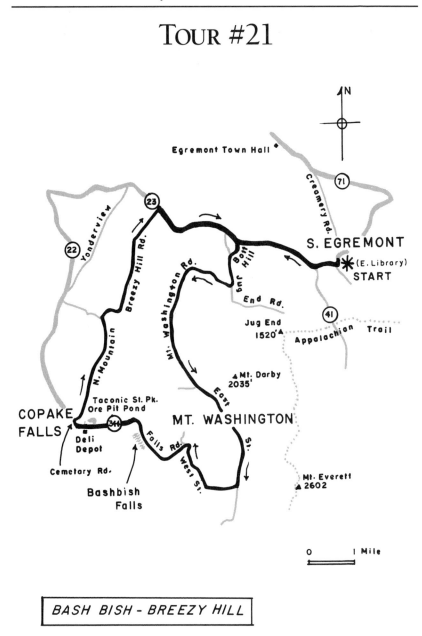

BASH BISH - BREEZY HILL

# BASH BISH — BREEZY HILL

**Mileage:** 24.4
**Time:** 1½ – 2½ hours
**Rating:** Challenging. 86 ft. per mile climbed. Total climbed: 2,090 ft.

**Description:** If you like climbing, this very scenic tour is for you. It has a lot of it, including 2.5 miles of a steady, 280-feet-per-mile ascent up Mount Washington Rd. and three miles of 130-feet-per-mile climbing on Breezy Hill Rd. Excellent views include Jug End Mountain and a panoramic view of the Taconic Mountain range and valley. Much of the tour is through sparsely populated farm country and forests of maple, pine, and hemlock. You'll ride down a beautiful gorge along Bash Bish Brook. One tricky, winding descent from the town of Mount Washington requires caution. But there's very little traffic, and the route is all on paved roads with some sections of patched pavement. Recommended for those in very good shape who have had a lot of hill-climbing experience.

**Options:** Pick berries (in season) at Blueberry Hill Farm. Visit Bash Bish Falls, the most spectacular waterfall in the Berkshires. Swim at Ore Pit Pond in Taconic State Park. (See Special Attractions chapter for descriptions.)

**Food and Drink:** Fill your water bottle(s) before you go. The first place to get more water is halfway through the ride at the drinking fountain in Taconic Park.

Mom's Cafe, on Main St. (Rte. 23/41) in the middle of South Egremont, is my favorite place for breakfast or lunch. It has outstanding blueberry pancakes and sandwiches, and you can eat on the deck overlooking the creek that flows behind the restaurant.

Mom's Convenience Store is next door, if you want to get pretzels, Gatorade®, or other snacks and drinks. Such items are also available at the Depot Deli in Copake, N.Y., halfway through the tour.

**Parking:** The town of Egremont has generously offered use of South Egremont Free Library parking lot on Button Ball Ln., just south of Rte. 23/41, for cyclists' parking on weekends. On weekdays, however, please park elsewhere, because the space is needed for library patrons. As an alternative, the Egremont town hall parking lot on Rte.71 (see map) has ample space, and town officials are happy to have you park there.

## IS HE SKINNY DIPPING?
Reid "Nature Boy" Saunders cutting loose at Bash Bish.

## DIRECTIONS

**0.0 Mile**     **Starting at the intersection of Rte. 23/41 and Button Ball Ln. in South Egremont, go west through town on Rte. 23/41.** At the west end of town, Rte. 41 splits off and goes south. Continue on Rte. 23 west. The road is mildly hilly and a bit winding.

**2.2 Mile**     **Take a left onto Botthill Rd.** You'll recognize it by the empty red wooden building on the southwest corner.

           **Swing left onto Jug End Rd. at the bottom of the hill.** There's a great view of Jug End Mountain to the south after the turn.

**2.9 Mile**     **Turn right onto Mount Washington Rd. at the stop sign.** You now have a challenging, 2.5-mile climb. It's a steady uphill, with a 280-feet-per-mile climb for this stretch. The road then becomes gently rolling with flat downhill stretches through forests and past old farms and country homes. Blueberry Hill Farm is 5.4 miles from the turn onto Mt. Washington Rd. You can pick your own blueberries in season (late July through August).

**9.6 Mile**     **Go right onto Bash Bish Falls Rd.** just past the white Church of Christ. There's no road sign, but you'll see a sign pointing to Bash Bish Falls. This corner is actually the town of Mount Washington, even though there is nothing there other than the church.

           On Bash Bish Falls Rd., you'll start going downhill. This is a cool and shady ride through heavily forested land. The road winds downhill. Watch your speed coming down; there could be sand in the road, and there are several very tight curves with frost heaves, bumps, and cracks in the pavement. Take it slowly. The first

*Even though it's best to sit on a long climb, it's wise to stand occasionally for a few dozen pedal strokes. This increases comfort by changing body position and altering which muscles are bearing the strain.*

"600 Tips for Better Bicycling"
by the Editors of *Bicycling Magazine*

tight S-curve is followed by a tight C-curve, with a swing to left where a road comes in from the west. You'll cycle a winding stretch of road through the gorge along Bash Bish Brook. The gorge's heavily wooded sides are steep along the river for a mile or so.

At Mile 12.9 (3.3 miles from the church in Mt. Washington), there's a parking lot on the left. Leave your bike here and take the trail, which begins at the south corner of the lot, to Bash Bish Falls. Follow the arrow blazes on the trees. (See Special Attractions chapter for descriptions of trails around the falls.) Climb to the top of the rocks above the parking lot for a spectacular view of the valley and mountains to the west.

Back on the ride, it's a winding downhill for the next mile. The road name changes to Rte. 344 as you enter New York State. You'll pass another parking lot for Bash Bish Falls on the left before coming to Taconic State Park, across from the Depot Deli convenience store. This very clean and well maintained park, which is free to enter if you arrive by bike, has a spring-fed swimming hole called Ore Pit Pond. There's a diving platform, ladders for coming out, a raft, and a lifeguard. Very cool, clean, and invigorating water. You can fill your water bottle at the drinking fountain near the park's entrance or at the faucet in the changing house.

**15 Mile** **Take a right onto Cemetery Rd.** There's no road sign, but it's the first street past the Depot Deli and across from the white American Legion building.

**15.1 Mile** **Turn right onto North Mountain Rd.** when you come to the stop sign beside the cemetery. The road is patched pavement. You start to climb again, and your climb is rewarded by incredible views of the Taconic

*The best descending position balances your body on the bicycle without placing an excessive amount of weight on either wheel. Keep about half your weight on the pedals and half on the saddle.*

"Faster, Longer, Stronger! "
*Bicycling Magazine*

Mountains to the west and of the valley and mountains to the south and north. At the end of this two-mile stretch, there's a "Y" in the road.

**17 Mile**     **Go right onto Breezy Hill Rd.** The patched-pavement road climbs about 130 ft. per mile for the next three miles, followed by a short, breezy descent to Rte. 23.

**20 Mile**     **Take a right onto Rte. 23.** The road rolls gently uphill and has a good shoulder. You'll pass Catamount Ski Area and the Swiss Hutte restaurant on the right. A little further up, a 0.7-mile descent begins, where the road levels and then is predominantly rolling and downhill all the way to South Egremont.

**24.4 Mile**     **Turn right onto Button Ball Ln.**, and you're back to the library parking lot where the trip started.

# TOUR #22

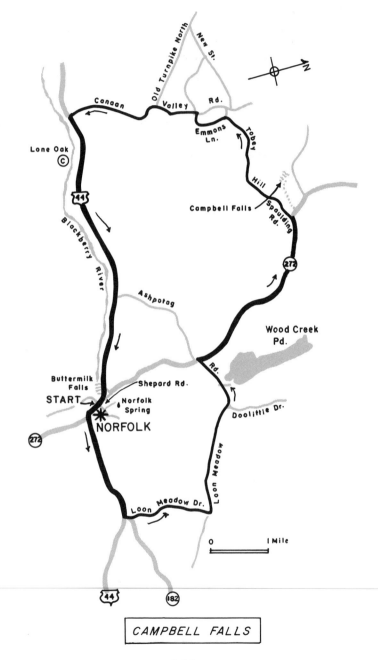

CAMPBELL FALLS

144

# CAMPBELL FALLS

**Mileage:** 15.8
**Time:** 1 – 2 hours
**Rating:** Challenging. 66 ft. per mile climbed. Total climbed: 1,040 ft.

**Description:** This tour features rolling hills through wooded country-side, complete with country homes and cattle farms. There are several challenging climbs on Rte. 272, on the first half of the ride, before coming to Campbell Falls State Park. The second half of the tour has moderately rolling and flat stretches, with a moderate climb near the end. All on paved roads with very little traffic.

**Options:** Hike, picnic, or cool off at Campbell Falls. Take a breather or picnic at Buttermilk Falls.

**Food and Drink:** Fill your bottle with spring water at Norfolk Spring on Shepard Rd.

**Parking:** On the side of Shepard Rd. by the field in Norfolk (see map).

## DIRECTIONS

If you like cool, natural spring water, fill your water bottle at Norfolk Spring. Look along the north side of the drive bordering the field, near where you parked on Shepard Rd. The water is coming out of what looks like a short, square, stone chimney, located just before the townhouse parking lot.

| | |
|---|---|
| **0.0 Mile** | **Starting at the corner of Rte. 272/44 and Shepard Rd., go east (left) into Norfolk.** |
| **0.1 Mile** | **Take a left onto Rte. 44 at the light, on the corner of the village green.** As it is a major road, this stretch has the most traffic. |
| **1.4 Mile** | **Turn left onto Rte. 182, then take another immediate left on Loon Meadow Rd.** You'll have several climbs over the next 2.5 miles. |
| **2.6 Mile** | **Take a left on Loon Meadow Rd. when you come to the "T" in the road.** |

**4.1 Mile** **At the fork after the stop sign, go left on Ashpotag Rd.** If you'd like to stop at Woods Creek Pond, look for a little paved road on the right as you descend a small hill. There's a sign, but it will be facing away from you, so you won't be able to read it.

**5 Mile** **Turn right on Rte. 272 when you come to the stop sign.** Hunker down — you'll start to climb right after the turn. The climbing continues, with some level and downhill stretches, for the next two miles.

**7.6 Mile** **Go left onto Spaulding Rd.** It's toward the bottom of a long descent, so keep your eyes open for it. Just after the turn onto Spaulding, you'll see the Campbell Falls State Park sign on your right. It's a ten-minute hike on a good path through the forest to the falls. You can pick up the trail at the west end of the field. It's the second trail, not the first one, you come to. It heads straight north. When you come to a clearing with a dirt road to the right, bear left to pick up the trail that heads down to the falls. There's a pool at the very bottom to cool your feet and other trails along the river for exploring.

**9.6 Mile** **Swing left on Emmons Ln. when you come to the "Y" in the road.** There is no road sign for Emmons Ln. Bear right when you come to the next bend.

**10.1 Mile** **When you come to the stop sign, take a left onto Canaan Valley Rd.**

**12.1 Mi** **Go left onto East Canaan Rd. (Rte. 44) when you come to the stop sign.** From here, look south for an excellent view of the Canaan Mountains.

---

*Weight your outside pedal when turning. As you approach a corner, stop pedaling with the outside pedal down (left pedal for a right turn; right pedal for a left), and put your weight on that foot. It increases your stability and enables you to go through corners safely and quickly.*

"Faster, Longer, Stronger!"
*Bicycling Magazine*

**15.7 Mile**     **Buttermilk Falls.** For a good place to picnic or relax, try Buttermilk Falls. To get there, go right on West Side Rd., just past the half-stone/half-stucco Immaculate Conception Church. About 0.1 mile down West Side Rd. there's a grassy patch on the right, with stone steps going down to the foot of the falls.

**15.8 Mile**     **Take a left onto Shepard Rd. to complete the tour.**

*"Thrusting my nose firmly between his teeth, I threw him heavily to the ground on top of me."*

Mark Twain
Summer resident of Norfolk, Connecticut

# TOUR #23

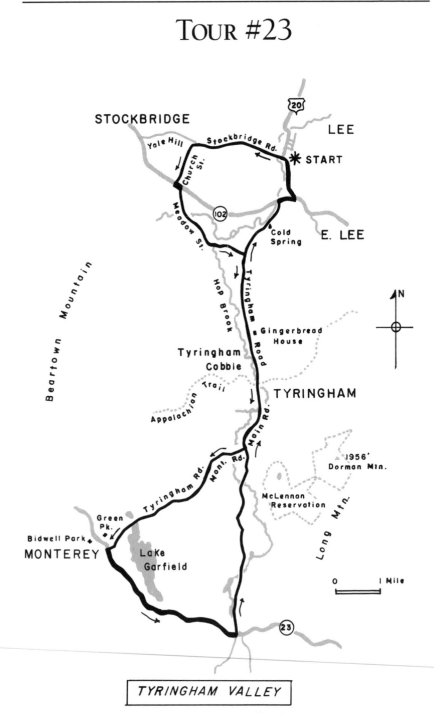

STOCKBRIDGE

LEE

Yale Hill

Stockbridge Rd.

START

Church St.

Meadow St.

102

Cold Spring

E. LEE

Beartown Mountain

Hop Brook

Tyringham Road

Gingerbread House

N

Tyringham Cobble

Appalachian Trail

TYRINGHAM

Main Rd.

1956' Dorman Mtn.

McLennan Reservation

Tyringham Rd.

Mont. Rd.

Long Mtn.

Green Pk.

Bidwell Park

MONTEREY

Lake Garfield

0        1 Mile

23

TYRINGHAM VALLEY

148

# TYRINGHAM VALLEY

*Down in the meadow and up on the height,*
*The breezes are blowing, the billows white.*
*In the elms and maples, the robins call,*
*And the great black crow sails over all,*
*In Tyringham, Tyringham Valley.*

— Richard Watson Gilder
Southern Berkshire poet

**Mileage:** 27.4
**Time:** 2 – 3½ hours
**Rating:** Moderate to challenging. 37 ft. per mile climbed. Total climbed: 1,010 ft. The ride is mostly easy but has one very (and I mean *very*) challenging 1.5-mile climb.

**Description:** Tyringham Valley has been called "the most beautiful valley in Massachusetts." This tour goes right down the valley, between the Beartown Mountain range on the west and Long Mountain on the east. There are majestic views, and you bike past handsome horse farms and fine country homes in this sparsely populated area.

The tour has stretches of moderately rolling road and one thigh-burner of a climb between Tyringham and Monterey. If you are in shape and want to test your hill-climbing technique — go for it! All well-paved roads.

**Options:** Visit fantastic, right-out-of-Hansel-and-Gretel, Kitson's Gingerbread House (Tyringham Galleries). Picnic in Bidwell Park. Quench your thirst with cool, pure water from Cold Spring. (See descriptions in Special Attractions chapter.)

**Food and Drink:** The first water-bottle fill is halfway through the ride at the drinking fountain in Greene Park, Monterey. I like to pick up a made-to-order sandwich and fruit from the Monterey General Store, take them down to Bidwell Park (a stone's throw down the road), and eat out on the rocks in the brook, listening to the lapping of the falling water and snoozing.

**Parking:** Park in the lot next to the village green in Lee (see map).

149

Jane McWhorter

## VIEW FROM TYRINGHAM COBBLE

## DIRECTIONS

**0.0 Mile**     **Starting in Lee at the village green, on the bend in Rte. 20, go west on Park St. (Stockbridge Rd.).** You cross Housatonic River and go up the short, steep hill past a golf course. The road then is rolling to flat to Church St.

**1.9 Mile**     **Take a left onto Church St.** You've got a breezy downhill.

**2.9 Mile**     **Turn left onto Rte. 102 when you come to the stop sign in South Lee.**

**3 Mile**     **Go right onto Meadow St.** and cross the Housatonic River. Meadow St. is the first right; you'll see a sign for Oak 'n Spruce Resort. Riding across the Housatonic's flood plain, you have a good view of the mountains to the east and south.

**5.1 Mile**     **Take a right onto Tyringham Rd. at the stop sign.** In this section, the ride is over moderately rolling hills, with outstanding mountain and valley views.

**7 Mile**     **Kitson's Gingerbread House** (Tyringham Gallery) is on the left 0.5 mile before you come to the quiet, little village of Tyringham. As you enter the village, you'll see a scrub-brush-covered, steep hill off to the right. Tyringham Cobble Park is at the top.

**9.3 Mile**     **Go right at Monterey Rd., 1.7 miles south of town.** The road dips down to the valley floor, and then you start the most challenging climb on this tour. This may well be the toughest climb you'll ever do in the Berkshires.

(Hey, let's focus on technique here: Breathe. Relax. Walk that bike right up the hill. Have fun with it — nothing lasts forever.)

When you get to the top, pat yourself on the back. You climbed 1.5 miles with 540 feet of altitude gain

*When climbing, think of yourself as pedaling across the stroke, rather than up and down. Strive to apply power from the back to the front. This maintains momentum while recruiting all your leg muscles.*

"600 Tips for Better Bicycling"
by the Editors of *Bicycling Magazine*

(that's 360 ft per mile). And if you enjoyed it, I've got a hundred-mile ride for you. It's the Greylock Century, and it's specially designed for masochistic types like you (and me). Look up the details in the "Resources" chapter under "Organized Rides."

The saving grace of this climb (for normal people) is that, coming back into the valley on the return leg, you go down an equal distance on a cooling, winding descent.

After the climb, the road is rolling and mostly downhill into Monterey.

**13.2 Mile**    **Turn left onto Rte. 23 when you come to the stop sign next to the white United Church of Christ.** (If you want to stop for food at the Monterey General Store or for water at Greene Park, take a right.)

**16.8 Mile**    **Take a left at Tyringham Main Rd.** The green and white sign on the corner indicates "Tyringham 6 miles." Keep a lookout for this intersection, as it's nondescript. On the corner on the right is a wooden-post fence and a small barn. On the left, there's a post-and-wire fence and a little horse stable.

The road rolls gently through thick maple forest and passes a couple of beaver ponds, followed by one mile of twisting downhill before opening out onto the broad Tyringham Valley. On the valley flat, you pass where the Appalachian Trail crosses the road. Further on, you'll pedal through the village of Tyringham.

**25.7 Mile**    **Cold Spring.** Keep your eyes peeled for the spring, because it's easy to whisk right by. Look for a widening on both sides of the road where cars have pulled off to park. There's a grey, stone, circular slab — the size of an easy chair — near the road on the right. Fill your bottle from the pipes behind it. Some people say the

*Reduce your need to brake on descents by sitting up to let your body catch the wind. This can take 10 mph off your speed.*

"600 Tips for Better Bicycling"
by the Editors of *Bicycling Magazine*

water has health-enhancing, invigorating properties, and folks come from miles around to fill up jugs for their home use. Enjoy!

**26.4 Mile** **Go right onto Rte. 20 at the stop sign. Then, almost immediately, make a left on Rte. 20 at the intersection.** Sign says "Interstate 90." Go through the intersection with the signal light, under the interstate's bridges, and continue into Lee on Rte. 20 west.

**27.4 Mile** **When Rte. 20 takes a sharp right turn you are back at the village green.** If you're in the mood, replenish your carbs with a Ben & Jerry's or Haagen-Dazs sundae at the classic 1950s-era soda fountain in McClelland's Pharmacy, across the street from Lee's County Court House (at the north end of the green).

*Fruit is your best snack choice for endurance and nutrition. It not only provides vitamins, minerals, and fiber, but it is all natural and almost all carbohydrates.*

# Tour #24

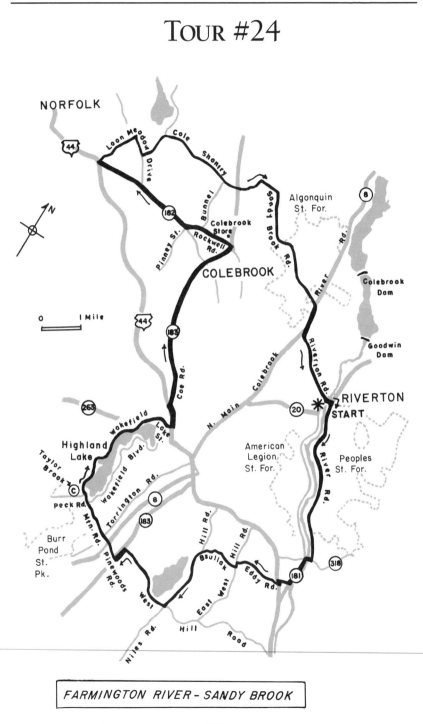

FARMINGTON RIVER - SANDY BROOK

# FARMINGTON RIVER — SANDY BROOK

**Mileage:** 38.4
**Time:** 2 $\frac{1}{2}$ – 4 hours
**Rating:** Challenging. 60 ft. per mile climbed. Total climbed: 2,320 ft.

**Description:** This is a great training ride, having plenty of climbing interspersed with long stretches of flat or downhill riding. The tour starts with a mellow ride along the picturesque rapids of the West Branch of the Farmington River (designated a Wild and Scenic River by the National Park Service) in Peoples State Forest. The route includes some long, moderate climbs and a few stretches of challenging climbing before coming to the flat ride along Highland Lake. There's also a long (4.5-mile), moderate uphill climb into the small town of Colebrook. The last section includes a long (6-mile) downhill ride along boulder-strewn Sandy Brook in Algonquin State Forest. All the roads are paved and in good shape, except for a two-mile stretch of Wakefield Blvd. around Highland Lake; this is patched pavement and tends to be rough and lumpy.

**Options:** Picnic in Riverton Park, in Peoples State Forest picnic area, or at any spot along the West Branch of the Farmington River. Swim in Highland Lake; cool off or picnic on Sandy Brook.

**Food and Drink:** Riverton General Store makes deli sandwiches to go and has a good selection of snack foods and drinks. The friendly folks there will fill your water bottle if you ask. You can also get water at Taylor Brook Campground (13 miles into the tour). In Winsted, there's Winsted Bread and Deli for drinks and snack food. Colebrook General Store (22 miles into the tour) also has made-to-order sandwiches, home-baked cookies, snack food, drinks, and water-bottle fills on request.

**Parking:** In the parking lot at Riverton Park, directly on Rte. 20 in Riverton, across from the Hitchcock Chair Factory (see map).

*Nick: "This is gonna be one dynamite ride!"*

*Joel: "My water bottle is full and I've got the power bars. Let's go!"*

## ■ DIRECTIONS

| | |
|---|---|
| 0.0 Mile | **Starting at Riverton Park, go east over the bridge.** |
| 0.1 Mile | **Take a right onto River Rd.** The road is rolling through the forest and along the river. If you want to picnic at the tables in the hemlock grove, stop at the state forest parking lot and walk back to the river. |
| 4.2 Mile | **Go right onto Rte. 318 when you come to the stop sign.** You'll go over a big, steel bridge. |
| 4.4 Mile | **When you come to the stop sign after crossing the river, turn left onto Rte. 181.** The road follows the river. |
| 5.3 Mile | **Take a right onto Morgan Brook Rd.** For the next four miles, it's generally uphill, with several short, steep climbs and some long, moderate ones. |
| 5.5 Mile | **Go left onto Rte. 44 at the stop sign.** |
| 5.7 Mile | **Turn right onto Eddy Rd., the first road on the right.** Now there's a fairly steep, 0.4-mile climb. |
| 6.9 Mile | **Take a left onto East-West Hill Rd. when you come to the stop sign.** There is no road sign on the corner. |
| 7 Mile | **Turn right onto Bsullak Rd., the first road to the right.** |
| 8 Mile | **Go left on West Hill Rd. (Niles Rd.) at the stop sign.** |
| 9.5 Mile | **When you reach the stop sign at the intersection, take a right on West Hill Rd.** The sign post will indicate that the road you've just been on is Niles Rd. West Hill Rd. is all paved but lumpy and patched in spots. |
| 11.5 Mile | **Take a left onto Rte. 183 at the stop sign.** |

*On a long ride, don't succumb to cravings for high-fat foods like chips, cakes, nuts, meats, and cheeses. They're less efficient as fuel and take longer to digest, thus creating competition between your stomach and muscles for valuable, oxygen-rich blood. In the end, your muscles will win, but your stomach won't take the loss well. Nausea and vomiting may result.*

"600 Tips for Better Bicycling"
by the Editors of *Bicycling Magazine*

| | |
|---|---|
| **11.9 Mile** | **Turn right onto Pinewoods Rd.** It goes downhill and passes under Rte. 8 before coming to a stop sign at Torrington Rd. |
| **12.5 Mile** | **Go straight across Torrington Rd. and onto Highland Lake Rd.** You start climbing right away, and the road goes through heavy forest in Burr Pond State Park. |
| **13.4 Mile** | **Take a right on Mountain Rd. at the junction of Peck and Mountain roads.** Taylor Brook Campground is down the road on the left. If you need water, ask at the cabin, and they'll let you fill up at the fountain. |
| **13.6 Mile** | **Go left onto Wakefield Blvd. when you come to the stop sign.** Here's a good stretch of flat to gently rolling road along Highland Lake. A tenth of a mile past the turn, you cross a little creek. On the right about 100 yards, there is a short path down to a swimming beach. The road further on is older pavement and is cracked, lumpy, and patched. |
| **16.7 Mile** | **Take a left onto Lake St., after going over the spill-way, and go all the way to the traffic light on Rte. 183/44.** |
| **17.1 Mile** | **Turn left onto Rte. 183.** You're at the western end of Winsted. Rte. 183 is a major road and often has lots of traffic, but you'll only be on it for about half a mile. Winsted Bread and Deli is on the right just after the turn. |
| **17.7 Mile** | **Go right onto Coe Rd. (Rte. 183 North).** The stretch up Coe Rd. is a steady, moderate uphill to the tiny town of Colebrook. Colebrook Store (and post office) is on the corner; you can't miss it. |
| **22.2 Mile** | **Take a left onto Rte. 182A (Rockwell Rd.) in the village of Colebrook.** |
| **23.5 Mile** | **Take a right onto Rte. 182 (Stillman Hill Rd.) when you come to the intersection.** You have some more climbing on this stretch. |
| **26.3 Mile** | **Turn right onto Loon Meadow Rd. just before coming to Rte. 44.** |
| **27.5 Mile** | **Go right on Doolittle Rd. at the stop sign.** This road is heavily wooded and winding. |
| **28.8 Mile** | **Go straight on Cole Rd. when you come to a sharp bend.** There's no road sign. (Doolittle Dr. goes to the left.) It's a winding and open ride down Cole Rd. |
| **30.8 Mile** | **When you get to the stop sign, take a left onto Shantry Rd.** |

**31.2 Mile**  **Go across Rte. 183 to Sandy Brook Rd.** It's all basically downhill from here; no more climbs. This prime stretch of road goes through Algonquin State Forest along the rapids of Sandy Brook. You can listen to the rushing water almost all the way. There are lots of good spots to picnic or rest. Look for places along the road where cars have pulled off; usually there are good pools nearby.

**35.6 Mile**  **Take a right on Rte. 8 (Colebrook River Rd.) when you come to the stop sign.**

**36.3 Mile**  **Go left onto Riverton Rd. and follow the river to Riverton Village.** This part of the route is a scenic, rolling road along the West Branch of the Farmington River. **Follow Rte. 20 to the left when you come to the stop sign in Riverton.** Pass Riverton General Store.

**38.1 Mile**  **Just beyond the store, on the right, is Riverton Park, where the tour began.**

*When you're well into a long ride and need to stop at a convenience store, your best food choices — with the best carbohydrate-to-fat/protein ratio — are fruit, pretzels (salt-free, if possible), fig bars, sports drinks, yogurt, and ice cream.*

# Tour #25

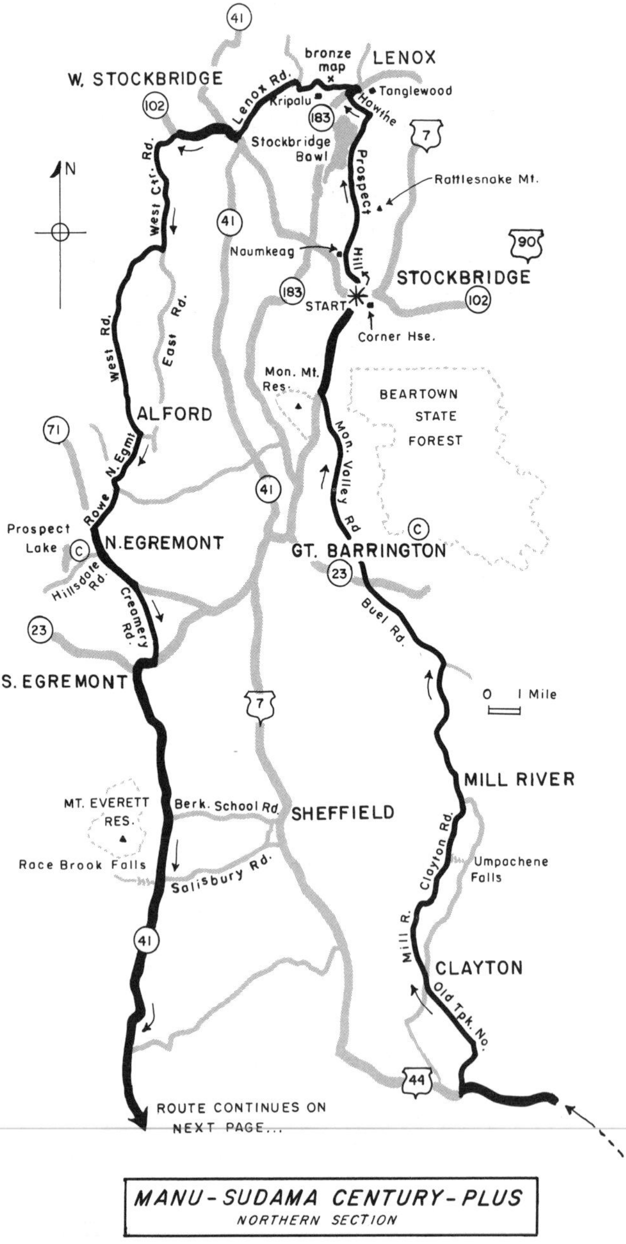
W. STOCKBRIDGE
LENOX
bronze map
Tanglewood
Lenox Rd.
Kripalu
Hawthe
Stockbridge Bowl
Prospect
Rattlesnake Mt.
West Ctr. Rd.
Naumkeag
Hill
STOCKBRIDGE
START
Corner Hse.
West Rd.
East Rd.
Mon. Mt. Res.
BEARTOWN STATE FOREST
ALFORD
Mon. Valley Rd
N. Egmt.
Rowe
Prospect Lake
N. EGREMONT
GT. BARRINGTON
Hillsdale Rd.
Creamery Rd.
Buel Rd.
S. EGREMONT
0 1 Mile
MILL RIVER
MT. EVERETT RES.
Berk. School Rd.
SHEFFIELD
Clayton Rd.
Race Brook Falls
Salisbury Rd.
Umpachene Falls
Mill R.
CLAYTON
Old Tpk. No.
ROUTE CONTINUES ON NEXT PAGE...
MANU-SUDAMA CENTURY-PLUS
NORTHERN SECTION

# Manu – Sudama
# Century-Plus

**Mileage:** 106
**Time:** 7 hours if you're a hot shot; 10 hours to three days if you're a tourist.
**Rating:** Challenging. 53.2 ft. per mile climbed. Total climbed: 5,640 ft.

**Description:** This is a challenging one-day ride. You can also make it a two- or three-day trip, if you stay at a bed and breakfast or motel, or camp along the route. (There are four campgrounds and plenty of accommodations to choose from. See the Places To Stay chapter for details).

There's plenty to see and do, and the scenery is magnificent, with many spectacular mountain/valley views, two waterfalls, three places to swim, and more places to picnic. The route passes quaint New England towns in both Massachusetts and Connecticut, country homes, horse ranches, and cattle farms. There are several challenging climbs and an equal number of descents, with plenty of gently to moderately rolling hills — even sections of flat road for good measure. The ride is named for two bicycling buddies, Manu and Sudama, who pioneered the route while living at Kripalu Center for Yoga and Health.

**Options:** Get a feel for the "Gilded Age" by taking a tour of the Naumkeag Estate mansion and gardens. See Nathaniel Hawthorne's Little Red House, where he lived and wrote after getting fired from his Customs House job in Boston. From the observation point at the Mountain Map, there's a panoramic view of the seven mountains. Hike to and picnic at Race Brook Falls. Swim or picnic at The Grove park. Ride across the old West Cornwall Covered Bridge. Skinny dip at Stillwater Pond. Picnic or rest at Buttermilk Falls. Swim, picnic, or sun on the rocks at Umpachene Falls. See some geological weirdness with a hike through Ice Glen. (See the Special Attractions chapter for details.)

**Food and Drink:** Water bottles can be filled in Stockbridge at the drinking fountain on Main St. next to the tourist booth at the route's start (0 mile); in Salisbury at The Kettle fountain next to town hall (39 mile); in Lakeville at a spigot at The Grove Park (41 mile); in Norfolk at the Battell Fountain on the green (town water) or at Norfolk Spring (80 mile). There are many restaurants and markets along

# Tour #25

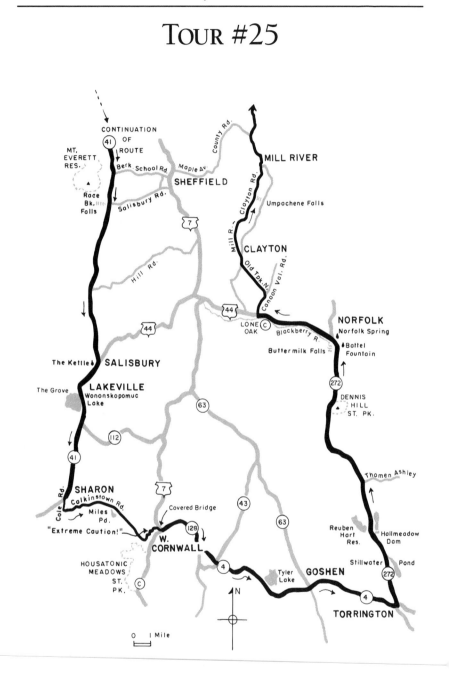

**MANU-SUDAMA CENTURY-PLUS**
SOUTHERN SECTION

the way. However, the stretch between West Cornwall and Norfolk (28 miles) doesn't have much in the way of food or drink, so stock up in West Cornwall.

**Parking:** Main St. in Stockbridge.

# DIRECTIONS

**0.0 Mile**   **Starting on the corner of Main and Pine streets in Stockbridge, go north on Pine.** Past the tennis courts, the road swings left and up the hill, and its name changes to Prospect Hill. Naumkeag Estate is on the left near the top. The road is rolling with one short grunt of a hill just past Lake Mahkeenac. (Right before this hill, you can see Kripalu Center to the north across the lake. It's the big, brick building on the side of the mountain.) Hawthorne's Little Red House is on the left across from Tanglewood Music Festival's Lion Gate.

**5.4 Mile**   **Take a right onto Rte. 183 when you come to the stop sign. Go left onto Richmond Rd. 0.1 mile further on.** The road is patched pavement and winds uphill with several tight curves. Stop at the **Bronze Mountain Map** for a panoramic view of seven mountains across the valley. The map is embedded in a rock on the left side of the road overlooking Shadowbrook (home of Kripalu Center for Yoga and Health). On the map are names and elevations for all the mountains you can see from this point.

**7.1 Mile**   **Go left onto Lenox Branch Rd.,** the first left you can take. Now it's a long downhill, with some rough spots and patched pavement.

**9.1 Mile**   **In West Stockbridge, turn left onto Swamp Rd. at the bottom of the hill at the stop sign and go right immediately on Rte.102/41.** The road crosses the Williams River and goes past its pond.

**9.3 Mile**   **Take a left onto Rte. 102,** where there's an old artillery cannon on the corner. After a short climb, you'll cross an overpass above the Massachusetts Turnpike.

**10.6 Mile**   **Turn left onto West Center Rd.** There's a sign here for "Kingmont." This is one of my favorite stretches of road. There are old farms in the valley between the mountains, and the rolling terrain curves delightfully. There's an open air chapel on the right about three miles from the turn onto West Center Rd. The original chapel building burned, but the spirit remains, and outdoor weddings are still held there.

**14 Mile**　**Go right onto West Alford Rd.** There's no road sign on the corner, but West Alford Rd. sweeps around downhill from a grassy triangle, which has a stop sign in it. The turn is just past a brown house, with a wooden deck, on the left.

**19 Mile**　**Take a right onto North Egremont Rd. when you come to the next grassy triangle.**

**20.4 Mile**　**Turn left at Green River Rd. at the stop sign.**

**20.6 Mile**　**Take a right onto Rowe Rd.** and head down the hill. A mile further on, there's a pebble beach on the left at the bridge over Green River — a good place to picnic or cool off.

**21.9 Mile**　**Go left when you come to the stop sign on Rte. 71.** There is no road sign on the corner, but you'll see one a short way down the road. Old Egremont Country Store is on the right less than 0.5 mile from the turn.

**23.6 Mile**　**Take a right onto Creamery Rd.** a little more than a mile past the store. Just before the turn, there's a sign saying, "Rte. 41," with an arrow pointing to the right. Go past Baldwin Hill Rd., which joins Rte. 71 just before Creamery Rd., and make a right onto Creamery.

**25.4 Mile**　**Take a right onto Rte. 23/41 when you come to the stop sign and ride through South Egremont.** Mom's Cafe and Mom's Convenience Store are on the left in the middle of town.

**26.1 Mile**　**Turn left on Rte. 41 just outside of town.** Note the views of mountains to the east, west, and south at dif-

---

*During the ride, start snacking in the first hour. Bananas, dates, and cookies are excellent. Nibble steadily to provide a constant supply of food energy and prevent upset stomach — almost sure to happen if you stuff down lots of food at once.*

"Ride Longer and Stronger"
*Bicycling Magazine*

ferent points. The road is rolling, with occasional flat stretches, all the way to Salisbury.

**31.4 Mile**   **Race Brook Falls.** If you want to hike to Race Brook Falls, look for the paved turn-out and sign on the right before you get to Salisbury Rd., and follow the trail to the falls.

**39 Mile**   **Swing right on Rte. 41 where it joins with Rte. 44** at the east end of Salisbury. The Village Store in the middle of town has a bike shop. You can fill your water bottle at The Kettle fountain (spring water) on the right past the big, white town hall at the west end of town.

**40.6 Mile**   **Go left on Rte. 41 south at the blinking light in Lakeville.** To stop for a swim, rest, or picnic at The Groves Park, turn right on Ethan Allen Rd. (you'll see the food shops), less than 0.1 mile past the turn. Bear right after the converted railroad station and go to the end of the road.

**Continue on Rte. 41 when you come to its intersection with Rte. 112.** From high points on the road, there are views of mountains to the south and west and of the lake below. Rte. 41 is also named "Sharon Rd." south of Lakeville.

**46 Mile**   **Take a left onto Cole Rd. Keep your eyes peeled for this one.** There is a small, black and white road sign in the grassy triangle on the right. Cole Rd. bears to the left, with an immediate short, steep climb.

**46.5 Mile**   **Go left onto Calkinstown Rd. when you come to the stop sign.** There's no sign on the corner. It's a winding, well-paved road with a few patches here and there. You'll climb 0.8 mile before starting a long descent. The road passes through the Niles Pond swamp, and its

*Spin moderate gears throughout the ride. By pedaling at a cadence of around 90 rpm, you'll delay the onset of leg muscle fatigue. Always shift before you start to strain, particularly on hills.*

"Ride Longer and Stronger"
*Bicycling Magazine*

name changes to West Cornwall Rd. The road is now mostly rolling, level, and downhill.

**51.5 Mile** **Use extreme caution for the next mile.** After you pass Surdan Mountain Rd., the road winds and is steep, with very tight curves and no shoulder. If it's wet or there is much traffic, it's particularly dangerous. Rte. 7 comes up abruptly at the bottom of a steep hill after a series of curves. Beware!

**52.4 Mile** **Go right onto Rte. 7 and take an immediate left on Rte. 128.** Cross the Housatonic River on the old wooden covered bridge, for which West Cornwall is famous. Cadwell's Classic Country Cooking, on the right after the bridge, has good food and moderate prices. The people there have always been happy to fill my water bottle. For munchies, there's an IGA supermarket at the other end of town and a small ice cream place off on the side road.

After town, you have a 0.8-mile climb along Mill Creek, and then the road is rolling with more uphill than down. 2.5 miles from West Cornwall, Rte. 128 swings left, and Rte. 125 goes straight. **Bear left and stay on Rte. 128 when Rte. 125 goes straight.**

**56.5 Mile** **Go straight across to Rte. 4 at the stop sign.** Heading down Rte. 4, you'll see the tour's most dramatic hill ahead of you. It's a straight, long, 1.5-mile climb to the Mohawk State Forest entrance. The road is then mostly rolling, with some even stretches, almost all the way to Torrington. Just before you get to Rte. 272, you have a screaming, breezy two-mile descent.

**Go left onto Rte. 272.** Stillwater Pond, on your right two miles from the turn, has some great places to swim. The most obvious one is down the bank from the dirt parking lot, but my favorite is a secluded spot beneath tall pines further down the road. Just before the orange diamond-shaped road sign with the curving arrow, there's a trail going off to the right. No houses or cabins on this end of the lake, and it's so private you can skinny-dip.

Rte. 272 to Norfolk has some moderate climbing, but is mostly mild terrain. As you come into the town of Norfolk, there's a fountain with a globe of the world and three fish spouting water into a basin. That's Battell Fountain, which has drinkable city water (there's a natural spring a little further up, if you prefer). A historical marker on the green tells about the town.

**80.2 Mile** **Go straight on Rte. 272 when you come to the stop sign at the corner of the green in Norfolk.** On the right, just past the stop sign, is a pharmacy. A stone's throw further on is the Apple House Grocery Store, which has a deli.

If you like cold, pure spring water, go to Norfolk Spring. Take a right on Shepard Rd., then a left just past the field. The spring head looks like a short, rectangular, stone chimney and is near the townhouse parking lot.

**Swing left onto Rte. 44 where routes 272 and 44 split.**

**84.7 Mile** **Turn right onto Canaan Valley Rd. just after crossing Whiting Creek.** You're back to very rural roads now, and there will be little traffic for the next 20 miles. The route goes up the valley 1.3 miles before coming to Old Turnpike North Rd.

**85.9 Mile** **Take a left onto Old Turnpike North Rd.** There's no street sign on the corner, but it's the first left you can take off Canaan Valley Rd. The road climbs up to the left, and there's a 35-mph sign on your right. Immediately you have a steady 0.4-mile climb through heavily shaded woods. This is followed by a long, even descent. Pass over the Konkapot River, then enjoy the descent all the way to the stop sign at the crossroads.

**87.9 Mile** **Go right when you come to the stop sign.** There is a white wooden sign in the bushes on the corner. Follow

---

*Stretch on the bike. At least once each half hour, stand and pedal for a minute. Then, while still out of the saddle, coast and move your hips forward, arching your back. Sit down and finish by doing several slow neck rolls and shoulder shrugs. You'll be surprised how fresh you feel.*

"Ride Longer and Stronger"
*Bicycling Magazine*

the arrow to Mill River. You are biking through the little town of Clayton, and 0.3 mile from the turn you'll come to a fork in the road, where there's another white wooden sign. **Stay to the left on Clayton-Mill River Rd. when the road splits.** This is a flat stretch through the valley, where you'll ride past a huge cornfield. A mile past Alum Hill Rd., Mill River-Clayton Rd. goes to the left and Konkapot Rd. to the right. There's a white wooden sign in the grassy triangle. Stay left on Mill River-Clayton Rd. You'll pass a sheep farm and a little further on  the road goes along the Konkapot River.

**91.5 Mile**  **If you want to stop at Umpachene Falls, turn right onto Umpachene Rd.** Only a plain, white, wooden, 4x4 post marker stuck in the ground at the corner on the right side marks the way. It's easy to miss it if you're not watching closely. Take the dirt road, across from Brewer Branch Rd., cross the bridge, and turn into the parking lot immediately on your right. Follow the sound of falling water to the falls.

**93.4 Mile**  **Continuing on Mill River-Clayton Rd., swing right across the bridge, then take an immediate left** in the middle of the town of Mill River. The sign on the corner has an arrow pointing left to Sheffield. Mill River General Merchandise store is immediately on your right. It's open 7:30-5:30 weekdays, 8:00-5:30 Saturday, and 9:00-noon on Sunday, and it carries essentials such as Gatorade®, sandwiches, and bananas.

The road now is a steady, moderately uphill climb. A half-mile north of town, Hartsville-Mill River Rd. splits off and goes right. Continue to the left, following the

---

*Vary your hand position every few minutes. Change your grip from the handlebar drops to the brake lever hoods to the top of the handlebar—and back again. This helps you avoid the upper body fatigue that comes from remaining in a rigid posture.*

"Ride Longer and Stronger"
*Bicycling Magazine*

sign to Great Barrington. You'll cross Konkapot River, the site of several old mills. On the right just before the bridge, there is a historical marker, which gives the mill's history. Two-tenths of a mile further on, the road splits around a wooded, grassy triangle. Keep to the right on Great Barrington-Mill River Rd.

**97 Mile** **When you come to the grassy triangle at the end of the road, go left onto Buel Rd.** This stretch is well paved and rolling.

**99.7 Mile** **Go straight across Rte. 23 to Monument Valley Rd. when you come to the stop sign.** From this valley road, you can see beautiful mountains. Toward the end of this stretch of road, look ahead and to the west for a view of Squaw Peak on Monument Mountain. The view from the summit of Monument Mountain is magnificent. If you're up to a hike, go left at Rte. 7, bike up to the Monument Mountain parking lot (about 0.25 mile on the right), and follow the trail. (See the Special Attractions chapter for more information.)

**104.3 Mile** **Take a right on Rte. 7 at the stop sign.**

**106.9 Mile** **Ice Glen.** For a hike up Ice Glen, turn right at Park St. ( a convenience store is on the corner), go to the end, cross the suspension bridge, and follow the blazes on the trees.

**107 Mile** **Back on Main St. in Stockbridge.** Congratulations! Pat yourself on the back — you're a bikin' animal!

*"Always bear in mind that your own resolution to succeed is more important than any other one thing."*

Abraham Lincoln

# Special
# Attractions

# SPECIAL ATTRACTIONS

COOL WALKIN' AT ICE GLEN

# ICE GLEN

*Veritable moss castles of gnomes and elves seem the tumbled boulders in the twilight of the gorge: all too sunless here for lover's tryst — not even golden Queen Summer succeeds in erasing the chill of his majesty the Frost-King's footsteps, yet by her commands beautiful fern-clusters line the yawning black rock caverns.*

That's how Katharine Abbott described Ice Glen in her book *Old Paths and Legends of the New England Border.*

Ice Glen is a curious geological formation in a deep, quarter-mile-long cleft in the rocks between Bear and Little mountains. Even in the middle of summer (particularly if the previous winter had heavy snowfall), you may find snow and ice in the crevices under the huge, jumbled boulders. Always a cool walk!

During the "Gilded Age," locals used to dress up on Hallowe'en and, with flaming torches, hike the trail just to be weird. As a matter of fact, the Laurel Hill Association has revived the tradition and now hosts an Ice Glen Walk with lanterns (no more torches) on Hallowe'en.

To get to Ice Glen, begin at the intersection of Park St. and Rte. 7 in Stockbridge and go east on Park St. to its end. There, a map by the bridge shows you the trail to the glen. Cross the Housatonic River and follow the path. The way is marked with blazes on the trees.

Give yourself 45 minutes to an hour for this hike, an exploration you can make day or night.

TOURS: on **25**; a short side trip from: **5, 9, 13, & 20**

# BARTHOLOMEW'S COBBLE

This National Natural Landmark takes its name from the high limestone knolls, or "cobbles," that rise above the Housatonic River. These outcroppings support an incredible concentration of plants, including several types of rare ferns.

Nature trails wind among gnarled, boulder-clinging trees in the forest above and along the grassy river-bottom grazing land called "Corbin's Neck." From high spots, you get great views of the Housatonic River valley.

This is one of the first places spring arrives in the Berkshires, and it has outstanding displays of the season's wildflowers. The combination of wooded hill, open farmland, and the meandering Housatonic River attracts a wide variety of birds; more than 200 species have been sighted here. Along the nature trail, the chickadees are so tame they've been known to eat sunflower seeds right out of human hands.

You can borrow the Bartholomew's Cobble guidebook from the conservation officer (on duty from Wednesday through Sunday during the summer season) for a self-guided tour. A cabin on one of the cobbles houses the Bailey Trailside Museum, which has displays describing the animals and plants, as well as a collection of Native American artifacts found in the area.

The cobble is a natural attractor for lightning, and this log cabin has been hit three times. On one occasion, the lightning blew a hole in the side of a wall and sent a chair hurling across the room to smash against the far wall. The splintered hole has been left as an exhibit.

Bartholomew's Cobble is open daily from 9 a.m. to 5 p.m., mid-April to mid-October; a small fee is charged.

**Location:** Bartholomew's Cobble is just west of Ashley Falls, MA, on the corner of Rannapo  and Weatogue Roads. For more information, contact The Trustees of Reservations, P.O. Box 792, Stockbridge, MA 01262. (413) 298-3239, or call the Cobble headquarters at (413) 229-8600.

TOURS: 4, 11, 16, & 17

# Bronze Mountain Map

This bronze plaque, imbedded in a rock, identifies and gives the elevations of the seven mountains you can see across the valley. Located just off Richmond Rd., above Shadowbrook (the building housing Kripalu Center), the site provides an outstanding panoramic view of Monument Mountain, Jacob's Ladder, Rattlesnake Mountain, and four other Berkshire mountains.

**Location:** The Bronze Mountain Map is on the south side of Richmond Rd., between Rte. 183 and Lenox Branch Rd.

Tours: 25

# BERKSHIRE NATIONAL FISH HATCHERY

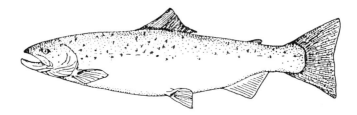

Atlantic salmon, "king of the game fish," once thrived in New England streams from the St. Croix River to the Housatonic. By the mid-1800s, dams, pollution, and overfishing had decimated their numbers. Through the efforts of several groups, including the U.S. Fish and Wildlife Service, salmon are returning to New England rivers. Although the numbers returning are small now, each year conditions improve—rivers are cleaner, and fish ladders are being constructed to give the fish access to new spawning areas—and the outlook for recovery is good.

In the holding pools of the Berkshire National Fish Hatchery, you can see mature salmon, which have been captured in New England rivers to be milked of their eggs for hatching elsewhere. And, if you arrive at feeding time, you may even get to feed these hungry whoppers. The Fish and Wildlife Service fish culturist on duty can tell you all about the restoration program. You're welcome to hike the trails on the hatchery's 36 acres bordering on the Konkapot River and to use the picnic tables.

The hatchery is open 9 a.m. to 5 p.m., daily. For more information, call (413) 528-4461.

**Location:** The Berkshire National Fish Hatchery is on Hatchery Rd. (River Rd.), between Rte. 23 and Rte. 57 in Hartsville, MA.

## TOURS: 10 & 14

# MONUMENT MOUNTAIN

William Cullen Bryant described his experience of this natural attraction in the poem *Monument Mountain:*

> . . . There, as thou stand'st,
> The haunts of men below thee, and around
> The mountain-summits, thy expanding heart
> Shall feel a kindred with that loftier world
> To which thou art translated, and partake
> The enlargement of thy vision.

Monument Mountain is one of the most distinctive peaks in the state. Its long, 1,700-foot high ridge of pinkish quartzite is scarcely 15 feet wide in some places. Hickey and Monument trails wind up to Squaw Peak, the summit.

The hillside is covered with red pine and, in June, with blooming mountain laurel. From the summit, there's a good view of the Housatonic River, Williams River, Konkapot Brook, and Green River. Lake Agawam shimmers to the northwest, and Beartown Mountain's long ridge stretches to the north and east.

Monument Trail passes a cairn of rocks (but you really have to look to find it) which was there before white men came to the valley. This is the "monument" after which the mountain is named. Some claim it's the burial place of a Native American woman who, unlucky in love, threw herself off the mountain (hence "Squaw Peak"). Others believe it was a territorial marker defining tribal boundaries.

At Monument Mountain, you can enjoy a great hike (1,642 feet above sea level) and a magnificent view from the summit. Just follow the trail indicated on the park sign. The park is open from dawn to dusk.

**Location:** Monument Mountain is on Rte. 7 between Great Barrington and Stockbridge.

For more information contact The Trustees of Reservations, P.O. Box 792, Stockbridge, MA 01262. (413) 298-3239.

TOURS: 20, 25

# Pfizer Limestone Quarry

The original quarry pit was begun in the 1940s to mine magnesium for the Manhattan Project (to create the first atomic bomb) during World War II. Men and trucks working at the bottom of this huge hole may look like toys. It's so deep a 14-story building could fit in the pit.

The rock taken out of the pit now is refined and used for commodities such as joint compound, stucco and plaster, stabilizer in asphalt shingles, and to make a white concrete-block material that is almost indistinguishable from stone.

Check out the site from the road, but don't cross the fence. The pit is dangerous, it's private property, and it's against federal regulations for non-authorized persons to be on the property.

**Location:** Pfizer Limestone Quarry is on Lower Rd., between Rte. 7 and Rte. 44, near Canaan, CT.

## Tours: 11, 17

# Bidwell Park

This pleasant, quiet, secluded park is on a shady bend in the Konkapot River. The site has a picnic table and small waterfall. It's only a short distance from the Monterey General Store, where you can get sandwiches and snack food to take with you for a picnic on the rocks in the creek. The park is so secluded, you probably won't be disturbed here by anyone, and the sound of the water going over the small dam and the rocks below it may lull you to sleep if you're in the mood for a snooze.

**Location:** Bidwell Park is in the village of Monterey, across Rte. 23 from the Grange Hall.

## Tours: 10, 14, 23

# River Park

On the Housatonic River, this park has picnic tables and an outhouse. From here, you can see a set of rapids where, during high water, kayakers practice slalom maneuvers through a set of gates hanging above the rapids. This is a good spot for a rest stop or picnic.

**Location:** River Park is on Dugway Rd. just west of Falls Village, CT.

Tours: 17

# WATERFALLS

FEELING THE RUSH
Campbell Falls after a rain.

# CAMPBELL FALLS

The Whiting River leaps and slides over rocks in a narrow gorge. The water falls in two great descents with a small pool or two in between and one at the bottom. Depending on how you approach the falls, you'll have either a long or a short walk, through towering pines and hemlocks, to this secluded place. You'll hear the sound of water cascading over the split-rock ledge before you come to the base of the falls.

This is an excellent place for cooling your feet (or more), and there's a good site for a picnic on the level, pine-carpeted area south of the falls. Although there are no picnic tables, several all-natural stumps and rocks suit the purpose.

If you like the sound of falling water, this is a great place to meditate or rest — dawn to dusk.

**Location:** Campbell Falls is off Norfolk Rd., south of Southfield, MA, just before Spaulding Rd.

TOURS: 19, 22

# UMPACHENE FALLS

This is one of my favorites. Umpachene Creek slides over bare rocks in a series of cascades down to a pool — large enough for a dip — before coursing on to join the Konkapot River. This is a fun place to cool off or rest. There are plenty of places to stretch out on the rocks and enjoy the sun, plus a picnic table. The park is open from dawn to dusk.

Umpachene Falls is named after a Mahican chief who had the foresight to ask Konkapot, the co-chief of his tribe, what would happen to their children if their land was sold to the newly arrived whites.

**Location:** The falls are on Umpachene Rd., just off Mill River-Clayton Rd., between Mill River and Clayton, MA.

TOURS: 6, 7, 14, 16, 19, 25

# RACE BROOK FALLS

This lithe watercourse hustles and darts among the rocks and under tree roots, breaking into smaller streamlets which race gracefully against each other and dash about the ferns and fallen trees, plunging from pool to pool before rejoining, splitting again, and going on their merry way. The music the streamlets make is delightful — tinkling, chortling, or gurgling, depending on what the rivulets are going over or under. Along the way, the streams cascade down five or six long rock faces. Use your imagination, and you can find magical places along the trail that may make you feel you've stumbled into a Tolkien story.

The brook is accessible from the Race Brook Trail, which you pick up from Rte. 41, south of Mt. Everett. Take the path to the right when you come to the fork in the trail — it's about a quarter-mile hike from the parking area — and follow it to the first cascade. For a spectacular view of the valley, climb to the top of the falls via the trail on the south side of the brook. Open anytime.

**Location:** Race Creek Brook is on the west side of Rte. 41, between Berkshire School Rd. and Salisbury Rd., south of South Egremont, MA.

Tours: **16, 25**

# BASH BISH FALLS

These are the most spectacular falls in the Berkshires. Bash Bish Brook flows through a rugged rocky gorge, with enormous hemlocks clinging to its sides, before making a drop of two hundred feet. The cascading water divides around a large, pulpit-like stone as it falls into the pool below.

Visitors have been known to swim in the pool at the base of the falls (at the time of this writing, it was designated "swim at your own risk"). The water is very cold, even in the hottest part of the summer. Big boulders below the pool are ideal for sunning and picnicking. There are several trails, including one which goes above the gorge leading to the falls. This trail takes you to the top of a perpendicular cliff called Profile Rock, which overlooks the gorge.

If you're a romantic at heart, you may try looking in the pool below for the "spirit profile" of a Native American maiden. According to a legend (of questionable origin), the beautiful squaw White Swan was the daughter of a witch who lived beneath the falls. The girl loved, and was married to, a handsome young brave. When she proved barren, her husband took another wife.

White Swan began to pine and brood by the falls, often gazing for hours into the water below. One day she heard the voice of her mother, whom she never knew while growing up, calling to her from beneath the cataract. With an answering cry of joy, she plunged over the cliff. At that moment, her husband came through the forest. He leaped in after her in a vain rescue attempt.

The next day the brave's body was found, but White Swan had disappeared. According to the legend, she and her mother still live behind the falls. If you are still a kid (at heart), or if you've gotten this far in life with your imagination still intact, you'll see White Swan's profile. And, if you listen, you can hear the falling water calling her nickname, "Bash Bish, Bash Bish."

The falls are open from dawn to dusk.

**Location:** Bash Bish Falls is in Mt. Washington State Forest, on Falls Rd. (Rte. 344 in NY) between West Rd. in MA and Rte. 22 in NY.

TOURS: 21

## LOOK FOR THE MAIDEN OR COOL YOUR HEELS
Bash Bish Falls

# BUTTERMILK FALLS

Norfolk Brook glides across the smooth, gray rocks on this beautiful small falls, which is right in the village of Norfolk, CT. Take the stone steps down from the small lawn off Westside St., a tenth of a mile south of Rte. 44. It's open anytime.

## TOURS: 11, 17

# GREAT FALLS

When the water is high on the Housatonic River, it creates a thundering sound as it falls into the rocky gorge at Great Falls. At other times of the year, there may be very little water going over the falls. When that happens, you can walk out into the wide, rocky riverbed among huge, pockmarked boulders, gouged-out crevaces, and tumbled rocks. In either case, there are great boulders on which to picnic or rest.

**Location:** On Housatonic River Rd., just north of the hydro-electric plant outside of Falls Village, CT.

## TOURS: 17

# NATURAL SPRINGS

For many, including me, nothing beats drinking fresh, cool, pure water to quench the thirst worked up on a long ride. And the best water comes from a spring — right out of the ground with all its earth energies intact, just as Mother Nature made it, unadulterated by human meddling. The following springs are routinely inspected by local health officials for purity. Don't buy bottled spring water at the store: get it direct!

# COLD SPRING

Pure water comes right out of the ground on the site. Considered by the town of Lee to be a very valuable natural resource, this spring is inspected every month and has always been found pure. It's been used for generations as the source of water during droughts, and folks come for miles around to fill their water jugs. Generations of housewives have used the water for drinking and cooking and for making pickles!

**Location:** Cold Spring is off Tyringham Main Rd., south of Lee, MA.

TOURS: 23

# Norfolk Spring

Norfolk Spring has been used for generations by local Norfolk towns-people, and jug-toting folks come from miles around to stock up with the pure water. The spring's water is tested quarterly by the town.

**Location:** Norfolk Spring can be found off Shepard Rd. in Norfolk, CT.

## Tours: 18, 22, 25

# The Kettle

The water in The Kettle comes from an underground spring on Mount Riga, and people from all over the tri-state area come here to fill their water bottles with what locals call "designer water." It's named The Kettle because the water used to flow into a huge iron kettle, which was forged locally in a blast furnace that also made cannon shot and smelted iron during the Revolutionary War. When the original kettle corroded over time, it was moved from the center of the road (where horses used to drink from it) to its present location, next to the town hall, and replaced with a locally cut granite bowl.

**Location:** The Kettle is on Main St. in Salisbury, CT.

## Tours: 17, 25

# SWIMMING

Eric Knudsen

## COOLIN' OFF AT UMPACHENE FALLS

If it's a hot day and you've worked up a sweat, cool off in the water! Following are descriptions of places perfect for dips in the water, splashing around, or diving; and still others are small and/or shallow pools just right for lying down in.

# KONKAPOT RAPIDS AND POOL

This beautiful pool is just below a series of rocky rapids. The water courses between ragged rock ledges and through a small gorge before emptying into the eight-foot-deep pool. Surrounded by hemlocks, birches, and maples, it's just a short distance down a trail from the road, yet it's perfectly secluded. This is an excellent place for a snooze, picnic, or swim.

**Location:** Konkapot rapids and pool are just off Hatchery Rd. (River Rd.) between Rte. 23 and Rte. 57 north of Hartsville, MA.

## TOURS: 10, 14

# THE GROVE

Lake swimming and sunning at the sandy beach are available at The Grove. Near the beach, there's a concession stand, which serves snacks and has changing rooms.

Set in a grove of tall, stately oaks on Wononskopomuc Lake, this park is managed by the towns of Salisbury and Lakeville. Picnic tables are on high ground beneath the oaks. There's a sandy beach with a lifeguard and a roped-off swimming area.

A fee is charged for non-residents, although if you arrive by bicycle it's only $1; when I offered to pay, the person at the concession stand waved away my dollar bill, telling me to keep it. This is a very friendly, clean, and attractive park.

**Location:** The Grove park is on the north shore of Wononskopomuc Lake, off Rte. 41 in Lakeville, CT.

## TOURS: 17, 25

UMPACHENE FALLS (see under "Waterfalls")

# STILLWATER POND

Surrounded by forest, and without houses or buildings of any kind on the north, this peaceful water is ideal for a swim. Stillwater Pond is very private and secluded, and cyclists of bolder persuasion have been known to skinny-dip here. (I have.) There's a wonderful fragrance of pine from the needles carpeting the ground at the edge of the lake.

Take Rte. 272 north from Rte. 4 until you see the curve sign, then follow the trail off to the right. There are other places you can pull off to swim before you get to this spot, but this is the nicest.

**Location:** Stillwater Pond is on the east side of Rte. 272 north of Rte. 4, north of Torrington.

## TOURS: 25

# GREEN RIVER

Green River is considered one of the cleanest rivers east of the Mississippi River, and there are several places to cool off in its beautiful, crystal-clear water.

• Just off Rowe Rd., between Rte. 71 and Green River Rd. downstream from the bridge crossing the river, there's a gravel bar and a pool big enough for taking a dip.

## TOURS: 3

• Off Rte. 23/41 between Great Barrington and South Egremont, there's a bridge crossing the river. East of the bridge, on the south side, there's a path next to a fire hydrant. Follow this to find many places to sun and cool off. The pools are mostly shallow, although there's one that's usually at least six feet deep, depending on water levels and time of year.

## TOURS: 1

• Off Seekonk Cross Rd., just past the airport runway, there are rapids and shallow pools (although, in the driest part of the summer, it may be too shallow). Or follow the paths further back to find a place that suits you.

## Tours: 15

• Off Hurlburt Rd., south of the Albert Schweitzer Center the road crosses the river. You can wade up the river to the west to find quiet, private pools.

## Tours: 3

# Ore Pit Pond

The water in Ore Pit Pond at Taconic Park is cool, invigorating, and clean. The swimming area has a raft and life guard and, in summer, there are usually lots of folks on the lawn sunning, reading, or watching kids near the pond. The park is free to enter if you arrive by bicycle, and there's a changing room with bathrooms. You can fill your water bottle at the fountain near the entrance. The Depot, a convenience store, is across the street.

**Location:** Taconic Park's Ore Pit Pond is on Rte. 344, just west of Bash Bish Falls.

## Tours: 21

# Sandy Brook

If you keep a lookout, you'll see several pools suitable for a cooling off in the river in Algonquin State Park along Sandy Brook Rd. Look for places beside the road where cars have pulled off to park. One nice spot is on the left, past Campbell Rd.

**Location:** on Sandy Brook Rd., between Rte. 8 and Rte. 183

## Tours: 24

# HIGHLAND LAKE

You can swim in Highland Lake along an undeveloped stretch of beach at the southwestern end of the lake. Often used by campers from Taylor Brook and Burr Pond State Park, it's a tenth of a mile from the turn onto Wakefield Boulevard. One hundred yards after the road crosses the little creek, take the short path through the woods on your right.

**Location:** The swimming area of Highland Lake is south of Winsted, CT, off Wakefield Blvd., at the southwestern corner of the lake.

## TOURS: 24

# SPECTACLE LAKE

This is a beautiful lake, surrounded by a forest of pine, birch, hemlock, and maple, with no buildings other than a few rustic cabins. If you're the bold type, this is a great place for a dip. But if you have an active imagination, you might want to wait for another spot to swim; after all, who knows what lurks in the dark depths? The lake bottom is sand, but the water is very dark, due to decaying vegetation.

The view of the lake from this spot can be very peaceful on a beautiful day, and even though the picnic table is dilapidated, it's a pleasant place to eat or rest.

**Location:** Spectacle Lake is on West Otis Rd., between Rte. 23 and Rte. 8, south of Otis, MA.

## TOURS: 10

# Buck River Swimming Hole

This pool is below a mild stretch of rapids on the Buck River. It's quite deep — even in the middle of summer — and very clear. The gnarled rock outcropping on the south side gives shade to part of the pool much of the day, so the water is cool all year. There are rocks for sunbathing and picnicking.

**Location:** Look for this Buck River swimming hole on the south side of Rte. 57, just past the Sandisfield School, between Sandisfield and New Boston, MA.

## Tours: 10

# Lake Mansfield

Lake Mansfield is shallow, so the water gets warm fairly early in the season. The park has a sandy beach, picnic tables, and a drinking fountain.

**Location:** The swimming area is on Lake Mansfield Rd., just outside of Great Barrington, MA.

## Tours: 15

KONKAPOT POOL

# CULTURAL ATTRACTIONS

# THE MOUNT

*On a slope overlooking the dark waters and densely wooded shores of Laurel Lake, we built a spacious and dignified house to which we gave the name of my great-grandfather's place, The Mount.*

These are the words Edith Wharton used to describe the summer residence she built in the Berkshires in 1902. She based the architecture and design on ideas she advocated in her books, *The Decoration of Houses* and *Italian Villas and Their Gardens*. Her influence on the development of the American interior design profession led literary critic Edmund Wilson to term her "not only one of the great pioneers, but also the poet of interior decoration." Lofty words — visit The Mount and see if you agree.

Wharton is considered, by many, to be America's premiere woman writer. She wrote 21 novels and novellas, 11 collections of short stories, and nine nonfiction books. These included the novels *The House of Mirth*, written at The Mount, and the classic *Ethan Frome*, set in the Berkshires. She received a Pulitzer Prize, the first woman ever to do so, for her book *The Age of Innocence*.

The Mount is now a National Historic Landmark, and the Edith Wharton Restoration, Inc., is in charge of preserving and restoring the mansion, its grounds, and gardens. Guided tours of the house and gardens last approximately one hour; the tour combines literary, historical, biographical, and design aspects of Wharton's life and writing. There's a book and gift shop on the property.

**Tour Schedule**:
May 25-June 20: Tuesday-Sunday, 10 a.m. to 5 p.m., with tours on the hour; last tour at 4 p.m.

*(continued)*

Courtesy of *The Berkshire Eagle*

EDITH WHARTON

June 21-September 2: Tuesday-Friday, tours at 10 a.m., 11 a.m., noon, and 3 p.m; last tour at 4 p.m.; Saturday and Sunday, tours at 9:30 a.m., 12:30 p.m., 3:00 and 4:00 p.m.

September 5-October 27: Thursday-Sunday, 10 a.m. to 5 p.m., with tours on the hour; last tour at 4 p.m.

Open Memorial Day, July 4th, Labor Day, and Columbus Day.

Admission: $4 adult; $3.50 senior citizen; $2.50 ages 13-19.

For more information, call (413) 637-1899

**Location:** The Mount is on Plunkett St. in Lenox, MA, at the southern junction of Rtes. 7 and 7A.

## Tours: 13

# CHESTERWOOD

If you've ever seen the statue of the seated President Lincoln, in the Lincoln Memorial in Washington D.C., here's your chance to find out about the statue's creator. Chesterwood is the estate of Daniel Chester French, who is also famous for the statue of the *Minute Man*, in Concord, Massachusetts. French created other fine works as well — some, like the Melville Memorial, are of angelic women and have a very dreamlike, romantic feel. Several are on display at Chesterwood.

In fact, Chesterwood houses nearly 500 pieces of sculpture — including molds, life-casts, and studies — and is one of the largest collections of fine art devoted to a single American sculptor and period. The site also includes French's Colonial Revival house, exhibits in the Barn Gallery, gardens, and rolling woodland trails, as well as his studio. There are guides to provide details on the artist and his work.

In French's studio, it's as if the artist just stepped out for a moment and will return shortly. His tools and partially completed works are around, including the lovely alabaster *Andromeda*. You can also see the railroad handcar and tracks he used to wheel his sculptures out of the studio so he could view them in natural sunlight.

Courtesy of Chesterwood

# THE ARTIST AND HIS WORK
Daniel Chester French outside his Chesterwood
studio with *Mourning Victory*

The trails are great, too. French cleared woodland paths to the north and west of his studio. A lower path is an easy 20-minute walk. The Ledges Trail is a vigorous hike over rocky ledges to an outlook in a hemlock grove. From there, you get a tri-state view of Monument Mountain and the surrounding Berkshire hills. As you hike, you'll come upon pieces of art by contemporary artists designed to mesh with the environment and natural forces (i.e., wind, rain, shadows, trees, etc.).

The gift shop has books and items relating to sculpture and historic preservation.

Open: May 1-October 31, daily, 10 a.m. to 5 p.m.
Fee: $4.50 for adults; $1 for children, 18 and younger
For further information, call (413) 298-3579.

**Location:** Chesterwood is on Williamsville Rd., just west of Rte. 183, off Mohawk Lake Road, two miles west of Stockbridge, in Glendale, MA.

## Tours: 5, 20

# NAUMKEAG

You can get a feel for the "Gilded Age" by touring this "Berkshire Cottage," a 26-room, gabled mansion. Naumkeag, which is Mahican for "place of rest," was the summer home of the Choate family. It was designed as a retreat from New York City life for Joseph Hodges Choate, attorney and ambassador to England, a man who successfully fought legal battles against the graduated income tax back in the 1880s.

The home is decorated with furniture spanning three centuries and beautiful Oriental rugs and tapestries. Taking a tour with one of the guides, it's easy to get a sense of the opulence in which the wealthy lived during that period of history.

Naumkeag's gardens are the masterpiece of landscape architect Fletcher Steele, who worked for more than 30 years on the gardens with Miss Mabel Choate. Stretch your legs and take a stroll — there are several themes from which to choose, including the peony terrace, the rose garden, the birch walk, or the Chinese garden with a pagoda, a stone Buddha, and Chinese dogs.

Guided tours are available. Naumkeag is on the National Register of Historic Places and is preserved through the work of The Trustees of Reservations. There is an admission fee.

House and gardens are open from late May through Labor Day, daily except Mondays. After Labor Day and through Columbus Day, they're open weekends and holidays only. Hours: 10 a.m. to 4:15 p.m.

For more information, call (413) 298-3239.

**Location:** Naumkeag sits on Prospect Hill in Stockbridge, MA.

## TOURS: 9, 13, 20, 25

# ALBERT SCHWEITZER CENTER

*No ray of sunlight is ever lost, but the green which it wakes into existence needs time to sprout, and it is not always granted to the sower to live to see the harvest.*

— Albert Schweitzer

At the height of a brilliant career in theology, philosophy, and music, Albert Schweitzer decided to devote his life to two aims: finding the basic principle of life, one which would satisfy both our reason and our spiritual needs; and spending the remainder of his life in direct service to other human beings.

After years of reflection and study, he arrived at the concept of "Reverence for Life," which he recognized as the basic principle of human ethics and environmental concerns.

Schweitzer's concern for nature was also put into practice as he realized his second aim — serving mankind. In his thirties, he studied medicine and, with his wife Helene, went to Gabon in Equatorial Africa to establish a hospital. As a doctor, he did not bring complex

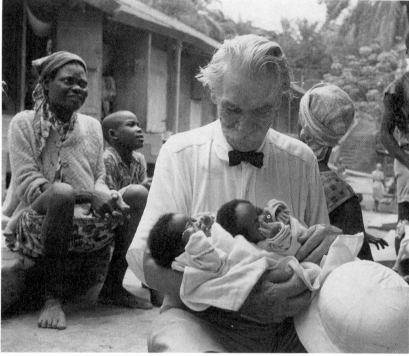

© Erica Anderson, Albert Schweitzer Center

*"Whatever kindness a man puts out into the world, works on the hearts and thoughts of his fellow men."*

Albert Schweitzer

medical technology to an unprepared continent, but adjusted his practice to the local environment. He was awarded the Nobel Peace Prize in 1953 for his work. The Albert Schweitzer Center was created to let people know about Dr. Schweitzer, his life, and work and to encourage others to incorporate "reverence for life" in their own lives. The Academy Award-winning film "Albert Schweitzer" is shown regularly at the center, and you can watch it (on video) when you visit. The center also has a museum, library, and archives. A path behind the center leads to a peaceful, wooded clearing, which has signs bearing quotations from Schweitzer. There are also pathways along Alford Brook, perfect for walks, meditation, or picnics. The center is open year-round, except Mondays and major holidays. From April 16-October 31, hours are Tuesday through Saturday, from 10 a.m. to 4 p.m., and Sunday from noon to 4 p.m. The rest of the year, it is open weekends from 11 a.m. to 4 p.m. For more information, call (413) 528-3124.

**Location:** The Albert Schweitzer Center is on Hurlburt Rd., between Great Barrington and North Egremont, MA.

TOURS: 3, 15, 20

# Henry Hudson Kitson's Gingerbread House

## (Tyringham Art Galleries)

Originally called the "Witch House"— and you'll know why when you see it — this attraction is right out of *Hansel and Gretel*. There is even a witch's face contoured into the side of the house. The roof of the studio is designed to reflect the rolling of the Berkshire hills.

The eccentric British sculptor, Sir Henry Kitson — famous for the *Puritan Maid* in Plymouth, Massachusetts; the *Continental Soldier* at Washington's headquarters in Newburgh, New York; and the *Indian Blessing* at Lebanon Springs, New York — built the Gingerbread House in the early 1930s, when he discovered the number of artists and sculptors living in the Berkshires.

After Kitson's death, the new owners, Ann and Donald Davis, turned the house into an art gallery. You can see the works of contemporary artists in the gallery and in the sculpture garden. There is a small admission fee.

It is open Labor Day through Memorial Day, and again during the fall foliage season, from 10 a.m. to 5 p.m. daily. For more information call (413) 243-0654 or 243-3260.

**Location:** The Gingerbread House is on Tyringham Main Rd., south of Rte. 102/20, just north of Tyringham, MA.

Tours: **23**

## LUNCH TIME FOR THE WICKED WITCH
Kitson's gingerbread house.

# NORMAN ROCKWELL MUSEUM

If you grew up with a copy of *The Saturday Evening Post* on the coffee table in your living room, visiting the Norman Rockwell Museum is bound to bring a wave of nostalgia. The warmth and humanness of Rockwell's artwork have touched millions, and it's no wonder he is considered America's best-loved illustrator.

The Norman Rockwell Museum houses the world's largest collection of Rockwell's works. Guided tours give pointers on key details in the paintings, how Rockwell developed his works, and colorful stories about the painter's personal life and his relationships with other residents of Stockbridge.

In 1969, about 5,000 people visited the museum in Stockbridge to see the handful of original works on display there. Now the annual visitor attendance is up to 145,000, and the museum can only exhibit 50 of its 500 works at a time. During peak season, the museum is crowded, and folks sometimes have to wait an hour or more for a tour. A new museum, large enough to house the entire collection, is being built (at the time of this writing) in nearby Glendale. It's scheduled to open in 1993.

The original museum is open all year, weekdays from 11 a.m. to 4 p.m., and on weekends and holidays from 10 a.m. to 5 p.m. The admission fee is adults $5, children $1. The museum's gift shop sells Rockwell books, prints, and postcards. For further information, call (413) 298-3822.

**Location:** Old Rockwell Museum is on the corner of Main St. and Elm in Stockbridge, MA. The New Museum is on Linwood Dr. off Rte.183 in Glendale, MA.

Rockwell was an avid cyclist, and each season the museum runs guided cycling tours along his favorite bike paths. See description of the "Tour de Rockwell" under "Organized Rides" in the Resources chapter.

TOURS: **5, 20**

# HISTORIC LANDMARKS

# SHAY'S REBELLION MONUMENT

A number of Berkshire farmers got very irritated when they returned to their homes after fighting in the Continental Army during the Revolutionary War only to discover themselves unjustly taxed by the government they had fought to establish. Furthermore, they had been paid for their service in a currency that was worthless, because the new nation wouldn't stand behind it. And even though the government would not accept the currency it had given the soldiers, it still demanded payment of debts. Many of the Berkshire soldiers were thrown into debtors' prison, because they couldn't pay in acceptable funds.

Daniel Shay, who had been a captain in the Continental Army and had fought at Bunker Hill, led an uprising against the injustice. He could be termed a true "rabble rouser," as his band's unsophisticated tactics included dragging local government officials out of their beds at night and beating them up. These rebels would show up whenever the government scheduled a court sitting to try debtors and would make enough of a ruckus to disrupt the proceedings. On one occasion, they also broke into the local jail to free prisoners confined for nonpayment of debts.

After one raid on the town of Stockbridge, about a hundred of Shay's men set off for Great Barrington. They made a tavern stop long enough to refresh themselves and then headed south. Government troops, led by Colonel Ashley, caught up with them south of South Egremont.

After ten minutes of fighting, the rebels broke and fled. Two men on each side were killed. That was the last battle of Shay's Rebellion. Several of the rebels were captured and tried at the Supreme Judicial Court in Great Barrington and sentenced to death for treason. Fortunately for them, the sentences were never carried out. Daniel Shay was pardoned.

However, the rebellion wasn't a total loss; Shay and his cause had a lot of sympathy from other residents in the Berkshires, and the unjust tax and debt laws were eventually changed.

The four-foot-high, rough-stone monument commemorating the rebellion sits on the corner of the field where the last battle took place.

**Location:** The monument is located on Sheffield-Egremont Rd., between South Egremont and Sheffield, MA.

## TOURS: 1, 16

# COLONEL ASHLEY HOUSE

This house, which Colonel Ashley designed and built, had well-seasoned oak and chestnut rafters and was considered the finest residence in pre-Revolutionary Sheffield. Ashley brought in woodworkers from across the colony to carve paneling and fashion the gracefully curved staircase. His study had a broad fireplace and hand-carved sunburst cupboard.

It was in this room that Ashley met with a group of his neighbors in early 1773 (some three years before Thomas Jefferson and associates drafted the Declaration of Independence in Philadelphia) to draft "The Sheffield Declaration," a statement of grievances against English rule. This document states that all people are "equal, free, and independent . . . and have a right to the undisturbed enjoyment of their lives, their liberty, and property."

That may have been the phrase Hannah Ashley's black slave, Mumbet, overheard and took to heart. She made a case for her own freedom and brought it to court. In a 1781 trial, Mumbet won her freedom and left the house forever. Her emancipation, bestowed in the court in Great Barrington, was instrumental in bringing about the abolition of slavery under the Bill of Rights.

The Colonel Ashley House is the oldest house in Berkshire County. It was restored and is being maintained by The Trustees of Reservations. Furnishings and household items date from the 18th and early 19th centuries and include special pottery and tool collections. There is also an herb garden on the property.

Colonel Ashley House is open for guided tours from Memorial Day weekend through Columbus Day, on weekends and holidays from 1-5 p.m. From the last Wednesday in June through Labor Day, it is open Wednesday-Sunday.

Admission fee is $3.50 for adults; $1 for children younger than 16. For further information, call (413) 229-8600.

**Location:** Colonel Ashley House is south of Sheffield, MA, on the south side of Cooper Hill Rd., just west of Rannapo Rd. on Bartholomew's Cobble.

## Tours: 4, 11, 16, 17

# MISSION HOUSE

A minister from Yale came alone to the wilderness to preach the gospel to the Native Americans of the Mahican tribe. Young and sincere, John Sergeant drew the Natives to him, and before long, a settlement was established.

That's how the town of Stockbridge began. Sergeant learned the Indian language and preached two sermons in the Native tongue on Sundays. In springtime, he went with the Natives to tap sugar maples. His written account is the first in the English language to pass on the method of the Native's sugar production.

The minister frequently met with Indians in the back of his simple cabin, spending long hours listening to their problems. Under Sergeant's leadership, the Stockbridge Mission flourished, and at one point the Governor of Massachusetts invited Sergeant and a delegation of Mahicans to come to Boston to effect a transfer of Stockbridge land to the whites. Needless to say, the Indians got the short end of the stick — they agreed to exchange a bale of pelts and fifty-two square miles of land for a church.

To please his wife Abigail, Reverend Sergeant built what is now called Mission House. The tall and ornate "Connecticut doorway," which serves as the dwelling's front entry, was carved in Westfield, CT, and dragged by oxen more than 50 miles over rugged terrain to Stockbridge. The doorway panels represent the ten commandments, an open Bible, and St. Andrew's Cross.

The Mission House has period furniture and household artifacts. There's a flower, herb and fruit garden designed by Fletcher Steele (the man who designed the gardens at Naumkeag) and, behind the house, a small museum of Native American artifacts.

The Trustees of Reservations maintain the Mission House now. It is open for guided tours from Memorial Day weekend through Columbus Day; Tuesday–Sunday and Monday holidays, 11 a.m. to 3:30 p.m. It is closed Tuesday after holidays. Admission is $3.50 for adults and $1 for children younger than 16.

**Location:** The Mission House is on the corner of Main and Sergeant streets in Stockbridge, MA.

TOURS: 5, 20

# OLDEST COVERED BRIDGE IN MASSACHUSETTS

Spanning the Housatonic River, east of Rte. 7, on Covered Bridge Ln., this attraction is just what its name suggests: the oldest covered bridge in Massachusetts. If you like covered bridges, you may want to visit this specimen. There's a picnic table near the bridge.

TOURS: 1

# West Cornwall Covered Bridge

On Rte. 128, just east of Rte. 4, this covered bridge spans the Housatonic River and is still fully functional. It was built of native oak in 1837, and it is located right on the edge of the village of West Cornwall, CT. During periods of high water, you can often see kayaks and canoes shooting the rapids beneath and downriver from the bridge.

TOURS: 25

# Indian Burial Ground

On the west side of Stockbridge village is a tree-shaded mound overlooking the golf course. Here a natural stone obelisk, taken from Ice Glen, was erected by the Laurel Hill Association as a monument to the Indians. On the face of it is the inscription, "The Ancient Burial Place of the Stockbridge Indians — 1734 — The Friends of our Fathers — 1877." From the knoll, there is an excellent view of the surrounding mountains.

**Location:** on Glendale Rd. just west of Church St. in Stockbridge, MA.

TOURS: 5

# Nathaniel Hawthorne's Little Red House

Overlooking Stockbridge Bowl and the distant mountains, this building is a reconstruction of the house in which Hawthorne lived after being fired from his job at a customs house in Boston. It was here that Hawthorne wrote some of his best works, including *House of Seven Gables*. Here also, he entertained his friend Herman Melville, who lived not far away in Pittsfield and was working on *Moby Dick* at the time.

**Location:** The Little Red School House is across from Tanglewood's Lion Gate on Hawthorne St., just south of Rte. 183, Stockbridge.

## Tours: 8, 13, 20, 25

# Beckley Furnace

For two hundred years, pig-iron production was the foremost industry of Canaan, CT. High-grade iron ore came from the mines in nearby Salisbury. The country was in a boom cycle, and carpenters, farmers, shipwrights, and railroaders needed the iron. Everything from nails to ships' anchors were smelted and forged here. The Beckley Furnace is a relic of this era.

The nearby, fast-flowing Blackberry River was harnessed to turn the turbines, which supplied energy to operate the air blast for the furnace. Part of the big, stone chimney remains. A sign in front of the chimney gives a detailed history of the iron-smelting period and the Beckley Furnace. You can also walk up a little trail past the furnace to the dam to picnic or explore, or to look for pocket-sized pig-iron ingots and slag glass along the bank of the river.

**Location:** Beckley Furnace is on the south side of Lower Rd., east of Rte. 7, just south of the intersection of Rte. 7 and Rte. 44 in Canaan, CT.

## TOURS: **11, 17**

# GENERAL STORES

BREAK TIME
Look for the homemade goodies.

Remember the old general store — the place you'd go to get penny candy (jaw breakers!), balsa-wood gliders, Superman comics, or red and white fishing bobbers? If you missed walking down creaking wooden floors, along narrow, dimly lit aisles, and past the dry goods, dusty fishing tackle, and the Red Man chewing tobacco, you can experience it here, now, in the Berkshires.

There are still some of these unsophisticated, eccentric places around, and tours in this book pass by many of them. You can also enjoy some great home-baked cookies, take a break on a wooden bench on the front porch, or knock off a postcard to a friend and mail it in the post office right in the store (some stores *are* the town's post office).

Many of the stores, often run for decades by the same family, also sell vegetables and fruit grown by farmers nearby or by the store owners themselves. No two country general stores are quite the same. Each has its own flavor and personality. Some are real classics; all are good places to stop for a taste of the rural. They're run by friendly folks, and most will be happy to fill your water bottle. The tours in this book go by the following stores:

Us Bonds General Store
Mill River General Store
Colebrook General Store
Monterey General Store
Stockbridge Country Store
Southfield General Store
New Boston General Store
North Egremont General Store
Riverton General Store
West Cornwall IGA

*Shoplifters will be shot and eaten.*

Sign above the door in Us Bonds
General Store, Otis, MA

# Resources

# BICYCLE RESOURCES

## RENTALS

The following shops rent bicycles:

| | |
|---|---|
| Plaine's Ski and Cycling Center | Pittsfield, MA |
| Main St. Sports and Leisure | Lenox, MA |
| The Bike Doctor | Ashley Falls, MA |
| The Village Shop | Salisbury, CT |

## SHOPS

### Massachusetts

**Lenox**

The Arcadian Shop
333 Pittsfield-Lenox Rd., (Rte. 7/20 north of Lenox)
Lenox, MA                                           (413) 637-3010

This is home base for the Berkshire Velo Club, and its evening group rides start here (see "Organized Rides" for schedule). The shop has an excellent selection of racing, touring, and off-road bikes, including Trek, Bridgestone, and Specialized models, as well as clothing (including general outdoor clothing and gear), parts, accessories, maps, and power bars. A mechanic is available. No bike rentals at this time.

Hours: 10 a.m. to 6 p.m., Monday through Saturday (to 9 p.m. on Thursday); noon to 5 p.m. on Sunday

Mean Wheels
55 Housatonic St.
Lenox, MA (off Rte. 7A)                             (413) 637-0644

This shop is run by two very knowledgeable and experienced cyclists, Ruth Wheeler and Cliff Hague. Road, touring, and off-road bikes, accessories, power bars, and parts are for sale. Mean Wheels specializes in Terry Road bikes for women; the shop also carries Klien, Marin, Off-Road, Iron Horse, and Fat Chance models. There's an in-house bike mechanic. No bike rentals.

Hours: 5 to 9 p.m., Monday, Tuesday, Wednesday, and Friday; 1 to 5 p.m. on Saturday

Main Street Sports & Leisure
102 Main St. (off Rte. 7A)
P.O. Box 2164
Lenox, MA 01240                                    (413) 637-4407
Here you can schedule private bike tours (both road and off-road) by
special arrangement. Rides are led by George Roberson, a cyclist/guide
with national competition experience. He will also teach biking techniques
and awarenesses if desired. Bike rentals available for $15 per half day,
$20 per full day, or two days for $30. Rate includes helmet.
Hours: 10 a.m. to 6 p.m. Monday through Saturday (Thursday evenings
until 8 p.m.); Sundays, 11 a.m. to 4 p.m.

**Pittsfield**

Plaine's Ski and Cycling Center
55 West Housatonic St.
Pittsfield, MA 01201                               (413) 499-0294
All major brands of racing, touring, and off-road bikes are for sale, as
is a wide selection of parts and accessories. In-house mechanics available. You can rent touring or mountain bikes for $15 for a 24-hour
period, but be prepared to put the charge on your VISA or MasterCard
or pay a $100 security deposit. Helmets are included in rental prices.
Hours: Open seven days a week — 9 a.m. to 6 p.m. Monday through
Saturday (Thursday till 9 p.m.); noon to 5 p.m. on Sunday

Ordinary Cycles
251 North St.
Pittsfield, MA 01201                               (413) 442-7225
This is the center point for serious bicycle racing in the Berkshires.
Informal group rides are held on Tuesday evenings in the summer.
Call Tom at the shop for details. The shop handles road, racing, tour-
ing, and off-road bikes sales, service, and accessories. Specializing in
Schwinn/Paramount, Bianchi, and Bridgestone bikes. There is an ex-
cellent in-house mechanic. No bike rentals at this time.
Hours: 9:30 a.m. to 5:30 p.m., Monday through Saturday

## Ashley Falls
The Bike Doctor
East Main St.
Ashley Falls, MA 01222                    (413) 229-2909

This shop carries new and used bikes, and there's a mechanic available. Rental of used bikes for $10 per day (no helmets available, so bring your own). Sales of Aerolite, Fuji, and Mt. Shasta bikes.

Hours: 9 a.m. to 5 p.m., Monday through Saturday

## Great Barrington
Harland Foster
15 Bridge St.
Great Barrington, MA 01230                    (413) 528-2100

This is a friendly country hardware store with its own bike shop and excellent in-house mechanic. It has bike sales, service, and accessories. Brands carried are Haro, Nishiki, Miyata, and Cycle Pro. No rentals at this time.

Hours: 7:30 a.m. to 5:30 p.m., Monday through Friday; 7:30 a.m. to 5 p.m., Saturday

# Connecticut
## Salisbury
The Village Store
Main St.
Salisbury, CT 06068                    (203) 435-9459

Here you'll find mountain and road bikes (Nishiki, Haro, Cannondale, and Ross), clothing, parts, and accessories. Mechanic is available. Rentals at $10 a day (no helmets).

Hours: 9 a.m. to 5 p.m., Monday through Saturday

## Torrington
Tommy's Bicycles
32-40 E. Main St. (Rte. 202)
Torrington, CT 06790                    (203) 482-2412

This is the grandaddy of bicycle shops, with more than 500 bikes on display, plus a full line of clothing, parts, and accessories. Experienced mechanics are available. All major brands carried. No bike rentals at this time.

Hours: 9 a.m. to 6 p.m., weekdays (to 9 p.m. on Thursday); 9 a.m. to 5:30 p.m., Saturday

Bike Express
corner of Rtes. 202 & 67
New Milford, CT 06776                              (203) 354-1466

This shop currently sponsors the Minoso Cycling Club. Bike Express
has a certified mechanic and one-day repairs available. It carries
clothes and accessories as well as Schwinn, Specialized, and Klien
bikes. No bike rentals at this time.

Hours: 10 a.m. to 5:30 p.m., Monday through Thursday; Friday till 7
p.m.; Saturday till 4 p.m.

# ORGANIZED RIDES & RACES
## Massachusetts

### Greylock Century

Are you a cycling masochist? If so, you're gonna love this race! There
are three major climbs — with the first being to the top of Mt. Greylock,
the highest point in Massachusetts. The other two climbs are just as
challenging.

This may be the toughest century you ever do. It's a friendly event,
though, with volunteers manning the three sag points with water,
sports drinks, homemade cookies, fruit, and encouragement! If you
finish, you'll have climbed more than 7,800 feet.

Some of the redeeming qualities of this ride are beautiful views of the
valley from the road up Mt. Greylock and a spectacular, seven-mile
winding descent on Rte. 2, the Mohawk Trail. The road winds down
through a gorge along the rapids of Cold River.

The ride's fee of $10 includes a T-shirt, if you finish. In 1991, the race
had 100 riders. It is sponsored by the Berkshire Velo Club and is
usually held the second Sunday in August. Contact the Arcadian
Shop, 333 Pittsfield-Lenox Rd., Lenox, MA 01240, (413) 637-3010,
for details and entry form.

### The Flat Century

The name is a joke; it's not flat at all — unless you compare it to the
Greylock Century! This is a more low-key event — a beautiful ride
through rolling hills, with magnificent mountain views. A highlight is
a stretch on the award-winning American Beauty Highway. The Flat
Century has spectacular scenery and well paved roads. It's a bring-
your-own-lunch affair. There's sag support with water, cookies, and
fruit between 70 and 80 miles.

The Flat is sponsored by the Berkshire Velo Club (BVC) and is usually held the second Sunday in July. Only a $5 entry fee; if you're a member of the club, it's free (annual dues for the BVC are just $5 per year). Contact the Arcadia Shop, 333 Pittsfield-Lenox Rd., Lenox, MA 01240, (413) 637-3010, for details and entry form.

Mark Mitchell

LEAD PACK
Rounding the bend in West Stockbridge.

## Josh Billings Runaground

*When a fellow gets to going down hill, it does seem as though everything has been greased for the occasion.*
— Josh Billings

When he spoke those words, Josh wasn't referring to the cyclists racing in the triathlon named after him. But if you do this race, you'll have your share of goin' downhill—and uphill, too.

It begins with a mass start of 500 or so cyclists and breaks into packs once you hit the first set of hills. If you've never been in a race where you can draft, you may enjoy the maneuvering and strategy this event invites. This triathlon, held the second weekend in September, has become a county institution. It's been held yearly since 1976, making it the oldest continuously run triathlon in the eastern United States and the oldest of its kind in the country.

More than 500 four-member teams and 100 ironwoman, ironman, and two-member teams compete in this bicycle-canoe-foot race. Because the bike is the first leg of the Josh, it's viewed as the most competitive event. The teams range from the very serious — some with semi-professional bicycle racers (many of whom are United States Cycling Federation Category II) — to just-for-fun folks.

The challenging, 27-mile bicycle leg starts in Great Barrington, courses the scenic Alford Valley, and goes through the centers of the towns of West Stockbridge and Stockbridge before ending with a hand-off of the sweatband to canoeists on Lake Mahkeenac (Stockbridge Bowl). They, in turn, hand off to the runners after paddling one and three-quarters times around the lake. The event is followed by a "bash," with food, drink, and live music at the Tanglewood Music Festival grounds.

All proceeds benefit Hillcrest Hospital's McGee Alcoholism Unit out-patient program. Fees are $60 per team and $35 per ironman (or woman). For more information and a race application, call Rich Woller at (413) 637-2906, or the Arcadia Shop at (413) 637-3010. (Also see the Josh Billings tour in the Tours chapter.)

If you'd like to do the bike leg of the race, but don't have partners for the canoe or run, you may be able to find a teammate by putting an ad in the local freebies — Shopper's Guide, (413) 528-0095, or Yankee Shopper, (413) 684-1373. Or, during the months before the race, check the ads for others who are looking for cyclists to complete their teams. These publications are available in markets and conven-ience stores, the ads are cheap, and they have a huge readership throughout the Berkshires. Many people find partners this way.

### "Tour de Rockwell" Tours

Norman Rockwell and his wife Molly were cyclists and had several favorite routes through the countryside around Stockbridge, Massa-chusetts. The Norman Rockwell Museum gives guided bicycle tours once a month, from June through October. Guides know the history and culture of the area as well as anecdotes from Rockwell's life, and they enjoy sharing them along the way.

There is a fee of $5 for adults and $2.50 for children; this includes a half-price ticket for admission to the Norman Rockwell Museum. For dates and times, call the Norman Rockwell Museum at (413) 298-4239.

## Berkshire Velo Club Weekly Rides

Every Thursday evening at 6 p.m., between the day Daylight Savings Time begins and the day it ends, a ride leaves from the parking lot of the Arcadian Shop in Lenox. This is a fast touring ride, with an average pace of about 15-17 mph.

A ride for more casual riders, also at 6 p.m. on Thursday evening, leaves from either Stockbridge Town Hall or in Lee.

Every second and fourth Thursday, a mountain-bike ride leaves from the Arcadia Shop parking lot.

Contact the Arcadian Shop for more information about any of these rides. (413) 637-3010.

## Berkshire Hiking Holidays (BHH)

This group has weekend through five-day mini-vacation packages, which include bicycle touring. BHH takes care of accommodations, food, and arranging entertainment and cultural sightseeing. For information on the schedules and custom-planned outings, contact Richard Woller at Berkshire Hiking Holidays, P.O. Box 2231, Lenox, MA 01240, (413) 499-9648.

# Connecticut

## Tour de Torrington

Here's some beautiful riding in northern Litchfield County, with lots of enthusiastic cyclists and a choice of distances: 15, 30, and 50 miles. In 1991, the tour had 300 riders, and it's expected to be larger each year.

All proceeds from the $25 entrance fee go to the Cancer Society. Chow down, at no charge, at the full picnic after the ride. The tour is held the first Sunday in August. Call Tim Grieco at (203) 482-2412 or write him c/o Tommy's Bike Shop, 32-40 E. Main St., Torrington, CT 06790, for more information or an entry form.

## The MacLean Stevens Prindle Memorial Ride

The ride includes an eight-mile loop around scenic Lake Waramaug, as well as a 25-miler and a hilly 50-miler going north through the Salisbury/Lakeville area. This is a very classy event, with the very best, all-natural, healthy food (it was supplied by Doc's Restaurant in 1991) at the picnic afterward. There's even a raffle, with prizes, at the picnic.

The tour marshalls and sag-wagon and safety-support volunteers are from the Minoso Cycling Club out of New Milford, Connecticut. The ride is named after a boy who died in a bicycle accident at Lake Waramaug. Proceeds from this ride go to the American Heart Association.

For the current year's date, entry form, or further information, contact Amy King at (203) 544-9537, or write to The MacLean Stevens Prindle Memorial Ride, American Heart Association Branch 533, 5 Brookside Dr., Wallingsford, CT 06492.

## Dog Days Triathlon

"We emphasize the fun nature of this triathlon," says Betsey Hallihan, the race organizer. Recreational as well as serious competitors are welcome to this low-key, family oriented bike-canoe-run race. The 17-mile bike leg comes after the run (4.6 miles) and canoe (2.5 miles), and is a three-lap ride around Long Pond to the finish line.

Divisions include two- and three-generation teams as well as a men's, women's, mixed, juniors', and seniors' divisions. Or you can enter as an ironman or ironwoman. Refreshments and ribbons are awarded after the race.

Entry forms are available at Village Store in Salisbury, Salisbury Bank and Trust, and On The Run Coffee Shop in Lakeville. The $12-per-person entrance fee includes a T-shirt. The race is put on by the Salisbury Winter Sports Club and is held in August. For race date, entry form or more information, contact Betsey Hallihan, P.O. Box 1661, Lakeville, CT 06039, (203) 824-5056.

## Minoso Rock and Roll Classic

This United States Cycling Federation (USCF) sanctioned race is held on the track of the world-famous Lime Rock Raceway during the summer and is sponsored by the Minoso Cycling Club. For more information, contact Scott Davis at (203) 354-4879.

## Minoso Cycling Club Weekly Rides

Every Saturday, club rides of varying distances leave from the green in New Milford, Connecticut. Once a month, there is a century ride. All levels of cyclists are welcome. For competitive riders, there are weekly time trials every Tuesday evening at 6:30 p.m. at Lake Waramaug. Call club president Scott Davis at (203) 354-4879, for more information.

# Bicycling Clubs & Organizations

Courtesy of *The Berkshire Eagle*

## High-Tech in 1884
E. H. Kennedy, President of the Berkshire County
Wheelmen, with his new bike.

### Berkshire Velo Club

For those who enjoy riding for fitness and enjoyment, this is a relaxed, fun club.

The Berkshire Velo Club (BVC) sponsors the Greylock Century and the Flat Century as well as weekly Thursday evening rides during the riding season (see under "Organized Rides").

Contact the Arcadian Shop in Lenox, (413) 637-3010, for information. Or contact club presidents Sue and Al Berzinis, 178 Hubbard St., Lenox, MA 01240, (413) 637-1718. (Sue and Al are tandem enthusiasts and welcome hearing from others using tandems or those interested in knowing more about tandem riding.)

## Berkshire Cycling Association

This is a club for racers; it is affiliated with the USCF. The club puts on one or two races in the Berkshires each biking season. For a racing calendar and information on training rides and clinics, contact Mike Tucker, 38 Springside Ave., Pittsfield, MA 01201, (413) 499-7236.

## League of American Wheelmen

Founded in 1880, this is the largest and oldest bicycle touring organization in the United States. League of American Wheelmen (L.A.W.) focuses on protecting the rights and promoting the interests of bicyclists. In the Southern Berkshires, there are two L.A.W. contacts who can answer questions about local rides and events:

- Massachusetts L.A.W Area Representative: Bob Steele, 24 Newell St., Pittsfield, MA 01201, (413) 499-1759
- Connecticut L.A.W. Ride Information Contact Tom Weidman, 2017 Boulevard, West Hartford, CT 06107, (203) 561-4264

The League has a strong national legislative and government relations program working to promote and protect the interests of cyclists, and it also has a nationwide network of bicycling clubs. It publishes *Bicycling USA* magazine (filled with helpful and entertaining news items, events calendar, feature articles, and columns written for the bicyclist) and the annual *Bicycling USA Almanac*. If you'd like more information on the League or would like to join, contact League of American Wheelmen, 6707 Whitestone Rd., Suite 209, Baltimore, MD 21207, (301) 539-3399.

## Minoso Cycling Club

This very active club is affiliated with the USCF. All levels of riders are welcome; annual dues are $15. Weekly club rides, with a range of distances, are held every Saturday. Time trials are held each Tuesday evening.

The club holds clinics on many aspects of cycling, including training, technique, and nutrition. It supports a community benefit event at least once a year and also puts on annual USCF-sanctioned races, including the Minoso Rock and Roll Classic at the race track at Lime Rock. This group is active in promoting bicycling safety in the community. For more information, contact Scott Davis at (203) 354-4879.

# BOOKS AND BROCHURES

The following books and maps are handy resources for cycle touring in the Southern Berkshires. Check for them in your local library or favorite bookstore, or order selected books and maps directly from **Freewheel Publications**. (See the order form at the end of the book.)

*The Berkshire Book: A Complete Guide,* by Jonathan Sternfield, offers a comprehensive guide to Berkshire County's historical, cultural, culinary, scenic, and recreational features and seasonal events. According to *New England Monthly,* this book "covers every aspect of Berkshire life — from early glaciation to the latest concert at Tanglewood. A must for every traveler's bookshelf." It's available for $14.95 at area bookstores or directly from the publisher, Berkshire House, Box 915, Great Barrington, MA 01230.

*The Berkshire Hills — A WPA Guide* is an unusual book giving a grass-roots look at the Berkshires. It's a compilation of local history, geography, and culture written during the 1930s by a group of government-employed writers. It also includes local lore, character sketches, maps, and photographs. Published in 1987, this 360-page paperback costs $11.95 and is available in bookstores in the Berkshires or directly from the publisher, Northeastern University Press, Boston, MA.

*The Berkshires Guide* is a thick, biannual listing of attractions, events, lodging, and dining, plus feature articles. It also includes simple maps for many of the towns in the Berkshires. For a copy of the guide, send $2.00, for postage and handling, to Country Hills Publishing, Inc., P.O. Box 860, Great Barrington, MA 01230.

*Discover the Berkshires* guide book is available free from the Berkshire Hills Visitors' Bureau. It has a comprehensive list of places to stay, eat, and shop, as well as tour operators and recreational opportunities in the Berkshires. You can pick up a copy at almost any inn, restaurant, or convenience store in the Southern Berkshires. Or, have one mailed to you at no charge by contacting The Berkshire Hills Visitors' Bureau, (413) 443-9186 (outside Massachusetts, call 1-800-BERKSHR), Berkshire Common, West St. Plaza, Pittsfield, MA 01201.

*Bicycling Magazine's Basic Maintenance and Repair,* by the editors of *Bicycling Magazine,* covers nearly every do-it-yourself procedure involved in caring for a bicycle. It shows how to true a wheel, service brakes, care for the gearing system, adjust derailleurs, and overhaul cranksets, hubs, headsets, and pedals. The 125-page paperback costs $6.95 (including postage) and is available from Rodale Press, Inc., 33 East Minor St., Emmaus, PA 18098.

*Training for Fitness and Endurance,* by the editors of *Bicycling Magazine,* includes information about how to stretch and warm up for a long ride and how to train for a century. It has tips on eating for peak performance and endurance, plus much more. The paperback has 122 pages and costs $6.95 (postage included). It's available from Rodale Press, Inc., 33 East Minor St., Emmaus, PA 18098.

*600 Tips For Better Bicycling,* by the editors of *Bicycling Magazine,* includes tips on how to train, long-distance touring, effective equipment, staying healthy, cycle commuting, what to eat, and more — from those who know best. It's a paperback with 124 pages, costs $6.95 (including postage), and is available from Rodale Press, Inc., 33 East Minor St., Emmaus, PA 18098.

*Bike Rides in the Berkshire Hills,* by Lewis Cuyler, has more than 30 bike rides, maps, background on Berkshire towns and cultural sites, and information about Berkshire natural history. It's available through Berkshire bookstores or directly from the publisher, Berkshire House Publishers, Box 915, Great Barrington, MA 01230. Published in 1991, it has 200 pages, with photos and maps. The paperback costs $8.95.

*The Old Farmers Almanac.* Using this to plan bike trips has made a believer out of me. Its own advertising says, "Containing, besides the large number of Astronomical Calculations and the Farmer's Calendar for every month in the year, a variety of New, Useful, and Entertaining Matter." It's available for $3.95 in book, convenience, or drug stores. Or call, toll free, 1-800-733-3000 to order by phone.

*The Spirit of Massachusetts Fall Foliage Guide* is a booklet available free from the Massachusetts Division of Tourism. In it, you'll find information about the foliage in different areas of the state, including places and ways to view foliage. Call the Fall Foliage Hotline to get a copy of the guide. During the season, you can call that number to find out the percentage of color and the expected peak dates. From Massachusetts, call 1-800-632-8038; from other Northeast states, call 1-800-343-9072; from all other states, call (617) 727-3201.

# MAPS

- Detailed road maps are available for **Berkshire County, MA,** ($3.25) and **Litchfield County, CT,** ($2.95) from Jimapco, Box 1137, Clifton Park, N.Y. 12065. Call 1-800-MAPS-123 to order by phone. Shipping is $3.25 per order. The maps can also be purchased in many local convenience stores, drugstores, and gas stations in the Southern Berkshires. These easy-to-read maps fold down to a handy size and have sufficient detail to make them very useful for cycling.

- A detailed **Berkshire County, MA, road map** is available for $5 from the Berkshire County Commission, County Courthouse, 76 East St., Pittsfield, MA 01201.

- A **Berkshire County Historical Map** is available for $1.50 from the Central Berkshire Chamber of Commerce, 66 West St., Pittsfield, MA 01201.

- **Vaughn Gray maps** are for those who like to explore. Available is one each for Berkshire County and Litchfield County. They're the most detailed road maps I've seen and include natural attractions such as waterfalls, natural springs, and state and local parks. Plus, they have artistic drawings of main historical features, beautifully done on parchment-like paper and suitable for mounting. These are such handsome maps, you may not want to fold them. I photocopied sections of mine and folded up the copies to take with me when I go exploring. Vaughn Gray maps are available in bookstores throughout the Southern Berkshires or directly from Vaughn Gray, Box 11, Glendale, MA 01229. Cost is $7 for the Berkshire County map and $6 for the Litchfield County map, with an additional $1.50 shipping per order. Maps come rolled in tubes.

# MEDICAL CARE — 24-HOUR EMERGENCY

## Massachusetts
**Berkshire Medical Center** — North St., Pittsfield, MA, (413) 499-4161

**Fairview Hospital** — 29 Lewis Avenue, Great Barrington, MA, (413) 528-0790

## Connecticut
**Charlotte Hungerford Hospital** — 540 Litchfield, Torrington, CT, (203) 496-6650

**Sharon Hospital** — West Main St., Sharon, CT, (203) 364-4111

**Winsted Memorial Hospital**—115 Spencer St., Winsted, CT, (203) 738-6600

# Tourist Information

## Massachusetts

**The Berkshire Hills Visitors' Bureau** is open Monday through Friday from 9 a.m. to 5 p.m. It has up-to-date tourist information, including accommodation vacancies during crunch periods, and can refer callers to inns and motels with space. The bureau is the source of the *Discover the Berkshires* guide book, which has a comprehensive list of places to stay, eat, and shop, as well as tour operators and recreational opportunities in the Berkshires. You can pick up a copy at almost any inn, restaurant, or convenience store in the Berkshires. Or, have one mailed to you at no charge by contacting the Berkshire Hills Visitors' Bureau, Berkshire Common, West St. Plaza, Pittsfield, MA 01201, phone (413) 443-9186 (outside Massachusetts, call 1-800-BERKSHR).

**Lenox Chamber of Commerce** is a very helpful walk-in center with an extensive pamphlet rack. It is also the site of the Berkshire Ticket Booth. Staff make referrals to local lodging places, which — during Tanglewood Music Festival season — include more than 50 private homes. The Lenox Chamber of Commerce is open year-round. In summer, hours are 10 a.m. to 4 p.m., Monday through Thursday; 10 a.m. to 6 p.m., Friday and Saturday; and 10 a.m. to 2 p.m., Sunday. In winter, the hours are Thursday through Saturday, 9:30 a.m. to 4:30 p.m., with a 24-hour answering machine. The chamber is located in the Lenox Academy Building, 75 Main St., Lenox, MA 01240, (413) 637-3646.

**Stockbridge Information Booth** (413) 298-3344. This is a kiosk-style booth on Main St. in Stockbridge. It's open daily in summer months (but only from noon to 2 p.m. on Sundays).

**Great Barrington Information Booth** is located at the southern edge of downtown Great Barrington on Main St. (Rtes. 23/7). (413) 528-1510. When commercial lodging rooms fill up, this resource refers visitors to private homes. It's open year-round: daily in summer from 9 a.m. to 5 p.m. (Fridays till 9 p.m.); it's closed Mondays and for lunch in winter.

**Lee Information Booth**, (413) 243-0852, is a seasonal wooden booth at the park in the middle of town on Main St.

**Massachusetts Department of Environmental Management** in Pittsfield will answer specific questions on local state forests and parks. (413) 442-8928

## Connecticut

**Litchfield Hills Visitors' Council.** The *Unwind in the Litchfield Hills* travel brochure — listing places to stay, restaurants, and cultural and scenic attractions in Litchfield County — is available here on request. The council provides maps, reservation services, and just about any information a visitor would seek. Contact Janet Serra for special requests. P.O. Box 1776, New Preston, CT 06777, (203) 868-2214

**Chamber of Commerce of Northwest Connecticut** will send a list of community attractions, sports, theaters, restaurants, lodging, and special events for the towns in northwest Connecticut. It also provides copies of the *Classic Connecticut Vacation Guide*. Contact the chamber at 333 Kennedy Dr., Suite 1, P.O. Box 59, Torrington, CT 06790.

# PLACES TO STAY

# PLACES TO STAY

I've included lodgings ranging from fine country inns and bed and breakfasts to rooms in private homes and campgrounds. In researching this chapter, I visited many lodgings in the Southern Berkshires. My selections are based on the friendliness of staff, apparent comfort, cleanliness, location, and the hosts' openness toward cyclists. I did not stay overnight at any of the places, so my choices are based on my impressions as a drop-in visitor. I am not attempting to evaluate or rate the accommodations (there are other books that do an excellent job of that); but I do want to give you enough pertinent information so you can make a choice that suits you.

To list these accommodations, I relied on my personal impressions, lodging guides put out by local chambers of commerce, and the individual inn/hotel keeper's literature. I gathered factual information as near as possible to this book's publication date — but in this rapidly changing world, "facts" do go out of date. You may want to check ahead with a phone call.

I'd be delighted to hear your evaluation of accommodations you use as a result of this book, and I'd be happy to include it in subsequent editions.

The selection here is by no means complete. There are many more fine lodgings available in the Southern Berkshires. For a wider selection of accommodations, as well as detailed descriptions and recommendations, get a copy of *The Berkshire Book* by Jonathan Sternfield. This excellent guide is available at local bookstores throughout the Berkshires or directly from the publisher. (See the Resources chapter for more information.)

Accommodations can also be found with the help of these tourist-service organizations:

| | |
|---|---|
| Berkshire Visitors Bureau | (800) 237-5747 |
| Bed & Breakfast USA | (413) 528-2113 |
| Berkshire Bed & Breakfast Connection | (413) 268-7244 |

Litchfield Hills Travel Council    (203) 868-2214
Covered Bridge Bed & Breakfast    (203) 672-6052
Lenox Chamber of Commerce*    (413) 637-3646

*(Note: Staff make referrals to local lodging places which, during Tanglewood Music Festival season, include more than 50 private homes.)

The following prices are based on a daily per-room rate, with double occupancy, during the on-season (summer and fall foliage). Off-season rates are 20 to 40 percent lower.

Inexpensive ................. up to $65
Moderate ................... $66 to $95
Expensive ............... $96 to $150

Add 8% state sales tax for accommodations in Connecticut and 9.7% in Massachusetts.

Many of the inns and bed-and-breakfasts (B&Bs) offer discount rates from time to time; it's worth calling. Also compare weekend and weekday rates; you can usually save a lot! The rate difference is as much as 30 percent. Plan ahead; many of the inns and B&Bs request advance reservations.

## LODGINGS

## Massachusetts

### Lenox

**The Village Inn**, with its colonial atmosphere, has been welcoming guests since 1771. It is an old, highly respected hostelry having 29 rooms with private baths. Full-scale restaurant serves breakfast, English tea, and dinner. Breakfast served on the porch in summer. The inn is famous for its afternoon English tea.

**Price:** inexpensive to expensive.
**Credit cards:** AE, CB, DC, MC, V
**Managers:** Clifford Rudisill and Ray Wilson.
**Address:**   Box 1810
16 Church St.
Lenox, MA 01240      (413) 637-0020
(located off Walker St. in the center of town)

**The Gables Inn** is the charming old home where Edith Wharton summered while The Mount, her "cottage," was being built. The air-conditioned inn is within walking distance of everything in the Lenox area — including Tanglewood Music Festival. It has 17 bedrooms, most with private bath. Continental breakfast. Pool.

**Price:** inexpensive to very expensive. Credit cards: AE, MC, V
**Manager:**    Frank Newton
103 Walker St.
Lenox, MA 01240                                    (413) 637-3416

**Birchwood Inn** is on a hill overlooking the village of Lenox. It has 10 rooms in the main house (eight with private bath) and two suites in the carriage house. A full country breakfast is served, plus wine and cheese in the afternoon. Birchwood Inn is listed on the National Register of Historic Places. Minimum stay of three nights required.

**Price:** moderate to very expensive.
**Credit cards:** MC, V
**Managers:** Arnold, Sandra, and Laura Hittleman
**Address:**    Box 2020
7 Hubbard St.
Lenox, MA 01240                                    (413) 637-2600
(located on the corner of Main St. and Hubbard)

**Candlelight Inn** is a gracious New England inn, with a homey atmosphere, located in the center of Lenox village. It has eight rooms furnished with antiques, private baths, and air conditioning. Continental breakfast included. There's a restaurant on the main floor and a fenced area in the back to store bikes.

**Price:** moderate to expensive.
**Credit cards:** AE, MC, V
**Managers:** Rebecca and John Hedgecock
**Address:**    53 Walker St.
Lenox, MA 01240                                    (413) 637-1555
(located on the corner of Walker and Church streets
near the village center)

**Kripalu Center for Yoga and Health.** You may wonder why I've included a yoga and health center, but this is such a great place to stay in the Berkshires, I wouldn't want you to miss the opportunity. The center offers many yoga and health-oriented programs, but you can also use it as a home base to cycle many of the tours in this book. Kripalu offers a lot of comforts, too — use the sauna or whirlpool, or get a professional massage or foot reflexology from the health services staff after your ride. You might enjoy taking a yoga class or "Dans-kinetics" (aerobic/yogic dancing) to loosen up and relax. *(continued)*

The center is run by members of the Kripalu Yoga Fellowship, and the staff are genuinely warm, friendly, and open — a fact to which I can attest, as many of these folks are my close friends, and I was on staff at the center for more than nine years. The resident staff at Kripalu have chosen a lifestyle of personal and spiritual integrity aimed at balancing mind, body, and spirit.

The food at Kripalu is outstanding — all natural, healthy, vegetarian, and delicious. Plenty of pasta dishes — including pizza, lasagna, and spaghetti — plus natural, whole-grain breads baked in-house and a fresh salad bar. All the meals are served from a buffet line and you can come back for seconds or thirds (or more) — obviously an advantage for carbohydrate-loading (or reloading).

Many of the staff (and guests) are active cyclists. If you were to check out the basement at the center, you'd find more than 250 cycles hanging from the walls!

Kripalu is housed in Shadowbrook, a former Jesuit novitiate on the 300-acre grounds that were once Andrew Carnegie's estate. The view from Shadowbrook is one of the best in the Berkshires. Looking at the panoramic sweep to the south across Mahkeenac Lake, you can easily see at least seven mountain ranges, some 30 or more miles away.

Accommodations range from beds in a dorm (segregated by sex) with hall bathrooms to private rooms with private baths. Kripalu also has a beach on Lake Mahkeenac for swimming. Call or write for a program guide.

**Price:** inexpensive to expensive. Introductory weekends from $65 (lodging and meals included).

**Credit cards:** MC, V

**Address:**   Box 793
Lenox, MA 01240          (800) 967-3577
(located at Shadowbrook on Rte. 183, just west of the main entrance to Tanglewood)

***All Seasons Motor Inn*** has 120 rooms, free HBO, air conditioning, phones, outdoor pool, and restaurant. There's no charge for an extra person in a room.

**Price:** inexpensive to moderate.

**Credit cards:** AE, D, DC, MC, V (groups talk to the manager, Greg Abbott, about corporate rate — approximately 20% less)

**Address:**   390 Pittsfield Rd.
Rte. 7
Lenox, MA 01240   (800) 622-9988, if calling in MA;
(800) 442-4201, if calling from outside MA

## Stockbridge

***Arbor Rose B&B*** sits on a hill overlooking an 1800's mill and mill-pond — perfect for swimming. There are five rooms in the large white house, two with private bath and the rest with shared bath. The attractive decor is highlighted by colorful paintings by the owner's mother, Suzette Alsop, a noted local artist.

**Price:** inexpensive to expensive.
**Credit Cards:** MC, V
**Owner:** Christina Alsop
**Address:**   Box 114
              Stockbridge, MA 01262                (413) 298-4744
              (located on Yale Hill Rd, off East Main St. — Rte. 102)

***The Red Lion Inn*** was an inn before the Revolutionary War, serving as a stagecoach stop on the route linking Albany, Hartford, and Boston. The current structure is the result of rebuilding after an 1895 fire. There's a big front porch on which to sit and watch Main St. life go by (and many do just that!). Featured in several Norman Rockwell paintings, the Red Lion Inn is right on a busy corner on Main Street in picturesque Stockbridge, so there's plenty of traffic, both human and auto, to watch.

The inn also has several cottages nearby. A pub called the Lion's Den offers nightly entertainment. And you can eat meals in the courtyard under the trees. There's also a pool.

**Price:** moderate to very expensive.
**Credit cards:** AE, D, DC, MC, V
**Manager:** Betsy Holtzinger
**Address:**   Main St.
              Stockbridge, MA 01262                (413) 298-5545
              (located at the village center, on the corner of Rtes. 7
              & 102)

***Woodside B&B*** is on an acre of land in the countryside — a contemporary, comfortable, and informal accommodation just outside the village of Stockbridge. Four rooms have shared baths in this newer home.

**Price:** inexpensive to moderate.
**Credit cards:** MC, V
**Manager:** Paula Schutzmann
**Address:**   Box 1096
              Stockbridge, MA 01262                (413) 298-4977
              (located on Rte. 102, just west of town)

## Lee

***Black Swan Inn.*** From the outside, this 52-room "inn" looks like a motel. But private balconies, colonial decor, its location on Laurel Lake, and a friendly atmosphere make it definitely inn-like. Some rooms even have hydratubs and canopy beds. The inn has a restaurant, swimming pool, exercise room, and sauna. Boat rentals are available, and the atrium restaurant has lake views.

**Price:** moderate to very expensive.
**Credit cards:** AE, CB, DC, MC, V, D
**Managers:** Sallie Kate and George Kish
**Address:**   Rte. 20 West
        Lee, MA 01238     (413) 234-2700 or (800) 876-SWAN
        (located on Laurel Lake, north of Lee)

***Morgan House*** is an attractive, former stagecoach inn with a friendly staff. It has small rooms but is high on hospitality. If you don't mind the sounds from the inn downstairs and traffic noise from the street, this place is great.

**Price:** inexpensive to expensive.
**Credit cards:** AE, CB, D, DC, MC, V
**Managers:** Beth and Bill Orford
**Address:**   33 Main St.
        Lee, MA 01238                    (413) 243-0181
        (located in the center of town)

***Prospect Hill House*** is a cape colonial on one acre at the end of a street. It offers a quiet setting and has four rooms, most with shared bath, plus a common room. Full breakfast provided.

**Price:** inexpensive.
**Credit cards:** none
**Managers:** Marge and Chuck Driscoll
**Address:**   1A South Prospect St.
        Lee, MA 01238                    (413) 243-3460
        (located just off Park St.)

***Super 8 Motel*** has 49 rooms, all with private baths. Non-smoking rooms, free coffee, and newspapers available. Free HBO and ESPN. You may rent a VCR.

**Price:** inexpensive to moderate.
**Credit cards:** AE, D, DC, MC, V
**Manager:** Nancy Davis
**Address:**   128 Housatonic St.
        Lee, MA 01238       (413) 243-0143 or (800) 800-8000
        (located on Rte. 20, just off the Massachusetts
        Turnpike at the south end of town)

## New Marlborough

***Millstones.*** This turn-of-the-century kennel-master's home was once part of the largest estate in town. The house now sits on seven groomed acres and has six bedrooms. Most rooms share a bath. The southside rooms overlook the hills sloping toward Connecticut. The public room has a piano and a collection of books and magazines.
**Price:** moderate.
**Credit cards:** none
**Managers:** Dorothy Mills and Beth Putnam
**Address:**   Box 1211
             Star Rte. 70
             New Marlborough, MA 01230          (413) 229-8488
             (located on Rte. 57, five and one-half miles east of Rte. 23)

***The Old Inn on the Green and Gedney Farm.*** The Old Inn is an 18th century establishment in the center of the quiet little village of New Marlborough. Rooms all share a bath. Gedney Farm, a short walk from the inn, is new. Eight two-level suites have been carved out of a Normandy-style barn, built turn-of-century as a showplace for Percheron stallions and Jersey cattle. Large bedrooms, with whirlpool tubs in the master baths. The restaurant in the inn is considered to be one of the finest in the Berkshires.
**Price:** moderate to very expensive.
**Credit cards:** MC, V
**Innkeepers:** Bradford Wagstaff and Leslie Miller
**Address:**   Star Rte. 70
             New Marlborough, MA 01230          (413) 229-3131
             (located on Rte. 57, in the center of the village)

***Red Bird Inn*** is a former stagecoach stop. This 18th century inn is located on a quiet country road and has rooms furnished with antiques, wide-plank floors, fireplaces, and old iron work. Some have private baths; some shared. Full breakfast served.
**Price:** moderate.
**Credit cards:** none
**Managers:** Don and Joyce Coffman
**Address:**   Box 592
             New Marlborough, MA 01230          (413) 229-2433
             (located on corner of Adsit Crosby Rd. and Rte. 57)

## Tyringham

***The Golden Goose*** is a white colonial with smallish rooms — three with private baths — and one studio apartment. Peaceful and quiet setting. There are a deck and picnic tables near the Appalachian

*(continued)*

Trail, and wine and cheese are served in the afternoon in the common room. Full breakfast provided.

**Price:** moderate
**Credit cards:** AE
**Managers:** Lilja Hinrichsen and Joe Rizzo
**Address:**    Box 336
            Tyringham, MA 01264                    (413) 243-3008
            (located on Main St. in the village)

### Great Barrington

***Arrawood Bed & Breakfast*** is in a Victorian home located on a residential street and has a warm, friendly atmosphere. A full country breakfast is provided.

**Price:** inexpensive to moderate.
**Credit cards:** none
**Managers:** Marilyn and Bill Newmark
**Address:**    105 Taconic Ave.
            Great Barrington, MA 01230              (413) 528-5868
            (located on the corner of Taconic Ave. and Oak St.)

***Elling's B&B.*** This six-room guest house sits above the Green River on a knoll surrounded by tall pines and maples. It offers great views of the fields and mountains from a house that was built before the Revolutionary War and which is one of the oldest in Great Barrington.

**Price:** moderate.
**Credit cards:** none
**Managers:** Jo and Ray Elling
**Address:**    RD3, Box 6
            Great Barrington, MA 01230              (413) 528-4130
            (located on a hill above Rte. 23, between South
            Egremont and Great Barrington)

***Littlejohn Manor B&B*** is a turn-of-the-century Victorian home and furnished partially with antiques. Four bedrooms all share several baths. There's a warm, friendly atmosphere and great breakfast, plus afternoon tea in the sitting room. It has an attractive flower and herb gardens.

**Prices:** moderate.
**Credit cards:** none
**Managers:** Herbert Littlejohn and Paul DuFour
**Address:**    Newsboy Monument Ln.
            Great Barrington, MA 01230              (413) 528-2882
            (located on the south side of Rte. 23, between Great
            Barrington and South Egremont)

***Seekonk Pines Inn B&B*** is a 150-year-old, former country estate surrounded by meadows and well-groomed acreage. It is furnished in Early American style and filled with personal touches, including family-made quilts and formal gardens for walking and resting. Healthy, filling breakfasts feature homegrown berries and whole grains. This accommodation also has a pool.

**Price:** moderate.
**Credit cards:** MC, V
**Managers:** Linda and Chris Best
**Address:** 142 Seekonk Cross Rd., Box 29A, RD1
Great Barrington, MA 01230 (413) 528-4192
(located on Rte. 23, between South Egremont and Great Barrington)

***Turning Point Inn*** is a very well-regarded lodging in a former stage-coach inn more than 200 years old. It has an informal atmosphere and serves a full vegetarian breakfast. There is also a new two-bedroom cottage. This is a no-smoking accommodation.

**Price:** moderate to expensive.
**Credit cards:** none
**Managers:** Jamie, Irving, and Shirley Yost
**Address:** RD2, Box 140
Great Barrington, MA 01230 (413) 528-4777
(located on Rte. 23, east of town)

***Mountain View Motel.*** A small motel with 17 units, each having a private bath or shower, cable TV, air conditioning, and in-room phone. A two-room suite for five is also available. Staff very friendly towards cyclists. Good mountain view.

**Price:** inexpensive to moderate; call for group rates.
**Credit cards:** MC, V, AE
**Hosts:** Elizabeth and Dick Watson
**Address:** State Rd., Route 23 East
Great Barrington, MA 01230 (413) 528-0250
(located just east of the junction of Rtes. 23 and 7, on the south side of the road)

## North Egremont

***Bread & Roses B&B.*** This 1800s farmhouse features five bedrooms, each with private bath and air conditioning, in a quiet rural area. There's also an extensive library and a porch overlooking the brook. Breakfasts can include items such as "French Toast Grand Marnier" and spinach and mushroom soufflé. This is a no-smoking accommodation. No children less than 12 years allowed. *(continued)*

Price: moderate.
Credit cards: none
Managers: Julie and Elliot Lowell
Address: Box 50, Star Rte. 65
        Great Barrington, MA 01230        (413) 528-1099
        (located on Rte. 71, half a mile from its junction with
        Rte. 23)

*Elm Court Inn* has immaculate, comfortable rooms above one of the more popular restaurants in the Southern Berkshires.

Price: moderate.
Credit cards: MC, V
Managers: U. and G. Bieri
Address: Rte. 71
        North Egremont, MA 01252        (413) 528-0325
        (located on Rte. 71 in North Egremont)

*Hidden Acres Bed & Breakfast.* Stone walls, massive trees, and five secluded acres offer peace and quiet at this rural B&B. Full country breakfast is served in the large country kitchen.

Price: moderate.
Credit cards: none
Managers: Daniel and Lorriane Miller
Address: RD 4, Box 150
        Great Barrington, MA 01230        (413) 528-1028
        (located on Tremont Dr., 0.9 mile north on Rowe Rd.
        from the corner of Rowe and Rte. 71)

**South Egremont**

*Baldwin Hill Farm B&B.* This working farm, in a very rural setting, includes a Victorian farmhouse turned B&B and many barns. It's very peaceful and quiet. Four rooms, one with private bath, have views across the fields to the mountains beyond. Full breakfast served. There is a pool.

Price: inexpensive to moderate.
Credit cards: MC, V
Owners: Richard and Priscilla Burdsall
Address: RD3, Box 125
        Great Barrington, MA 01230        (413) 528-4092
        (located on the side of Baldwin Hill North/South Rd.,
        north of the village)

*The Egremont Inn* is a historic inn built in the 1780s. It's located on a side street in the center of the village, has low ceilings, fireplaces,

*(continued)*

broad porches, and 21 rooms furnished with antiques. Its fine restaurant is located on the main floor. Beautiful scenery and a swimming pool.

**Price:** moderate to expensive.
**Credit cards:** D, MC, V
**Manager:** John Black
**Address:** Old Sheffield Rd.
South Egremont, MA 01258 (413) 528-2111
(located on Old Sheffield Rd, off Rte. 23)

### Sheffield

*A Unique Bed & Breakfast Inn.* Four guest rooms, all with private baths, are available in this log home at the foothills of Mount Everett. Full breakfast served.

**Price:** moderate to expensive.
**Credit cards:** MC, V
**Manager:** May Stendardi
**Address:** Box 729
Sheffield, MA 01257 (413) 229-3363
(located on Rte. 41, several miles north of the Connecticut/ Massachusetts state line)

*Centuryhurst Bed & Breakfast.* This grand old home, nestled among tall trees, is listed on the National Register of Historic Places. Four guest rooms share two baths. Continental breakfast is served. There is a swimming pool, and this is a no-smoking establishment.

**Price:** moderate.
**Credit cards:** AE, MC, V
**Managers:** Ronald and Judith Timm
**Address:** Box 486
Sheffield, MA 01257 (413) 229-8131
(located on Main St.– Rte. 7– in town)

*Stagecoach Hill Inn* was built in the early 1800s as a stagecoach stop. There are choice rooms in the main house or small chalets, all with private baths. The inn also has an English pub, a restaurant, and a swimming pool.

**Price:** inexpensive to moderate.
**Credit cards:** AE, CB, DC, MC, V
**Manager:** Danielle Pedretti
**Address:** Rte. 41
Sheffield, MA 01257 (413) 229-8585
(located on Rte. 41, several miles north of Lakeville, Connecticut)

***Ivanhoe Country House*** is along one of the most scenic roads of the Southern Berkshires and nestled at the base of Race Mountain. The Appalachian Trail passes nearby. It has comfortable rooms, all with private bath. Continental breakfast provided. Golden retrievers are raised on the property, and there is a swimming pool. There are many fine restaurants in the area.

**Price:** moderate to expensive.
**Credit cards:** none
**Managers:** Carole and Dick Maghery
**Address:**  RD1, Box 158
Sheffield, MA 01257        (413) 229-2143
(located on Rte. 41, four miles south of Rte. 23)

***Orchard Shade.*** This house, built in the 1840s, has operated as bed-and-breakfast since 1888. It's furnished with antiques, and the large screened-in porch is perfect for relaxing.

**Price:** inexpensive.
**Credit cards:** AE, MC, V
**Owners:** Debbie and Henry Thornton
**Address:**  Box 669
Sheffield, MA 01257        (413) 229-8463
(located on Maple Ave., off Main St.– Rte. 7–
at the north end of town)

## Ashley Falls

***Ridgeview Motor Court*** is ten little cabins on a quiet country road. It's rustic, simple, and attractive.

**Price:** inexpensive.
**Credit cards:** none
**Managers:** Anthony and Andrea Cavalier
**Address:**  Rte. 7A, Box 74
Ashley Falls, MA 01257        (413) 229-8080
(located on Rte. 7A, south of Sheffield village)

## New Boston

***New Boston Inn.*** Built in the early 1700s, this old stagecoach stop has been serving travellers since 1737. It's listed on National Register of Historic Places and is considered to be Berkshire County's oldest inn. It has low ceilings, wide-board floors, and eight guest rooms. Rooms have private baths and are decorated with early pine furniture. There's evidence that a ghost resides at the inn (according to a report in *Yankee Magazine*). Some have seen the Irish maiden, dressed in

*(continued)*

bridal black, who was shot by a scorned suitor in an upstairs room. There's a place to store bikes in the annex.

**Price:** generally expensive, but inexpensive economy rooms are also available.
**Credit cards:** AE, MC, V
**Innkeepers:** Anne and Bill McCarthy
**Address:** Box 120
Sandisfield, MA 01255            (413) 258-4477
(located at the corner of Rtes. 8 and 57, in the village of New Boston)

## Connecticut

### Salisbury

**Salisbury Inn** is more like a motel than an inn. It offers inexpensive, clean rooms — and as many as desired can sleep in a room. Some rooms are set up with double beds, some with queen or king, and at least one room with three beds. The restaurant's food has had very favorable reviews in *The New York Times*; Caribbean cuisine is a specialty here.

**Price:** inexpensive to moderate.
**Credit cards:** AE, MC, V
**Host:** Frank Godin
**Address:** Route 44
Salisbury, CT 06068           (203) 824-7797
(located on Route 44, between Salisbury and Canaan)

**Under Mountain Inn** is a 1730s colonial home set on three acres. It is very British in character, as the owner is retired from the British Merchant Navy. The food is English, with items such as steak and kidney pie, bangers and mash, shepherd's pie, and fish and chips. The inn has 11 rooms furnished with antiques and private baths. Afternoon tea is served. Many British books are in the parlor. This inn has been featured in *Travel & Leisure*, *Conde Nast Traveler*, and *Country Inns* magazines. Non-smoking rooms available.

**Price:** moderate to very expensive.
**Credit cards:** AE, D, MC, V
**Owners:** Peter and Marged Higginson
**Address:** 482 Under Mountain Rd. (Rte. 41)
Salisbury, CT 06068           (203) 435-0242
(located on Rte. 41, four miles north of Salisbury village)

**The White Hart Inn.** The owners have restored this formerly abandoned and derelict landmark into a very attractive inn. The oldest portions of the inn were built prior to 1810, when a farmhouse was converted to a tavern. There are 26 rooms, each with private bath, air conditioning, phones, and cable TV.

**Price:** moderate to very expensive.
**Credit cards:** AE, CB, DC, MC, V
**Owner/managers:** Terry and Juliet Moore
**Address:**  The Village Green
        Box 385
        Salisbury, CT 06068          (203) 435-0030
        (located at the intersection of Rtes. 41 and 44
        in the village)

## Lakeville

**Yesterday's Yankee B&B.** This home, with its period-furnished rooms, was built in 1774. The hosts are warm and friendly, and the rooms are comfortable. Breakfast includes home baking and fresh fruit.

**Price:**  moderate. Twin size roll-a-way beds available for an additional $20. Call for special rates.
**Credit cards:** MC, V
**Hosts:** Doris and Dick Alexander
**Address:**  Rte. 44 East
        Salisbury, CT 06068          (203) 435-9539
        (located on Rte. 44, east of the intersection of Rtes. 44
        and 41 in the village)

## Norfolk

**Manor House B&B.** This elegant Victorian Tudor estate, transformed into a bed-and-breakfast, is included in Fodor's *50 Best in the U.S.A.* It is very comfortable, and the hosts are friendly. Deluxe, full breakfasts include homemade bread with honey harvested from the hosts' own hives. This is a real bargain for accommodations in this price range.

**Price:** moderate to expensive.
**Credit cards:** MC, V
**Hosts:** Diane and Henry Tremblay
**Address:**  P.O. Box 447
        Maple Ave.
        Norfolk, CT 06058          (203) 542-5690
        (located on Maple Ave, north of Rte. 44 in town)

**Mountain View Inn,** housed in a Victorian mansion, has 11 guest rooms, most with private baths. There are also a parlor, piano bar, and lounge. Maxfield's Restaurant, which is in the house, offers breakfast, lunch, and dinner.

**Price:** inexpensive to expensive. Special packages available.
**Credit cards:** MC, V, AE, Discover
**Innkeepers:** Michelle and Alan Sloane
**Address:** Rte. 272

      Norfolk, CT 06058               (203) 542-5595

      (located just south of the village green, on Rte. 272)

**Riverton**

**Old Riverton Inn** originally opened in 1796 as a stagecoach stop on the route between Hartford, Connecticut, and Albany, New York. It now has a quiet atmosphere and fine dining in the restaurant. The inn has 12 rooms, each with private bath and color cable TV. There is a locked garage for storing bikes.

**Price:** inexpensive to expensive.
**Credit cards:** MC, V, AE, Diner's Club
**Innkeepers:** Mark and Pauline Telford
**Address:** Rte. 20, Box 6

      Riverton, CT 06065             (203) 379-8678

      (located on Rte. 20, just east of the bridge across the West Branch of the Farmington River)

# CAMPGROUNDS

OUT OF THE SADDLE
Nick "Bubba" Zito pitching camp.

## Massachusetts

**Beartown State Forest** is near Great Barrington, Stockbridge, and Lee. You can camp on the shores of, and swim in, pristine Benedict Pond. The Appalachian Trail passes just south of the campsites. There's a lot of wildlife in the 10,870-acre forest, and you may catch glimpses of beaver and deer.

**Camping Facilities:** 12 campsites, unimproved toilets, water, picnic tables, and fireplaces available. No showers. There are also 12 sites for self-contained vehicles. There is one group campsite, which accommodates 100 persons maximum. It is only available to non-profit groups, and reservations are required.

**Fees:** $8 per night for individual campsites; $16 per night for group campsite

**Camping Season:** mid-May through Columbus Day

**Directions:** Massachusetts Turnpike, Exit 2, Rte. 102 west, to Rte. 7 south, to Rte. 23, east to Monterey. Follow signs.

**Address:** P.O. Box 97, Blue Hill Rd.
Monterey, MA 01245 (413) 528-0904

*October Mountain State Forest* is north of Lee and east of Lenox. This 16,000-acre forest has campsites on the hillside facing the west, plus miles of scenic trails — including the Appalachian, which runs through the forest.

**Camping Facilities:** 50 campsites, flush toilets, showers, picnic tables, water, fireplaces, and dumping station available.

**Fee:** $12 per night.

**Camping Season:** mid-May through mid-October

**Directions:** Massachusetts Turnpike, Exit 2, Rte. 20 west. Follow signs.

**Address:** Woodland Rd.
Lee, MA 01238 (413) 243-1778

*Prospect Lake Park.* This is a very clean and well-laid-out park, with plenty of tall pines and two lake beaches.

**Camping Facilities:** 150 wooded, shaded or sunny campsites, with 22 on the waterfront. Picnic tables, water, and fire rings available, plus flush toilets, hot showers, camp store, recreation hall, snack bar, pub, and laundry room. There are several cabins furnished with kitchens and baths.

**Fees:** campsites $17.75 to $22.00 per night (for two persons); cabins $50 to 75 per night. For reservations, call or write.

**Camping Season:** first weekend in May through Columbus Day

**Directions:** west 0.75 mile on Prospect Lake Rd. from Rte. 71 in North Egremont

**Address:** Prospect Lake Rd.
P.O. Box 78
North Egremont, MA 01252 (413) 528-4158

*Sandisfield State Forest* is a 7,785-acre forest located south of Monterey and east of New Marlborough. Wilderness camping is available at 12 designated campsites, which are a short hike from the parking area.

**Fee:** $3 per night

**Camping Season:** year round

**Directions:** Massachusetts Turnpike, Exit 2, Rte. 102, Rte. 7 south, Rte. 23 east, Rte. 57 south. Follow signs.

**Address:** West St.
Sandisfield, MA 01255 (413) 258-4774

*Tolland State Forest.* Here, you can camp beneath tall pine trees right on the shore of 1,000-acre Otis Reservoir.

**Camping Facilities:** 90 campsites, with flush toilets and water. There are five group campsites, each accommodating 25 persons maximum. They are only available to non-profit groups, and reservations are required. Call or write for reservations.

**Fees:** $12 per night for individual campsites; $16 per night for group campsites (available for non-profit groups only).

**Camping Season:** mid-May through mid-October

**Directions:** Rte. 23, or Rte. 8 to Reservoir Rd. Follow signs.

**Address:**  P.O. Box 342, Rte. 8
East Otis, MA 01029                    (413) 269-6002

## Connecticut

*Burr Pond State Park* is south of Winsted. Reservations can be made by writing directly to the campground.

**Camping Facilities:** 40 wooded sites, with flush toilets, water, picnic tables, fireplaces, and additional attractions.

**Fee:** $9 per night per campsite

**Camping Season:** Memorial Day through Labor Day

**Directions:** Torrington Rd., east on Mountain Rd., south on Peck Rd.

**Address:**  385 Burr Mountain Rd.
Torrington, CT 06790                    (203) 379-0172

*Housatonic Meadows State Park* is between Cornwall Bridge and West Cornwall.

**Camping Facilities:** 104 sites in a rustic setting near the Housatonic River. Flush toilets and showers available. Reservations can be made by writing directly to the campground.

**Fee:** $9 per night per campsite

**Camping Season:** Memorial Day through Labor Day

**Directions:** one mile north of Cornwall Bridge on Rte. 7

**Address:**  Cornwall Bridge, CT 06754          (203) 672-6772

*American Legion State Forest.* Camp beneath tall pines along the West Branch of the Farmington River. Reservations may be made by writing directly to the campground.

**Camping Facilities:** 30 sites, with flush toilets and showers.

**Fee:** $9 per night per campsite.

**Camping Season:** Memorial Day through Labor Day

*(continued)*

**Directions**: midway between Pleasant Valley and Riverton on West River Rd.

**Address:** P.O. Box 161
Pleasant Valley, CT 06063                    (203) 379-0922

*Lone Oaks Campsites*, the largest in the area, is between Canaan and Norfolk.

**Camping Facilities**: more than 500 sites, from tent sites to large RV sites. Flush toilets, hot showers, store, and on-site trailer rentals available. Recreational facilities include a dance hall, recreation hall, two swimming pools, and nightly live entertainment.

**Fee**: $18-30 per night per site (for four persons). For reservations, call the toll-free number.

**Camping Season**: April 15 through October 15

**Directions**: on Rte. 44, four miles east of Canaan

**Address:** Rte. 44
East Canaan, CT 06024                    (800) 422-2267

# New York

*Taconic State Park.* This 5,000-acre park runs along the borders of New York, Massachusetts, and Connecticut.

**Camping Facilities**: more than 100 sites, including tent, platform, and trailer and RV sites. Each has a picnic table and campfire ring. Washrooms with flush toilets and a shower house are nearby. For reservations, call their toll-free number, (800) 456-2267. There are also cabins. Both rustic (unheated, with cold running water) and cottage (hot running water, flush toilets, showers, fireplaces, stove, and refrigerator) are available.

**Fees**: campsites, $10 per night (six people per site) plus a $6.25 reservation fee; cabins — rustic $44.50 per night (for four persons), cottage $51 per night (two bedrooms — four persons) and $62.50 per night (three bedrooms — six persons). There is also a $9.40 reservation fee for the cabins.

**Camping Season**: from the first Friday on or after May 10 through the last Sunday on or before October 31

**Directions**: in Copake Falls, east of Rte. 22 on Rte. 344

**Address:** Copake Falls, NY 12517-0100                    (518) 329-3993

# Appendix

# Appendix

# PREPARING YOUR BICYCLE FOR TRANSPORT

## Disassembling Your Bicycle for Shipping

1. Shift the gears so that the cables are slack.
2. Deflate the tires halfway for more shock-absorbing capability.
3. Remove the seat and seat post as a unit.
4. Remove the front wheel, cut a small block of wood to fit between the front-fork dropouts, and tape in place.
5. Remove the brake cables from the brake levers.
6. Remove the handlebars and stem as a unit.
7. Remove the pedals. (Remember that the left pedal is a left-hand thread; the right is a standard right-hand thread.)
8. Tie or tape the front wheel to the right side of the frame, padding between the wheel and frame with cardboard. Turn the crank arms parallel with the box bottom and tape in place.
9. Make two 6-inch square "washers" of several layers of cardboard with a center hole. Tape these in place over the exposed front axle end and the end of the rear axle opposite the derailleur.
10. Unbolt the rear derailleur (but don't disconnect the cables) and tape it to the rear wheel spokes below its normal position so it doesn't stick out past the frame.
11. Cradle the handlebars and stem over the top tube or around the fork and head tube, if space permits.
12. Lower your bicycle into the box.

## Preparing the Box

1. Cut five pieces of cardboard, each about one foot in length and wide enough to fit snugly across the inside width of your box. Form tightly rolled shock-absorption tubes, and fit them so that they span the width of the box.
2. Place one tube inside the box near where the lower end of the front fork will be. Place two tubes, slightly flattened to fit, through the rear wheel and tape them inplace. Place other tubes where the

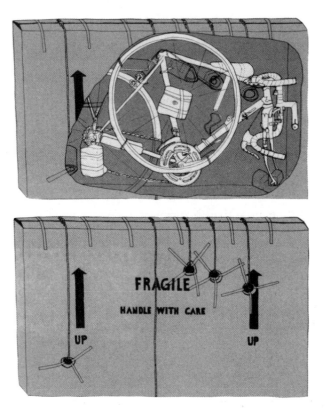

frame top and down tubes meet, through the front wheel spokes, and below the top tube, toward the front of the bike. Tape each in place.

3. Add cardboard pads wherever any remaining sharp or fragile parts might contact the box. Anchor the cross-bracing cardboard tubes further by punching holes in the box sides to match the tube centers, and running rope through the tubes and holes. The rope will help hold the tubes in place and can also serve as handles.

4. Wrap the saddle, pedals, and any other parts you've removed in newspaper or cloth and secure them inside the box.

5. Seal the box with tape and clearly label it with your name, destination, and home return address.

Reprinted with permission from BikeCentennial,
P.O. Box 8308, Missoula, MT 59807

## Bike Cases and Bags

Rugged, reliable bike cases and bags are available from:

Performance Bicycle
Box 2741
Chapel Hill, NC 27514
(800) 727-2453

Rhode Gear
765 Allens Ave.
Providence, RI 02905
(401) 941-1700

Bike Nashbar
4111 Simon Rd.
Youngstown, OH 44512-1343
(800) 627-4227

# Appendix

# ABOUT THE AUTHOR

Photo by Debra Howard

Steve Lyons, a resident of Housatonic, Massachusetts, is no stranger to traveling. His love for exploring has taken him from coast to coast in the United States, through Europe, the Mid-East and Asia, and around the world — literally. He has authored over a dozen magazine and newspaper articles on traveling. Over the last nine years, Lyons has been exploring the Berkshires by bicycle. A long-time triathlete, he also enjoys the camaraderie of organized rides and races, including the Josh Billings Runaground Race and the Greylock Century in the Berkshires.

When not bicycling, exploring, or writing, you may find him at Kripalu Center for Yoga and Holistic Health, in Lenox, Massachusetts, where he works as a massage therapist.

He is a member of the League of American Wheelmen, the Rails to Trails Conservancy and BikeCentennial.

# Index

# Index

# Index

# Index

# ORDER FORM

Freewheel Publications
P.O. Box 2322, Lenox, MA 01240
The following books and maps are handy resources for cycle touring in the Southern Berkshires. Check for them in your local library or favorite bookstore or order them directly from **Freewheel Publications**.
**See the book and map descriptions in the Resources Chapter.**
Please send me the following books:

| Quantity | | Amount | |
|---|---|---|---|
| _____ | **The Bicyclist's Guide to the Southern Berkshires**, by Steve Lyons | $16.95 | _____ |
| _____ | **The Berkshire Book: A Complete Guide**, by Jonathan Sternfield | $14.95 | _____ |
| _____ | **The Berkshire Hills—A WPA Guide**, Northeastern University Press | $11.95 | _____ |
| _____ | **Jimapco Map of Berkshire County, MA** | $3.25 | _____ |
| _____ | **Jimapco Map of Litchfield County, CT** | $2.95 | _____ |
| _____ | **Vaughn Gray Map of Berkshire County, MA** (includes shipping) | $8.50 | _____ |
| _____ | **Vaughn Gray Map of Litchfield County, CT** (includes shipping) | $7.50 | _____ |

Total for books/maps  _____
Shipping: $2.00 first book  _____
75 cents each additional book or map  _____
Massachusetts residents please add 6% sales tax  _____
AMOUNT ENCLOSED (U.S. FUNDS)  _____

**I understand that I may return any book or map for a full-refund if not satisfied.**

Name: _____

Address:_____

City: _____ State: _____ Zip: _____

____ I can't wait 3-4 weeks for Book Rate. Here is $3.50 for Air Mail.

# ORDER FORM

Freewheel Publications
P.O. Box 2322, Lenox, MA 01240
The following books and maps are handy resources for cycle touring in the Southern Berkshires. Check for them in your local library or favorite bookstore or order them directly from **Freewheel Publications**.
**See the book and map descriptions in the Resources Chapter.**
Please send me the following books:

| Quantity | | Amount | |
|---|---|---|---|
| _____ | **The Bicyclist's Guide to the Southern Berkshires**, by Steve Lyons | $16.95 | _____ |
| _____ | **The Berkshire Book: A Complete Guide**, by Jonathan Sternfield | $14.95 | _____ |
| _____ | **The Berkshire Hills—A WPA Guide**, Northeastern University Press | $11.95 | _____ |
| _____ | **Jimapco Map of Berkshire County, MA** | $3.25 | _____ |
| _____ | **Jimapco Map of Litchfield County, CT** | $2.95 | _____ |
| _____ | **Vaughn Gray Map of Berkshire County, MA** (includes shipping) | $8.50 | _____ |
| _____ | **Vaughn Gray Map of Litchfield County, CT** (includes shipping) | $7.50 | _____ |

Total for books/maps _____
Shipping: $2.00 first book _____
75 cents each additional book or map _____
Massachusetts residents please add 6% sales tax _____
AMOUNT ENCLOSED (U.S. FUNDS) _____

**I understand that I may return any book or map for a full-refund if not satisfied.**

Name: _____

Address:_____

City: _____ State: _____ Zip: _____

____ I can't wait 3-4 weeks for Book Rate. Here is $3.50 for Air Mail.

W9-AHR-340

# SECRET DUBLIN

## AN UNUSUAL GUIDE

Pól Ó Conghaile

JONGLEZ PUBLISHING

**Pól Ó Conghaile** is a travel writer based in Dublin.
He is Travel Editor at *The Irish Independent* & Independent.ie,
and a regular contributor to *National Geographic Traveller*
and *Cara Magazine* and as well as national TV and radio in
Ireland.
He has been voted Irish Travel Journalist of the Year an
unprecedented five times, and continues to travel widely
in Ireland and overseas in search of new stories and
adventures. However far he travels, his favourite city
and return destination remain the same: Dublin.

Follow Pól on Twitter at @poloconghaile,
or visit www.poloconghaile.com

«Secret Dublin» was voted 'Travel Book of the Year'
at the Travel Extra Irish Travel Journalism Awards 2013

We have taken great pleasure in drawing up
*Secret Dublin - an unusual guide* and hope that
through its guidance you will, like us, continue
to discover unusual, hidden or little-known aspects
of the city.
Descriptions of certain places are accompanied
by thematic sections highlighting historical details
or anecdotes as an aid to understanding the city
in all its complexity.
*Secret Dublin - an unusual guide* also draws
attention to the multitude of details found in places
that we may pass every day without noticing.
These are an invitation to look more closely at the
urban landscape and, more generally, a means of
seeing our own city with the curiosity and attention
that we often display while travelling elsewhere …


Comments on this guidebook and its contents,
as well as information on places we may not have
mentioned, are more than welcome and will enrich
future editions.
Don't hesitate to contact us:
• Jonglez Publishing, 17, boulevard du Roi,
  78000 Versailles, France
• E-mail: info@jonglezpublishing.com

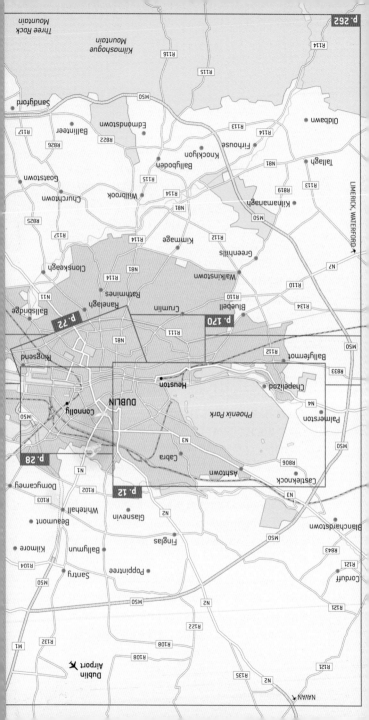

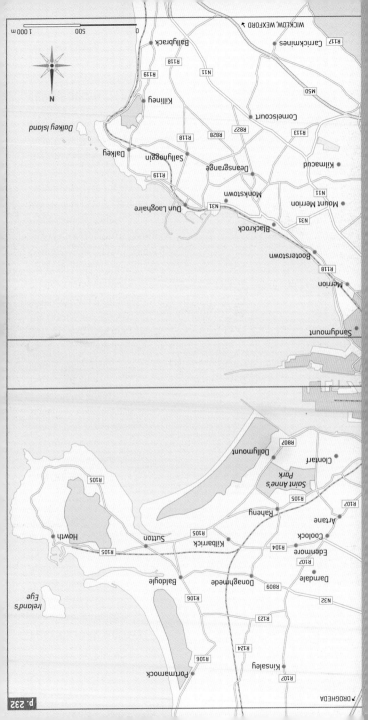

# CONTENTS

# CONTENTS

## WOOD QUAY TO WAR MEMORIAL

# PHOENIX PARK & QUAYS

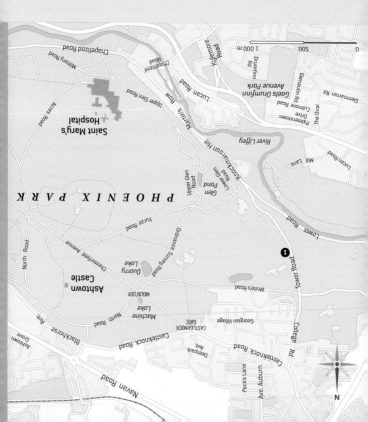

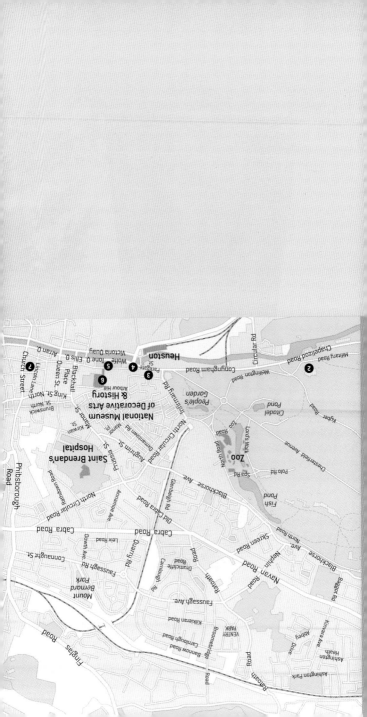

# CLOCK TOWER, FARMLEIGH ❶

Farmleigh House & Gardens, Phoenix Park, Dublin 8
- 01 815-5900
- www.farmleigh.ie
- Open: Daily 10am–6pm (last admission 5pm)
- Admission: free
- Transport: Dublin Bus stop 1670 is at the Castleknock gate to Phoenix Park. The 37 from Baggott Street (via Suffolk Street) stops here (15-min. walk)

**F**armleigh is a 51-hectare estate cocooned within the Phoenix Park. Developed over several decades by Edward Cecil Guinness (Lord Iveagh, 1847–1927), the house and gardens were bought by the Irish government in 1999 and have since hosted Queen Elizabeth II and Emperor Akihito of Japan, among other official visitors. Wildly eclectic interiors, a Dutch-style sunken garden, a Boathouse Café and an art gallery are all open to the public, but the most unusual feature of all, perhaps, is the Victorian Clock Tower.

> *Mister Guinness has a clock ...*

> *Mister Guinness has a clock*
> *And on its top a weathercock*
> *To show the people Castleknock*

So goes a local ditty celebrating the 37m landmark, which can also be spotted by eagle-eyed drivers passing across the West Link toll bridge. The tower is said to have been the work of the Guinness Brewery's engineering department, and its east and west faces both bear clocks adorned with cast-iron dials and copper hands. Surprisingly, however, the "Clock" Tower also contains an 8,183-litre water tank. Hidden away at balcony level, this tank once provided a private water supply for the estate, pumped via a weir built into the River Liffey at the Strawberry Beds, a mile-long (1.6km) millrace, and a turbine that both pumped water and generated electricity for Farmleigh. The bridge that was constructed to carry the lines over the river can still be seen – albeit in a dilapidated state – near the Angler's Rest pub.

The Clock Tower is reached via the pathways leading south-east from the house. Short, steep steps lead through a sumptuous series of mature trees towards its base and a doorway topped by a granite stone into which the date "1880" has been carved. Views from the balcony are said to be breathtaking, stretching as far as Malahide to the north and the Dublin Mountains to the south, although it was closed when Secret Dublin paid a visit. The clock has remained in perfect working order since it was assembled by the celebrated Sir Howard Grubb, who also provided the instrumental equipment for the great roof at Dunsink Observatory. Today, however, its weights are raised electrically.

## MAGAZINE FORT

Phoenix Park, Dublin
- 01 677-0095
- www.phoenixpark.ie
- Open: Phoenix Park is open 24/7, year-round
- Admission: free
- Transport: Dublin Buses 25 and 26 stop at the Chapelizod Gate, Parkgate Street and the Islandbridge Turnstile, which are closest to the magazine fort

*Dublin's only remaining fort*

The Phoenix Park is one of the largest enclosed recreational spaces of any European capital and there's no shortage of things to do within its 1,752 acres: Dublin Zoo, Farmleigh House & Estate, Áras an Uachtaráin and Ashtown Castle are all located here. Hidden away in the south-east of the park, however, is a more unusual attraction. Here, sunk into the hilltop site where Sir Edward Fisher built the original Phoenix Lodge in 1611, you'll find the decaying remains of a magazine fort. It dates from 1734, when the Duke of Dorset directed that a powder magazine be provided for Dublin: Fisher's Lodge

was knocked down and the star-shaped structure was installed in its place. Its dubious merits drew a stinging satirical response from Dean Jonathan Swift, who was inspired to whip out his notebook after encountering the building. "Behold, a proof of Irish sense," he wrote. "Here Irish wit is seen; when nothing's left that's worth defence, we build a magazine." The words are said to be the last Swift ever wrote, though they did little to stop the development. In 1801 an additional wing was added to the fort to accommodate troops.

The magazine fort has seen some action, though not the kind for which it was intended. Irish Volunteers captured it during the Easter Rising of 1916 and the IRA raided the Irish army's stocks here on 23 December 1939. The so-called "Christmas Raid" saw more than 1 million rounds removed from the fort in over a dozen lorries – though the audacious heist was followed by a disastrous aftermath (for the IRA, at least). Several arrests were made, most of the ammunition was recovered and an outraged Dáil voted to extend a new Emergency Powers Act to provide for the internment of Irish citizens at detention camps in the Curragh.

In recent years, access to the fort's interior was forbidden due to its instability, but that changed in 2016 when the OPW opened it up for limited guided tours during conservation works. At the time of going to press, there were no long-term plans for a visitor attraction, but walkers can still follow a trail around the earthen defences that echo its star-like shape. At their sharpest points, the outer walls look almost like the prows of ships, and the tall, redbrick chimneys seem to play on the Wellington Monument beyond.

House Wine White
Moupellier 3€21.50
Chardonnay G1 €5.75
South Africa

Taloumbar Blanc
Chile Bt2150
G1 €5.75

GUINNESS

# "BONGO" RYAN'S BOOTH

**3**

Ryan's, 28 Parkgate Street, Dublin 8
• 01 677-6097
• www.fxbuckley.ie/ryans-victorian-pub/
• Open: Mon-Thurs 12pm-11.30pm, Fri & Sat 12pm-12.30am,
Sun 12.30pm-12am.
• Transport: Luas, Heuston (Red Line; 5-min. walk); Dublin Bus stops 1474
and 7078 are nearby on Parkgate Street

*A vessel
of Victoriana*

**D**ublin has its vessels of Victoriana, but few follow through with the level of detail and deliciousness on display at Ryan's of Parkgate Street. Established in 1886, the pub's oak and mahogany bar, antique engraved mirrors and tantalising snugs – hidden behind mirrored partitions towards the rear of the premises – are just the entrées.

Look out for the old gas lamps on the counters, clutching their orbs of light with artistry and elegance. Or the tiny brass match lighters fixed to counters and windowsills throughout the pub. In years gone by, punters would have struck matches against these as handily as they struck up conversations with each other, and one can only imagine the fug of smoke drawing down over the mirrors and mahogany. There are brass foot rails, tobacco drawers, whiskey casks, and the snugs even have little bells for summoning the barmen. These whispery little booths date back to an era when it was frowned on for a lady to enter a pub, but their privacy also appealed to passing priests and policemen. Today, they're listed by Dublin City Council and have been booked over the years by U2, among others.

Best of all is the booth once occupied by Willie "Bongo" Ryan. Set right in the heart of the mahogany bar, this is where the Limerick man sat taking money from, and issuing change to, his barmen. It's a plum spot and the endless mirrors must have enabled him to keep an eye on every nook and cranny of his bar. Above the booth, a mechanical clock burrows right through the woodwork. Made in Germany, it's said to be the oldest two-faced indoor clock in the country, and "Bongo" traditionally set it five minutes fast, allowing his patrons a few precious moments of grace before catching their trains out of Heuston station.

Today, those patrons are likely to be lawyers from the nearby Criminal Courts of Justice, GAA (Gaelic Athletic Association) fans wetting their beaks before a match at Croke Park, diners enjoying a swift aperitif before repairing to the steakhouse upstairs, or the odd tourist, delighted to have stumbled across this Victorian time warp. Step inside, delight in the detail and lament the fact that the snugs are taken. It's like a visit to Dublin, c. 1886 – all that's missing is "Bongo" himself.

## ANNA LIVIA

**4**

Croppies Memorial Park, Wolfe Tone Quay, Dublin 8
• 01 222-5278
• www.dublincity.ie
• Open: Dec & Jan: 10am–5pm. Feb & Nov: 10am–5.30pm.
Mar & Oct: 10am–6.30pm. April & Sept: 10am–8.30pm.
May & Aug: 10am–9.30pm. June & July: 10am–10pm
• Transport: Luas, Heuston (Red Line; 5-min. walk); Dublin Bus stops 1474 and 7078 are nearby on Parkgate Street

*The Floozy in the Jacuzzi*

**D**ublin has erected its fair share of controversial public artworks, but Éamonn O'Doherty's *Anna Livia* may well have been the most controversial of all. Commissioned by Michael Smurfit for the Dublin Millennium celebrations of 1988, the statue was embedded in the middle of a busy pedestrian island on O'Connell Street and rapidly became a focal point for praise, ridicule, mischief and anti-social behaviour in equal measure.

*Anna Livia*, 18 ft (5.5 m) long and reclining in a gushing fountain, was designed to symbolise the River Liffey (her name evokes Anna Livia Plurabelle, a character fulfilling a similar function in Joyce's *Finnegans Wake*). The artistic merits of the bronze figure were not obvious to all, however, and as is their wont, Dubliners soon brought her down to earth with a nickname – "the Floozy in the Jacuzzi". Over time, Gardaí and City Council workers despaired of the hoards of people cavorting on the fountain's edges, the constant stream of litter tossed into its water, the baths taken during sunny spells, and the foam parties whipped up whenever someone emptied a bottle of washing-up liquid into the mix. *Anna Livia* was finally removed during the redevelopment of O'Connell Street in 2001, replaced by the more masculine *Dublin Spire* ("the Stiletto in the Ghetto") and dispatched into storage at St Anne's Park in Raheny.

Unbeknown to many, however, this sculpture has since experienced a second coming. In 2011 *Anna Livia* was taken out of storage and transported down the Liffey on a barge to her new home in Croppies Memorial Park. This small, flowery triangle at the intersection of Benburb Street and Wolfe Tone Quay was formerly part of the military recreation grounds at Collins Barracks, and as a public park, measures barely 0.25 hectares. O'Doherty's sculpture has been lowered into position in a curvy, ornamental pond and, with the odd duck for company, looks currently to be enjoying a very relaxed retirement.

## THE CROPPIES ACRE

**⑤**

Benburb Street, Dublin 7
• 01 702-8811
• www.heritageireland.ie
• Transport: Luas, National Museum (Red Line); Dublin Buses 37, 38 and
39 stop nearby

> *Last
> resting place
> of the rebels*

**D**evelopment space comes at a premium in Dublin's city centre, but one prime acre of land will never be built upon. Set between the former Collins Barracks and Eilis Quay, this quiet retreat is the last resting place of hundreds of rebels from the 1798 Rebellion.

The Croppies Acre is so-called for the Croppy Boys who fought in 1798. "Croppy" refers to the closely cropped hairstyles worn by many of them – a style borrowed from French revolutionaries who cut their hair to distinguish themselves from wig-wearing aristocrats. After the Rebellion, up to 300 of those captured, hanged and beheaded were thrown into a mass grave – or Croppy Pit – on this land. (At the time, the area between Collins Barracks and the River Liffey would have consisted of marshy wasteland.) The Rebellion itself, mounted by United Irishmen against British Rule, saw tens of thousands of deaths and innumerable atrocities – the hairstyle that gave the Croppy Boys an identity also served to identify them for capture. A granite slab bearing the simple legend "1798" was erected by the Irish army in 1985, with the land officially opened as a memorial park on the bicentenary of the Rebellion in 1998.

The Croppies Acre was also the site of one of Dublin's best-known soup kitchens during the Famine. Established by the famous French chef, Alexis Soyer (appointed by the British government to dispense meals at a low cost to the Exchequer), the soup kitchen began operating in 1847 and within five months had served some 1 million meals, as Frank Hopkins writes in *Hidden Dublin: Deadbeats, Dossers and Decent Skins* (Mercier Press, 2007). Soup was dispensed from a 300-gallon (1,364-litre) boiler at the centre of a wooden building, with people admitted in lots signalled by the ringing of a bell. Renowned though Soyer was as a chef, however, there were complaints that his soup actually harmed some people suffering from dysentery …

## ARTEFACTS IN STORAGE ❻

National Museum of Ireland – Decorative Arts & History, Collins Barracks, Benburb Street, Dublin 7
- 01 677-7444
- www.museum.ie
- Open: Tues–Sat 10am–5pm, Sun 2pm–5pm. Closed Mon
- Admission: free
- Transport: Luas, Museum (Red Line); Dublin Bus Stop 1475 is nearby on Wolfe Tone Quay

*Opening
the archives*

For the first time in the history of Ireland's National Museum, artefacts kept in storage are accessible to everyone. Not all artefacts, of course – but enough to make you feel like a curator for an afternoon, thanks to the museum's hugely impressive "visible storage" facility at Collins Barracks.

"What's in Store?" is an open-storage exhibition showcasing some of the museum's finest collections of glass, silver, pewter, brass, enamel and Asian applied arts. The Asian collections – including priceless lacquer, jade, ivory, statuary and metalwork – have not been on view since the museum opened at Collins Barracks in 1997. You can also see some of the ceramics collection, including 18th-century delftware, Belleek, Carrigaline and a brilliant collection of 18th- and 19th-century glass from Dublin, Cork, Belfast and Waterford. Much of the glass from the latter half of the 19th century is linked to the Pugh Glassworks, which produced a wide range of domestic and industrial glass from its Marlborough Street premises. Pugh brought a rare artistry and craft to its products, thanks to highly talented engravers like Franz Tieze and Joseph Eisert. In fact, no flint glass manufacture took place in Ireland from the closing of this facility in 1890 to the opening of Waterford Crystal (then Glass) in 1947.

Elsewhere, watch out for the row of Japanese samurai, ivories and enamels – including warrior armour dating from the Edo period (1600–1868). Exploring another aisle, you might stumble across archaeological glass, including Roman treasures from the second century BC. Or perhaps some vintage scientific instruments: watches, octants, sextants, telescopes and other devices from the 18th and 19th centuries, for instance. It's a whole other way of viewing a museum, and a brilliant complement to the more traditional displays.

# BURIAL CRYPTS

**7**

St Michan's Church, Church Street, Dublin 7
• 01 872-4154
• stmichan@iol.ie
• Open: Tours run throughout the year. Summer: Mon–Fri 10am–12.45pm
and 2pm–4.30pm, Sat 10am–12.45pm. Winter: Mon–Fri 12.30pm–
3.30pm, Sat 10am–12.45pm • Admission: €6/€4
• Transport: Dublin Bus stops 1615 and 1616 are right outside St.
Michan's; Luas, Four Courts (Red Line; 5-min. walk)

*The
mummies
of St Michan's*

Fancy touching the finger of a 650-year-old Crusader? Provided your tour group is small enough and you butter up your guide, that's just one of the experiences that could await you in the crypts beneath St Michan's Church. The dry atmosphere in the limestone vaults has caused dozens of bodies to mummify, and visitors have descended through padlocked iron doors in the graveyard to see them since Victorian times. Most famous of all is The Crusader, a frighteningly well-preserved specimen whose hands and fingers have been worn to a leathery shine by visitors stroking them, which is said to bring good luck.

Dating from 1685, St Michan's is said to be the oldest parish church north of the River Liffey. Its exterior is dull and its interior unshowy – though there are some fine wooden galleries and several items of interest, including an 18th-century baptismal font, an organ on which Handel is said to have practised before debuting his Messiah, and the original altar frontal from Dublin Castle's Chapel Royal – rescued from a market stall in the Liberties. But let's not kid ourselves: the main event is what lies beneath, hidden away in five ancient burial vaults.

Of course, crypts wouldn't be crypts without their share of myths and legends, and St Michan's doesn't disappoint in this regard. Modern science has cast doubts on the most famous (it doesn't take a maths whizz to work out that a 650-year-old Crusader would be too young for the Crusades), but there's plenty of verified history here too. One of the vaults contains the musty coffins of the Sheares brothers, for example – hung, drawn and quartered for their role in the 1798 Rebellion. Another houses the Earls of Leitrim. All the coffins are ornately decorated save for one: that of the Third Earl, William Sydney Clements, a ruthless landlord who was assassinated in Milford, Co. Donegal, in 1878.

There's a spot of showbiz to the tour, too. A wise-cracking guide leads visitors through stout iron doors down into the netherworld, sprinkling his historical script with gallows humour. He's quite upfront about the mysteries behind the mummies. Why is one missing a hand and both of its feet, for example? How old are they exactly? And if you win the lotto after touching the lucky Crusader's hand, will you oblige the guide with a 15 per cent cut?

# CENTRE NORTH

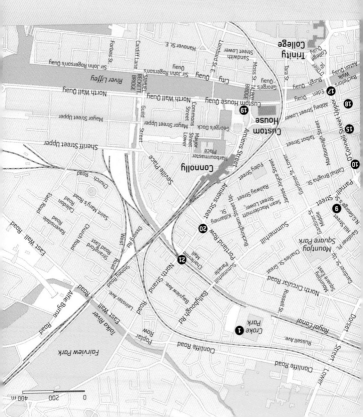

# MURDER AND THE GAA MUSEUM ❶

Croke Park Stadium, Cusack Stand entrance (off St Joseph's Ave.)
• 01 819-2323
• www.crokepark.ie
• Open: Jan–May & Sept–Dec: Mon–Sat 9.30am–5pm, Sun & Bank
Holidays, 10.30am–5pm. June–Aug: Mon–Sat 9.30am–6pm, Sun & Bank
Holidays, 10.30am–5pm
• Transport: Connolly DART station (15–20-min. walk); Dublin Bus stops
499 and 500 are nearby on Summerhill Parade

*From a hurling murder to Muhammad Ali's shorts*

It's surprising that more people aren't killed playing hurling. Think about it … 30 sinewy athletes battling against each other with axe-shaped sticks and a sliotar (hard leather ball) belted about at speeds of up to 180kmph.

"It looks like there's a bit of a shemozzle in the parallelogram," as commentator Micheál Ó hEithir once quipped … although it mostly stops short of murder.

Mostly. Croke Park is Ireland's 82,300-capacity sporting cathedral, and though inter-county games are highlights, there's a lot more to it than live action. A brilliant suite of stadium and rooftop tours rivals those at the Nou Camp or Old Trafford, and buried deep beneath the Cusack Stand you'll find a GAA Museum that really should be better known. Displays range from historical artefacts (check out Michael Cusack's blackthorn stick, or the ref's whistle from the Bloody Sunday massacre of 1920) to famous kits and medals; from halls-of-fame and interactive sporting challenges to the Liam McCarthy and Sam Maguire cups themselves. Croke Park has been known to host other sports too, as Muhammad Ali's shorts and gloves from a 1972 bout with Al "Blue" Lewis attest.

Amidst all of this is displayed a yellowing document, a handwritten witness statement describing a trial in 1785. It recounts the actions of one Michael Brennan during a hurling match in Co. Laois that year. Brennan "came behind the back of Patrick McDarby and with the flatt of his hurl … he gave a desperate stroak of same on the head," the statement reads. "McDarby fell

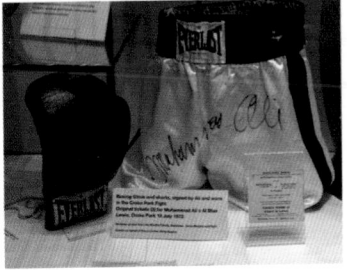

upon his face upon the Ground with his armes and legs extended … in a few minutes some people came up and turned [him onto] his back and then he was immediately blooded and heard several people then say he was killed and would never recover." Thankfully, today's athletes wear helmets.

# RIVERRUN GARDEN

②

Phibsborough Library, Blacquiere Bridge, off North Circular Road, Dublin 7
• 01 830-4341
• www.dublincity.ie
• Open: Mon–Wed 12.45pm–4pm, 4.45pm–8pm; Tues, Thurs, Fri, Sat, 10am–1pm, 2pm–5pm; closed Sun. The garden is visible beside the entrance gates at all times
• Admission: free
• Transport: Dublin Bus stops 81, 82 and 796 are nearby

> **The Dublin UNESCO City of Literature Garden**

James Joyce certainly got around Dublin City. And slowly but surely, memorials to the author are getting around it too. One of the most recent is the Dublin UNESCO City of Literature Garden, occupying a modest corner of Phibsborough Library's front lawn.

In spite of its grand title, the Riverrun Garden is still relatively unknown. It was designed to celebrate Dublin's being chosen as one of a handful of UNESCO World Cities of Literature in 2011 and was launched at that year's Bloom Festival in Phoenix Park. Bord Bia, the Irish Food Board, invited the City Council to exhibit, and the result, designed by the City Council's Parks & Landscape Services Division, went on to win two prizes – a Silver Medal and Best Overall Small Garden in Show. Poets like Gabriel Rosenstock and Anne Leahy read from their work here during Bloom, and after festivities wrapped at the Phoenix Park, the garden was transplanted to today's permanent location in Phibsborough.

On the face of it, Riverrun would appear to be a pretty straightforward celebration of Joyce's *Finnegans Wake*. Through the flowery space circles a miniature "river" (when it's working), with various inscriptions linking the book's opening sentence and unfinished closing line: "A way a lone a last a loved a long the riverrun, past Eve and Adam's, from swerve of shore to bend of bay, brings us by a commodius vicus of recirculation back to Howth Castle and Environs." But there's more to it: the stones were salvaged from old city streets and buildings; the tree echoes the traditional gathering place for storytellers of yore, and a sculpture by Leo Higgins is reflected in the pool – as communities are reflected in the stories they tell.

In the words of its creators, "The garden is symbolic of Dublin's ability to reinvent itself."

# BLESSINGTON STREET BASIN ❸

Blessington Street, Phibsborough, Dublin 7
• 01 830-0833; 01 222-5278 • www.dublincity.ie
• Open: Daylight hours • Admission: free
• Transport: Connolly DART station (15–20-min. walk); Dublin Bus stops 189 and 196 (Phibsborough Road). The basin is a 10-min. walk from O'Connell Street

"

## Dublin's
## Secret Garden

Looking for an off-radar park recommendation in Dublin? The Iveagh Gardens may be the stock tip, but this waterside oasis is the genuine hidden gem. Measuring just 0.75 hectares, the Blessington Street Basin is a short stroll from O'Connell Street, squirrelled away at the end of a beat-up street, yet almost totally unknown to Dubliners. Dating from 1810, when it opened with the aim of providing clean water to Dublin's northside, the park draws its supply from the Royal Canal. Though officially named "the Royal George Reservoir" in honour of King George III, locals have always preferred "the basin". It no longer serves as a reservoir, however, offering a hush-hush little haven to visitors and local wildlife instead.

After walking past the gritty Georgian ghosts of Blessington Street, the trees, water and leafy central island come on like a bloom in spring – with perimeter paths peppered with benches, Victorian-style lampposts, a fountain that spumes sporadically and the basin itself, bubbling with birdlife, waterfowl, butterflies, bats and fish. Sealed off by stone walls and circled by the terraces, chimneys and spires of Phibsborough, it's quite the surprise package.

Although capable of holding some 4 million gallons of water, it was only a matter of time before a burgeoning city required even more, and the Blessington Street Basin saw its function change after the introduction of the Vartry Reservoir in 1868. For the next century, its water went on to supply the Jameson and Powers' whiskey distilleries in the city, and it was formally opened as a public park in 1891. "During the months when the roads are hard and dusty, and country walking is not always agreeable, a retreat, shaded, cool, and somewhat ornamented, must be appreciated," noted a contemporary editorial in *The Irish Times*.

The present-day park layout is thanks to an inspired renovation in the early 1990s, when the fountain, railings and seating were added, and the manmade island bolstered to become a wildlife habitat. Watch out, too, for the park-keeper's lodge just inside the main entrance. Dating from 1811, its Tudor-style gables, colourful window boxes and pert chimneystacks are a perfect little pick-me-up after the dispiriting approach along Blessington Street.

## ST MARY'S CHAPEL OF EASE ❹

St Mary's Place, Broadstone, Dublin 7
• Open: Not officially open to visitors, as the building is occupied by several businesses. Potential customers may be able to make an appointment, however
• Transport: Connolly Street DART station (20–25-min. walk); Dublin Bus stops 191 and 194, along the Western Way, are a short walk from St Mary's Place

### The Black Church

C ould this be the spookiest church in Dublin? Dating from 1830, the "Black Church" got its nickname thanks to the calp limestone used in its construction – on wet days, it seems to take on a darkly ominous guise. The sense of foreboding is further ramped up by the hypodermic spires and slit-like windows of John Semple's Gothic Revival design. But that's not all. According to local lore, if you're brave (or foolish) enough to walk around St Mary's three times in an anti-clockwise direction at midnight, the devil will appear to steal your soul.

Austin Clarke, who grew up nearby, named a volume of his memoirs after St Mary's – its title, *Twice Round the Black Church*, falls just short of the circuits required to summon Old Nick. "My childhood years were spent under the shadow of an edifice known locally as The Black Church," the poet wrote. "This Protestant Church on the north side of Dublin was grim and forbidding in appearance, and its popular name in the neighbourhood, with all its theological implications, was apt. Even before the age of reason, I was dimly aware of the *odium theologicum*, and when the sound of Sunday singing came faintly from the lancets behind the iron railing, I expected to see the devil loom terrifically from the leads."

Similarly, in James Joyce's *Ulysses*, there is a moment when Leopold Bloom experiences the sins of the past (real or imagined) rising against him in a medley of voices, including "a form of clandestine marriage with at least one woman in the shadow of the Black Church".

St Mary's was deconsecrated in the 1960s, ostensibly because of the diminishing numbers at its services (a "chapel of ease" is a secondary church in a parish, built for parishioners based further away from the principal place of worship). Today it's home to several businesses, and though not officially open to visitors, potential customers may be able to glimpse the interior by making an appointment with one of them. The most notable feature is Semple's extraordinary parabolic arch, a flowing design that seems to blur the distinctions between walls and ceiling, adding further to the Black Church's intrigue.

# 12 HENRIETTA STREET ❺

Off Bolton Street, Dublin 1
• Open: By appointment for small arts and cultural groups (keeptheduck@gmail.com)
• Admission: varies
• Transport: Tara Street or Connolly DART stations (20-min. walk); Luas, Jervis Street (Red Line; 10-min. walk); Dublin Bus stops 8 and 10 are nearby on Granby Row

> *Georgian Dublin's most fashionable address*

It's one of the city's great mysteries. How can the architecture of Georgian Dublin be feted all over the world; how can its regal redbrick terraces and elegant set-piece squares be so celebrated in travel guides, while Henrietta Street is left to rot?

This, after all, is "the single most intact and important architectural collection of individual houses – as a street – in the city", according to Dublin City Council's conservation plan. As an architectural site, the cobbled, early 18th-century street is "as important to the record of settlement in these islands as... Clonmacnoise or Wood Quay." And yet, over time, Henrietta Street has fallen into disrepair, its crumbling houses only surviving thanks to the passion of a handful of residents and other committed parties. It's a short walk from O'Connell Street, but it feels like a Georgian galleon, adrift in an inner-city sea.

Named after the Duchess of Grafton, Henrietta Street was laid out between the 1720s and 1740s and for decades remained one of Dublin's most fashionable addresses. Early residents included four All Ireland Primates and two Speakers of the House of Commons, although things gradually went to seed in the late 19th and early 20th centuries – a period during which the houses were subdivided into tenements, with grand staircases and other fittings torn out to create space, and valuable chimneypieces sold. Nor is the street helped by its status as a cul-de-sac, rear-ended by the unsympathetically angled King's Inns. A tenement museum is currently being developed by Dublin City Council at No.14 (facebook.com/14henriettastreet)… watch this space.

In the meantime, small groups can visit No. 12 Henrietta Street by appointment, or by signing up to occasional events like those run by @ TheDrawingRoom (thedrawingroom.ie) or Contemporary Music Centre (cmc.ie). Originally designed by Edward Lovett Pearce, the townhouse was substantially altered over the centuries – not least when it was subdivided into tenements – but remains a breathtaking glimpse of faded Georgian grandeur. Since he bought it in 1982, the owner has stabilised and restored No.12 with minimal intervention, leaving sash windows, plaster friezes and tall ceilings to mix and match with ebbing paint, worn-down wood and creaking replaces. "Persons loitering or dancing on the stairs will be prosecuted," reads an old sign, painted in the first-floor stairwell.

## THE HUNGRY TREE

**6**

Temple Gardens, King's Inns, Dublin 7
• 01 874-4840
• www.kingsinns.ie; www.treecouncil.ie
• Open: 7am–7.30pm (or later)
• Transport: Dublin Bus stops 1613, 1614 and 1619 are nearby on Constitution Hill. The stops are served by the 83 and 83a routes between Kimmage and Harristown

> ## An "arboricultural curiosity"

**N**ature's revenge. The passage of time. Human folly. It's tempting to ascribe all manner of symbolic interpretations to this cartoonish phenomenon in Temple Gardens.

The Hungry Tree greets walkers, barristers and benchers as they enter the gardens at King's Inns from the south gate. It's a graphic spectacle: a hapless bench apparently being eaten alive by a London plane tree. The bench, like the others scattered about this handsome park, dates from the early 19th century. The plane's slow-motion gastronomic exploits have seen it listed as a heritage tree by the Tree Council of Ireland – alongside specimens like the 400-year-old mulberry at the Teacher Training College in Rathmines, reputed to be Dublin's oldest tree, and the Autograph Tree, a copper beech inscribed with the initials of visitors ranging from W. B. Yeats to George Bernard Shaw, in Coole Park, Co. Galway. Standing 21m high and measuring 3.5m in girth, the Hungry Tree is listed on the Heritage Tree Database as an "arboricultural curiosity". That senior members of an Inn of Court are known as "benchers" only adds to its delight.

Inns of Court traditionally provided law students with accommodation, meals and tuition over the course of their studies. The King's Inns were designed by James Gandon and built in the early 1800s, although the Honorable Society of King's Inns (the governing body for barristers in Ireland) goes way back to the reign of Henry VIII – it was founded in 1541. Temple Gardens were opened to the public in the late 19th century, creating not only a welcome amenity for the working-class suburb in which they are set, but a handy short cut between Broadstone and Henrietta Street. The short cut is yet another surprise – an echoing, cobblestoned courtyard bookended by a triumphal arch added by architect Francis Johnson.

## STAINED GLASS ROOM ❼

Dublin City Gallery, The Hugh Lane, Parnell Square North, Dublin 1
• 01 222-5550 • www.hughlane.ie
• Open: Tues—Thurs 10am—6pm; Fri & Sat 10am—5pm; Sun 11am—5pm. Closed Mondays.
• Admission: free
• Transport: Dart (Tara/Connolly Street; 15-min. walk). Luas: Abbey Street (10-min. walk). Dublin Bus Stops 8, 10, 461 and 4726 are all nearby on Parnell Square

> *The gallery within a gallery...*

I t's the Hugh Lane's gallery-within-a-gallery. To step into the Stained Glass Room in the Dublin City Gallery is to step momentarily into a whole other dimension – a whispery, church-like, and ridiculously beautiful room that twinkles like a heavenly disco ball.

The room is easy to miss if you're rushing towards more famous exhibits – Francis Bacon's cluttered studio, for example, or Jack B Yeats' stunning 'There is No Night'. But what's inside is unforgettable. The gallery's stained glass collection includes kaleidoscopic works by the likes of Harry Clarke, Evie Hone, James Scanlon, Wilhelmina Geddes and Paul Bony, backlit so gorgeously you could giggle. Stained glass has floated in and out of fashion in Irish arts circles over the years, but when you see a collection like this gathered together, when you can bask in its blooming colours, florid storytelling and intricate craftsmanship, the magic is plain to see.

The highlight is Harry Clarke's 'The Eve of St. Agnes'. Dating from 1924, this work consists of 22 small panels - each depicting a stanza of Keats's poem of the same title. The panels, split between two windows, tell the story of Madeline, a young heroine prevented from meeting her love because he is the sworn enemy of her family. According to an old superstition, however, virgin girls carrying out certain rituals on the eve of St. Agnes' feast day (January 20th) will see their loves come to them. So it transpires for Madeline, whom Clarke depicts in various panels lying 'lily-white' in her bed, watched over by her lover, and in scarcely disguised erotic union ('like a throbbing star… into her dream he melted…'), before their escape together into the storm. Phew!

To many, this is Clarke's (1889-1931) masterpiece, a beautiful and romantic work as sensual as the poem on which it is based. It's the highlight of a hidden room just crying out for a visit on a first date, Valentine's Day, or for anyone intending to get down on one knee…

---

More Harry Clarke windows can be seen in another unusual location – Bewley's Café on Grafton Street, where six magnificent examples were commissioned by Ernest Bewley and completed just prior to Clarke's death in 1931. You'll find them in the ground floor tearooms.

---

# LETTER FROM BRENDAN BEHAN ❽

Dublin Writers' Museum, 18 Parnell Square, Dublin 1
• 01 872-2077 • www.writersmuseum.com
• Open: Mon–Sat 9.45am–4.45pm, Sun and public holidays 11am–4.30pm
• Admission: Adults €7.50, children €4.70, family ticket €18
• Transport: Tara Street and Connolly DART stations (15-min. walk); Luas, Abbey Street (Red Line; 10–15-min. walk); Dublin Buses 10, 11, 13, 16 and 19 stop nearby

> *A great place for a quiet piss-up*

In an age of instant messaging, there's something irresistibly nostalgic about an old-fashioned letter. All the more so when that letter was written by Brendan Behan (1923–64).

"It's a screwy kind of place," the author says of Los Angeles, writing home to his half-brother, Rory Furlong, in May 1961. Across several pages of Montecito Hotel letterhead on display in the Dublin Writers' Museum, Behan goes on to describe the "Irish" airs played for him at Frank Sinatra's club and a fit-looking Fred Astaire ("still looks a lean forty"). He ranks LA as a poor cousin to New York. Sunset Boulevard, he concludes, is "oddly enough in its own reprehensible way... not unlike [Crumlin's] Sundrive Road." Broadway, on the other hand, is "a great place for a quiet piss-up", though he wonders whether the Dublin papers carried news of his exploits: "They only seem to know when I'm in jail or dying."

That tended to be the way of it with Behan. Once his literary legacy had been secured by works such as *The Quare Fellow* (1956) and *The Hostage* (1958), the bellicose Dubliner went about drinking his way through a golden age of literature in the city. Behan famously described himself as "a drinker with a writing problem", and true enough, his boozy behaviour won him more fame and notoriety than anything he committed to the page. He died, after collapsing at a bar, aged just 41.

His letter from LA is one of the highlights of the Dublin Writers' Museum, a good first port of call for those interested in exploring the city's literary heritage. The exhibits here – laid out in a fusty series of Georgian rooms – feature several other curiosities, including a telephone used by Samuel Beckett (perhaps Godot said he'd call?), Austin Clarke's desk, and stanzas of the Great Hunger written in Patrick Kavanagh's own hand. Living writers, alas, are conspicuous by their absence. Not that Behan would have minded, judging by his ebullient signing-off. "Tell Seán I said fuck Gargarin [sic] and Shepard," he writes, dismissing two great astronauts of the time. "Hollywood and Broadway are space enough for your loving brother, Brendan."

# NO. 7 ECCLES STREET FRONT DOOR    ⑨

James Joyce Centre, 35 North Great George's Street, Dublin 1
- 01 878-8547
- www.jamesjoyce.ie
- Open: Tues–Sat 10am–5pm, Sun 12 noon–5pm
- Admission: €5/€4
- Transport: Tara Street and Connolly DART stations (10-min. walk); Dublin Buses 120, 4, 40b, 40d, 7, 7d and 8 stop at bus stop 4725 on nearby O'Connell Street

> **The most famous door in Irish fiction...**

**S**tep through the front door of 35 North Great George's Street, and you'll find a local literary treasure: the James Joyce Centre. But there's a more interesting front door in the backyard.

No. 7 Eccles Street was the fictional home of Leopold Bloom, the central character in James Joyce's *Ulysses*. Although Joyce himself only stayed at the address for one night in 1909, it is central to his novel. It is here that we meet Bloom as he prepares breakfast in bed for his wife, Molly. It is from here that he leaves on his peregrinations around the city, and to here that he returns in the wee hours, famously forgetting his front-door key.

"Why was he doubly irritated?"

"Because he had forgotten and because he remembered that he had reminded himself twice not to forget."

In 1909 Joyce had watched as his friend John Francis Byrne, who lived at No. 7, similarly climbed over the front railings having forgotten his latch key. The events of that day obviously made an impression: Byrne and Bloom share the same height and weight.

Today, the front door to No. 7 is kept under an awning. It's an underwhelming setting, to say the least, but at least it is a setting. In the 1960s, the Georgian terrace incorporating No. 7 Eccles Street was razed to facilitate the expanding Mater Private Hospital. The door was only rescued thanks to the intervention of Patrick Kavanagh, Flann O'Brien and John Francis Ryan, owner of The Bailey pub. By all accounts, their negotiations to buy the door almost collapsed after the nuns who owned the land learned of its connection with "that pagan writer", but the transaction went ahead, and the door was taken to The Bailey, where it remained until its donation to the James Joyce Centre.

Today, reunited with its stone frame, the portal to No. 7 looks strangely distressed. The knocker and handles are rusty, the paint chipped, the wood cracking in places – hardly befitting the most famous front door in Irish fiction. But it's as moving a memorial to "the mummy and the daddy" of Irish writers, as Frank McGuinness dubs Joyce in a video upstairs, as you'll find in his native city.

May God keep me this instant,
keep men safe and watch over them on their journeys
in Memory of Eugene Lawlor Rock Chipper
RIP

## THE CAB DRIVERS' SHRINE ❿

O'Connell Street, Dublin 2
• Transport: Tara Street or Connolly DART stations (5-10-min. walk); Luas,
Abbey Street (Red Line; 5-min. walk); Dublin Bus stops 4496 and 6059
are nearby on O'Connell Street

*Erected
by ordinary
Dubliners*

The taxi drivers at the northern end of O'Connell Street are as much a fixture of Dublin's main street as the GPO or the O'Connell Monument. Walk past day or night, and you'll find a cabal of cabbies lining up opposite the Savoy Cinema – sharing gossip, sucking on cigarettes, reading papers or honking horns to move the line along.

Just as much a fixture, though less noticed, is the statue of Jesus at the head of the rank. Standing on a granite plinth, encased in a PVC box, Christ is depicted with arms outstretched and Sacred Heart blooming like a flower in the centre of His chest. He stands on a rock painted with stars – look closely, and you'll not only see spots of blood in His palms, but toenails painted a pale peach. Despite its modern casing, the statue has been here since the Civil War, when horse-drawn cab drivers helped to rescue goods and furniture from shops set ablaze on O'Connell Street. The salvaged goods were left in the centre of the street for shop-owners to reclaim them, the story goes, but nobody came for the Sacred Heart. The cabbies duly got some boxes from Moore Street and set it up as a temporary shrine. To this day, it remains the only memento of fighting on the street.

"May God bless the taxi driver's [sic], keep them safe and watch over them on there journey's [sic]," the current plaque reads. "In Memory of Eugene Lawlor, Rank Organiser, RIP."

Its colours and grammar have made the shrine the subject of some pretty snarky comments over the years. While it's true that it won't end up in the Saatchi Gallery, the more you look at it, the more touching it becomes. The grammar is so obviously atrocious, it seems to underline the endearing honesty of it all. There's no poetry or pretence, and Christ Himself is modest, in contrast to the bronze depictions of O'Connell, Parnell and others nearby – not to mention the 120m spire.

"For ages I thought this was some poncy modern art exhibit," as one passer-by posted on Yelp. "Then I got a closer look at it. It's actually quite a touching memorial ... it's also nice to know that a community, like the taxi drivers, can have their values represented right in the heart of the city."

# WILLIAMS & WOODS BUILDING

**⑪**

26 King's Inn Street, Dublin 1
• www.chocolatefactory.ie
• Open: 8am–4pm (café)
• Admission: free entry to café customers
• Transport: Luas, Jervis Street (Red Line), 5–10-min. walk

> *A hip
> hideaway
> in Dublin's first
> poured-concrete
> building*

I t's one of the most satisfying surprises in the inner city. There you are, strolling through an urban fudge of modern apartments, car parks and commercial developments when – bam! – a glorious maverick of a corner building comes into view. Williams & Woods was Dublin's first poured-concrete building, a former jam and marmalade factory run by a company that once supplied the city with its fix of Toblerone, Silvermints, 'Buttercup' toffees and the Irish Coffee Bar, among other brands.

It dates from 1910, with the original sign beautifully preserved on an angled corner … more than can be said for Williams & Woods' old HQ, an 18th-century hospital that was demolished after the company sold it in 1978 (a cinema occupies the site today).

Today, after years as a storage warehouse, the building has been given a new lease of life as the Chocolate Factory, a hive of studios housing photographers, designers, dancers, architects, up-cyclers, urban farmers and even a kung-fu academy.

It's an inspirational space, and the visitor may leave wondering why more of Dublin's neglected built heritage couldn't be rebooted in the same way. So many characterful old buildings with stories to tell are boarded up, sprouting weeds and falling into treacherous condition as politics, legal issues and plain old shenanigans play out.

Visitors can't tour the Chocolate Factory's studios, but everyone is welcome at the funky Blas Café situated in the wide-open, ground-floor space downstairs. Pared-back woods, big old iron-framed windows, lamps fashioned from cymbals and drums and a rolling gallery of artworks all serve as a setting for a loose and tasty menu (try the bacon and egg breakfast bap or the free-range chicken chipotle on sourdough). It's a hip space that will get you thinking about Dublin's social history all over again.

# BRERETON'S PAWNBROKERS

⑫

108 Capel Street, Dublin 1
• 01 872-6759
• www.johnbreretonjewellers.ie
• Open: Mon, Tues, Thurs & Fri 9am–5.30pm, Sat 9am–7pm. Closed Wed
• Transport: Tara Street DART station (20-min. walk); Luas, Jervis (Red Line; 5–10-min. walk); Dublin Bus stops 312 and 1479 are nearby on Ormond and Wellington Quays

" **T**he shop creaked with the weight of other people's sorrows."

*Three brass balls*

So writes E. L. Wallant in his novel, *The Pawnbroker* (HBJ, 1978). The quote is repeated in Jim Fitzpatrick's *Three Brass Balls: The Story of the Irish Pawnshop* (Collins Press, 2001) and the words will surely echo as you descend into the clinical basement of No. 108 Capel Street.

This is the address of Brereton's jewellery shop, but as the three vintage spheres suspended above its awning suggest, it's also one of Dublin's last remaining pawnshops. Golden spheres as a symbol of pawnbroking originated with the Medici family of Florence, whose bank was the largest in Europe in the 15th century. They also evoke the patron saint of pawnbrokers, St Nicholas of Myra, whom legend says once helped a man with three daughters, but no money to provide them with a dowry, by throwing three golden purses into his house. There's no Santa Claus in the basement at Brereton's, however. Just the fluorescent-edgy environment of a modern-day pawnshop, with security glass and sparse counters offset by a big old pledge book, some framed pawn tickets dating back to 1904, and of course, a window full of slightly sad-looking jewellery and trinkets – a golden bulldog with bejewelled collar (€595) here, a golden chain bearing the word "Mum" (€295) there.

John Brereton established his business in 1916, and a fourth generation runs the family's shops on Capel Street, O'Connell Street and Grafton Street today. At the time, Dublin was crawling with pawnbrokers, with as many as 50 "people's banks" surviving into the 1930s. Customers raised funds by selling everything from artificial limbs to their Sunday best ("for the pawnbroker, even the most ridiculous pledge would be accepted if he knew his customer", Fitzpatrick writes). Only three remain today, however – you'll also find brass balls hanging outside Carthy's of Marlborough Street and Kearns of Queen Street.

---

Capel Street looks just a few years from ruin, but this unique thoroughfare was once a fashionable address, and even a short walk throws up all sorts of gems. Former Taoiseach Seán Lemass was born at No. 2, there are some fine Georgian townhouses, and the Victorian shopfronts include John McNeill's (No. 140) – today a pub, but formerly the music shop that made the bugle which sounded the Charge of the Light Brigade (1854).

# RENATUS HARRIS ORGAN

**⓭**

The Church, Jervis Street, Dublin 1
• 01 828-0102
• www.thechurch.ie
• Open: Bar from 10.30am; Gallery Restaurant from 5.30pm
• Transport: Tara Street and Connolly DART stations (10-min. walk); Luas, Jervis Street (Red Line); Dublin Bus stops 312 and 1479 are nearby on the quays

*Where religion meets R & B*

**M**ost visitors to The Church, it's probably fair to say, are expecting house and R&B rather than a Renatus Harris organ once played by George Frederick Handel. But this beautifully restored instrument isn't the only surprising feature among the interiors of this well-known pub, restaurant and nightclub in the former St Mary's Church on Jervis Street.

In its former life, the superpub was a Protestant church. Dating from 1702, the building took its name from a medieval monastery that once sprawled north of the River Liffey and seems to have predominantly been the work of William Robinson, the architect responsible for Kilmainham's Royal Hospital. St Mary's was the first church in Dublin to boast a gallery, and that feature remains in place today, with restaurant tables overlooking a long bar at ground level, and the early 18th-century organ that is the building's centrepiece. A couple of chipped keys aside, the instrument is largely unaltered since it was played by Handel, who debuted his *Messiah* in Dublin and lived for a time on nearby Abbey Street. It was designed by the master English organ-maker Renatus Harris (1652–1724), and today, its golden pipes form an extraordinary backdrop to one of the biggest drinking spaces in the city. In fact, diners can sit right up beside the ivory keys and stop knobs once tinkled upon by Handel himself.

The church, which was refurbished in the 2000s, contains several other artefacts. There's a bust of Arthur Guinness to celebrate his marriage here in 1761. A stained glass window is framed with Portland stone. A baptismal font may have captured water from the brows of Seán O'Casey and Wolfe Tone, who were among 25,000 souls christened at St Mary's. The Cellar nightclub now haunts the former crypts, and wooden floorboards leading from the gallery into a glass-enclosed tower connected to the building were rescued from the Adelphi Cinema. Prior to its demolition in 1995, the Adelphi had hosted performances from The Beatles, Johnny Cash and Roy Orbison, among countless other legends. Their names are listed here.

# CHAPTER HOUSE, ST MARY'S ABBEY ⓮

Meetinghouse Lane, off Capel Street, Dublin 1
• 01 833-1618 • www.heritageireland.ie
• Open: Hours and dates vary (check website for details)
• Admission: free
• Transport: Tara Street DART station (20-min. walk); Luas, Jervis (Red Line; 5–10-min. walk); Dublin Bus stops 312 and 1479 are nearby on Ormond and Wellington Quays

> *The most historic spot in all Dublin*

**W**ere it not for the clues in the street names, you'd hardly know St Mary's Abbey had ever existed. Abbey Street, Mary's Lane, Capel Street, Mary Street – all hark back to a Cistercian monastery that was once among the most important in medieval Ireland, but today is reduced to a single chapter house and slype (covered passageway) buried in the inner city.

St Mary's was founded in 1139 as a daughter house of the Benedictine Order of Savigny in France, but adopted the Cistercian rule just eight years later. This was a time of rapid expansion for the order, and by 1228 the Cistercians had 34 monasteries throughout Ireland. St Mary's was easily the richest – thanks to its proximity to the emerging city of Dublin and the monks' own genius for contemporary technology, engineering, farming and business. It also played a historic role in the affairs of the State: as Dublin had no suitable public buildings at the time, the abbey hosted meetings of the King's Irish Council. Indeed, it was here that Thomas Fitzgerald flung down his Sword of State in renouncing his allegiance to King Henry VIII.

"We are standing in the historic council chamber of St Mary's Abbey where Silken Thomas proclaimed himself a rebel in 1534," as Ned Lambert whispers in the "Wandering Rocks" chapter of Joyce's *Ulysses*. "This is the most historic spot in all Dublin."

You wouldn't think it today. After Henry VIII's dissolution of the monasteries in 1539, St Mary's was granted to the Earl of Desmond "for the keeping of his horses and train". After that, it was cannibalised by the city as a quarry (some of its stone is incorporated in Grattan Bridge, and a section of its cloister has been found in a wall on Cook Street).

So the great monastery vanished – except for one tantalising space. Somehow, the chapter house where monks would have met after morning mass (and indeed, the very room where Silken Thomas sealed his fate) survives. Secreted away, several metres below street level on Meetinghouse Lane, you'll find a remarkable heritage attraction (extensive works were being carried out during Secret Dublin's latest update, so check the website before visiting). Its ceiling is like an elegant ribcage, with bays of vaulting supported by triple-shafted corbels. Mock-ups of lancet windows are set into the east wall. Display boards continue into a small section of the slype. It's at once Dublin's best-kept secret and its most shameful cautionary tale.

# GPO WITNESS HISTORY & COURTYARD ⓯

GPO, O'Connell Street, Dublin 1
• 01 872-1916 • www.gpowitnesshistory.ie
• Open: Mon–Fri 9am–5.30pm, Sat & Sun 10am–5.30pm. Closed on
public holidays (but not Bank Holidays). Guided tours available
• Admission: €10 (adults), €5 (children over 5), €25 (family)
• Transport: DART (Tara Street or Connolly station, 10-min. walk); Luas
(Red Line, Abbey Street, 2-min. walk); Dublin Bus stops 4496 and 6059
are nearby on O'Connell Street

*The spiritual heart of Dublin*

**E**very Dubliner knows the GPO's iconic façade. It was here, on 24 April 1916, that Padraig Pearse read the Proclamation of the Irish Republic. The building's columns and Portland stone portico were the only parts of the General Post Office still standing after the Easter Rising and naturally, 100 years later, it played a central role in the Irish state's centenary commemorations.

But the GPO's central courtyard? That's not so familiar. To access this space, visitors need to buy a ticket for one of the city's newest "visitor experiences", GPO Witness History. It's worth the outlay.

Passing into the historic building's basement, interactive displays quickly immerse you in the stories of this controversial rebellion – from its social and political context to its momentous aftermath, from big names to the small moments too (personal artefacts include Éamonn Ceannt's razor and Countess Markievicz's leather-bound prayer book). A 15-minute audiovisual experience brings to life the circumstances that led to the Rising, including the cultural revival and struggle for Home Rule. There are lots of touchscreens and video booths too.

The courtyard comes as the visitor journey ascends back to ground level. Beautifully remodelled ahead of the 2016 commemorations, its brickwork is crisp, its vaulted and sash windows intricate, its rooftops seeming almost to be pierced by the spire, which soars 120m above O'Connell Street outside.

It's easy to imagine the horses and mail carts that would have passed through the yard in bygone times, and a nicely understated art installation by Barbara Knezevic features 40 shards of rock mirrored on stainless steel. They Are of Us All remembers the 40 children killed during the Easter Rising. For a fleeting moment, standing dead centre in such a symbolic space, it feels like you're at the spiritual heart of the city.

Afterwards, of course, you exit through a gift shop. What the 1916 leaders would have thought of the t-shirts, key-rings and tea towels commemorating their struggle we will never know, but the bright and cheerful café is a bonus. Grab a coffee overlooking the courtyard, while the crowds pile up and down O'Connell Street oblivious to its very existence.

# HIPPOCAMPUS LAMPS

**16**

Grattan Bridge, Dublin 2
• Transport: Tara Street DART station (15-min. walk); Luas, Jervis Street (Red Line; 5–10-min. walk); Dublin Bus stops 312 and 1479 are nearby on the quays

*Henry Grattan's Hippocampi*

**D**ubliners widely refer to it as Capel Street Bridge, but the stone and cast-iron structure straddling the Liffey between Capel Street and Parliament Street is in fact named after Henry Grattan (1746–1820). It dates from the 1870s, when its precursor was adapted to include cast-iron supports, footpaths on either side of the road and ornate street furniture – including several of the city's most intriguing cast-iron lamp standards.

The pale green lamps, set at intervals along the railings, are each propped up by a pair of curvy seahorses – or more correctly, Hippocampi. Bearing the head and forequarters of a horse and the tail of a fish, these powerful creatures are best known from Greek and Roman mythology, where they pull Poseidon and Neptune's sea-chariots. However, "Capel" is also pleasingly similar to the Irish word for horse (*capall*), and water horses also feature in Celtic mythology, where shape-shifting beasts like the *each-uisce* and Kelpie are described as luring humans to their deaths in the lakes and streams they haunt.

Evocative as the cast-iron Hippocampi are, however, they're much more likely to be simple symbols of Dublin's status as a maritime port. For much of the 18th century, Capel Street (actually named for Arthur Capel, the First Earl of Essex) was the city's primary thoroughfare and one of its most fashionable addresses. At that time, the Custom House was located on Essex Quay at the site of the present-day Clarence Hotel, and hard as it is to imagine today, the area would have run thick with ships and sails. Several features of the bridge have come and gone over the years – from a statue of George I on horseback to Continental-style kiosks erected in the noughties – but the Hippocampi have survived.

Two similar cast-iron Hippocampi can be found flanking the statue of Henry Grattan on College Green. Sculpted by John Henry Foley and erected in 1874, the statue was originally surrounded by four such lamps, but they were removed several decades ago.

# BULLET HOLES
# IN THE O'CONNELL MONUMENT

**17**

O'Connell Street, Dublin 1
• Transport: Dart (Tara Street or Connolly Street DART stations); Luas,
(Luas, Abbey Street (Red Line); Dublin Bus; Dublin Bus stops 271, 273 and
others are nearby on O'Connell Street.

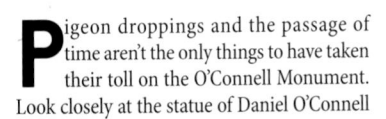

*A legacy
of the 1916
Rebellion...*

Pigeon droppings and the passage of time aren't the only things to have taken their toll on the O'Connell Monument. Look closely at the statue of Daniel O'Connell on his granite plinth, at the bronze figures swarming about in the frieze below, at the four winged victories above the base. They're peppered with dozens of small holes, drilled by whizzing bullets.

The bullet holes are a legacy of the 1916 Rebellion and the turbulence that followed, including the Irish War of Independence and the Civil War that erupted after the establishment of the Free State in 1922. Clearly, the intersection of O'Connell Street and the city quays hasn't just been a busy junction for traffic. During the course of recent restoration works, no fewer than 10 bullet holes were identified in the 12m-high figure of O'Connell alone, two of which pierced his head. In total, there are approximately 30 bullet holes in the monument.

Daniel O'Connell was one of Ireland's towering historical figures. Following his death in 1847, the committee responsible for the monument resolved that it should memorialise "O'Connell in his whole character and career, from the cradle to the grave, so as to embrace the whole nation". Though a fund was established soon after his funeral, it wasn't until 1882 that the result – to a design by John Henry Foley – was officially unveiled: O'Connell tops the plinth, with four winged victories representing patriotism, courage, eloquence and fidelity at the bottom. Sandwiched between the two is a frieze of some 30 figures, including the Maid of Erin, her breast punctured by perhaps the most visible of the bullet strikes.

What would the Great Emancipator have felt about his statue being showered in a hail of gunfire? In truth, O'Connell was no stranger to weaponry. In 1815 he was even challenged to a duel by John D'Esterre, a member of Dublin Corporation, which ended with D'Esterre being mortally wounded by a shot to the hip. Tradition holds that the memory haunted O'Connell for the rest of his life – so much so that he wore a black glove on his right hand when receiving Holy Communion.

It's not only Dublin's grandest monument that bears O'Connell's name, of course. O'Connell Street itself is Dublin's widest boulevard, and bullet holes are only the start of its secrets.

## COMPETITION LETTERBOXES  **18**

Independent House, Middle Abbey Street, Dublin 1
• Transport: Tara Street and Connolly DART stations (5–10-min. walk);
Luas, Abbey Street (Red Line); Dublin Bus Stops 271, 310 and 4496 are
nearby on O'Connell Street

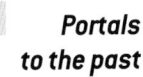

*Portals
to the past*

**A**lthough today's postal address finds Independent News & Media on Talbot Street, the building historically associated with the group is Independent House.

Dating from 1924, this was the headquarters of the *Irish Independent*, *Evening Herald* and *Sunday Independent* for almost 80 years before the group relocated. It was sold in an off-market deal for €26 million in 2003, but languished for several years before being acquired for less than a quarter of that amount by retail group Primark in 2013. According to *The Irish Times*, the building was earmarked to become part of a "Northern Quarter" retail district, but like so many other Celtic Tiger confections, it fell foul of recession when the banks took over Arnotts Department Store in 2010. Although the newspapers and their staff have decamped, several nostalgic traces remain. The newspaper titles can still be seen on the building's façade, for example. A copper-framed clock protrudes from the middle of four recessed columns, connected to the third storey by a precarious-looking access bridge. Most evocative of all, at street level, are the little hooded letterboxes once used for correspondence, classified ads and competitions. These have weathered less well, with the surrounding brass plate having grown patchy and the script succumbing to rust. Nevertheless, there's something romantic about them, with social media having rendered snail mail from readers all but extinct.

Independent News & Media wasn't the first company to run newspapers

from Middle Abbey Street, of course. This block had previously been home to *The Nation*, a nationalist newspaper founded by Thomas Davis, Charles Gavan Duffy and John Blake Dillon in 1842, as a bronze plaque beside the letterboxes recalls. What becomes of Independent House, its clock and letterboxes remains to be seen, although it is a protected structure.

CR TERCH M CHRISTAIN
CUSTOM HOUSE QUAY

# FREE FLOW

**19**

North Wall Quay, Dublin Docklands
• Transport: Tara Street DART station (10-min. walk); Luas, George's Dock (Red Line; 5–10-min. walk); Dublin Bus stops 6252 and 2499 are nearby at Sean O'Casey Bridge

*A surreptitious movement towards the sea ...*

**D**ublin's Docklands aren't the first place you'd associate with art in the city. Nevertheless, there's a surprising collection of public commissions lining the quays in the area. A bronze linesman hauls a rope on City Quay. Reflective sequins mask a Bord Gáis installation near The O2, recalling the banded wrapping of the freight containers once common on the River Liffey. Rowan Gillespie's *Famine* haunts Custom House Quay.

Most surprising of all is Rachel Joynt's *Free Flow* (2005), an installation of 900 small, internally lit glass cobbles set along a section of the north quays stretching from the Custom House to North Wall. Joynt's other public works in Dublin include *People's Island* (1988), a collection of footprints and birds' feet set in bronze in a busy traffic island on O'Connell Bridge, and *Arc Hive* (2003), a series of honeycomb-like grids inlaid into the floor of Pearse Street Library. *Free Flow* conveys the same sense of discovery and detail; it's a sculpture stumbled upon underfoot, coaxing passers-by to engage first with the pavement, then with the place. Peppered along North Wall Quay, the light fixtures hide away hundreds of silver and copper fish, suspended within stainless steel halos. The lights themselves are watery shades of green and blue, helping to suggest "an almost surreptitious movement towards the sea", as the artist puts it. They recall *Starboard* (2001), Joynt's translucent ship plan on Gregg's Quay in Belfast, as well as *Mothership* (1999), her cast bronze sea urchin at Sandycove.

The sense of discovery in her public art "is paramount", Joynt has said. "I don't want a sign telling people what to do," as she explained in a recent piece in the *Irish Arts Review*. And that's exactly what makes *Free Flow* such a stumbled-upon delight.

## THE FIVE LAMPS  ⑳

Junction of Portland Row & Strand Street, Dublin
• Transport: Connolly DART station (5-min. walk); Luas, Connolly (Red Line; 5-min. walk); Dublin Bus stops 516 and 619 are nearby

*Hang yer bollix off it!*

At first glance, there appears to be little doubt as to how the Five Lamps got its name. The landmark stands at a busy junction in the north inner-city, with the five lamps sprouting from its cast-iron column echoing the five streets – Portland Row, North Strand Road, Seville Place, Amiens Street and Killarney Street – that intersect around it.

It's a key reference point for directions in the area. "Carry on past the Five Lamps," someone might say. Or "It's not far from the Five Lamps." Friends, sporting teams, walking groups and countless others have used the landmark as a rendezvous point; there's a city arts festival and brewery named after it, and it's said that no-one born north of the Five Lamps can really call themselves a true Dubliner. Others delight in pointing out the black-and-gold standard, before delivering one of the city's greatest quips: "Hang yer bollix off it."

The Five Lamps refer to more than the five-point junction, however. Dating from the late 1800s, they were originally erected as a memorial to General Henry Hall, a celebrated veteran of the British Army's campaigns in India. As Christine Casey writes in *Dublin* (Yale University Press, 2005), Hall is said to have "raised a corps among a wild race of Imhairs, whom he civilised by inducing them to abandon their habits of murder and infanticide." Afterwards, he settled in Galway, and the monument is said to commemorate five key battles fought on the subcontinent. The Five Lamps survived the fallout from another great battle in 1941, when German aircraft bombed Dublin's North Strand – a small memorial park to the 28 people killed and 90 injured on that fateful occasion, together with a colourful wall mural, can be found nearby on Amiens Street.

As you get closer to the lamppost, look out for four lions' heads on its column. These survive from a time when the original gas-lit fixture incorporated a fountain. Water spurted from the lions' mouths into four basins at its base, drinking cups were chained to the structure, and both humans and horses would have enjoyed a passing sup. Sadly, though the elegant lamp standard survives, it seems rather at sea today amid an ugly jumble of CCTV poles, traffic lights and street signage, not to mention the mélange of derelict buildings and charmless modern apartment and commercial blocks surrounding it.

# ROYAL CANAL & LOCKKEEPER'S COTTAGE  **㉑**

Newcomen Bridge, North Strand Road, Dublin 1
• Transport: Connolly DART station (10–15-min. walk); Luas, Connolly (Red Line; 10–15-min. walk); Dublin Bus stops 516 and 618 are on North Strand Road

> *The Auld Triangle went jingle jangle ...*

**O**nce upon a time, canals were the motorways of Ireland. In their heyday, horse-drawn barges carried tens of thousands of passengers and hundreds of thousands of tonnes of freight along the Royal Canal and Grand Canal every year. Over time, of course, railways and roads went on to replace these watery thoroughfares, and today their fates are mixed. The Grand Canal is an idyllic vision of greenery, sculptures and cycle paths as it approaches the Liffey, but the Royal Canal is the forgotten child. Since its closure, restoration has been slow.

The Royal Canal dates from 1789, although poor surveying meant it didn't reach the River Shannon until 27 years (and 47 locks) later. Its outlet at the River Liffey can be seen at Spencer Dock, built by the Midland Great Western Railway Company, but there's another fascinating piece of built heritage at the first lock. Just beneath Newcomen Bridge on the North Strand Road, a few metres from the hulking Croke Park, sits a two-room lockkeeper's cottage dating from the 1790s. In recent years, the cottage had been rented by a family who took pride in its upkeep – smart white paint, splashy flowers and wooden shutters delighted passers-by. Going to press it was unoccupied, with Waterways Ireland considering a number of options for its future use. Block out the surrounding clutter of billboards, railway lines and flats, and the scene looks very similar to how it might have done over 200 years ago, when keepers living in the cottage tended the gates, beams and chamber of the double lock.

From Newcomen Bridge, it's possible to follow the canal west towards Ashtown. Scenery along the route ranges from leafy to bleak and unforgiving – most notably as it passes the walls of Mountjoy Prison. This is where Brendan Behan famously set his Auld Triangle, going "jingle jangle / All along the banks of the Royal Canal". Walking beneath the stands of Croke Park, imagine the rousing rendition performed by Bono and The Edge during U2's 360° Tour, when they dedicated the ballad to perhaps its finest interpreter – Ronnie Drew of The Dubliners.

Further along, at the seventh lock, the parallel railway line switches to the south side of the canal and follows it all the way to Ballinea Bridge, west of Mullingar.

# CENTRE SOUTH

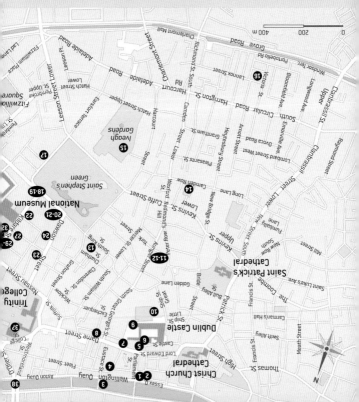

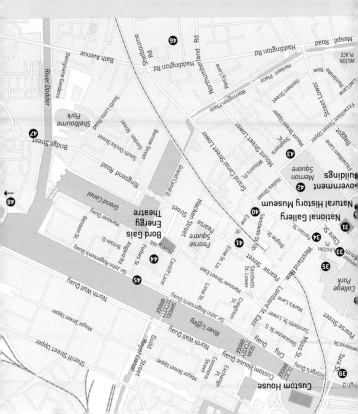

## SUNLIGHT CHAMBERS FRIEZES ❶

Parliament Street & Essex Quay, Dublin 2
• Transport: Tara Street DART station (5-min. walk); Luas, Jervis Street (Red Line; 5-min. walk); Dublin Bus stops 1443, 1479 and 2912 are nearby

*The story of soap*

Stand at the south-east corner of Grattan Bridge and look back towards the corner of Parliament Street and Essex Quay. Block out the trundling Dublin buses, perhaps the duvet of grey sky overhead and you could – just for a moment – be in mercantile Italy.

The building facing you, Sunlight Chambers, is one of the most unusual in Dublin. Dating from 1901, it was designed by Edward Ould (the architect of Liverpool's Port Sunlight) in Italianate style and is most notable for the ceramic friezes between storeys: sunny splashes of colour crafted by the sculptor and potter, Conrad Dressler. From a distance, you'd assume the friezes depict classical scenes. But no. The building was constructed as the Irish headquarters of Lever Brothers, the British soap and detergent manufacturers (Sunlight was one of its brands at the time) and the terracotta curiosities pay homage to the art of a good scrub. Look closely, and you'll see washerwomen cleaning clothes, merchants haggling for oils and smellies, labourers ploughing fields, women drawing water from a well. "The story of soap", as it has been described, is quite the counterpoint to dear old dirty Dublin.

Above the friezes, the building's overhanging eaves are unlike any of its neighbours'. There's also a tiled roof and the top two storeys are arcaded. Apparently, Sunlight Chambers met with opposition from Irish architects and builders at the time (Ould was British), with *The Irish Builder* journal dubbing it the ugliest building in Dublin. This is hardly the case, but as Lisa Cassidy points out in her "Built Dublin" blog, Sunlight Chambers isn't all squeaky-clean. The forced labour used to extract palm oil in the Belgian Congo – a key ingredient in Lever Brothers' products – doesn't conjure up scenes quite as rosy as those unfolding across the friezes. According to Jules Marchal's book, *Lord Leverhulme's Ghosts* (Verso, 2008), forced labour reduced the population of the colony by half, accounting for more deaths than the Holocaust.

Today, the building is occupied by M. E. Hanahoe solicitors, who commissioned a complete restoration in the late 1990s. Architects Gilroy McMahon consulted widely in conserving and cleaning up the stone and ceramics, resulting in the beautiful colours of today.

# ISOLDE'S TOWER

Exchange Street Lower, Dublin 8
• Transport: Tara Street DART station (5–10-min. walk); Dublin Bus stop
1443; Luas, Jervis Street (Red Line; 5–10-min. walk)

> *The hidden heart of Dublin's medieval defences*

It's an Irish solution to an Irish problem. During the development of a new apartment complex, the foundations of a cornerstone of Dublin's 13th-century city walls are discovered. What to do? Why, after an admirable excavation, you build around and above them, of course – leaving passers-by to view the neglected results in a dank basement pit through a rusty metal grid.

But here's the thing. Despite its shameful presentation (beer cans and cigarette butts are scattered throughout the stagnant pond), Isolde's Tower still sucks you in. The more you stare into that dankness, the more you see. Discovered in 1993 during an archeological dig on behalf of Temple Bar Properties, the foundations belong to a tower built as part of an extension to the city walls in Anglo-Norman Dublin. The tower is 4m thick, and though the surviving stones stand at barely half that height, you can still get a sense of the seriousness of any potential attack from the River Liffey. In its heyday, the tower projected into the river at up to 12m in height, serving as a first line of defence – not to mention a grisly backdrop for the display of criminals' heads on spikes. Along with a range of post-medieval pottery, several skulls were discovered in river silt during the excavation.

Isolde's Tower is named for the daughter of the sixth-century King Aonghus – her ill-fated love for an English lord inspired the legend of Tristan and Iseult (or Isolde). It was demolished in the late 17th century – ironically, another period during which Dublin's medieval defences were hindering its "modern" development. Its foundations lay buried until discovered during excavations for the soulless bank of apartments in whose bowels they skulk on today's Exchange Street Lower. As Dublin City Council does not control the site, its hands have been tied in arresting its deterioration – the "exhibit" is regularly blocked by wheelie bins, and a thoughtful set of railings designed

by artist Grace Weir has been allowed to rust. The tower itself is regularly flooded. Sigh!

# THE RIVER PODDLE

Wellington Quay, Dublin 2
• Transport: Tara Street, DART station (15-min. walk); Luas, Jervis Street (Red Line; 5–10-min. walk); Dublin Bus stops 312 and 1479 are nearby on the quays

*Dublin's underground river*

The River Liffey is Dublin's iconic waterway, flowing through the city centre and cleaving apart its great north–south divide. But there are other rivers coursing through the cityscape, including one running almost entirely underground: the River Poddle.

The best way to catch a glimpse of Dublin's shyest river is to stand on the boardwalk at Ormond Quay. Looking across the Liffey towards Wellington Quay, you'll make out a small arched opening in the quay wall, guarded by a murky, weed-strewn gate. This is the main outfall for the Poddle and is best viewed at low tide, when you get the full effect of its trickle emerging from the tunnel. The Poddle wasn't always hidden, of course. In medieval times, the river formed the moat around Dublin Castle, converging with the Liffey in a tidal pool at the site of today's Dubh Linn Gardens. This "black pool" is where the Vikings are likely to have moored their ships, and of course, it gave the city its name. Rising in Cookstown and flowing through Tempelogue and Kimmage before it hit the medieval city centre, the Poddle was an important source of fresh water for the developing city, and its estuary (which would have covered the area around Crane Lane and Essex Street in today's Temple Bar) remained a feature of the cityscape until it first began to be filled and culverted in the early 17th century.

This twisting, turning subterranean river is central to Dublin's heritage and lore. In 1592 it aided Red Hugh O'Donnell's escape from Dublin Castle. The Poddle is also believed to be the same "River Sáile" from the ballad made famous by The Dubliners. "Salach" is an Irish word meaning "dirty", which would have been a good description of the river before it was fully enclosed during the 18th and 19th centuries. Today, fully 4km of the river is culverted, and though not publicly accessible, you can follow its course above ground from Ship Street to Palace Street, where it bifurcates, with one channel passing under the Olympia Theatre, before reuniting once again to exit the brick tunnel at Wellington Quay.

# GUITAR, RORY GALLAGHER CORNER ❹

Temple Bar, Dublin 2
• Transport: Tara Street DART station (5–10-min. walk); Dublin Bus stop
312 is nearby on Wellington Quay

> *It's got
> a kind
> of tattoo quality
> about it ...*

**B**lues legend Rory Gallagher (1948–95)
inspired huge devotion, both during
his life and after. In fact, were you
so inclined, you could undertake a Rory
Gallagher-themed tour of the country. Think
of the bronze statue and tribute festivals in his
hometown of Ballyshannon, Co. Donegal, his
grave in Ballincollig, Co. Cork, or Crowley's Music Centre – where Gallagher
bought his famous Fender Stratocaster, a 1961 Sunburst model that was
reputedly the first in Ireland.

That Stratocaster has since been retired by Rory's brother, Donal Gallagher,
but you can find a copy of it in a rather unusual place: attached to the wall
on the corner of Meeting House Square and Essex Street in Temple Bar. The
intersection here has been known as Rory Gallagher Corner since the area was
developed, but it wasn't until the mid-noughties that a planning application
was lodged on behalf of Dublin's music equipment stores to erect a memorial
to the Donegal musician. Dublin City Council gave its blessing in 2006, and
despite fears that the corner would become a shrine for fans who couldn't resist
showering it with graffiti, it's been respected ever since.

The original guitar is almost as famous as the bluesman himself. Gallagher
picked his Fender (serial no. 64351) second-hand after its first owner – a
showband guitarist – returned it because he had ordered red. "It was in good
condition when I bought it, but it's got so battered now it's got a kind of tattoo
quality about it," Gallagher later said. "There's now a theory that the less paint
or varnish on a guitar, acoustic or electric, the better. The wood breathes more.
But it's all psychological. I just like the sound of it." The Strat was stolen from
the back of a tour van in 1961 (the theft featured on RTÉ's *Garda Patrol*), but
despite lying abandoned in a ditch for days, it suffered no lasting damage.

According to Gallagher's official website, the guitar's wear and tear
(faithfully reproduced in bronze on this Temple Bar street corner) was partly
due to the high acidic content of its owner's rare blood group. "So when Rory
sweated on stage – and he sweated buckets – it was like paint stripper."

Fender has since made a tribute model of the priceless instrument.

# CITY HALL MURALS

City Hall, Dame Street, Dublin 2
- 01 222-2204
- www.dublincity.ie/dublincityhall
- Open: Mon–Sat 10am–5.15pm
- Admission: free
- Transport: Tara Street DART station (10-min. walk); Dublin Bus stop 1934 is on Dame Street nearby

*A hidden history of Dublin*

Most cities tell their stories in words. And Lord knows, Dublin – one of a handful of UNESCO Cities of Literature – is no slouch in that regard. But did you know that its story is told in pictures too? Step into the rotunda of City Hall and look up. As your eyes adapt to the light, you'll make out 12 panels under the ornate dome depicting historic scenes and the heraldic arms of the provinces.

The murals, measuring about 2.5x1.2m, were proposed by James Ward in 1913. Ward was head of the Dublin Metropolitan School of Art and he saw the project as a way to gain some hands-on experience for his students. Permission was granted by Dublin Corporation with the proviso that the subject matter relate to the history of the city (which it did). Eight, now slightly murky, figurative panels portray key legends and scenes from Dublin's past. In "Irishmen oppose the landing of the Viking fleet 841AD", for example, a stoic central figure rallies his troops as Scandinavian longships approach. "Brian Boru addressing his army before the Battle of Clontarf 1014AD" stresses Ireland's Catholic heritage. It depicts Boru on horseback, bearing a small crucifix with a milky-hued Jesus slumped on its wood. Boru himself looks like Gandalf the White.

All the subjects are medieval, which doubtless protected them from political controversy at the time, but they are of course open to interpretation. It's easy to see struggles with Viking invaders, for instance, as echoing the conflicts under English rule. City Hall is no Sistine Chapel, but the more you absorb yourself in the murals, the more layers they reveal ... even if Ward's students didn't always feel the same way. Indeed, a young Harry Clarke – as Philip McEvansoneya wrote in *The Irish Arts Review* – is said to have grown "heartily sick" of the tedious and time-consuming nature of the work.

City Hall was built between 1769 and 1779 as the Royal Exchange – a financial hub for the city's merchants. Dublin Corporation purchased the building in 1851 and it went on to host the funerals of Charles Stewart Parnell and Michael Collins, among others – even doing a stint as temporary HQ of the Irish Provisional Government. In the vaults, you'll find "The Story of the Capital", an interactive exhibition tracing the history of the city from Viking and Norman times to the present day.

# LADY JUSTICE

**6**

Dublin Castle, Dublin 2
• Transport: Tara Street DART station (10–15-min. walk); Luas,
St Stephen's Green (Green Line; 5-min. walk); Dublin Bus stop 1934 is
nearby

*Justice
is blind ...
or is it?*

L ady Justice has some very simple symbolism to get right. Personifying justice, she must hold a sword and a balanced set of scales representing truth and fairness. She should face the people. And she is often blindfolded, representing her impartiality and her ability to make judgments without regard for class, wealth or identity.

So why does Dublin's old dear get it so wrong? Standing atop the entrance to Dublin Castle's upper yard off Castle Street, just beside the 18th-century Bedford Tower, Lady Justice shows her back to the city. Her eyes are wide open. Look closely and you may even notice that her scales are tipped ever-so-slightly to one side.

The statue has been controversial, it turns out, ever since John Van Nost sculpted it at the behest of the British authorities in 1751. "The Lady Justice, consider her station, her face to the castle, her arse to the nation," is the popular saying. And while the leaning scales may be explained by rain dripping down

the statue's arm into one of the pans, there's a rather delicious irony in the fact that they lean towards the side of the castle housing the tax offices, as the excellent city blog Come Here To Me (comeheretome.com) points out. Nor will it be lost on Dubliners that Lady Justice looks over both the historic centre of administration in the city, and the site of the famous tribunals of inquiry into corrupt payments to politicians.

Perhaps her smile shows a little more insight and wisdom than she is credited with.

## SICK & INDIGENT ROOMKEEPERS' SOCIETY ❼

2 Palace Street, Dublin 2
- 01 667-6213
- www.roomkeepers.com
- Transport: Tara Street DART station (10–15-min. walk); Luas, St Stephen's Green (Green Line; 15-min. walk); Dublin Bus stops 1934, 1935 and 2003 are nearby

> **Dublin's oldest surviving charity**

The late 1700s may have been a golden age for architecture in Dublin, but they also saw some desperate poverty and squalor – with countless families in the inner city crammed into appalling conditions rife with filth, disease and little prospect of improvement.

The Sick & Indigent Roomkeepers' Society was established in 1790 to alleviate the plight of Dubliners who had fallen ill or become destitute through no fault of their own. In the absence of a system of public welfare, this motley crew of concerned citizens – including grocers, a schoolmaster, a stonecutter, a carpenter and a pawnbroker in their ranks – developed a fund to relieve "the honest poor", as *The Irish Times* later termed them, providing temporary aid in the form of fuel, rent, tools or equipment. It was a successful initiative, with donations swelling to the point where it became one of the leading charities of the 19th century – organising balls, temperance picnics and, in 1855, moving into these striking premises, set just a few metres from the pedestrian entrance to Dublin Castle on Palace Street.

The building itself is a Georgian gem, the only surviving 18th-century structure on the street (apart from the castle gate), and one with a knack for surprising Dubliners who stumble across it. Although the charity vacated No. 2 for smaller offices on Leeson Street in the late 1990s, its name remains emblazoned in bold and quirky letters across the facade, striking a contrasting note to the cosy Chez Max bistro tucked away beside it. As well as its charitable history, the house is a former home of Irish State physician Robert Emmet, whose son and namesake was executed after a failed rebellion in 1803. The British military occupied it in 1921, and recently, its unusual appeal was echoed in the name of Americana-influenced Dublin band, The Sick and Indigent Song Club.

The Sick & Indigent Roomkeepers' Society is the oldest surviving charity in the city, although operations have scaled back significantly since its heyday. In recent years, No. 2 has been home to architectural historian Peter Pearson and actor, playwright and producer Daniel Reardon.

# STAG'S HEAD MOSAIC

Dame Court, Dame Street, Dublin 2
• 01 679-3687
• www.louisfitzgerald.com (Stag's Head)
• Transport: Tara Street DART station (5–10-min. walk); Luas, St Stephen's Green (Green Line; 5–10-min. walk); Dublin Bus stops 1358 and 1278 are nearby

*You couldn't buy advertising like it*

As welcome mats go, this is rather special. Strolling along Dame Street, look down as you pass the covert little alleyway opposite the Central Bank. A colourful mosaic of a stag's head is set into the pavement, with a stark black arrow directing you towards Dame Court. Follow that arrow down the rabbit hole and you'll end up at the Stag's Head pub.

Although there have been taverns on this street corner since the late 1700s, the Stag's Head dates in its current form from 1895, when businessman George Tyson planned a Victorian pub that might compare favourably "with the best establishments of its kind either in London or any other part of England," as Turtle Bunbury writes in *The Irish Pub* (Thames & Hudson). Its regular customers – a motley mix of blow-ins, Trinity College students, theatre types and suits from the nearby stock exchange – would surely agree that he succeeded. Behind the redbrick façade lies a gorgeously opulent time capsule, with an original Aberdeen granite bar, studded banquettes, bevelled mirrors, ancient whiskey casks, a whispery snug (the old Victorian "Smoke Room") and mahogany panelling all contributing atmospherics. Oh, and just in case you need reminding of where you are, there's a colossal stag's head mounted over the main bar, and several colourful animals set into the pub's stained glass panels and lamps.

The Stag's Head has its stories, of course – like the time Quentin Tarantino is said to have been refused service for pulling rank. He wasn't the only Hollywood star to visit – *Educating Rita* (1983) and *A Man of No Importance* (1994) were filmed here too. The pub has even featured on a postage stamp.

The original Dame Street mosaic was removed for refurbishment in the early noughties, prompting an outcry from those who noticed. Thankfully, it has since been returned to its rightful place, though eagle-eyed Dubliners might notice that it is now a little further from the alley and the "wrong" way round. The none-too-subtle arrow is also a new addition. The alley is as grotty as the pub is grand (you can skip the puke and pee by taking the long way around via South Great George's Street), but let's not quibble over minor details. There's gold at the end of the rainbow, however you get there.

'*I like to pay taxes. With them I buy civilization.*'

Oliver Wendell Holmes Jr

'*Is maith liom cánacha a íoc. Ceannaím sibhialtacht leo.*'

Oliver Wendell Holmes Jr

# REVENUE MUSEUM

Dublin Castle, Dublin 2
• 01 863-5601 • www.revenue.ie
• Open: Mon–Fri 10am–4pm • Admission: free
• Transport: Tara Street DART station (10–15-min. walk); Luas, St Stephen's Green (Green Line; 5-min. walk); Dublin Bus stop 1934 is nearby

> *They were not received with joy*

Two things are certain in life: death and taxes. And while Dublin doesn't have a museum dedicated to the former, it does have one for the latter – hidden away behind the chapel at Dublin Castle. A revenue museum may sound like a dull proposition, but it's a surprisingly absorbing visit – and unlike the subjects of its displays, it won't cost you a penny.

Inside, a series of moodily lit cases traces the history of Irish tax collection back into the annals (some of Ireland's earliest written records – as in many countries – concern the collection of taxes and duties). Income tax was first introduced by Gladstone's government in 1853, but there have been all manner of charges down through the ages – from stamp duty to customs and excise levies, VAT and even a hearth tax, introduced in 1664 in the form of a two shilling charge on every hearth in a dwelling. Window tax followed in the early 1800s, famously prompting many poorer households to install half-doors in an effort to circumvent a charge they dubbed "daylight robbery". Needless to say, those tasked with collecting taxes have faced their fair share of hostility as a result, and the museum also gives a sense of the camaraderie shared by Revenue employees. One display, discussing the illegal distilling of poitín, describes the large numbers of police dispatched to the wilds of Donegal and Mayo, where "they were not received with joy". It's a beautiful little understatement.

Other highlights include an 18th-century chest used to convey taxes and duties, a burnt book rescued from the Custom House fire of 1922, a case of counterfeit goods (including remarkably good copies of Timberland boots, Durex condoms and a Burberry handbag) and the first-ever set of accounts published by Ireland's Revenue Commissioners, for the year ended 31 March 1923. The handwriting is impeccably neat, evoking the "dextrous drafters/of sub-sections, pluggers of loopholes;/custodians of the frosted public hatches" described so memorably by another revenue man, the poet Dennis O'Driscoll.

"One of life's little certainties is taxation," as one dispiriting display quips. Though there are two sides to every story, as a very personable museum attendant will tell you. "It's pretty handy all the same to have the guards and nurses," he winks.

## CHESTER BEATTY ROOF GARDEN ⑩

Chester Beatty Library, Dublin Castle, Dublin 2
• 01 407-0750
• www.cbl.ie
• Open: March – Oct: Mon–Fri 10am–5pm, Sat 11am–5pm, Sun 1pm–
5pm. Nov – Feb: Tues–Sat 10am–5pm, Sat 11am–5pm, Sun 1pm–5pm
(Closed Mondays)
• Admission: free
• Transport: Tara Street DART station (10–15-min. walk); Luas, Stephen's
Green (Green Line; 5-min. walk); Dublin Bus stop 1934 is nearby

**An oasis of calm in the city centre**

Understandably for a city that is rained upon so often, Dublin doesn't really "do" roof gardens. That's not to say roof gardens are not "done", of course – as this peachy patch atop the Chester Beatty Library in Dublin Castle attests.

The rooftop garden is an oasis of calm in a busy city centre. Split into a series of different surfaces – gravel, ornamental grasses, stone and hardwood – the small space commands some lovely views over the Dubh Linn Gardens below, and the sprawl of Dublin Castle beyond. Freely accessible through the museum (though backpacks, food and cameras must be checked), its close-knit timber trellises give the feeling as much of a fancy backyard as a rooftop

project. The plants creeping up these wooden barriers are slowly transforming them into green walls, though the carefully positioned "windows" will remain, preserving the bird's-eye views over the cityscape. Creative use of indigenous materials creates the overall sense of a contemporary Irish garden, but there's also a Japanese feel to the layout, with its emphasis on harmony and lack of a single dominating feature. Wisteria, silver birch, honeysuckle, bamboo, clematis and heather are just some of the plants adding colour. It's the perfect setting for the Library's Qigong classes, too!

Beneath this rooftop oasis lies Dublin's most under-appreciated museum. The Chester Beatty may be "one of the finest small museums in the world", according to the Washington Post, but locals have been slower to give it a go. Step inside the door, however, and you're hooked. Beatty's collection of manuscripts, prints, icons, miniatures, early printed books and objets d'art is considered the most valuable gift ever given to the Irish nation, with Chinese jade books, dragon robes worn by emperors, papyrus gospels dating from AD 150, clay tablets from Babylon and the earliest known copies of the Book of Revelation just some of the highlights. Throw in a surprising menu of Middle Eastern food at the Silk Road Café, not to mention a beautifully airy atrium, and you have the makings of a very interesting afternoon.

# OUR LADY OF DUBLIN

**⓫**

Whitefriar Street Church (original) & St Mary's Abbey (replica)
56 Aungier Street, Dublin 2
• 01 475-8821 • www.carmelites.ie
• Open: Mon–Fri 8am–6pm, Sun 8am–7.30pm • Admission: free
• Transport: Tara Street DART station (20-min. walk); Luas, Harcourt
Street (Green Line; 10-min. walk); Dublin Bus stop 1354 is close to the
church on Aungier Street

*The Black
Madonna
of Dublin*

The Church of Our Lady of Mount Carmel ("Whitefriar" stems from the white cloaks worn by the Carmelites, who were first recorded here in 1274) is home to a fascinating collection of shrines and memorabilia. Most fascinating of all is that dedicated to Our Lady of Dublin.

At its heart is a 16th-century oak statue of the Virgin Mary and the Infant Jesus, its blackened colour offset by an explosion of golden mosaic tiles and white marble. The statue is originally believed to have belonged to St Mary's Abbey, a wealthy Cistercian monastery that played a central role in the affairs of the State until its dissolution under Henry VIII. A statue of the Madonna comparable to some of the contemporary pieces at Westminster Abbey's Henry VII Chapel is said to have held pride of place in the abbey's church (a replica can be seen today in the Chapter House on Meetinghouse Lane). When St Mary's was surrendered, tradition has it that the statue was disguised as a pig trough in a nearby inn yard to avoid detection. This isn't as unlikely as it sounds: statues of the period were commonly hollowed-out to reduce their weight and prevent warping and splitting of the wood.

The mysterious Madonna next found a home in a chapel on St Mary's Lane, as the story goes, before making its way to a second-hand shop on Capel Street. There, it was spotted by the Carmelite, Fr John Spratt, and brought to Whitefriar Street in 1824. The statue is said to be the only one of its kind in Dublin to have escaped destruction following the Reformation, although Our Lady's jewel-bedecked headpiece was not part of the purchase – the original silver crown ("a double-arched crown such as appears on the coins of Henry VII") is believed to have been sold and melted down.

As well as its many shrines, Whitefriar Street Church houses several displays in its entrance corridor, including the story of Noel Purcell's famous words, uttered to a Carmelite priest as he lay on his deathbed at the Adelaide Hospital: "Tell the Gaffer that Purcell is ready when He is."

# ST VALENTINE'S RELICS & THE BLESSING OF THE RINGS  ⑫

Whitefriar Street Church, 56 Aungier Street, Dublin 2
• 01 475-8821
• www.carmelites.ie
• Open: Mon–Fri 8am–6pm, Sun 8am–7.30pm
• Admission: free
• Transport: Dublin Bus stop 4456 is at the Carmelite priory on Aungier Street

> *Love's final resting place*

**Y**ou can look for love anywhere, but the odds of finding it are that bit higher at a rather unexpected location: the Church of Our Lady of Mount Carmel. Better known as the Whitefriar Street Church, one of its shrines contains a life-size statue of a saint, together with his relics.

His name? St Valentine.

The brass inscription is beautifully matter-of-fact. "This shrine contains the sacred body of Saint Valentinus the Martyr," it reads. "Together with a small vessel tinged with his blood." The relics are contained in a small wooden box tied with a red silk ribbon and sealed with wax. The box is contained within a casket bearing the papal coat of arms of Gregory XVI. The casket is contained within a glass display in a marble alcove. The inner box remains unopened.

So how did St Valentine end up in Dublin? In 1835 John Spratt paid a visit to Rome. The Irish Carmelite's reputation as a preacher preceded him, so when he spoke at the famous Church of the Gesù, the elite of Rome flocked to hear him and offer tokens of their esteem. Intriguingly, one such token came from Pope Gregory XVI himself: the remains of St Valentine. The remains had been "taken out of the cemetery of St Hippolytus in the Tiburtine Way," according to a plaque on the casket, and they arrived in Dublin on 10 November 1836. Although placed in storage for a time after Fr Spratt's death, a shrine was constructed in the 1950s, complete with a carved statue of the saint.

Today's shrine is found in a little alcove to the right of the altar. Above it you'll see a spiral-bound notebook in which visitors can write their petitions. "Thank you for helping Natalie and I sort out our troubles," reads one, with a smiley-face after the name. "I'm never going to let her go. I love her forever and ever." Other entries ask St Valentine to bless their families, to help couples looking for a home and to intercede for lonely souls in their search for company.

On St Valentine's Day, couples are also welcome to attend a ceremony that includes a blessing of rings. Every 14 February, the reliquary is removed from the shrine and placed before the high altar; afterwards, you can buy a little souvenir at the shop by the entrance.

# GAIETY THEATRE HAND PRINTS

**⓭**

South King Street, off Grafton Street, Dublin 2
- 01 679-5622
- www.gaietytheatre.ie
- Transport: Tara Street DART station (10–15-min. walk); Luas, St Stephen's Green (Green Line); Dublin Bus stops 790, 791 and 5034 are nearby on St Stephen's Green and Dawson Street

*Stars in the sidewalk*

**M**ost visitors to the Gaiety are looking at the stars, so they could be forgiven for missing the array of plaques at their feet. Cast in bronze outside the theatre's Venetian façade, the collection of handprints is a who's-who of performers, including Luciano Pavarotti, Brian Friel, Peter Ustinov, Bernadette Greevy and John B. Keane … all of whom have graced the famous stage.

Like a souvenir-sized version of the collection at Grauman's Chinese Theatre in Hollywood, the handprints are a strangely endearing memento of the celebs they celebrate. The shiny, tactile prints almost invite you to stoop down, try your own paws for size and wriggle your fingers about in the cool, bronze indentations. It's far more personal than your standard stars in the sidewalk.

Pavarotti's prints are the *coup de grâce*. The Italian legend first sang here in 1963, during a Dublin Grand Opera Society performance of *Rigoletto*. He went on to become a star at Covent Garden, of course, but on South King Street, Pavarotti was "just another good young kid on the block making his way," as Opera Ireland archivist Paddy Brennan recalled after the tenor's death in 2007 – revealing that the great man joined a theatre troupe for a kickabout in Phoenix Park. "He was a bloody great footballer," Brennan told *The Irish Independent*. "He was a big man … but as a young fellow, he had legs like a ballet dancer." Pavarotti's hands were cast for posterity in 2001.

Since her own opening night on 27 November 1871, the Grand Old Lady has been one of Dublin's best-known and most beautiful theatre spaces. A populist programme of opera, ballet, dance, drama, pantos and musicals has been taken to heart by Dubliners, providing a playful complement to the more literary fare of the Gate and Abbey theatres. The handprints of Irish stars like Maureen Potter, Twink, Niall Toibín, Ronnie Drew, Milo O'Shea, Des Keogh and Rosaleen Linehan take pride of place on the pavement outside, but even international stars realise the generosity of the tribute.

"Well, I'm immortal," as Rupert Everett said, leaving his handprints after *The Judas Kiss* in 2012. "Everyday it rains on Dublin, I'll be able to think about it raining onto my little hands …"

# ST KEVIN'S PARK

**⓮**

Camden Row, Dublin 8
• 01 661-2369
• www.dublincity.ie
• Open: Daylight hours
• Admission: free
• Transport: Tara Street DART station (20-min. walk); Luas, Charlemont or Harcourt Street (Green Line; 5-min. walk); Dublin Bus stops 1285 and 1353 are nearby on Wexford Street

> *The perfect place to bring a book ... or a body-snatcher*

**D**ublin has its well-known parks and its lesser-known parks.

St Kevin's is definitely one of the latter, a leafy little oasis set in a former churchyard off Wexford Street. It's a gorgeous little pocket of peace, no more than a stone's throw from the perky pubs, venues and restaurants of Wexford Street. The snoozing local or office worker spotted here with a book or a sandwich always looks like the cat that got the cream.

Though St Kevin's is a small park, it's not that tiny – there's plenty of space for strolling and sitting along the lawns and pathways under its ash, yew, birch and elder trees. At its heart is the shell of an 18th-century church where Arthur Wellesley, the first Duke of Wellington, is said to have been baptised – though the only new life in evidence today is hidden away in the thatch of ivy covering its limestone, where birds nest and late summer and autumn flowers provide nectar for bees, butterflies and wasps. Indeed, 19 bird and three bat species have been spotted here, according to Dublin City Council's Parks Division.

In spite of the teeming wildlife, the park's cemetery contains plenty of death. By now, most of its gravestones have been stacked upright against perimeter walls, but several of the more prominent examples remain in situ, including that of Thomas Moore's family. In the church, a secret grave is said to mark the burial place of Archbishop Dermot O'Hurley, a religious figure hanged for treason in 1584 after enduring horrific torture. A memorial at the south-east corner of the building goes into some detail: "[This] included roasting the archbishop's legs in two boots filled with boiling pitch and oil." Perhaps O'Hurley is resting more easily since his beatification by Pope John Paul II in 1992.

Like many old city cemeteries, St Kevin's was targeted by body-snatchers – opportunistic grave robbers who stole freshly buried corpses to supply city medical schools in the decades leading up to the Anatomy Act of 1831. Rumour has it that the souls whose headstones were rearranged have stayed to haunt the place.

# IVEAGH GARDENS ⓯

Clonmel Street, off Harcourt Street, Dublin 2 (main entrance)
• 01 475-7816
• www.iveaghgardens.ie
• Open: Mon–Sat 8am, Sun & Bank Holidays 10am. Gates close at 3.30pm (Dec & Jan), 4pm (Nov & Feb), 6pm (March–Oct)
• Admission: free
• Transport: Transport: Luas (Green Line) stops at Stephen's Green nearby

T hey're just a few hundred yards from Stephen's Green. In summer, they host concerts attended by thousands. The dogs on the street know them. Yet somehow, the Iveagh Gardens remain one of Dublin's best-kept secrets.

> *One of Dublin's best-kept secrets*

Why? One answer is their invisibility. Though not much smaller than Stephen's Green, the gardens' access points are well hidden – through small gates stashed away behind the National Concert Hall, on Hatch Street, and behind an old house on Clonmel Street, for example. Wander off the beaten track, however, and you're soon rewarded with a gorgeous and leafy arrangement of sunken lawns and set pieces – from waterfalls and fountains to short, squirrel-spotted woodland walks, rockeries, a rustic grotto and cascade, a rosarium whose collection dates back over 150 years, and a sundial within a souvenir-sized yew maze … all less than five minutes on foot from Grafton Street.

The Iveagh Gardens began life as part of "Leeson's Fields", an uncultivated swathe of land fanning out south of the mansion once owned by the wealthy Leeson family. After Harcourt Street was laid out in the late 18th century, the Earl of Clonmell bought 11 acres of the fields as a garden for his house

(today's No. 17) – a subterranean passage built between house and gardens is still believed to exist. The gardens fell in and out of favour while leased for public use in the early 19th century, before being bought by Benjamin Lee Guinness as a garden for his townhouse (Iveagh House, on Stephen's Green), and transformed into their current layout by landscape gardener Ninian Niven ahead of the Great Exhibition of 1865.

A subsequent Lord Iveagh gifted them to the Irish state and, thankfully, any temptation to build on this lovely city "lung" has been resisted. To this day, trivia fans may be tickled to know that the sunken lawn remains the only purpose-built archery ground in the country.

## IRISH JEWISH MUSEUM

**16**

3 Walworth Road, Dublin 8
• 01 453-1797 • www.jewishmuseum.ie
• Open: May–Sept: Tues, Thurs & Sun 11am–3pm. Oct–April: Sun 10.30am–2.30pm. Group bookings by arrangement
• Admission: free
• Transport: Luas (Green Line) stops at Charlemont Place and Harcourt Street, both a 10–15-min. walk away. Several Dublin Bus routes stop at nearby Richmond Street South and Rathmines Road Lower

*Portobello was once known as "Little Jerusalem"*

Ireland's Jewish community reached its peak in the 1940s, with some 5,000 members. Today, that number has fallen to around 1,500, according to an Irish Jewish Museum that provides a fusty but fascinating insight into their heritage in the heart of Portobello. Wentworth Road, with its Victorian redbricks, feels like an unlikely location for a museum – but Portobello was once known as "Little Jerusalem" and hummed with synagogues, schools, homes and kosher businesses (the Bretzel Bakery survives on nearby Lennox Street, albeit under new management). At No. 3, a modest red doorway bears an intercom that visitors are invited to "Please Ring": inside, you'll find a ground floor crammed with display cases and a restored, first-floor synagogue strewn

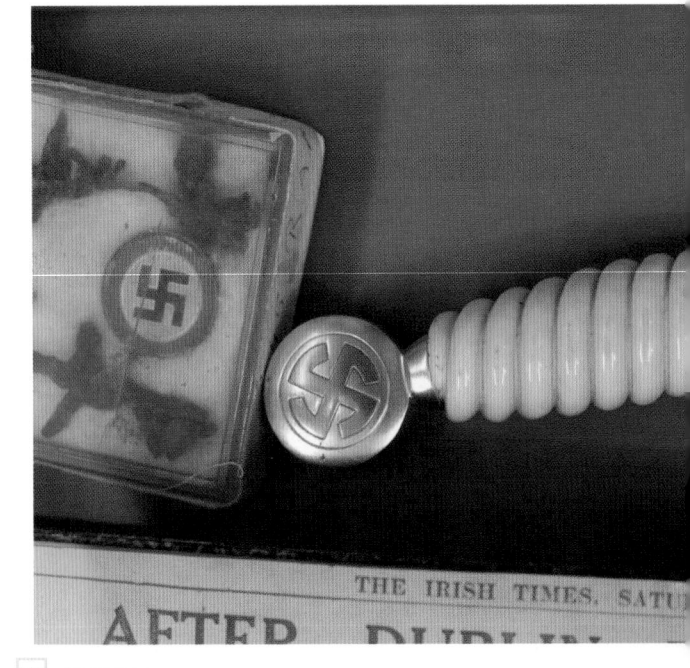

with ark covers and Torah scrolls. At first, it all feels a bit stuffy and dated, but the more moseying and nosing about you do, the more intimate it becomes. A curator's letter welcoming visitors dates from 1989. Yellowing election posters, photographs and news clippings recall well-known Dublin politicians like Robert Briscoe and his son Ben, or Mervyn Taylor. There are identity cards, mementos of old Jewish businesses, a wooden Victorian shopping basket and a recreated kitchen – complete with two separate sinks and draining boards for meat and dairy. A display devoted to James Joyce's *Ulysses* also highlights the fact that Leopold Bloom was a Jew, born on Upper Clanbrassil Street.

A case of World War II artefacts makes a deep impression. Among other items, it contains a yellow Star of David arm patch; a copy of the marriage certificate of Ester Steinberg, the only known Irish victim of the Holocaust; pieces of bomb shrapnel recovered from the damaged Greenville Hall Synagogue; and a Nazi dagger with brass swastika and ivory handle. On closer inspection, this chilling keepsake turns out to bear a hopeful inscription – as an accompanying *Irish Times* article explains. It was gifted to the museum by Moris Block, a Jewish Dubliner who served with the British Army and spent the final days of the war in Dusseldorf. There, he helped three German Jews who had spent much of the war hiding in a basement, and one of them inscribed the dagger as a thank-you. "To my friend Moris Block in memory A Fischmann", it reads, alongside a Star of David dated 1945.

**hopeful**

A curious inscription
displayed in a Dublin
Jewish brotherhood a
trauma of the Holoca

JANUARY 4. 1941.

Upstairs in the Irish-Jewish Mus

# IRISH MARBLE PANELS

**17**

Dept of Justice & Equality, 51 St Stephen's Green, Dublin 2
• 01 674-4999
• www.justice.ie
• Open: Office hours
• Admission: free
• Transport: Pearse Street DART station (5–10-min. walk); Dublin Bus
stops 843 and 844 are close to No. 51 St Stephen's Green East

*Rock 'n' Roll at the Department of Justice*

I f you're you're looking for justice, 51 St Stephen's Green may or may not deliver. If you're looking for a surprise collection of Irish marble, on the other hand, then the lobby of the Department of Justice and Equality comes through every time.

The building itself sits on the site of the 17th-century residence of the Monck family. It was rebuilt around 1760 by George Paul Monck, as an information handout explains (Rocque's maps of 1756 and 1773 describe this side of the Green as Monks' Walk). In the early 1800s it came to be known as the Lord Chancellor's House after it was acquired by Lord Mannors, a former Lord Chancellor of Ireland. In 1848, 51 St Stephen's Green was purchased by the government and turned into a Museum of Irish Industry, and it's from this period that the 40 samples of Irish marble in the lobby appear to date. They arrived thanks to museum director Sir Robert Kane, who wished "to promote the commercial potential of Ireland's quarries and natural resources", as Mary Mulvihill wrote in her offbeat guide to the city, *Ingenious Ireland*.

The range of colours used in the panels is quietly breathtaking and certainly succeeds in showcasing the variety of Irish stone. Not all of it is marble, however. There are sleek black samples from Kilkenny, evocative of night skies pinpricked with stars. There is pale green Connemara marble, rippling with the echoes of ancient geological forces. But fully 34 of the panels are in fact polished limestone. The secret is out ...

# HUGUENOT CEMETERY

**(18)**

27 St Stephen's Green, Dublin 2
• Transport: Pearse Street DART station (10 min. walk); Luas, St Stephen's Green (5 min. walk); Dublin Bus stop 768 is directly outside the Huguenot cemetery on Merrion Row

*A surprise cemetery ...*

**M**errion Row is a short strip of prime Dublin real estate, stretching from the Shelbourne Hotel at one end to Doheny & Nesbitt's pub at the other. That's why, hemmed in between two modern office buildings, it's such a surprise to find a gate bearing the inscription: "Huguenot Cemetery, 1693". Beyond the gate, colourful trees drip down over the decaying headstones. In spring, the plots are covered in a carpet of bluebells, making the city-centre scene even more unlikely.

The Huguenots were French Protestants who fled their country after the Edict of Nantes (1598) was revoked in 1685. The edict had promoted a more tolerant approach by a Catholic country to Calvinists and other minority religious communities, but was rolled back by Louis XIV, prompting an exodus. Sensing an opportunity, James Butler, the first Duke of Ormonde and Lord Lieutenant of Ireland, extended an invitation, hoping that Ireland's economy would benefit from Huguenot skills and industry. This it did, as new arrivals quickly became a dynamic community in Dublin. Settling in the Liberties, they soon enjoyed commercial success in textiles, finance, wine importation, watch-making and other businesses, supplemented by a reputation for integrity ... as attested by the saying, "As honest as a Huguenot".

The cemetery became a designated French burial ground in 1693. Its gates are now closed to visitors, but it's so small you can see everything through the railings anyway, including the inscriptions on several graves, and a large marble panel naming 240 or so souls buried within – if not quite from A to Z, then at least from Afée to Plantier de Montvert. Du Bédat is a name that crops up in James Joyce's *Ulysses*. "Wouldn't mind being a waiter in a swell hotel," Bloom daydreams. "Tips, evening dress, halfnaked ladies. May I tempt you to a little more filleted lemon sole, miss Dubedat? Yes, do bedad. And she did bedad. Huguenot name I expect that." Though Joyce would certainly have been familiar with the cemetery, it's hard to say if this plot inspired that particular rumination, however. There are Du Bedat tombs in Mount Jerome also.

The Huguenot cemetery closed in 1901. After falling into ruin in the 1980s, it was restored by the French Ministry of Foreign Affairs and is today cared for by Dublin City Council. Before you leave, check the inscription, where Huguenot is misspelled as "Hughenot". Joycean pun or stonemason's mistake?

# THE SHELBOURNE HOTEL MUSEUM ⓳

27 St Stephen's Green, Dublin 2
- 01 663-4500
- www.theshelbourne.com
- Open: Restricted to hotel guests and customers
- Transport: Pearse Street DART station (10-min. walk); Luas, St Stephen's Green (5-min. walk); Dublin Bus stop 768 is directly outside the Huguenot cemetery on Merrion Row

*A secret museum*

The Shelbourne Hotel is one of Dublin's *grand dame* institutions, a sparkling old Georgian building on the corner of St Stephen's Green. That much is obvious.

The history hidden within these walls is more of a mystery. Sure, we all know that the Irish Constitution was drafted here in 1922, in Room 112, under the chairmanship of Michael Collins. You may also know that Peter O'Toole once famously bathed in champagne at the hotel and that celebrity guests have ranged from Charlie Chaplin to JFK and the Rolling Stones. But were you aware that, squirrelled away in a corner of the reception lobby, there is a tiny museum dedicated to its history?

The museum, which can be visited by guests of the hotel (or customers enjoying, say, afternoon tea in the Lord Mayor's Lounge, dinner in the Saddle Room or cocktails in the bar), is a small-but-perfectly-formed testament to some of the most famous moments in the Shelbourne's storied career. Check out the colour photograph of Princess Grace of Monaco in her salon, for instance – the pink flowers in her hair play effortlessly off an off-the-shoulder evening gown. Take a minute to inspect the original deeds of the hotel, which opened in 1824, and a draft copy of the Constitution. There are items of gleaming silverware, letters from guests including former Irish Taoiseach, Charles J. Haughey (when he signed off, in 1952, the future Taoiseach was a young accountant with Haughey, Boland & Guiney). There are shelves of fusty, leather-bound guest registers, and a spotless pair of white gloves is even provided, should modern-day guests wish to turn the pages and flick back through the years.

Food features prominently – there's a civilised eight-course menu from 1926, including "Jambon d'Irlande au Clicquot", for example. After enjoying the hotel's hospitality, not everybody went gently into the good night, however. A letter from the South African Rugby Tour of 1952 refers to a cheque for £716 enclosed "for damages of furniture incurred during the visit of the above Team to your hotel". Given what the Springboks do to opposing teams, one can only imagine what they did to the opulent interiors and tasteful furniture of this 19th-century establishment.

A small step is all it takes to pass from the inner sanctum of the hotel into this little glass time capsule. And all for the price of a cocktail …

# BEN DUNNE'S BULLETS

**20**

Little Museum of Dublin, 15 St Stephen's Green, Dublin 2
• 01 661-1000
• www.littlemuseum.ie
• Open: Mon–Sun 9.30am–5pm, Thurs 9.30am–8pm
• Admission: €8/€6
• Transport: Luas, St Stephen's Green (Green Line); Pearse/Tara Street DART stations (10–15-min. walk); Dublin Buses stopping nearby include 7b, 11, 116, 118, 14, 142, 145, 15 and 46a

**Thank God
I am free ...**

Hookers, cocaine, whizz business deals and payments to politicians ... Ben Dunne's life has had more ups and downs than a yo-yo in a lift. But surely nothing in the straight-talking entrepreneur's chequered career could compare with the events of 16 October 1981.

On that day, Dunne was on his way to open a new Dunnes Stores in Northern Ireland when he was seized by four masked gunmen and held prisoner for several days. The Irish Republican Army (IRA) demanded a ransom of £500,000, which it has been alleged (although not confirmed) his father, Ben Dunne Snr, paid to secure his release. The 34-year-old was eventually freed after television appeals and several meetings with the kidnappers by Fr Dermot McCarthy. Police on both sides of the Irish border sealed off escape routes in the area before Dunne was found outside a church on the border at Cullyhanna, Co. Armagh. "He was dishevelled, bearded and seemed to be quite roughed over, although not injured in any way," a Belfast reporter told the *Herald Tribune* at the time. "All he could say was 'Thank God I am free. You don't know how glad I am.'"

Before his release, on 22 October, two of Dunne's abductors handed him a couple of bullets, telling him that they could have been used on him and Fr McCarthy if the police had closed in. Afterwards, Dunne had the bullets mounted on a piece of stone from the Armagh cemetery where he had been held captive. They have since been donated to the Little Museum of Dublin, where you'll find them in a locked cabinet alongside a smorgasbord of other quirky artefacts from the city's 20th-century history – from rooms dedicated to U2 to a chunky old bus ticket machine.

Close by to Ben Dunne's bullets, look out for a facsimile of James Joyce's death mask. Joyce was 58 when he died in a Zurich hospital, following surgery for a perforated ulcer. The Irish government declined Nora Joyce's offer to permit the repatriation of his remains (Nora hit back by leaving his Finnegans Wake papers to the British Museum). Although you'll find another death mask at the Joyce Centre on Eccles Street, the author himself is buried in a grave in Fluntern Cemetery in Zurich.

GET THE
FULL FACTS?

REPEAL
SECTION 3

OF THE BROADCASTING A

Abbeville Honey, 1980s. Charles Haughey kept bees at his country house in Kinsealy. He gave jars of the honey they produced to family and friends... to keep them sweet!

SUNDAY BUSINESS POST

FINANCIAL, POLITICAL AND ECONOMIC NEWSPAPER

£260m
meat
plan
axed

# HAUGHEY'S HONEY POT

**㉑**

Little Museum of Dublin, 15 St Stephen's Green, Dublin 2
• 01 661-1000
• www.littlemuseum.ie
• Open: Mon–Sun 9.30am–5pm, Thurs 9.30am–8pm
• Admission: €8/€6
• Transport: Luas, St Stephen's Green (Green Line); Pearse/Tara Street
DART stations (10–15-min. walk); Dublin Buses stopping nearby include
7b, 11, 116, 118, 14, 142, 145, 15 and 46a

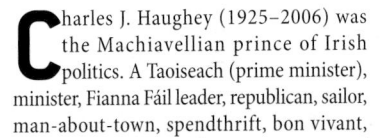

*A little
something
to keep them
sweet*

**C**harles J. Haughey (1925–2006) was the Machiavellian prince of Irish politics. A Taoiseach (prime minister), minister, Fianna Fáil leader, republican, sailor, man-about-town, spendthrift, bon vivant, phone-tapper, Charvet shirt-wearer, patron of the arts and brass-balled hypocrite who told Ireland it was living "way beyond [its] means" while himself enjoying a flash lifestyle way beyond his political salary – here was a personality as divisive as it was dominant over several decades in Irish politics.

"A consummate vote-getter, it was often said that he came from every county in Ireland," as we are told (he was actually born in Castlebar). "But he made his home in Dublin."

Millions of words have been written, and no small number of portraits painted, of a man who would have been a shoe-in as Ireland's most controversial 20th-century politician until the economic ground fell from beneath Irish feet in recent years. As is often the case with larger-than-life public figures, however, it's not the big books and TV series that get to the essence of C. J. Haughey. In many cases, it's the smaller things – such as this inconspicuous-looking jar of Abbeville honey, mounted in a glass case in the Little Museum of Dublin. Few people know that Haughey was an avid bee-keeper, collecting honey from the hives at Abbeville, his Georgian mansion in Kinsealy, Co. Dublin. Fewer still are aware that he made a habit of gifting that honey to family and friends in jars such as the one on display ..."to keep them sweet". Such a tiny jar, and yet it says so much.

The artefact – if you could call it that – was presented to the museum by Seán Haughey, son of the former Taoiseach, and it hangs in the middle of a wall jam-packed with Dublin lore. Other political items that catch the eye are Mary Robinson's poster from the 1990 presidential elections, a gift box from former Dublin Lord Mayor Alfie Byrne and Bertie Ahern's first election flyer from 1977. But few leave such a strong impression as the Haughey-related artefacts. As well as the honeypot, they include a monochrome portrait by Colman Doyle, and a painting that hung above Haughey's desk in Kinsealy for almost 40 years: "Think Big," it exhorts. Whatever else you think about the man, he certainly did that.

## ERIN & LUGH

22

Dept of Jobs, Enterprise & Innovation, 23 Kildare Street, Dublin 2
• Transport: Pearse Street DART station (5–10-min. walk); Luas, St
Stephen's Green (Green Line; 10-min. walk); Dublin Bus stops 746, 747
and 4350 are located on Kildare Street

*Art Deco
Dublin*

**D**ublin, it's fair to say, is not known for its Art Deco treasures. But here's a humdinger: "The most distinguished Government office building to be commissioned after the establishment of the Free State," as Christine Casey describes it in *Dublin* (Yale University Press, 2005).

Completed in 1942 to a design by J. R. Barrett, the steel-framed building, which originally housed the Department of Industry and Commerce, somehow manages to combine dramatic bas-reliefs, a five-storey window, domineering keystones, weighty bronze gates and a ministerial balcony without completely dominating its Georgian neighbours. The limestone reliefs are by Gabriel Hayes, who designed Ireland's old 1p and 2p coins, and they bring a touch of Soviet propaganda to the fledgling Irish state – featuring stoic men in profile, working hard with hammers, wrenches, wheels and shovels as they cobble, mill, craft and manufacture high up above the passers-by. The most impressive six-pack belongs to Lugh, who appears to be tossing planes from a lintel above the Kildare Street entrance. His angular nose has been chipped, though so strappingly is the Celtic god of light portrayed, you'd doubt he even noticed. Overlooking all of this, atop the five-storey window with its Art Deco glazing, is Erin – the female embodiment of Ireland and a stern-faced woman on a mission. Along with the keystone depicting Brendan the Navigator around the corner, she was carved in situ.

Sadly, members of the public are not allowed inside today's Department of Jobs, Enterprise and Innovation. But you can rest easy in the knowledge that the minister of the day works in a walnut-panelled office with marble chimneypieces. This was the first Irish government building specifically designed for its purpose, and for all the unintentional comedy value, its Art Deco chevrons, zigzags and receding planes make a beautifully austere impression.

# K1 TELEPHONE BOOTH

**㉓**

Dawson Street, Dublin 2
• Transport: Pearse Street and Tara Street DART stations (10-min. walk);
Luas, St Stephen's Green (Green Line; 5–10-min. walk); Dublin Bus stops
792 and 5034 are nearby

> ## *For whom the bell tolls ...*

I n one brief leap, public phone booths seem to have jumped from street corners to the endangered species list. Mobile phones and morphing technologies have transformed these once ubiquitous booths into disconnected time machines.

Despite all this, halfway up the eastern side of Dawson Street, one of the few remaining K1 kiosks still stands in its original location. Dating from the 1920s, K1s were the predecessors of the UK Post Office's much-loved red booth (K1 stands for Kiosk Number 1). This one is believed to date from around 1925, which makes it one of the earliest in Ireland. It takes the form of a concrete structure adorned with a green wooden door, glass panels and eye-catching original trimmings, such as the brass door handle and a thick leather door-strap inside. Further booths were rolled out by the Department of Posts and Telegraphs during the late 1920s (a second K1 survives in the village of Foxrock), with something of a boom witnessed in the run-up to Dublin's hosting of the Eucharistic Congress in 1932. For decades afterwards, a succession of phone-box designs would become a fixture of villages, towns and cities throughout the country, serving as little TARDISes in which a few coins kept Ireland connected.

Indeed, hard as it is to believe nowadays, many Irish households were without a landline as recently as the late 1970s and early 1980s. The growing penetration of household and subsequently mobile phones, however, set them adrift. In 2009 almost half the public phone booths in Ireland were removed by Eircom after it emerged that usage had plummeted by some 80 per cent in the previous five years.

All of which makes the K1 kiosk on Dawson Street pretty much a museum piece. Stand inside, shut out the traffic and listen to the clink of coins. The phone itself may or may not be working when you visit – though perhaps that's no harm given the €2 "min. fee" notice that flashes across the display. In time-honoured fashion, the interior also smells like (ahem) a wet dog. Close your

eyes, hold your nose and prepare for a trip through time.

# THOMAS MOORE'S HARP

24

Royal Irish Academy, 19 Dawson Street, Dublin 2
• 01 609-0620
• www.ria.ie
• Open: Mon–Thurs 10am–5.30pm; Fri 10am-5.30pm.
• Admission: free
• Transport: Pearse & Tara Street DART stations (10-min. walk); Luas,
St Stephen's Green (Green Line; 5–10-min. walk); Dublin Bus stops
792 and 5034 are nearby

**A musical treat...**

The oldest surviving harp in Ireland is found in the Old Library at Trinity College, but Thomas Moore's shamrock-strewn antique at the Royal Irish Academy (RIA) is just as interesting, if less widely known. Dating from 1821, it's an original "Royal Portable Harp", which maker John Egan invented by combining the mechanisms of Erard pedal harps, the dital buttons traditionally found on harp-lutes and the curvaceous shape of the ancient Irish harp, or cláirseach. Portable harps, festooned with elaborate hand painted shamrocks, were hugely popular in the society drawing rooms of 19th-century Dublin and London.

Egan presented this particular instrument to Thomas Moore (1779 – 1852), the Irish poet and songwriter. Moore was considered Ireland's national bard and, at the peak of his popularity, a copy of his "Irish Melodies" would have been found in households all over the country. Ditties like "The Meeting of the Waters" and "The Last Rose of Summer" won him international recognition and he published several biographies – though he's also remembered as one of the men responsible for burning Lord Byron's memoirs. His misty visions of Ireland have their critics, of course, and there's a mischievous moment in *Ulysses* when Leopold Bloom pauses by Moore's statue next to the former public urinal on College Green: "They did right to put him up over a urinal: meeting of the waters."

Moore's harp is found in a glass display case towards the rear of the library's exhibition area, painted green and tickled with golden shamrocks. It was restrung in 1879, as the RIA's notes explain, and played in these very rooms during the centenary celebrations of the bard's birth that year. "Nor did we believe that from an instrument of the size such power, pathos and tenderness could be produced," reported the *Freeman's Journal*. "A more touching or a affecting musical treat could not be possible afforded to an Irishman."

Nor is it the only Moore memorabilia on display: 1,200 of the bard's books were presented to the RIA after his death – "a typical gentleman scholar's library of the early 19th century" that remains virtually intact in the Council Room, also known as the Moore Library. A bust of Moore by Thomas Kirk (1868) can also be seen, as can a portrait over the fireplace.

# McCLINTOCK'S POLAR BEAR ㉕

Natural History Museum, Merrion Square, Dublin 2
- 01 677-7444 • www.museum.ie
- Open: Tues–Sat 10am–5pm, Sun 2pm–5pm, closed Mon
- Admission: free
- Transport: Pearse Street DART station (5–10-min. walk); Luas,
St Stephen's Green (Green Line; 10–15-min. walk); Dublin Bus stop 2811
is right outside the museum

*The bear with the bullet hole*

It almost looks like a third eye. But the black hole in the forehead of the Natural History Museum's polar bear was carved by a bullet. It's a pretty direct reminder of the fact that the stuffed animals on display here were once... well, animals. Not to mention the fact that the Victorian passion for collecting them left a legacy of destruction as much as education.

The museum's polar bear was shot in the late 1850s during an expedition in the Canadian Arctic led by Francis Leopold McClintock (1819–1907). Hailing from Drogheda, Co. Louth, McClintock was a veteran of Arctic travel and his mission was to track down the remains of an ill-fated exhibition led years previously by Sir John Franklin. Franklin disappeared while attempting to chart a section of the Northwest Passage in 1847 – losing his entire crew of 130 to starvation, hypothermia and disease after their icebound ships were abandoned in the inhospitable climate. McClintock's team found several bodies, in addition to written records and artefacts from Franklin's party, and brought back among his souvenirs the skin of a polar bear – the one displayed in the museum. Look for the musk ox and calf on the first floor nearby – these also come courtesy of McClintock, whose team shot and ate them as they trekked across the Canadian Arctic.

Beginning with a collection bought by the Royal Dublin Society in 1792, the Natural History Museum's teeming display cases of minerals, animals, fish and insects quickly expanded thanks to regular donations and moved to the current building in 1857. Over 10,000 specimens are on display today in a museum that, although clearly dated and fusty, holds a special place in the hearts of Dubliners. It's as enjoyable for its Victoriana as its wildlife, and its education team has come up with some super programmes for families and schoolchildren.

McClintock's polar bear isn't the only celebrity on show – other animals came thanks to such famous explorers as Thomas Heazle, whose statue can be seen at the front of the building, and luminaries like King George V, who donated the Bengal Tiger in 1913.

---

For a museum that feels like it should be displayed in a Victorian cabinet of its own, this one isn't shy of keeping up with the times. Spotticus, a male giraffe installed in 2003, even has his own Twitter account: you can follow his tweets on @SpotticusNH.

# PRINCE ALBERT MEMORIAL

Leinster Lawn, Dublin 2
• Transport: Pearse Street DART station (5-min. walk); Luas, St Stephen's Green (Green Line; 10–15-min. walk); Dublin Bus stops 2810 and 2811 are on Merrion Square West

> *Dublin's only royal monument*

I t's a puzzle fit for a pub quiz. Where is Dublin's only surviving royal monument? The answer lies hidden away in the lawn of Leinster House, where a black-bronze statue of Prince Albert stands with its back to the Natural History Museum.

The monument has done well to survive at all. In 1929, after all, Dublin's statue of William III in College Green was blown up. Another royal likeness, that of Queen Victoria, was removed from its pitch outside Leinster House in 1947 and stored for decades before eventually making its way to a second life in Sydney in the 1980s. No other imperial monuments remain on public display in the capital – which makes this one all the more remarkable.

The prospect of a memorial to Prince Albert was first mooted in the early 1860s, when the Dublin Prince Albert Statue Committee sought to erect their tribute in Stephen's Green, which they hoped would open to the public as "Albert Park". After a parliamentary bill knocked that on the head, the ancient city junction of College Green was proposed, and in turn slammed by Irish nationalists. "In the coming days of revolutionary conflict, if an Albert statue should cumber the ground in College Green, it could easily be pulled down, and the bronze would come in handy for the casting of bullets or cannon for the patriot army," as one Fenian told T. D. O'Sullivan, author of *Troubled Times in Irish Politics* (1905). Today's statue of Henry Grattan took pride of place in that particular location in 1875.

In the end, Prince Albert was sculpted by John Henry Foley – the man behind both the Albert Memorial in London's Kensington Gardens and the Daniel O'Connell Monument on O'Connell Street – and placed on Leinster Lawn in 1872. Queen Victoria was not impressed, as James Loughlin writes in *The British Monarchy and Ireland, 1800 to the Present* (2011): "Victoria, obsessed with grief over Albert's death throughout the 1860s, perceived an insult she would not forget." The sentiment went both ways, however. After repeated threats by Republicans, the statue was moved from a central spot on the lawn to its current protected site in 1924.

# FREEMASON'S HALL  ㉗

17 Molesworth Street, Dublin 2
• 01 676-1337
• www.freemason.ie
• Open: Guided tours Mon–Fri 2.30pm (June, July & Aug). Otherwise by appointment
• Admission: €2
• Transport: Pearse Street DART station (10-min. walk); Luas, St Stephen's Green (Green Line; 5–10-min. walk); Dublin Bus stops 792, 5034 and others are on Dawson Street

> *The HQ of freemasonry in Ireland*

Irish freemasonry has a long and proud tradition. There's evidence of freemasons in the country as long as 500 years ago – and its Grand Lodge, established in 1725, is the second oldest in the world (the Grand Lodge of England was founded in 1717).

Freemason's Hall itself dates from the late 1860s and, as you'd expect from the HQ of Irish freemasonry, everything about the building is steeped in ceremony, symbol and exactitude. From dramatic set pieces like the Grand Lodge Room to the furtive squares and compasses hiding in door knockers, seatbacks and lapel pins, every centimetre of Edward Holmes' Victorian design reflects its masonic purpose. Despite the secret society stereotypes, tours are surprisingly open – taking in the Prince Masons' Room, the Egyptian-themed Hand Chapter Room, the Knights Templar Preceptory Room, a ground-floor museum and the undisputed highlight: the Grand Lodge Room. This is a dizzying piece of theatre, with velvet thrones surrounded by heavy drapes, studded leather benches and gilt-framed portraits of bigwig freemasons like Albert, Prince of Wales, and Augustus Fitzgerald, the Third Duke of Leinster. The black-and-white squared carpet is slightly disorienting, piling on the sense of drama as you access an esoteric organisation's inner sanctum.

Lodges from all over Ireland meet at Freemasons' Hall, but the best thing about the tour is the openness of the guides, who'll happily debunk any theories regarding the Illuminati, human lizards or fake moon landings. Arcane rituals are central, of course ("They're what sets us apart from a golf club") and it's true that there are secret handshakes, or "grips", though membership is open to all men who believe in a Supreme Being.

Despite the stuffiness, membership is enjoying a boom in Ireland. Our guide attributed this partly to the Dan Brown phenomenon, but intrigue, theatre and ritual play their part too. "It's boy scouts for big boys," as he put it. "And we've got nothing to hide."

# SINÉAD O'CONNOR'S "NO SECOND TROY"    28

The National Library, 2/3 Kildare Street, Dublin 2
• 01 603-0200 • www.nli.ie/yeats • Open: Main Library exhibitions:
Mon–Wed 9.30am–7.45pm, Thurs & Fri 9.30am–4.45pm, Sat 9.30am–
4.30pm, Sun 1pm–5pm • Admission: free
• Transport: Pearse Street DART station (5–10-min. walk); Luas, St
Stephen's Green (Green Line; 10-min. walk); Dublin Bus stops 746, 747
and 4350 are located nearby on Kildare Street

> **Beauty like a tightened bow ...**

The National Library's Yeats exhibition offers an award-winning insight into the life and work of Ireland's most famous poet – both through notebooks, manuscripts and artefacts donated by his late wife and son, and a series of audio-visual enclaves featuring snippets of sound and film.

Best of all are the inspired matches of modern voices with classic poems – read aloud and played on a loop in a hushed, octagonal space accompanied by images on screen (lake isles, Sligo scenery, Maud Gonne and the like). Seamus Heaney and Theo Dorgan are among them, but the big surprise, and absolute highlight, is Sinéad O'Connor's reading of "No Second Troy".

W. B. Yeats's short, taut poem poses a series of rhetorical questions about his muse ("Why should I blame her that she filled my days with misery ...") and is almost universally known by people schooled in Ireland thanks to its inclusion in the Leaving Certificate anthology, *Soundings* (Gill & MacMillan, 1969). O'Connor's voice blows its cobwebs away with every syllable. Freshly enunciating the familiar lines, her tone fluctuates from a hardness underlined by her Dublin accent, to a syrupy sensuality, to a wounded vulnerability heightened by the listener's intimate knowledge of her own controversial life. It's an inspired pairing of voice and verse, breathing new life into old words:

> *What could have made her peaceful with a mind*
> *That nobleness made simple as a fire,*
> *With beauty like a tightened bow ...*

---

Dating from 1890, the National Library's architectural highlight is undoubtedly its main reading room (visitors can peek, as long as they don't disturb diligent readers beneath the dome).

But there are hidden gems to be found elsewhere in the building too. Look out for the owl symbolising Wisdom in the Front Hall's mosaic floor, or the wooden fire surrounds carved by Carlo Cambi of Siena. Even the toilets are worth a visit (check out the armchairs) in a building with the lofty aim of collecting, preserving and promoting "the larger universe of recorded knowledge". Phew.

---

# COLLECTION OF MEDICAL INSTRUMENTS ㉙

Royal College of Physicians, 6 Kildare Street, Dublin 2
• 01 669-8801
• www.rcpi.ie
• Open: by appointment
• Admission: free
• Transport: Pearse Street DART station (5–10-min. walk); Luas, St Stephen's Green (Green Line; 10-min. walk); Dublin Bus stops 746, 747 and 4350 are nearby on Kildare Street

*Weird and wonderful*

The Royal College of Physicians of Ireland (RCPI) dates back to 1654, when Dr John Stearne founded his Fraternity of Physicians of Trinity Hall. A Royal Charter followed from King Charles II in 1667 and the college has gone on to amass probably Ireland's finest medical library.

Books aren't the only artefacts in its heritage collection, however. In the basement of this grand building on Kildare Street, you'll also find a weird and wonderful stash of medical instruments. Displayed behind glass, there's a mahogany medical case that once belonged to William Robert Kerans (1836–1914), an army surgeon who saw action in China during the Taiping Rebellion of 1860 and Egypt during the Urabi Revolt of 1882. There are obstetrical instruments dating from the 1700s, with one accompanying note describing a ghastly device designed "to perforate the head of an infant, in order to lessen the size of it, by evacuating part of the brain". There's a brass and ivory enema kit that slots into a discreet wooden case to avoid embarrassment (bound in leather to resemble a book, it even has the title *Morning Exercise* on the spine). There's a homeopathic guide from Leath & Ross, the first manufacturers of such medicines in Britain, and a facsimile notice from the National Association for the Prevention of Tuberculosis, warning the public: "Do not spit!"

No. 6 Kildare Street itself was designed by William Murray, and constructed after a fire destroyed the original Kildare Street Club premises in 1860. It was completed in 1864, a year behind schedule – look closely and you'll find "1863" set into plasterwork, stained glass and other features throughout the interiors. Visitors are in for a treat, with a grand series of restored Victorian rooms stretching deep beyond the façade. They culminate in Corrigan Hall, a converted racquet hall whose high wooden ceiling was erected without nails.

Napoleon commonly gave presents and mementos to his friends. Given the conditions of his captivity on St. Helena he had few possessions and as a result he presented a number of personal items to O'Meara as a testament to their friendship. These included Napoleon's toothbrush and some soap.

Also on display is a small lancet used by O'Meara to bleed Napoleon. While on St. Helena Napoleon's health suffered considerably, and O'Meara's skills were frequently needed. At the time bloodletting was a common treatment for a wide variety of diseases.

Napoleon died of cancer of the stomach. At the time there were suggestions that he had been poisoned using arsenic while on St. Helena. Recent research has refuted this showing that although there were high levels of arsenic in his body, they occurred across his lifetime suggesting that Napoleon took arsenic medicinally.

# NAPOLEON'S TOOTHBRUSH

Royal College of Physicians of Ireland, 6 Kildare Street, Dublin 2
• 01 669-8801 • www.rcpi.ie
• Open: by appointment
• Admission: free
• Transport: Pearse Street DART station (5–10-min. walk); Luas, St Stephen's Green (Green Line; 10-min. walk); Dublin Bus stops 746, 747 and 4350 are nearby on Kildare Street

> *The emperor and the Irishman*

**N**apoleon is known all over the world. Barry Edward O'Meara, not so much. Still, the Irish physician's close friendship with the French emperor was such that Napoleon not only trusted him to take notes for a posthumous diary, but gifted him some extraordinary personal effects – including his toothbrush and a pair of personalised snuffboxes.

The items, along with a small lancet used by O'Meara to bleed Napoleon, are found in a modest display case in a hallway of the Royal College of Physicians (RCPI) on Kildare Street. They date back to Napoleon's time on St Helena, where he was imprisoned after his surrender at the Battle of Waterloo in 1815. O'Meara, an army doctor who hailed from Dublin, was senior surgeon on the HMS *Bellerophon*, and Napoleon requested his presence on the island as his personal physician. During their time on St Helena, the emperor and the Irishman became close friends, with Napoleon encouraging O'Meara to keep a diary ("Doctor, it will make you a fortune, but please do not publish until I am dead," he said). When O'Meara was dismissed from the island in 1818, he told the Admiralty that Napoleon needed to be brought to England for proper treatment – a gesture that saw him dismissed from the navy, lose his pension and struck from the medical register. Not one to let a situation get the better of him, O'Meara responded by establishing himself as a dentist, displaying Napoleon's wisdom tooth in his shop window. When the emperor died in 1821, his prediction came to pass: O'Meara published a diary based on his notes, and it won him fame and fortune.

O'Meara's mementos were dispersed after his death, but reunited by another Irish surgeon, Sir Frederick Conway Dwyer (1860–1935). When Conway

Dwyer died, they were presented to the RCPI, where further evidence of Napoleon's personality cult can be found lodged between the antlers of a tiny wooden deer head. The cube of wood is said to be a piece of the emperor's coffin, dating from 1841 when his body was exhumed from St Helena.

# PORTRAIT OF DOÑA ANTONIA ZÁRATE

**31**

National Gallery, Merrion Square, Dublin 1
• 01 661-5133 • www.nationalgallery.ie
• Open: Mon–Sat 9.15am–5.30pm (but late opening Thurs until 8.30pm),
Sun 11am–5.30pm • Admission: free
• Transport: Pearse Street DART station (5-min. walk); Dublin Bus routes
4, 5, 6, 7, 7a, 39/a, 46a, 13a, 44, 48a and 45 all stop nearby on Merrion
Square

*Silent
witness
to an art heist*

**S**he looks a little vacant, sitting there. Curly locks, a black gown and lace mantilla contrast sumptuously with her lemon-yellow damask settee. But however you might describe this sultry Spanish actress, Doña Antonia Zárate seems a million miles from skulduggery of any sort.

That wasn't the case on the night of 26 April 1974. "That painting means a great deal to me for two reasons," as Lady Clementine Beit later explained. "Alfred was standing beneath it when he proposed to me, and we were tied up under it during the Dugdale raid."

Sir Alfred and Lady Clementine Beit owned the Goya. In 1952 this dashing couple had bought Russborough House, a magnificent Palladian mansion near Blessington, Co. Wicklow, specifically to house their art collection. Mick Jagger, Fred Astaire and Jackie Kennedy were just some of the guests who enjoyed the paintings over the years... but there were uninvited guests too. Russborough was raided several times during the Beits' tenure – including a heist by IRA members led by rogue British heiress, Rose Dugdale, in 1974. On that occasion, Sir Alfred and Lady Beit were tied up in their salon and pistol whipped as their *Portrait of Doña Antonia Zárate* was cut from its frame with a screwdriver. Luckily, the Beits survived and their paintings were recovered. In 1987 the couple donated a large portion of their collection to the National Gallery, in what was described as "one of the most magnificent [donations] ever received by any museum, anywhere". Goya's portrait was included, despite being missing at the time – it was stolen once again, along with a tranche of other paintings, in a 1986 raid by Dublin gangster Martin "The General" Cahill. It was only after a police sting in Antwerp several years later that Doña Antonia Zárate finally made it to the gallery walls.

"This is one of Goya's most striking female portraits," the gallery blub reports. Though few – if any – of the visitors shuffling past know anything of her 20th-century adventures.

---

The Beit Collection isn't the National Gallery's only donation of international significance. In 1900 its governors and guardians accepted from Henry Vaughan a bequest of 31 watercolours by J. M. W. Turner... on the condition that they be shown only during the month of January.

---

## THE ANIMAL CARVINGS OF KILDARE STREET 32

The National Library, 2/3 Kildare Street, Dublin 2
• 01 603-0200
• www.nli.ie
• Admission: free
• Transport: Pearse Street DART station (5–10-min. walk); Dublin Bus stops 746, 747 and 4350 stop nearby on Kildare Street

*Monkey business*

"A generation of men is like a generation of leaves." So runs a quote by Homer inside the National Library's exhibition space on Kildare Street. Judging by the carvings at the base of the columns outside its sash windows, however, not everyone takes such a poetic view.

In a former life, this wing of the library served as the Kildare Street Club – a gentleman's clique attended by the upper crust of Dublin society. Strangely, however, the carvings anchoring its columns depict birds of prey, a dog chasing a rabbit and, best of all, three squawking monkeys playing billiards. What gives? The craftsmen responsible for the carvings were the O'Shea brothers, Cork-born stonemasons who rose to fame in 19th-century Dublin (they also worked on Trinity College's Museum building). Members of the Kildare Club would no doubt have enjoyed billiards, among other pursuits – leading one to wonder whether the O'Sheas were conspiring with them in a joke. Or perhaps they were making a subtle comment on an evolving British Empire? Similar monkeys carved by the brothers were removed from the Oxford Museum during the fallout following the publication of Darwin's *On the Origin of Species*, as Anto Howard writes in *Slow Dublin* (Hardie Grant Publishing, 2010). At the time, outraged critics refused to believe that man could have descended from the primates.

Most tempting is the theory suggesting that the animals are a sly dig at the privileged members who would have swanned about inside. The Kildare Club "represents all that is respectable", George Moore once said. "That is to say, those who are gifted with that oyster-like capacity for understanding … that they should continue to get fat in the bed in which they were born."

Monkey business, in other words.

# FINN'S HOTEL SIGN

Leinster Street South, Dublin 2
• Transport: Pearse Street DART station (5-min. walk); Luas, St Stephen's Green (Green Line; 10- min. walk); Dublin Bus stops 404, 405, 406 and 494 are a short walk away

*A Memory of the Artist as a Young Man ...*

**B**ack in the early 1990s, a Dublin scholar discovered the literary equivalent of Tutankhamun's tomb. Or so he thought. Danis Rose had been working on a critical edition of *Finnegans Wake* when he claimed to have unearthed an unknown work by James Joyce … a series of sketches written between *Ulysses* and *Finnegans Wake* and which he believed were to be titled "Finn's Hotel".

Although other scholars had known about the sketches, most had held that they were early drafts of *Finnegans Wake*. Based on his reading of freshly released letters, however, Rose argued otherwise. "There can be no doubt that 'Finn's Hotel' should be viewed apart from any other work, as a place that Joyce went to after *Ulysses* and from whence he came to *Finnegans Wake*," he told the *New York Times*. Objections by the Joyce Estate meant that the stories were never published in their own right, however, and the controversial scholar's theory failed to launch.

Whatever the truth about the sketches, the real Finn's Hotel did play a significant role in Joyce's life. Overlooking Trinity College on Leinster Street South, Finn's harboured a small warren of rooms that sprawled over two redbrick houses, and though it no longer exists today, the hotel's sign is still painted on the terrace's gable end. Joycean enthusiasts fondly remember Finn's because it was here that the author first set eyes on Nora Barnacle, the love of his life. Barnacle worked as a chambermaid at Finn's and later stopped to talk to the 22-year-old on Nassau Street. Their first date took place on 16 June 1904 – the day on which *Ulysses* is set and Bloomsday celebrated. The sign was carefully restored during a recent refurbishment of the buildings.

In subsequent years, Joyce would revisit the hotel – described by his biographer, Richard Ellmann, as "a slightly exalted boarding house" – when he returned to Dublin as part of a business venture aiming to establish the Volta cinema on Mary Street. He asked a waitress there to show him Nora's room and rapturously recounted the experience in a letter to his sweetheart. Like Three Kings kneeling before the manger, he gushed, "I had brought my errors and follies and sins and wondering and longing to lay them at the little bed in which a young girl had dreamed of me."

# SWENY'S CHEMIST

**34**

1 Lincoln Place, Dublin 2
- 087 713-2157 (11am-5pm); 085 814-6713 (after 5pm)
- www.sweny.ie
- Open: Mon–Sat 11am–5pm
- Admission: free
- Transport: Pearse Street DART station (5-min. walk); Dublin Bus stops 408 and 2809 are nearby on Clare Street and Westland Row, respectively

> *The literary pharmacy*

James Joyce was nothing if not fastidious. Were Dublin to be destroyed, the author is said to have believed it could be rebuilt from the pages of *Ulysses*. And so much has changed since the novel was first published in 1922 that Joyce's masterpiece is indeed starting to look as much like a record of the Edwardian cityscape as a work of fiction. Nelson's Pillar, the red light district of Monto, 7 Eccles Street and Barney Kiernan's pub are just a handful of its locations that have disappeared.

Sweny's Chemist is a notable survivor. Dating from 1847, this little pharmacy crops up in *Ulysses* when Leopold Bloom calls to collect a prescription for his wife, Molly. "He waited by the counter, inhaling the keen reek of drugs, the dusty dry smell of sponges and loofahs. Lot of time taken up telling your aches and pains," he thinks. "Chemists rarely move. Their green and gold beacon jars too heavy to stir ... Smell almost cure you like the dentist's doorbell." Although his prescription is not ready, Bloom does leave with a bar of lemon soap – the sweet scent of which has proved irresistible. In 1904 Joyce himself is known to have visited the same premises to consult with pharmacist Frederick William Sweny, and he drew heavily from memory in recreating the fusty interior.

Sweny's shut up shop in 2009, and for a time looked like it too might join the city's growing list of lost literary locations. Fortunately, however, a group of Joycean enthusiasts stepped in, negotiated a rent, staffed it on a voluntary basis and have managed to keep it going by selling books, postcards, curios – and yes, bars of lemon soap. Regular readings of *Dubliners*, *Ulysses* and *Finnegans Wake* are held, but what's most remarkable is that the interior remains almost exactly as Bloom and Joyce would have experienced it over a century ago. Rich mahogany counters take up most of the floor space. Blue bottles and bric-a-brac gather dust on dark shelves. In the old dispensary drawers, unclaimed prescriptions bound in brown paper and string date back to 1903.

Despite the city-centre traffic, bustling footsteps and whining alarms outside, you get completely caught up in the words and the world of the books. For a moment, the city is rebuilt.

# ZOOLOGY MUSEUM

**35**

Zoology Dept., Trinity College, Dublin 2
• 01 896-1366
• www.tcd.ie/zoology
• Open: by appointment
• Admission: free
• Transport: Pearse Street DART station (5-min. walk); Luas, St Stephen's Green (Green Line; 10–15-min. walk); Dublin Bus stops 405, 494, 2809 and others are nearby

*A brilliant and bizarre little collection*

It's a museum that should be in a museum. Squirrelled away amid the offices, labs and lecture rooms of Trinity College's Zoology Department, this brilliant and bizarre little collection contains everything from a stuffed auk to the skeleton of an elephant. It's like someone kidnapped a corner of the Natural History Museum ... without telling a soul.

Little known though it is, the Zoological Museum has a long tradition. A collection begun over 250 years ago was once one of the most important teaching museums of its day – prompting a purpose-built building in 1876. Today's visit is confined to a small corner of the first floor, but at least the museum's short-term future looks bright, with a refurbishment recently achieved thanks to generous donations and an enthusiastic curator.

Browsing the display cases, you'll find spectacular creatures in various states of preservation: insects on pins, fish in formaldehyde, specimens in jars, a stuffed Tanzanian Wolf rivalling any of the smaller mounts in the National Museum's 'Dead Zoo' up the road. The Great Auk is the only species with the "dubious privilege" of a precisely known point of extinction, visitors learn: on 22 June 1844 the last remaining pair was strangled and cast into a boat off the south-west tip of Iceland. Warming to the theme, Trinity's specimen was the last of its kind to have been recorded in Ireland (found swimming off the Co. Waterford coast in 1834). The Board of the university even granted a "great auk pension" of £50 a year to the ornithologist who donated it.

Across the room stands the skeleton of "Prince Tom", an Asian elephant donated to Dublin Zoo by the Duke of Edinburgh. Upon its death in 1882, the animal was transferred on a float to Trinity College, where it was enthusiastically dissected "with the aid of shears, ropes and pulleys", in the words of Catherine De Courcy, author of *Dublin Zoo: An Illustrated History* (Collins Press, 2009).

Don't miss the stuffed Great Indian Rhino, either – a display panel informs us that the animal was "confused in the past with the mythical unicorn".

# MUSEUM BUILDING

**36**

Trinity College, Dublin 2
• 01 896-1477 •www.tcd.ie/geology
• Open: Mon–Fri 10am–5pm
• Admission: free
• Transport: Pearse Street DART station (5-min. walk); Luas, St Stephen's Green (Green Line; 10–15-min. walk); Dublin Bus stops 405, 494, 2809 and others are nearby

*Trinity's rock stars ...*

T rinity's Museum Building, home to its Geology Department, was inspired by the Venetian-Byzantine style of architecture. Built between 1853 and 1857 to designs by Thomas Deane and Benjamin Woodward, its ground-floor hall is a beautiful piece of work, and can be visited by the public on weekdays.

Faced with Caen limestone, the inner walls here feature carvings by the O'Shea brothers (who gathered fresh flowers as their models), columns and balustrades containing examples of Irish marbles and Cornish serpentine, and an arching dome constructed from blue, red and yellow enamelled bricks. Right inside the door, you can't miss the male and female Irish elk (*Megaloceros giganteus*) skeletons, but continue nosing about and you'll also find several additional displays – ranging from fossilised *Chirotherium* footprints to an illustration of life's evolution on Earth.

All are from the university's Geological Museum – a collection of over 100,000 specimens ranging from meteorites to fossils, dinosaur bones and mineral collections drawn from the three rock types: igneous, metamorphic and sedimentary. The collection dates from 1777, and indeed, the Museum Building was purpose-built in the 1850s to house it and the university's growing stock of geological, botanical, ethnographical, zoological, engineering and other wonders. As the campus evolved, however, the collections were dispersed, and locating them is today something of a treasure hunt.

In recent times, the Geology Museum has lurked in an upper-story hideaway. To see its rock stars, visitors followed a sequence of signs up a series of shrinking stairways before eventually arriving in a stuffy room lined with old display cases. Here, you could pore over everything from corals to cephalopods under the watchful eyes of a red deer skeleton and a wooden model of a pterodactyl. Displays also dealt with Irish industrial minerals and included some fascinating trinkets, such as a pair of 18th-century tokens (valued at a halfpenny each) from the Avoca Mines… as well as a few glittering handfuls of industrial diamonds.

During the latest update of Secret Dublin, the Geology Museum was closed pending relocation. The Museum Building, however, remains as magnificently intriguing as ever.

# CHALLONER'S CORNER ③⑦

Front Square, Trinity College, Dublin 2
• 01 896-1000 • www.tcd.ie/visitors
• Transport: Tara Street & Pearse Street DART stations (5-min. walk); Luas,
St Stephen's Green (Green Line) and Abbey Street (Red Line) (5-min. walk)

> **Dublin's smallest cemetery**

Trinity College isn't short on ceremony. Or celebrated alumni, for that matter. Which is one reason it's surprising to find this tiny cemetery squirrelled away in such an inconspicuous nook off Front Square. Set at waist-height above an ATM in a passageway between the College Chapel and Dining Hall, it's almost as if it was hidden on purpose.

That's part of its charm, of course. Said to be Dublin's smallest cemetery, Challoner's Corner takes its name from Luke Challoner, one of Trinity's first Fellows and a leading light in the years following its establishment in 1592. Challoner's private book collection formed the basis of the Old Library here, and he developed it further over the course of several purchasing trips to London with James Usher, a future Archbishop of Armagh. A monument from his tomb can be seen in the little enclosure, though you'll have less luck with the faded inscription. Originally housed in the old College Chapel, the monument was moved outdoors when the building was replaced in 1798 and the elements have taken their toll (there is said to have been an alabaster figure, but any trace of it has long since weathered away). A translation of Challoner's Latin epitaph, from *Fuller's Church History of Britain* (1665), reads:

*This tomb within it here contains,*
*Of Chalnor the said remains;*
*By whose prayer, and helping hand,*
*This House erected here doth stand.*

Among the other former Provosts and Fellows remembered here are John Sterne (1660–1745), who built the Printing House, and George Browne, whose death in 1699 was partly the result of an injury sustained during a college riot. Browne's is the overblown mural tablet flanked with Corinthian columns, though its lengthy Latin inscription makes no reference to his being struck by a brickbat while on his way to admonish some students …

Not that it's all ancient history. Select souls continue to have their epitaphs cast in stone at Challoner's Corner – hence the memorials to former Provosts William Arthur Watts, who died in 2010, and Francis Stewart Leland Lyons, who passed away in 1983. Despite its forgotten feel, the souvenir-sized cemetery has a quiet dignity – tidily kept as it is, and surrounded by leafy bushes, scholarly stone, and memorials almost close enough to touch. It's hard to believe the busy city centre junction of College Green is just footsteps away.

THIS PLAQUE COMMEMORATES
FR. PAT NOISE
ADVISOR TO PEADAR CLANCEY.

HE DIED UNDER SUSPICIOUS
CIRCUMSTANCES WHEN HIS
CARRIAGE PLUNGED INTO THE
LIFFEY ON AUGUST 10TH 1919.

ERECTED BY
THE HSTI

# PLAQUE FOR FATHER PAT NOISE

**38**

O'Connell Bridge, Dublin 2
• Transport: Tara Street DART station (5-min. walk); Luas, Abbey Street (Red Line); numerous Dublin Buses stop along O'Connell Street and the quays

> ## The craic
> ## with the plaque

Father Pat Noise was a priest who died under suspicious circumstances when his carriage plunged into the River Liffey on 10 August 1919.

Or was he? Certainly, the small bronze plaque embedded in the west side of O'Connell Bridge appears to commemorate a real man. But in fact, it's a hoax. Snugly designed to fit a space once occupied by a control box for the city's ill-fated Millennium Clock, the plaque was installed in broad daylight in 2004 and lay unnoticed by Dublin City Council for two years. "It is certainly very unusual for this to happen," Council representatives told the *Sunday Tribune*, which first brought it to their attention. After examining the unauthorised memorial, the Council stated that it would be removed.

Father Noise, whose profile features in relief on the plaque, is described as "an advisor to Peadar Clancy" – a real-life Irish Republican who fought in the Easter Rising and was killed in Dublin Castle on Bloody Sunday (21 November 1920). It has been suggested that "Pat Noise" is a play on the Latin for "Our Father" (*Pater Noster*). Video footage later supplied by the hoaxers, which apparently shows them installing the plaque on this busy bridge, described it as a tribute to their father. The plaque states that it was "erected by the HSTI" – a playfully rude anagram opening it up to all sorts of interpretation. Is the plaque a comment on Ireland's dubious tradition of spending public money on projects like the Millennium Clock, which was festooned with weeds within weeks of its installation? Is it a comment on Irish Republicanism, the Catholic Church, or a simple act of mischief that encapsulates the Irish love of a good giggle, an imaginative prank and pulling a fast one on the authorities?

It's a memorial to sheer persistence, too. After the Council removed the plaque in 2007, a replacement appeared within months. That, too, was threatened with removal, until a growing show of public support prompted a south-east area committee vote to retain it.

Critics decry a juvenile act of vandalism, but it remains in place today.

## CON HOULIHAN'S "SHRINE"

**39**

Mulligan's Pub, 2 Poolbeg Street, Dublin 2
• 01 677-5582
• www.mulligans.ie
• Open: Mon–Thurs 10am–11.30pm, Fri, Sat 10am–12.30am,
Sun 12.30pm–11pm
• Transport: Tara Street DART station (2-min. walk); Luas, Abbey Street
(Red Line; 5-min. walk); several Dublin Bus stops are nearby on Hawkins
Street and D'Olier Street

*"He's loved
by young
and old ..."*

Thanks to its grubby elegance and blistering literary credentials, Mulligan's is one of the most hallowed drinking holes in Dublin. Push through the doors on Poolbeg Street, and all it takes is a magical little moment for your eyes to adjust, for dark spaces awash with worn-down counters, oily wallpaper, gas lamp fittings and cracked leather stools to emerge.

It feels like it has always been thus: when John Mulligan leased the premises in 1854; when James Joyce staged a back parlour arm wrestle in his short story, "Counterparts"; when a young JFK sank a pint in 1945; when Julia Roberts recently pulled up a pew.

Famous as its visitors have been, it speaks volumes about the place that none of them are celebrated in cheesy memorials on the walls. None of them, that is, except Con Houlihan. He gets not only a photograph, but a veritable shrine.

Houlihan (1925–2012) was a sports writer who churned out such colourful, funny and transcendent work for the Irish Press Group – and later for Independent Newspapers – that he ranked in the public imagination alongside literary lights like Behan, Kavanagh and Flann O'Brien (indeed, all four are captured in pavement plaques outside another of Houlihan's favourite haunts, The Palace). The Kerryman was also a giant of the Dublin pub scene, and the mounted photograph here captures him at his "office" with customary glass of brandy and milk in hand. Houlihan regularly composed his copy in Mulligan's, and even lodged cheques behind the bar. As a fellow sports journalist, Ian O'Riordan of *The Irish Times*, put it after Houlihan's death at 86: "Even after a hard day's night he would – sometimes astonishingly – be at his desk before dawn to handwrite his column."

"Con Houlihan is the greatest living sports journalist," runs a quote from John B. Keane on the shrine – a hodgepodge of wood, brass and the odd typo that's all the more endearing for its gaudiness. "When he entered the sporting scene, the cobwebs of bias and bigotry were blown away by the pure breath of his vision and honesty. I played rugby against him but drank porter with him. We were useful enough players but we excelled at the other …"

At the bottom, a poem by Brendan Kennelly concludes:

*He's loved by young and old,*
*He's [sic] words are bright and true*
*Making the thoughtless think, The humourless laugh*
*Now that's a hard thing to do …*

# ARCHER'S GARAGE

**40**

Fenian Street, Dublin 1
• Transport: Pearse Street DART station (5-min. walk); Dublin Buses 120, 27x, 4, 7 and 8 stop at bus stop 408 on nearby Merrion Square

> *The building that rose from the dead*

**D**ublin is full of beautiful architecture. Like any big city, however, it is also blighted by hundreds (some might say thousands) of horrendous architectural crimes.

Think of the row of Georgian town houses demolished to make way for the ESB office block on Fitzwilliam Street. Ponder the loss of No. 7 Eccles Street, one of the most famous addresses in world literature. Consider the destruction of the former Theatre Royal in 1962 to make way for Hawkins House, the sickly-looking Department of Health HQ. Even the famed Wide Streets Commission razed much of the city's medieval fabric, stealthily creating arteries like modern-day Parliament Street, "with workmen reportedly removing roofs from sleeping inhabitants", as Niall McCullough writes in *Dublin: An Urban History* (Lilliput, 2007).

For a short time following one weekend in June 1999, it looked as if Archer's Garage was to be the latest casualty of rampant development. An ambitious, art deco-inspired building that turned a nifty corner on Fenian Street, Archer's was the first building in Ireland to be constructed from reinforced concrete… not to mention fitted with funky fluorescent lighting. Designed by Arnold Francis Hendy and dating from the late 1940s, it sold and serviced Ford automobiles in its day, but by the late 1990s was the only remaining building on a site earmarked for a new apartment complex. Despite being Grade 1 listed, Archer's was destroyed by contractors working for a well-known Dublin developer while city watchdogs (and eagle-eyed citizens) were off-duty, enjoying a Bank Holiday weekend.

A public outcry duly ensued, with Dublin City Council ordering the developer to restore the garage or risk a hefty fine and/or imprisonment. Archer's quickly became a poster child for a reckless style of development in the city and an endemic slowness to recognise and adequately protect Dublin's 20th-century architecture. It took fully five years to finally be reinstated.

If you drive by the corner of Fenian and Sandwith Streets today, don't bother pulling into the garage for a can of oil (inviting though the forecourt, with its thick white supporting column, may seem). The chalk-white building now forms the entrance to an adjoining office block and is occupied by a bank. It's not a perfect replica of the original – whose merits Dublin wags would no doubt have disputed in the first place – but it is a testimony to one victory against cavalier developers.

For fans of architecture, Archer's will always be the building that rose from the dead.

# DUBLIN CITY ARCHIVES ④

128–144 Pearse Street, Dublin 2
• 01 674-4999 • www.dublincity.ie
• Open: Mon–Thurs 10am–8pm, Fri–Sat 10am–5pm. Closed Sun
• Admission: free
• Transport: Pearse Street DART station (5-min. walk); Dublin Bus stops 351 and 398 are outside and opposite the library building, respectively

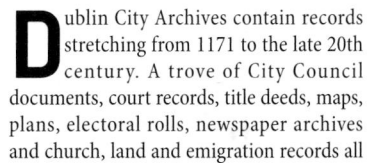

**Nelson's head and Bang Bang's Colt 45**

**D**ublin City Archives contain records stretching from 1171 to the late 20th century. A trove of City Council documents, court records, title deeds, maps, plans, electoral rolls, newspaper archives and church, land and emigration records all document the development of Dublin over the centuries. Anyone can visit, provided they bring the ID necessary to obtain a research card at the desk and abide by the rules – no photos, pens, food or phones.

It's not just paper records, either. A torch from the 2012 London Olympics is on display, and Nelson's head stands on a plinth in the corner of the reading room. Not his actual head, mind you – but that of the 13ft (4m) figure that came crashing to earth when the IRA blew up Nelson's Pillar on O'Connell Street in 1966. "There was an almighty flash and a sound like a clap of thunder," as a local taxi man, stopped at nearby traffic lights, recalls in a contemporary news story displayed alongside. "I just had time to get out." The head took a battering, but remains remarkably intact considering the height from which it fell – not to mention a previous, ill-fated attempt by UCD (University College Dublin) students to melt it in the 1950s. For all the effort to destroy him, Nelson still keeps his one good eye on the citizens in this room.

Another item in the archives – humbler, but just as engaging – is the Colt 45 once brandished by Thomas "Bang Bang" Dudley (1906–89). Bang Bang "shot" thousands of people around Dublin, but was never held to account for his crimes. The reason? His "gun" was a church key. "He used to shoot me with that every day," says Leo Magee, a porter working at the archives and one of many Dubliners with fond memories of Dudley's cowboy antics in cinemas, trams and on streets throughout the city. "With a final theatrical flourish, a victorious Bang Bang would then gallop off into the distance, slapping his rear end as if he were on a horse," as Paul Drury recalled recently in a feature for the *Irish Daily Mail*.

"The whole city was mine," Dudley told another paper, the *Evening Press*, in 1979. And scouring through the books and records here, it's hard not to feel the same way.

# OLD DUBLIN LAMPPOSTS ㊷

Merrion Square Park, Dublin 2
- 01 661-2369
- www.dublincity.ie
- Open: Dec, Jan: 10am–5pm. Feb, Nov: 10am–5.30pm. Mar, Oct: 10am–6.30pm. April, Sept: 10am–8.30pm. May, Aug: 10am–9.30pm. June, July: 10am–10pm
- Transport: Pearse Street DART station (5-min. walk); Dublin Bus stops 408, 494 and 2810 are close to Clare Street and the north-west entrance

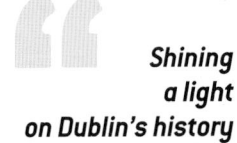

> **Shining a light on Dublin's history**

**M**errion Square isn't just a historical park. It's also something of an outdoor museum, stashing away curiosities from the Dublin of yesteryear. Those stones edging its pathways? They're cobbles rescued from old city streets. Those elegant gas lamps, watching over the walks, monuments, playgrounds and gardens? They're bygone city standards, restored by Dublin City Council as an exhibition of public lighting through the ages.

The lamps are especially evocative, with vibrant green and red paint adding a splash of colour to the ornate cast-iron designs. Walking around (there's a numbered map by the entrance on Merrion Square East), you'll find Sugar Stick Lamps, Swan-Necked Lamps, Bodega Lamps, Mallet Lamps, Square Arc Lamps … and many more. Some can be traced back to their original locations, as with the gas lamp from 114 Grafton Street or the pillar lamp from 1A Percy Place. Others are preserved like extinct species, bearing the names of long-forgotten manufacturers: Ross & Walpole, for instance, who also supplied ironwork for the Guinness Brewery in the 1880s. There are no individual information panels, so the best way to follow the trail is to shoot a picture of the map and seek out the 25 or so lamps from there.

Merrion Square itself dates back to 1762, when its first townhouses were built. Early plans show a double line of trees around the perimeter – by the early 1800s, this was enclosed with railings. Though mainly housing offices today, the Georgian square used to be one of Dublin's most fashionable addresses – former residents included Oscar Wilde (at No.1, across from which you'll find his coy sculpture by Danny Osborne), Daniel O'Connell (No. 58) and W. B. Yeats (No. 82). All would have held keys to what was then a private park.

In 1930 the Catholic Church bought the green space with the intention of building a cathedral. That never came to pass, and one of the city's finest oases became a public park on its transferral to Dublin City Council in 1974.

# IRISH ARCHITECTURAL ARCHIVE   **43**

45 Merrion Square, Dublin 2
• 01 663-3040
• www.iarc.ie
• Open: Tues–Fri 10am–5pm
• Admission: free
• Transport: Pearse Street DART station (10-min. walk); Luas, St Stephen's Green (Green Line; 10–15-min. walk); Dublin Bus stops 409 and 493 are nearby on Merrion Square North

> *The largest body of historical architectural records in Ireland*

The Irish Architectural Archive collects and preserves the records of Irish architecture – from its earliest structures to contemporary buildings – and, as an independent limited company with charitable status, those records are freely available for anyone to consult.

The place to do that is a fitting one: the largest terraced townhouse on Merrion Square. This Georgian building dates from 1795, and after stepping through the automatic glass-door gateway, visitors arrive in a drawing room doused in natural light from several sash windows. This is the first exhibition space, with recent displays including models of buildings designed by Eileen Gray (1878–1976), a Wexford-born architect most famous for E-1027, the holiday home she created with Jean Badovici on the French Riviera. Pushing through to a darker room inside, glass cabinets and subtle lighting might throw illumination on the work of architects like Pugin, for example, or on subjects ranging from Dublin's social housing to its Georgian interiors or the restoration of Christ Church Cathedral. Items in the collections range from books, pamphlets and drawings to the thousands of files created by larger practises.

Taken together, the archive's trove is the largest body of historical architectural records in Ireland, with over 250,000 drawings, 400,000-plus photographs and an extensive reference library in its care. Visitors can also access a huge range of books and periodicals, as well as early printed texts, using the catalogues and public-access terminals in the reading room.

# CHIMNEY PARK

Off Grand Canal Square, Dublin 2
• Transport: Pearse Street and Grand Canal Dock DART stations (both
a 10–15-min. walk); Luas, Spencer Dock (Red Line: 10–15-min. walk);
Dublin Bus stops 7512, 7076 and 7077 are nearby

*A smokin' inner-city oasis*

Joined-up thinking can never be taken for granted in a city. Yet here, tucked away just a few steps from the evolving urban landscape of Grand Canal Square, is a sandy little space that looks and feels like it was designed by the people, for the people.

Chimney Park opened in 2009, just after the Celtic Tiger was snared in a merciless trap of recession. At the time, it was clear the South Docklands could no longer be the soaring city quarter that planners and developers had dreamed up in the noughties. Certain landmark buildings got in before the financiers pulled out, however – including The Marker, a five-star hotel designed by Manuel Aires Mateus, and the Grand Canal Theatre, an ambitious centrepiece realised in signature style by Daniel Libeskind. Concealed behind the former (and beside the latter) is where you'll find the modest little Chimney Park.

Revolving around a restored redbrick chimney on the former Dublin Gasworks site, this appears at first glance to be a casual space. But don't be fooled: a huge amount of consultation with stakeholders and local parties went into a design that shines in the detail. Closer inspection of the playground reveals unusual touches like mirrored walls and clever little grip-bricks inserted into the base of the chimney – transforming it into a climbing wall. Children from the local City Quay National School even created a special poem, "Talking Chimney", which has been engraved into the park benches. All that remains is for people to find it …

---

Dublin's South Docklands are criss-crossed by some of the most evocative street names in the city. Look out for Blood Stoney Road, for example, named for the pioneering former port engineer, Bindon Blood Stoney. Nearby, Lazer Lane stems from "Lazaretto", which recalls the former nearby quarantine stations for lepers and sailors.

Best of all, perhaps, is Misery Hill – apparently deriving its name from a time when corpses from the gallows at Baggot street "were strung up to rot as a warning to other troublemakers", as Turtle Bunbury writes in *Dublin Docklands – An Urban Voyage* (Montague, 2008).

# DIVING BELL

**45**

Sir John Rogerson's Quay, Dublin 2
- Open: 24/7
- Admission: free
- Transport: Pearse Street and Grand Canal Dock DART stations are both a 10–15-min. walk away; Dublin Bus stops 7512, 7076 and 7077 are nearby

*Dublin's Docklands belle*

For years, it looked like it was destined for the scrapheap, but this big, brash and bright-orange chunk of metal on Sir John Rogerson's Quay turned out to be treasure rather than trash. Until its recent refurbishment, how many passers-by would have known that the unlikely looking device was, in fact, originally designed as a diving bell for dredging the Liffey channel?

Following a four-month restoration in 2015, the Diving Bell is now a visitor attraction. Pedestrians who once peered into its portholes can today step inside, absorbing its unlikely history through a series of interpretive panels. The bell dates back to 1860, they learn, when it was designed by the brilliantly named Bindon Blood Stoney (the former port engineer, memorialised in nearby Blood Stoney Street). At the time, Dublin Port was undergoing an expansion, with deep-water quays deemed necessary to facilitate the growing number of steam ships seeking to access the city. Instead of using traditional cofferdam techniques to construct the new docks, Stoney came up with the radical solution of laying prefabricated concrete slabs on a seabed and then flattening them by using a diving bell hung from a floating barge. The bell's 20-ft-square [1.86 sq. m] airlocked chamber and access shaft are now elevated, allowing visitors to step into the space where pods of men would have worked in shifts. If you think it's claustrophobic today, just imagine what it was like back then – a hot chamber, in which workers often suffered ear traumas in the compressed air (although there are no records of fatalities or serious mishaps).

Stoney's was a remarkable achievement – right down to the large-scale use of concrete, a technique in its infancy at the time (the deep-water quays built on his watch are still capable of receiving the largest ships entering the port). The bell itself was used right up to the 1950s, when shifts were at least alleviated by electric light and a telephone, according to Cormac F. Lowth, writing in *The International Journal of Diving History*. According to Lowth, "One of the few perks of working in the diving bell was to find a few plump flatfish that had been left behind on the bottom when the water receded, for [the men's] supper."

# NATIONAL PRINT MUSEUM

Garrison Chapel, Beggars Bush Barracks, Haddington Road, Dublin 4
- 01 660-3770
- www.nationalprintmuseum.ie
- Open: Mon–Fri 9am–5pm, Sat–Sun 2pm–5pm. Closed Bank Holiday weekends
- Admission: free. Guided tours €3.50/€2
- Transport: Lansdowne Road DART station (10–15-min. walk)

**P**rint may be a medium in decline; this unusual jewel is anything but. Hidden away in a former chapel at Beggars Bush Barracks, the National Print Museum "collects, documents, preserves, exhibits, interprets and makes accessible the material evidence of the printing craft, and fosters associated skills of the craft, in Ireland." A wordy remit – and aptly so.

*"Imagine what the world would be like without it ..."*

This is a working museum. Visit during term, and you might find schoolkids making posters, punching holes or folding origami printers' hats. You may be lucky enough to catch a retired printer demonstrating the machines he maintains. Guides are on hand to give tours ("Print was an even more important invention than the internet," one says in passing) and you may even spot a student from the National College of Art and Design (NCAD) harnessing ideas for a letterpress project.

The history of printing dates all the way back to AD 105, when China's T'sai Lun developed paper from the shredded bark of a mulberry tree. In 1493 Johannes Gutenberg invented the printing press as we know it, and new technologies again came to the fore in the 1980s, when computers propelled print into the 21st century. Visitors to the museum can learn about the printing process, typefaces and the apprenticeships through which the craft was passed on, and even peruse one of the few surviving copies of the 1916 Proclamation of the Irish Republic. Typeset and printed in secrecy on an old Wharfedale stop-cylinder press (like the one on display in the museum), this is an intriguing document not just from a historical point of view, but also as a record of the resourcefulness of the men who printed it. With a shortage in type supply, they mixed fonts, printed the document in two halves, used sealing wax to turn a "P" into the "R" of "Republic" (check out the slightly fatter slanted leg) and worked late into the night that Easter Sunday. Only about 30 of the 1,000 original copies survive.

The museum has a clear message. Print may be dying in a digital age, physical newspapers and books may be fighting for their very survival, but the craft continues. "Spend a week noting every printed item and object that you encounter or use," it says. "Then imagine what the world would be like without them. What a dull world it would be."

# CELTIC REVIVAL SYMBOLS

**(47)**

The Oarsman, Ringsend, Dublin 4
• 01 668-9360
• www.theoarsman.ie
• Sun–Thurs 12 noon–11.30pm, Fri & Sat 12 noon to 12.30am
• Transport: Dublin Bus stops 356 and 392 are nearby on Bridge Street
and are served by routes 1 and 47; Grand Canal Dock DART station
(15-min. walk)

> *Romantic nationalism in Ringsend*

Ringsend is one of Dublin's forgotten inner-city suburbs, an outlier that never seems to have enough heritage, shops or restaurants to draw much interest from the city centre.

At its heart, however, lies Dublin's last surviving example of stuccowork portraying the ideals of romantic nationalism on a public house. You'll find it in the pediment of The Oarsman, a Victorian pub lying just across the road from St Patrick's Church. The decorative work takes the form of a roundel containing three quintessential symbols of Irishness – a round tower, a Celtic cross and an Irish wolfhound – in true Celtic Revival style. What looks at first like whimsy is in fact the work of James Comerford and William Burnett, the renowned 19th-century stucco artists also responsible for the famed (though sadly defunct) Irish House on the Liffey quays. The simplistic, almost cartoonish depiction of the romantic nationalist symbols is a style that would have been popular in the city when it was created in the 1880s. It was commissioned when the pub was owned by William Tunney, and remained in place as the name changed from McCluskey's to McCarthy's and eventually its current incarnation as The Oarsman.

Inside, the pub is a nicely preserved Victorian oasis. Original features like whiskey casks with brass taps, a cast-iron support column, vintage grandfather clock and worn wooden floors all add authenticity and character, with the pick of the seating just inside a picture window overlooking the church. Today's Oarsman is a gastro-pub, and you can order up specials ranging from cheese and meat boards to burgers and chargrilled halloumi cheese. There are regular traditional music sessions, too.

## GREAT SOUTH WALL

Pigeon House Road, Ringsend, Dublin 4
• Transport: Dublin Bus 18 (Sandymount/Palmerstown) stops at Seán O'Moore Road

*A direct line into Dublin Bay*

D on't let first impressions fool you. Access to the Great South Wall is via one of the ugliest, smelliest and most industrial roads in the city. But that's just one of the factors that make it so special. Remember the scene towards the end of *The Shawshank Redemption* (1994), when Tim Robbins tunnels out of the prison, crawling through some 450m of subterranean shit pipes to taste freedom? It's kind of like that, only without the prison sentence.

Turning off the southside roundabout near the East Link toll bridge, take the first turn left into the industrial site. You'll pass scrapyards, power plants, container yards and a stinking sewage pond before the Pigeon House Road finally spits you out onto the capital's least-known stretch of coastline. Here, drive on round the Poolbeg Power Station until you come almost to the foot of the enormous Pigeon House Towers – the red-and-white-striped sentinels looking out over Dublin Bay. The Great South Wall stretches a couple of kilometres out into the bay, like a zip-line or a giant uvula ending at the Poolbeg Lighthouse. Park up, and you can enjoy a walk that transports you out into stunning views of the cityscape, the Howth peninsula, the Sugar Loaf in Wicklow, even Terminal 2 at Dublin Airport. Looking back towards Dublin from the end of the wall is an exhilarating sensation, especially on a windy day. Ferries and container ships pass on their way into Dublin Port. Kitesurfers billow about, like exotic birds. You're right in the middle of the bay.

The Great South Wall dates from 1716, when an original wood and gravel bulwark was commissioned to shelter incoming ships and combat the silting that plagued Dublin Bay. A stone version followed, using massive granite slabs from quarries at Dalkey. At the time of its completion in 1795, the 5km structure was one of the longest sea walls in the world – though much of it has since been gobbled up by Dublin's docklands. Despite its length, sand continued to thwart the shipping channel, so a sister wall (the Bull Wall) was constructed on the north side of the bay in 1824. Built after a survey by Captain William Bligh (of *Mutiny on the Bounty* fame), it combined with the Great South Wall to harness retreating tides, successfully scouring sand back out from the channel.

It's not only a hike, but a fascinating history lesson.

# WOOD QUAY TO WAR MEMORIAL

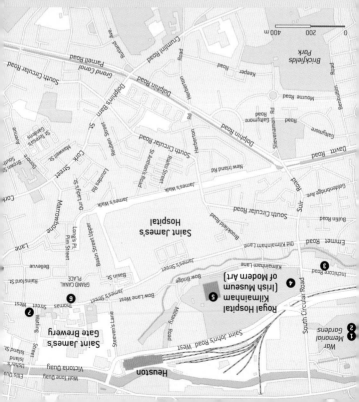

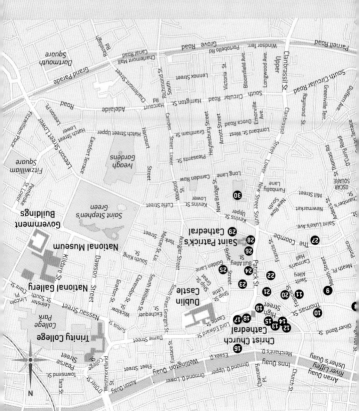

# GUILLEMONT GINCHY CROSS

War Memorial Gardens, Islandbridge, Dublin 8
- 01 475-7816
- www.heritageireland.ie
- Open: Mon–Fri 8am–sunset, Sat & Sun 10am–sunset. Access to bookrooms by appointment
- Admission: free
- Transport: Dublin Bus 51, 68, 69 from Aston Quay

*Sombre souvenirs from the Somme*

**O**n 9 September 1916 some of the bloodiest fighting of the Somme campaign was brought to a close when the 16th Irish Division captured the villages of Guillemont and Ginchy. By then, the surrounding landscape had been transformed into a wasteland, so much so that an elm cross erected some months later, built from a beam of a shattered farmhouse in Flanders, would have been one of the few intact items – natural or manmade – for kilometres around.

Today, that cross stands hidden away within one of two granite bookrooms in the War Memorial Gardens. Call ahead for one of the attendants to open the metal doors, and a shaft of light spills inside, illuminating a tall, dark Celtic cross stretching some 4m in height inside. The Guillemont Ginchy Cross, as it is known, was made in December 1916 by the pioneer battalion of the 16th Irish Division, whose title and emblem – a shamrock – are engraved onto the crossbeam. A metal plate down the front surface appears to hold the wood together, and is spotted with smaller souvenir crosses pinned with paper poppies – mementos from visiting veterans and their families. Behind it hang several poppy wreaths.

According to a bronze plaque in the room, the memorial was placed on the Somme battlefield, between the villages of Ginchy and Guillemont, in February 1917. A sepia-tinted photograph shows the cross on its original site, with a

small footnote reminding visitors of the terrible toll taken by this battle: during the capture of the two towns, the Irish Division's casualties amounted to 236 officers and 4,091 other ranks. The cross remained on the battlefield for nine years before being replaced by an Irish granite cross erected in church grounds at Guillemont in 1926. It was brought to Ireland "with due reverence" in 1937.

# IRELAND'S MEMORIAL RECORDS

**❷**

War Memorial Gardens, Islandbridge, Dublin 8
• 01 475-7816
• www.heritageireland.ie
• Open: Mon–Fri 8am–sunset, Sat & Sun 10am–sunset. Access to bookrooms by appointment
• Admission: free
• Transport: Dublin Bus 51, 68 and 69 from Aston Quay

*Harry Clarke's hidden gem*

Ireland's War Memorial Gardens are well known, both as a stately commemoration of the soldiers who died in the First World War and as one of four Irish gardens designed by Sir Edwin Lutyens. Sunken rose gardens, sculpted lawns and pristine ornamental features combine to make a gorgeous space in which to play, pray or wallow.

Less well known are the two granite bookrooms at the gardens' heart. To access these, you need to call the park attendant in advance – or chance your luck on arrival – and once a time has been arranged, the attendant will meet you with a key. It's a rigmarole, but a very worthwhile one. Inside the southern pavilion, you'll find glass-topped cabinets containing *Ireland's Memorial Records* – eight volumes in which the names of Irish soldiers who died in the Great War are inscribed. Ireland might have been neutral, but that didn't stop 49,435 men from "falling" between 1914 and 1918. Almost every town and village lost someone.

Soldiers are listed alphabetically in short entries along with their rank, regiment, place of birth and the date and cause of their death ("killed in action", "died of wounds" and so on). The books are illustrated by Harry Clarke – the Arts & Crafts artist whose stained glass shines so beautifully elsewhere. Here, though lacking his usual vibrant explosions of colour, you'll find Clarke's signature artistry applied to a title page depicting Hibernia with her torch, wolfhound and harp, and margins strewn with Celtic symbols, silhouettes of soldiers and battlefield scenes. Hard as it may be to feel an emotional connection with men who died a century ago, the care in these books certainly succeeds in honouring them.

The volumes date from 1923, when 100 copies were commissioned following an appeal to gather the names of the Irish dead after the Great War. Published by Maunsel & Roberts, the books employed the best of contemporary Irish craftsmanship and were housed in the War Memorial Gardens when they opened in 1940 – ironically, just as another generation of young men were dying in the Second World War. Queen Elizabeth and Prince Philip visited in 2011 and their signatures are also on display.

## KILMAINHAM MADONNA

**3**

Kilmainham Gaol, Inchicore Road, Dublin 8
- 01 453-5984
- www.heritageireland.ie, www.kilmainhamgaolmuseum.ie
- Open: January-December: 9.30am–5.30pm; last tour leaves at 4.15pm; closed December 24, 25, 26.
- Admission: €7/€3
- Transport: Luas, Suir Road (Red Line); Dublin Bus 69 and 79 from Aston Quay, and 13 and 40 from O'Connell Street, stop on Inchicore Road

*Art behind bars*

**K**ilmainham Gaol made its mark on thousands of prisoners between the 1780s and 1920s, including many key figures from Irish history. But some also made their mark on the goal.

One of its most famous female political prisoners was Grace Gifford (1888–1955), a Dublin-born artist and cartoonist best known for her relationship with the nationalist, Joseph Plunkett. Gifford was born a Protestant, but decided to become a Catholic after meeting the deeply religious Plunkett (his middle name was Mary, after the Blessed Virgin). The couple's wedding date was set for Easter Sunday of 1916 – rather inauspiciously, as it turned out, given Plunkett's leadership role in the 1916 Rising. When he was condemned to death, his fiancée brought a wedding ring to the chapel at Kilmainham Gaol, where the couple were married on the eve of his execution, 3 May. Gifford later returned as a prisoner in her own right, spending three months in "A" Wing as a member of the anti-Treaty IRA. It was during this time that she painted the Kilmainham Madonna, a glowing mural of the Virgin and Child in pencil and watercolour that, deliberately or not, evokes her husband's name.

After being closed in 1923, Kilmainham Gaol lay abandoned for decades. During this time, the elements took their toll on Gifford's work, along with other historic graffiti, so the mural on view today is a 1966 restoration, painted by Thomas Ryan, later a President of the Royal Hibernian Academy of Arts. How accurately Ryan's retouching reflects the original is unclear, as Anne Clare writes in *Unlikely Rebels: The Gifford Girls and the Fight for Irish Freedom* (Mercier, 2011). "He decided to change the Virgin's cloak from blue to red, and though she herself lacks the free-flowing gracefulness that characterised the original, the artist still avoided the relative lifelessness of the 20th-century Italian Madonnas." You can decide for yourself by peering through the spy hole in Gifford's cell door during a guided tour.

## BULLY'S ACRE

**④**

Military Road, Kilmainham, Dublin 8
• Open: Military Historian and author Paul O'Brien runs occasional summer tours of Bully's Acre, or groups can book tours by appointment by emailing Paulf.obrien@opw.ie
• Transport: Luas, Heuston (Red Line; 5-min. walk); Dublin Bus stop 2640 is nearby on the Inchicore Road

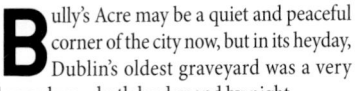

> **Dublin's oldest graveyard**

**B**ully's Acre may be a quiet and peaceful corner of the city now, but in its heyday, Dublin's oldest graveyard was a very busy place – both by day and by night.

Set just inside the Royal Hospital's Kilmainham gate, the 2.4 hectare site has a long history. Bully's Acre was the location of a 12th-century priory founded by the Knights of St John of Jerusalem, and before that, Brian Boru and his troops are believed to have camped here before the Battle of Clontarf in 1014. Earlier still, it was the site of a monastery founded by St Maigneann (after whom Kilmainham, or *Cill Maigneann*, is named). "Bully" is probably a corruption of the word "bailiff". As it was common ground, hundreds of thousands of people were laid to rest here over the centuries – "monks, knights, princes and citizens", as an explanatory plaque puts it. Among them were the Irish nationalist leader Robert Emmet (for all of a few days), boxer Dan Donnelly and possibly even the sons of Brian Boru, who were killed at Clontarf. About 70 gravestones remain.

Bully's Acre was a favourite haunt of bodysnatchers. Indeed, Dan Donnelly's was one of countless corpses exhumed by the grave robbers supplying city surgeons with material for dissection in the 18th and early 19th centuries. "An abundant supply is obtained for all Dublin schools from the burying ground commonly know as Bully's Acre," as a medical student writing to *The Lancet* – quoted by Frank Hopkins in *Rare Old Dublin* (Marino, 2002) – claimed in 1830. "There is no watch on this ground and subjects are to be got with great facility." Public outrage led to the return of Donnelly's body (albeit minus an arm), but he was an exception – at the height of the trade, disinterred corpses were even being exported to the UK.

In 1832 Bully's Acre was finally closed to the public because of a cholera epidemic. If the gates are closed, the best spot for a view of the remaining headstones – which include a granite cross shaft dating from the 10th century – is halfway along the eastern wall, where it dips to a height of some 1.2m, giving a clear view over the leafy paddock inside.

## ORDER OF THE GARTER MOTTO ❺

Royal Hospital, Military Road, Kilmainham, Dublin 8
- 01 612-9903
- www.rhk.ie; imma.ie
- Open: Tues–Sat 10am–5.30pm, Wed 10.30am–5.30pm, Sun 12 noon–5.30pm
- Admission: free
- Transport: Luas, Heuston (Red Line; 10-min. walk); Dublin Bus stops 2637 and 2638 are nearby on St John's Road West, just after Heuston station

> *"Evil be to him who evil thinks"*

There's a story told about Edward III (1312–77) and a young woman he is said to have admired, the Countess of Salisbury. While attending a ball in Calais, the countess accidentally dropped her garter, provoking the amusement of the assembled company. Edward III, defending the lady's honour, is said to have picked up the garter, tied it around his own leg and pledged to found an order of knighthood in its name.

"*Honi soit qui mal y pense*," he exclaimed. "Evil be to him who evil thinks."

Garters and evil may be far from the mind of visitors to the Royal Hospital. Built as a home for retired soldiers in 1684, this is one of the finest buildings of its period in Ireland – as well as the home of IMMA, the Irish Museum of Modern Art. Look closely at the steeple over the Great Hall, however, and you'll see a coat of arms under the pediment facing the formal gardens. It belongs to the Duke of Ormond, who commissioned the building, and is encircled by the same words: *Honi soit qui mal y pense.*

Although the story linking Edward III and the countess is probably untrue, the Order of the Garter – with its motto, also translated as "Shamed be he who thinks evil of it" – is very real indeed. The oldest and most senior British order of chivalry, it honours those who have held public office, contributed to national life or served the sovereign personally (it's exclusive too, with numbers limited to 24, plus Royal Knights, at any one time). The order was founded by Edward III in 1348, although the garter itself is more likely to represent a belt or arming buckle, with the knot symbolising ties of loyalty, than a racy piece of underwear. James Butler, the Duke of Ormond, was a Knight of the Garter, hence his use of the motto at Kilmainham.

In an interesting footnote, Butler's grandson – also called James – was appointed a Knight of the Order of the Garter a few months after succeeding to the dukedom in 1688. After he was accused of supporting the Jacobite rising of 1715, however, his honours were extinguished. Butler's banner as a Knight of the Garter was taken down in St George's Chapel, in what remains the last formal degradation from the order, on 12 July 1716.

## CAMINO STARTING POINT ❻

St James's Church, James's Street, Dublin 8
- 01 453-1143
- www.stjamesparish.ie
- Open: Sacristy: Mon–Fri 10am–12pm
- Transport: Dublin Bus stops 1941 and 1996 are nearby on James Street. Both stops are served by routes 123, 13 and 40, travelling east or west

> *"May the road rise to meet you"*

To modern pilgrims, the Camino de Santiago de Compostela (or Way of St James) is a trail that begins in southern France or northern Spain and ends at St James's reputed burial site at the Cathedral of Santiago de Compostela in Galicia.

Medieval pilgrims setting off on the Camino wouldn't have been privy to the delights of budget airlines, however. They viewed their journeys as beginning once they left home. In Ireland, the traditional starting (or departure) point on the Camino was St James's Gate, where a shrine to the saint was located at the western entrance to the city. Pilgrims had their passports stamped here before setting sail for northern Spain and, though few people now realise it, that tradition has never stopped. Camino passports can still be bought and stamped in Dublin today.

The main place to do this is St James's Church, outside of which hangs a small blue tile featuring a scallop – traditionally the emblem of St James, and carried by pilgrims both for symbolic and practical reasons, such as scooping water from springs. In the sacristy here, you can purchase a passport featuring an Irish blessing ("May the road rise to meet you"). The church's stamp is included too – one of many that pilgrims will collect at towns or *refugios* along their way, and which serve as proof of their journey once they reach Santiago. Passports can also be ordered online from the Camino Society Ireland (www.caminosociety.ie), as can a specially designed Guinness stamp from the Storehouse nearby.

---

Other Camino links in the city can be seen in the remains of the old chapter house at Christ Church, which would have been used to receive pilgrims; Bulloch Castle in Dalkey, where monks provided accommodation for travellers next to what was then Ireland's main port; and street names like Lazer Lane, which recall old quarantine stations for lepers.

St James's Church itself dates from 1844, when Daniel O'Connell – whose carved head can be seen wearing an Irish crown outside the main entrance – laid its foundation stone.

## ST PATRICK'S TOWER & PEAR TREE ❼

Digital Hub, Thomas Street, Dublin 8
• 01 489-6200
• www.thedigitalhub.ie
• Open: working hours (reception is just inside the Thomas Street gate)
• Admission: free
• Transport: Dublin Bus stops 1940 and 1997 are nearby at the junction of Thomas and Watling Streets; Luas, Museum (Red Line; 10-min. walk)

> *The ghost of whiskey distilleries past*

**G**uinness isn't the only drinks superpower associated with Dublin. Two years before Arthur Guinness signed his historic lease at St James's Gate, fellow businessman Peter Roe had bought a substantial site for a whiskey distillery nearby on Thomas Street. It did a bomb too, sprawling over 17 acres (nearly 7 hectares) and producing some 2 million gallons (7.57 million litres) of whiskey a year at its peak. Whiskey from the Roe Distillery was exported as far afield as Australia, and brought the family enough wealth to allow them to bankroll the refurbishment of Christ Church Cathedral in the 1880s. By that time, according to the Ireland Whiskey Trail (www.irelandwhiskeytrail.com), its output was almost twice that of Jameson's and was "probably the highest of any distillery in the world at that time".

Sadly, the 20th century was less successful, with the distillers ceasing production in 1926 and Guinness taking over the site in 1949. Mention the name "Roe" today, and the reaction is "Huh?" In its day, however, it would have carried as much weight as the black stuff.

Roe's distillery buildings were demolished in stages – making way for housing, car parks, office buildings for Guinness and so on. But one striking structure remains. Just inside the Thomas Street entrance to the Digital Hub, a 150ft (46m) windmill stands almost unchanged (save for its blades) since 1757. At the time of its construction, this was the largest smock windmill in Europe, and its distinctive copper-clad cupola would have been visible for miles around. Look closely at the onion-shaped dome, and you'll see a flat, 4ft-high (1.2m) depiction of St Patrick bearing a crozier and mitre. It's the reason the structure is also known as St Patrick's Tower.

Another feature of note is the pear tree at the windmill's base. Bolted to a wall for support, the tree is said to have been planted early in the 19th century, when it would have stood alongside the tower at the heart of the brewery. It's on the Tree Council of Ireland's list of heritage trees because of its unusual location and habitat value. There's no access to the windmill itself, but autumn visits to the pear tree may prove more fruitful …

## ROBERT EMMET'S WHEREABOUTS ⑧

St Catherine's Church, Thomas Street, Dublin 8
• Transport: Tara Street DART station (20-min. walk); Luas, Four Courts
(Red Line; 15-min. walk); Dublin Bus stops 1939 and 1998 are nearby on
Thomas Street

> **"Let
> no man write
> my epitaph ..."**

As political oratory goes, Robert Emmet's speech from the dock takes some beating: "When my country takes her place among the nations of the earth, then – and not until then – let my epitaph be written." Over 200 years since it was delivered, the speech continues to retain its force and its 25-year-old author has become central to Irish nationalist lore.

Emmet was executed on 20 September 1803 at a gallows erected outside St Catherine's Church on Thomas Street. Dressed in black, the United Irishman is said to have handed his watch to the executioner and hung for 30 minutes before his light frame finally succumbed. Afterwards, according to an account in *History Ireland* magazine, he was decapitated on a butcher's block, with the hangman holding up the bloody head for the assembled crowds to witness. A monument outside St Catherine's honours the patriot, but it's the less-heralded plaque at ground-level in front of the railings that people tend to miss – a heavily chipped stone highlighting the site of Emmet's death "at the roadway opposite this tablet".

Emmet's failed rebellion was only the beginning of his legend, of course. After a brief burial at Bully's Acre, his body was disinterred and whisked away to an unknown location. Various theories exist as to where this was – some favour the former Emmet family vault at St Peter's Church (now demolished) on Aungier Street; others the vaults of St Michan's; still others the grounds of the Priory in Rathfarnham, then home to his sweetheart Sarah Curran, but now a housing estate. Ireland may have taken her place among the nations, but without a body, it may be quite some time before that epitaph can finally be written.

Although the whereabouts of Robert Emmet's body remain a mystery, several of the United Irishman's personal effects survive. In the National Museum at Collins Barracks, you'll find his emerald ring and leather notebook, for example. Emmet's writing desk is also owned by The Brazen Head, where he took rooms. Ironically, both he and his hangman drank at the pub, and after his death, according to Aubrey Malone's *Historic Pubs of Dublin* (New Island Books, 2001), morbid patrons took to watching the latter drink before requesting their drinks "from the hangman's glass".

Most gruesome of all, displayed at the Pearse Museum in Rathfarnham is the thick-set and heavily marked block on which Emmet is said to have been executed.

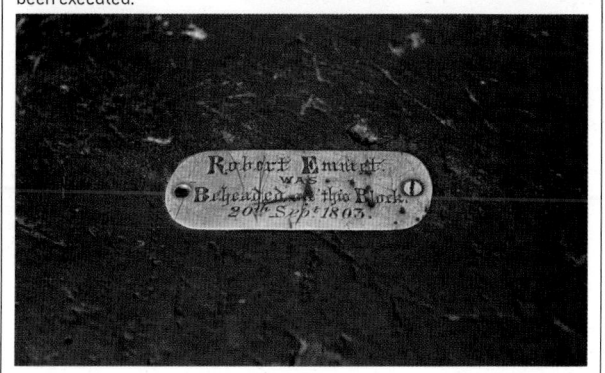

## OUR LADY OF LOURDES GROTTO ⑨

St Catherine's Church, Meath Street, Dublin 8
- 01 454-3356
- www.meathstreetparish.ie
- Admission: free
- Transport: Tara Street DART station (25-min. walk); Dublin Bus stops 5025 and 7412 (5-min. walk); Luas, Harcourt Street (Red Line; 15–20-min. walk)

*Dublin's "Grotto Lotto"*

**S**et outside the medieval walls of the city, Dublin's Liberties were traditionally answerable to several masters and placed under the protection of several saints. Even today, the area retains the feel of a world unto itself – a place where salt-of-the-earth traders rub shoulders with art and design students or rock 'n' roll residents like Imelda May, amidst a jumble of centuries-old churches, squiffy pubs and hip new cafes.

At the heart of the Liberties is St Catherine's, one of the oldest parishes in the city and a place where the Catholic faith continues to run deep. Dip down the alleyway beside the church on Meath Street, for instance, and you'll find a grotto dedicated to Our Lady of Lourdes. A church or shrine dedicated to St Catherine of Alexandria is said to have existed in this area of Dublin since Hiberno-Norse times, and today, stones have been stacked up into a cave-like formation. One section contains a recessed statue of Our Lady, another a little alcove where devotees light candles and reflect on a framed prayer.

"O ever immaculate virgin mother of Mary," it begins. "You know my wants, my troubles, my sufferings. Deign to cast on me a look of pity …"

Mary herself is dressed in flowing blue and white, glancing skywards with a halo of glowing lights about her head and a golden string of rosary beads draped over her arm. Bouquets of flowers lie scattered about her feet, left by locals who trickle in and out through the day. Some stop a few feet back, whispering a Hail Mary under their breath. Others venture closer, perhaps popping a coin in the candle box. The 21st century seems a world away.

Beside the grotto, look out for the little souvenir and card shop, where you can buy mass cards, trinkets and tickets for the weekly "Grotto Lotto". Prizes worth several hundred euros go to weekly winners, with profits funnelled into church fundraising.

---

The foundation stone for St Catherine's Church was laid in 1852, but look up and you'll notice the spire is in a rather different, Art Deco style. It was added in 1958.

## MOSAICS OF JOHN'S LANE CHURCH ⑩

Church of St Augustine & St John, 94 Thomas Street, Dublin 8
• 01 677-0393
• www.johnslane.ie
• Open: Mon–Fri 10am–5pm, Sat 10am–6pm, Sun 8.30am–1pm
• Admission: free
• Transport: Tara Street DART station (20–25-min. walk); Dublin Bus stop 1938 is nearby; Luas, Four Courts (Red Line; 5–10-min. walk)

> *A poem*
> *in stone ...*

John's Lane Church makes an instant impression. Rising up near the ancient junction of Cornmarket, its red sandstone, granite and limestone façade tapers into a French Gothic steeple that remains, at over 60m, the tallest in the city. Although not as well-known as the nearby cathedrals, Pugin's design is one of the finest pieces of ecclesiastical architecture in the city – indeed, Ruskin is said to have dubbed it "a poem in stone".

Oohs and aahs abound. Outside, look for the 12 apostles in the nooks of the tower carved by James Pearse, father of the patriots Padraig and Willie. Inside, a soaring suite of arches and pillars carries the eye towards a bloom of stained

glass windows and an altar cut from Carrara marble. The contrast with the hustle and bustle of the Liberties is titillating. In a couple of bounds, you pass from a vigorous throng of arts students, from busy locals and street vendors selling everything from hula hoops to kitchen roll, into a sanctified space full of votive lights, carved confessional booths and twinkling shrines. John's Lane Church is no museum space, either. Visit during working hours, and you'll find a congregation kneeling with their priest, a cleaner running her mop across the marble, or hear the hushed verses of a rosary.

Amid all of this, it's easy to overlook the Shrine of Our Lady of Good Counsel. Set to the right of the altar as you face it, the little enclave is home to some breath-taking mosaics – with countless flecks of coloured glass and tiles arranged into crisp depictions of the Nativity and the Annunciation. An intricate take on the Augustinian crest is embedded into the floor; a painting of Mary and the infant Jesus forms the centrepiece above.

Dating from 1898, the enclave was tended throughout the 20th century by the "Knights of the Shrine", who worked as ushers and stewards during novenas and other special devotions to Our Lady. Only a handful of these Knights remains – you might spot one or two at the annual Triduum (three-day devotion) to Our lady in April or during special prayers on Wednesdays at 11am.

More intricate mosaics can be found in the Shrine of St Rita of Cascia (under the Harry Clarke window) and the Shrine of the Sacred Heart.

# GRAFFITI IN TIVOLI STREET CAR PARK  ⓫

142–143 Francis Street, Dublin 8
• www.tivolicarpark.com
• www.allcitygraffiti.com
• Transport: Tara Street DART station (20-min. walk); Dublin Bus stops 1938 and 1937 are nearby; Luas, St Stephen's Green (Red Line; 15-min. walk)

***Dublin's al fresco art gallery***

I t's the last thing you'd expect to see on Francis Street. There you are, moseying past the derelict Iveagh Market, dipping in and out of an Aladdin's cave of antique shops, when all of a sudden, you encounter a mischievous granny stencilled onto a wall, with a spray can and walking stick in her hand. "I don't wanna grow up!" she screams.

Turn into the Tivoli Theatre car park behind the unlikely artwork, however, and the graffiti really takes off. Splashed across the walls of warehouses are dozens upon dozens of works of art – turning a vacant lot into an outdoor gallery. As you sidestep between parked cars, skips, wheelie bins and the general detritus of urban life, one piece after another reveals itself. Depending on when you visit, you might find vibrant tags; a snorting bull; an urban cowboy whose side profile dwarfs passers-by; or images such as two pigeons cavorting under the heading: "Anywhere is Paradise with You" – the work of Steve Powers, a New-York-based artist better known as ESPO, who travelled to Ireland from the US on a Fulbright Scholarship several years ago.

The setting is perfect – a rambling, derelict space overlooked by the ugly arse-ends of buildings, themselves bedecked with fire escapes, drainpipes, barbed wire and window bars. In the near distance is the soaring steeple of St Augustine & St John's Church. At the car park entrance, a recent slogan read: "You can look down on me, as long as you look at me." It was also by ESPO, as was another piece depicting a sinking *Titanic*, with a speech bubble puffing from its funnels: "Don't give up on us baby!" It may be a nasty, backstage parking lot, but the graffiti lifts it off the page, transforming the car park into a blooming gallery of street art.

---

How does the graffiti come to be here? Every year, the car park hosts graffiti jams run by All City, with live graffiti writing from Irish and international artists, BMX demos, skater courses, live music and DJs further re-imagining this rundown inner-city pocket.

## THE 40 STEPS

**⑫**

Cook Street, Dublin 8
• Transport: Tara Street DART station (15–20-min. walk); Luas, Four Courts (Red Line; 10-min. walk); Dublin Bus stops 1937 and 2001 are nearby on High Street

*The gateway to hell*

The faithful in Dublin's old churches worked hard to get into heaven, but the road to hell was all downhill. Literally. A medieval shortcut skirting around St Audeon's Church meant 40 steps was all it took for 18th-century citizens to descend from the heights of Cornmarket to a squalid pocket of brothels, taverns and laneways colloquially known as "Hell".

Stretching from Cook Street towards Fishamble Street, "Hell" ran thick with criminals, outcasts and ne'er-do-wells – one of the most famous was Darkey Kelly, a notorious madame who ran the Maiden Tower brothel. As the story goes, Kelly became pregnant with the child of Dublin Sheriff, Simon Luttrell, and pressed him for financial support. Gentleman as he was, Luttrell denied all knowledge of the child and upped the ante by accusing his lover of witchcraft and infanticide. In 1761 Kelly was burnt at the stake in front of a baying mob, although the baby's body was never produced. She hasn't gone away, either – sightings of Darkey Kelly's ghost have been reported at the 40 Steps in the ominous passageway where abandoned babies were once left at the side of St Audeon's Church.

Interestingly, contemporary newspaper reports appear to suggest that Kelly may have been executed for another reason. Several bodies were discovered hidden in the vaults of her brothel, according to a recent rereading of reports by the producers of *No Smoke Without Hellfire* on Dublin's South 93.9FM. Kelly may not have been a witch, in other words, but she may well have been Ireland's first serial killer. Welcome to hell, indeed.

Even today, the 40 Steps retain a dank, spooky atmosphere. No matter how bright the day, the thickness of the old city walls casts a pall over the bottom steps, and a long portion of the slipway is hidden from view – a fact that has not only proven attractive to historical criminals and drug addicts, but their contemporaries too. Be careful.

## PORTLESTER CHAPEL AND CENOTAPH   **13**

St Audoen's Church, High Street, Dublin 8
• 01 677-0088
• www.heritageireland.ie
• Open: May–Oct: daily 9.30am–5.30pm
• Admission: free
• Transport: Tara Street DART station (15–20-min. walk); Luas, Four Courts (Red Line; 10-min. walk); Dublin Bus stops 1937 and 2001 are nearby on High Street

> **A secret city centre space**

**D**ating from 1181, St Audoen's is named after the patron saint of Normandy, St Ouen. But it doesn't take much nosing around this wonderful mash-up of medieval churches and chapels to find another name standing out: that of Roland FitzEustace, Lord Porlester.

In its golden age, St Audoen's was a wealthy parish in the commercial heart of Dublin. Burial here was a plum posthumous status symbol, and names like Usher, Sparke and Duff can still be found carved into large and wordy tombstones. FitzEustace, however – who was appointed Lord Chancellor of Ireland by both Edward IV and later Henry VII – went a step further. In 1455 he built his own private chapel. Hidden away just to the right of the visitor centre entrance, you'll find the space hemmed in by an elegant miscellany of medieval walls, Romanesque arches and the towering bulk of the neighbouring Catholic church. The chapel has been shorn of its roof since 1773, and an information panel includes a fading reproduction of George Petrie's "Hanging Washing in Lord Portlester's Chapel", a painting of a woman stringing garments along lines across the arcade. It's a blithe, almost pastoral scene, remarkable for the fact that it takes place bang in the middle of Dublin.

The chapel and chancel were vested in the Board of Public Works in 1880, the panel goes on to reveal, at a time when the windows and arches were repaired and the tombstones laid horizontally.

The centrepiece of Portlester's chapel was a striking cenotaph. It was moved inside for protection many years ago, and today you'll find it in the bell tower, where recumbent effigies depict the baron in medieval knight's garb, with a sword hung from his hip, wife at his side and a loyal dog at his feet. Portlester commissioned it during his lifetime, but he is actually buried in Kilcullen, Co. Kildare.

## MEDIEVAL LANEWAY

**⑭**

St Audeon's Church, High Street, Dublin 8
• 01 677-0088
• www.heritageireland.ie
• Open: May–Oct: daily 9.30am – 5.30pm
• Admission: free
• Transport: Tara Street DART station (15–20-min. walk); Luas, Four Courts (Red Line; 10-min. walk); Dublin Bus stops 1937 and 2001 are nearby on High Street

> *The only excavated example in the city*

You can view St Audeon's Church from above on High Street or from below on Cook Street, but neither gives a clue as to the layers of history hidden within. Dublin's only remaining medieval parish church dates from the 12th century (and possibly even before) and is riddled with nooks and crannies, with aisles, chapels, towers, tombs and monuments.

Right in the middle of St Anne's Chapel, you'll even find an excavated section of a 12th-century laneway. Dublin would have been braided with cobbled lanes when the medieval church was built, of course, but this claims to be the city's only excavated example showing a surviving section in its unaltered state. Discovered during the early 1990s, the lane is thought to have run close to the wall of the original church, and beneath the extensions that were added in subsequent centuries. It continued downhill towards the River Liffey, passing through St Audeon's Arch in the old city walls. Although only a short section is on display, curving slightly as its dark stones dip back underground, it's easy to imagine the pitter-patter of ancient feet. High Street and St Audeon's lay at the crossroads of medieval Dublin and all manner of tradespeople, laymen, priests and even pilgrims getting their passports stamped before embarking on the Camino would have used the timeless thoroughfare.

St Audeon's is at once a working parish church, and an Office of Public Works (OPW) heritage site. That's the beauty of a visit: in the Church of Ireland aisle, you'll find a spotless altar and an 11th-century baptismal font. Parallel to it in the Guild Chapel of St Anne, there's an exhibition on the medieval guilds that thrived in the church's heyday, with displays including a handful of instruments from the guild of barber surgeons – among which is a cauterising tool.

"The yron is most excellent but that it is offensive to the eye and bringeth the patient to great sorrowe and dread of the burning and the smart," reads a contemporary account.

## HOLY WATER STOOPS

**15**

St Audeon's Catholic Church, High Street, Dublin 8
• 087 239-3235
• www.kosciol-dublin.pl
• Transport: Tara Street DART station (15–20-min. walk); Luas, Four Courts (Red Line; 10-min. walk); Dublin Bus stops 1937 and 2001 are nearby on High Street

*Symbolic seashells*

**D**ating from 1846, St Audeon's Catholic Church (as distinct from the Church of Ireland next door) is home to the Polish Chaplaincy in Ireland. Several minor gems are found inside, including a handcrafted Walker organ dating from 1861 and a statue of the Infant Jesus carved by Pietro Bonanni in 1847, but the most unusual are just outside the door. Holy water stoops set either side of St Audeon's front entrance are actually enormous clamshells, fished from the Pacific Ocean in 1917, as the story goes, and brought back to Dublin by a seaman whose brother was one of the parish priests working in the church at the time.

Shells are not an uncommon motif in churches, of course. Throughout antiquity, hinged species like the scallop and clam have symbolised fertility and the female – both as protective and nurturing forms, and more explicitly as emblems of the vulva. The scallop, for instance, was the symbol of Venus. Although it's not mentioned in the bible, Christian tradition also has it that John used a clamshell to baptize Jesus, and shells can often be found decorating baptismal fonts or used to pour Holy Water over babies. Giant clams are the world's largest molluscs, living in the wild for a century or more and weighing up to 200kg in their prime. In some cases, giant specimens like those at St Audeon's are even used as baptismal fonts.

Although made from stone, a 12th-century baptismal font featuring a seashell carved on its aisle-facing side is still in use at St Audeon's Church of Ireland next door.

> Visitors may linger at its unique holy water stoops today, but taking one's time wasn't always the St Audeon's way. This church was where, from the 1950s, Father "Flash" Kavanagh was reputed to say the fastest Sunday mass in the city, freeing parishioners in time for The Sunday Game!

## WOOD QUAY AMPHITHEATRE ⑯

Dublin City Council Civic Offices, Wood Quay, Dublin 8
• www.dublincityartsoffice.ie
• Open: Daylight hours (park)
• Admission: free
• Transport: Tara Street DART station (15-min. walk); Dublin Bus stops 2001 (High Street) and 1444 (Wood Quay) are serviced by numerous routes from the city centre

**Echoes of history**

**D**ublin's Civic Offices are its most controversial buildings. Built atop of one of the most significant Viking archaeological sites in Europe, architect Sam Stephenson's brutalist-style "bunker" structures are as bull-headed a symbol of "progress" as you'll find in the city.

They didn't go up without a fight. As construction loomed in the late 1970s, officialdom locked horns with an outraged Irish public in an unprecedented way. Up to 20,000 protestors, including the young (future President) Mary Robinson, took to the streets in "Save Wood Quay" marches. As excavations continued, Professor F.X. Martin and his "Friends of Medieval Dublin" even occupied the site. In the end, the campaign failed, excavated treasures went to the National Museum and two of four planned "bunkers" were built (the river-facing block by Scott Tallon Walker was added in 1994). Arguably, however, Ireland's attitude towards preserving its heritage had changed for ever.

Moseying through the park and pathways linking the buildings today, the historical footnote springs to life. Was the right decision made? What was the alternative? Parts of the landscaping do evoke some optimism – especially the public amphitheatre that nestles up against the "bunkers". Rows of granite seating and a raised, circular stage surrounded by grass verges set a sweet scene for a picnic or coffee, and in summer, the amphitheatre hosts outdoor events. Opera in the Open, for example, is a Dublin City Council initiative presenting live performances every Thursday lunchtime during August. Other one-off events take place from time to time – on Culture Night in September, for instance. Lurking in the building behind is the indoor Wood Quay Venue, a basement meeting and exhibition space that incorporates a stretch of 12th-century city walls uncovered during the construction.

> If you fancy venting your frustration, do it in the centre circle of the amphitheatre. Shout, or sing, in this exact spot, and your voice will echo in the most surprising way. Step out of the circle and the echo ends. It's a space that resonates in more ways than one.

# THE CAT & THE RAT                                    **17**

Christ Church Crypt, Christchurch, Dublin 2
• 01 677-8099
• www.christchurchdublin.ie
• Open: April-Sept: Mon–Sat 9.30am–7pm, Sun 12.30-2.30pm & 4.30pm
– 7pm; March & Oct: Mon–Sat 9.30am–6pm, Sun 12.30–2.30pm;
4.30–6pm. Nov–Feb: Mon-Sat 9.30am–5pm. Sept–May: Sun 12.30–
2.30pm. Closed 26 Dec
• Admission: €6/€2
• Transport: Tara Street DART station (10–15-min. walk); Luas, Smithfield
(10-min. walk); Dublin Bus stops 2002 and 2035 are nearby on Lord
Edward Street and Nicholas Street

*Tom & Jerry*

**C**hrist Church Cathedral is one of the stand-out structures in Dublin, a granite chandelier of a centrepiece that could hold its own in any city on earth. Although founded by the Hiberno-Norse King Sitric in 1028, today's architecture has been heavily influenced by extensive Victorian restorations. It's sometimes hard to tell whether you're looking at an elegant Anglo-Norman original, a Victorian pastiche – or what's really the case, a spectacular hodgepodge of both.

One part of the building that hasn't been interfered with is the crypt. The oldest surviving structure in Dublin stretches under both the nave and choir of the cathedral, and its nooks and crannies are home to some unique treasures: a plate gifted by William of Orange after the Battle of the Boyne (1690), medieval city stocks dating from 1670 (they were once used to punish criminals on Christ Church Place) and the reputed tomb of Strongbow among them. Most surprising of all, however, are the mummified cat and mouse displayed in a glass case. The parched, leathery creatures were found trapped in one of the church's organ pipes in the 1860s, where local lore suggests they became stuck during a high-speed chase and were subsequently preserved in the dry atmosphere of the crypt. Tom & Jerry, as they are known, were discovered during a servicing of the organ and went on to find themselves name-checked in James Joyce's *Finnegans Wake*, where a character is described as "stuck as that cat to that mouse in that tube of that Christchurch organ".

While you're browsing through the crypt's motley artefacts, take a moment to look around at the arches and columns supporting this 12th-century maze. Many centuries after their construction, they continue to take the weight of the entire cathedral.

On 13 April 1742 Handel's *Messiah* debuted at Neal's Musick Hall. The oratorio was rapturously received by an audience in which ladies wore dresses without hoops to make room "for more company". A plaque commemorating the event can be seen at the George Frederic Handel Hotel, outside of which anniversary performances take place every April.

# SYNOD HALL BRIDGE (18)

Winetavern Street, Dublin 8
- 01 677-8099; www.christchurchdublin.ie
- 01 679-4611; www.dublinia.ie
- Open: Christ Church: April-Sept: Mon–Sat 9.30am–7pm, Sun 12.30-2.30pm & 4.30pm – 7pm; March & Oct: Mon–Sat 9.30am–6pm, Sun 12.30–2.30pm; 4.30–6pm. Nov–Feb: Mon-Sat 9.30am–5pm. Sept–May: Sun 12.30–2.30pm. Closed 26 Dec
  Dublinia: Mar–Sept: 10am–6.30pm. Oct–Feb: 10am–5.30pm
- Admission: Christ Church €6/€2; Dublinia: €8.50/€5.50; Combined ticket €13.25/€6.25
- Transport: Tara Street DART station (10–15-min. walk); Luas, Smithfield (Red Line; 10-min. walk); Dublin Bus stops 2002 and 2035 are nearby on Lord Edward Street and Nicholas Street

*From Vikings to vaults*

For a city that is rained upon so often, Dublin doesn't really "do" covered walkways. When it does, however, it does them in style – as with this arching, integrated bridge linking Christ Church Cathedral and its former Synod Hall over Winetavern Street.

The bridge dates back to the 1870s, when it was added during extensive renovations undertaken by George Edmund Street. This was also when the Synod Hall was built around the former St Michael's Church – the two buildings were unrelated at the time and Street designed the Synod Hall to incorporate St Michael's original 12th-century tower. The hall itself was "large and prosaic", as Christine Casey describes it in *Dublin* (Yale University Press, 2005), but the bridge is an unexpected delight. Caen stone walls and a timber roof are offset by a series of leaded stained glass windows that let in floods of pixelated light whenever there's a blast of sunshine. On one wall, a shining plaque remembers Henry Roe, the wealthy distiller at whose "sole expense" the Synod Hall was erected. It's a surprising and atmospheric treat enhanced by the sense of remove from the busy stream of cars and buses passing below.

Today, the Synod Hall is occupied by Dublinia, an interactive exhibition about the medieval city. Combined tickets can be bought for Dublinia and Christ Church, allowing visitors to exit the exhibition on an upper floor, cross over the bridge and descend via the smooth limestone steps into the cathedral. Alternatively, one can access the structure via Christ Church itself, though confusingly, Dublinia cannot be entered from the east this way.

## TAILORS' HALL ⑲

An Taisce, Back Lane, Dublin 8
- 01 454-1786
- www.antaisce.org
- Admission: free (office hours, by appointment)
- Transport: Tara Street DART station (15-min. walk); Dublin Bus 2001 stops nearby on high Street

> *The Back Lane Parliament*

Just a single medieval guildhall survives in Dublin. Squirrelled away in the aptly named Back Lane, off High Street, the two-storey building is today home to An Taisce, the National Trust for Ireland.

Without its intervention, it's unlikely that Tailors' Hall would be here at all.

The building dates from 1706, when the Guild of Merchant Tailors established it as its headquarters and meeting place. Back then, Dublin was a radically different city. Today's High Street streams with six lanes of traffic, and busy junctions make it tough work for pedestrians. When the city's tailors visited their HQ, however, they would have come at it through a tight-knit neighbourhood dotted with markets, tanneries, taverns, breweries and linen shops, with long-vanished names like Cutpurse Row and Handkerchief Alley (a small chunk of the old City Walls remains on Lamb Alley). Tailors met here until 1841, and in their day were an influential guild. "They had the right, for instance, to seize the cloths of tailors who were not members of the guild but were selling in the city," as Peter Pearson writes in *The Heart of Dublin* (O'Brien Press, 2000). But, of course, that was then.

This is now. Over the years, Cornmarket and the junctions near Christ Church were overhauled. Whole streets were razed; others widened and re-landscaped. Tailors' Hall went through various different uses – as an army barracks, hostel and courthouse, for instance – before being left to rot. An Taisce's restoration is a minor miracle, and a deserved winner of the Europa Nostra Award 1988.

So what can you see today? Entering via a passageway off Back Lane, rich red brick and surprisingly grand arched windows hint at the history within. The Great Hall contains a minstrels' gallery with a sparse, wrought-iron balustrade and large marble fireplace (look for the 18th-century engravings; sadly, the central tablet has been stolen). Black and white photos illustrate the sorry condition in which Tailors' Hall lay before restoration, and an enormous hearth anchors the basement. It's not just about built heritage, either. In 1792 Wolfe Tone, James Napper Tandy and others met here during a campaign against the Penal Laws, leading to its nickname: the Back Lane Parliament.

## LORD IVEAGH'S LIKENESS  ⓴

Iveagh Market, 22–27 Francis Street, Dublin 8
• Transport: Dublin Bus stop 2383 is on nearby Patrick Street, with stop 7413 also nearby at The Coombe; Luas, Harcourt Street (Green Line; 15-min. walk)

*Lord Iveagh's "impish" grin*

**S**ir Edward Cecil Guinness (1847–1927), also known as Lord Iveagh, certainly made his mark on Dublin. But could this kooky-looking keystone, set into one of the arches ringing the Iveagh Markets, be the most personal mark of all?

The figure is one of several carved into the keystones on the former market building. The keystones represent the continents, according to Christine Casey's *Dublin* (Yale University Press, 2005), but Pat Liddy, the legendary Dublin author and tour guide, has suggested that the "impish grin" of the bearded figure appearing to wink at passers-by from the corner of Francis Street and Dean Swift Square is that of Lord Iveagh, who founded the Iveagh Trust to provide affordable housing in Dublin and London.

The Iveagh Trust was established in 1890 and its legacy in Dublin is astonishing. Overlooking St Patrick's Park (created by Sir Benjamin Guinness), you'll find a beautiful complex of buildings including the Iveagh Trust Flats, the famous "Bayno" where local children played, and the Iveagh Baths, which housed a swimming pool for residents. The Iveagh Market dates from 1906, when it was commissioned to accommodate street traders who had lost their old market rights after inner-city slums were cleared. Designed by Frederick G. Hicks, the covered market was for traders selling old clothes, fish, fruit and vegetables, and was built on a site formerly occupied by Sweetman's Brewery. Beyond its brick and stone façade lies a market hall with a perimeter gallery perched on cast-iron columns.

The market continued in operation until the 1990s but has lain sadly derelict for some time. A redevelopment scheme was mooted, but Ireland's recent economic nosedive appears to have put that on hold.

Though the building's fortunes have waxed and waned, the winking keystone remains. Perhaps it knows something we don't?

## CITY WALLS

Power's Square, off St Nicholas Street, Dublin 8
• Transport: Tara Street DART station (20-min. walk); Luas, St Stephen's
Green (Green Line; 10-min. walk); Dublin Bus 49 stops nearby on St
Nicholas Street

*If
these walls
could talk ...*

**A**t first glance, Power's Square seems noteworthy only for its pretty inner-city gardens. Take a closer look at the trees and blooms marking the eastern end of this tiny enclave, however, and you'll see a 4m wedge of stone hiding in plain sight. It's as solid a chunk of history as you'll find in the city – a surviving section of the old City Walls.

The 68m stretch of the old wall alignment, altered over time but still containing some of its original masonry, is one of few remaining sections of Dublin's medieval defences. Other sections, such as the early mural defences on Cook Street, the 83m stretch at Ship Street Lower and the monument-style remnant on Lamb Alley at Cornmarket, may be better known – but similarly to Power's Square, they survived because they were incorporated into later property boundaries. Without that, all would have long since vanished.

Most of the remaining City Walls, which John Perrot's survey of 1585 describes as having measured between 4.8m and 6.7m high and between 1.22m and 2m wide, are buried beneath the modern city. Remnants have been found during archaeological investigations at City Hall, Dublin Castle, Werburgh Street, Nicholas Street, Winetavern Street, Augustine Street and Usher's Quay among other locations. A section of the early mural defences survives in the basement of Dublin's Civic Offices at Wood Quay. Dublin Castle's Record Tower is another survivor, as is the base of Bermingham Tower and the foundations of the Powder Tower, which visitors can see in an underground chamber during castle tours. Elsewhere, the remains of Genevel's Tower are preserved within an underground chamber at Ross Road, although not currently accessible to the public. On Exchange Street Lower, the base of Isolde's Tower can also be seen in a murky holding area beneath an apartment block.

If you're interested in learning more about the route of the City Walls, it's possible to follow the "virtual" perimeter via a series of granite markers dotted at various points around the historic city centre. Bronze plaques on the markers contain an outline of the medieval city, with metal spots denoting the location of particular towers and gates.

## CHURCH OF ST NICHOLAS OF MYRA (WITHOUT) 22

Francis Street, Dublin 8
• 01 454-0387
• www.francisstreetparish.ie
• Open: Mon–Fri 10am–12pm
• Transport: Dublin Bus stop 2383 is on nearby Patrick Street, with stop 7413 also nearby at The Coombe; Luas, Harcourt Street (Green Line; 15-min. walk)

*Santa Claus and the Axe Murderers*

To step into the Church of St Nicholas of Myra is to step back in time.

Arrive around 10.30am midweek, just after mass has wound up, and you'll find a small congregation intoning the rosary. Old women massage their beads with waxy, wrinkled fingers, while around them, a suprisingly beautiful interior blooms like a flower.

Dating from 1829, the church has its origins in a 13th-century Franciscan monastery. The "Without" part of its title refers to the fact that it lay outside the medieval city walls, as distinct from the Church of St Nicholas of Myra (Within). Hidden away in a sprawl of inner-city housing, its immaculately maintained interior is dotted with little alcoves and shrines, bright statues of Jesus, Mary, Joseph and St Anthony. Over the altar, a Pietà by sculptor John Hogan shows Christ laid out after his crucifixion, his mother about to cup his head in her hands. Rich stained-glass windows include Harry Clarke's depiction of the marriage of Mary and Joseph, and St Nicholas of Myra with three golden satchels and an anchor at his feet – hinting at his role as Santa Claus and the patron saint of sailors. Pews line up neatly beneath a beautifully ornate ceiling, raspberry-pink recessed panels pick up the curtains in the confessional booths, and a line of plaster friezes skirts behind the altar and its flickering candles. A thought for the day reads: "One of the secrets of life is to make stepping stones out of stumbling blocks."

On your way into the building, don't miss its map of medieval Dublin. It shows the locations of various churches dedicated to St Nicholas through the ages, along with a hilarious illustration from Giraldus Cambrensis's *Topography of Ireland* (1188). Entitled "Irishmen Demonstrate the Axe", it depicts a crazy-eyed savage who, despite the presence of an eminently chop-able tree, "demonstrates" his tool by lodging it in his colleague's forehead.

---

Like its namesake beyond the old city walls, the Church of St Nicholas (Within) has a long history dating back to the 11th century. Its fortunes ebbed and flowed over the centuries, and sadly, all that remains of it today is a bricked-up portion of its entrance at the junction of Nicholas Street and Christchurch Place, by the city's Peace Park.

## BRONZE PLAQUES (23)

Nicholas Street, Bride Street, Bride Road, & Ross Road, Dublin 8
• www.chrisreidartist.com
• Transport: Tara Street DART station (20-min. walk); Luas, Harcourt Street (Green Line; 10-min. walk); Dublin Bus stops 2385 and 2310 are nearby

**"I'll cure you myself"** " I never really had a conversation with my father. Sometime in the 1960s he caught me mitching from school and gave me an awful hiding. Ripped the clothes off me, lashed me with the belt and punched me in the eyes."

It's the kind of revelation you'd wince at in a book, an interview, or perhaps were it to be delivered in confidence over a cup of tea or a pint. And yet here they are … the same words, cast in bronze in a plaque set into the walls of Nicholas Street. Nor are they alone. Keep your eyes peeled as you walk past the redbrick Victorian flats of Bride Street, Bride Road and Ross Road, and you'll find 20 or so others set into the streetscape. Sobering confessions, nuggets of social history and memories of the rare ol' times: these are walls that really do talk.

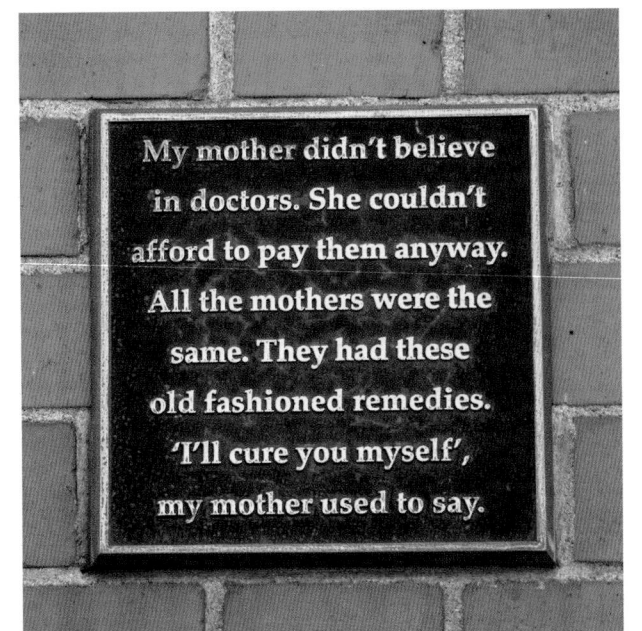

My mother didn't believe in doctors. She couldn't afford to pay them anyway. All the mothers were the same. They had these old fashioned remedies. 'I'll cure you myself', my mother used to say.

The plaques are based on recordings made by artist Chris Reid with local residents and installed as a commission under Dublin City Council's Public Art Programme. By casting them in bronze, and giving them a heritage-style appearance you might normally associate with official tributes or memorials, Reid further emphasises the fact that voices like these are so rarely heard. One local remarks on how good it would be if a community centre were to be built in the area. Others remember camaraderie in the pubs, local men taking bets as they tossed coins into a pot behind the Iveagh Baths, neighbours teaming up to wash their stairs, or the local ragman who tricked kids into swapping valuable clothes for goldfish.

Professor Declan McGonagle of the University of Ulster has suggested that the results "ventilate history from within". And certainly, these insights into a world out of sight for so many Dubliners can be startling in their simplicity. "My mother didn't believe in doctors," another reads. "She couldn't afford to pay them anyway. All the mothers were the same. They had these old-fashioned remedies. 'I'll cure you myself,' my mother used to say."

Since installing the plaques in 2009, Reid has published a book – *Heirlooms & Hand-me-downs* – that develops the stories and memories.

## THE MUSEUM FLAT

**(24)**

3B Iveagh Trust, Patrick Street, Dublin 8
• 01 454-2312 • liamfinegan@theiveaghtrust.ie
• Open: Small groups by appointment
• Transport: Tara Street DART station (20-min. walk); Luas, Harcourt Street (Green Line, 10-min.walk); Dublin Bus stops 2385 and 2310 are nearby

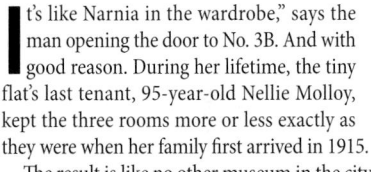

*The flat that's frozen in time*

" It's like Narnia in the wardrobe," says the man opening the door to No. 3B. And with good reason. During her lifetime, the tiny flat's last tenant, 95-year-old Nellie Molloy, kept the three rooms more or less exactly as they were when her family first arrived in 1915.

The result is like no other museum in the city: a living space frozen in time. At the heart of the sitting room stands an old Lambert range, still set with newspaper for kindling. Above it, there is a brass rail for hanging clothes, with a tasselled yellow drape hiding stove brushes. Lace curtains veil sash windows and quaint, floral wallpaper is bedecked with old family portraits, religious images, crucifixes and various icons like the Infant of Prague. The Iveagh Trust tried to modernise 3B several times (there is no bathroom or running water), but Nellie always refused – preferring her space as her family had kept it and perhaps fearing she might not get it back after a refurbishment. Old crockery remains in the cupboard. Nellie's dresser is peppered with hairclips, perfume and Holy Water. Above it, a little cushion is riddled with clothes pins.

The Iveagh Trust dates from 1890, when it was established by Sir Edward Cecil Guinness to provide affordable housing in Dublin and London. No. 3B was first let in 1904; Nellie's father, a British Army veteran named Henry Molloy, signed his tenancy agreement on 7 June 1915. Nellie and her four siblings slept in one bedroom – boys and girls separated by a curtain hung from a brass rail. Their parents took the other bedroom, sleeping beneath a large shrine to the Virgin Mary whose base Henry had decorated with a brass skirting fashioned from old artillery shells. The stand-up piano in the living room is no ornament – the family loved their hooleys, and wedding breakfasts in the flat were regularly followed by sing-songs.

As a young woman, Nellie worked for a linen company in Harold's Cross, even serving as shop steward before finally leaving to look after her aging mother. She never had a partner or children and, during the 1940s, is said to have declined an offer of marriage from "a disappointed Kilkenny man". She died on 29 October 2002, 35 years to the day after her mother. After discussions with her family, the Iveagh Trust purchased the contents of her flat, maintaining it as a museum that grows more magical with every passing year.

# GULLIVER'S TRAVELS  ㉕

Golden Lane & Bride Street, Dublin 8
• Transport: Tara Street DART station (15-min. walk); Dublin Bus stop 2383
(2–3-min. walk); Luas, St Stephen's Green (Green Line; 5–10-min. walk)

> ## Storied figures in stone

Jonathan Swift didn't just make his mark on St Patrick's Cathedral. A short distance away from the great building where Swift served as dean from 1713 to 1745, one of his most famous works is celebrated in a series of roundels embedded into the façades of council-built apartments along Golden Lane and Bride Street. Eight separate ceramic disks depict scenes from his classic novel, *Gulliver's Travels*.

As public housing goes, this is some of the best Dublin has to offer. The apartments were built by the then Dublin Corporation in 1998, a sturdy redbrick phalanx garnished with glass block corners, white steel railings and the figurative casts. The roundels followed as the buildings were nearing completion and are the work of Terry Cartin of Cartin Ceramics. Cartin researched the images in the Gilbert Library on Pearse Street before moulding and manipulating the clay, firing it at up to 1,200 degrees, and fitting the pieces together from a cherry picker during a scorching summer ("It was bloody hot," he recalls). The end results are much loved by residents of the apartments and a creative way of linking this part of Dublin with a great work of satirical literature. Swift's masterpiece was published in 1726 and scenes such as that depicting Gulliver waking to find his arms, legs and hair tied down by the tiny citizens of Lilliput, the giant kissing the queen's hand through her window, or pulling enemy ships with his hands, will be instantly recognisable to anyone who has read the book.

## ST PATRICK'S WELL

**26**

St Patrick's Park, Patrick Street, Dublin 8
• 01 475-5435
• www.dublincity.ie
• Transport: Luas, St Stephen's Green (Green Line; 5-min. walk); Dublin Bus stops 2383 and 2385 are nearby on Patrick Street

*A subterranean secret in St Patrick's Park*

**V**ery little concrete information exists about the life of St Patrick, but that hasn't stopped stories about the saint cropping up all over Ireland – from sombre sites like Croagh Patrick, where he spent time in the wilderness; or Down Cathedral, where he is reputedly buried; to quirky hits like the Holy Well at Struell, where he is said to have sung psalms all night … while naked.

In Dublin, tradition has it that St Patrick baptised the first Irish Christians in a well – thought to have been located around the site of the present-day St Patrick's Park. Presumably, the saint would have drawn water for his task from the River Poddle, which flows underground today, and a small parish church that stood on an island between two branches of the river was the original St Patrick's. The church was raised to cathedral status in 1213, and remains one of the quintessential Dublin visits today. Both it and the park were the beneficiaries of Guinness largesse, with Sir Benjamin Guinness spending a fortune restoring the cathedral in the 1860s, and Sir Edward Cecil Guinness, Lord Iveagh, developing St Patrick's Park, which was completed in 1904. Within it, in a small bed of shrubs, you'll find a stone plaque indicating that "near here" was the "reputed site" of St Patrick's Well.

This isn't just fanciful thinking. In 1901 building works beside the cathedral unearthed six Celtic grave slabs. Subsequently dated to the 10th century, one

of the granite slabs seems to have covered the remains of an ancient well. Two can be seen inside the cathedral today, where a plaque dates them to between 800 and 1100. The stone on the left is the one to look out for, resting on a plinth that declares it to have been found six feet [1.28m] below the surface on the traditional site of St Patrick's Well. Sadly, there is no information as to whether the saint was naked on his visit.

# THE COOMBE MONUMENT                                     ㉗

The Coombe, Dublin 8
• Transport: Dublin Bus stop 5025; Luas, Harcourt Street (Green Line; 15-min. walk)

> *Dublin characters, cast in stone*

Towards the end of 1825, two women and their newborn babies perished in heavy snow while attempting to reach the Rotunda Hospital. When their heart-wrenching story became public knowledge, a number of "benevolent and well-disposed people" clubbed together to found the Coombe Lying-In (Maternity) Hospital for the relief of poor women. History was made.

So we learn from the plaque affixed to this Dublin monument – a striking portico that looks like it's been beamed down next to a housing development along the Coombe. In fact, it's the other way round – the portico pre-dates the housing development and it served as the entrance to the Coombe Hospital until the institution moved to its present-day location in Dolphin's Barn in 1967. Although the hospital itself dates back to 1770, the maternity service for which it's known wasn't founded until 1826, when £100 was donated in memory of those two unfortunate Dublin mothers. After its relocation, the old hospital building was demolished to make way for today's modern redbrick development, with the granite portico restored by Dublin Corporation as a memorial to mothers who gave birth "to future citizens of Ireland" at the hospital, as well as to its staff and friends.

Those citizens have been a colourful bunch, if the steps to the rear of the portico are anything to judge by. Look closely and you'll see the names of several local characters inscribed in the stone: men like P. J. "Johnny Forty Coats" Marlow (who wore three or four overcoats no matter what the weather), Skin the Rasher, Shell Shock Joe, The Tuggers, the Hairy Yank, Lady Hogan, the Prince of Denmark, the Earl of Dalcashin, Bugler Dunner, Jembo No Toes and perhaps most beloved of all – Thomas "Bang Bang" Dudley.

Bang Bang's nickname stems from the mock shoot-outs he staged with his "gun" – a large church key. He was a lifelong fan of cowboy movies and locals regularly humoured him by returning fire on the streets. "Despite progressive eye disease, Bang Bang maintained his daily beat in the city, frequently causing mayhem by jumping onto buses, slapping his rear end as if he was on a horse," the *Irish Independent*'s obituary reported after his death in 1989.

# RUSH LAMP

**28**

St Patrick's Cathedral, St Patrick's Close, Dublin 8
- 01 453-9472
- www.stpatrickscathedral.ie
- Open: Mar–Oct: Mon–Fri 9.30am–5pm, Sat 9.30am–6pm, Sun 9am–10.30am, 12.30pm–2.30pm, 4.30pm–6pm. Nov–Feb: Mon–Fri 9.30am–5pm, Sat 9.30am–5pm, Sun 9am–10.30am, 12.30pm–2.30pm
- Admission: €6/€5
- Transport: Luas (Green Line) (5–10-min. walk from St Stephen's Green); Dublin Buses 49, 54a, 27, 56a, 77a and 150 all stop next to St Patrick's Cathedral

> **The light of Dean Swift's life …**

There are many mementos of Jonathan Swift at St Patrick's Cathedral. Swift famously served as dean here from 1713 until his death in 1745, and along with the pulpit from which he preached, visitors can see two rather pointy-nosed death masks, Swift's grave, a cast of his skull and a table at which he celebrated the Eucharist in his country parish in Co. Meath. Given his reputation as a writer, it's not surprising to find the cathedral in possession of some early editions, too.

Swift was almost 78 when he died, a ridiculously old age for the time, leading to speculation that his penchant for exercise and cleanliness may have paid a healthy dividend. "At a time when people rarely washed, Swift was obsessed with cleanliness," we are told. "He also exercised every day. In pleasant weather, he walked or went horseback riding. When bad weather kept him inside, Swift raced up and down the three sets of stairs in the Deanery." Talk about being ahead of the curve.

The most evocative artefact of all, however, is one of the least remarked upon. You'll find it in the cabinet alongside his waxy death mask – it's a rush lamp, by the light of which Swift and his closest friend, Esther Johnson (known as Stella), are said to have read together. At the time, rush lamps were regarded as lights for the poor – their flames coaxed from reeds soaked in flammable substances, such as wax, rather than more expensive candles. Swift never married, and scholars have debated the exact nature of his relationship with his muse, but he clearly delighted in Stella's company, writing to her daily when he was away in London, and composing ditties too. "Since I first saw thee at 16/The brightest virgin on the green/So little is thy form declined/Made up so largely in thy mind," as he wrote on her 34th birthday. The affection was repaid – Stella, who first met Swift when he worked for Sir William Temple on his estate in Surrey, moved to Ireland to be nearer the dean.

Whatever the nature of their relationship, there's something irresistibly romantic about this little rush lamp. Can't you imagine the pair huddled up together in a cavernous cathedral interior? Stella died, aged just 46, in 1728 (we are not privy to her exercise regime). Overcome with grief, Swift moved out of his usual rooms to avoid seeing her funeral lights in the cathedral windows.

# MARSH'S LIBRARY

**㉙**

St Patrick's Close, Dublin 8
• 01 454-3511
• www.marshlibrary.ie
• Open: Weekdays 9.30am–5pm, Sat 10am–1pm, Sun 10am-5pm. Closed Tues, Sun. Reading room by appointment only
• Admission: €3/€2, children U16 go free
• Transport: Luas (Green Line) (5–10-min. walk from St Stephen's Green); Dublin Buses 49, 54a, 27, 56a, 77a and 150 all stop next to St Patrick's Cathedral

*Ireland's first public library*

I
t may be Ireland's first public library, but there's a sizeable portion of Dubliners who have never heard of – let alone visited – the squirrelled-away Marsh's Library on St Patrick's Close.

The library is named after Archbishop Narcissus March (1638–1713), under whom it was built in 1701. Designed by Sir William Robinson, the architect responsible for the Royal Hospital at Kilmainham, its collection of 25,000 books is a picture-perfect example of how a fusty old library should be. Step through the ivy-strewn entrance arch, mosey up the dank steps, ring the bell and finally you are ushered into the hushed interior. Pay €3 to the gatekeeper and allow your eyes a moment to adjust to the rich palette of browns: the oak bookcases, the lettered gables, the beautifully tactile leather-bound books themselves. It feels like the kind of room in which you might stumble upon a lost literary secret, an ancient cure or the beginnings of a murder mystery (some of the books even bear bullet holes from the 1916 Easter Rising).

The books themselves date largely from the 16th to the 18th centuries and cover religion, medicine, law, travel, science, mathematics, music and classical literature. They range from hefty tomes to tiny curiosities: a small collection of verse, for instance, contains a poem to Queen Elizabeth I by Sir Walter Raleigh. Marsh's Library also contains some 300 manuscripts, with one "Lives of the Irish Saints" dating from 1400, and a Hebrew tome printed in 1491 bearing a note in the archbishop's own hand: *"Liber rarissimus"* (rare book). There are even special "cages" interspersed with the bookshelves – in times gone by, readers were locked into them while perusing rare books.

This is more than just a collection of old books, however. "Please try me!" reads a note in a ledger, inviting visitors to try the collection of quills. There's a death mask of Jonathan Swift and a skull cast of his friend and muse, Stella. Regular exhibitions based around themes in the books open up whole worlds of mystery and delight – such as the amazingly random "Anatomical Account of the Elephant Accidentally Burnt in Dublin on Friday, June 17, in the Year 1681". Who knew?

Among the relics, you may stumble across Narcissus Marsh himself. As the story goes, the archbishop was distraught when his niece, Grace, ran away to marry in secret. Grace wrote a letter to her uncle, which she stashed in the pages of one of his books, but Marsh was reportedly never able to locate it.

To this day, his ghost continues the search…

# THE CABBAGE GARDENS

**㉚**

Cathedral Lane, off Kevin Street, Dublin 8
• 01 222-5278 • www.dublincity.ie
• Open: Daily. Dec & Jan: 10am–5pm. Feb & Nov: 10am–5.30pm. March &
Oct: 10am–6.30pm. April & Sept: 10am–8.30pm. May & Aug: 10am–
9.30pm. June & July: 10am–10pm
• Admission: free
• Transport: Dublin Bus stop 2311 is nearby on Kevin Street Upper: it's
served by the 150, 151, 27, 26a and 77a bus routes; Luas, Harcourt St
(Green Line; 10-min. walk)

*"Think of God and follow me"*

**D**espite the earthy title, this is not the place to come for a head of cabbage.
Located at the top of Cathedral Lane, the Cabbage Gardens are in fact a small park named for the fact that Oliver Cromwell and his soldiers are said to have cultivated the vegetables here after their arrival on these shores in 1649. Cabbages hadn't been grown in Ireland before this time, so they must have seemed pretty exotic (Cathedral Lane itself was known as Cabbage Garden Lane until 1792). Today, however, you'll find a lung of green space surrounded by stacked gravestones, council flats and a five-a-side pitch.

The gravestones came after the cabbages – they date back to 1666, when the gardens were granted as a cemetery to the Parish of St Nicholas Without by the Dean and Chapter of St Patrick's Cathedral. Many local parishioners were buried there (as an information sign explains), including shoemakers, clothiers, grocers and timber merchants. In 1681 they were joined by French Huguenots, who leased a narrow strip of land in the north-western corner of the gardens. One of the most famous is David Digues La Touche des Rompières, who founded La Touche Bank – the precursor of today's Bank of Ireland – with fellow weaver Nathaniel Kane in 1722. He was buried here in 1745. Although Dublin City Council moved dozens of gravestones to the edge of the park when they opened it to the public in 1982, many inscriptions are still clearly legible today. A headstone erected by Henry Medcalfe "of the Poddle" in memory of his 20-year-old son John, for example, carries the jolly reminder:

*Passengers as you pass by*
*As you are now so once was I*
*As I am now so shall you be*
*Think of God and follow me*

Sadly, judging by the deteriorating state of the headstones, such messages may not be visible for much longer. Memorials in the north-western corner in particular have been thrashed by vandals, leaving their stone breaking apart, their inscriptions crumbling and their legacies collapsing into gravel littered with broken glass and cigarette butts.

# OUTSIDE THE CENTRE - NORTH

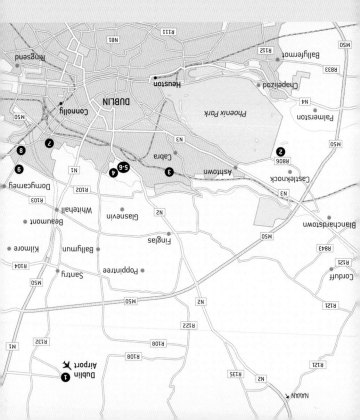

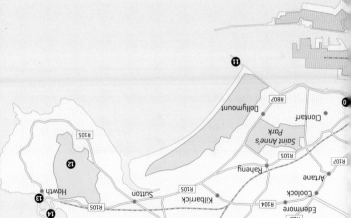

## OLD TERMINAL BUILDING ❶

Dublin Airport, Co. Dublin
• www.dublinairport.com
• There are guided tours of the original terminal during Open House Dublin, the Irish Architecture Foundation's annual open day (openhousedublin.com)
• Transport: Dublin Bus's Airlink 747 service connects Dublin Airport with several city stops, as do bus routes 16, 41 and 102. Private coach services are also in operation

*The golden age of Irish air travel*

Dublin Airport officially opened for business on 19 January 1940, when a propeller-driven Aer Lingus Lockheed 14 departed for Liverpool on a chilly Thursday morning.

Since then, the airport has mushroomed into a sprawling complex capable of processing 30 million passengers a year. The original building has been swallowed up in a spaghetti of terminals, runways, taxiways, access roads and office buildings, but passengers walking the skybridge between Terminal 1 and Pier D can steal a glimpse at the toothpaste-white façade and surgically curvy architecture in all their nostalgic glory. Surprisingly, the modernist jewel remains a working building, housing DAA offices, the Met Office's airport presence and some passenger boarding gates – so it's effectively still in use as a terminal.

Work on the building began in the late 1930s, to a design by Desmond FitzGerald. The tiered floors echo the form of a great ocean liner, and the building's form curved deliberately to present a long façade towards taxiing aircraft, and a shorter concave to arriving passengers – seeming to embrace them as they arrived at the door. Inside, check-in desks faced out into a double-height foyer, visitors were free to access the balconies as a viewing platform, and the staircase, with its travertine steps and brass railings, survives. The same cannot be said, alas, for a restaurant (run by the legendary Johnny Opperman) that once looked out onto the airfield, or the dances held here at night – something almost impossible to imagine today. But then, this was a time of handwritten tickets, going-away suits and security-free zones; a golden age of air travel immortalised on Dublin Airport's Pinterest site (pinterest.com/dublinairport). When Dublin's first transatlantic flight took off in 1958, Eamon de Valera quoted Charles Lindbergh: "In any development of transatlantic travel, Ireland holds the key."

Of course, it wasn't all romance. Air travel was notoriously expensive before the days of budget airlines, and many of those passing through this beautiful Old Terminal Building would have been emigrating – some never to return. Over time, Dublin's trickle of flights became a flood. Built to accommodate just 100,000 passengers a year, the original building was well and truly outgrown by the late 1950s, when a new North Terminal was added.

## DUNSINK OBSERVATORY

Castleknock, Dublin 15
• 01 440-6656
• www.dunsink.dias.ie
• Admission: free on open nights (7.30pm, first and third Wed from Oct to March – register ahead to attend)

*That pot of gold under a dump*

**D**riving deep into the suburbs of Castleknock, you mightn't expect to find the oldest purpose-built scientific research centre in Ireland. But that's exactly what Dunsink Observatory is.

Dating from 1785, when it opened as a facility for Trinity College, Dunsink is best known as the workplace of the great William Rowan Hamilton (1805–65), but it has its quirkier stories too.

The observatory is today part of the Dublin Institute for Advanced Studies, and although not open to the public per se, it is used for public outreach – hosting events during Science Week in November, for example, as well as open nights supported by the Irish Astronomical Society (irishastrosoc.org) on the first and third Wednesdays of winter months (October to March). These tend to include talks, Q&As and, weather permitting, the chance to gaze through the historic Grubb Telescope in the South Dome – it dates from 1868, a time when the Rathmines firm was exporting telescopes all over the world.

Inside the house itself, a line-up of old clocks evokes the observatory's former role in setting Ireland's time standard (some 25 minutes and 21 seconds behind GMT).

### Nixon's "goodwill moon rocks"

If you do attend a talk, you might ask how a lunar rock reportedly worth up to €4 million ended up in the nearby rubbish dump. The story dates back to Richard Nixon's presidency, when hundreds of moon rocks were sent as gifts around the world following the final Apollo landing expedition. Ireland's was kept in Dunsink Observatory, but got lost following a fire on 3 October 1977. In an interview with the BBC, a scientist who worked at Dunsink at the time claimed that the rock had been deposited with the rest of the rubble into Dunsink landfill nearby. "That pot of gold under a dump" is how Joseph Gutheinz Jr, a Texas-based lawyer and former NASA agent, described it to the BBC.

Finding the pea-sized treasure would be almost impossible, of course, but Dubliners can take some comfort in the fact that they are not alone – almost half of Nixon's "goodwill moon rocks" are said to be unaccounted for.

## BROOME BRIDGE

Broombridge Station, Cabra, Dublin 7
• Transport: Dublin Bus stops 286 and 828 are nearby on Carnlough Road;
Broombridge station is about 10 min. by Commuter service from Connolly
station

> *An equation etched in stone*

On 16 October 1843, Sir William Rowan Hamilton was struck by "a flash of genius" while walking along the banks of the Royal Canal. In that moment, as commemorated by a plaque on Broom Bridge, the physicist, astronomer and mathematician conceived of the fundamental formula for quaternion multiplication "and cut it on a stone of this bridge".

Archimedes had his "Eureka" moment in the bath. Hamilton (1805–65) had his while out walking with his wife. For years, the Dubliner had been pondering how to extend complex numbers to three dimensions, but suddenly he struck upon the idea of using four dimensions instead. "A very curious train of mathematical speculation occurred to me," as he wrote in a letter the following day. Pulling out a pocketknife, Hamilton cut his formula into the stone:

$$i^2+j^2+k^2 = ijk = -1$$

![Stone plaque on Broom Bridge reading: "Here as he walked by on the 16th of October 1843 Sir William Rowan Hamilton in a flash of genius discovered the fundamental formula for quaternion multiplication $i^2 = j^2 = k^2 = ijk = -1$ & cut it on a stone of this bridge"]

In 1958 a memorial plaque was unveiled by Éamon de Valera, himself a keen mathematician who had spent hours as a young man scouring the bridge for evidence of the equation. His search was in vain. "The weather had done its work," as Prof. Annraoí de Paor of UCD, who was present at the unveiling, recalls in his essay "An Unworldly Scholar".

Quaternions, four-dimensional numbers to which the commutative law of multiplication does not apply, blew algebra wide open. Hamilton's discovery paved the way for several major scientific breakthroughs, including the development of vector analysis and the theory of electromagnetic waves. Even today, as a mathematical shorthand for rotation calculations in 4D, quaternions are central to movie special effects, the control of spacecraft and computer graphics – they were used to create Lara Croft in the computer game, "Tomb Raider", for example. But Hamilton didn't stop there. He also invented biquaternions, made major contributions in mechanics, optics and geometry, and was knighted in 1835.

Sadly, Broome Bridge is not such an inspiring setting today. Sandwiched between a railway station and an industrial estate, its stony hump is regularly festooned with litter and graffiti and brightened only by the occasional duck or swan. A Hamilton walk is held annually on 16 October, however, setting out from his former base at Dunsink Observatory.

# WITTGENSTEIN'S STEP

**4**

National Botanic Gardens, Glasnevin, Dublin 9
• 01 857-0909 (visitor centre)
• www.botanicgardens.ie
• Open: Winter (second-last Sunday in October to last Sunday in February): Mon–Fri 9am–4.30pm, weekends & public holidays 10am–4.30pm. Summer (first Sunday in March to last Sunday of October): Mon–Fri 9am–5pm, weekends & public holidays 10am–6pm
• Admission: free
• Transport: Dublin Bus routes 4 and 9 (from O'Connell Street) and 83 (Kimmage/Harristown)

> *"When the sun shines in my brain ..."*

The National Botanic Gardens are home to some 17,000 plant species, but just as exotic is this modest bronze plaque found in its Victorian palm house. It marks the spot (or step, to be precise) where Ludwig Wittgenstein (1889–1951) came to sit and write in his notebook during a short but very productive stay in Dublin over the course of a winter in the late 1940s.

During his stay, the Viennese philosopher roomed at the Ross Hotel on Parkgate Street. He is said to have liked Dublin – describing it as having the air of "a real capital city" – and during the winter of 1948 he spent time writing, thinking, walking, enjoying black coffee and omelettes at Bewley's of Grafton Street and relaxing with his good friend, the Irish physicist Dr Con Drury, according to Richard Wall's book, *Wittgenstein in Dublin* (Reaktion Books, 2000). His stay appears to have been fruitful, too. "When I came here I found to my surprise that I could work again; and as I'm anxious to make hay during the very short period when the sun shines in my brain, I've decided … to stay here where I've got a warm and quiet room," the philosopher wrote in a letter dated 6 November 1948. Wittgenstein was troubled by health issues that winter, but not enough to prevent regular visits to the National Botanic Gardens, whose Victorian palm house may have reminded him of Vienna. Sitting inside this lovely spaceship of a structure, he would have been insulated from the chilly weather, and it's tempting to imagine him working on his posthumously published work, *Philosophical Investigations* (1953). Strangely for an author seen by many as the greatest philosopher of the 20th century, Wittgenstein only had a single book – the 75-page *Tractatus Logico-Philosophicus* – published during his lifetime.

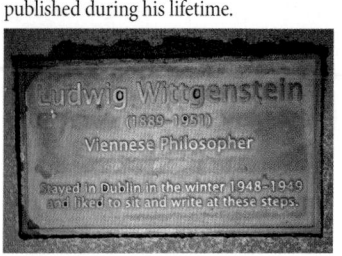

The National Botanic Gardens, which date from 1795, are home to Ireland's richest plant collection. Over 300 of its specimens are rare or endangered, with six technically extinct in the wild. The palm house was erected in 1883 after a previous structure was damaged in a storm.

# DANIEL O'CONNELL'S CRYPT

**5**

Glasnevin Cemetery, Finglas Road, Dublin 11
- 01 882-6500 • www.glasnevintrust.ie
- Open: Access by guided tour only. Tours leave at 11.30am and 2.30pm year-round, with an extra slot at 1pm during summer
- Admission: €12 (tickets include tours and museum access)
- Transport: Dublin Bus 140 from O'Connell Street

> "My body to Ireland, my soul to heaven, my heart to Rome"

A 170-ft (52m) granite tower marking the burial place of Daniel O'Connell (1775–1847) dominates Glasnevin Cemetery. It's impossible to avoid George Petrie's monument when you enter the cemetery gates – indeed, as the highest round tower in Ireland, the structure is visible for several kilometres around. What lies beneath, however, is another story.

Although routinely locked to the public, visitors can gain access to O'Connell's crypt by joining a guided tour of the cemetery. The crypt has recently been restored after lying closed for more than a decade and features a Kilkenny marble altar inscribed with a Durrow Cross as its centrepiece. The tomb is contained within a room decorated with a swirling mix of Christian and Celtic symbols, a mosaic-tiled floor and a sculpted scene of the Crucifixion. Also featured, in gold lettering on a green band, is O'Connell's dying wish: "My body to Ireland, my soul to heaven, my heart to Rome." The Liberator passed away in Genoa while on a pilgrimage to the Italian capital, and in accordance with his wishes, his heart continued on to the Irish College in Rome while his body was interred at Glasnevin. Strangely, the oak and lead-lined coffin lies within easy reach through several shamrock-shaped holes in the stone. It's said that touching it brings the visitor luck, and around the edges that are easiest to access, the wood has been worn smooth. If you bend down and peer right into the recesses, a cross and inscription can be made out, covered in a layer of dust. The access feels extraordinary – especially since the monument was the target of a suspected loyalist bomb attack in the 1970s.

O'Connell, renowned for his success in securing Catholic emancipation, was also responsible for the establishment of the non-denominational Glasnevin Cemetery in 1832. At the time, Irish Catholics had no dedicated cemeteries of their own, and the lands were acquired to lay to rest "people of all religion and none". Several members of O'Connell's family have also been interred beneath the tower – somewhat unsettlingly, their wooden coffins can be seen stacked on top of each other in a little room branching off the main crypt.

## MICHAEL COLLINS' SECRET ADMIRER ❻

Glasnevin Cemetery, Finglas Road, Dublin 11
- 01 882-6500
- www.glasnevintrust.ie
- Open: Mon–Fri 10am–5pm, Sun & Bank Holidays 11am–5pm
- Admission: free (tours and museum access: €12)
- Transport: Dublin Bus route 140 departs from O'Connell Street

*The Big Fella's blooms*

Some 1.2 million souls are buried at Glasnevin Cemetery, ranging from political leaders like Daniel O'Connell, Charles Stewart Parnell and Éamon de Valera to nameless victims of Ireland's famine and cholera outbreaks. For sheer star power, however, none can match the cult of Michael Collins (1890–1922) – Glasnevin's most visited grave.

Set just behind the cemetery's distinctive museum and cafe, the grave and cross are bedecked with an explosion of flowers that seems to refresh itself on a daily basis. "It's got nothing to do with us," a guide says, describing the constant procession of visitors bearing blooms, cards and even love letters to the last resting place of the charismatic hero, who was assassinated at the age of 32. Many of the fresh flowers are sent or personally delivered, the guide reveals, by a mysterious French lady. "I think her name is Véronique."

Indeed it is. The *Sunday Independent* recently identified Véronique Crombé, a museum guide and lecturer from Paris, as Collins' secret admirer. In an interview with the newspaper, Crombé described the "overwhelming" desire she has to keep his memory alive – a desire sparked when she first saw Neil Jordan's movie, *Michael Collins* (1996). On 22 August 2000, the anniversary of Collins' death at Béal na Bláth, Crombé felt the inexplicable need to rush into a cathedral to light a candle. "The 22nd, the date he was shot dead, was the decisive moment which helped me understand that definitely, sooner or later, I would have to go to Ireland to know more and that going to his grave would show me the way. That Michael himself was drawing me to continue on his story." Her first visit to Glasnevin had a profound effect, she says. "It was the start of something that is still with me. When a person dies young, an energy is left behind. An energy surrounding things left undone."

Crombé sends flowers from France on St. Patrick's Day and significant anniversaries, but she's not alone in her devotion. For years, Collins's grave had been looked after by another admirer, Dennis Lenihan. Several other men, united by a passion for history and the same respect for Collins, have now joined him - including James Langton, Paul Callery, Ronnie Daly, Paul Fleming and Rod Dennison. The "mysterious French lady" has a romantic appeal, Véronique concedes, but she urges us not to forget the dedication of her friends.

BVILT
IN THE
YEAR
5618

# JEWISH CEMETERY

❼

67 Fairview Strand, Dublin 3
• Open: If you're lucky
• Transport: Clontarf Road DART station (10–15-min. walk); Dublin Bus
123 stops at bus stop 4518 on Fairview Strand at Richmond Road

> **Built
> in the year 5618**

"**B**uilt in the year 5618". If ever a plaque was designed to grab your attention, this is it. Even its context is mystifying. It's set into the wall of a tiny gatehouse that looks ready to float off at any moment, like Mr Fredricksen's house in the film *Up*. What's the story?

First off, don't worry. Fairview Strand is not a blip in the space–time continuum: 5618 is a date from the Hebrew calendar, which is based on lunar months. The equivalent year in the Gregorian calendar is 1857, when the lodge was constructed. And beyond it lies Fairview's Jewish cemetery.

The cemetery itself dates from 1718, when it was leased from Captain Chichester Phillips of Drumcondra Castle. It was bought outright in 1748, "as a leasehold for 1,000 years at the annual rent of one peppercorn", as Diarmuid G. Hiney writes in the *Dublin Historical Record* (Vol. 50, No. 2, 1997), and served as a burial ground for Jews living in Dublin until 1900, when a larger cemetery opened in Dolphin's Barn. Though the area feels rather grimy today, and the surrounding walls are sporadically tagged with graffiti, Fairview Strand was once a fashionable area with fine views of Dublin Bay. Only a handful of burials took place after 1900, the last of which was in 1958.

The lodge was built to house a caretaker. Walls were added for greater privacy and to protect against grave-robbers – a scourge of Dublin cemeteries at the time. "In 1839, laws of the Dublin Jewish Congregation stated that after every burial, bodies should be watched for a week," Hiney writes. "A quaint anecdote is told about the headstone of Solomon Cohen which disappeared, and one of his sons on visiting a Christian friend in the area noted that his father was buried in the chimney breast." One wonders if Mr Cohen's remains still lie in the listed building …

Today, the Dublin Jewish Board of Guardians maintains the tiny plot, with the assistance of resident caretakers. "The best I can tell you is to knock at the door," Secret Dublin was told in the off-licence nearby (we received no answer). Intriguingly, a window above the "5618" plaque is spotted with Catholic icons like the Infant of Prague, the Virgin Mary and St Anthony … it looks like an Irish household of the 1950s, complete with lace curtain. If you don't get an answer either, here's a tip: take the no. 123 double-decker bus along the road and peer over the wall, bypassing all the formalities.

# 15 MARINO CRESCENT

Marino Crescent, Clontarf, Dublin 3
• Transport: Clontarf Road DART station (2–3 min. walk); bus stop 613 is nearby on Howth Road, beside Marino Crescent

*Bram Stoker's birthplace*

Clontarf has its castle – an atmospheric hotel with its origins in a Norman defensive structure built by Hugh de Lacy in 1172. Much as fans might wish it, however, *Dracula*'s author wasn't born there. In fact, Bram Stoker arrived in a humbler, though no less interesting abode at 15 Marino Crescent.

Visit the Crescent today and you'll find a leafy residential street curving round the agreeable oval of Bram Stoker Park. No gargoyles, turrets or coffins … just an elegant terrace of Georgian villas dating back to 1792. They've had mixed fortunes since – some of the houses are still handsome; others just look happy to be there. No. 15, where Bram was born to Abraham Stoker and Charlotte Mathilda Blake Thornley in 1847, is definitely one of the latter. Sandwiched between its taller siblings, the three-storey-over-basement affair looks modest, even plain, thanks to its featureless façade. At a stretch, the chimney stacks could be viewed as fang-like – but really, the only thing vampiric about this villa is its blood-red door. There's no literary plaque, and it has been privately owned since Stoker's day.

As the house is a private residence, visitors cannot venture inside. But it's titillating, nevertheless, to think that the author of *Dracula* was born here. The third of seven children, Stoker was a sickly child and lay bedridden with a mystery illness until he was 7. "I was naturally thoughtful, and the leisure of long illness gave opportunity for many thoughts which were fruitful according to their kind in later years," he would write. During these early years, could his mother have begun passing on horror stories of cholera victims buried alive in her native Sligo? It's tempting to think so …

Interestingly, Stoker also married a resident of Marino Crescent: Florence Balcombe, who counted Oscar Wilde among her suitors, had lived at No. 1.

---

Despite its links with Stoker, Marino Crescent's nickname – "Spite Row" – has nothing to do with Dracula. In fact, it dates from the late 1700s, when a developer involved in a spat with Lord Charlemont, the owner of the Marino estate and the nearby Casino, built it in such a way as to obstruct his views of Dublin Bay. The Earl was unimpressed, if not undead.

# THE CASINO AT MARINO  ❾

Cherrymount Crescent, off Malahide Road, Marino, Dublin 3
• 01 833-1618 • www.heritageireland.ie
• Open: March to October (check website for dates). Opening hours:
10am–5pm (March, May & October), 10am-6pm (June-September).
Public tours on the hour. • Admission: €4/€2
• Transport: Clontarf DART station (15-min. walk); Dublin Bus routes 14, 27,
27a, 27b and 128 (from Eden Quay) and 42 and 43 (from Abbey St Lower)
stop at bus stop 665 on Malahide Road

*A small
house
with a big
reputation*

I t's Dublin's littlest big house. Or perhaps Dublin's biggest little house. Either way, there's no doubting the Casino's selling point. Designed by Sir William Chambers as a flight of fancy for James Caulfield, the First Earl of Charlemont, the "small house" measures barely 4m² in total.

Here's the surprise, however. Though it looks like a folly, and despite having only a handful of visible windows, the Casino actually contains 16 rooms. Not only that, but they're breathtakingly rich in both subtlety and design. Together, its interiors and exterior amount to "one of the most fascinating essays in stone in Ireland," as David Newman Johnson has put it in the *Irish Arts Review*.

As with many young aristocrats of his day, Caulfield was inspired on a Grand Tour of Europe, and he returned to Dublin determined to build an estate with Italian flair. It was fashionable at the time to adorn estates with garden temples, hunting lodges, hermitages and the like – but the Casino, begun in 1760 and completed over the course of two decades, was a more unusual miniature. By all accounts, Charlemont and Chambers spared little cost in its construction. The Casino's principal floor takes the form of a Greek cross, surrounded by a dozen or so Doric columns. Its Portland stone carvings are beautifully rendered, the rooftop urns mask a pair of chimneys, and inside – another surprise – there are two storeys and a basement, containing eight vaulted servants' rooms. In the attic, you'll find Lord Charlemont's State Bedroom, complete with Ionic columns.

After falling into neglect during the latter half of the 18th century, the Casino was acquired by the State and painstakingly restored to the excellent condition in which it is found today. Plasterwork, friezes, inlaid floors, rosewood mahogany doors – the depth of detailing ensures that, 250 years on, the house is regarded as one of the most exquisite neoclassical garden temples in Europe.

Charlemont opened his park to the public, allowing locals to admire the Casino and its spectacular views over Dublin Bay. Not everyone was enthralled, however. Lead was stolen on several occasions from the building's roof, and Marino Crescent (close to Clontarf DART station) was built with the deliberate intention of spoiling Charlemont's view. Its nickname? "Spite Row".

## ST ANTHONY'S HALL

**(10)**

Clontarf Road, Dublin 3
- 01 833-3459
- www.stanthonysclontarf.ie
- Transport: Clontarf DART station (10-min. walk); Dublin Bus routes 130 and 32x stop at bus stops 1737 and 1742 on Clontarf Road

*Birthplace of the nation?*

**W**here exactly is the birthplace of the modern Irish nation? The GPO, where Padraig Pearse read the Proclamation of the Republic in April 1916? Kilmainham Gaol, where the leaders of that Rising were executed? The Shelbourne Hotel, where the constitution was drafted in 1922?

Or perhaps somewhere rather less grandiose. Say, a town hall in Clontarf?

At first glance, St Anthony's Hall appears more like a church. Indeed, this was its function for several decades before the present-day parish church (to the rear) was built in 1975. Prior to 1925, however, it served as a town hall and was let out by Dublin Corporation for various purposes – concerts, movies, dances and the like. One of those events was held to raise money for Peadar Kearney, author of the national anthem, after he shot himself in the foot during rifle practice with the Irish Republican Brotherhood's Dublin Brigade.

Members of the IRB also used the space to congregate for some years, with a key meeting held on Sunday, 16 January 1916. Behind closed doors that evening, the Supreme Council of the IRB made a decision that was to change the course of Irish history – albeit unbeknownst to many of those present. The military council had been edging towards setting Easter Sunday as a date for a rising in the city, and at this meeting, Sean McDermott moved that the IRB should rise "at the earliest possible time". One of those present "recalled [Padraig] Pearse hinting about Easter, and somebody replying that it was a busy time for farmers," as Austen Ogran writes in his biography of James Connolly. "The Supreme Council assented in ignorance of the plans for Easter Sunday." History was made.

In 1998, alas, a substantial portion of the former town hall was demolished – including the historic room where the IRB decided to authorise the Easter Rising.

---

Two years before the Easter Rising, Clontarf had been the location for another skirmish that might well have influenced the course of history. In 1914 Volunteers running guns from Howth were intercepted at Clontarf by a force of police and soldiers. "A parley took place," as Michael Collins told the author Hayden Talbot. Shots were fired, and one of the Volunteers was bayoneted.

"By this time there was only the front rank of our force anywhere in sight! The rest of us ... had disappeared across the fields! And so not one gun was lost!"

# REALT NA MARA

Bull Island, Clontarf, Co. Dublin
• Transport: Dart (Clontarf Road Dart Station, 30-min. walk), Dublin Bus stops 1751 and 1727 are nearby on Clontarf Road, serviced by the 130 bus from Lower Abbey Street.

*Star of the sea...*

I n 1950, Dublin dockers began paying instalments of a shilling into a fund created for the construction of a memorial to Our Lady in Dublin Bay. When a guinea (21 shillings) had been amassed, they were issued with a signed certificate: a document that hung proudly in many houses.

Delays finding a site meant that Clontarf's soaring 'Realt na Mara' ('Star of the Sea') wasn't erected until 1972, but all those thousands of shillings were put to good use in the end.

Set at the end of the North Bull Wall, reached after crossing Bull Island's iconic single-lane wooden bridge, the walk out to 'Realt na Mara' is as nostalgic as it is bracing. Along the way, you'll pass old bathing areas and spot kite-surfers and exotic birds hovering over Dollymount Strand (sometimes, it's hard to distinguish between the two). Our Lady herself lies at the walk's endpoint, a windy spot where views extend to Howth, the Pigeon House Towers and Bray Head. Perched 70-foot atop of a concrete tripod, she watches over Dublin Bay – hands borne outwards, palms turned upwards. Twelve cut-glass stars from Waterford Crystal are embedded in her halo, glistening in the sun. Even without the Catholic context, the sense of an angel watching over the water is strangely comforting. At night, the Star of the Sea is floodlit from beneath, making a beautiful sight from Clontarf's prom.

---

Until 200 years ago, Bull Island didn't exist. The island only emerged, in fact, when sea walls were built to combat silting problems in Dublin Bay. North and South Walls forced receding tides to carve silt from the Liffey channel, and in time, the residue accumulated next to the North Bull.

With its long, sandy beach, Dubliners quickly embraced the mushrooming island as an amenity, and today, Bull Island hosts a golf club and Nature Reserve teeming with tens of thousands of birds. Brent Geese, Grey Plover, Redshank, Oyster Catchers and Curlew can all be found in the mudflats, salt marshes and dunes of what is now a UNESCO Biosphere Reserve.

---

# MUCK ROCK

⑫

Howth, Co. Dublin

• Transport: Howth DART station (5–10-min. walk); Dublin Buses 31 and 31a serve bus stop 557 at Howth Road DART station, a short walk from the turn-off to Howth Castle

*Pirates, warriors and stunning views*

**M**ost hikers coming to Howth head for the Cliff Path or Tramline loops. But beautiful as they are, there's another tramp that takes you to views that top the lot.

To access Muck Rock, walk west from the harbour and pass through the gates of Howth Castle. Dating in its current form from the 16th century, the castle has been home to the Gaisford-St Lawrence family for hundreds of years and runs a cookery school in the old kitchens. Tradition has it that Grace O'Malley, the pirate queen, landed at Howth around 1757 and called in at the castle in the hope of dining there and obtaining supplies. The gates were closed to her, however. Greatly offended, O'Malley abducted Lord Howth's heir and took him to Co. Mayo. He was returned on the promise that the gates would never be shut at dinner time and that a place would always be laid at the table for an unexpected guest. That extra place continues to be laid to this very day.

To get to the rock, continue to the Deer Park Hotel, following the golf course to the right of the building until the pathway enters the thickets of rhododendron at its base. This is easier at some times of year, and in some types of weather, than others (it's not for its cleanliness and ease of access that the hill is known as Muck Rock). As you walk, watch out for Aideen's Grave, a collapsed portal tomb dating from megalithic times, said to be named after the wife of Oscar na Fianna. Oscar, a legendary warrior, was the son of Oisín and Niamh (of Tir na nÓg) and the grandson of Fionn Mac Cumhaill. His death caused his grandfather to weep for the first (and only) time in his life, and Aideen to die of grief. Oisín is said to have built the tomb at Howth, the capstone for which weighs over 70 tonnes. It has long since collapsed, giving the appearance of a huddle of rocks, or some ancient husk.

Winding up the hill, you'll eventually pass through the leaves to a stunning view of Dublin Bay. On a clear day, you can see as far as the Mourne Mountains from here. Even in poor weather, you can make out the kitesurfers on Dollymount Strand and the Martello Tower on Ireland's Eye offshore. The tiny island can be reached via ferry from the East Pier, with a hidden beach offering one of the best picnic spots in the city, its stacks teeming with seabirds – including puffin, terns and guillemots.

Not a bad return for a walk up a muddy rock.

# YE OLDE HURDY GURDY MUSEUM ⓭

Martello Tower, Howth, Co. Dublin
- 086 815-4189
- hurdygurdyradiomuseum.wordpress.com
- Open: May–Oct: 11am–4pm. Nov–April (weekends only) 11am–4pm
- Admission: €5/€3 (children free)
- Transport: Howth DART station (5–10-min. walk); Dublin Bus routes 31 and 31a serve bus stop 557 at Howth Road Dart Station (10-min. walk)

*E10MAR*
*calling*

**A**hurdy gurdy may officially be a musical instrument, but ever since former Taoiseach Seán Lemass walked into the studios of Radio Eireann one day in the 1950s, asking the controller "How's the hurdy gurdy?", it has taken on a life of its own.

Well, it has in the mind of Pat Herbert, anyway. Herbert is the owner of Ye Olde Hurdy Gurdy Museum, a fascinating collection of vintage radios and communications devices housed in a hilltop Martello tower in Howth. Having grown up in Co. Mayo, he traces his own love affair with radio back to an afternoon spent listening to the 1947 All-Ireland Football Final as it was broadcast live from New York. Collecting went on to become a passion.

On display are all manner of curios. Stacks of historic devices line the 8ft-thick (2.4m) walls of the tower – a 1940s Marconi here, a 1920s crystal radio there. A Paris Aerial looks like a framed photograph of Rita Hayworth until it's turned around to reveal wires, dials and instructions for gaining reception. Based on an aerial designed by the French underground movement as an answer to Germany's jamming of BBC news bulletins during the Second World War, it went on to become a novelty household device. Other whimsical creations are designed to look like spice racks, chameleons or cars. There are beautifully retro TV and radio all-in-ones, old valve machines, a 110-year-old Edison phonograph and 1950s trannies made to look like ladies' handbags. Most spellbinding of all, perhaps, is the actual Heathkit Apache ham radio set that brought first word of the Niemba ambush to General Seán McEoin. On 8 November 1960, eleven Irish soldiers were ambushed by Baluba tribesmen while on peacekeeping duties in the Congo. Nine were killed, and news of their fate was delivered to the Chief of Staff on this very machine.

The Martello tower in which Herbert's collection is displayed also has its place in the history of Irish radio and communications. Lee De Forest, the American radio pioneer, experimented with transmissions here in 1903 and it later housed a Marconi station. Today, the tower and museum are home to an amateur radio station with the call sign "EI0MAR".

# GEORGE IV'S FOOTPRINTS

West Pier, Howth
• Transport: Howth DART station (5–10-min. walk); Dublin Buses 31 and 31a stop at bus stop 557 at Howth Road DART station, a short walk from the West Pier

*King-sized boots to fill*

I t's fair to say that history hasn't been kind to King George IV (reigned 1820–30). But then George IV wasn't exactly kind to history. "One of the idlest monarchs ever to ascend to a throne," is how Irish historian Turtle Bunbury puts it. From shortly after his birth in 1762, when the attending courtier declared him to be a girl, to his death in 1830, the king was variously described as lazy, inept, drunk, corpulent, absurd, vain, fitful, cruel, indulgent, dissolute, a national joke and an inveterate spendthrift.

In 1821, shortly after his coronation, George IV visited Ireland, where he is said to have staggered off the boat at Howth in a state of intoxication. He had apparently gorged himself on goose pie and Irish whiskey during the crossing, after which his landing footprints – pointy-toed and dainty of heel – were cast on the West Pier by stonemason Robert Campbell. From there, the king went on to wow the Irish population, as Bunbury writes, "by drinking toasts, shaking people by the hand, and calling them all Jack and Tom … like a popular candidate come down upon an electioneering trip."

Almost 200 years later, the footprints remain on the pier – "16 paces in this direction", as a sign helpfully points out – and are regularly filled with rain and/ or seawater. They barely hint at the catastrophes that preceded and followed the brief moment during which the casts were taken.

George was as renowned for his extravagant lifestyle as his disastrous marriage. In fact, his wife, Caroline of Brunswick, died just five days before he landed at Howth – though the monarch not only saw fit to continue with his travel plans, but remained abroad during her funeral. Pressing business included visiting his mistress, Elizabeth Conyngham, at Slane Castle. "It is believed that the reason the road from Dublin to Slane is one of the straightest roads in Ireland is because it was so designed to speed him on his journey," as Henry Conyngham, the Eighth Marquess Conyngham, writes on his website. To this day, the bedroom he slept in at Slane is known as the King's Room.

Needless to say, George IV is remembered almost wholly without sympathy. Although his visit to Ireland was a success, Robert Huish wrote in his biography of 1831 that he had contributed more "to the demoralisation of society than any prince recorded in the pages of history".

# OUTSIDE THE CENTRE - SOUTH

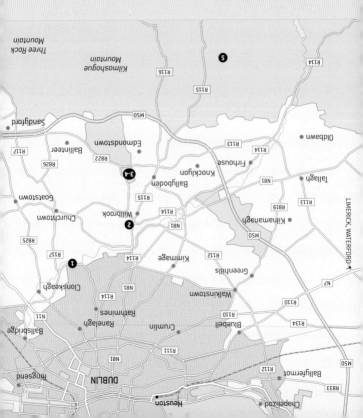

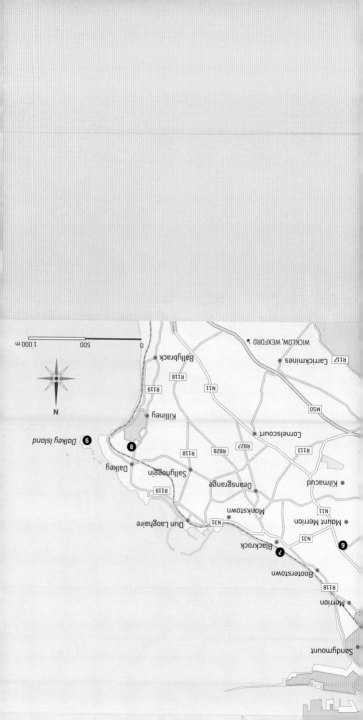

# THE DODDER RHINO

**❶**

Classon's Bridge, Milltown Road, Dublin 6
• Transport: Dublin Bus stops 2817 and 2898 are a 10-min. walk away on
Milltown Road, near the intersection with Dundrum Road

*We couldn't
get a hippo*

T he River Dodder is renowned for its
wildlife. Gushing through Tempelogue,
Bushy Park, Milltown and Donnybrook
before joining the Liffey at Ringsend, it's
possible to see otter, kingfisher, bats, brown
trout and cormorants along its course. And, erm … rhino.

Or at least, one rhino. He's made of bronze, bolted to a concrete platform in
the water just west of Classon's Bridge and shrouded in mystery. The sculpture
is said to have appeared overnight in 2002, but nobody seems to have claimed
responsibility or ownership (officially, at any rate). Staff at the Dropping Well
pub, which overlooks the river at the junction of the Milltown and Churchtown
roads, won't be drawn on the beast's provenance. "We couldn't get a hippo," was
the cryptic response when Secret Dublin made inquiries …

The pub has, however, come up with a name – "Woody" – apparently decided
upon following a customer competition. The rhino has also been known to don
a Santa hat at Christmas, so perhaps it's not completely outlandish to suggest
a publicity stunt. Extinction does not appear to be on the cards either. Despite
being knocked over by floods and having debris regularly festooned about his
hooves, the Dodder Rhino recently celebrated his tenth anniversary.

The Dropping Well itself was first licensed during the Great Famine in 1847
– not just as a pub, but a community morgue. During those years, a steady trail
of starving and disease-ridden souls would have walked and communed along
the riverbanks here, so twinning the two must have made sense to John Howe,
the pub's original owner. Today, you'll find tables in the dining area with views
over the river, a granite bridge named after John Classon (who built it and the
sawmill that once stood on the site of the pub) and, of course, Woody the rhino.

# RATHFARNHAM CASTLE

②

Rathfarnham, Dublin 14
- 01 493-9462
- www.heritageireland.ie
- www.rathfarnhamcastle.ie
- Open: Wed-Sun 9.30am-5.30pm (year-round)
- Admission: €4/€2
- Transport:Dublin Buses routes 16, 16A, 17 and 17A stop by Rathfarnham Castle

*A fascinating fortified house*

In 1912 Fr. Frank Browne was a Jesuit trainee and passenger on the RMS *Titanic*. He travelled out of Southampton on the first leg of the ship's maiden voyage, taking dozens of photographs that have gone on to become iconic records of the liner and its passengers.

He never got further than Cobh, however. Although Browne had been invited to remain for the full journey, when *Titanic* dropped anchor off the coast of Cork a brusque telegram from his Provincial was waiting. "GET OFF THAT SHIP", it said: 1,517 passengers and crew went on to lose their lives, while Browne disembarked with his treasure trove.

That's just one of the fascinating facts popping up on a tour of Rathfarnham Castle, an unusual suburban heritage gem that just gets more intriguing the deeper you look. The castle dates from 1583, when it was built for Adam Loftus (1533–1605), the former Archbishop of Dublin, Lord Chancellor of Ireland and first Provost of Trinity College. It's probably the earliest example of a "fortified house" built in Ireland. Such buildings, as the OPW's website (rathfarnhamcastle.ie) outlines, mark a significant stage in the transition from military castles to country houses in Ireland – going some way to explaining the castle's weird, hybrid appearance, which is further underscored by its toothpaste-white lime rendering.

The original fortified building, with its flanker towers, was substantially remodelled by Henry Loftus, the Earl of Ely (1709–83). Further, 20th-century wings (now demolished) were added by the Jesuits, who bought the building in 1913, a year after the *Titanic* sank, using it as a seminary and retreat right up to the 1980s. Browne spent time living at the castle, taking many photographs of it (you can view some in the South Dublin County Library digital archive at source.southdublinlibraries.ie). Highlights of today's sparse, but beautifully restored interiors, range from original rococo stuccowork to 16th-century gun loops and sweeping spaces like the first-floor ballroom. Look out for a small passageway dubbed "Apollo Sunburst Passage" – its ceiling is the work of William Chambers, while the roundels over the doors were designed by James "Athenian" Stuart. This is the only house in Ireland where designs by the two can be seen in one place. The secret histories just keep on coming.

# HUDSON'S FOLLIES

**3**

St Enda's Park, Grange Road, Rathfarnham, Co. Dublin
- 01 493-4208
- www.pearsemuseum.ie
- Open: Nov-Jan 9am-4.30pm; Feb 9am-5.30pm, Mar 9am-6pm, April 9am-8pm, May-August 9am-9pm, Sept 9am-8pm, Oct 9am-6pm. From 10am at weekends and on holidays
- Admission: free
- Transport: Dublin Bus 16 stops opposite the park on Grange Road

> **Robert Emmet's courting grounds**

**S**ay the words "park" and "Rathfarnham" and one place comes to mind: Marlay Park has been a playground for generations of locals, hosting everything from buggy-pushers to summer rock concerts to hikers setting off on the Wicklow Way. But there's another park nearby – 33 hectares of greenery that are arguably more beautiful, and certainly more intriguing.

St Enda's Park was laid out in the late 18th century by Edward Hudson (1743–1821), a wealthy dentist with a practice on Grafton Street. He bought the property, christened it "The Hermitage" and set about dotting the woodland paths with a unique collection of follies based on Irish field monuments. They are still there today. Follow the meandering trails through the trees, and you'll come across a hermit's cave, an Ogham stone, a vaulted archway, a ruined abbey and a stone watchtower. There's a faux hermitage, built from a jumble of stones in the eastern woodlands. Its doorway is locked today, but a room inside contains an arched recess and a stone bench, and a dolmen outside doubles up as a picnic table.

Such follies might be dismissed as an elaborate waste of money, of course – were it not for the romance of one particular local tradition. Hudson is said to have allowed the Irish nationalist leader Robert Emmet to meet secretly with his sweetheart Sarah Curran in the grounds (Curran's family lived nearby, and the avenue forming the northern border of the park is named after her today), so it's tempting to imagine the pair whispering amid the ruins. After their clandestine courtship, the couple became engaged in 1802, though their romance was cut short after Emmet's ill-fated rebellion of that year. He was captured as he attempted to visit Curran in Rathfarnham and subsequently executed – on a butcher's block.

That same block – so it is claimed – can be found in the Pearse Museum today. The museum is housed in Hudson's old mansion, which later became Padraig Pearse's home and boarding school for boys. Pearse renamed "The Hermitage" as "St Enda's Park" in 1910.

# PEARSE BIRTHPLACE & MUSEUM ❹

Birthplace: 27 Pearse Street, Dublin 2
Museum: St Enda's Park, Rathfarnham
• 01 493-4208 • www.pearsemuseum.ie
• Museum: Nov-Jan Mon-Sat 9.30am-4pm; Feb Mon-Sat, 9.30am-4pm;
March-Oct Mon-Sat 9.30am-5pm. On Sundays and bank holidays,
the museum opens at 10am
• Admission: free
• Birthplace: Pearse Street DART station (5-min. walk)
• Museum: Dublin Bus 16 stops opposite St Enda's Park on Grange Road

> *Schools and shopfronts*

**P**adraig Pearse (1879–1916) was one of the main leaders of the Easter Rising, but there's no statue commemorating him in Dublin. He's not alone – of the seven signatories of the Proclamation of the Irish Republic, James Connolly is the only one with a statue in the city centre. Pearse, however, is remembered in other places and ways.

Visit Glasnevin Cemetery and you might chance upon re-enactments of his oration at the graveside of Jeremiah O'Donovan Rossa ("Ireland unfree shall never be at peace …"). Stop at 27 Pearse Street, and you'll find a restored Victorian shopfront carrying the name of his father's stonemasonry business (Padraig and his brother Willie were born in the building, which today houses the Ireland Institute for Historical and Cultural Studies). Venture into St Enda's Park in Rathfarnham, and you'll discover one of the best small museums in the city.

The Georgian building at the centre of the park was Pearse's home for a time, and the setting for his bilingual boarding school for boys. St Enda's (or Scoil Éanna) began life in Ranelagh as a cultural nationalist experiment, using new methods of teaching Irish, literature, history, music, nature studies and physical education. It moved to Rathfarnham in 1910 and, a few cordoning ropes aside, it looks like the boys left only yesterday – an old dorm contains rows of iron-frame beds laid out under high ceilings, there's a sparse school chapel, and Pearse's study retains his desk and chair. Artefacts include a cannonball from the siege of Limerick, a print depicting the torture of Anne Devlin, historic swords and pistols, and even the gruesome butcher's block on which Robert Emmet is said to have been beheaded.

St Enda's was widely deemed a success, though not everyone was impressed with the way things were run. "The regime in the school was strict, the living conditions were Spartan, and the food was scarce," recalled one former pupil. It ran into financial difficulties before the Rising, although these were assuaged when donations piled in after Padraig, Willie and two other teachers were executed in 1916. The school finally closed in 1935.

**Acknowledgements**
Our thanks to Catherine McCluskey (Visit Dublin), the OPW (with special thanks to Catherine O'Connor and Patricia Ryan), Dublin Civic Trust, Dublinia, The National Museum of Ireland, Dublin City Council, Harriet Wheelock (RCPI), The National Gallery of Ireland, Dr Jason McElligott (Marsh's Library), Liam Finegan (Iveagh Trust), Dr. Mary Clark and Leo Magee (Dublin City Archives), Rhona Delaney, Denis McIntyre, Rev. Gillian Wharton, Paul O'Kane (Dublin Airport), Jana Gough, Robert Poynton, Niamh Connolly, Prof. Annraoí de Paor, John McKeown and Éanna Rowe (Waterways Ireland). The author also wishes to thank Lynnea, Rosa and Sam Connolly, without whose love and patience this book would not have been possible.

**Photography credits:**
All photos by **Pól Ó Conghaile**, with the exception of Stained Glass Room (Collection: Dublin City Gallery The Hugh Lane), Goya's Portrait of Dona Antonia Zarate (National Gallery of Ireland), and the Old Terminal Building (courtesy of Dublin Airport).

Maps: **Cyrille Suss** - Layout design: **Roland Deloi** - Layout: **Iperbole** - Proofreading: **Jana Gough** and **Kimberly Bess**

© **JONGLEZ** 2017
Registration of copyright: March 2017 – Edition: 03
ISBN: 978-2-36195-177-1
Printed in Bulgaria by Multiprint

# NOTES

and artefacts like arrowheads, axes and pottery have also been unearthed, pointing to Neolithic and Bronze Age activity. One excavation of a Neolithic midden even found the skeleton of an adult male whose skull had been filled with periwinkle shells. Strange as it may seem, Dalkey Island (the literal Irish translation of "Deilginis" is "thorny island") has also been used for farming.

The island's Martello tower and battery date from 1804, when they were built as part of a broader system of coastal defences against Napoleonic invasion. The garrison remained here long after the threat passed – in fact, the British military is said to have paid soldiers for many years "for their idleness", during which time they integrated into Dalkey society, marrying local girls, raising families and keeping goats, as an information sign reveals. St Begnet's ruins date from the 10th century (the little church is named after an Irish princess said to have fled an unwanted suitor to embrace Christianity in Britain). The island is also home to tern colonies and populations of wild goats, rabbits and brown rats. The most exciting wildlife to spot on a visit, however, are the local dolphins and seals, which can regularly be seen playing about in the sound – one of the most biologically diverse areas on the east coast. Prison never felt so free.

# DALKEY ISLAND

**9**

Dalkey, Co. Dublin
• Transport: Dalkey DART station (10–15-min. walk); Dublin Bus stops 3057 and 3058 are a 10–15-min. walk away in Dalkey Village

> ## The "thorny island"

t's like a reverse Alcatraz – an island lying just 300m off the coast of South Dublin, so close you're tempted to dive off the pier and swim across. Nobody does, however, because the postcard-pretty Dalkey Island lies on the other side of a treacherous sound.

There are ways and means of getting there, of course. In summer, local fishermen can be hired for €10/person or so for the return journey out of Coliemore Harbour. Kayaking companies also run guided tours from Bulloch Harbour, paddling out over surprisingly clear waters to explore the Martello tower, St Begnet's Church and an old gun battery on the island. Although measuring just 25 acres (some 16 hectares) in size, Dalkey Island hosted some of the first Stone Age settlers on Ireland's east coast,

# THE METALS & DALKEY QUARRY

**8**

Dalkey Avenue, Dalkey, Co. Dublin
• Transport: Dalkey DART station (10-min. walk); Dublin Bus stops 3057 and 3058 are a 5-min. walk away on Ulverton Road. Routes 7d, 8 and 59 serve the area

*In the footsteps of funiculars*

**D**riving along Dalkey Avenue, it's very easy to miss The Metals. One reason for this is the disconcerting name: what sounds like an industrial site, or a sculptural installation, is in fact a thin little footpath. Slicing through this leafy suburb, its granite slabs are the only clue to a history that has left an indelible mark on Dublin Bay and the city streets.

The Metals are the former route of a funicular railway. Built in 1817, the system was designed to transport granite from Dalkey Quarry to Dublin Bay and, at its peak, 250 wagonloads of stone traversed the 3-mile (4.8km) distance every day. Each train bore about 18 tonnes of rock in three wagons, with empty trucks hauled back up on a parallel line, and horses taking over for the final stretch to the harbour. By 1823, some 1,000 workers and their families were living in the area and the village had 37 pubs. Conditions were not as salubrious as the modern-day suburb might suggest, however – many workers lived in cabins without running water, there were outbreaks of cholera, and dangerous work "led to many losses of eye, limbs and even lives", according to an information sign. The results of their labour, however, remain on magnificent display today – in the harbour, the flagstones of Dublin's streets and as far afield as the Basilica of St John the Baptist in St John's, Newfoundland.

If you follow the laneway up to the quarry itself, it's still possible to see marks made by the chains in the great granite slabs. That isn't all. The views from the hilltop are amazing – stretching from Dun Laoghaire harbour past the South Bull Wall towards Howth (both the harbour and the wall were built using stone from this spot). Venture into the old quarry itself, and it's like walking through a miniature National Park. In sunny weather, granite crystals sparkle underfoot and climbers crawl all over the sheer slabs rising up from the earth.

Quarrying at Dalkey ended in 1917 and today the land forms part of Killiney Park.

# SEASIDE BATHS ❼

Blackrock, Dun Laoghaire, Sandymount, Clontarf
• Transport: Blackrock Baths: Blackrock DART station (2-min. walk); Dun Laoghaire Baths: Dun Laoghaire DART station (10-min. walk); Clontarf Baths: Clontarf DART station (10-min. walk); Sandymount Baths: Sydney Parade DART station (10-min. walk)

*The original infinity pools*

There's a fading bronze plaque by the railway bridge in Blackrock. It's half-turquoise now, in the way that only bronze can go, but you can still make out the inscription. It commemorates Eddie Heron (1910–85), for 35 years the undefeated diving champion of Ireland.

"His skill, grace and courage will never be equalled," the plaque states.

A few steps below the bridge lies the derelict site of some of Heron's greatest dives. The Blackrock Baths, originally built in 1839 and for almost 150 years a magnet for bathing and watersports in the area, are today a crumbling ruin. In its heyday, this facility accommodated up to 1,000 spectators at swimming galas, diving contests, water polo matches and the Tailteann Games. But it has been abandoned since the mid-1980s and finally lost its iconic diving boards in 2012, when Dun Laoghaire Rathdown County Council demolished most of the surviving structure because of safety concerns. Believers still hope the baths will reopen, but silted up, tagged with graffiti, worn down by wrecking balls and bashed by "the ravages of the sea", that day seems further off than ever.

There's a similar story – albeit one with a happier ending – in Dun Laoghaire. The public baths there date from 1843; at their peak, they offered not just sea and freshwater pools, but children's facilities and medical installations using sulphur, seaweed and hot seawater. They fell into ruin after closing in 1997, but were spruced up in "ice-cream" colours recently, thanks to Dulux's Let's Colour project (they're directly across from the Holy Hatch at Teddy's). Councillors have since voted to redevelop them in the form of a jetty and small urban beach. Going to press, similar plans were afoot to refurbish the dilapidated baths in Clontarf.

Meanwhile, another hulk on Sandymount Strand looks least likely to be rescued. These sea baths were once linked to the coast by a 75m iron and timber pier, but all that remains today is a discarded husk of concrete, set adrift in the sand.

# SPIRITUAL SIGNS ❻

St Thomas's Church, Foster Avenue, Co. Dublin
• 01 288-7118
• www.booterstown.dublin.anglican.org
• Open: Sun services (check website for times) are open to all
• Transport: Dublin Bus stop 2009 and 2070 are nearby on the Stillorgan Road

> **"This sign will change. God's love remains"**

**C**ould these be the most thought-provoking traffic lights in Dublin?

Set at the junction of Fosters Avenue and the N11 Stillorgan Road, a red light stops you beside a blue sign bearing a spiritual message with a difference. "Seven days without prayer makes one weak," it might read. Or: "This sign will change. God's love remains." Not long ago, motorists could have learned that "When God saw you, it was love at first sight."

Or what about: "Jesus is my rock and I am ready to roll …"?

The sign belongs to St Thomas's Church, dating from 1874 and today run by the Anglican parishes of Booterstown and Mount Merrion. The church interior, which can be seen at morning mass on most Sundays, contains several features of interest – including a stained-glass window designed by Evie Hone. But the exuberant signs out front are what lodge most in the mind. "The idea is to make people think, to give them a smile, to help them feel positive, encouraged or a bit upbeat," explains parish rector, Rev. Gillian Wharton. The first sign went up in the 1990s and they're changed around once a year. "Different messages have different aims," Wharton explains ("Jesus the carpenter is looking for joiners" is her own favourite). "We don't want to seem like we're proselytising – that's the absolute opposite of what we want to do. But the sign is in such a prime location that people will often drop in suggestions through the letterbox. We've even had people emailing [ideas] from overseas."

The fun and creativity doesn't stop there. The parish holds a "Sausage Service" in St Philip & St James' Church once a month, offering young people involved in Sunday sports the chance to worship quickly and informally before scooting over to the parish centre for sausages and potato wedges. A blessing of the animals takes place on the fourth Sunday in May, with parishioners bringing cats, dogs, rabbits, gerbils, guinea pigs, budgies, hens, hamsters and a host of other pets to the church to be blessed. "Quiet Christmas" is another novel service responding to a need: held the Sunday before Christmas at St Thomas's, it's aimed at parishioners "who do not want to do the whole razzmatazz thing" on the day itself.

Before you know it, the lights are green and you're on your way again.

# THE HELL FIRE CLUB

**5**

Montpelier Hill, Dublin Mountains
• 01 201-1187
• www.dublinmountains.ie
• Open: The car park is open from 7am-9pm (April-Sept) and 8am-5pm (Oct -March)
• Transport: The Hell Fire car park and forest entrance are situated about 6.5km south of Rathfarnham on the R115 to Glencullen

*A forest
with a fright*

Hell is the last place one wants to end up on a hike. But it's a very live possibility in the Dublin Mountains – if legends about Montpelier Lodge are to be believed.

The building, squatting eerily atop Montpelier Hill, was originally built as a hunting lodge by William Conolly, Speaker of the Irish House of Commons, around 1725. In his day, Conolly was the richest commoner in Ireland (his principal residence was Castletown House in Cellbridge, Co. Kildare) and he certainly picked his spot: the views from 390m above Dublin City and Bay are sensational. After Conolly's death in 1729, however, legend tells of the lodge coming to be occupied by "wild young gentlemen" who had been barred from a tavern in the city. It's hard to separate truth from tradition at this stage, but the Hell Fire Club went on to earn itself a historical reputation as one of the most debauched dens of iniquity, gambling, drinking and satanism on the island.

The stories are legion. One suggests a Stone Age tomb was destroyed during the construction of the hunting lodge (during a recent archaeological dig, a rare discovery of megalithic art was made on a stone unearthed at the site). Others tell of dogs refusing to enter, of black masses, poltergeists interrupting late-night drinking parties, of the ghostly whiff of brimstone and the occasional appearance of the devil himself. The Hell Fire Club (motto: "Do as you will") is also said to be haunted by a black cat, the ghost of a creature ritually scalded with *scaltheen* (a cocktail of whiskey and butter) back in its horrible heyday. One of the club's most famous members was Richard Whaley, who is believed to have gone even further, dousing a servant in brandy and setting him ablaze in 1740. In the ensuing chaos, the building caught fire, Whaley leapt out of the window and several drunken bucks lost their lives.

There's no doubt that Montpelier Lodge's reputation colours a visit. It's a blackened bunker of a building, seeming almost to crouch down in the grass. Inside, clammy walls are covered in ancient and modern graffiti, and floors are littered with piles of earth, twigs and broken glass. You can climb upstairs to the first storey, where fireplaces snake through the walls up into holes in the charred roof and metal bars protect the open windows. A visitor centre is reportedly in the works, but for now, the Hell Fire Club is definitely a day-time excursion ...